The Crazy Ladies GUIDE to ENTERTAINING AT HOME

- Distribute ashtrays and cigarettes throughout apartment
- Mix martinis and keep in orange juice bottle in refrig
- Mix Scotch sours and keep in grapefruit juice bottle in refrig
- Prepare hors d'oeuvres, cover with alum foil, keep in refrig
- Set hair and put in Norform
- Sit under dryer while Norform dissolves (wear panties)
- Bathe breasts in cold water, then take hot shower
- Remove rollers from hair and put in diaphragm
- Put on body stocking
- Put on makeup and comb out hair (use new silver eyeshadow)
- Put on pink satin harem pajamas, luminescent pink & lavender earrings, pink vinyl mules
- Put records on hi-fi
- Man with ice cubes should deliver now
- Take hors d'oeuvres out of refrig and set on living-room table
- Drink martini and wait for first guest to arrive
- Try to keep heart from pounding every time doorbell rings and

it might be Jack Bailey

The Crazy Ladies

JOYCE ELBERT

A SIGNET BOOK from

NEW AMERICAN LIBRARY

This is a reprint of a hardcover edition published by New American Library

SIGNET TRADEMARK REG. U.S. PAT. OFF. AND FOREIGN COUNTRIES
REGISTERED TRADEMARK—MARCA REGISTRADA
HECHO EN CHICAGO, U.S.A.

SIGNET, SIGNET CLASSIC, MENTOR, PLUME, MERIDIAN AND NAL BOOKS *are published by New American Library, 1633 Broadway, New York, New York 10019*

FIRST PRINTING, JANUARY, 1970

26 27 28 29 30 31 32 33 34

PRINTED IN THE UNITED STATES OF AMERICA

With special thanks to Lee Karr
for his technical assistance

To Robert A. Gutwillig

Part 1

CHAPTER ONE

Simone Georgette Lassitier was twenty-four years old and lived on smashing Fifty-Seventh Street not far from the Russian Tea Room. Being superstitious about numbers she had a habit of subtracting twenty-four from fifty-seven to see what significance the resultant figure, thirty-three, could possibly have for her. At various times she had concluded that:

1) She would get married at thirty-three
2) Divorced at thirty-three
3) Go mad at thirty-three (*Mon Dieu, c'est la schizophrénie*)
4) Die (from mysterious and unanalyzed causes) at thirty-three
5) Move to Thirty-Third Street
6) Have six children (three plus three)
7) Have nine children (three times three)
8) Have zero children (three minus three)

She never bothered to add twenty-four and fifty-seven because it hardly seemed likely that the figure eighty-one would have any bearing upon her life. She would certainly never live to eighty-one, and she did not think it likely that she would move to Eighty-First Street. Although she knew that the East Eighties encompassed a great deal more than Yorkville, it was the German section nonetheless that struck her as representative of that entire area, and being staunchly French she was opposed to anything even vaguely German. A behavioral psychologist who later came all over her new

Mr. Mort dress had once taken her to a Bavarian restaurant for dinner, and the sight of Moselblümchen on the wine list was enough to make her tongue turn green for the next week.

Simone's apartment on Fifty-Seventh Street was tiny but cheap. Mr. Lewis, who owned the thrift fur shop downstairs, told her that two sisters had lived in the apartment for so many years that one finally died of old age in the other's arms. Grief had driven the surviving sister out and Simone could see why. There would be no escape from one's memories in an apartment this small.

When the sister moved she left all furniture behind, as a result of which Simone had inherited two bunk beds, two bureaus that had been painted a lemon yellow and sat on either side of the bottom bed, a drop-leaf table, and two folding chairs, as well as two creaking rockers with seat cushions that had faded pictures of foreign cars on them.

The kitchen, a narrow cubicle off the main room, was papered in a peeling green, orange, and pink flower design that owed a great deal to Gauguin. There was no oven, only a hotplate. When Simone had first come to look at the apartment this bothered her more than anything else. How would she be be able to warm up her TV dinners without an oven?

"At this rent you don't have to bother with that TV crap," the agent had told her. "You can eat porterhouse."

"They now come with soup and apple crunch," Simone replied remorsefully.

She had signed the lease anyway. The bunk beds arranged so ingeniously, one above the other, made her think she was in the cabin of a ship on its way to Rio, or Östersund, or Mozambique, or one of those places, and after she had been living in the apartment for a while she even figured out how to warm up her favorite TV dinners. It was really very simple. You put them in a large skillet, covered the skillet, and turned on the gas. True, they did not heat as evenly as in an oven and sometimes a cold lump would be found in the mashed potatoes, but at moments like those Simone pretended that Sugarloaf Mountain was just about to come into view, the anticipation of which made one cold potato lump seem a foolish and trivial inconvenience.

It was six months since Simone had first moved in, and having survived the summer months without benefit of either an air-conditioner or fan, she was now, in January, braving the perils of a niggardly heating and hot water system. The first thing she did when she came home from work was to bathe and be quick about it. If she waited too long, the other tenants would have used up the supply of hot water and that meant no shower until the following morning. Going to sleep grimy was a distasteful business to Simone and she did her best to see that this happened as infrequently as possible.

Going to sleep itself was more a necessity than either a desire or a need. At ten o'clock every evening an icy chill descended upon the one radiator and one riser in the room. It was then that Simone would put on two flannel nightgowns, jump into bed, pull all the blankets tight around her, and pray for spring. To ensure additional warmth she piled the following things on top of the blankets: a bear rug she had bought in the Village, a guanaco coat she had bought wholesale from her employer, and a hot pink mohair coat she had charged at Lord & Taylor's Young New Yorker Shop (still unpaid for). She was grateful for Chou-Chou, her toy poodle, who feeling the bite, too, jumped in beside her and breathed warmly into her neck all night long.

Last month she realized she had been wasting her time sleeping in the lower bunk bed. It was infinitely more cozy up above, so now every evening she drank a cup of hot chocolate (occasionally spiked with an inexpensive brandy), and then climbed the ladder to her nest near the ceiling, carrying a squealing Chou-Chou in her arms. Before long the street and traffic noises would lull her to sleep beneath layers of flannel, rugs, and coats, a small dog nestled comfortably in her arms.

Simone's worst fear before falling off to sleep was that she would wake up in the middle of the night and have to go to the bathroom. When this did, in fact, happen, she tried her best to ignore the urge. It made her shiver just to think of getting out of bed and climbing down the ladder and going into the icy bathroom with its leaking window. Sometimes she succeeded in cajoling herself back to sleep until morning, sometimes sleep stubbornly eluded her until she had relieved herself, and once the worst thing of all happened. She peed in bed in her sleep. Luckily there was one of those cotton pads under the bottom sheet or she might have ruined the mattress. As it was she had to get up in the middle of the night and make the whole damn bed over, throwing the soiled sheet into the bathtub until morning. After that, she did not try to inhibit any urinary urges no matter what the temperature in the apartment, no matter what the hour, no matter what her inclination. Perhaps there was something colder in the world than a urine-soaked sheet on a cold night, but if so Simone hoped she would never find out what it was.

When morning came Simone felt as though she had been miraculously spared for another day. Awakened by the alarm bell and a burst of smothering steam heat, she would gasp and choke her way to the kitchen cubicle to boil water for the camomile tea that she bought down the street at Vim & Vigor. While she waited for the water to come to a boil she fed Chou-Chou one of the many revolting dog foods on the market, trying not to look at the wretched stuff as she put it in his dish, for fear of gagging. It invariably amazed her when Chou-Chou licked the plate clean, stood up for a second on his hind legs as though waiting to be congratulated, and then ran to the front door to be taken out.

The dog was an incurable optimist. Either that, she had decided, or an idiot. Maybe both. He never learned. He would stand at the door, his clump of a black tail jiggling, his button eyes imploring her to get the leash despite the fact that experience should have taught him by now that there would be no outing for at least another hour. Sometimes in exasperation Simone would say to him, "Stupid dog, would you like me to walk down Fifty-Seventh Street in my two flannel nightgowns and slipper-socks?" The emphatic up and down movement of his brainless little head could only mean that Chou-Chou saw nothing wrong in that. Simone would then press her thumbs over her ear lobes and wave both hands at him like an imbecile, crying, "Aaaaaaaah, *chien.* Aaaaaaaah, *stupide,*" at the same time sticking out her tongue and rolling her eyes. The only effect this had upon Chou-Chou was to make him get an instant erection.

"So provocative am I," Simone had once commented in disgust to the peeling Gauguin on the kitchen wall, as she smashed a baby cockroach with the back of a skillet. By then the water in the tinny saucepan she had bought at the 5&10 would have come to a boil and she would pour it into her dear little 5&10 cup. She was certain that somewhere, probably not far away, an American girl on the breakfast route was taking equal pleasure in her imported Limoges china. After Simone had been in the United States for a while she began to realize how frequently one person's exoticism turned out to be another person's Woolworth.

But put it off or not, there was still the day ahead. A kaleidoscope of a day. Was there any other kind? Simone did not allow herself to think about that too much, she did not like to *think* (thoughts, conjectures, conclusions—did they really matter? were they really more important than non-thoughts, nonconjectures, etc? she suspected not). No, the thing to do was get dressed very fast, put on eye makeup, face makeup, makeup makeup, and beauty spots, glitter shadow, blush, and always the hair. Hair! Simone sometimes wanted to die because of her hair. Would anybody believe that? It was true, though. One day she would strangle herself with it. The verdict still rankled: her hair had no body. "Too fine," said the stylist at Charles of the Ritz, sighing into his bottle of straightening lotion. "Too fine, not enough bounce, my dear *mademoiselle. Mes regrets.*" Wafty hair, if there was such a word (had she invented it? she despised it). To make her descent complete, they sold her a fall, and there was a marvelous wafty irony there, too. It was dyed *French* hair.

"Wouldn't it be funny if it was originally my mother's hair?" Simone asked the saleslady who stood behind the hairpiece counter, counting her commission in human heads.

The saleslady regarded her impassively from violet-shadowed eyes, and said, "You can make it higher in front by stuffing tissue paper under the crown."

Simone felt inadequate wearing someone else's hair (even her mother's), inadequate and a wee bit Ophelia-ish, and yet she did wear it to work practically every day. She had become quite expert at fastening the obscene thing to her deprived head. First she took a clump of her own pale brown hair, a clump right in front, and pushed it to one side with a bobby pin, then she made a kind of spit curl arrangement with two bobby pins farther back on her head, that was home base; onto the spit curl she hooked the comb of the fall itself. Then she brushed back the clump of her own hair to cover 1) home base, and 2) the beginning line of Mother's hair. *Et voilà.* A new, strong, sturdy, bouncy, lovely, shiny, pale-brown, dyed head is Simone's, and for only one hundred and fifty dollars (partially paid for).

Chou-Chou thought the fall was a funny thing. He liked to bite it.

Over her no-bra and *peut-être* slip, came the work dress. It was a uniform really. Simone owned three of them and they were all identical: sleeveless, black, unadorned sheaths, with a tiny slit down the center back seam to allow for greater freedom of leg movement. In the showroom, sometimes the uniform was left on, when modeling a South African lamb mini-coat, for example, or an Ethiopian kidskin motorcycle jacket, to be easily removed when modeling a natural palomino suit, or a hamster at-home outfit. Fun furs came in a wide variety of kicky styles, as Simone had discovered when she'd gone to work for Mini-Furs, Inc., almost a year ago.

I am a model.

It was only when she stepped out on Fifty-Seventh Street to walk le dog (he only became le dog on Fifty-Seventh Street) that Simone remembered who she was and then she slouched better beneath the shades that tickled the tips of her Fabergé eyelashes. Parading past Little Carnegie, Marboro Books, Mary's Thrift Shop, E. H. Friedricks Company, Place Elegante, Bard's Footwear, Galleria & Deli, Hubert Drugs, Dale's Lingerie, Hotel Great Northern, and Chase Manhattan, she was no longer a girl who had once peed in bed, who wore fake hair, who had no money, no drive, no ambition, no husband, no boyfriend, no lover, who was going to kill herself any minute, who slept in two flannel nightgowns, who was beautiful. Beautiful? Yes. And to think that overnight she had nearly forgotten. One glance in the windowpane of Place Elegante (antiques, children's boutique) reminded her of her outward self, that wonderful girl in the hooded guanaco, carrying the Gucci bag was—*she, me, I, it, her*—a perfectly delicious-looking stranger leading a small dog on a B. Altman leash. She leaned forward to kiss her reflection discreetly. The windowpane was cold.

Simone never watched Chou-Chou when he did his duty. "Yes," she told people, "when Chou-Chou does his duty I turn away and think of Panama. Why Panama? Because it is supposed to be so unpleasant."

Secretly, she thought of Cap d'Antibes.

Mr. Lewis was still selling mink and sable boas for twenty-nine and sixty-nine dollars, and the mailman was a double spy. Simone suspected that while delivering the mail he deftly took fingerprint samples off all the boxes. Somewhere in Moscow every nuance of her index finger was intimate knowledge. That did not bother her so much as the fact that her monthly copy of *Elle* arrived ragged and obviously pre-looked-at (if not preread) by the other mailmen at the post office who had neither the ambition nor the inclination to be double spies. She rather admired her mailman for being so unscrupulously enterprising. Her father had been a spy of sorts during the war, a minor spy, and yet they had shot him anyway. Her mother had said, "He was captured and shot by the Boche when you were only one year old." It seemed he used to hide his camera in his fishing net and take photos of the German installations along the Normandy coast. He gave the photos to the local mailman and that was the end of it, the end of him as it turned out one day. Simone had been wary of mailmen ever since and she wondered how this one would fare when he was finally caught by some cunning American intelligence agent with his collection of fingerprint samples. Simone barely remembered the war. She was too young. A German officer had once slept downstairs on their sofa. He was very polite. He said that Calvados was a marvelous drink. He said that Pont l'Évêque was a marvelous cheese. He said that the French were marvelous people. *Tant pis* we have to kill them from time to time.

The mailman's name was Mr. Salinger but he was not related to the famous writer, or so he claimed. In between her double spy conjecturings, it occurred to Simone that he might actually be *the* Salinger gathering material for a new book. Why not? According to her only literary friend, Edwin L. Kuberstein, nobody knew what the son of a bitch looked like since he refused to be photographed. He hid in an attic in a house somewhere in New England and ate nails. That is, when he wasn't delivering mail on Fifty-Seventh Street. Several days ago he had handed Simone a tiny white envelope as she returned from her morning outing with le dog.

"Is that all you have for me?" she asked, feeling slighted by the junk-mail people (*I want my junk!*).

"I'm afraid so, Miss Lassitier."

"Franny and Zooey."

"Excuse me?"

Simone gave him an X-ray look. To her disappointment, he seemed genuinely perplexed. Perhaps he was exactly what he appeared to be: a plain old mailman (actually, he was quite young). A civil servant. A bona fide United States government employee with flat feet and corns, who, along with his other mailmen compatriots, had cornered the Epsom salt market.

"It looks like an invitation."

"What does?" Simone asked, wondering whether he had had plastic surgery on his face.

"Your little letter."

"Oh I rarely get invited anywhere these days, Mr. Salinger."

"A pretty girl like you. I'll bet you get lots of invitations."

"Honestly, I don't."

"I'll bet you go to parties and discotheques and those places every night."

"Give my regards to the Glass family."

"I don't deliver their mail. That's Reilly's route."

When Simone got upstairs and removed Chou-Chou's collar and leash, she opened the envelope. It did indeed contain an invitation. On the front of the invitation it said *PARTY* in big lopsided letters and there were drawings of cocktail glasses and bottles of liquor dancing drunkenly in the air against a pale pink background. Inside it said:

Date: Wednesday, January 21st
Time: After 8 P.M.
Place: 32½ East 38th Street (Apt. 7-J)

It was signed by Simone's ex-roommate, Anita, and there was a handwritten note on the bottom. "Do come. I have a plethora of men." Simone did not know what *plethora* meant and she further knew that Anita knew she would not know. It was typical of Miss Norforms to try to be superior by using a word that sounded like an obscure pulmonary disorder. When they had lived together Anita used to learn a new word every week. She claimed it helped her in her work. Anita was an airline stewardess with a flair for languages and a penchant for champagne.

"I have a penchant for champagne," she had announced to Simone one day.

"Is that your new word for the week?"

"Yes. It means a strong leaning, attraction, or inclination."

What Anita really had a penchant for was every unmarried executive coming up the ramp with an attaché case in one hand and the *Wall Street Journal* in the other. Simone had not seen or spoken to Anita in quite a few months and she wondered what had prompted her to give a party. Somewhere, somehow, on some devious level, some man was directly responsible. Simone was dying to know how seriously involved he was with Anita.

Simone had never met a girl who wanted to get married more desperately than Anita and it amazed her that Anita had not yet achieved her singular ambition. She worked so hard at it that perhaps she frightened them off. Her obsession had frightened off Simone and finally broken up their roommate relationship. Anita was forever running to Ginori's and mentally buying Venetian caviar servers, silver brandy warmers, Steuben goblets, and Sèvres dinner service for her future home, and then coming back to the two-and-a-half room flat in Murray Hill and describing each projected purchase in infinite detail to Simone.

Anita's other favorite haunt was Bloomingdale's furniture

floor. One day she talked Simone into going there with her. A salesman addressed Anita as "*Mrs.* Schuler," at which point Anita firmly pressed Simone's arm. She later explained that one got better service if one appeared to be married.

"It enhances your buying power in the eyes of sales people," she told Simone. "Did you see that copy of an *acajou* chest of drawers with fluted pilasters?"

"Where did you learn all that stuff?"

"I'm studying eighteenth-century antiques," Anita said. "I plan to have a walnut *poudreuse* in my bedroom."

After a while Simone could not take it any more. Anita had become a furniture and objet d'art catalog. "I saw the most elegant fei ts'ui boudoir clock in Paris yesterday. The dial is jade, the numerals are gold. Don't you think it will look stunning above my serpentine fireplace?"

And meanwhile they were eating canned chili off a card table and wondering how they were going to pay the rent that month. Since the apartment had been Anita's to begin with, Simone said she would move out. The parting had been amicable. Anita admitted at the last moment that perhaps it was all for the best since Chou-Chou got on her nerves.

"The only animal I truly like is a lion by Rodin. I saw it at Ostertag's. It was standing on a griotte marble base."

Simone felt relieved to have her own place once more and not be forced to listen to rapturous descriptions of the latest bronze Doré mount that Anita had just unearthed. Poor Anita. Apparently it was not so easy to get over growing up in Cleveland, Ohio, particularly if your father came from Frankfurt and happened to be a pork butcher to boot.

There were evenings when Simone did not go to sleep in two flannel nightgowns at ten o'clock, evenings when she camped out in strangers' beds, or went to discotheques wearing a paper dress trimmed with paper pompons that she would later cut into washcloth squares (her secret wish was to be married to a throwaway man in a throwaway paper wedding gown and spend her honeymoon on the moon), evenings dreaming at underground movies, evenings when she had cocktail dates, dinner dates, after-dinner dates, after-after-dinner dates, when she zoomed uptown, downtown, crosstown, sextown, undresstown, or staydressedanddoitanywaytown (penises had an interesting way of sticking their heads out), dancing, moaning, drinking, motorcycling, smoking, screaming, and never coming. "No," she had a habit of saying to a man right at the start. "I never come." Like some people never drink martinis.

There was nothing she would not do in bed if it struck her as amusing at the moment. One time she had let a computer programmer fuck her in the ass with an A&P hotdog. Then they had boiled the hotdog and eaten it. It did not taste bad. Count on mustard.

Yes indeed, men had done strange things to her. She had done strange things. Once a man picked her up as she was strolling through Central Park, and invited her back to his place for a drink. He lived not far away. Six days later and six pounds lighter she had finally been released. Well it hadn't been terrible exactly, not as terrible as it could have been, she supposed, except that she did not think it was so amusing to be gone down on for such a long period of time. After a while it hurt. And he wouldn't stop. She kept telling him he had no imagination but he didn't care; that made him slurp away all the more. At last, she gave up and asked if it would be all right if she read a book to take her mind off things. He said okay, but unfortunately he liked only one writer: J. D. Salinger. Yes, that was her first introduction to her literary friend, Edwin L. Kuberstein, and the novels of J. D. S.

Another time she went to bed with a dental assistant who called her *kid* and had an unfortunate stammer. In the middle of the night he was heard to say, "K-k-k-k-k-iss me, k-k-k-k-k-iddd, I'm c-c-c-c-c-oming." A Negro recording star who took her to St. Martin's for a couple of weeks in the sun and then insisted that she stay in the stall shower with him most of the time and soap his erection. A Greek businessman named Stamos who reeked of ouzo and had a thing about electric toothbrushes. A market research analyst who cried a lot late at night.

It was sad. Simone became bored. She stopped going to bed with everybody. It bothered her to keep doling out money for the pill when she was leading such a virtuous life, but since things like that were liable to change any minute she dutifully continued to swallow the little white and pink darlings every morning, at the same time wondering who was going to break her self-imposed fast. She was tired of crazies. She wished she could meet a nice normal neurosurgeon, instead of men who wore Hawaiian shirts and tried to shoot Redi-Whip up her vagina . . .

It had been another kaleidoscope day for Simone at Mini-Furs, Inc., on Seventh Avenue, and in order to take her mind off the senseless things that were happening all around her she fastened her thoughts on what to wear to Anita's party that evening. In between modeling green mole pantsuits for a buyer from Atlanta and running down to the optometrist's storefront office to pick up Mr. Swern's new contact lenses, Simone decided upon her brown and white plumed mini with the matching white-plumed wig (a minor fortune charged at Bonwit's and still unpaid for), and nothing underneath except a Pursette to keep out the cold. In the window next to the optometrist was a cardboard photograph of an attractive brunette wearing a black Persian lamb coat. A cardboard man was looking at her admiringly. Underneath it said: Men notice a girl in Persian lamb.

Back upstairs in the showroom, the buyer from Atlanta had wanted to be shown what Mr. Swern had in Argentine spotted cat.

"Go get the horizontal coat with the leather trim," Mr. Swern told Simone. The buyer from Atlanta was not so sure of the horizontal coat with the leather trim.

"Maybe you should look at our selection of sheared Chinese weasel," Mr. Swern suggested.

Now, at nine-thirty that evening, having bathed and douched (yes, God, I'm clean all over), Simone secured her fishnet stockings with four flesh-colored band-aids and wondered whether it might not be too late to learn how to live with a normal man. Besides, to the best of her recollection she had never met one. Was that possible? Wait. What about that married space salesman who lived in Camden? He was relatively . . . then she remembered his tendency to telephone on weekends and ask her to describe her underwear, dribble dribble. Oh they fooled you at the beginning. The more sane they appeared, the nuttier they usually turned out to be. Like the electronics engineer who wanted her to do it to herself with a candle while he watched. She didn't even mind that so much but no candle was big enough for him. Besides she was terrified that at any second he was going to light the other end and sit gleefully by while hot wax dripped onto her more delicate regions.

She had no reason to think that anyone she met at Anita's party would be much of an improvement over previous nuts. Still she refused to relinquish hope. Perhaps without knowing it she had been building up all this time to a quiet anthropology student with an aging mother and a serious outlook. "Can the study of other people's cultures help us to understand modern society and its dilemmas, or the prospects of the future?" he might say to her in just a little while, his eyes peering intently at her from behind higher education glasses. And when they made love it would be an ethereal experience, two bodies floating far far above the earthbound crassness they both so grandly disdained.

It was nine-thirty. Simone sprayed herself lavishly with Ma Griffe, stuck Chou-Chou in her brown tote bag, and walked across the street to the Russian Tea Room. The bartender remembered Chou-Chou from the last time.

"We're going to a party," Simone said, "but we're a little early. Could we please have a Brandy Alexander."

She was not unaware of the man seated two stools away. He was in his fifties and wore an open shirt with a paisley ascot, a safari jacket, and a small pointed beard.

"A party," he said, "how quaint."

When she did not answer, he asked whether she lived in the neighborhood, but before she could reply he said that, of course, she must, it was the only civilized neighborhood in New York. There was nobody on the stool between them and he slid over.

"Why don't you take me to your party?" he suggested. "You could fold me up and put me in your bag along with the little monster. By the way, dear, your left eyelash is crooked."

"The glue sticks."

"That's a property of glue, dear."

Simone did not like him. He was probably a jockstrap fanatic, last seen in some famous baritone's Carnegie Hall bureau drawer inhaling musty fragrances that would eventually prove too much for his weakened lungs. She drank the Brandy Alexander quickly and paid the bartender.

"Or we could go to my place and I will perform my little sonata for you."

On his limp penis, no doubt. "I really don't think it's a good idea," Simone said. "Not with your pulmonary disorder."

Out on the street once more she hailed a cab and gave the driver Anita's Murray Hill address. The party should be well under way by now. She wondered if she would know any of the men. She wondered if any of the men would be interesting. She wondered if any of the men would be interested in *her*.

"Watch out, *schmuck*!" the driver yelled to a jaywalking drunk.

Simone leaned back against the cold January seat as the taxi swung down Fifth Avenue and wondered if any of the men (among that plethora Anita was expecting) would turn out to be even vaguely, even prosaically, even *repulsively* N**O**R**M**A**L.

When Beverly Northrop's husband told her, three days ago, that he had invited his publisher to their home for dinner Wednesday evening, Beverly said, "Oh darling, not prime ribs and baked po again?"

"No, darling," Peter said. "Tony's tastes are truly international. This is your great chance to plan something exotic. In fact, darling, it can't be exotic enough. Tony spent years in Florence. You know the type. Dreadful snob."

Beverly thought this last remark very amusing coming from Peter, who, when put on the carpet for his heretical inclinations by the minister of The Cathedral, firmly said, "I must correct you, Dr. Freemont. I am not entirely without faith."

"Well then," Dr. Freemont replied, "perhaps you can tell me what you do believe in."

"Gladly, sir. In Harvard and my family."

Which at the time Beverly thought was quite sweet of Peter. But that was over two years ago, before Peter, Jr., was born, before their daughter turned into a little monster, before Peter had gone to work for Tony Elliot. If Dr. Freemont asked him the same question today, Beverly wondered what Peter's answer would be. His secret answer, that is. Peter had changed so much in the past couple of years that sometimes Beverly felt she did not know him anymore, could not trace him back to the shy student she had fallen in love with when she was an undergraduate at Wellesley.

She would never have fallen in love with Peter had she met him in Salt Lake City. She found it difficult even to imagine Peter in Salt Lake City, although he had, in fact, been there twice: the first time for their wedding, and the second time when her father died. She remembered taking Peter on a brief walking tour of Mormon country. She remembered him standing on Temple Square appraising the seagull monument (the world's only monument to a bird) with that lowered-lid look of his, that so very *Eastern* look. Yes, Peter was so Eastern and the East was so foreign to her. Even now, after having lived here for eleven years, Beverly still felt like an incurable stranger to this flat and colorless land, and she often wished that her father had let her go to the University of Utah where she would have been close to home, close to everyone and everything she loved, but he had said she should widen her horizons, go East, young lady, step out into the world, leave the womb. For she was shy, too.

At Wellesley she had dormed in the Tower, the girl in Tower East who had fallen in love with the boy in the high room at Beck Hall. Years later when their daughter was born, Beverly writhed and moaned at Mineola hospital and for some reason, for no reason, for every reason, she realized (in between contractions) that she had fallen in love with and married Peter Bennett Northrop III of Brookline, Mass., the way a French girl visiting the United States for the first time might fall in love with an American boy—for protective coloring and also because it was just a little bit exotic.

Exotic, too, was the house they subsequently bought, a fifteen-room Tudor castle in the estate section of Garden City. It made no sense, that house.

Really now, doesn't it make sense, Mother? (Beverly had written to her mother the day that Peter signed all the boring real estate papers). Now we have our very own retreat, complete with turrets, peaks, cornices, stained glass windows, heavily paneled doors, and even the most beautiful multicolored slate roof that I want to slide down in the worst way, but Peter won't let me, says I will break my neck. The house is far too elegant for us, I told Peter so, but he wouldn't listen. Says it fits us handsomely because it costs ninety thousand dollars and we are people who should live in a ninety-thousand-dollar house because, damn it, we can bloody well afford to, dear girl (which he sometimes but not often calls me), because we are bloody RICH.

Her mother had never really liked Peter and her mother wasn't even a Mormon. Her father had vaguely liked Peter and he was only a Jack-Mormon (drank, smoked, seldom worshiped, and had the most vibrant way of greeting total strangers on State Street: "Good morning, Sir!" with that proud, outgoing manner one rarely, if ever, encountered in the East). Peter was not exactly the most likable person in the world; he was far too intolerant of too many things, and to make matters worse did not take the trouble of hiding his intolerance. But then, he was shy, too. That was what most people missed altogether. They would have forgiven him, Beverly frequently thought, if only they knew how hard it was for him to get about in the world. That was their great common bond, their great common failing, their Beverly and Peter *bête noire*, their precious, indestructible, inimitable timidity, their lie to the world, their shelter and their fortress.

They went to Paris for their honeymoon and Peter was shy

at the Lancaster. Then they went to Cannes and he was shy at the Carlton, which did not prevent them from becoming very fashionably Cannois, he in his white dinner jacket, she in her lime Givenchy, both tanned to a coffee-cream. Then they went to another Carlton in another city in another country: Alicante on the southeast coast of Spain where they drank rosado and walked out in the middle of a bullfight. Walking out was Peter's idea. Beverly did not care one way or another, although she was curious why he deemed it so important to leave at that particular moment. It was not the most uninteresting moment. The matador was about to place the banderillas himself and that apparently meant a great deal to a great many of the spectators. There was a birdlike grace about the way the matador arched his body and then swooped down upon the uncertain bull, that swooping motion was quite beautiful, Beverly thought, particularly beautiful because of the dazzling emerald green costume, tight tight was how it fit, a second skin, but Peter had touched her arm, and said, "*Vamonos,*" the only Spanish word in his vocabulary.

"But why?" she asked him later when they stopped for still more rosado at a shady café.

"It's a fag's sport, you know. That is, if you're an American. Sorry but I refuse to be reverent and romantic about the so-called art of bullfighting. Think we've had enough of those two reactions anyway in terms of bulls and men who fight them with handkerchiefs stuffed into their pants. Tired of looking at dumb bulls and make believe balls, darling. I prefer the real thing and I don't think the real thing exists in Spain, not now, hasn't for a long time; the country is too damn out of step with the rest of the world, too sleepy, too dark. No camp at all."

Shy people were often bitter, frustrated people, Beverly decided as they silently walked back to the ubiquitous Carlton where another episode of their bed life unfolded. Peter had excited her from the start. At Cambridge they used to make love in his high room at Beck Hall and one night he tried to strangle her with his belt. No, not really tried, pretended to be really trying. It was a gesture of perversion, a kind of moral statement that he seemed to be striving to express. She did not take it literally because she knew it was not literally intended, but nonetheless it unedged her a little, since her reaction to this quasi-strangling was going to determine many important things. She acted a little afraid, a little contemptuous, a little aroused. Peter wanted control of her, and in that one distilled moment she obliquely made it clear that he would have it for as long as he wished ("I love you," he then said for the very first time). While Beverly did not fully comprehend the nature of his fantasies, she was sympathetic to them and yielding. Peter would be her first and her last lover. There was something so special about him that she could not conceive of trading him in for any other man, ever. She loved the way he looked. Spare and wiry, which she was anything but. Her breasts were large with great pink nipples, her hips were ample, she had what Peter (drawing from God-knew-what fund of knowledge) referred to as "a sublime Cuban posterior" that he would ultimately become very familiar with.

At first she had felt herself to be too large for Peter, too massive. Would she one day inadvertently crush him to death in her sleep? But he had soothed her doubts on that score.

"We all tend to have an exquisite appreciation of our own physical peculiarities," he said, "a touchiness about them which has a way of developing a compensatory taste in us for opposite peculiarities in the other sex."

Beverly felt better after that, more encouraged to parade around his room unclothed without the need to apologize for her flesh. Peter liked to watch her. His eyes would harden. She used to wonder what he was thinking but did not dare ask for fear of what the answer might be. He drove her nipples mad, at times she thought they would burst, they swelled so. He could not keep his hands off them, his mouth off them, he wanted her hands on them too, both their hands together in the Hotel Carlton in Alicante, but hers under his until she was so wet that she thought she would drown in her own oozing moisture. Her body was absolutely weightless and yet every part of her was distended. The heat was unbelievable. She could hear herself making strange crying sounds.

Finally he was inside her, he had pushed a pillow under her, a sad guitar strummed on the street outside, *es tipico el ambiente,* and Beverly lay on the bed in a lackadaisical fashion, legs sluttily sprawled low which Peter liked but which was really not too good for her because her clitoris was unusually high (he had missed it altogether the first couple of times they made love), and in that flat, tending downward in spite of the pillow position, she could not become too aroused but it aroused her mentally to see the effect that her affected sprawl had upon him. Once his excitement had been established Beverly raised her legs because by then he was running safe and the change would not disturb him and would vastly help her. It was important that she get her legs up up. More pillows were needed. The two of them would expire one day in a mountain of percale snow, their legs touching the ugly ceiling light fixture.

When Beverly's orgasm started she would have killed anyone who, for any reason, might have interrupted it. One day she would be an old lady (was that possible? and yet she would be old because she was durable) and she would remember the amazing feeling that by seconds preceded the orgasm itself, a feeling so intense and at the same time so fragile and tenuous, heralded by a taste in the mouth (another hormonal taste heralded her period), but she could not describe it, that feeling, could not describe it in words, perhaps colors? alternating electric reds and blues, sizzling, dazzling, racing to a final sweltering muffled scream.

Much of the time Beverly got on top. That position was really better for them because Peter's peter was not all that big. It went in tighter, harder if she got on top. At first she did not know how to move and she was a little embarrassed about that, particularly when she caught his glance. Peter, eyeballs-awake seeing her awkwardness initiated the rhythm that she would thankfully follow, but after a while she began to understand how to initiate it herself and she found a tremendous amount of excitement in being the pseudoaggressor (maybe it was real, though) while Peter lay beneath her, a willing and lovely conspirator as she foamed over his lithe, young boy's body. Men had nipples too, she rather surprisingly discovered. And sensations therein. Tweak. He liked it. Tweak tweak.

They sexually grew up together so that after eight years of marriage and two children, they had finally made first grade. There was a milk and cookie aspect to their lovemaking that Beverly sensed but did not know how to explain, let alone rectify, and that made her feel funny. Very often Peter lost his erection right in the middle of everything, and she felt desolate then, vaguely wanted to kill him, or herself, but she did her best not to act concerned for fear of unnerving him all the more. The more he lost his erections (they were last seen roaming around the North Shore of Long Island, giddily directionless), the more resourceful he became in terms of things they could and should *do*. He had never entirely given up his strangling fantasy and sometimes he wanted her to strangle him with a tinted stocking: "The pink?" "No, angel, the blue": which she cooperatively did but it bored her.

Or he would go down on her which seemed to excite him

tremendously and often resulted in a workable erection. She came quite a few times that way and was very fond of it on its own terms but not as a substitute for his actually being *in* her. Also, as soon as she came that way she immediately wanted him in her, the sense of vacancy was urgent, she really needed to be filled and at once. That was why for Beverly masturbation proved so unsatisfying, the terrible gnawing vacancy afterward. What could she do? Stick a carrot in? And yet, supposedly, some women did. She preferred not to think of that, let alone those other things she had heard about that were actually manufactured for the express purpose of . . . they had a disgusting name too that she had managed to forget, thank God. Peter had told her about the "devices," as he referred to them, wanted her to get one and fuck him in the ass with it but for the first time she refused one of her husband's requests, said she would not do it, could not, would vomit.

"Well then," he said, "I will do it to you."

"Not with one of those things you won't."

"No, sweet, with my very own thing."

It did not feel bad but not as good as the other way. However, Peter loved it, just loved it, he could not get enough of it, and finally it began to depress Beverly but she let him go on because, well, he was her husband, first and only lover, father of her children, focus of her life, and what could she say? It would pass, she told herself, but it didn't. Then one day he got the job he had been after, a reporter of all things for a fashion newspaper, Tony Elliot's paper, and it passed. So did practically everything else, in fact. Their once active bed life seemed to grind to a loud and abrupt halt. Peter apparently had lost interest. When he was asleep, Beverly would cry. When he was awake she would try to arouse him. Sometimes she succeeded and they would have a go at it, always in the ass now, but it was so depressing that Beverly felt worse than before.

When they woke up Wednesday, the day that Tony Elliot was coming to dinner, Peter said to her, "You're getting rather plump, darling. Do you know that?"

"I'm the same as I've always been," she replied, feeling a bit stupid about her answer.

"Please wear your black sheath tonight. I'm very fond of the way that dress looks on you."

"Doesn't Tony Elliot like well-rounded ladies?"

"I don't know or give a damn what kind of ladies Tony likes. I do know what I like, though."

Beverly felt familiarly abused. "I was rather under the impression that you liked *me*."

"I am mad about you, darling, and that's why I wish you would try to shed a few pounds."

"A shed is a place of shelter. It's where they keep corn."

"Don't be tedious at seven o'clock in the morning."

"Peter, do you think I look older than my age?"

"How old are you these days?" he asked, reaching for a cigarette (another new habit of his, smoking upon arising).

"If I didn't know you were kidding . . ."

"You know how rotten I am when it comes to figures," he said.

"Except plump ones?"

"You said that, darling, not I."

"Really, Peter, I'm almost twenty-nine and you damn well know it."

"Really, Peter," he cruelly mimicked her. He wasn't even good at it. "Lose ten pounds and you'll lose five years."

Tears lurked in Beverly's blue eyes. She had reddish-brown hair and a faint smattering of freckles, a pert nose.

"Women with your coloring should never cry," Peter pointed out. "Brunettes can sob successfully, blondes can whimper and look attractive, but a redhead . . . out of luck, it destroys the capillaries. It really does, darling."

"Please kiss me, Peter."

He kissed her gently, dispassionately.

"Couldn't we . . . ?" she said.

"I think you've turned into a little nymphomaniac, darling."

"But we almost never, any more."

She remembered Alicante and the sad guitar and did not give a damn about her capillaries. Tears were sweet, satisfying, swell. Beverly did not know how to cope any longer. Garden City had become her womb, what irony. Her poor father had wanted her to leave womb-like Salt Lake City and so what? What for? All she had done was trade it in for a suitable Eastern substitute and proceed to burrow. She glanced occasionally at the paper that Peter wrote for. She really did not understand that paper, its direction, its attitudes, why, in fact, it even existed. Was it some kind of joke? She could understand *Vogue* or *Harper's Bazaar* because they were so extravagantly lush, those women in those unwearable clothes in those unthinkable stances in those green dynel après-swim-ski wigs. Yes it was amusing, diverting, seven-foot-tall West Indian models could be accepted the way one accepted a son's Batman fancies, but Peter's paper was something else again. It demanded another kind of attention, another kind of reaction. It was more immediate (being a newspaper, albeit a weekly), it did not have the glossiness nor the expensive four-color artwork of a magazine, it was not as Batmanish, it could not be so readily passed off as an editor's surrealistic dream, it photographed real(?) women in their real St. Laurent, Cardin, Courrèges, Chanel, Givenchy, Ungaro, Galanos, Bill Blass, Norell clothes, in real restaurants in real world capitals, leading chic wealthy important trivial enviable international desperate lunching-out lives upon shad roe, caviar and blini, Blue Point oysters, striped bass in champagne sauce, fettucini, steak au poivre, petits pois, forever Campari espresso mousse. But how thin they were, those forever lunching-out women. Did they really eat the food they ordered or did they order it to make certain that their culinary selections would be dutifully recorded in next week's issue of *The Rag?*

Beverly lunched a great deal of the time at the Cherry Valley Country Club, upon a small steak, small potato, small salad, and twelve martinis. Well, that was an exaggeration. But those ladies constantly reported on in *The Rag,* did they not, too, drink a great deal? Beverly liked being high. It soothed her.

"I mean," she said to Peter at 7:20 A.M. Wednesday morning, "they look so lousy in most of the photos, those lunching-out ladies, they look half bombed, and what do they do when they leave Caravelle and the Colony? Where do they go in their original Courrègeses and Chanels?"

Peter said she was being vicious, admitting however that the ladies she referred to were pretty cunty when you got right down to it but they were newsworthy, and they set the fashion pace these days and who was he to wonder why. Besides which some of them were okay, they tried to be real people (whatever that was).

Beverly rarely came to town. Garden City had everything. She shopped at Lord & Taylor's there. She was a size twelve.

"Once a relatively slender size, now inflated," was Peter's comment. "Size five is the size. Twelve for tanks."

She only weighed one hundred and thirty-six pounds, which did not seem bad for five feet seven inches.

"Should probably weigh one hundred and eleven," Peter said.

Beverly did not know how he came up with these strange conclusions, nor why. He wanted to humiliate her. Would he humiliate her in front of Tony Elliot? At 7:30 A.M. Peter repeated his dictum of several days ago: "Tony's tastes in food are truly international."

At 7:30 P.M. (while Simone was eating a canned hamburger, cold, prefatory to Anita's party) Beverly and her Negro housekeeper were taking the main course of one of *Life*'s Great Dinners out of the Northrop's family-sized General Electric oven. It was the Choucroute Garni, which turned out to be a nauseating concoction of sauerkraut and various horrible sausages, but Beverly had determined that it should be international enough even for Tony Elliot's tastes. According to *Life*'s informative notes, the dish originated in the border region of Alsace which "puts a French touch on German cooking."

"Prime ribs and baked po," Margaret, the housekeeper, said mournfully to Beverly as they regarded the pungent sauerkraut platter.

"It's too late to think about things like that now, Margaret."

"Yes, Ma'am. It certainly is."

"However, Mr. Elliot is a world traveler. I'm sure he will appreciate our little foreign specialty."

"I'm going to buy a bottle of Airwick first thing in the morning," Margaret said, "or we'll never get the sauerkraut smell out of this house, that's for sure."

"We shouldn't have put the pie together so soon. *Life* says the crust may get soggy."

Beverly liked to affect a camaraderie with Margaret when it came to culinary matters, just as though they were on equal footing.

"If you'll pardon my saying so, Mrs. Northrop, *Life* is the soggy one. How did they ever dream up a meal like this?"

It had not been a particularly difficult meal to prepare, but it had been difficult tracking down the motley ingredients that were called for. The kielbasa, for instance. *Life* said that that was a garlic-flavored sausage, and if it could not be located, it was all right to substitute Kosher frankfurters. Kielbasa most definitely could not be located at any of Garden City's finer meat markets. No indeedy. Polite clerks gagged discreetly at the other end of the telephone when Beverly made her exotic request, and she finally had no choice but to send Margaret to a Kosher butcher in Roslyn for the damned frankfurter substitutes. Margaret resented the assignment. She said "the girl" should go. Beverly pointed out that "the girl" did not know how to drive, and that settled it, at least in this one particular instance.

Margaret did not like "the girl" and was fond of telling Beverly that "the girl" was overpaid.

"She's not worth fourteen dollars a day, Mrs. Northrop," Margaret had said the first week "the girl" was hired. "I've been watching her polish your fine Baker chairs and she doesn't use *muscle*."

Beverly did not know what she would do without Margaret, who had been with them for as long as they had been in Garden City, who slept in and kept the children out of her hair, although now that Sally had started kindergarten the house was relatively quiet until two in the afternoon when she returned with her exuberant tales of school lore. Margaret recieved forty-five dollars a week but, of course, she had two rooms and a private bath on the top floor of the castle. Beverly had once gone up to Margaret's quarters when Margaret had been conspicuously absent for some period of time, to find her rolling convulsively around on the beige wall-to-wall carpeting, having an attack of some mysterious nature and hoarsely crying, "Soda soda." Beverly did not understand. She assumed that Margaret wanted a coke, and Peter, Jr., had drunk the last one about ten minutes before.

"I can give you a ginger ale," she told the distraught woman.

"Soda soda," Margaret wailed.

Apparently in Margaret's lexicon, ginger ale was not soda.

"How about a nice cold No-Cal?"

Margaret simply kept repeating, "Soda soda," while clutching at her stomach until it finally came home to Beverly that the poor woman was having a gas attack of momentous proportions and was trying to indicate bicarbonate of soda. Why hadn't Margaret said so in the first place? The incident had since become a cherished family anecdote.

"Mr. Elliot is going to need plenty of soda after this dinner," Margaret informed Beverly, who was trying to smell the sauerkraut without actually inhaling the unusual aroma. *Life* had suggested using a quarter of a cup of gin in the sauerkraut if juniper berries, which the recipe originally called for, were hard to come by. Beverly thought that the gin was a lovely idea. In addition to gin, the lowly sauerkraut had been simmering for hours in white wine, bouillon, parsley, carrots, onions, peppercorns, blanched bacon bits, and bay leaves.

"I have a hunch Mr. Northrop and I will need some soda, too," Beverly replied. "However, it all seems to look and smell the way *Life* says it's supposed to look and smell, and they should know. I'm going back to the dining room now. You can take away the soup plates and bring in the Liebfraumilch."

Beverly had defied *Life* on that last score. They firmly proposed beer as an accompaniment to the Choucroute Garni, but that was going too far. What would the world traveler, Tony Elliot, think of them if they served him Rheingold at dinner? Mr. Smiley at the liquor shop on Seventh Street had heartily recommended the Liebfraumilch, saying that it seemed to come from the same general region as the main course. Beverly replied that indeed it did and ordered two bottles to be sent over chilled.

Tony Elliot was finishing the last of *Life*'s puréed mushroom soup which Margaret had garnished with paper thin slices of lemon, according to directions.

"Very good," he said. "Very delicious. Very unusual to be served a homemade soup these days."

"Thank you, Tony."

Beverly felt awkward calling him Tony but he had most graciously insisted that she do so. Everything about Tony Elliot was gracious. His manner, his voice, his bearing, his oxford blue shirt and double-breasted pinstriped suit. Gracious and impeccable. He was a small thin man in his early forties, with very clear, almost brilliant blue eyes. All three of us have blue eyes, Beverly thought for no particular reason. She did not like Tony Elliot and she did not know why. He had been extremely complimentary to her from the moment he arrived. He said she was a brave woman to wear a black dress these days, and he admired courage.

"It's Peter's favorite dress," she admitted, wondering whether the deep V-neckline wasn't just a bit out of style. And yet who would know more about such fashion details than Peter himself?

"One never sees a cleavage any more," Peter remarked. "Cut outs under the arm and across the navel, yes, but no cleavages. Frankly, I miss them."

As Margaret removed the Sèvres soup plates, Beverly caught Tony Elliot looking down the deep V of her dress, and she blushed in spite of herself. Perhaps the poor man was sick to death of all those skinny lunching-out ladies with their anemic chests squeezed into size six Norells. Beverly was proud of her breasts. They were not only large, they stood up, and after two children also. She was a 36-B. Even at Wellesley she had been a 36-A. She once overheard a girl on campus refer to her as "Miss Big Tits of 1918," but she passed it off as jealousy since the girl was built like a boy on top. During her pregnancies Beverly's breasts had ballooned to gigantic proportions. Peter warned her that she would be raped on the street one day if she weren't careful. That was during her second pregnancy, which had produced Peter, Jr., a little over two years ago. Directly after Peter, Jr., was born Peter quit his job at *Time,* where he claimed he was getting nowhere, and went to work for Tony Elliot, publisher and founder of *The Rag.* Why Tony had chosen such a distasteful name for a fashion newspaper, Beverly still could not figure out.

"Ah," Tony said, as Margaret appeared with the wine. "How delightful. Liebfraumilch."

"I hope you like it," Beverly said.

"It happens to be one of my favorites."

"Darling, I smell the most incredible smells," Peter said. "You never did tell me what exotic delicacy you and Margaret have whipped up for dinner."

"I wanted it to be a surprise."

"If it's only half as delightful a surprise as the soup that preceded it, I will be enthralled," Tony said.

"It's a rather unusual dish," Beverly explained. "Unusual for us at any rate. Most of the time we eat very simply. Steaks, chops, a rib roast, that sort of thing. Peter claims he's too sated after those business lunches to have room in his stomach for anything rich. Some evenings he has a Ritz cracker with cottage cheese for dinner. Would you believe that?"

"Darling," Peter said, smiling, "don't give away all our domestic secrets, shall we? Some things should be held sacred." He tasted the wine. "I leave the final judgment to our eminent wine expert, Mr. Elliot."

Peter filled Beverly's glass and then Tony's.

"It's quite good," Tony said, raising his glass. "I propose a toast: to the consummation of unfulfilled desire."

"I'll drink to that," Peter said.

Beverly was sorry that she had had two martinis before dinner instead of one. A familiar throbbing above her left eye could mean only one thing—the onset of another migraine attack.

"Darling," Peter said to her, "aren't you going to join us in our toast?"

She touched her forehead lightly as though the pain could be whisked away by the merest, the most delicate finger pressure.

"In a moment. Please excuse me. I'm afraid I must take one of my pills. I feel a headache coming on."

Peter and Tony rose as she left the table to go up to the second floor where she kept her prescription bottle.

"I'm sorry you're feeling badly," Tony said.

"Terrible shame, darling."

"I'll only be a second," Beverly said. "Please drink your wine."

"She suffers terribly from those bloody headaches," Peter was saying to Tony as she left the room. Tony looked properly sympathetic.

Upstairs in her very own private bathroom Beverly swallowed two of the pills and prayed that they would work. Sometimes they warded off the attack altogether, but at other times they only effected a halfway cure. Her doctor could not explain the reason for that. "Medical science does not have the answer to everything," he was fond of saying. Beverly had her own hunches on the subject, most of which had to do with the strength of the anxiety that precipitated the attack, for she was convinced that anxiety was a catalytic agent in the migraine headache field, and (another hunch) that it was an anxiety which for one reason or another could not be openly accepted by the sufferer, an anxiety so painful that even the blinding migraine pain was preferable, if that could be believed. What was she anxious about? Certainly not that stupid Choucroute Garni, that was too ludicrous. No, it was Tony Elliot, something about those brilliant blue eyes, something . . . she could not squelch the thought, something fishy.

Margaret was bringing in the watercress salad with mustard vinaigrette dressing as Beverly returned to the dining room. The salad looked tempting, darkly green, refreshing. Perhaps the meal would be a great success after all. Perhaps one day Peter would love her as he used to. Perhaps she would stop getting migraine headaches. Perhaps Tony Elliot would turn out to be the dearest man in the world.

"Are you feeling better, darling?" Peter asked, as he held her chair.

"Yes. A bit." The nausea that accompanied these headaches had just begun to build up, it was a thick, acrid, terrible taste.

"The wine might help," Tony suggested. "It's a soothing wine, I've discovered. Please do try some."

"I feel so foolish spoiling our dinner like this. I feel so childish."

Childish, unwomanly, vulnerable. She remembered sobbing uncontrollably at the hospital the first time a nurse had shaved off her pubic hairs in preparation for childbirth. She had known of course that she would be shaved but the advance knowledge did not change anything, because suddenly when she looked down at herself she was eight years old and in her mother's clutches again, and the tears would not stop. In the weeks after Sally was born she cried every time she went to the bathroom and saw herself.

"That page-four replate missed the city editions yesterday," Peter was saying to Tony.

"I'm seriously considering changing printers," Tony said. "The half-tones have been so inexcusably bad that it's madness not to change. The question is, who to change *to?* But that's another subject and hardly appropriate at this point."

Margaret appeared once more in her white half-apron carrying a heaping platter of Choucroute Garni at a most precarious angle. For some reason that Beverly would never understand Margaret had managed to arrange the platter maniacally imbalanced: the pork butt and assorted sausages were all piled on one side leaning heavily downward, while the much less weighty sauerkraut sat on the other side breathing gin into the air.

Peter gave the dish his famous lowered-lid look. "Darling, what on earth *is* it?"

Between the combined Choucroute and migraine nausea, Beverly did not dare open her mouth to answer him for fear of vomiting, Margaret, playing the martyr, empathetically raised her eyes to the heavenly crystal chandeliers, thereby absolving herself of all responsibility for this *thing* that she had been forced against her better judgment to publicly present. The whites of her eyes against the black of her face made an interesting Franz Kline, Beverly thought, feeling very cultured as a result of having twice taken the Tuesday morning bus tour from Garden City to the gallery circuit in Manhattan for instant art appreciation.

Choking back waves of nausea, she said, "This happens to be a rather popular regional dish from Alsace . . ." at which point one of the Kosher frankfurters rolled off the imbalanced platter onto Tony Elliot's gracious, immaculate, pinstriped lap.

Had Anita Schuler known Beverly she would have envied her in spite of everything.

Had Beverly known she was considered enviable by a younger, more beautiful woman, she would have been surprised. "You don't know the half of it."

"Yes, but at least you're married."

"And I could say, at least you're free."

"Free for *what?*"

Free to be unhappy, not even Beverly's kind of unhappy, but unhappy in a vacuum, unhappy by herself, it was the worst, the most dismal kind of unhappy.

Anita had been in New York for two years and hopelessly in love with Jack Bailey for one of those years when she decided to give a party and invite the bastard (the vacuum was beginning to stretch, its yawns drove her crazy). A party was the only strategy she could think of, after months of hard thinking, that might result in close proximity to Jack once more because if she waited for him to resume their faded romance she might wait until the year two thousand.

She wondered why it had taken her so long to come up with the party maneuver. Her brain must have been pickled these last bleak months. A briny brain that had just begun to function again, to make a guest list, to plan the food she would serve, to approximate the number of bottles of liquor she would need for the number of people who might ultimately show up. It was only after she had plunged into the actual preparations that she started to realize what a convoluted business it all was.

Convoluted, she had rehearsed before the full-length mirror at the airline hotel in Madrid the very morning of the party: *rolled or wound together, one part upon another as leaves in a bud.*

When Anita began to invite people to the party last week a series of surprises awaited her, unpleasant surprises, unlikely surprises, unbelievable surprises. The telephone which she had always regarded as a compassionate lifeline to the outer world turned into a cruel and merciless instrument.

Surprise #1: "Hi, this is Anita. I'd like to invite you to a party I'm giving next Wednesday evening."

"Next Wednesday? Oh I'm sorry but Lewis and I are going to the theater. We have tickets for *Man of La Mancha*. I'm so thrilled, I can hardly wait."

"Why don't you drop by after the show? I'm sure the party will still be going strong."

"We'd love to but we're meeting some friends at Sardi's

for supper and then we're all going over to Arthur. I just adore Arthur, don't you?"

Surprise #2: "Hi, this is Anita Schuler. I'm giving a party next Wednesday evening. Do you think you can make it?"

"Anita Schuler?"

"I met you through Simone Lassitier. You took me to dinner at Le Moal. Remember?"

"Oh sure, the sexy airline stewardess. Honey, I appreciate the invitation but it just so happens that I'm getting married next Wednesday afternoon. In fact I'm a little bombed at the moment. The nervous groom, dig?"

Surprise #3: "Hi, this is Anita. I've decided to give a party next Wednesday and I was hoping you'd be able to come."

"Huh?"

"What's the matter? Did I wake you?"

"Yeah."

"I'm terribly sorry. Why don't I call you back in a couple of hours?"

"D'ac."

Surprise #4: "Hi, this is Anita Schuler. How would you like to come to a party I'm giving next Wednesday night?"

"Now isn't that rotten luck? I have to fly to Cleveland on Wednesday. Big convention and all that jazz. Wait a minim. You're from Cleveland, aren't you? I'll bet you know lots of cute girls there. How about doing an old lech a favor and fixing me up with a couple of hot telephone numbers?"

Surprise #5: "Hi, this is Anita Schuler. Can you come next Wednesday?"

"Not that it's any of your business but I can come any damn day of the week I feel like it. In fact I have been known to have multiple orgasms, and in the snappiest circles too."

"I'm sorry. I meant to say, can you come to my party next Wednesday?"

"Wednesday is a hell of a long way off. Why don't you give me all the dope and I'll try to make it. No promises. You never know what may turn up between now and then."

Surprise #6: "Hi, this is Anita. I hope I didn't get you at a bad time."

"As a matter of fact, you did. I have a long distance call on the other line. I'll call you back when I'm through."

Surprise #7: "Hi, this is Anita Schuler. How would you like to come to a little party I'm throwing next Wednesday night?"

"Do you expect to have enough men?"

"I certainly hope so."

"The last party I went to there were four women to every man. Four beautiful, ravishing women to every crummy shithead man. I've never felt so put down in my life. When you've finished inviting everyone, give me a ring and let me know how the total picture shapes up. I simply couldn't face another social catastrophe. My analyst says it's lousy for my ego."

Surprise #8: "Hi, this is Anita. Are you free next Wednesday evening? I'm giving a party, I think."

"You *think?*"

"Well it's so hard to line up people. Have you given a party recently?"

"What for? So a bunch of freeloaders can drink all my booze and put cigarettes out in my trailing ivy?"

"I don't have trailing ivy."

"They'll think of something else rotten to do. Count on it. Take a piece of advice from an old friend. Make sure you have a fire extinguisher handy. I'm not kidding. My new twenty-dollar-a-yard drapes once went up in a burst of flames thanks to some drunken pyromaniac."

"I appreciate your concern but you haven't said whether you can make it."

"Afraid not. Wednesdays are out for me. That's my AA night. Watch those cigs."

Surprise #9: "Hi, this is Anita Schuler. I'm throwing a big wonderful marvelous fascinating party next Wednesday night. How would you like to join the fun?"

"It sounds kind of noisy for my taste. You can't hear yourself think at those things, let alone talk. Now if you were having a small, *intime* affair with just a couple of close friends . . ."

Surprise #10: "Hi, this is Anita. I've decided to invite a couple of close friends over next Wednesday evening. Do you think you'll be able to join us?"

"Four days ago I would have jumped at the opportunity, but I've fallen in love since then. In love. Can you imagine? There's still a man in this rotten city you can fall in love *with?*"

"That's marvelous. Bring him along."

"Are you kidding? So some other girl can get her hands on him while I'm discussing Vietnam with her boring date? No thanks. This one, doll, I'm keeping under wraps until I see a three-carat ring on you know which finger."

It was absolutely unbelievable. Who could imagine that

someone trying to give a party in New York would run into so many peculiar roadblocks? In Cleveland if someone gave a party everybody who was invited and could walk came to it. They were only too happy to come, and why not? Free entertainment, free liquor, free food, free fun. They not only showed up, you usually couldn't get them to leave, you practically had to throw them out, and even then they called you for weeks afterward to tell you what a marvelous time they had had: "Hey, party girl, that *was* a dinger."

It was easy to give a party in your hometown. Everyone was rooting for you, they were on your side, they wanted you to succeed, to give a good party, a great party, a memorable party, because in a sense it was their party, too. They felt an almost civic kind of coresponsibility. When you gave a party in your hometown you were extending a warm, friendly, convivial invitation to your fellowman.

In New York you might as well be trying to sell poisoned peanuts for all the cooperation or enthusiasm you provoked. Had it not been for a sudden inspiration that came to Anita directly after surprise #10 she might have junked the whole venture, Jack Bailey or not, but it occurred to her at that point that perhaps her method of invitation was wrong, her telephone approach doomed to failure. Perhaps the thing to do was invite everyone by mail.

"Why didn't I think of that before?" she asked the two women in the Matisse print that hung over her convertible sofa. But they did not look up from their conversation; they went right on talking to each other against the backdrop of their Moorish screen.

The greeting card shop on Thirty-Ninth Street had a wide assortment of party invitations. Anita chose the one with cocktail glasses and bottles dancing in midair mainly because it had such a gay, giddy, self-confident quality about it, exactly the quality she wished to convey to her prospective guests.

"Two packs," the man at the cash register said. "Two dollars."

It came to a total of forty invitations. It was cheaper than telephoning people, it was less time consuming, it was certainly less humiliating. Anita also suspected that it would produce better results, since by mail you let people decide what they were going to do in their own good time as opposed to forcing a decision out of them on the telephone at a moment when their minds might be taken up with other matters.

At the bottom of the invitation she sent to Jack Bailey she

wrote, "Bring a girl if you like. Or come alone. But please do come."

On the flight back from Madrid Wednesday morning a passenger stole her cap and she decided that if Jack showed up with a girl she would poison the two of them on the spot. However, she doubted if he would. Men were funny about things like that. They rarely had the nerve to bring a new girl to an ex-girlfriend's party.

The flight that was supposed to land at JFK at nine-thirty was late, thanks to thirteen air traffic controllers who wanted their place in the sun along with the garbage collectors. By noon Anita was so nervous that she went out and bought a new antiperspirant guaranteed on the label to be "99.8% effective or your money back." She remembered the first time she had nearly ruined a brand new airline blouse with copious stains under the arms; it happened immediately after her initial meeting with Jack Bailey, captain of her flight to Cairo that day.

When she brought the blouse to her local cleaner, she said, "I don't understand it. I've never perspired heavily before."

"What's his name?" asked the cleaner with a smile-smirk.

"I'm afraid I don't know what you're talking about."

"No offense, Miss, it's just that when some people get all worked up . . ."

"It was an extremely hot day," she said, putting an end to the conversation. "That's all."

"Whatever you say, Miss."

How dare he presume? The indignity of it. Here she was still aglow with the memory of Jack Bailey's voice, the curve of his lip, those deep-set, enigmatic eyes (did women love any other kind?), the anticipation of what it would feel like to be embraced by those expansive shoulders, and this bald-headed cleaning man had the nerve to intrude upon her reveries by playing armchair psychologist with her. She wondered how many girls before her had felt as she did when they presented various bits of soiled clothing that spelled out their dark and intimate secrets.

From then on Anita had the cleaner send a boy to pick up and deliver all her wearables. Dealing directly with tradesmen had always struck her as an unpleasant business anyway and this experience clinched it. When she was married she would have servants to take care of such things for her. When she was married to Jack Bailey she would have servants and a walnut *poudreuse* in her bedroom . . . and she would not have to work any more.

Being a stewardess had lost most of its charm for Anita a long time ago. She once explained to a curious date, "The reasons for becoming a stewardess and the reasons for remaining one vary tremendously. At least they have in my case."

He was a young corporation lawyer who could not hang onto an erection for more than three seconds flat, and he asked her during dinner what the essential difference was.

"I became a stewardess because it seemed like a glamorous thing to do and also because I wanted to travel. I still want to travel but a lot of the glamour has worn off. When we work, we work hard and we work crazy irregular hours, particularly flying internationally as I do now, being up all night, sleeping in the morning, having to get dressed in the middle of the afternoon when I haven't had enough sleep, sleeping in a different bed in a different hotel in a different city, all of which could be great if the layovers were longer, but they aren't and we don't have time to explore a city or get to know any of the people or really do very much except maybe squeeze in a little shopping. Stewardesses are the greatest shoppers in the world."

He fed her a breakstick, and said, "Why do you stay with it? It doesn't sound as though you like it very much."

"I do and I don't. Before I became a stewardess I contemplated being a secretary in Cleveland but I didn't think I could stand a routine nine-to-five job. You know, seeing the same people every day, going to the same office, eating lunch at the same time with pretty much the same friends. Flying becomes an addiction after you've been at it a while. On the one hand you want to stop, yet you also realize that you've become accustomed to it as a way of life. You're *accustomed* to feeling tired. In fact, you're so accustomed to it that you don't even know how tired you are until you take a vacation and lead a regular life for a few weeks and suddenly you feel so good, so healthy, so energetic, so alive. I mean, most of the time we walk around either in a daze where nothing bothers us, or else we're all nervous and wound up, ready to snap at any second. When you shift constantly from one state to another, after a while you become a little anesthetized."

"It sounds awful."

"It's like being high."

"Is that why you're not drinking? Because you're high to begin with?"

"Something like that."

There was no point in telling him that she was still bloated from the flight and that drinking made her bloat all the more. She had gotten back from London only that morning and it would take until tomorrow morning at least before the bloating subsided. Nobody knew why the girls swelled up during flight, although Jack Bailey had told her the Air Force was doing a study on it. She wished they would hurry up with their conclusions and recommendations because the only thing worse than bloating was never knowing when to expect her period. She had long ago given up relying upon the traditional twenty-eight day cycle. It made no sense at all as far as she was concerned. Five days late, eleven days early, she never knew when the damn bloody thing was going to strike so she stopped trying to anticipate it. Every occupation had its hazards and if hers were more discomforting than most, they were also more unusual and therefore more exotic. Although Anita would not have admitted it to anyone, her greatest fear was being labeled commonplace and she did as much as she could, in every area that she could, to make certain she would never be stuck with that particular tag.

Her appearance, for instance.

Blond, blonder, blondest.

The airline that Anita worked for had finally, after months of bitter debate, issued a new regulation governing the color of its stewardesses' hair. They had decreed that if a girl wished to lighten or darken her natural hair color, three shades was the most she could go in either direction.

Upon hearing the good news several weeks ago Anita promptly set out for the Elizabeth Arden salon during a layover in Paris, and being a medium blond to begin with emerged several hours later a shimmering ash blond. If anything the extra blondness tended to soften the already soft contours of her face. It gave her a pale, luminescent glow which was reflected in her amber eyes, eyes that looked out upon the world of men with their very sure, very knowing, very female gaze that seemed to say, "Tell me now, how can I please you? What can I do? All you have to do is *tell* me."

Even as a child she had had the eyes of a woman. She remembered a small color photograph in the family album, which could not have been taken when she was more than seven or eight years old. In it she wore a dusty pink sweater and a matching dusty pink beret, and she was smiling beneath half-closed eyes. The first time her mother had shown the album to visiting relatives one of the men—a distant cousin—came out with a long wolf whistle and said,

"Jeepers creepers, where'd you get those peepers? Oh boy, is this kid going to be a knockout. Watch out, folks!"

Anita had always felt more grownup than the other girls of her age who seemed scarcely aware of their sex. She sometimes thought she had been born aware. She *liked* being a girl and was puzzled by her friends' tomboy pursuits and aspirations. At home her father kiddingly used to call her "little mother" because even at a young age she showed a marked maternal bent. Being the oldest of four children, she had a way of treating the others with a great deal of tender solicitude and concern, almost as if they were her children rather than her brother and sisters. Their mother was sick a great deal and this gave Anita a bona fide opportunity to exercise her maternal talents which she lost no time in taking advantage of. She loved dressing her younger brother and two sisters, feeding them, bathing them, kissing them, reading to them, even worrying over them. "She *fusses* too much," her brother Kurt once complained to their father. "I'm not a kid any more. Make her stop."

Everyone in the family just naturally assumed that Anita would be married at an early age. Her entire childhood, adolescence, and young womanhood seemed to point unequivocally in that direction. One only had to look at Anita to decide that she had been born for the express purpose of fulfilling the role of wife and mother. When questioned about her hopes and plans for the future, she would smile dreamily and say, "Oh of course I want to get married. When the right man comes along."

In high school she could have had the pick of the crop. She was by far the most popular and sought-after girl. All the other girls envied her. Boys poked each other when she went by in her pale yellow sweater and tweed skirt, her blond hair swinging casually above proud shoulders. She managed to become a cheer leader even though it took her longer than the other girls to learn the new steps, and she was often behind them in her timing. She won the role of pretty, seventeen-year-old Anya in the senior class presentation of *The Cherry Orchard* and gave an adequate if not inspired performance. She was chosen to be prom queen (her favorite role by far) and upon graduation was voted, "The girl who has everything in abundance: beauty, charm, wisdom. May she use her gifts well."

What gifts, she wondered? (At one time she had briefly contemplated becoming a nurse but instinct told her she did not have the stomach for blood and guts crudities.) She decided to get laid. She had held out up until that point because she wanted to be a virgin during her high school days. She did not know why; it just seemed important that she remain physically intact until she received her diploma. The lucky man was Terry Radomski, pitcher for the school baseball team, who had been after her since the summer before. One day that summer his family was up at the lake and they had spent an afternoon in his parents' bed, naked, and he had pleaded with her.

"Please, honey. I'll be gentle. It won't hurt as much as you think. You'll see."

She explained that it wasn't the pain she was worried about (which was not entirely true) but that she had to remain a virgin until graduation. He was rubbing a small button of flesh that she later came to identify as her clitoris, when she told him that.

"But that's not for another six months!" he shouted, abruptly removing his hand.

"I know," she said, "but that's the way it is."

"Are you nuts or something? I mean why in hell did you take off all your clothes if you didn't intend to go through with it?"

"I'm sorry if I misled you, but I just can't do it. I wouldn't feel right. Don't you understand? I just *can't*."

"Understand? I'll tell you what I understand. This."

He waved a very large erection right under her delicate nose.

"Do you see that? Well how do you think I feel at this point? If I weren't such a gentleman, I'd ram the damn thing right up your ass, you cunt."

Nobody had ever spoken to her like that before. His rage was frightening. His condemnation was even more frightening. She started to cry.

"Oh knock it off," he said, suddenly weary. "Put your clothes on. I'll take you home."

"I feel so terrible, I mean for your sake. I feel so bad about . . . *it*." She stole a quick, embarrassed glance at his still enlarged penis. "Isn't there anything I can do for you? Anything beside you-know-what?"

A slow smile erased the angry lines on Terry Radomski's lean seventeen-year-old face. "Now that you mention it, honey, it just so happens there is a little something you might consider. That is, if you're really worried about your Uncle Terry's well-being."

"Oh I am worried. Honestly I am."

"Take it in your mouth."

She was so startled that all she could say was, "What?"

"This."

"I don't—"

She never got to finish the sentence. She had never had a penis in her mouth before. It was a strange experience. She closed her eyes so she wouldn't have to see anything. That way it would almost be like a dream tomorrow, a slow, wavery, blurry, violet dream that didn't count at all, because it was a dream and dreams didn't count, they weren't real life, they were things you imagined and then forgot about because they were so unimportant, so insignificant, so meaningless, so essentially *dream*like, so senseless, so painless. Her mouth began to ache but she did not stop, she just kept right on going until she had anesthetized the ache and didn't feel anything, didn't hear anything except Terry's voice far away saying strange, soothing things in a strange, tense voice that didn't sound like Terry's voice at all, wasn't Terry, wasn't her, wasn't them, wasn't anyone or anything remotely recognizable. And then it happened. Very suddenly her mouth was full of it, full of some warm bitter liquid that had no place to go. She nearly gagged.

"Swallow it, honey. It's got vitamins."

She had a wild urge to spit the terrible stuff out on the floor, on the floor of his parents' bedroom where it would lie in an ignominious puddle until they came home from the lake, suntanned and healthy, and found this grim present from their darling son. Being fastidious, however, Anita swallowed it and smiled.

"Now that wasn't so bad, was it?" he asked.

She bravely shook her head. "No, it wasn't."

Oddly enough as soon as she had swallowed it she felt an overwhelming sense of satisfaction, almost of pride, as though she had just done something very original and clever. She wondered whether other girls did what she had done. She wondered whether they did it better. She wondered whether they swallowed it, too.

"You have unexpected talents," Terry said, ruffling her hair.

"Did you like it?"

"What do you think?"

He looked so happy, so peaceful, so pleased with her that she became very pleased too. "I'm glad," she said, smiling at him.

"You're a great little cocksucker."

It was not the first compliment Anita had received, but perhaps the most unusual. It was not the first act of service she had ever performed, but very definitely the most significant.

When Terry relieved her of her virginity six months later it was almost an anticlimax to preceding events. She bled less than she had expected. It hurt less than she had expected. She enjoyed it less than she had expected. In fact, everything about it was *less*. Less blood, less pain, less pleasure. Was this what the big mystery was all about? She could not believe it. Maybe something was wrong with her. But Terry said that she was doing just fine, that with some girls it took awhile before they warmed up to it or acquired a taste for it.

"It's like alcohol," he pointed out. "The first time you think you're going to puke but pretty soon it starts tasting good. At least that's the way some girls react to sex. It's different with men."

"Why?"

"I don't know. Men just like it right away," said the voice of authority. "They don't need a breaking in period."

"Maybe I'll never get broken in."

"We'll practice a lot. Everything's going to be all right. You'll see."

"Maybe I'm frigid."

"Just keep practicing these contraction things I told you about and leave everything else to your Uncle Terry. You don't pitch no hit, no run games without a lot of practice, honey. Remember that."

That was seven years and one month ago. Anita had never forgotten it. The evening of her party things went smoothly because she had practiced in advance exactly what she was going to do and in what order she was going to do it. Her chronological list of preparations looked like this:

- Distribute ashtrays and cigarettes throughout apartment
- Mix martinis and keep in orange juice bottle in refrig
- Mix Scotch sours and keep in grapefruit juice bottle in refrig
- Prepare hors d'oeuvres, cover with alum foil, keep in refrig
- Set hair and put in Norforms
- Sit under dryer while Norform dissolves (wear panties)
- Bathe breasts in cold water, then take hot shower
- Remove rollers from hair and put in diaphragm
- Put on body stocking

- Put on makeup and comb out hair (use new silver eye-shadow)
- Put on pink satin harem pajamas, luminescent pink & lavender earrings, pink vinyl mules
- Put records on hi-fi
- Man with ice cubes should deliver now
- Take hors d'oeuvres out of refrig and set on living-room table
- Drink martini and wait for first guest to arrive
- Try to keep heart from pounding every time doorbell rings and it might be Jack Bailey

Anita was getting a bit fed up with bathing her breasts in cold water, and sometimes she wondered whether the hydrotherapy treatment would ever work on her. She had been at it for nearly a month now and her breasts were still as small as when she had started, despite the theory that cold water was supposed to stimulate them and make them swell. At least that was what one of the women's magazines said.

Tonight she decided to try the superhydrotherapy treatment which she reserved for special occasions. This included throwing a handful of salt and a few ice cubes into the cold water. Salt was supposed to firm the breasts. Anita then dipped a terry towel into the freezing saline solution in her bathroom sink and bravely began to massage herself. As she massaged, shivering, she chanted, "One day I will have a cleavage, one day I will have a cleavage, one day I will have a cleavage, please God."

The hot shower immediately afterward was a merciful release.

At the diaphragm stage of her preparations, Anita fumbled a bit. Practice or not she would never get used to putting the damn thing in. If only she could take the pill like everyone else, she thought, but with her flying-bloating condition it was out of the question. She had tried the pill briefly, and although her breasts swelled to interesting proportions, so, unfortunately, did her stomach. It was like being doubly bloated, she looked as though she were in her fifth month, and she had no choice but to give up the pill. To make matters even more depressing, just recently her diaphragm size had gotten larger.

"I am promoting you," said the nearsighted gynecologist, moving her up from a Ramses 70 to a 75.

The diaphragm slipped off the plastic inserter and landed on her blue bathroom rug. She had to wash it, reapply the jelly, and try again. She succeeded the second time and remembered the good doctor's advice about feeling inside to make sure that it was in *right*. It always felt a little strange to be sticking her hand in such a delicate region, particularly with her Fabulous Fake fingernails, but what could a girl do? Well, the cavern was growing, no doubt about it. She would not be at all surprised if one day an entire Latin American army marched right in there and set up a junta government, not surprised in the least. And it was all Jack Bailey's fault, because even though she had not been to bed with him since he dumped her last October Anita felt certain that he was directly responsible for her unfortunate growth.

His penis was so big that the first time she saw it erect, she screamed. Jack thought she had lost her mind. She kept jabbering, "It will never go in, never never never." Guess what? It went in (and came out through her ear). The terrible thing was that after it was in, they couldn't move, they just lay there locked together like Siamese twins waiting for someone to come and sever whatever it was that people severed with Siamese twins. After attempting a few unsuccessful and scream-producing thrusts, Bailey said they would have to try a different position. He suggested that she lie down on her stomach.

"You're not going to do it to me in the . . ." She searched frantically for a discreet word. If he ever did that, she would have diarrhea for the next five months.

"No I'm not," Jack said. "Now lie down on your stomach like a good girl."

"Yes, Captain."

It turned out to be a pretty groovy position and not painful at all. She had never done it that way before, yet it seemed immediately obvious that a man would have to be on the large side to do it like that because otherwise it would never *reach*. The only unpleasant part was that she felt like a dog, but she quickly banished such thoughts from her mind. Also, she couldn't see Jack's face. There was something detached and impersonal, almost indecent, about doing it with your back to the man, and something exciting too. Anita had never felt so wonderfully degraded in her life.

For some reason Jack couldn't seem to come and he stopped. Then he started to kiss her on the stomach (she could not think of it as her *belly*, it seemed too disgusting), and before she knew what was happening his head was down between her thighs.

"That's dirty," she said with a self-conscious laugh.

"It sure is. Don't you stewardesses ever douche?"

"I use Bidinettes."

"That's only for the outside area. What about inside?"

"Well, I . . ."

"Oh shit. Didn't your mother tell you anything at all about feminine hygiene?"

The next day Anita asked another stewardess what she used and the girl recommended Norforms because they were easier and more pleasant than sticking a tube thing *up there.* When Anita reported this great germicidal discovery to Jack on their next date he said he would give her his opinion later on, after he had a chance to personally check out the effectiveness of the Norforms treatment. His verdict was encouraging. Apparently the little triangular suppositories really worked.

And yet she had lost him anyway. Just when they seemed to be getting along so well, he dropped out of sight. No explanation, no nothing. Silence. She caught glimpses of him at the airport from time to time and on two different occasions they worked the same flight together. He was friendly but distant. One of the other stewardesses told her that he was dating an English girl he had met in London.

"You know the type," the stewardess said. "With hair down to her ankles and her skirt up to her navel."

Anita wondered whether they sold Norforms in London. At that point she could have supplied the entire city with the contents from her medicine chest. It was bad enough that Jack Bailey had walked out on her just when she started to have orgasms with him, but he might have done it before she went to the expense of stocking up on a six months' supply of a girl's best pharmaceutical friend.

The man with the ice cubes had come and gone, and Anita had reached the martini stage of her list when the downstairs doorbell rang. It was ten to eight, early even for an anxious party goer, since her invitations that clearly specified "after eight." As she pressed the buzzer she proceeded automatically to the last item on her list: try to keep heart from pounding. She tried but to no avail. A man's step could plainly be heard coming out of the elevator and down the hall in the direction of her apartment. She had checked with Crew Sked when she first started to plan the party last week, and they told her that Jack was due back in New York at six-thirty tonight which meant it could conceivably be him if he had decided to come directly from the airport. Assuming he could. Nobody came directly from the airport anymore. It was impossible thanks to the lunacy that was taking place in all those control towers.

"Please, God, let it be him," she silently prayed.

She opened the door to a man she had never laid eyes on in her life. He was about five foot eleven and quite attractive, with very dark hair and a dazzling smile. He wore a navy blazer, navy and white striped tie, gray skinny trousers, and no coat despite the thirteen degree weather.

"You must be Anita Schuler," he said, glancing at her breasts which still quivered slightly from all that hydrotherapy business. "Am I early?"

"Yes," she said. "A little."

"My watch has been running fast."

"I'm a bit confused," she admitted. "I don't believe I know you."

"And I'm a bit embarrassed. You see, I'm a neighbor of Jack Bailey, I have the apartment above him, and Jack happened to tell me about the party. He said he was pretty sure you wouldn't mind having an extra man. You don't mind, do you?"

"Oh no. No. Not at all."

He seemed visibly relieved. "That's good because I'm not in the habit of going around crashing parties. Really I'm not."

"I'm sure you're not." His obvious shyness was engaging. "Isn't Jack planning to come?"

"Oh sure. He'll be along later." The man smiled again. "He thought I might keep you company in the meantime."

Then he handed her the paper bag he had been holding. It contained an expensive bottle of Scotch, lavishly gift wrapped.

"Thank you," she said. "Please come in. I've been sitting here by myself sipping a martini, waiting for the others to arrive."

Her heart was pounding no more. It rested within her, strangely still. Jack Bailey would soon be there, in the same room with her, close to her, ecstatically close. She felt infinitely grateful to this shy stranger for bringing her such marvelous news.

"Something tells me that I haven't properly introduced myself," he said, following her into the apartment. "My name is Robert Fingerhood."

She held out her hand. "Hello, Robert Fingerhood. And welcome."

A light flickered briefly in his dark eyes, a gleam that hinted at another side of his nature, assertive, insistent, not contradictory but complementary to his modest façade. Cat and mouse, she thought, not knowing why. He shook her hand.

"Did anyone ever tell you that you're an exceptionally beautiful girl?"

At ten to eight Wednesday evening, Lou Marron was seated at her desk in the living room of her East Seventies garden apartment. She was wearing an art nouveau pullover and a pair of tight lavender stretch pants, and was feeling very square and out of it. Even her abbreviated Sassoon cut was becoming (if it had not already become) quite Coney Island, which meant she would have to do something about her hair and *fast*.

Any minute now Tony Elliot would take her aside and looking at her with those psychedelic blue eyes of his would say, "It was terribly nice at first, so clean and geometric, but perhaps now it's just a wee bit Coney Island. Perhaps, Lou, you should try something a little more *marrant*. We can't have you going around with an outdated head. After all, you are our star female reporter."

"Am I really?" she would say. "I thought Peter Northrop is."

Is? Or was?

For Peter had been Tony Elliot's darling of all possible darlings on *The Rag,* his very own special assignment boy, his slave and undoubtedly his tormentor (could anybody be one and not the other? Lou suspected not). She hated Peter Northrop with a passion verging on lunacy, she had dreams of killing him, long glistening knives danced in her dreams before making their final, fatal plunge into his incredibly lean middle. Lou had an X-ray eye and could see through clothes, could see through Brooks suits to absolutely spare stomachs with not an extra ounce of flesh on them. At times she was convinced that Peter wore a panty girdle. It would have rosebuds on it and dainty blue-for-boy leaves. But then she knew she was being even more crazily vicious than necessary, since there was no reason in the world why a young man of thirty-two had to be paunchy, was there?

David Swern was paunchy, but David was fifty-six, old enough to be Peter's father, her father. David was sweet. She loved him. Loved. Hated. How simple-minded she was. Or was that life? Passion could be so easily diverted from channel to channel and Lou had been diverting it since she was born. She often wondered what it would be like to have a low-keyed, tranquil kind of personality and outlook, she could not even conceive of what it would feel like, how one would feel upon awakening at, say, eight in the morning like a sane person and having a sane cup of coffee, even saner piece of toast, instead of pole-vaulting out of bed at 3 A.M. to drink pink Pierre Marcel champagne (NYS), which she bought chilled in tiny five-ounce bottles, and to watch 1935 movies with Constance Bennett while her cat aptly named Mr. Crazy raced and howled throughout the apartment and tried to eat the goldfish who had no name at all, and as a consequence only a very tenuous identity. She kept the goldfish in an oversized brandy snifter which sat on the top shelf of her bookcase. Mr. Crazy sharpened his nails on one side of the bookcase, inasmuch as most of the furniture in the living room was of the plastic, see-through variety (Lou had inflated it with her vacuum cleaner). When Mr. Crazy was really bad his name was changed to Mr. Lunatic Asylum. He knew that when Lou called him Mr. Lunatic Asylum he was in serious trouble, but did that stop the beast? Only made him worse. That was why Lou liked him: he had plenty of nerve and was a born rebel. She identified with Mr. L. A.

Once David said to her: "The cat is in love with you."

She laughed but it was true. The cat was jealous of her, jealous of any man who visited her, but not jealous of women.

"How can he tell when it's a woman?" David wanted to know.

"He has eyes."

"But how does he know the difference? What if a woman came in wearing slacks? Would he think it was a man?"

"Or you could put on a dress," Lou said, laughing, "and we'll make the transvestite test. Want to?"

David wouldn't, he said he didn't care that much and besides he'd feel like a fool trying to get into one of her skimpy dresses. All the seams would burst. Lou controlled herself from saying that if he were really a sport he would wear one of his wife's half-size *shmattes*. She controlled herself because, as with the Peter Northrop panty-girdle fantasy, she was being just plain vicious. Mrs. Swern was probably an attractive woman who ate cottage cheese platters at Schrafft's and dressed intelligently in dark, simple, unfat clothes, with lots of corset things to keep her together. And really what was so terrible about that? After all, Mrs. Swern was in her fifties but then so were Marlene Dietrich and Loretta Young etcetera. It was a subject that fascinated Lou. Aging. One's physical concept of oneself. Lou had long ago decided that she would never grow old, meaning not old-old.

"And why is that?" David had asked her, amused.

"Because I'm busy playing *Daddy's Little Girl* all week long, every week of the year, on The Million Dollar Movie, that's why, sweetheart."

"You're only twenty-seven," he said. "In ten years you'll think differently."

"No I won't. I refuse to grow up. It would spoil my act."

"Don't grow up," David said. "I love you the way you are."

"Do you really?"

"Really."

"Serioso?"

"Serioso."

"Why?"

He sighed. "Why do you always ask me *why?*"

"Because I haven't grow up. Da-da."

That Da-da business tickled David. She had called him that from the start because otherwise he would have begun to get Middle of the Night, Fredric March anxieties and spend hours in boring Freudian thoughts about her childlike dependency upon a dirty old man. This way at least the thing was out in the open and they could be funny about it. Lou felt that she did not have the time nor the energy to harbor underground guilts. Just cough them up and to hell with it. They would all be pushing up daisies soon anyway. That was the ironic part. Even if she didn't have her aging anxiety she was going to die young thanks to the fact that Red China would eventually obliterate the decadent Western world. As a result of mass obliteration fear, the decadent Western world had become even more decadent. Boys turned into girls before revolutions and vice-versa. Why, if it weren't for Red China *The Rag* wouldn't exist. Some day when she was more professionally secure (as the germ warfare commandant) she must be sure to tell that to Tony Elliot, who had voted for Goldwater.

She would say, "You're netting two million a year thanks to those Chinese restaurant Communists you're so militant about and you're so dumb, kiddo, that you don't even know it."

The time would come when she would spit into Tony Elliot's psychedelic eye and laugh. When she told that to David he said there was a great deal of hostility in her.

"I know," she answered, "but don't automatically jump to paranoia conclusions. I mean, some days they *are* all after you."

She did not know who she hated more: Peter Northrop or Tony Elliot, but she suspected that Peter was a shade ahead mainly because he was smarter and therefore more dangerous than Tony, who relied heavily upon advisers. On the other hand, Tony was smart enough to know which advisers to rely upon. That was something. If he gave her the column (THE COLUMN! IT WAS LIKE SEX! IT WAS BETTER THAN SEX!), she would forgive him everything, the dear sweet man. She would take it all back. She would light a candle at St. Peter's. She would repent. She would kiss Tony Elliot's funny little feet and tell him how absolutely marvelous and brilliant he was (the filthy fascist), how she had always admired him, how she had always adored working for him, even when he made her do the obituaries and all the p.r. rewrites. If he gave Peter Northrop the column . . . no, she refused to think about it. If that happened she would be pole-vaulting out of bed almost before she got in and *feeding* the goldfish to Mr. Lunatic Asylum, who would not have been Mr. Crazy for weeks, the poor vicariously demented animal.

Office gossip had it that Tony was going to announce his column decision very shortly. Office gossip was only fifty-fifty reliable, however. One never knew what to believe. Lou remembered the last rumor: Tony Elliot was selling his stock and getting rid of *The Rag*. The bathrooms at the office did a landslide business when that one was floating around. Employees were so nervous they were coming to work at eight in the morning to make sure that the building was still there, not to mention their desks. It was sheer, unadulterated panic. The reporter who covered the fur market, Lou's old stamping grounds, got so frantic one afternoon that he ran into the ladies' room instead of the men's room. He told Lou later that it wasn't even a mistake. It was just that the men's room was too far away and he had weak sphincter muscles. Luckily only a switchboard operator in her bedroom slippers and a nitwit from circulation happened to be in there at the moment or he would have been a little embarrassed. Everybody gave him funny looks after that but he said what the hell did he care? It was better than crapping in the middle of the news floor right next to the teletype machine, wasn't it? Lou said she supposed so but she tried to stay away from him from then on.

The rumor of Tony selling out continued to persist with all sorts of weird variations, such as Peter Northrop was buying *The Rag* with his Brookline money and would shortly fire his enemies, of whom he had many. Lou didn't sleep for two weeks when that one was circulating and the goldfish lived a precarious minute-to-minute life. When that particular version died down, somebody on the city desk said he heard that Tony Elliot was going to move *The Rag* to Pennslyvania to get away from the New York union problems and that anybody who wanted to move to Pennsylvania was by all means welcome to come along. Employees who had just bought homes or put a lot of money into snazzy apartment decorations were seen staring longingly out the office windows onto the Lexington Avenue pavement, stories below. The dining-out editor who was a built-in furniture fanatic slept at his desk on top of the copy paper and even ordered an electric percolator from Macy's so he wouldn't have to call down for coffee for fear his voice would break on the telephone.

And then nothing happened. It all just died down and crept away, leaving nothing behind except a publishing company of twitching maniacs. That was why Lou did not know whether to believe the current rumor about Tony Elliot making his column decision *very shortly*. Some days she believed it and some days she didn't, which was probably the worst reaction of all, because as a result of the horrendous uncertainty she had started to throw up every morning. She had not thrown up since she was a child and had to go to school, which she loathed. She had known then that she was throwing up in anticipation of school (William Cullen Bryant grade school in Philadelphia, the same school her daughter was going to now) because she never threw up on weekends. And now it was starting all over again. Regressionarini. Actually, she felt pretty good after the vomit, purged and clear-eyed, ready for nameless catastrophes. Still it was revolting to see last evening's dinner sitting in the toilet bowl, the courses all mixed up. Lou tried not to look. Scope helped.

But the reason Lou was feeling so square and out of it (at the very moment that Anita was welcoming shy Robert Fingerhood to her party) was because of the difficulty she was having in putting down that afternoon's interview on paper. Being the lingerie editor, most of the time she was confined to writing about single-wired brassieres and the newest spandex girdles, but every once in a while Tony Elliot got bighearted and let her do feature stuff with a by-line. She religiously clipped and saved her articles in a professional-type brochure, which she looked at when she was depressed and needed her ego bolstered.

Lou needed her ego bolstered this very minute because the person she had interviewed that afternoon was a painter named Steve Omaha and she really did not understand anything about painters. They frightened her in a way. Their frame of reference was completely alien to her, but Tony Elliot had a big thing about painters, whom he felt were very significant influences in the world of haute couture (St. Laurent doing the Mondrian-mother bit a few seasons back, as one not so slight example), and besides painting was so very *in* these days, American painting in particular. After years of taking a back seat to the venerable Paris school, de Kooning and Pollock had finally broken through the French *snobisme* and brought American painters into the limelight in the early Fifties.

"It destroyed a lot of American painters," Tony told her one day when he was expounding on his painter-fashion hangup, in his roving expounding manner, which was a direct thumb in the nose at sequitur thinking, let alone speech. "The reason it destroyed them—and I'm talking about a guy who was born around 1920—is because when he signed up to be a shmeerer he also signed up to be a loser. Financially speaking. So it attracted a lot of visually oriented masochists in this country. Then Pollock and de Kooning pulled the rug out from under them. My God, the masochists thought, I might be rich! Famous! Me!! Little old nothing me. How can I stand it? I must have my failure. I *demand* my failure. What happened is that the stronger personalities persevered and the weaker ones died like flies. That is, their painting became so horrible that nobody with half a head would show it. You see the deviousness of all this? When suddenly some of these poor American bastards realized that they were painting FOR MONEY it completely shattered all their corny languishing-in-a-garret copouts. The new generation of painters are something else. When they sign up for *la vie bohème* they know damn well that there's a good chance of making it in a very caviar world. Pollock died for the minimal art boys. That's what it amounts to."

Which made Lou more confused than ever because she just was sort of not interested in painters, although she knew she should be since it was obviously *the* thing to be. Tony Elliot was a good barometer of *the* thing to be. She tried to hide her ignorance from him, as well as her basic disinterest in a subject that eluded her: art. Lou liked to be able to put her finger on things, to be able to dissect and evaluate, and there was nothing she could put her finger on with any degree of confidence in the New York art world, which was international anyway.

She would much rather have been sent to interview the owner of a new London boutique, or a mad-eyed movie star, in fact anybody seemed preferable to Steve Omaha who turned out to have a great bushy black moustache, a mod suit, and a very internal way of talking. Painters, she had discovered even with her limited experience, did that. They completely dispensed with phatic conversation, which, for a reporter, was a damned helpful thing. It saved oodles of time. They got right down to whatever happened to be on their minds at the moment.

Somebody named General Budenny (pronounced Boo-doh-nyi) was very much on Steve Omaha's mind that afternoon when Lou visited him at his loft in the flower district. Cavanaugh, *The Rag*'s star photographer, accompanied her on the mission. Cav liked painters. He said they had élan. Lou liked Cav because Cav hated Tony Elliot but was so clever at dissimulation that Tony thought Cav loved him. *The Rag* was just one big pool of insidious intrigue, but then Lou suspected that most offices were. Offices were sexy for that reason. All that muted tension floating around.

"General Budenny was the general in command of the Red Cossack Cavalry Division during the Russian Revolution. In 1918 he was made commander of the Soviet Army." Steve Omaha seemed to think this over. "After 1918 there was a lag, a time lag. I saw pictures of him at the library. He was shown at the race track in Moscow with his family. His wife was pretty elegant, you know. In 1941 he was appointed Marshal of the Soviet Union in command of the Southern Front. There were three prominent marshals who at that time stopped the Nazi offensive and he was one of the leading geniuses in the Soviet hierarchy. He was the most brilliant soldier in the Soviet Union, and that's the last I heard of him."

Lou and Cav looked at each other. Steve Omaha caught the look.

"You're wondering what I'm getting at. Well, here's the whole point. I was told by two authorities in the field that I absolutely without a doubt resemble General Budenny. Do you understand the signifcance?"

Cav took a shot of Steve Omaha standing in front of an

immense triptych of Humphrey Bogart, Mary Astor, and Sidney Greenstreet all mounted on cavalry horses, smoking Tiparillos.

"Is this a recent painting?" Lou asked.

"Yes. Do you like it? Some days I like it and some days I wonder. But here's the thing about General Budenny. If I identify with him because of the close resemblance, then instead of being a downtrodden painter I'm suddenly a general in command of a cavalry division, leading armies into battle and things like that."

Steve Omaha looked at the triptych. "Maybe I should have made them Lucky Strikes. What do you think?"

Cav took a shot of Steve Omaha looking perplexed in his mod suit.

"I'm leading armies, you understand," Steve Omaha said. "I lead them to Riker's in the morning." He laughed for the first time. "No, I lead them to the *paintings*, my paintings. That's what I do. You see there is definitely an identification that takes place when you are told you resemble someone absolutely, I think it's Walter Mittyism in a way. Besides I would rather resemble General Budenny than my father who was a junk dealer. My grandfather, though, was a different kettle of fish, he was a sergeant in the Russian cavalry. He preceded General Budenny. I'M IN LOVE WITH GENERAL BUDENNY! He was a Red Russian, he must have come from fairly humble origins himself even though he rode. I used to ride even before I found out about General Budenny."

"How would you describe your painting?" Lou asked.

"Why describe it when you're looking right at it?"

"Is it Pop? I thought Pop was dead."

"No, it's not Pop. It's a different thing. Actually it goes back to David. Dahveeeeeed. Do you like all those *Art News* explanations about influences and traditions? I don't like them. They bore the shit out of me."

"Do you feel an affinity with General Budenny because you both come from humble origins?"

"Yes, but I was never a general, I was in the infantry, I was a Pfc. in the war. I'm forty-three. Do I look forty-three?"

He looked at himself carefully in a cracked mirror that hung over the refrigerator. "I think I look pretty good for forty-three but who knows? We're all so vain. I was in the D-Day invasion. I remember coming across the Channel, I remember how incredibly seasick I was, all that pitching and rolling. You would think we would have been scared out of our minds approaching enemy-held territory but we made jokes, even I was making jokes as lousy as I felt. We talked about all the girls we were going to screw when we got to Paris and were heroes. One of the guys had even managed to get hold of a pair of nylons for the first French sweetie he screwed. Can you imagine? Here we are about to take part in the greatest invasion of all time and this nut is carrying a pair of nylon stockings in his pocket. Five minutes later he was dead. I saw him fall down in the water, face down. The waves broke over him. You know what I did? It's crazy because the noise from shells or mortar bombs, I don't know which, but the noise was unbelievable, I'm standing practically up to my neck in water and I took the nylons out of this poor dead bastard's pocket and that's how I landed on the beach. That's how I happened to pick out the name Omaha for myself. That's where we landed, Bloody Omaha. I wish I had known about General Budenny then, but it's too late to change now. I've got a bit of a reputation. Maybe I could call myself Steve Omaha Budenny. Does that make sense?"

"Yes I think so." She had only the vaguest idea what he was raving about, but when she played back the tape later that evening she might be able to make sense out of it. She certainly hoped so.

"Is it true," Lou asked, "that you're going to have a show at Leo Castelli's very soon?"

"It's not definite. Maybe I'll have a show at Goldowski's. Maybe Janis. I'm going to make a big scene. That's what I'm holding out for. A *succès fou.* Here's how I started out today. First I drank two Bloody Marys, that was a mistake. Then I went and talked to Martha Jackson. Martha might give me a show. I've been highly recommended to her. Then I went to see the ladies at the Park East Synagogue, I have a couple of paintings hanging there. Oh they're so sweet, the Rabbi's wife. Then I went to a friend's opening and saw everybody I knew. That was pretty depressing."

"Who are your favorite painters?" Lou asked.

"I used to like Cézanne, but I got over that. It changes you know. Your influences change. I'm very big these days on David. Dahveeeeed. Do you know his work?"

"No, I'm afraid not."

"He painted Marat in the bathtub and did a sketch of Marie Antoninette on her way to the guillotine."

"What do you like about his work?"

"There's a grandeur about it. He had plenty of guts. He

was a big despot during the Reign of Terror after the Revolution. They couldn't cut off enough heads for Dahveeeeed. Actually when you get right down to it, he was a monster."

Cav was having a good time with the Sonja Henie painting. Steve Omaha had painted her twirling on black ice, wearing a Russian Cavalry uniform. The name Budenny ran across the painting in a thin wavery black script.

"Sonja Henie likes Budenny too," Steve Omaha said. "Have you noticed? They go to Riker's a lot. I know the manager."

So that now, five hours after the screwball interview, was it any wonder, Lou wondered, that she was having a difficult time writing the piece? She envied Cav. All he had to do was go back to the office and develop the pictures, then select the ones he thought most suitable. Her process of selection seemed infinitely more torturous. When she had asked Steve Omaha what he thought about mini-skirts he said, "I like them very much. I really like them on girls with big fat legs. I think that's sexy. I like girls with big fat legs. There's nothing like it when a girl with big fat legs wraps them around you. It's like being in heaven. You're very pretty but your legs are so slender."

"Actually, they're not," Lou started to say. Her legs, being slightly on the heavy side, were her one major physical embarrassment.

But Steve Omaha paid no attention to the interruption. "Everybody wants to be slender these days. I might lose ten pounds myself. And here's another thing about mini-skirts. Which came first—the pill or the miniskirt? Think about that."

In addition to Lou's writing problem, there was a time problem. She was supposed to have dinner this evening with David, *her* David, and he said he would call her at eight. It was nearly eight now and the particular slant of the Steve Omaha piece still eluded her. How could she tie in Omaha with fashion? Too bad he was a Russian. The Russian influence was already well under way as a result of the *Zhivago* movie. It would hardly be original to capitalize on that. Of course she could always use Steve Omaha's obsession with General Budenny as one more emphatic manifestation of the current Russian influence on fashion but that seemed not too brilliant an idea. Why the hell wasn't Omaha a Cherokee Indian or an ex-Australian sheepherder? Where did Tony Elliot find these people anyway? The terrible part was that she absolutely had to write something sharp because everything she wrote these days (and feature material most of all) would prove or not prove to Tony how right she was for the column.

The column! Lou became sexually steamed up just thinking of it. She wished David were a better lover but tonight almost anyone would do, not really, that was an exaggeration, but when she became column-aroused she simply had to make love. She would insist that they make love before going out to dinner, in fact screw dinner. The minute he walked in the door she would open his fly, that should get her message across fast. What if he couldn't get an erection? She would go down on him until he did. She didn't much mind going down on David because his penis was not too big and neither was her mouth. A dentist had once kidded her about it, suggested that she use a child's toothbrush to reach the back molars, smirk smirk. Men with large penises thought she was a washout in the going down department and they were right because even though her intent was good she could not sustain it, and then sometimes she inadvertently bit them. It wasn't her fault. Her teeth got in the way. Besides, it was not her favorite form of sex activity by a long shot. She merely did it as an accommodation. It sure turned the bastards on, though.

As for that sixty-nine business, that was even worse, that was strictly for the birds. She told someone once: "I have never been fond of cooperative endeavors." When you were both chewing each other up at the same time, there was too much to concentrate upon, energies were too dispersed. And you couldn't tell what the other person's reaction was to what you were doing because he was so far away, so incommunicado, so you just went on in a vacuum hoping that things were working out okay. Who could come in that uncomfortable position anyhow? It was so awkward until you got everything adjusted right and everything had to be so right, bodies at precise angles, it was like plane geometry, one degree off and the whole exercise was a big fiasco. It was dopey, that sixty-nine stuff, juvenile; she had contempt for men who really went for it.

No, the thing to do was FUCK. Column-fucking. If David ever knew some of the thoughts she had when they made love he would surely be discouraged. Here the poor man probably figured that all kinds of unspeakable images were flashing across her depraved brain, when in reality she was envisioning her column on page four of *The Rag. Lou's*

Lulus. Tony Elliot himself had suggested the title. To torture her, of course, to make her think she stood a better than even chance of landing the plum. She wondered what title he had suggested to Peter. *Peter's Peckers?*

"Mr. Crazy is on the immediate verge of becoming Mr. Lunatic Asylum," she told the cat, "unless he stops this madness."

Mr. Crazy hated it when Lou sat down at her desk to write because he knew that the degree to which he was being ignored was far more absolute than when she was immersed in any other kind of activity. When she sat down at her desk to write, Mr. Crazy tried to sit on top of the typewriter so that she couldn't work. Or he would race around the room and knock things over to distract her. He was ingenious. At the moment he was trying to devour the goldfish.

"Mr. Crazy isn't a real person," she called out. "Cats aren't real people. Only people are real people."

He responded to the inflection in her voice. He knew when he was about to become Mr. Lunatic Asylum. It wouldn't be tonight though, because just then she got up from her desk to go into the kitchen to see what time it was. When she saw that it was a quarter after eight she sat down on the see-through plastic armchair, not the desk chair. The fact that David still had not called was unusual as he was easily the most punctual man she had ever known. She was very punctual, too, and it happened to be a quality she appreciated in people. She did not understand men who said they would call you at eight but never really meant it, they meant they would call *around* eight or maybe nine or maybe not at all. That was why Lou was so grateful to have David, even if he wasn't the most proficient lover on the island of Manhattan. They had been together for almost two years now and she had become increasingly grateful to him during that time, grateful for his being there, for being reliable, for being so kind.

Everybody at the office knew about her and David, and Peter Northrop once asked her whether she didn't find it anxiety-causing to be involved with a married man.

"On the contrary," she said. "Because at least with a married man you know where he is when he's not with you. He's with his wife. It's simple. But a single man could be anywhere, with any one of a number of wild mini-skirters."

"That's an angle," Peter admitted.

"Married men treat you better, too."

He gave her brand new Kohinoor mink a significant look. "So I see."

"I don't just mean gifts. I mean in general."

And then she said no more about it, she would never say any more to Peter Northrop about David's generosity because the mink coat was a pebble in a pond compared to the fact that David gave her money every month for her daughter Joan, who lived with Lou's parents in West Philadelphia, who thought Lou's parents were her real parents, who thought Lou was her older, glamorous sister with a big New York career job. David gave her one hundred dollars a month, which Lou's parents gratefully accepted, asking no questions. They imagined that she made a great deal more money than she actually did, because she told them that she did. *The Rag* was not exactly famous for paying exorbitant salaries but how could her parents know that? They had fanciful and unrealistic notions about the salary level of a roving reporter and Lou let them hang on to those notions. Her father would be shocked if he ever found out that she was having an affair with a married man three years his senior, shocked and disbelieving.

Lou's parents' naïveté was a convenient thing for her. She knew how their minds worked in this matter, or at least she was pretty certain that she knew: after giving birth to an illegitimate child at the age of seventeen she had bitterly renounced the world of men and turned all her energies toward a journalistic career, work, work, and more work was what they imagined their repentant daughter's life to be. In a sense they weren't far from wrong, but neither were they one hundred percent right for there still was David Swern to take into consideration. Dear David. She relied upon him so and never more so than recently, what with this persistent nagging column decision still hanging in midair, driving her and Mr. Crazy crazy. The only person she could talk to about it freely, openly, was David. He was the only one who understood, who sympathized with her anxieties, who was totally on her side, who believed in her, who would make love to her shortly and not go out to dinner if that was what she wanted.

It was almost a quarter to nine when the telephone rang.

"Lillian was taken ill," David said, his voice harassed. "That's why I haven't called before. She got another one of those attacks and I had to stay with her until the doctor arrived. He's with her now."

"Is it very serious?" Lou asked.

"I don't know, baby. I won't know until I talk to the doctor."

"Oh, David, I'm so sorry."

"So am I. Sorry about everything. Lillian, of course, and sorry that I won't be able to see you tonight. I was looking forward to it."

"I was, too."

"Did you have a good day?" he asked.

"No. I had a terrible day." And she was about to have a terrible night. Maybe she would call up someone, but *who?*

"I have to go now," David said. "I hear the doctor coming out. I'll speak to you tomorrow. If she's better, maybe we can meet for lunch. I have something for you."

"What?"

"Wait until tomorrow."

"David . . . please try not to worry too much. She's had these attacks before. I'm sure she'll be all right."

"I hope so."

"Please don't worry."

"I won't."

"David?"

"Yes?"

"I love you."

"I love you, too, baby."

"Okay," Lou said, "I'll speak to you tomorrow and remember that I have my fingers crossed about Lillian."

"You're a sweet kid."

"Goodnight."

"Goodnight," David said.

Lou looked down at her lavender stretch pants and art nouveau pullover, she looked at the typewriter on the desk with the blank piece of paper in it, she looked at Mr. Crazy, who looked back at her knowing that something was up. His antenna told him that desertion was imminent.

"You're right, Mr. Crazy," Lou said.

She would change into her silver lace micro-mini over the Rudi Gernreich slip, throw on her Kohinoor mink, and scoot down to Elaine's to see what the action was. It was no fun being column-aroused without a man to put out the fire, no fun at all, particularly when she had still to get a line on the Steve Omaha piece. Records helped. She chose one by The Electric Prunes and began to play it on the Magnavox that David had given her last Christmas. As she slipped out of the lavender pants she did a fast frug in her Van Raalte bikini briefs.

"I've got a hot date with General Budenny at Elaine's," she told Mr. Crazy, who had begun to race and howl at the top of his lungs, at last on his way to very definitely becoming Mr. Lunatic Asylum for the rest of his deserted evening.

❁ CHAPTER TWO ❁

The two girls delicately kissed each other on the cheek, careful not to disturb their respective makeup.

"Rima, The Bird Girl," Anita Schuler said.

"Miss Norforms," Simone Lassitier said.

They smiled. They laughed at their old funny-bitchy nicknames for each other. When they had been roommates six months ago they had barely been able to put up with each other, but now they were no longer apartment involved they felt a mutual generosity of spirit, a loving nostalgia, a tenderness that had previously been lacking. It seemed to Simone that Anita in her pink satin harem pajamas, pink and lavender earrings, and pink vinyl mules looked more beautiful than the last time she had seen her, the luminescent glow which had always been there was even more pronounced now, even more madonnalike was her inward fire, and Simone concluded that it could only be love.

On the other hand, Anita was a Cancer and Cancers were forever walking around with that dreamy, saint expression on their faces as though they had just spotted another vision of God on some remote and deserted hillside. Kneeling in submissive ecstasy. That was Simone's impression of the Cancer personality, a personality that she very frankly felt a bit contemptuous of. All those water signs (Cancer, Pisces, Scorpio) aroused her contempt because she, as a Libra, was air, lofty, above it all, soaring in the stratosphere, not kneeling on a lowly hillside. Then Simone realized that she was being bitchy and being bitchy was definitely not supposed to be a characteristic of Libra, the scales, the balance, the great lover of peace and harmony.

"I love peace and harmony," Simone said to herself, wondering just how much there was to this astrology business after all, wondering whether if she had her horoscope charted it would not turn out that she had Aries in the ascendancy which would allow her to be as bitchy as she liked.

"I was afraid you'd never get here," Anita said to her.

"I didn't mean to be late, but you know how terrified I am of arriving first."

"Don't worry about that. Practically everyone I've invited has already shown up. Everyone, that is, except Jack."

"Jack who?"

Simone followed Anita through the crowded and noisy living room of weaving couples. The dancing was spirited, Chagall dancing, flying, girls were dancing in turquoise body shirts and orange bubble skirts, in swingy tents, in art nouveau paper shifts, in hot pink mini-zip shifts, in fur and vinyl jumpsuits, in see-through, no-bra midis, in little sweater dresses and up to the little girl knee stockings, in fabulous gold burnooses, emerald lounging pajamas, in silver cutout suits, in white mink bunny bonnets, in . . . and into Anita's tiny bedroom off the hallway for coat depositing and gossip.

"Jack Bailey, of course," Anita said.

Oh, God, was Simone's reaction, is she still hung up on *him?*

"I thought that was all over," she said as discreetly as possible.

"Well it is all over, but . . ."

Anita firmly closed the door to the bedroom, closing out the party sounds, and taking Simone's guanaco coat, laid it carefully on top of the tall pile of coats on the double bed. Simone noted that the same chenille chartreuse spread covered the bed as when she had lived in the apartment and slept on the Castro Convertible in the living room. Simone did not like chenille spreads, they reminded her of Forest Hills, where she had once worked as cook(!) and nursemaid(!) for a perfectly despicable family that was very big on chenille spreads, wax grapes, and artificial potted palms.

"Jack and I did break up last October," Anita said. "I told you all about it, the way he just pulled out so unexpectedly, but we're still on friendly terms and to tell the truth, Simone, I can't get over him. It's awful but I just can't stop thinking of him."

"Is that why you decided to give a party? So you could invite him?"

Anita nodded miserably. "And I sure wish to hell he would get here. I'm so nervous that even my new antiperspirant isn't working right. By the way, I love your dress. Where did you buy it?"

"Bonwit's. I owe them a fortune."

"Not again?" Anita said.

Simone laughed. "No. Still. But let's not talk about money, it's too boring. Are the pajamas new? They're marvelous."

"Do you really like them?"

"I adore them. What are you wearing underneath?"

"A Hollywood Vassarette. It's got booster pads."

"I don't understand why you're so obsessed with your breasts. It's very chic these days to be on the small side."

"That's easy for you to say. You've got a cleavage, even if it's not visible at the moment. Aren't you wearing a bra?"

"I'm not wearing a thing underneath," Simone said, "except a Pursette."

"Well at least you're not pregnant for a change."

"How do you know?"

"I always assume that when a girl has her period she's not pregnant."

"I don't have my period."

Anita looked very confused (Simone felt very pleased). "Then what's the Pursette for?"

"It keeps me warm."

"You're as nutty as ever," Anita said.

"I'm a Libra," Simone said in a nutty voice, striking a nutty pose. "We're very fanciful people you know."

She moved over to the mirror above Anita's Salvation Army bureau to check her white plumed wig. It seemed to be all right, not on the verge of falling off or tipping ignominiously to one side as it had a way of doing in her nightmares. She took a Fresh-Up out of her tote bag and dabbed it over her face, threw it away in Anita's plastic chartreuse wastebasket that had a picture of the Eiffel Tower on it. Chou-Chou made a small, whimpering sound.

"You've brought Chou-Chou!" Anita said. "I didn't notice him before. How are you, Chou-Chou, darling? Come here, little boy, let me look at you."

Anita took Chou-Chou from the bag and pretended to kiss him, making sure to hold him as far away from her as possible. Simone recalled Anita telling her that the only animal she had ever liked was a stone lion by Rodin, and she smiled to herself at Anita's attempt to be affectionate to the dog. It was sweet of her, Simone concluded, she's trying to be nice to him for my sake and that counts for something.

"I hope you don't mind my bringing the dog," she said, feeling very insincere, "but I hate to leave him at home in the evening. He's home by himself all day long and he gets so lonely. He won't be any bother. He'll stay in the bag."

"Of course I don't mind," Anita said, putting Chou-Chou back in the tote. "I'm delighted to see him again. He's so cute. I wish I could get a pet but with my crazy job it's out of the question. Are you still working for that fun fur manufacturer?"

"Oh yes and it's so dull. I was going to look for something else a while back but then Mr. Swern gave me a raise, so I decided to stay on. Sometimes I feel as though nothing ever changes. Mr. Swern is still involved with that newspaper woman I told you about. Even that hasn't changed."

"You mean the one he refers to by a fake name?"

"Yes, as though I'm so stupid I don't know what her real name is."

"What is her real name?"

"Lou Marron. I told you once. She writes for that dizzy fashion paper, *The Rag*. She's always calling Mr. Swern from the Caravelle and telling him what Baby Jane Holzer is having for lunch. Sometimes I think that's why his stomach gets so upset, listening to all that disgusting food talk all the time. It's enough to upset anyone's stomach."

"I like food," Anita said. "It wouldn't disgust me."

"You see what I mean?" Simone lifted her brown and white plumed mini to check the band-aids that were holding up her fishnets (she thought of her father and his camera). "That's exactly what I mean. Nothing ever changes. You still like food. Mr. Swern is still managing to get it up for that disgusting Lou Marron. I'm still walking five miles a day in that lousy showroom. Habit habit habit habit habit habit habit habit habit habit habit . . ."

"Are you going to get hysterical and ruin my party?"

"I'm sorry, but aren't you bored working for that airline? Serving all that disgusting food?"

"Of course I'm bored," Anita said, "but what would I do if I quit? Working as a secretary seems even more depressing. Sitting in an office all day, banging away on an IBM electric. I just don't think I could stand it at this point. I've gotten a raise too. Big deal. I now make four-fifty a month but I manage to get in as much overtime as I can so it's not too terrible financially."

The two girls looked at each other.

"Do you think we'll ever get married?" Anita asked.

"*You* will," Simone said.

"No, *you* will because you don't even want to."

"I want to."

"Not like me."

That was true. "Perhaps not as much as you do, but I think that someday it would be nice to be Mrs. Somebody."

"I'm a year older than you," Anita said. "Do you realize that? I was twenty-five in July. Twenty-five. I can't believe it. I always thought I'd be married and have at least one child by twenty-five. What if I'm not married by thirty? I'll kill myself."

Anita was always threatening to kill herself. Simone had stopped taking her threats seriously a long time ago.

"You should have your horoscope charted," Simone said, checking out her eyelashes now (everything about me is fake, she thought). "Then you'll know which months or which years are your best marriage bets and you'll stop knocking yourself out the rest of the time. Remember, our destiny is in the stars. You can't fight these things."

"You know I don't believe all that astrology crap."

"Perhaps that's why you never got anywhere with Jack Bailey. You never found out whether his sun was in conjunction with your moon. You might be wasting all your energy on a man whose sun is not right for you."

"That's the craziest thing I've ever heard."

Kneeling on a hillside, Simone thought, despite the fact that Anita had made a corner for herself at the edge of the bed and was sitting there, perfectly upright, looking perfectly beautiful and very very blond even if she wasn't having more fun.

"And what about you?" Anita asked. "Have you been seeing anyone recently?"

"No. Nobody. I've become a hermit."

"What happened to that computer programmer you were so crazy about?"

"He drifted off into the night."

In a moment of wild abandon Simone had told Anita about the computer man and the A&P hotdog business, and had regretted it ever since because apparently Anita never recovered from the shock value of that sordid little incident. Simone wondered what Anita was like in bed. She suspected that Anita lay there like a sack of wheat, moving barely enough to spread her legs at the appropriate moment. Anita had once told her that she bleached her pubic hairs to match the hair on her head and whenever Simone thought of Anita in bed she always thought of a sack of wheat with lots of curly blond pubic hairs at the bottom, but actually she found it very hard to think of Anita in bed at all, it was too unlikely a mental image, too out of keeping with Anita's kneeling-on-a-hillside personality. Anita once said that Jack Bailey was the first man to go down on her which definitely struck Simone as peculiar since she knew that Anita had been screwing around since she graduated from high school.

"Do you mean in all those years nobody else ever tried?" she asked Anita.

"Oh they tried but I wouldn't let them."

"Why not?"

"It seemed a funny thing to do. I was embarrassed."

"What were you embarrassed about?"

"I can't explain. It just seemed like an odd thing to do."

And that was all Anita would say on the subject. Simone wondered what had prompted her to allow Jack Bailey to enter where other men had failed to tread, but getting meaningful answers out of Anita when it came to sex was like pulling a dead horse and after that she had not even bothered to try to pinpoint the compelling quality of Captain Bailey. The only thing she could come up with was that maybe Jack had an inferior sense of smell and didn't mind all that bleach.

"Are there any interesting men out there?" she asked Anita now.

"I would say so, but I'm not sure that you would find them interesting. You do have rather unusual tastes, you know."

"That's not true, at least not any longer. I mean, maybe I did used to get involved with bananaheads but all I'm looking for these days is a normal man."

"A normal man? You? I don't believe it. Besides there aren't any."

"I've already reached that conclusion," Simone said. "But I keep hoping, never give up hope. Really I'm so tired of loonies, aren't you?"

"Why do you think I'm still interested in Jack?"

Because he can't smell bleach. "Why?"

"Because compared to most of the creeps walking around these days, he's relatively sane."

"But he's twenty years older than you."

"I don't care. He's sane."

Simone had met Jack Bailey on several occasions when she and Anita were roommates and although he had never personally appealed to her she did have to admit that he seemed quite sane. However there was a meanness about him, his lips were too thin, something that turned her off, perhaps meanness was the wrong word, hardness might be more like it. He had always struck Simone as a man who had very few illusions about life, who knew exactly where he was headed and who needed nobody to go along with him. She wondered what it was about him that Anita found so fascinatingly irresistible. Rejection?

"Anyhow, they're all impotent," Simone said, sticking the tote bag with Chou-Chou in it on the floor next to the radiator so the dog would be warm.

"Who's impotent?" Anita asked.

"All the men in New York."

"Jack Bailey isn't."

"Well," Simone said, sticking to her guns, "all the men I meet are. And if they're not impotent their penises are so small that they might just as well use their fingers and get the same results. Is Bailey on the large side?"

"You know I don't like to talk about sex details," Anita reminded her, thinking once more of her unfortunate diaphragm growth. Jack Bailey had really screwed her, but good. Now that he had made her so large she couldn't go to bed with a man with a small penis even if she wanted to because of all that extra space there would be floating around, but she was damned if she would admit that to Simone who was probably still very tight and small thanks to those finger penises she was always complaining about. It was no use. No matter what you did, you lost, Anita decided, as she opened the door and led Rima, The Bird Girl, into the weaving, bobbing party room.

The first person Simone noticed among all the weaving, bobbing people was a man standing perfectly still, almost solemnly still, reflective.

"Who is *that?*" she asked Anita.

"Somebody named Robert Fingerhood. He's kind of cute, isn't he?"

"He sure is. How do you know him?"

"Actually, I don't. He crashed the party, but in a very polite way. He's a neighbor of Jack's. Come on, I'll introduce you. Do you want to be introduced?"

"Oh yes. He looks so normal."

"What if Jack doesn't show up after all?"

"What if that normal-looking man turns out to be a mirror fetishist?"

"Or what if he shows up with another girl?"

"What if he has a finger penis?"

"I'll kill myself," Anita said.

"I'll join you," Simone said.

"What's a mirror fetishist?"

"The kind who likes to look in a mirror while he's doing it to you."

"I never met one of those."

"You're lucky," Simone said, sticking out her 34-A chest as discreetly as she could in anticipation of being introduced to a new (hopefully N*O*R*M*A*L) man. She was somewhat chagrined to note that while Robert Fingerhood dutifully shook hands with her and smiled an enchanting smile, his primary interest seemed to be the luminescent Anita.

"How very nice to meet you," he said to Simone, shifting his gaze to Anita who had shifted her gaze to the electric clock, which pointed ignominiously to five after ten (Beverly and Peter were just saying goodnight to Tony Elliot, and Lou Marron was making a big entrance at Elaine's in her Kohinoor mink).

"Are you sure Jack said he'd be here?" Anita asked Robert Fingerhood.

"That's what he told me."

"I certainly wish he would hurry up."

"Not everyone is as eagerly punctual as I am," Robert said. "And believe me, I've been put down for it many times."

"I wouldn't put you down," Anita said. "I prefer it to the so-called cool, five-hours-late arrival. According to Crew Sked Jack was due back in New York at six-thirty tonight. That's when you could rely on Crew Sked. Forget it now. Excuse me, but I have to change the records not to mention my head."

"What's the matter with her?" Robert asked Simone as Anita walked off.

"Isn't it obvious? She's in love."

"With Jack Bailey?"

"Of course. She's been in love with him for over a year now."

"I had no idea. I just met Anita for the first time tonight."

"I know. She told me that you crashed the party."

Robert Fingerhood looked at her very directly. "I'm glad now that I did."

"Why don't we get a drink?"

Simone appreciated the fact that Robert was able to make a fast maneuver switch, for although he had apparently been very much interested in Anita, as soon as he was informed that Anita was very much interested in Jack Bailey, Robert promptly changed course and became very much interested in Simone. It seemed like a realistic move to Simone, and being extremely unrealistic herself she appreciated it all the more. Two unrealistic people together was her idea of utter bedlam. And yet, while she would always aim for the Robert Fingerhoods of the world, with their finger upon the daily pulse of the earth, she would still inwardly continue to find her soulmates in those who were as disorganized, as impractical, as childishly romantic as she. It was, finally, Simone's ultimate dilemma: to identify with a man and be playpen delirious, or to seek her emotional opposite and be adult dissatisfied. Simone knew that up to a point she was dealing here with two extremes, that people *per se* were not that extreme, that people were individuals subject to many and varied nuances of behavior and therefore could not be categorized as conveniently as she would perhaps like to categorize them, that it was naïve and self-defeating of her to insist upon such categorization, but in spite of all that (yes, *in spite* of it) certain boundaries did exist, there was a certain kind of demarcation line which separated the two camps and although she might persist in her search for the N*O*R*-M*A*L man, she wondered whether she was not destined to end up with her exact, or almost exact emotional counterpart. Which did absolutely nothing at the moment to undermine her interest in the attentive Mr. Fingerhood.

"Here we are," he said, leading her to Anita's makeshift kitchenette bar. "Now what would you like? I see that there's Scotch, vodka, and bourbon."

Not accustomed to drinking, Simone felt a bit woozy after the one Brandy Alexander at the Russian Tea Room. "Oh, why don't you mix them all together and throw in lots of ice and ginger ale?"

"Very well."

Although amused by her capriciousness, he would still indulge her in it. She liked him for that. If there was one thing she could not take at this stage in her life it was another Baptist minister, do this, don't do that, no, not that way, this way. She had had enough of those quasi-educational types with their authoritarian outlook and hard breathing.

"What do you *do?*" she said to Robert Fingerhood, who was busily mixing together Scotch, vodka, and bourbon. "Workwise, that is."

"I'm a psychologist. A clinical psychologist. And this is one hell of a stiff drink. Don't say I didn't warn you."

"How nice."

"Which? The drink or my profession?"

"Both."

Simone had no idea what a clinical psychologist was but at least it sounded N*O*R*M*A*L. Was it possible that after twenty-four years her dreams were finally coming true, that she had finally managed to meet a man—

1) Who would not be impotent?

2) Who would not have a finger penis (even though his last name was Fingerhood)?

3) Whose refrigerator would not be suggestively stocked with cans of Redi-Whip and/or A&P hotdogs?

4) Who would not insist that she fuck herself with a candle?

5) Who would not go down on her for six days running while in self-defense she was forced to read the collected works of J. D. Salinger?

6) Who would not turn out to be a mirror fetishist of the worst, the most exquisitely rigid order ("No honey, move it to the right, that's too far, honey, remember we want to see everything.")?

The last character had been a photographer for girlie magazines last seen shot to death in his studio, his chin slumped over the blowup of a brownish nipple. Aside from his obsessive voyeurism he had been rather sweet, considerate, generous, but Simone stopped seeing him anyway. After a while he got on her nerves. They never made love like ordinary people in an ordinary dim, if not dark, room. Oh no, not Mr. Big Eyes. Every session was like a professional photographic sitting. The lights had to be just so, the music had to be just so (Billie Holliday alternating with Ray Charles), the bedcovers had to be just so, the clothes she wore had to be just so. Why, he wouldn't even let her get completely undressed, which was amusing at first but later after she had seen him a couple of times she asked whether it would be okay with him if she took off her garter belt, stockings, and boots, to which he replied, "What? And ruin everything?" Then he would arrange the goddamn mirror and the whole madness would begin all over again. Sometimes Simone wondered who had shot him. Probably another girl whom he had driven crazy by not letting her take off her garter belt. Those things itched after a while, which was one of the main reasons Simone had since dispensed with them altogether.

The girl in the turquoise body shirt and orange bubble skirt entered the kitchenette, and said, "Is there any Diet-Rite around? Would somebody please check the refrig for some Diet-Rite?"

Robert Fingerhood obligingly opened the refrigerator. "Sorry but you're out of luck," he said. "Would you like some ginger ale?"

"Are you kidding?"

"I'm afraid that's all there is."

"What kind of party is that? No Diet-Rite, no pot. This girl has got to be kidding, baby."

A man in a splashy Tom Wolfe tie entered the kitchenette and tapped the girl on the shoulder. "Come on. They're playing 'Dang Me.' "

"I'll dang you any time, baby."

As Simone sipped her triple-threat drink, Robert Fingerhood made himself a very weak Scotch on the rocks, then they found a corner for themselves in the living room near the window and watched everybody dance. After "Dang Me" a record called "The Dangling Conversation" began to play on the hi-fi. Simon and Garfunkel were the singers and they kept singing something about the borders of our lives and either the superficial side or the superficial size. Simone could not make out which it was and actually what did it matter? The record was generally not too clear, or perhaps it was the player which Anita once told her had only one tube. Clear or not, Simon and Garfunkel were restful, their quiet, chanting voices gave the dancers a chance to rest and recoup their energies before The Rolling Stones or The Happenings started to blare forth once more and all the girls in vinyl jumpsuits and white mink bunny bonnets and fabulous gold burnooses jumped up and started their writhing weaving bobbing contortions once more.

"Do you like to dance?" Simone asked Robert Fingerhood.

"No, not particularly. Do you?"

"No, not particularly," she lied.

Simone loved to dance, she was a natural dancer, her body was slender, fluid, and people were forever telling her that she looked as though she were made for dancing. She had even devised a special leaping dance of her own which she privately titled, "Rima's Dance." But under the circumstances, she thought it more prudent not to admit to her proclivities. Robert might goodnaturedly suggest that she find herself a dancing partner from among the men in the room, and at the moment she did not want to leave his side for fear that another girl would latch onto him.

"What *do* you like to do?" Robert asked.

She felt like saying "fuck," but she managed to control herself. "I like to listen to fables. Tell me a fable, please."

Robert's very dark brown eyes looked into her very light blue ones. "Let's see now. Do you know the story of *The Little Prince?*"

"No."

"Would you like to hear it?"

Maybe she would marry Robert Fingerhood and carry endless charge plates and charge endless clothes that she would not have to worry about paying for. "Yes, I would, but before you start, please tell me one thing. What zodiac sign are you?"

"Aries."

"Not only was he potentially N*O*R*M*A*L but he was an Aries to boot! Simone could have expired on the spot. Aries and Libra was a beautiful combination, exquisite, a real astrological match if there ever was one.

"Of course, we'll have to have our horoscopes charted," she said. "One's sun sign isn't everything, you know. We have to find out about our moons, too."

"We'll do that later," he said, smiling another of those gorgeous smiles. "Right now we're going to talk about *The Little Prince*. Ready?"

But Simone was so busy marveling over the Aries-Libra hookup that she missed the beginning of Robert's story. When she caught up to him he was talking about a drawing that the author of *The Little Prince* had made when he was a child.

"The adults that he showed the drawing to thought he had drawn a hat when in reality it was a picture of a boa constrictor digesting an elephant."

"Yes?" Simone said, thinking about the beauty of an air and fire relationship, and at the same time trying desperately to remember whether any fire signs she had gone to bed with had small penises.

"The drawing incident was Saint-Exupéry's first disillusionment with the sensible adult world. As a result he had nobody to talk to until his plane crashed in the Sahara Desert and he met the little prince whose first words to him were, 'Draw me a sheep.' Since Saint-Exupéry had never drawn a sheep in his life he drew the boa constrictor digesting an elephant, but the little prince (spotting the drawing for what it was) said that elephants were too big because on his planet everything was very, very small. Well, finally, after several unsuccessful sheep drawings Saint-Exupéry drew a box and the little prince was very delighted."

The girl in the turquoise body shirt and orange bubble skirt was now weaving-dancing with an Englishman who had hair down to his shoulders. Simone could tell he was English because of the ridge in his nose. Next to the Germans, she hated the English most.

"Why was he delighted?" she asked.

"Because the sheep was inside the box," Robert Fingerhood explained. "Sleeping."

Something at this point told Simone that Fingerhood might not be so N*O*R*M*A*L after all, but she simply said, "I see."

"How's that for a fable?"

"Is that the end?"

"No, it goes on and on, but I won't. Fables should be kept short. How would you like to come back to my place? I have a bottle of Moët *brut* in the refrigerator."

Simone liked the fact that he didn't waste any time. She approved heartily of the direct approach. Why beat around the bush? Why forestall the inevitable catastrophe?

"Wait here," she said. "I'll go get my coat."

"You're not leaving so soon," Anita said, looking very alarmed, the anxious-hostess look. "The party's just getting started."

"We're going back to his place," Simone whispered in Anita's ear. "And you know what for, my darling Miss Norforms."

"You're incorrigible."

"Is that your new word for the week?"

Robert helped Simone on with her coat while Anita stood anxiously by wondering whether this was the beginning of a mass exodus. They were standing in the parquet-floor hallway when the doorbell rang and a blond man wearing an airline pilot's uniform, cap and all, entered carrying a weekend bag in one hand and a bottle of Beefeater's in the other.

"Jack!" Anita cried.

"Hi, honey." He kissed Anita on the cheek. "Sorry to be so

late but our takeoff was delayed for a change. Count on holding patterns and I've come direct from the airport. What else do you want to know?"

Then he spotted Simone and Robert standing side by side.

"Well, well. The doctor and the teeny bopper. My God, what a match."

"Hello, Jack," Simone said, still thinking that his lips were too thin. He probably did terrible sadistic things to Anita that she would never hear about.

"We hate to run," Robert said.

"You're running with quite a girl," Jack said.

"How do you know?" Simone said.

"Anita told me about the computer programmer."

"What computer programmer?" Robert said.

"Never mind," Simone said, giving Anita the dirtiest look she could dredge up. "Let's go."

Anita had a big mouth and lousy taste in men, that was Simone's conclusion. She could not, for instance, imagine what Anita saw in Jack Bailey, who to the best of her knowledge had never said an interesting thing in his life. According to Anita, though, he made up for that in bed.

"What does he do that's so marvelous?" Simone used to ask her but Anita would not say. Simone did notice, however, that after a night with Jack Bailey Anita invariably walked around with little bruise marks on her arms.

"Why do you have those disgusting marks?" Simone would ask. "Does he pinch you?"

Anita denied that Jack Bailey had ever pinched her and then she clammed up, which made Simone more curious than ever. Perhaps he used a small metal instrument, like a plier, on Anita's delicate flesh, although why that should be so pleasurable, Simone could not figure out. She, personally, had no interest whatsoever in going to bed with Jack Bailey, even if he was as large as she suspected. When she and Anita had lived together, Anita used to go to Jack's apartment to make love. Had they made love in Anita's chartreuse bedroom, Simone would have peeked through the keyhole to get the complete, definitive picture, and she was sorry now, very sorry indeed that she had not been able to talk Anita into letting her have a free show, because the fact was that other people's sex lives fascinated her. Perhaps that was why she had put up with the girlie photographer for as long as she did: they both were basically voyeurs, although in comparison to him she was a dull amateur. When the detectives had come to question her about his murder (it was just like a scene out of *Burke's Law*) she said that she most certainly could imagine any number of girls knocking him off, but the police were on the wrong track if they thought that *she* was the guilty party. The reason they were on the wrong track, she explained to Detective #1, was because they should be concentrating their efforts on nonvoyeur type girls. That type would be much more apt to put a bullet through Mr. Big Eyes' head than she would because that type might get pretty violent at being asked to masturbate in front of those damn floodlights in the studio, whereas she just thought it was not a terribly amusing thing to do. Detective #1 had looked at Detective #2 in a funny way at that and then they very politely thanked her, left, and were never heard from again. She had never before realized how polite the New York City police were.

"Where do you live?" Simone asked Robert Fingerhood.

They were in his car, a sports convertible, going south on Park.

"We're almost there. You'll see in a minute."

It turned out to be a street off Third, possibly Twenty-Fifth? Twenty-Sixth? The neighborhood was so darkened that she had missed the street signs altogether. She would not like to live in a neighborhood like this, it was so dark, so quiet, so dissimilar to the ebullience of Fifty-Seventh Street, where it was never dark or quiet, where there were all those lovely shops and restaurants and the (wonderful) Russian Tea Room, patronized by men with gorgeous profiles. Simone's secret dream was to move into the Russian Tea Room and live there forever on blinis and beluga caviar and vodka mists, surrounded for the rest of her life by men with gorgeous profiles.

"Here we are," Robert Fingerhood said, as they got off the small, self-service elevator in a modest brick apartment house.

"Jack Bailey lives directly beneath me."

Simone wondered whether Robert had been living here when Jack Bailey was busily banging Anita last summer and doing those terrible plier things to her. If he had, he might have heard some interesting sounds drifting out of Jack's bedroom window.

"Are you really a doctor?" she asked Robert, as he unlocked the door to 5–E. "Jack referred to you as a doctor before."

"I'm not a doctor *yet*," Mr. Fingerhood said, "but I will be as soon as I finish my dissertation."

"When will that be?"

Switching on a light, he said, "Oh, very soon."

The apartment! Well, the apartment was . . . no, Simone could not even begin to absorb it, the decor, the wildness of it, the jungle aspect, the entire stage-set quality, oh, it would take a minute for this one to sink in.

"What is your dissertation about?" she asked, wondering whether she was really in 5-E or in a tropical Mexican village; there were jaguar skins on the walls, there was some mysterious animal rug on the floor, there were tall, lush plants that seemed to tremble in the still, Mexican night.

"I don't believe I could go into the nature of the dissertation at this point," Robert said, "but I will tell you the title and that at least can give you an idea. It's called: *The relationship between the rate of the subject's maternal heartbeat and the rate of sexual intromission that is optimal in achieving orgasm.*"

"I never come," Simone said.

Robert looked at her as though he had heard wrong. "Never?" he asked with a miserable smile.

There was even a natural hemp hammock and a stuffed owl perched on a wood sculpture branch that hung precariously over the hammock.

"No, never," she replied.

Robert's dark eyes seemed to be doing some rapid calculating, all kinds of odd things were going on behind them, schemes, plans, plots, mathematical pyrotechnics, and Simone just hoped that whatever he came up with as a hopeful cure for her noncoming affliction was not too bizarre by nature because she was just a wee bit fetish fatigued at this point in her life. Then she noticed the whip. It stood in a corner, barely identifiable. Someone else might have taken it for a skinny umbrella or a snake standing up but Simone had been through too much in her twenty-four years to make either of those foolish mistakes. An ominous cloud began to descend upon her earlier optimism. Oh-oh, she thought, looking casually around to see if there happened to be any collected works by a novelist she had not read before. She threw herself into the natural hemp hammock and began to rock back and forth, waiting for Robert to emerge from the kitchen. When he finally did he was carrying a chilled bottle of Moët *brut* and two sparkling glasses.

"I feel like I'm in a jungle or a Tennessee Williams play," Simone said. "It's marvelous. I love it."

Robert set the champagne and the glasses down on what appeared to serve as a small endtable. Unlike the whip, Simone could not identify this peculiar grayish object and she was afraid to ask what it was. Of one thing, though, she felt virtually certain: it had unusual organic origins that she was in no big rush to define. Then Robert leaned over her reclining hammock form and kissed her on the lips, sticking his tongue so far down her mouth that she could feel the sensation in her stomach.

Simone hated to be kissed. "I, I . . ." She managed to get out a few squeals of displeasure in between his persistent kisses. "I, I, really I don't . . ."

When he finally released her she said, "If I take off all my clothes, do you promise to stop kissing me?"

"Sure I'll stop. Why don't you take them off in the bedroom? We can have the champagne there, too."

That did not seem like a bad idea to Simone, who would do practically anything to stop a man from kissing her. When a man kissed her she felt as though she had her face in a can of worms, ugly crawly creepy worms. She thankfully followed Robert Fingerhood into the bedroom, not knowing what she was in store for. The bedroom! My God! It was just one big immense bed with so little floor space around it that a fat person could not possibly have gotten through. There were some built-in shelves behind the bed, containing a radio, some magazines, two books, a box of Kleenex, an old can of beer, and an object that looked like an electric razor. Simone unzipped her brown and white plumed mini down the back and stepped out of it, leaving it on the narrow floor space.

"That was quick," Robert said, getting out of his jockey shorts. "Don't you ever wear underwear?"

"What the hell for?"

He had an erection a mile long which he wasted no time in trying to put inside her but it would not go in. "Something's blocking the way," he said at last. "What's in there anyway?"

She was breathing so hard that it took her a moment to pull herself together and remember the Pursette. "Just a minute. I'll be right back."

She went into the bathroom (would you believe toilet paper on a stuffed moose's antler???) and flushed the Pursette down the toilet. Then she gargled with some of Robert's Reef and then for some reason she suddenly remembered that she had left Chou-Chou in the tote bag sitting on the floor in Anita's bedroom next to the radiator. Simone knew she had a terrible tendency to be absent minded but she had never before left behind both a bag *and* a dog, and she could only wonder whether there was something about Robert Fingerhood, some magnetic, compelling quality that might account for such a dual lapse of memory on her part. Poor Chou-Chou. He must be so miserable in his abandonment. She felt so awful about her negligence even if it was unintentional, and spitting out the Reef into Robert's cracked sink, she promised herself that she would go and pick the dog up first thing in the morning before she went to work; maybe she would even take poor neglected Chou-Chou to work with her.

"I've gotten rid of the obstruction," she informed Robert as she dove into the immense whiteness of the bed. "How about a little champagne?"

He poured two glasses and handed her one. "Here's to depravity," he said, swallowing his in one gulp.

Something told Simone that another strange episode in her strange-enough life was about to unfold. Oh, yes, another chapter was definitely in the making, there was really no question of that in her mind. The champagne was good, it stung just right. She belched discreetly and drank more because Robert had refilled both their glasses. Oh, he was sneaky, but still she wondered what the peculiarity would be when it finally manifested itself. In fact, she was so curious that she hoped it didn't take too long, because she had a very low anxiety threshold (a social worker had told her that; he was a Eurasian who ate Tums a great deal, maybe that was why she thought of him now in between belches), but most of all she hoped that the peculiarity, whatever the hell it was, would not turn out to be boring old hat, that would be truly terrible. Imagine, Mama, yesterday's used up fetish!

Robert Fingerhood placed his champagne glass on the shelf behind the bed and picked up what had looked to Simone like an electric razor. In the dimness of the room she managed to make out the name on it: Vibrette.

"Have you ever used a vibrator before?" Mr.-about-to-become-Dr. Fingerhood asked, smiling another gorgeous, tempting, seductively entrancing smile as he plugged the fascinating appliance into an outlet behind the bed and gave Simone lots of brand-new-fetish glances.

After the heavily paneled door in the castle in Garden City finally closed upon Tony Elliot, Beverly sighed, and said, "Well, darling, I'm glad that that's over with."

"Why, darling?" Peter asked. "Didn't you like Tony?"

That strange fishy man. "It wasn't that I didn't *like* him."

"In that case, what was it?"

"It was . . ." Beverly touched her forehead. "I'm afraid my pills aren't working this time."

"Yes, your migraine. I'd nearly forgotten, darling."

"Darling, how could you forget?"

"Now don't play the martyr. You've had these attacks before and you've survived beautifully. You'll survive this one."

"Of course, I will. I think I'll go help Margaret in the kitchen."

"That's precisely what I mean. Why martyr yourself by helping Margaret when you're feeling so rotten?"

"It will take my mind off my head, not to mention that terrible meal."

"Oh I don't know. I suspect that Tony found it very amusing."

"He must have quite a sense of humor."

"That he does," Peter said with a faint smile as though remembering another amusing incident in the life of Tony Elliot, one that Beverly would never hear about.

Beverly kissed her husband on the cheek. "I'll be up shortly."

"I think I might read for a while," Peter said. "Don't rush."

"You know, darling, you don't get enough sleep these days."

"You know, darling, you're getting to be a pain in the ass."

"All I said was—"

"Don't compound it."

"But Peter, I—"

"Go help Margaret."

Beverly did not know how it had evolved, her erstwhile solution to these growing clashes with Peter, she did not know how she had happened to hit upon it or what in fact it actually meant, and she did not want to know, but whenever Peter surprised her with a barbed verbal attack she silently said the following to herself, having memorized it (again for reasons she did not understand) when she was a child:

"Jeconiah was the father of Shealtiel, Shealtiel of Zerubbabel, Zerubbabel of Abiud, Abiud of Eliakim, Eliakim of Azor, Azor of Zadok, Zadok of Achim, Achim of Eliud, Eliud of Eleazar, Eleazar of Matthan, Matthan of Jacob, Jacob of Joseph, the husband of Mary, who gave birth to Jesus called Messiah."

And then she felt better. A little. She felt even better than a little when she went into her beautiful buttercup yellow kitchen and watched the efficient Margaret send Choucroute

Garni stained dishes through the gleaming dishwasher, watched her stack them on the rack on the drainboard, watched Margaret's broad capable hands dry each dish and cup and glass with extra loving care. Beverly just liked to sit on the caned stool next to the General Electric oven and watch the wheels of progress turn round and round in her own kitchen, except of course, that it was not such progress at that because tomorrow Margaret would be drying differently stained dishes and cups and glasses, and the day after and the day after that, and was there really any end to it, any meaning to it, any point to it all, now was there?

Lately that was the question Beverly had begun to ask herself. Late at night while Peter slept and dreamed his own private dreams she would lie awake and wonder whether she was going to spend the next twenty years of her life watching her husband sleep while she lay awake, watching Margaret dry dishes while she sat on the caned stool next to the oven, useless.

Beverly had nothing to do. Boredom stimulates the clitoris.

And then something else occurred to her one day. She had not minded having nothing to do so long as Peter had been making love to her, but during these past couple of years when he had practically stopped (except for a few unsatisfactory interludes) she felt worthless, meaningless, and she began to wonder whether her only function, her only reason for being was of a sexual nature, was that all she was good for? And why had she been so easily, almost gratefully satisfied with it? Perhaps because without it she was dissatisfied with everything.

Sex. It seemed so far away now, so foreign to her, an activity she could not believe she had once participated in with such regular frequency that she had altogether taken it for granted, assumed it would last forever and instead it had one day abruptly died and for all she knew been buried deep in the earth behind her naïve and trusting back. She could see the shovels hurling dirt at a furiously rapid rate of speed, cover up the telltale signs of sensuality and nobody will ever know that they once existed.

But the body remembers. That was another of Beverly's thoughts when Peter lay peacefully sleeping off husbandly responsibility—that the body like the brain had a memory and could only be tricked for so long before it demanded its due. However, as Beverly saw it, the question was: what could she do to give it its due? Resisting the possibility of other men (but for how long, she wondered?), she had begun to drink.

Margaret knew about the drinking and accepted it, the way a servant might accept a crippled mistress. Even now without a previous word of conversation between them, Margaret said, "Shall I pour you a little drink, Mrs. Northrop?"

"It's not good for my head."

"Maybe a little cognac would be soothing."

"You shouldn't encourage me, you know."

"Yes, Ma'am."

"On the other hand," Beverly said, thinking of Peter reading upstairs in bed, shutting her out, "maybe a little cognac."

Drinking was terrible for her head and cognac worst of all but she did not care, feeling so terrible to begin with. Children were supposed to help, give one a sense of oneself, of motherhood, of responsibility, of importance, a feeling of worthiness, and they did up to a point. Without her children Beverly felt she would truly die yet children were not enough, never, they finally never were, money and maid-help did not count. *De trop.*

For again there was Margaret, there was kindergarten until one o'clock for Sally, there were naps for small Peter, there was cookie and milk time (overseen by Margaret), there was ubiquitous retreat for Beverly if she wished it. She could go to her room and not be disturbed for as long as she wished; she could go to the country club for lunch, for drinks, or simply for the sake of going there; she could go shopping for a new dress, cashmere sweater, shoes, scarves, gloves, tweed skirts (was Garden City the Fifth Avenue of Long Island for nothing? No, sighed Lord & Taylor, Saks, Best's, Peck & Peck, and Andrew Geller in gentle but firm unison, no no); she could have her hair done a new way and read the latest *Vogue;* she could call Betty or Eunice or Kitty or Patsy or Sandy or Dee Dee or Gigi or Marni and they would taaaaaaaaalk; she could do volunteer work at the Nassau Hospital thrift shop, or go chat with the Cathedral Ladies at the rummage shop, she could . . . she could do anything she damned well pleased but it had finally hit Beverly that she didn't feel like doing anything except make love to her husband who at present wasn't having any.

"Do you feel any better, Mrs. Northrop?"

"Better and worse. All at the same time." She held out her empty glass, noting the expression of concern on Margaret's dark brown face. "Pour, please."

She was nearly twenty-nine and if she kept up this drinking, she would lose her looks for sure. Beverly thought about that. At thirty-five she might be a bloated lush, one of those ludicrous women teetering around, uncoordinated, uncaring, unfit for anything except the next martini and the next one after that. What should she do? Go on the wagon of course, but she lacked the incentive. It wasn't that she lacked the will power but rather that she saw no reason to apply the will power and make it stick. For the sake of her children. Okay, that was a bona fide incentive, or at least it should be and yet it wasn't. Did that make her a lousy mother? Probably it did from the outside looking in, but she was inside looking the other way and all she knew was that the children were extensions of Peter and without Peter they lost a great deal of significance. They were still very important to her but not *as* important and she couldn't help that. If that made her a lousy mother, then that was what she was.

Maybe if the children were older, she often thought, more fully formed, more grown up, she would be able to regard them more as individuals and less as extensions, but there they were aged two and five, why Peter, Jr., barely talked at all and Sally was a curious little girl whom perhaps Beverly would never understand, Sally was so brave and unshy, so extroverted, so fearless, spunky would be the right word, and Beverly had been just the opposite when she was a child. In fact, sometimes she felt as though she were the child and Sally the mother.

Once Sally said to her, "You know, Mommy, your hem is too long"—the sort of remark that was not at all uncommon for a five-year-old child to solemnly make, but Beverly had felt threatened, she felt as though it were her own mother rather than her daughter speaking, chastising, reprimanding, and she had an almost uncontrollable urge to send the skirt to the tailor on Franklin Avenue for instant shortening. But in reply to Sally all she said was, "I like it the way it is, darling. It's the right length for me."

And that ended that except for remembering having once told her own mother that a certain pair of shoes did not look right with a certain dress that her mother owned, and her mother had coolly replied, "Oh, yes, it looks fine, darling. This color goes with everything." And the child Beverly had bowed to maternal authority, had felt (she recalled now) that that authority was unswerving and unswayable, when for all she knew her mother might have felt just as doubtful as she felt when Sally had criticized her hem length, and probably at the same time Sally had thought that *she* was the voice of maternal authority, unswerving and unswayable, and was it a role that mothers kept enacting all their lives and children kept believing until they, too, became mothers themselves and repeated the lie of pretense with their children?

"Pour, please."

"Perhaps if you went upstairs and lied down, you'd feel better, Mrs. Northrop."

"I plan to do that eventually, Margaret, but in the meantime . . ." she waved her empty glass.

It was true that lying down was about the best remedy for a migraine, just lie down on your back and try not to rock the boat, try to keep the recurrent waves of nausea at bay, lie still and don't move, don't think. There were two framed pictures on Beverly's buttercup kitchen wall. One was a delicate flower print and the other was a kindergarten drawing that Sally had made several months ago, showing the face of a girl with a starlike object planted above her left eyebrow. When Sally had come home with the drawing Beverly asked her what the object was.

"It's a fly," Sally said.

"Why does the girl have a fly on her face?"

"Because she's *outside*, Mommy."

The purity of her daughter's logic impressed itself upon Beverly who had never felt so muddled in her life as she had these last two years, ever since Peter started working for Tony Elliot and all but stopped making love to her. At first, she was bewildered by her husband's abrupt withdrawal, then confused, then depressed, then hysterical, then bewildered all over again, until at last the individual emotions wore themselves out and fused into one massive leadlike emotion that she could no longer define. She could not think straight any more, she did not know what to do, she could not find her way out of the maze, she was trapped, and only one solution kept coming back to her with logical persistence: have an affair with another man.

It seemed to Beverly like a simpleminded enough solution except for the fact that she had no idea whom to have the affair with. These things were more easily contemplated than executed. She supposed that if she put her mind to it she could manage to wrangle some sort of lovemaking out of the husband of Betty or Eunice or Kitty or Patsy or Sandy or Dee Dee or Gigi or Marni, but the amount of effort she would have to put forth seemed almost beyond her and that was really the debilitating aspect of her sexless position: she felt utterly sexless. She felt as though someone had sewn her vagina together twenty-five years ago and it would never open again or function normally. It was an iceberg feeling, frozen, dead. At times she cried, a sort of dead, dry crying, as juiceless as she was. All her mucous membranes had dried up and it was all Peter's fault. He, on the other hand, seemed to be in marvelous spirits, as though her demise had made him strong.

Beverly sometimes wondered whether husbands and wives killed each other off like that. Sandy once told her that at the beginning of her marriage her husband had been bothered by a faulty digestion, whereas she was capable of consuming seven-course meals without the slightest twinge of stomach upset. Then gradually an interesting thing started to happen. Sandy began to get worse in the digestion department until after a decade of marriage their roles had become completely reversed, Sandy ending up with bleeding ulcers and a restricted diet while her husband went around boasting of his "genetically strong constitution."

"I'm going upstairs," Beverly announced. "Goodnight, Margaret."

"Goodnight, Mrs. Northrop. I'm sorry about the way that platter tipped on me and got Mr. Elliot all greasy."

"It was my fault, Margaret. It was my fault for planning that catastrophic meal to begin with."

"Thank you, Mrs. Northrop."

"Airwick first thing in the morning."

Margaret laughed. "I won't forget."

The body remembers. Beverly felt like a prisoner going to her execution, as she climbed the robin blue carpeted stairs to the second floor where the hangman awaited her. As usual Peter had thrown the blankets on the floor and was partially covered by the top sheet, his wiry, hairless chest and a book bared to the world. He was reading *Remembrance of Things Past,* the story of Beverly's present life.

"Are you still reading that book?"

"Obviously," he said.

That was the kind of answer she got from Peter these days, she could not get to him at all. There had to be another woman. There was no other explanation for his rejection of her, there could be no other, and once she had asked him whether he was involved with someone else.

"No," he had said.

"Then why don't you make love to me any more?"

He had shrugged. "Perhaps I don't care to any more."

It was his insolence more than anything that drove Beverly mad. Had he apologized, had he said he was tired, depressed, debilitated, had he lied she might have forgiven him a little, but not shy Peter, shy people did not need to lie, their shyness was their lie to the world. Then why did she persist in thinking that there was another woman? Beverly could answer her own question: because another woman was less threatening to cope with than nothing; she could begin to compete with another woman but how could she compete with nothingness? She prayed that there was another woman, someone whose identity would shortly be made known to her. She would like to see her, examine the opposition, prepare for combat. The only woman she could conjure up as the possible party was the one in Peter's office, that reporter he pretended to disdain. Last week he had again made a sneering reference to "that bitch, Marron," and instead of asking him what he meant Beverly wondered what Lou Marron's body was like and why Peter preferred it to hers.

Under questioning Peter admitted that Lou was thin but what had that to do with it? It was not her body that concerned him (he said), it was the sheer bitchiness of her, the horrid possibility that Tony Elliot might give Marron the column instead of giving it to him. That was the way Peter referred to her, never as Lou, or Lou Marron, or Miss Marron, but simply Marron, as though she were a man. Beverly found this very suspect.

"Tony Elliot seems quite fond of you," she said now as she removed her black, V-necked sheath in front of the oval mirror.

"Yes, he does, doesn't he?" Peter said without looking up at his wife who stood observing herself in her black lace brassiere with the cutout part that revealed her large pink nipples, and the black half slip under which an Olga panty girdle slyly lurked. It was at the beginning of their marriage that Peter had voiced his objections to brassieres, and while Beverly could appreciate his attitude she defended her necessity to wear the damn nuisances inasmuch as her breasts were so large.

"They joggle without a bra," she explained.

"Let them, then."

But she could not, she felt too wanton without the support she was accustomed to and being braless ruined her silhouette in clothes, for even though her breasts were relatively high considering their size they did slump to a certain degree which was only natural. Their sheer weight had to bring them somewhat down (it was like the problem of support involved in bridge building, Peter once said), and that was how they happened to hit upon cutting out the nipple part of her brassieres which Beverly herself did very cunningly with a curved cuticle scissors, because that way she had her support in clothes, and Peter knowing what was going on underneath the façade had his fun.

In the old days when they were still very erotically involved Peter would come directly home from work and they would drink a couple of Scotches in the music room (it was cozier there than the more formal living room, and Peter liked the baby grand). Then they would lock the door and Beverly would remove her sweater or dress, and usually it was a sweater, so that after a tiring day in noisy Manhattan Peter could suck her nipples in the blissful quiet of their Garden City retreat. His tongue absolutely drove her wild. He would fasten first upon one breast and harden the nipple to the point where Beverly thought she would have an orgasm even before his probing fingers reached beneath her flimsy panties and began their tantalizing exploration. The panties would soon be flung on the forest green wall-to-wall carpet and Peter's mouth would soon be softly sucking one nipple in the cutout brassiere, one hand would be teasing the other nipple, and his second hand would be rubbing her clitoris which by then was moist and distended, and at that threefold moment in the music room Beverly would think: this, finally, is what I live for, this is what makes it all worthwhile.

After a few moments of unendurable pleasure Peter would transfer his mouth to the other nipple and he would place Beverly's hand upon the abandoned one, guiding her hand with his so that she could feel for herself its taut hotness. He liked to seat her on the cool piano stool and make her lift her skirt over his elegant head and explore her throbbing clitoris with his tongue that was still nipple-hot and thirsty for the moisture that flowed shamelessly out of her. When his lips closed around her like that, his hands would creep up to her supplicating nipples and play with them very lightly, driving her to a state of such maniacal passion that she longed to cry out her ecstasy but Peter would not let her. He would not let her move too much either, not just then. He did not restrain her for fear that her outbursts might be heard by Margaret, or "the girl," or Sally (Peter, Jr., was not yet born), but rather because he wished to heighten their mutual pleasure by virtue of holding back its uninhibited expression. It was only when tension reached the torrential stage that Peter allowed her to put on her sweater and panties, and then with shaking legs Beverly would follow him up to their bedroom to consummate languidly the foreplay of lovemaking.

"Peter," Beverly said now, "remember when we used to make love in the music room when we were first married?"

"Of course, I remember. Why do you ask?"

"I was just wondering why we stopped. I don't even remember stopping, but one day it was gone."

"Things like that can't go on forever."

"Why not?"

"People grow up."

Is this what they had grown up to? Abstinence? What kind of growth was that? She looked at her husband for further explanation but none seemed to be forthcoming. Beverly suddenly felt tired, defeated, and she began to remove her nylons, they were just plain beige nylons not those crazy textured patterned things all the Twiggys were wearing in *The Rag*. Beverly could not compete with those skinny Twiggy shapes, nor did she want to. She liked her voluptuous body even if voluptuousness were *passé*. She liked it and she would not change it for all the Lou Marron thinness in all the Twiggy world. Some women were not meant to be thin, was Beverly's feeling, their bones demanded flesh, their personalities insisted upon it. Beverly debated a moment and then slipped out of the Olga panty girdle before slipping out of the black half slip. She tossed the panty girdle on the dusty pink carpet. That advertising baffled her: who cared if there really was an Olga behind every Olga, who gave a damn? Then she tossed the half slip after it and confronted Peter in only her black lace cutout brassiere, her full white body trembling in the dusty pinkness of the room.

"Darling, are you having an affair with that Marron woman?"

"What a ridiculous idea. Marron! Where do you get such ideas?"

"It's not *where,* it's *why.*"

"Very well," he said obligingly. "Why do you get such ideas?"

"Because in this case it seems like the only logical explanation."

"To what may I ask?"

"Your not making love to me."

"I make love to you," he said, buried beneath Proust.

"When? Once a year?"

"Beverly, please don't exaggerate. You know it's much more frequent than that."

She sat down beside him on the bed, barely able to voice the question that had been on her mind for a long time now. "Peter, do I repel you?"

He put the book aside and looked up at her. "Why do you think such things? No, you don't repel me. Why do you pursue a subject that I am obviously not interested in?"

"I don't know what else to do. I want to get to the bottom of our problem and the only way I can do that is to find out what your feelings are. That's why it's so important that you be honest with me. If you're tired of me, say so. If I repel you, tell me. But don't just lie there reading a book, ignoring me, pretending that everything between us is fine when I know that it isn't. Peter, I'm a woman. I can't live like this much longer."

"You're going to become hysterical any minute. I can hear it in your voice. Darling, you should take a tranquilizer."

"I'm sick of taking tranquilizers. There's only one tranquilizer that interests me and you've managed to deprive me of it quite effectively."

"Oh, Christ, are we back to that again?"

"Back?!" Beverly shouted. "Did you say *back?* We've never left it. What's there to leave? How can you leave it? What the hell are you talking about, you lunatic? How can you just lie there reading Proust?"

In one swift motion she knocked the book out of his hand, it landed on the carpet on top of her Olga. [Oh there was significance in that combination: did Proust care if there was an Olga behind every Olga? But of course.]

"You see?" Peter said, very matter of factly. "You've become hysterical just as I predicted."

She would kill him. That was what it finally amounted to. One day she would just kill him. Beverly suddenly understood murder for the first time in her life. Before this it was an unfamiliar commodity she read about in the newspapers, one which had no bearing upon her daily existence since people who killed people were not people that she, Beverly Fields Northrop III, normally associated with. They were cranks, nuts, madmen, Martians removed from her polite world of Stewart Avenue and the Cherry Valley Country Club. Until that second people who killed people were as remote to her as people who lived in rat-infested slums; they were dream-like creatures and now she was potentially one of them, she had entered the dream giving it a *déjà vu* reality that was more frightening than anything she had ever encountered to date. But if it was frightening, it was thrilling, too, because murder was (misplaced) passion, at least her particular brand of murder would be. She could feel her blood heating up. She could see the *Daily News* headlines. She could imagine young secretaries on the subway reading about the latest suburban scandal. She could visualize the shocked reaction of her Garden City friends. She could anticipate what she would say to the police.

"I was bored."

Murder was exciting. She would say that, too. She would say it was exciting because at least something was *happening*, and nothing had happened in her life for so long, absolutely nothing. Proust and Olga were very happy together, they were kissing.

Beverly got up and ran out of the room and nearly fell down the robin blue stairway, into the living room, into the bar, and poured a glass of Dewar's minus ice, water, soda, regret, and drank it down as fast as she could. Margaret was nowhere in sight or sound. Beverly had a fast, apprehensive thought about Margaret possibly not having looked in on Peter, Jr., and Sally to see if they were all right before going up to her quarters on the third floor for the night. Of course, Margaret had looked in (she cajoled herself). Count on Margaret. Beverly did count on her, there was nobody else in the immediate cast of characters that she could count on, not herself, not Peter, not her friends . . . DeeDee and Marni and Gigi, did she know anything about them, anything that really mattered, did they know her? The only person she ever thought she knew was Peter, and now she had to admit she was wrong about him. The betrayal had soured her life. If she had been wrong about Peter, perhaps she was wrong about everyone, everything. Yes, she would have to think it all over again, but how could she have been so wrong? Why was Proust kissing a girdle designer? Who said it had to make sense? Ahhhhhhh.

"Take off that ridiculous brassiere," Peter said when she returned to the bedroom with a second glass of Scotch in her hand. "That brassiere was yesterday. Don't you understand anything?"

Beverly's headache had left her, she now realized. "I'll tell you what I understand, you bastard. This."

She tossed the undiluted Scotch in his surprised face, then she threw the empty glass across the room where it smashed to pieces against the W & J Sloane chest of drawers. Then she laughed. It was a very loud jagged sound, her laughter. It seemed to bounce off the pink and gray wallpaper and reverberate in her ear. Laughter, pain, frustration, drunkenness, despair, fury. Beverly felt diseased both in body and in mind. Leaping upon Peter she slapped him as hard as she could before he caught her hand in his and pinned her down on the bed.

He was perceptibly trembling with rage. "Very well, you crazy cunt, spread your legs."

"I despise you," she said, trying to reach for him again, to slap him, punch him, kick him, scratch him, claw him, anything to hurt him, but he was too quick for her.

"I'll tie you to the bed if you don't lie still," he said. "Believe me, I will. Now be a good girl and do what I say."

His voice chilled her. It was so calm, so detached, so unemotional, so alien, not at all the voice of the man she had been living with for eight years.

"First," he went on in the same tone, "take off your brassiere and place it on the night table, no throwing now, no theatrics, or you'll be tied to this bed for a week. I mean it, Beverly."

He released her hands and allowed her to unsnap the hooks of her brassiere. For a second she wavered, tempted to fling it in his face, but plain animal fear stopped her, a premonition of disaster if she should indulge her inclination.

"Fine," Peter said, as though he were speaking to a child. "Now I am going to lie down on my back and I want you to sit on top of me, on my thighs. Don't lie on me, just sit, and keep your legs back."

They exchanged places and Peter lay down flat on the bed, his penis, she noticed, quite enlarged by now, and following instructions Beverly sat down on the upper part of his thighs, barely touching the rodlike organ that she prayed would shortly be inside her. Instead, they remained in that position for several minutes, unmoving, untalking, Beverly's legs tucked back beneath her, her torso very slightly arched forward, eagerly waiting, until she could bear it no longer.

"Peter, I—"

"Be quiet."

"But Peter—"

"I said, be quiet."

"I will not be quiet!"

Reaching out he smashed her across the face with such force that she nearly fell backward in shock. Immediately tears dimmed her great blue eyes but she dared not open her mouth to speak for fear of a second reprisal. She choked back the tears as best she could and wondered what in her life had brought her to this incomprehensible episode. Trying to control herself, she remained perfectly still for what seemed like an eternity in time when all of a sudden Peter reached out and smashed her across the face again, the blow this time striking her with an even greater intensity than the first one, being even less expected than the first one. In one convulsive movement she rolled off his thighs and collapsed into great heaving sobs. Peter did not touch her nor did he say a word. Instead he got out of bed, picked his book off the floor, got back into bed, and turned the pages to where he had left off. It took Beverly several minutes to stop crying, to wipe her eyes, to absorb the new turn of events. At first she could not believe what was happening. Surely he was not going to lie there and read his book, not now, not so casually, so disdainfully.

"Peter, I'm sorry if I . . ."

She stopped because she did not know how to finish the sentence. She did not know what she was sorry about, and yet a great undefined sorrow seemed to weigh upon her.

"Go to sleep, Beverly."

Sleep? How could she sleep? He must be mad. "But I thought that we were . . ."

"We were until you turned into a hissing scorpion."

"I'm sorry I threw the drink at you."

He said nothing.

"I'm sorry I slapped you."

He still said nothing.

"Peter, really I'm sorry."

"Good."

Was that all he had to say? Her cheeks still smarted from his cruel blows, but now in the aftermath Beverly realized that she was leaking wet and thoroughly aroused. Was he going to ignore her for the rest of the night? She could bear anything but that, she could even bear being hit again, anything, anything was preferable to this negation. She moved closer to him.

"Peter, I love you."

He patted her bare shoulder. "Go to sleep."

"Kiss me."

He kissed her very sweetly on the lips. "Now go to sleep and I'll wake you up in the middle of the night."

He was true to his word. Hours later when the room was quite dark and the world very still, Beverly sleepily felt her husband's finger upon her clitoris, and a minute later he had entered her still moist recesses and was moving against her with a ruthless energy she had never before known, his movements had the quality of a strange ritualistic dance. More fully awake now, she started to move with him (he was lying on his side behind her), she moved against him with her great rounded hips, pushing them as far back against him as she could and at the same time opening herself wider and still wider for him until she felt that initial shudder of ecstasy begin its slow race through every part of her sweating, agonized body. The sweat was pouring out of her, out of every enlarged pore in her wet skin, and she was exquisitely aware of a man's fingers moving across her breasts and down her bunched up stomach, across her full thighs that now quivered and shook with rapid rhythmic convulsions, his fingers at last coming to rest on the raised triangle of hairs at the very second that Beverly's body heaved and fell in one long piercing cry of excruciating pleasure.

Toward morning as daylight began to invade the darkened bedroom Beverly awakened and sensed danger. Peter was sleeping quietly on the far side of the bed. She hugged her warm, glowing body as though to reassure herself that her fears were without foundation, but they persisted nonetheless. The ecstasy of a few hours before was somehow tempered by the certain deadly knowledge that something in her life had changed overnight and would never again be the same.

Anita was sorry to see Simone and that cute Robert Fingerhood leave her party so early. She was more than sorry, in fact, she resented their leaving. After all the preparatory trouble she had gone to it did not seem fair that people should feel free to pick themselves up arbitrarily, just when things were getting under way, and go off into the night, guiltless, as though they owed their hostess no debt of courtesy at all.

It was particularly insulting in this instance because Anita had always considered Simone a friend of hers. She would have expected Simone to behave in a more thoughtful fashion, and yet when had Simone ever thought about anyone except herself? When the two girls lived together it was always Anita who tried to maintain a certain practical balance in the household. She knew she could not count on Simone to do so because Simone was giddy, inconsiderate, utterly self-indulgent. Anita remembered the morning Simone woke up first and drank all the orange juice in the refrigerator. There must have been at least half a quart that she blithely finished off, leaving absolutely nothing for Anita.

"I couldn't help it, I was dying of thirst," was Simone's explanation.

Or the time Simone borrowed Anita's new Fiorentina suede T-straps that cost forty-five dollars at Saks, and came back from her date with the shoes scuffed and water stained.

"What did you do?" Anita asked her the next day. "Make love in the bathtub?"

"No, in the sink, and afterwards he drank a glass of water and some of it dripped."

"In the sink? What a crazy thing to do. Why did you have to do it in the sink?"

"Because he took me to a party and it was the only available place."

"Couldn't you wait until you went back to his apartment?" Anita asked, wondering whether sandpaper would remove the blotchy water stains.

"It wasn't that I couldn't *wait*. I've just always wanted to get laid in a sink."

"Don't you ever think of anyone but yourself? You know how much the shoes cost. The least you could have done was taken them off."

"Please don't be angry at me. *J'ai une gueule de bois* from all that damn drinking. And I'm sorry about the shoes, Anita, really I am."

But Simone wasn't sorry that she might have ruined a brand new pair of shoes, Anita could see that. She was merely sorry that she was being reprimanded for her misbehavior in her morning-after hungover state.

"You certainly know some strange men," Anita said. "I don't understand where you dig them up."

"If I had someone who cared for me, I wouldn't do these things," Simone said in her most winsome manner, in her most appealing French-accented voice. "You don't know how lucky you are that you have Jack. You don't know how many nuts there are in New York."

"Thanks to you, I'm beginning to find out."

"It wasn't bad in the sink," Simone said, looking thoughtful. "He had strong thighs. Also you don't have to go dripping into the bathroom afterward to wash, since you're right there. It's convenient in a way."

"I prefer a nice soft mattress myelf. And so does Jack, I'm happy to say."

It was with Jack that Anita had the first orgasm of her life. She wondered whether she would ever have one with any other man and somehow she doubted it. She had read somewhere that once a woman developed the ability to have orgasms she could have them with almost any man who made love to her, since the ability depended upon the woman's receptiveness rather than the man's technical know-how, and up to a point Anita agreed with that theory. She agreed that a woman had to be receptive, truly receptive, and in a state of blissful surrender for the miracle to take place, and that was why Anita felt so strongly about Jack Bailey—she did not think she would ever be in that same intensified state with another man, she could not imagine it. There was just something about Jack. It was not what he did in bed, it was what he was, the way he looked, his body, the texture of his skin.

That was why Anita could not discuss sexual matters with Simone, why she refused to discuss them. Simone's entire attitude was childish, infantile. Simone always wanted to know the specific technical details, as though those could help her overcome her stubborn frigidity. Anita once tried to tell her that the mechanics of lovemaking were subsidiary to the quality of emotion felt, but Simone just looked at her as though she had two heads. Anita finally felt sorry for Simone. Getting laid in the sink was no solution, but Simone would not understand that. In her desperation she would go on trying every outlandish position, getting herself involved in every freak situation that came her way, wondering all the while why none of them brought her the satisfaction she so desperately craved (Robert Fingerhood was at the moment showing Simone his vibrator, which much to her chagrin he had no intention of using just then).

Anita came back to the party present just as Jack Bailey returned from the kitchenette bar with a tall glass of something bubbly brown in his hand.

"Jack," she said, "I'm so glad you could make it tonight. I was afraid you might never get here."

"I'm a sucker for a party. You know that."

His gaze wandered across the room, his glint blue eyes taking it all in in one sweeping glance. Jack was from Nevada and he had once told her that killers in the old wild West invariably had blue eyes, and Anita believed it.

"It's been so long since I've seen you," she said. "How have you been?"

"Pretty good. No complaints. And you?"

"Oh, just marvelous." She wondered if she sounded convincing. "I've been meeting lots of people and going out, oh, you know, plays and movies and concerts and discotheques and things. There's so much to do in New York."

"Yes," he said, sipping his drink. "Isn't there?"

She debated whether she should bring up the English girl he was supposedly seeing, but something told her that no matter how tactfully she mentioned it she would only sound jealous and probing, two qualities that she knew Jack despised.

"I hear you've been flying to London lately," she said instead. "Do you like that flight?"

"I like London."

"But now you've switched to Paris."

He smiled, if it could be called a smile; it was more of a lopsided smirk. "I like Paris, too. I like to move around. The same place gets dull after a while."

The same woman, too, was what he meant. Was that why he had left her last October, because he needed variety? Or was it something specific she had done, perhaps something she had failed to do, some need of his that she had not met? Anita had to find out. She could even accept his rejection of her if only she knew the reason. It was the not knowing that had driven her crazy these last few months, the endless conjecturing, the wondering, all the conclusions arrived at which were not conclusions at all without Jack's stamp of authorization.

"Have you ever been through the Sainte-Chapelle in Paris?" he asked her.

"No. Have you?"

"I spent the morning there today. You know it used to be a church for members of the royal household. Before the revolution of 1789, of course."

"I didn't know that."

She looked at him. He had removed his pilot's jacket and cap, and standing beside her in his plain white shirt and dark trousers he might have been a waiter. What was it about him that she found so attractive? He was not really good looking, his features were too beat up, his hairline was receding, there was a ruddy quality to his face that at times deepened into an almost angry red, and yet he had an elegant kind of symmetry, the way he walked, he walked like a man who had just gotten off a horse, Anita had never seen an Eastern man walk that way, it was a sort of Gary Cooper saunter, something about the way the hips moved, and it had an irresistible charm for Anita, who, when they were still involved, was happy just to sit and watch him languidly walk across the room, naked.

"What's amazing about Sainte-Chapelle is that all of that beautiful stained glass should have managed to survive two catastrophic wars. You should go there the next time you're in Paris. It's an eerie feeling climbing the stone staircase to the chapel on the second floor, your footsteps following in the footsteps of Louis XIV three centuries later."

"It sounds very interesting."

"Not interesting. Inspiring."

"That's what I meant."

Anita respected Jack's absorption in places and things that she knew could never equally absorb her. She felt this quality in him to be an intrinsic part of his masculinity. He was easily the most masculine man she had ever met and yet if someone had asked her to explain why, she would not be able to, perhaps it was something that could not be successfully explained, only felt. Jack had a world of his own. That was part of it. And he had been around so much, he had known so many women, he had been married twice, he had a fourteen-year-old son living with his first wife near Las Vegas, he had fought in three wars. Anita was in love with the fabric of his past, as well as the more immediate physical shock of his presence.

It sounded crazy but just looking at his arms excited her. He had rolled up the sleeves of his shirt, revealing strong muscular arms, even the veins that ran the length of his arms aroused her desire, they seemed to throb with vitality. Jack appeared much thinner in clothes than he actually was ("I dress skinny," he had once remarked). His chest was deep. Anita used to like to rest her head on it (did it remind her of her father's chest?). His shoulders were broad, heavy, she felt they would protect her in all emergencies. She was not attracted to men who were too lean. Peter Northrop's lean body would not excite her when she finally encountered it. No, there was something thrilling to Anita about a certain amount of weight on top of her when she made love, a feeling of being slightly crushed. Her satisfaction demanded that density of force, that pressure, and there were times when she used to wonder whether she really cared about Jack's mind, what his thoughts were, his dreams, whether she knew him at all, had ever examined his soul, or if it was only the sheer physical impact of him that she had fallen in love with, the mirage of him, for she had to admit to herself one day that she did not listen when he spoke, at least not to his words or the facts they conveyed, but rather to the way he spoke, the rhythm of his voice, the enthusiasm he revealed in talking about, say, a Sainte-Chapelle, which apparently meant a great deal to him and next to nothing to her. Yet she would happily let him go on for an hour if he wished, he could not bore her no matter what he spoke about, he could stand there and recite the Greek alphabet backward and she would be mesmerized by his sheer presence.

That, Anita decided, was the mystery of love, the elusiveness of it, the eternal riddle that people were forever trying to solve. *Why?* Why do we fall in love with this person and not that one? Everyone was so busy analyzing the components of love, dissecting a piece here, chipping away at a motive there, it was ridiculous; they were trying to bring logic to something that would forever escape the rational mind. Love could only be explained by the senses. That finally was what it amounted to, and if someone at that very moment were to ask Anita why she was in love with Jack Bailey she would not be ashamed to say, "Because I like the way he walks across the room."

The doorbell buzzed and she excused herself to Jack, saying, "I'll be back in a second."

What she really felt like saying was, "Please don't go away, don't leave me, don't flirt with another girl." What if he should walk off into the night with the girl in the vinyl jumpsuit? (Anita despised herself for having invited that girl.) They had been looking at each other a moment ago, she now realized with the delayed double take of unpleasant awareness. It was imperative that Jack stay with her after all the others were gone and the party had collapsed into a pile of debris; it was imperative that he make love to her tonight (she had waited for him so long!), that she sleep beside him once more and listen to his quiet, even breathing. She loved him so much that she could not believe he did not love her a little. It would not be human if he didn't.

"Anita, darling. You look divine as usual. I'd almost forgotten what a smashing creature you are."

"Ian, dear. I'm so glad you could come."

Ian Clarke kissed her on the cheek, and whispered. "Will you let me stay over tonight if I promise to behave myself? Dare I hope?"

She laughed, at the same time realizing that her diaphragm felt funny. She wondered if it had gotten dislodged since she put it in hours ago. She must be sure to check it out just as soon as she made Ian a drink and introduced him to at least one person.

"Ian, you're such a faker."

"It's part of my charm."

Ian Clarke was a tall Englishman in his late twenties, mod haircut, a perennially quizzical expression on his face and a rather spindly physique. Yet he was attractive in a way, there was an alert, birdlike quality about him that held a certain appeal. Still like most of his countrymen he depressed Anita. She had never been able to make anything out of the English, determine what they were really like, perhaps their façade was the message after all and nothing more profound lay beyond.

Anita had gone to bed with Ian several times the winter before and it was the kind of formal and polite lovemaking that could not be classified as terrible because nothing terrible had happened, and yet nothing marvelous nor interesting had happened either. Instead there had been a staginess about the act, almost as though they were giving an instructive lesson to a vast student body on the mechanics of sexual intercourse. Not only that but one of Ian's hip bones got in her way, it jutted into her flesh at a most uncomfortable angle and although she tried to move her body so as to dislodge it, all she succeeded in doing was transferring the jut to another part of her highly sensitive flesh.

The reason she had gone to bed with Ian to begin with was to try to get her mind off Jack Bailey. She had just then met Jack and could see all the danger signals in herself of falling hopelessly in love with him, without seeing any signal at all from Jack that he might eventually feel the same way toward her. However, after several nights with England's gift to the colonies, she was ready to face whatever catastrophe awaited her in the arms of Jack Bailey; not only was she ready, she was positively looking forward to it, and as soon as she and Jack had gotten over several serious hurdles (his unmanageable penis, her germicidal problem) they settled down to the best lovemaking of Anita's life, not to mention the production of her very first orgasm.

Anita remembered that orgasmic moment in shamefaced detail. She was so beyond herself with the significance of what was happening that she screamed out at the top of her lungs, "Oh God fuck me fuck me please don't stop!" and then had been so horrified by the sound of her own words that even as the convulsive spasms shook her body she felt her face turn hot and red with abject humiliation.

As the relationship with Jack wore on, several things happened to dim Anita's subsequent enjoyment. First, there was the invincible feeling that Jack expected her to take more of the initiative, to somehow be more resourceful, more energetic in bed, and she really did not know how or what precisely to do beyond repeating her old high school success with Terry Radomski in the going down department. Jack seemed to enjoy her attempts up to a point but sometimes she sensed annoyance on his part, and once he brusquely pushed her head away, and said, "Not now, honey." That bewildered her as much as did his tacit but undeniable expectations of her.

"What is it that you want me to do?" she finally asked him.

"Just for a change of pace, honey, why don't you get on top?"

To please him Anita did as he suggested but she did not enjoy it. She did not know what to do when she got on top, and it did not seem like a natural position for a woman to assume. She resented his having suggested it at all but she nonetheless bravely attempted to simulate an excitement that she did not feel. Her thought at the time was that she would obediently accede to whatever demands Jack Bailey made of her until . . . well, why should she be ashamed of her motives? They were valid enough. Until she became Mrs. Jack Bailey and could pick and choose her forms of enjoyment.

Another basis of dissension between them was Jack wanting to make love to her when she had her period. Anita had never heard of such a thing. She was shocked. She was so shocked that she even repeated the incident to Simone who was living with her at the time, but Simone had a callous reaction to say the least.

"Oh, that's not so terrible," Simone remarked. "Wait until he wants to eat you when you have your period."

It was at that point that Anita decided Simone was completely depraved and beyond help, although in a surge of painful envy she found herself wondering whether Simone was not far better off than she, more liberated, less bound by rigid notions of this is right and that is wrong, and yet Anita *was* bound by them, tied, out of step with a world that seemed to have no consideration for the corny old-fashioned virtues she prized so dearly. Anita felt that she had been denied her birthright of wifehood and motherhood, and instead was expected to jump around in bed like a sex-crazed lunatic whose thoughts went no farther than the next orgasm. But her thoughts did go farther. Sexual intimacy was not something she took lightly, it was a giving of a very precious, the most precious, part of herself and she could not give it in a vacuum of unadulterated hedonism. No, that was not for her, her sexual desire and her marital aspirations were inextricably interwoven and she felt there was little, if anything, she could do about it. In desperation, she had tried to explain her feelings to Jack.

"I'm sorry, honey," he said by way of reply, "but I've been divorced twice and I have no intention of becoming a three-time alimony loser."

"I know that I could make you happy."

"Happiness is constipating."

(Pilots were hung up on shit) "Is that all you have to say on the subject?"

"Isn't that enough?"

"But aren't you lonely living by yourself?" (She was planning all the gourmet meals she would prepare for him when they were man and wife . . . boeuf bourguignon, cervelle au beurre noir, chicken paprikash, mussels ravigote, her mouth watered at the tantalizing prospect of matrimony).

"Loneliness is not an unnatural state," Jack informed her. "Marriage is."

"I'll take a Scotch and water, if I may," Ian said to her now.

Sex and liquor, liquor and sex. Was that all men ever thought about? When she returned with Ian's drink, she asked him if there was any particular girl he wanted to be introduced to.

"In other words, you're turning me down for yourself?" he said mockingly.

That was another thing about the English she disliked, their compulsive humor. They were forever making jokes, thinking themselves very witty and clever even when their remarks were palpable fictions, for the fact was that Ian was not at all interested in her, he was looking for a girl with money, he had told her so himself. After the first time they made love, he said, "You're a lovely piece of ass. It's unfortunate that you're a poor working girl."

When she asked him what he meant by that, he propped himself up on one spindly elbow and very matter-of-factly said, "That's what I'm looking for in this country, luv, a girl with money. You don't think I want to go on working at that dreadful network for the rest of my natural life, do you?"

Anita said she supposed not, feeling all the while terribly insulted that he should have chosen that tender moment to let her know that no matter what she did, she would simply not *do*. There was nothing worse, she realized, than being insulted when you were naked; in a condition of undress all insults carried a double thrust.

"You really are a bastard," she told him, and it occurred to her, not without some degree of pride, that it was the first time in her life she had ever said that to a man.

"Now don't get angry merely because I'm being honest for a change. There's no point in people deluding each other, particularly when serious economic factors are involved, now is there?"

Anita felt too insulted to answer, too insulted even to cry, too depressed at being written off for monetary reasons, or were they social status reasons, too? After all, what was a stewardess but a glorified waitress in the sky, despite inflated recruitment advertising to the contrary? She could have accepted Ian's telling her that he did not go for blondes, or that her breasts were too small to suit him, or that she looked too much like his mother for comfort, but to be discarded because she had no money, no income, no inheritance, was almost more than she could bear. It seemed so undemocratic a rejection, so un-American, and she had to remind herself that Ian was not an American and did not have American values. It was on that last score that she finally managed to excuse and forgive his blunt dismissal of her.

"Are you still at the network?" she asked him now, deciding that in his black turtleneck pullover and handsome tweed jacket he looked the best she had ever seen him.

"Yes. Dreary business after all this time and getting drearier by the minute. And you? Are you still serving eight course meals over the Atlantic and warming up cranky babies' formulas?"

"Status quo."

Oddly enough she no longer felt any bitterness toward Ian, perhaps because seeing him tonight for the first time in a year she realized how vulnerable he was in his own way, how unfulfilled, how basically unhappy working at a job he disdained (assistant director on a daytime television quiz show, appropriately enough named "Quiz"), and still in search of the American heiress of his dreams who, apparently, was not as easy to come by as he must have imagined when he left the shores of England three years ago.

"What's new in the romance department?" Ian asked. "What have you been up to since the last time I saw you? Are you in love?"

"Yes."

"I take it then that the lucky fellow is here tonight."

"Yes."

But where? For a second Anita panicked until she spotted Jack emerge from the bathroom and then head directly toward the girl in the vinyl jumpsuit, then with a nod of agreement the two of them moved out onto the floor to dance their teasing, nontouching dance and Anita felt a heavy weight descend upon her, their dancing was like long distance lovemaking, tempting, exciting, everything. Oh, God, Jack had once stuck his finger up her ass. Now why should she think of that now? Because it had hurt and so did this tease-dance? Maybe maybe.

"Ian, would you please get me a drink?"

"Of course. What would you like?"

"Vodka and ice, please."

"Back in a jiffy."

"Thanks."

But he hesitated. "You look a bit *gênée* suddenly. Are you all right?"

"Oh yes, just slightly warm. It is warm in here, isn't it?"

"I'm going to get you that drink and then I'm going to open a window," Ian said, looking concerned.

He had never looked concerned about her at any time during the course of their brief affair, and Anita wondered whether he was able to feel that way now because of the fact that sex was no longer an issue between them, nor was love, marriage. It struck her as interesting that only when all the important man-woman considerations were conveniently out of the picture was he able to respond to her with simple human compassion.

"I made it rather strong," Ian said, handing her a glass. "You look as though you might need it."

"I do."

"Is he giving you a rough time?"

"Yes. Yes, he is."

She took a large swallow of the icy vodka, then another. The glass she was drinking from had once held damson plum jelly. It was an old glass left over from her roommate days with Simone. In fact, it was Simone who had bought the jelly, which she used to spread on zwieback as an accompaniment to her morning coffee. Anita wondered how Simone was making out with Robert Fingerhood. Perhaps they would fall in love and get married and Simone would ask her to be maid of honor. Perhaps every girl she knew would get married before she did. Just last week one of the senior stewardesses had announced her engagement. She was thirty-five if she was a day and not even very goodlooking, horsey really. One of the other stewardesses had said, "I'll bet she does something funny in bed."

Anita finished the vodka and went to get another as Ian struggled with the window which had not been opened in months, as the Supremes began to sing "Stop in the Name of Love."

"Do you feel any better?" he asked when she returned from the kitchenette with the jelly glass refilled.

("Do you feel any better, Mrs. Northrop?" Margaret was asking Beverly in the buttercup yellow kitchen).

"The air helps," Anita said.

"Which one is he?"

"He's dancing with the vinyl jumpsuit."

"Not bad."

"Yes, he is attractive."

"I meant the girl."

"Don't rub it in."

"Oh sorry. Tactless of me. But you're much more attractive, you know. Really you are. I'm not just flattering you."

"You're sweet."

"No, I'm not. I'm a bastard and you bloody well know it."

"Perhaps but you're being very sweet tonight."

"Ladies in distress have always appealed to my chivalrous nature. We English are stuck with the legend of our romantic past."

Haven't I been good to you, haven't I been sweet to you?
Stop in the name of love before you break my heart
Think it o-o-ver, think it o-o-ver.

"Sometimes I think I never should have left Cleveland," Anita said.

"What is it like, your Cleveland?"

"It's horrid. It's probably the worst city in America."

"Why is that?"

"Because it's so ugly. It's one of the ugliest cities I've ever seen. All the people there think about is making money."

"I suspect that's not confined to Cleveland. Believe they do that everywhere these days."

"The girl Jack is dancing with is loaded."

"How can you tell? She looks pretty sober to me."

"No, not drunk. Rich. Very rich."

Ian began to get that dollar sign gleam in his calculating

eye. "You don't say. Now why didn't you tell me that before?"

"I was saving it as a surprise."

He instinctively smoothed his mod haircut and brushed an imaginary speck of something off his tweed jacket. "Stand by for action, my darling. By the way what kind of money is it? Something solid I hope."

Think it o-o-ver, think it o-o-ver

"Real estate," Anita said.

"You're a love. See you later."

Think it o-o-ver, think it o-o-ver

If Ian's maneuver proved successful, that would not necessarily prevent Jack from approaching or being approached by any of the other girls. She had to grab him before he was grabbed by the girl in the hot pink mini-zip shift, or the girl in the see-through no-bra midi, the one in the gold burnoose was easily the most beautiful girl there, she had great almond eyes and a flawless complexion, the girl in the swingy tent was cute, gamine, the turquoise body shirt and orange bubble skirt girl was striking if not conventionally pretty, yes they all had something, some distinctive individualistic quality that could not be overlooked, there were so many attractive women in New York, the competition was awesome, Anita felt overwhelmed by it. Why should Jack choose her when there were so many others more attractive, more vital than she? Even the least attractive girl in the room, the one in the skinny sweater dress, managed to hold her own by virtue of having the shortest haircut and the most dazzling eyeshadow, an avocado shade of green which zippy color schemed with the lavender and purple stripes of her dress. Anita's own pink satin harem pajamas seemed almost mundane in contrast to the exoticisms surrounding her, and she wished now that she had chosen something different to wear, perhaps she should have bought one of those metal dresses that clanged. Nobody in the room was wearing metal, she observed, probably because it was still very expensive, Paco. The Supremes were off into "Honey Boy."

He's sugar he's spice he's everything that's nice
He's my honey boy my ever loving pride and joy
Mmm mmm mmm, Mmm mmm

Were the Supremes happy, Anita wondered, was anyone?

His kisses are his claim to fame, honey boy is his name
I'd rather have a minute of his time than all the gold
in the Fort Knox mine, Mmm, mmm mmm, Mmm mmm mmm

Jack loved to make love to music. He had once been a musician years years ago, tenor sax, what else? But not very good at it. WOR rock and roll was the station they used to make love to.

"Uninterrupted by commercials."

That was what Jack said the first time and was saying again hours later, party people gone. She had grabbed him away from all the others all right and was grabbing him now, but they were both incredibly drunk and doing things at strange angles. There were minutes when Anita cried, screamed out her pent up anger, collapsed into curled up foetus positions, because although he was here now he was here by default and she knew it, she would never have him, no matter what she did, never never never never never never never, not only would he never marry her but he might never phone her again. At least she had had the brains to check her diaphragm before and make sure that it was in right, maybe she shouldn't have checked it, she had always wanted Jack's child but Jack himself had to be part of the deal or it was no deal as far as she was concerned.

"Keep your legs down," he said.

She remembered one time they had taken a bath together and sailed toy boats on iridescent bubbles and she wondered what those serious-faced passengers ("We're ditching in the Atlantic, folks") would think if they could have tuned in on their captain and star stewardess playing with toy boats in a bathtub and soaping each other's genitals. Then they had dried off and dusted talcum powder on themselves and drunk champagne and spent the rest of the afternoon in the Palace Hotel in Madrid making looooove and saying that they really should go to the Prado and look at the Velázquez things, but room service was so much nicer than *Las Meninas,* gazpacho with tiny chopped up bits of cucumber floating on the red, buttery veal and vino and oh why were all the good times *yesterday?*

Think it o-o-ver, think it o-o-ver

"You're moving too fast," Jack said.

Jack liked her skin, buttery veal, but she was not mysterious enough for him, she did not create an aura. Also Ian would probably never speak to her again when he found out that the girl in the vinyl jumpsuit didn't have a cent to her name beyond next week's paycheck (she taught Latin languages at a high school in Westchester). He would be furious with her but what did she care about spindly Ian with his unfortunate jutting hipbone? She had to have her hair bleached soon, the roots were showing. Did people ever grow up or only deceive each other with earnest daytime faces that collapsed in bathtubs and toy boats? Lies, everyone told everyone else the most absurd lies about themselves and were afraid not to believe what they were hearing ("We're ditching in the Atlantic, folks"). The Palace Hotel was marvelous, Anita wanted to spend the rest of her life there in regal gowns being fawned upon by waiters stiffly wheeling in silver carts of buttery veal. Who cared about reality?

"I do."

She did because she had to face it, she was going to call the hairdresser first thing in the morning, her roots made her insecure. So did her breasts, she could see *she* would never get anywhere with hydrotherapy. Maybe the only solution was a silicone implant (one thousand dollars, which she did not have), for now that she had taken off her Hollywood Vassarette, her breasts had no character at all. She blamed it all on that filthy pork her father was eternally dealing in, hog merchant. She was a pig. It would all be better tomorrow, there would be blue birds over the Terminal Tower tomorrow when the world was free.

"There'll be love and laughter and peace ever after."

That was what Jack had once sung to her but she didn't recognize the song or know what he meant, a generation separated them. She suspected that if Jack ever did marry again, it would be a woman close to his own age, which was ironic because most men wanted young girls. Anita knew she really didn't care about sex, it was a device to entice, marriage was what she cared about.

"I love it," she moaned.

Even having achieved her first orgasm last year did not mean as much to her as it should have. She dreamed of dishwashers and baby clothes. She hoped that Simone and Robert Fingerhood would not fall in love, she would be too jealous. Jack was going to come before she did this time, she couldn't come, she was too insecure about her roots. Perhaps some women were melting sexpots who thrived upon eroticism but she was not one of them. Jack was absolutely panting and out of his mind with orgasm tremors. Beast, pig, no, no she loved him but what did it mean? Misery. He came so much that she would drip for hours, the room smelled of semen, the sheets were damp, it was all inside her, one hundred thousand potential babies who would never see the light of day thanks to Ramses 75, what would future men say to her?

"It's like fucking a paper bag."

Too small upstairs and too big downstairs.

The story of Anita's life.

Chou-Chou whimpered in Simone's tote bag next to the radiator and in his sleep Peter Northrop said, "Marcel Proust was a *yentah*."

Lou smoked too much.

As she walked the few blocks from her garden apartment to Elaine's on Second Avenue, she had a strong almost overwhelming desire for a Gauloise but she did not allow herself to light one. For one thing she felt vulgar smoking in the street, but mainly she had decided to cut down on smoking in general, it was too typical a career girl hangup and she could not bear the thought of being typical anything, it was too frightening a thought, one which she had fled from all her life just as she had fled from Philadelphia shortly after her daughter was born.

The delivery was by cesarean section and now, ten years later, Lou physically bore the memory of birth in the form of a long-since whitened scar that made a jagged vertical line down her abdomen. She felt at times that God had overseen the placing of that scar in order to remind her constantly of past blunders. Before David, whenever she went to bed with a man she would explain away the scar by saying that she once was operated on for peritonitis and then she would make a little joke out of it all by adding:

"That was the way Sherwood Anderson died, you know. He swallowed a cocktail toothpick on a cruise ship to South America and it fatally pierced his peritoneum. Can you imagine? After a lifetime of suffering, to be killed by a lousy toothpick?"

And men would smile and feel sorry for poor Sherwood Anderson rather than poor Lou Marron, which was precisely her purpose in telling the anecdote. She could not stand being pitied, not because she was strong and above pity but because she was weak in ways that possibly only David knew about and any show of pity merely served to reinforce that lurking sense of weakness which for the most part she successfully managed to hide from the eyes of the world.

It was freezing cold on Second Avenue and Lou felt grateful for the Kohinoor mink that David had given her last year on her twenty-seventh birthday. In only six more months she would be twenty-eight and what had she really accomplished? She was nobody, nothing, not a great success in work, no success at all in terms of love or marriage. The years had gone so quickly. Soon she would be thirty and would probably have to start dyeing her hair, which already showed a couple of prematurely gray hairs mixed in among the black.

That reminded her of Tony Elliot's advice about changing her hairstyle, but the question was what to change it to? One had to anticipate future trends rather than go along with current ones which were bound to become quickly outdated. This meant that since straight hair, either long or short, was the present vogue there would soon be a return to curly hair, particularly since clothes were so spare and geometric these days. Curly hair could add a softness of contrast that was now lacking in the overall fashion picture. But Lou looked terrible in curly hair, her face was too long for it, her features too sharp. Curly hair looked good on pert-faced, small-featured women with small dolls' heads. She did not have that kind of head. She had once tried curly hair via a permanent, years ago when she first came to New York, and the result was catastrophic. She had not been able to recognize herself and neither had anybody else.

"You must be kidding," was the consensus. "You *have* to be kidding, Lou."

They were right, she finally decided, she was kidding herself. Well, she would just have to think about it some more, surely there was some solution that would fit the bill. And for a second, as she pushed open the door to Elaine's, she felt a tremulous surge of regret that instead of the protective warmth of a husband and children she had somewhere along the way chosen the precarious existence of a highly competitive career that made her subject to the whims and fancies of men like Tony Elliot. And yet at the same time she knew that because of everything she was the choice had been inevitable; there was a drive within her that could not be satisfied by a husband and children, and had she married she would surely have made a mess of it, her heart would not have been in it, she would have been bored. But perhaps someday when she was older, more secure in her work, perhaps then she might meet someone, love someone, perhaps . . . or perhaps it was already too late.

"Hi there."

The bartender waved to her over the throng of people crowding the popular bar, people all pushed together, jammed together in a warm mass of cigarette smoke and iced drinks, people talking, people waiting for people to talk to, people killing time, people searching for escape, for companionship, for affection, for sex. Lou suddenly remembered her initial motive for coming here. A man. Someone to spend the night with and take her mind off everything, off Tony Elliot and the column, off that horrible Peter Northrop, off the Steve Omaha piece that she had yet to write, off her illegitimate daughter who was lost to her forever, off the jagged scar that marred her slender body, off David and his ailing wife.

"I believe it's a Lou Marron, indeed I do."

"Indeed you are right," she replied in the same lighthearted tone to the man who had appeared at her side out of nowhere.

He was a playwright with a couple of medium East Village successes to his credit and he was reputed to be gauging his next piece of work for the Broadway stage. His name was Arnold or Arthur or Albert, it was embarrassing but she never could remember which. Physically he was a breezy, stocky type who looked more like a shoe salesman than a writer of dramatic tragedies, but as Lou had long ago discovered creative people often saved their aspirational selves for their work and publicly presented the self they were at that moment, the self they were either trying to overcome or somehow modify. Their personal projection to the world was their being, their work (hopefully) represented their becoming. She knew that she tended to appear outwardly very serious, intense at times, whereas her writing struck a light, frivolous, blasé note, a note implying she had things wrapped up with such utter control that people who did not know any better automatically believed that was the way she was. It occurred to her now that Peter Northrop for all of his sardonic and trivial stances wrote with greater depth and far less frivolity than she.

"Can I buy you a drink?" Arnold (or Arthur or Albert) asked.

"Yes, thank you."

"What would you like?"

"A bottle of wine."

The couple standing to her left had overheard the exchange and laughed. Arnold turned a bit red. Was he being made a fool of? Or should he consider her request a campy kind of thing and go along with it for fun, proving that he could not be so easily threatened by unlikely demands as it might appear, that he too had a sense of the absurd?

"White or red?" he asked her.

"White, please."

"Half a bottle of Orvieto," he told the bartender. "For the lady."

The bartender appeared with a chilled bottle and poured an inch or so into a glass, awaiting her approval. She did not taste it but waved her hand in acceptance, *"Ça va."*

The bartender looked at Arnold and shrugged. Who could figure out women? Arnold shrugged back, pleased to have gained an ally in this foolish role he found himself playing.

"Would you like some?" Lou asked him.

"No thanks. I'm quite happy with my Scotch."

Lou did not know why she had done it, what had prompted her to order the wine, some misplaced vindictiveness that she was taking out on poor innocent Arnold (or Arthur or Albert). Whatever his name was, however, he would not do, not for the night, not for any night as far as she was concerned, he was too bovine even if he did write dark bathroom tragedies about the unhappy state of mankind. If she went to bed with him she would do something awful, like burst out laughing just when he started to come, or insist that he go home immediately afterward without explaining why. She could be cruel with men, had been cruel (although not at the beginning) and always felt terribly depressed later.

Excerpt from an old diary of Lou's written shortly after her twentieth birthday:

> My need to be sexually involved versus my fear of melting. Here is the dichotomy: on the one hand unbounded passion, on the other self-containment, work, emotions in order. My inability to reconcile the two levels of being. How classic a case I am! I want an ordered existence, a comfortable relationship with a man, then I can think, read, write. At the same time I want wild eroticism, uncertainty, no writing or reading or thinking at all, hedonism. I do not like to be driven to

extreme states of erotic dependence. They frighten me. To hear my own voice unleased in orgasm is frightening beyond belief. A wild animal. I sink, melt. The fear of being a slave. I feel that my orgasms when they finally come (because they have been kept so carefully in check for so long) are wilder, deeper, more unruly than other people's. What egotism. And yet I can't help it, I believe it. I go into such a lunatic and uncontrollable state that I am destroyed for days afterward. I don't want to do anything except lie around and listen to popular torch songs and feel miserable. My body is on fire but my mind is a blank. I need more but more doesn't help, it only makes all the rest worse. I could stay in bed for a million days and at the same time know it is my doom. Is there no reconciliation?

Lou looked up at the colorful Paris Review posters above Elaine's bar, then she looked at her playwright friend and smiled politely, then she caught the eye of a couple having dinner at a table farther back in the room. Odd that she had not noticed them when she came in. They were a comfortable couple to be with, they made her feel at ease, they accepted certain things that other people might not so casually accept, her relationship with David for one thing, and they did it without asking questions or casting doubts. She wanted to go over and sit with them but now that she had ordered this bottle of wine she felt temporarily obligated to Arnold and she resented her shortsightedness.

"Do you know them?" she asked him, nodding toward the couple having dinner.

"No. Afraid not."

"They're awfully nice, they're really wonderful people."

"Do you want to join them?"

"Well, it would be nice. I haven't seen them in quite a while."

"Go ahead then."

"Won't you come with me?"

He appraised her coolly. "You don't really want me to."

"That's not true."

"I suspect it is."

"Look, I'm sorry if I—"

"You know," he said, "you're really rather a bitch."

"Ciao, bambino."

"*Bambino* yourself."

"Lou!" the couple at the table said in unison.

"Hello," she said. "It's good to see you again."

"So good to see *you,*" the woman said. "Where is David?"

For she frequently came here with him, it was one of their favorite places. "He's home with his wife tonight. She's sick for a change."

They regarded her above the fettucini as though to gauge the exactitude of her despair. Was David's wife truly sick, or was there another ominous reason that he was not with Lou tonight? Were they having difficulties? Had they perhaps rashly broken up? Having been reasonably happily married for so many years themselves, this couple often sought a vicarious excitement and conflict in the lives of their less stable friends, without actually wishing them any unhappiness or bad fortune.

"I hope it's nothing serious," the man said.

"The doctor says it's colitis."

"That could be serious."

"I don't think it is in this case, I don't know. David doesn't think it is. The doctor says it's basically a nervous affliction. Very often they recommend psychotherapy."

"Would you like to join us for dinner?" the woman asked, as their eyes met in the tacit acknowledgment of betrayed wives being naturally reduced to nervous afflictions of one sort or another.

"Thanks but I couldn't eat a thing. After David phoned to break our date tonight I made a chicken sandwich at home," she lied, wondering why her lies were always so exquisitely precise: why chicken, for instance, and not roast beef? "I'm not the least bit hungry but I'd like to join you if I may."

"Please, dear, sit down," the man said, getting up and pulling out a chair for her.

"Thank you."

"You'll never gain any weight eating a chicken sandwich for dinner," the woman said, not unkindly.

Lou regarded her with a keen combination eye—the female eyeball here, the fashion reporter eyeball peering out over there.

"But I wouldn't like to gain weight," she said, slipping out of the white, black-streaked mink, and pouring some of the Orvieto into her empty wine glass. "I feel much better if I'm thin, more energetic, I work better, the nerve endings are closer to the skin."

She stopped, self-consciously afraid that her mention of energy would in some way reveal the clue to the nature of tonight's restless sexual quest. And yet why shouldn't she be in search of a lover, ten lovers if that was what she wanted? What was wrong about it? David was married. David was fifty-six years old. David did not live with her. She loved David but David was not hers. She suspected that if she ever did marry, she would remain faithful because to cheat on a husband was like cheating on oneself, a husband was so much a part of oneself, a possession almost. *My* husband.

"How come the vino?" the man asked.

It occurred to Lou that this was the first time she had ever been alone with the two of them, in the past David had always been present to round out the group, balance it, and in his absence she felt an odd intimacy with each of them, with both of them. She felt closer to them and at the same time more vulnerable.

"Arnold bought it for me," she said.

"You mean the guy at the bar?"

"Yes. Do you know him?"

"No," the man said, doing fork things with his fettucini. "But his name is Albert."

"I never can remember. It's so embarrassing."

"He's an easy guy to forget."

"I think he's rather nice," the woman said. "Sort of lost and floundering but at least he admits it, he doesn't have that put-on pretentiousness that so many—"

"He's a fucking bore," the man said, "and so are his plays."

"I thought you said you didn't know him," Lou said.

"Oh I've spoken to him once or twice at parties."

The man was a very successful lawyer and the woman had been his secretary before they were married. Now they had two children and the woman stayed home and took care of them. They had a lovely apartment with a terrace on the East River Drive. Lou had never thought about it before but she found herself wondering whether the woman was bored, whether the man had a girlfriend on the side, whether their marriage was as happy as she had always imagined, or was she merely projecting her own insecurities and anxieties?

"What are you folks doing after dinner?" she asked. "I was thinking of going down to Cheetah or The Electric Circus. I'm all keyed up from that damned office. I thought maybe I could dance away my frustrations."

"Why don't you come with us instead?" the man suggested. "We're going to an opening at the Jewish. There's an Yves Klein exhibition."

"Yes, do come," the woman said. "It might be fun. Klein is

the one who used to put paint on people and then roll them around on the canvas. Also, he held his wedding reception at the Coupole."

"He can't be all bad. I'd love to go." Then she told them about having interviewed Steve Omaha that afternoon. "This is certainly my day for art. Did I tell you that David bought two Braque lithos last week? He's becoming quite a collector."

"He and Jaques Kaplan," the man said. "The hip furriers are getting to be like dentists in the collecting department."

The Jewish Museum on Ninety-Second Street was jammed with exotic people, it was simply crawling with them. The whole thing was like some sort of freak fashion show that Lou might have expected to find at Arthur or Trude Heller's (which was out to begin with), but not here, and there was Cav off in one corner snapping away for all he was worth accompanied by a newcomer to *The Rag,* a young girl reporter assiduously taking notes for next week's issue (Tony Elliot didn't miss a trick, you had to say that for the bastard). It was the kind of third-rate reporter assignment Lou used to get stuck with when she first started working for the paper, and she felt a surge of satisfaction at this tangible testimony to the fact that she had indeed moved up the career ladder no matter how column-frustrated she'd been feeling lately. She waved at Cav who was wearing a purple velvet tie and a bright orange jacket. He beckoned her over, and she hesitated for a moment, wondering what had happened to the couple she came with, but they were lost somewhere in the vast frenetic shuffle of butterfly legs and bared milky skin and feather boas and mean pantsuits and gold empire nightgowns.

"This is a happening," Cav informed her. "Too bad Klein isn't alive to witness the spectacle. I'll bet he'd have given anything to be able to roll this bunch around on a nice clean twenty foot canvas."

He took a shot of a man whose entire head was painted blue and had the words *Homage to Yves Klein* running across his forehead in neat white letters. Then he took a shot of a stringy-haired girl with sequined eyelashes, wearing a thrift shop outfit. Then he said to Lou, "We're going to cut. Enough is plenty. See you tomorrow."

After they left Lou debated whether to stay awhile, go someplace else, try to locate her wandering friends, or perhaps go home and put Vitacream on her face and watch "The Johnny Carson Show." She had not arrived a a decision when a tall Negro in a vanilla suit said hello and introduced himself to her.

"I'm Marshall—"

She failed to catch his last name. "Hi. I'm Lou Marron."

"I was watching you from across the room. You looked a little lost."

"I wouldn't have thought it possible to *see* anybody across this room."

"It is quite a crowd, isn't it?"

"Overwhelming. And you, are you a painter?"

He laughed as though this were terribly amusing. "I hate to disappoint you but I work for The First National City Bank. I'm in the personal loan department."

"It's no disappointment," she said, wondering why these things happened to her. "I was just telling some people who seem to have disappeared that I've had my fill of painters and paintings for the day." Then she explained about her job and the Steve Omaha interview. "I think I was shanghaied into coming here. Frankly, I would have preferred some place quiet like the Bus Terminal."

"Would you like to go to Trude Heller's?"

"Why not?"

Leave it to her to meet a square spade. The personal loan department! Was he kidding? Oh well in spite of his WASP aspirations perhaps he would turn out to be okay in the sack. Who could ever tell about these things? They were so damned mysterious. Some men talked a good bed game and then when you actually got them there they were complete washouts, duds, ninnies. They didn't know what to do, or if they did know they didn't have the essential equipment to do it with. He had large feet. That was an encouraging sign. And as the taxi headed down Fifth, Lou wondered what Peter Northrop was like in bed, that rotten AC-DC bastard. There was something about men who made it both ways, something attractive . . . what? . . . zzzzz . . . maybe she should have gone home alone and put Vitacream on her face and gone to sleep . . . zzzzz . . . maybe.

"Good evening," the man at the door at Trude Heller's said. "A table for two?"

"Please," said Marshall, looking very dignified and proper, at the crummiest discotheque in town.

The discotheque dancers were perched on a high ledge behind the band, two girls and a boy, the girls were wearing maroon vinyl miniskirts and the boy was wearing a striped shirt and very tight white pants, and they were all gyrating-dancing all by themselves together, their faces significantly blank, their bodies jerking and moving to the loud, dissonant, hypnotic music, as psychedelic lights flashed on and off across the room, and couples were gyrating-dancing on the floor. There was a hypnotic spell here, an other-world quality of being lost on Mars after the ultimate earth explosion and seeing new life through pink and lavender radiation glasses.

Lou was glad she was with a Negro, even if he did work for The First National City Bank. He lent an appropriate élan to the situation. Negroes were so in these days, it made her feel hip. The neighborhood she had grown up in in Philadelphia had become almost completely black within the last ten years and her parents had since moved to Spruce Street, which was closer to downtown and still almost completely white. She remembered her childhood in the house on Catherine Street, which was now occupied by a Negro family. One day recently she had taken a taxi to her old neighborhood and told the driver just to drive around slowly because all she wanted to do was look at yesterday. Staning there on her old front porch (where she as a child had once stood) was a little Negro girl bouncing a ball, playing by herself. A my name is Anna and my husband's name is Adam, we come from Alabama and we sell apples. B my name is Betty and . . .

"Those fine old houses," the white cab driver said nostalgically. "They were sold for a song."

"What would you like to drink?" Marshall asked.

"A double Scotch, please."

"Two double Scotches," he told the waiter.

"There's no point in ordering singles in this place," Lou explained. "The waiters are so busy that they don't have a chance to get back to you for ages."

She wondered whether Stokely Carmichael and H. Rap Brown drank Scotch. She had never met a Negro who didn't. An Englishman could go to hell in the tropics because that was exoticism, but a Negro had to drink Scotch and wear vanilla suits. Everybody aimed for what they weren't, including herself. Knocked up at seventeen, too dumb to know what to do about it, too terrified to tell her parents until it was too late to do anything about it except have the baby, and all the while hoping that the poor terrified high school boy was going to marry her, so now here she sat pretending to be chic, hip, in, sophisticated, successful and very much New York with it. And to a girl in Des Moines she would pass for exactly that, but what did it really mean in terms of the way she *felt?* One of the existentialist writers had said,

"We are what we have done." But what if you did all sorts of superficially convincing things and still *felt* like a knocked-up seventeen-year-old girl? Oh, there was a gap there.

"Would you like to dance?" Marshall said.

"Sure."

He wasn't a bad dancer, but uninspired and somewhat self-conscious. He would probably turn out to be the only untalented Negro in New York. No rhythm. She wished she were with David. She wondered what David was doing just then, probably he was asleep. He and his wife had separate bedrooms and he once told her that when he couldn't sleep he read late into the night. They lived on West End Avenue in one of those great old-time buildings with thick walls and labyrinthian apartments that just were not built any more, all those secret dens and hiding place rooms. Still the Upper West Side depressed Lou terribly. The streets were too long. Tony Elliot had told her that that was why the Upper West Side had such a depressing effect upon people, the streets were easily twice the length of the average Upper East Side street and there was a Chirico gloominess about them, a fear that one would never get to the end of a block, the blocks seemed to stretch so interminably.

"The Upper West Side," Tony Elliot said, "is really Chirico's *Melancholy and Mystery of a Street*, painted, I believe, in 1914."

After two more double Scotches and more uninspired dancing, Lou suggested that they leave. "I'm getting sleepy," she said.

"So am I."

"I'll buy you a nightcap at my place."

"I'll accept."

He put his arm around her in the taxi going uptown and she wondered how much longer it would be before they were making love. Probably not very long at all. She was nervous, she always felt a little nervous in advance, but not the least bit nervous once things got under way. In that sense she was like an actress who trembles and shakes in the wings waiting for her cue, but then is fine the minute she steps out on stage. It was the anticipation that made her nervous. Lou's panties felt damp already. The minute he touched her there he would know that she had been ready for quite a while, ready and eager, anxious to get going, to go and to come.

Lou rarely had trouble achieving an orgasm and she did not know why it seemed to be such a momentous problem for so many women. If a man did not do what she liked, she would tell him what she wanted, and she suspected that most women were too shy or embarrassed to make their subtle sexual needs known, the fools. After all why bother going to bed with a man in the first place, if you intended to cheat yourself out of the ultimate reward? Other things about certain women' attitudes surprised her too, such as an obsessive concern with penis sizes. Unless a man were minuscule (which she had encountered only once, thank God), any penis would do, it was a matter of knowing what to do with it. There was always a position that did the trick, a modus vivendi to be worked out. Most women, Lou felt, were too romantic about these matters and not practical enough. They were too ashamed to admit their needs, too stupidly compliant about too many things, melting hothouse flowers, the way she once was.

She would never again be a sexual slave, she would never again allow herself to become so erotically dependent upon a man that it destroyed the fabric of her life, no, never again. That was why she had developed a technique for coming. It was *her* technique, the man was only a necessary instrument, and that was also why any normally endowed man would do. Beautiful bodies. Flabby bodies. Big shoulders. No shoulders. She no longer cared about such considerations. Her own release of pleasure was what she was after and fuck the aesthetics.

"Play with me," she told Marshall when they were finally in bed in Lou's mauve wallpapered bedroom with the wavery Klee print over the dressing table. All female orgasms began with the clitoris and she didn't give a shit what the so-called manual experts said about the vaginal variety. The clitoris was the trigger to female orgasms and it didn't matter to Lou whether the man did it through finger manipulation or with his tongue. Either one was okay just so long as he did it for the necessary period of time. Unfortunately that time period varied from person to person, or even with the same person under different circumstances, but it rarely took longer than ten minutes for Lou to reach a significant stage of arousal and then she wanted the man inside her, needed him inside.

"Do you like it?" Marshall asked, his dark skin gleaming in the dimly lit room, his somber brown eyes fastened upon her.

"Yes, I love it. Please don't stop."

At least he had found the button right off. Some men were amazingly inept in that department, they just foundered around rubbing in all the wrong places until she gently but firmly guided their fingers (or tongues) to where X marked the spot. "*There,*" she would say. But Marshall needed no such guidance, she was happy to discover, and she sensed that he seemed desirous of pleasing her. He probably felt he had to live up to the inflated legend of the great black stud and for her sake she hoped so.

"I want to be inside you," he murmured.

"Not yet."

"Okay."

"Please don't stop."

"No, baby."

"It feels marvelous."

"I'll do anything you want," he said.

"You're doing exactly what I want. Don't stop."

But then when she was ready to have him inside her, he wasn't. He had lost his erection.

"Oh, no," she moaned.

If she didn't come tonight, she would never be able to write that goddamn Steve Ohama piece. The image of Steve wading through waisthigh water in the English Channel flashed across her mind, shells and bloody bodies all around him, the fear of unknown German installations, death and terror surrounding our D-Day hero, and then later the General Budenny hangup, Sidney Greenstreet smoking a Tiparillo on horseback, and Steve's passion for mini-skirted girls with big fat legs wrapped around him. What a crappy assignment, none of it fit, it was all a disparate mess. Cossack in the water. Lou in the soup. Marshall in a bag. Everything was very up tight, goddamn it, goddamn this black son of a bitch she had picked up. Black coffee. No, not really. Much more on the *café au lait* side, as opposed to the only other Negro she had gone to bed with (in Philadelphia—where else?), who was quite chocolate.

"White women expect so much of me," he said in the darkness. "Sometimes it's too much to live up to."

She put both arms around him and began to kiss him softly on the lips, then she let one hand wander down to his poor limp cock, which she just as softly began to massage. She'd get this guy hard if it was the last act of her life, hard and in her. She could feel her own orgasm hovering on the edge, and she just hoped that by an inadvertent movement she would not come like this, in a vacuum. It was so much more pleasurable to feel that force inside her as she came. Fuck Steve Omaha, Peter Northrop, and Tony Elliot, fuck them all, relief was just around the corner. She could feel him hardening in her hand, hooray. He had a long, thin one. She preferred the shorter, thicker type, they hit the sides better, it was a more pulsating sensation, but long and thin would do very nicely tonight and finally finally Marshall had gotten on top and entered her and was moving against her with slow pelvic gyrations.

"You don't have much of an ass, baby," he said, grabbing her by the buttocks.

At that second Lou's breathing turned into quick harsh gasps, which culminated seconds later in a sharp cry of marvelous beautiful wonderful delirious relief.

CHAPTER THREE

It was shortly after 6 A.M. Thursday morning when Simone woke up in Robert Fingerhood's leviathan bed and thought of Normandy. It was January in New York but Normandy in spring was a dream vision of rosy apple blossoms, there were thick wooded hills, lush pastures, sleek cattle, Percheron mares, prosperous farms, fertile soil, a mild climate, and Simone envisioned herself sitting underneath a rosy apple tree, staring at a cloudless sky, dreaming.

That was one version of Normandy anyway, the popular travelogue version. Whenever Simone chanced to read something about Normandy these days that was the way it sounded, that and the thick cream, golden butter, fragrant cheeses, a cuisine *à la crème*, and always included in the glowing description was special emphasis upon the region's famed Calvados, guaranteed to warm even the harshest of souls.

But Simone's village of Port-en-Bessin (population approximately 1,300 according to the latest *Guide Bleu*) was on the coast and, therefore, a different story altogether. It was a fishing port. One saw masts on one side of the main street while on the other were a couple of small shops, a couple of small cafés, and the eternal Hotel de la Marine facing the harbor where her mother worked as a waitress, serving the water's catch of skate, crab, squid, eel, lobster, scallops, and mackerel to complacent diners who calmly ignored the sound of the port's foghorn.

Fish and fishermen. That was how Simone remembered Normandy, *her* Normandy. There were other things she did not remember because she had been too young when they took place, but having been told about them so many times in the years that followed, having been told about them in the blunt yet picturesque detail characteristic of her people, they were a part of her memories, they had become an intrinsic part of her personal nostalgia . . . a line of American soldiers stood waist deep in the water, a landing craft burned nearby, the water was as gray as the gray foggy sky, the lighthouse and the long west jetty burned through quite clearly in Simone's mind, and the rows of cliffs where the Orne came down to the Channel, summer villas on the slopes overlooking the town were destroyed by American artillery fire, and a German officer snored on her mother's sofa downstairs in the sparse living room.

Fortunately Port-en-Bessin had been only very slightly damaged on D–Day. For a year before the Allied invasion the Germans had worked with their usual industrious zeal to improve the port, clear the mudbanks, dredge the boat basins, perfect the harbor as much as they could in order to use it for flak barges that would eventually participate in the invasion of England. As a result of all this improvement activity it became rapidly clear to the townspeople that the Germans did not expect an attack on that part of the French coast, for if they had they would have made the port absolutely unfit for use in capture. Instead like the robots they were ("Calais is where the attack will come!" screamed Hitler, and even Rommel with his sharp tactical mind finally capitulated to this misguided belief), they unwittingly helped the Allied invasionary forces by presenting them on that sixth day of June with a perfectly lovely, perfectly accessible harbor. The Normans with their dry humor loved the irony of that. They were still chuckling about it in 1959, the year that Simone turned sixteen and turned her back on Port-en-Bessin forever.

Robert Fingerhood stirred in his sleep, then opened a cautious eye. "Hi," he said. "Good morning."

"Hi."

"Did you sleep well?"

"Oh, yes," Simone said. "Very well."

"I woke up at one point during the night and you were curled into a little ball."

"I love you," she murmured, not really meaning it but thinking it was a nice thing to say, so affectionate really, and warm, just the way she felt.

He looked troubled, though. Was he used to strange girls waking up in his bed the morning after and bleating out their love for him? Did he feel guilty because he did not love them back? Or only disturbed for lack of the proper thing to say in return, a reassuring and yet not binding thing?

"You're a wonderful lover," Simone said.

Looking at her very tenderly, he replied, "I thought it was *you*."

"That's sweet."

More tartly now: "Shall we kill each other with kindness?"

He could be cruel, she saw that. "Yes. Please. I want you to kill me." Simone loved the idea of being demolished by a man. Then she would not have to prove anything to anyone anymore, she would not have to be anything or do anything, and losing her looks wouldn't matter.

"You're a beautiful girl," he said, as though reading her mind.

She wasn't, not really. She knew her flaws only too well, her nose was too short, her face was too round, but she had worked hard to overcome the flaws with careful makeup, the right hairstyle, and as a result of her efforts she gave the impression of being beautiful. Hair. She still would kill herself as a result of her hair inadequacy, mother's fall or no. A triumph on one hand and a defeat on the other—the careful and successful camouflage job she had performed on herself made her feel constantly wary of being found out for the faker she was.

"More beautiful than Anita?" she asked. It was time for coquettishness.

"Why bring her into it?"

"I saw the interest," Simone said shrewdly.

"It's gone now, all gone."

"C'est vrai?"

He mimicked her rather high-pitched voice. *"C'est vrai."*

"Anita has a nice body," Simone admitted, more secure now. "But she wears padded brassieres. Don't ever say I told you. She's very funny about it." Women would sell each other out at a moment's notice, she thought.

As though on cue Robert reached over and put his hands on her lovely breasts. "Padded brassieres are obscene. They should be outlawed."

Simone would not have admitted it to save her life but she had practically no sensation in her breasts, her nipples were sort of dead or something, and whenever a man reminded her of that unpleasant fact (as Robert by his action was reminding her now) she promptly changed the subject.

"Where do you work?" she asked him.

"At The Child Guidance Center. It's a private clinic."

"Is it in Manhattan?"

"Yes. On Park and Sixty-Fourth."

"Does that mean you work with children?"

"And with their parents, too."

Since he was still massaging her nipples, she started to pant a little so he wouldn't feel absolutely unsuccessful. Maybe she was a lesbian. She felt almost nothing when a man fucked her, it was terrible, just a slight dispersed stirring at first, then absolutely nothing.

"What did you say you were? I mean, did?"

"I'm a psychologist."

"What's the difference between a psychologist and a psychoanalyst?"

"They employ different modalities of treatment."

She knew he was a good lover even if she hadn't felt anything. She had been to bed with so many men she could tell the difference between good and bad; she might not be able to *feel* the difference but she had ways of judging, mental standards of evaluation, she knew who the freakouts were, and Robert Fingerhood wasn't. At last she had met a N*O*R*M*A*L man and the funny thing was she kind of missed all that lunatic freakiness. Why, he hadn't even used the vibrator on her. He disappointed her there. Why show it to her if he didn't intend to use it? Maybe that was the way she would finally come: vibrating herself with Vibrette.

One day last summer not long after she had moved into her tiny Russian Tea Room apartment she had met two hairdressers at Hubert Drugs and taken them back to her place. They made it every which way. The freakouts had fucked each other, too. She hated to admit it but the entire experience excited her beyond words. Put me at the end of the daisy chain, I'm expecting a phone call. It was really weird, those three entangled bodies, and the feminine hairdresser whimpering all sorts of profanities, stealing her act. They were all stoned out of their heads on pot, really quite deranged, but she had enjoyed it because it seemed very real, it seemed that was the way things should be even when they insisted that she screw herself with a carrot (being health minded, luckily she had some). She liked them, they were as nutty as she; she liked it when one went down on her while she went down on the other. She liked being the connection, she liked it so much she nearly came. They were certainly nicer than the steel guitar player who had begged her to pee on him in the bathtub. She laughed at that. But did it anyway. Why not? It seemed to give him so much pleasure.

"What's the difference between a psychologist and a psychiatrist?" she asked Robert Fingerhood.

"Psychiatrists have a somatic orientation."

She did not understand a word he was saying.

"Also they're shorter than psychologists," he added.

"Who is?"

"Are. Psychiatrists."

"Why is that?"

"They had shorter fathers."

Her ignorance amused him, probably made him feel important and professionally secure. Simone was not particularly interested in a man's occupation, it seemed quite irrelevant, the only reason she asked questions was because she had learned from experience that it flattered men, but she didn't care what their answers were. They could have said anything and it would have made the same difference to her. No. What she was interested in was their bedtime behavior. Robert was a tender lover, gentle but passionate. Also he had a really gigantic penis, she'd have bet anything it was longer than Jack Bailey's (she and Anita could draw diagrams the next time they got together), and she was fascinated by the way Robert came. Men had different styles of coming. Some were very sneaky, you didn't even know they had come, you just figured they'd gotten soft for some inexplicable reason, it kind of leaked out of them. But with Robert it was a whole rock and roll production; he went through heaven and hell, his entire body shook and his face got a crazy laughing look on it. Simone liked to watch men's faces when they came; it embarrassed them but what could they do about it? They usually tried to turn away but she relentlessly followed them and watched. Like with the two hairdressers. It was a small enough satisfaction. She knew she couldn't come because she was so narcissistic, at least that was what someone had once told her. The midget.

"Oh baby baby baby baby baby baby baby."

Robert Fingerhood seemed to be having a great morning orgasm. It was all up inside her, gummed together again. It was unfortunate that she had left her purse at Anita's, since there was a spare Pursette in it which she could now use to plug up the dike. Simone did not know how she had gotten along before she discovered Pursettes, they were so small and easy to carry around.

"What time is it?" she asked him a few minutes later when he had detached himself.

He turned to look at the clock on the shelf behind the bed. "Twenty to seven."

She would have to leave soon. She had to stop by Anita's and pick up Chou-Chou, go home, shower, and change her clothes. She didn't feel like leaving, not at all. She felt safe with Robert. He would protect her, he had a very protective nature, he was covering her with the blankets this very minute, instinctively trying to keep her warm. The two hairdressers would have let her freeze to death, they didn't care. And yet they had excited her. She kept remembering that. When it was all over the three of them smoked Madison Little Cigars. Genuine cork-tipped, it said on the package.

"Do you have to go to work?" Robert asked.

"Yes. Unfortunately."

"What do you do?"

"I model for a fun fur manufacturer. Coats and dresses and suits and ponchos and evening pajamas and things."

"Is it fun?"

"No it's a bore, but I don't know how to do anything else. I can't type or take shorthand or any of that."

"Do you mean they make dresses out of fur these days?"

"Oh yes. They make everything. Yesterday I showed a black calf A-line suit with a monkey border to a buyer from Atlanta."

"Couldn't your knowledge of French help you get a better job?"

Jobs. There it was again. Was that all anyone in New York ever thought about?

"I suppose so," she admitted, "but I don't really care that much. The whole idea of jobs depresses me. They seem so *de trop, stupide*."

"Except when you have to pay the rent."

He had propped himself up on two pillows against the wall and lay stretched out now with his body above the covers, his legs crossing over her covered body at right angles.

"What would you do if you could do anything you wanted?" he asked.

"Go to South America. Have you ever been to South America?"

"No."

"Rima, The Bird Girl, lived in South America. In the jungle."

"Who's she?"

"Didn't you ever read *Green Mansions?*" she asked, in amazement.

"Afraid not."

He might know all about psychiatrists being shorter than psychologists (or was it the other way round?), but he had never read the greatest book in the world! That was the trouble with these intellectual types, they knew all the wrong things.

"Rima lived in the jungle and commanded all the animals. She could speak to birds." Simone pointed to last night's plumed mini-dress and plumed wig, which lay ignominiously on the narrow floor space. "That's who I was supposed to be at Anita's party. Rima, The Bird Girl."

"You should have told me before," he said with a friendly smile.

"Maybe some day I'll get to South America. I saw a travel poster in a skin store on Seventh Avenue the other day. The New York Fur Club has a tour going there soon. The picture on the poster shows a girl leaning out of a window with wooden shutters. She's supposed to be in Peru and she's waving. The tour goes to Rio, São Paulo, Buenos Aires, and Lima."

"Can't you afford it?"

"No. I owe Bonwit Teller nine hundred dollars. I'm afraid they're going to arrest me any day now."

"That's a good reason to leave the country."

But Simone was being very serious about her predicament. "I try to give them fifty dollars a month, but at that rate it will take me another year and a half to get in the clear. Isn't that disgusting? I can't afford to give them more than fifty because I only make a hundred a week and I have a lot of hidden expenses."

She had happened to hit upon the term "hidden expenses" when she found herself dead broke once three days after payday. Not being able to account for the disappearance of her entire paycheck she concluded that she must have hidden expenses somewhere, the money had gone someplace, and some day she was damn well going to sit down and figure out exactly what those hidden expenses were, the sneaky little devils. To tide her over until the following payday she had to borrow twenty dollars from Mr. Lewis, who owned the thrift fur shop downstairs and was raking in a modest fortune in mink and sable boas.

Mr. Lewis shook his head sadly and said he didn't know what young girls did with their money these days, they were all like his daughter, extravagant, careless, impractical. They should have had his experiences slaving in sweatshops when he first came to this country from the Ukraine many years ago. If they had done that, they would know what work and money really meant, they would understand values.

Sometimes Simone thought it was almost not worth borrowing money from Mr. Lewis, if she had to listen to dire lectures about his early days of deprivation and poverty. She could have told him a few early day stories herself, but why compound the gloom he had already created? There was no point in dwelling upon past misfortunes, that was Simone's firm conviction. It didn't make sense to relive those things, the whole point was to keep going and be optimistic about the future. People like Mr. Lewis and Anita thought she was shallow and unsympathetic to have that kind of attitude, but Simone felt they were the shallow ones, and cowardly, too, clinging to the tragedies of yesterday in order to put off the possibility of today's and tomorrow's great good luck.

Robert turned tentatively toward her. "How would you like to move in with me?"

For a second Simone was not sure she had heard right. "Excuse me?"

"I'm asking you to come live with me," Robert said, looking perfectly serious and even a little apprehensive that his offer might be rejected.

Simone's immediate reaction was to jump up to a sitting position, the covers falling off her exquisitely proportioned body as she did so.

"Do you mean it."

"Of course I mean it."

"I can't believe it! Oh, I'd love to live with you!" Then she gazed at him like a frightened animal. "You're not kidding, are you?"

"I mean it I mean it I mean it. I'm not kidding I'm not kidding I'm not kidding."

Simone clapped her hands joyfully. "Oh, this is wonderful. *Oh, que je suis contente.*"

She suspected she could live very happily with Robert Fingerhood. He was so nice, so considerate (even if he didn't use the Vibrette). And also then she wouldn't have to pay rent, phone, or electric bills, all that money down the drain, and she could pay off Bonwit's in only a few months, maybe even save enough money for the South American tour. There were all sorts of exciting possibilities. In time she might be able to quit working altogether and stay home and set her terrible hair and read books about faraway places and cook tasty casseroles during the day, pending Robert's return from The Child Guidance Center in the evening. The fact that Simone had never cooked a casserole in her life did not faze her one bit, a girl had to start somewhere. Actually her past attempts at cooking anything had been total catastrophes. That family she briefly worked for in Forest Hills used to clutch their stomachs every evening in glazed disbelief that she had managed to pass herself off to them as a competent cook. Ah, but that was yesterday. Dim drab yesterday. Anita and Mr. Lewis just didn't know a thing about the connection between persistent optimism and resultant good luck, that was all she could say, and that was saying a mouthful!

"If I come live with you, it means Chou-Chou, too," she reminded Robert. "My dog."

"That's okay."

Simone flung her arms around Robert and kissed him gratefully on the lips. As she did so she felt a faint stirring of desire within herself, and she wondered whether in her case sensuality might not be more prompted by a show of kindness on the part of the man, rather than upon any so-called erotic act he might choose to perform. Perhaps the reason she had never been able to have an orgasm was because no man had been particularly kind to her. Perhaps tenderness was the key word to the whole business. Tenderness and consideration. Perhaps the female nature instinctively protected itself against erotic inclinations when these other essential qualities were lacking. Perhaps she was normal after all!

In a heady rush of self-discovery and illumination Simone covered Robert's face with a hundred thankful kisses, and this time when she said, "I love you," she had a hunch that if she didn't quite mean it yet, she very shortly would.

Later that morning Simone discovered (to her regret) that her employer David Swern, the customer's man of Mini-Furs, Inc., fell into the same gloomy-minded category as both Anita and Mr. Lewis when it came to the sphere of futuristic thinking. She was in such a state of wild elation by the time she got to the showroom that she simply had to tell someone about her great good fortune. Ordinarily she would have spoken to the other two models she worked with, but one of them was out that day with the curse and it looked as though the other was going to be tied up all morning with canvas fittings in the designer's back room. *Tant pis.*

Simone could not contain herself until the afternoon, her

personal publicity release simply would not wait, and she did not feel close enough to the bookkeeper, a fortyish blonde with overteased hair, to tell her anything about her private life; the firm's two salesmen while basically sympathetic, kindly men were not worldly enough, she felt, to be made the recipients of her compelling Robert Fingerhood news.

So that when she found herself alone in the showroom with Mr. Swern in the middle of the morning after a private customer had screamed about linings and stormed out, Simone decided to strike while she had the chance. Mr. Swern was seated in one of the brown simulated-leather booths at the far end of the room, drinking his second container of black, saccharined coffee for the day, and staring idly off into space. Simone had heard from the bookkeeper that his wife had had another attack last night and she wondered now whether his thoughts were with her, poor man. His handsome gray hair, which usually had a silver sheen to it, seemed drab today, unkempt. His mouth was sad. Even his perennial suntan looked as though it had faded a shade or two overnight. Still—

"You probably aren't interested, Mr. Swern, but I just have to tell someone—"

The attractive, middle-aged man looked up. "Tell someone what?"

Mr. Swern had an unfortunate tendency to jump the gun on everyone's train of thought, and apparently personal sadness did nothing to interfere with this tendency. It was a kind of anxiety on his part, Simone had concluded some time ago, rather than a reflection of rudeness. That was why she forgave him for it.

"I'm in love, Mr. Swern."

Mr. Swern gave her a wary, dark-eyed, Jewish look. "For your sake I hope he's more substantial than that rock-and-roll nut you were running around with last summer."

In a moment of abandon she had told Mr. Swern about the steel guitar player and that peeing business last July, and then wondered why she found it so easy to confide in him. Perhaps because her own father would have been about Mr. Swern's age if he were alive, and also because in spite of a caustic façade Simone instinctively knew that Mr. Swern was a softie at heart.

But even if her instincts hadn't been quite up to par, one of the younger salesmen in the firm once told Simone that Mr. Swern had never quite recovered from the shock of seeing his old world of quality furs change before his eyes into the current world of nutty fun furs. It seemed that for years Mr. Swern used to manufacture the most expensive mink and sable coats for elegant fur salons all over the country.

"He prided himself upon the quality of his product," the salesman said. "Then, the market changed. Youth came on the scene. Out with quality, in with camp. So, whereas in the past a man like David Swern would revel in the lush skins of a flowing wild mink evening coat, now the poor s.o.b. has to sit and smile at flying squirrel ponchos and civet micro-minis."

"Robert is not only more substantial," Simone said proudly to her employer, "he's the first **N*O*R*M*A*L** man I've ever met in my life."

"I should have ordered a toasted English with the coffee," Mr. Swern said. "I'm meeting Miss O'Hara for lunch but she can't make it until one-thirty. Those reporters really work hard, you know, it's not such fun and games the way they run around all day interviewing people. Something else: I just realized what with all the hysteria last night, I never ate dinner. How do you like that?"

Simone did not like it at all. Not only was he disinterested in her Robert Fingerhood news, but there was his wife at home suffering from loneliness and painful colitis attacks and here sat her husband talking casually about toasted Englishes and lunches with girlfriends he referred to by make-believe names.

"I'm sorry to hear that Mrs. Swern isn't feeling well," Simone said, discreetly avoiding the Miss O'Hara subject. "I heard she had an attack last night. How is she today?"

"She's resting comfortably, as they say in hospitals."

"I'm glad to hear that. Would you like me to order a toasted English for you?"

"No. Forget it. I should lose a couple of pounds anyway. I'm getting a roll around the middle. But don't let me stop you. Finish your story. You're in love and . . . what? What is this guy like? Who is he? What does he do?"

"He's a clinical psychologist and he lives in the most marvelous apartment. He's asked me to move in with him and I've accepted!"

"Does he have any money?"

Money. Jobs. There it was again. "He might not have any money, Mr. Swern, but he has a Mexican hammock and a stuffed owl in his living room."

"That's dandy. That's just dandy." Mr. Swern looked at

her with infinite pity mingled with a dash of wholesome contempt. "Did you ever hear of anyone trading in a stuffed owl for twenty shares of AT&T?"

"All you ever think about is money. That's all anybody in New York ever thinks about. Well, I think it's disgusting!"

"What's this character's name?" Mr. Swern asked, overlooking her outburst.

"Robert Fingerhood."

"Fingerhood?" Mr. Swern was at last impressed. "That's Jewish."

That possibility had not occured to Simone. "I guess so."

Mr. Swern seemed infinitely more interested in Simone's newest romance now that he had discovered they shared the same religious faith. "Well, well," he said. "In that case maybe something will come of it. You need someone solid. A wild kid like you."

While Simone felt sympathetic toward most Jews she had met, she nevertheless harbored a peculiar underlying feeling that if you turned one of them over, really over, you would unearth a Nazi. The same maniacal quality of obsession characterized them both. Zzzzzzz snored the stolid German officer on her mother's sofa. One day when he was awake he offered her an orange sweet. "Don't eat it," her mother hissed, "it's probably poisoned." The minute her mother turned her back Simone gulped down the candy and waited to die. Then nothing happened.

"What makes you think that because he's Jewish he's solid?" she asked Mr. Swern.

Pepe, the firm's designer, chose that moment to interrupt the conversation. He darted into the showroom holding an Ethiopian kidskin pantsuit that was still in the unfinished stages, a look of sharp distress on his face.

"David," he said, "there's something wrong with this jacket. Or maybe it's the way Helen is built." Helen was the model he was working with in back. "Maybe we should fit this garment on Simone."

"Try it on, dear," Mr. Swern said. "I'll take a look."

"Helen is too short for this jacket," David Swern said when Simone stood before him in the brown and white, double-breasted ensemble. "Simone has the right proportions from shoulder to hip."

Pepe nodded at her. "Okay, you can take it off."

She started to follow him into the back room to remove the pantsuit when Mr. Swern motioned to her to wait.

"I'd like you to do me a favor," he said. "It's a good thing

I remembered it. As soon as you slip out of that thing, take five dollars from petty cash and run up to Cartier's, you know where they are. I want you to pick up an emerald and rose quartz bracelet they're holding for me. Would you do that like a good girl?"

This was one day that Miss O'Hara was going to get more for lunch than lunch, Simone could see that. And meanwhile up at the West End Avenue apartment poor Mrs. Swern was drinking warm milk through a straw and taking her medicine. Men were such hypocrites, even nice men like David Swern. But Simone knew that it was hardly her place to tell him what to do or not do. She was in no position, no position of authority at all, and it made her mad. Glancing contemptuously at the half-finished, but already elegant kid jacket she was wearing, she said, "I think it's disgusting to kill animals for money."

Mr. Swern honored her with his first smile of the day. "At least I don't stuff them," he pointed out.

When Beverly woke up Thursday morning, Peter was gone. She looked at the electric clock that sat on top of the W & J Sloane chest of drawers. It was 10:07. Margaret would have taken Sally to school, returned to feed Peter, Jr., and by now was undoubtedly going about her household chores.

Margaret had a day for everything. Today being Thursday was polishing-the-silver day. Margaret polished with Gorham. Beverly hallucinated with cold fear. I am losing my mind, she thought, nothing makes sense any more, the symbols don't represent anything. A husband, two beautiful children, the castle, Margaret polishing the silver, money, position, and none of it, *none* of it meant a goddamn thing. Beverly wanted to die. The hideousness of last night's lovemaking, the violence, had impressed itself upon her in her sleep. The crack of Peter's hand across her face was surely responsible for many bad dreams. She could not specifically remember the dreams, but a heavy weight hung over her in her now-awake state and she vaguely recalled gnarled fingers and tall gray mountains in her dreams, sensations of slipping, falling. She was in love with a woman, she did not remember what the woman looked like nor who she was supposed to be, but the love impression lingered, and at one point the woman said, "You'll see, I'll be nice to you, wait and see."

Brazilian music hovered at the edge of the dream, carnival time and painted masks, multicolored hysteria reigned in Rio, and suddenly Beverly wanted to be free, she wanted to be a young virginal girl again without responsibility, a girl who went to carnivals wearing a midnight blue mask, a window for watchful eyes, eyes that would meet other eyes, meet and touch, later to kiss but only with eyes. Eye-kissing was delicious, Beverly thought. She and Peter had eye-kissed at the beginning at Cambridge and for several years afterward, too. His eyes were even bluer than her own, brighter. Hers were grayblue but his were clear clear blue. There was a touch of madness about them at times, they seemed to go up in his head like the eyes of people in religious exultation, madmen in psychic combat.

She thought of Peter soon to be lunching at the Harvard Club. Well, maybe, she didn't know. He told her that he ate there quite often. Did he take Lou Marron to lunch from time to time (every day?)? Beverly had never dared ask her husband, did not have the nerve to ask, she was too fearful of what his reply would be. If he said yes, she would be convinced they were having an affair. If he said no, she would be convinced he was lying. Either way she couldn't win. Cowards never won anything anyway except a measure of their own cowardly shame when they looked at themselves in the mirror, as Beverly was looking now.

But what was there to see? A twenty-eight-year-old woman who had just awakened and not yet pulled herself together (who might never pull herself together). The hair part was nice, it was really Beverly's best feature and she took pride in it, it hung thick and heavy in all its reddish-brown lushness, but being a redhead had terrible disadvantages. Beverly had all the typical redhead problems, the freckles, the skin that could not, would not take the sun. It burned, blistered, and peeled, and she had long ago given up trying to ever acquire even the semblance of a tan, the sun would never reward her for her efforts, all it would do was give her more freckles, as if she didn't have enough to begin with.

Freckles had been a terrible source of anguish to her when she was in her teens, and once on the sly behind her mother's back she sent away for a lotion which according to the advertisement, if assiduously applied, was guaranteed to remove all those unwanted small brown blemishes. The lotion had been advertised in the back pages of some flashy movie magazine that she bought one day specifically to read the headline story about why Elizabeth Taylor was so happily married to Michael Wilding. Beverly thought that Elizabeth Taylor, with her black hair and unfreckled skin, was the most beautiful girl she had ever seen. Any girl who didn't have freckles must by necessity be happy, was Beverly's feeling at the time, and anyone as beautiful as Elizabeth Taylor must be doubly happy. Which as subsequent events pointed out only went to show how little one person ever knew about another person's happiness, movie stars or not.

The freckle cure did not work. All it did was give Beverly an itch. And then, too, it smelled funny. It had a sharp vinegar smell and one morning her mother asked her what she was using on herself that made her smell so suddenly strange. In a moment of panic Beverly said it was a new skin cleansing formula that her best friend had recommended, it really cleansed *deep* (she said) and prevented the outbreak of blackheads, and was very good for the skin in addition because it contained vitamins. Her mother laughed at that. "Vitamins!" she said, contemptuously. "You smell like a cheap salad dressing."

Beverly was terrified of her mother who was beautiful, not as beautiful, of course, as Elizabeth Taylor but almost, and the same brunette type, too. Her mother certainly wasn't plagued by freckles, her mother had flawless skin, neither too light nor too dark, perfect actually, skintight smooth. There were some things that could never be changed, Beverly had realized then with the kind of sick, sinking feeling that is a by-product of recognition of inevitability, and skin was one of those unchangeables. It was a very dismal, hopeless realization. No matter what she did the rest of her life, no matter what she became or didn't become, no matter how happy she was or how miserable, how rich, how poor, how loved or unloved, no matter what—she would have freckles until the day she died.

"Get going, get going!" shrieked the myna bird downstairs from its cage in the music room.

Those were the only words he knew. Peter had bought the bird several months ago without giving Beverly previous warning. That was Peter's style. One evening he just arrived in Garden City on the 6:42 with a bird cage in his hand and a small black bird with an orange beak fluttering nervously around inside.

"The only time birds talk is in the morning," Peter informed her. "I'm going to teach him a few rousing morning words. You'll see."

She did not doubt it for a second, she never doubted anything Peter said. Peter was not one of those off-the-top-of-the-head talkers. When he said something he meant it.

Besides what did she know about the habits or inclinations of myna birds. Maybe it was easy as hell to teach them rousing morning words. So that several days later when Beverly was having coffee in the sunlit kitchen and the bird shrieked out, "Get going, get going!" it was immediately clear to her that Peter had planted the very words in the bird's mouth that he himself wished to express. There was something grotesque to Beverly about hearing her husband's sentiments come screeching out of that small black feathered thing, something repellent, hideous really. It was just the sort of stunt that Peter with his dark humor would be expected to pull off, it was absolutely typical of him.

Beverly did not feel well. She stuck out her tongue. The reflection in the mirror confirmed her suspicions. Her tongue was distinctly coated an unhealthy shade of grayish-white and it was no wonder. The taste of last night's wretched meal still lingered in her mouth. She vaguely contemplated canceling their subscription to *Life*.

"Get going, get going!"

And then, too, her period was late, which always made her feel not up to par. What was par anyway? Beverly no longer knew. If she wasn't suffering from one ailment, it was another. Migraine headaches, hangovers, upset stomachs, overdue period tension. Her breasts were painfully swollen, a premenstrual symptom that she dreaded each month. Another ache to add to the growing list. The funny part was that she looked like the proverbial picture of health; she really did, robust, all but glowing. She wondered how she managed to pull off that cute little trick. It was a miracle considering how lousy she felt most of the time.

A faint throbbing at her temples reminded her of the migraine attack she had succeeded in warding off last evening. Or had she succeeded? Maybe the pill she took had not altogether knocked out the lurking pain, maybe she should take another one this very minute as added insurance. That seemed like a good idea. She went into the dusty pink bathroom and swallowed one of the little pain killers with a glass of water. The water tasted terrible, it tasted like that terrible sauerkraut mess she and Margaret had so laboriously prepared. She brushed her teeth and gargled with Reef hoping to get rid of the foul taste.

Then she weighed herself on the pink Detecto scale. The arrow pointed ignominiously to one hundred and thirty-seven. She had gained a pound. But she never ate! Well, practically never. And when she did eat she was so god-damned careful. A small broiled steak. Cottage cheese (ugh). An occasional *omelette aux fines herbes.* All good solid, supposedly slenderizing protein. How could anyone gain a pound on a diet like that? It was the liquor, of course. She simply had to cut down. As soon as she thought of liquor she wanted a drink immediately, she wanted one now. What the hell did she care what Margaret thought? Margaret was a servant. Peter didn't care what servants thought; their thoughts didn't bother him in the least; he was completely oblivious to such considerations, but then Peter had been brought up surrounded by servants. Dinner, he once told her, was always served by a Negro man servant who wore immaculate white gloves. Beverly's family would hardly be considered poor (her father had been a successful gynecologist) but compared to Peter's Brookline family they were slobs. The opinions of servants bothered her, she wanted to come off well in their eyes, to be considered a lady. She would never be a lady, Olivia de Havilland was a lady, maybe that's what Peter should have married—a lady, someone very soignée and elegant. She was too rustic for that crap.

"Get going, get going!"

"Oh, shut up," Beverly said, as she walked back to the bedroom to dress for the boring day ahead.

It was still cold out. The windows were frosted. Beverly chose her pale blue Hadley cashmere pullover and the blue and green tweed A–line skirt. She would wear her Andrew Geller walking pumps with the stacked heel even though nobody in Garden City ever walked anywhere. Garden City was like Beverly Hills in that respect, people were just not seen walking around the streets. Beverly drove her Mercedes everywhere, and everywhere usually amounted to a five-minute drive. It was one of the nicest things about Garden City ("The community of gracious living," according to their chamber of commerce)—compactness, all of one's necessities and luxuries only a five-minute drive away and not a parking meter in town.

A wave of dizziness swept over Beverly as she fastened her stockings to the garters on her panty girdle. Peter said that nobody wore panty girdles any more and that if she lost ten pounds, she would be wise to buy herself a couple of wispy garter belts at Lord & Taylor. But why this dizziness? She felt shaky suddenly, and weak. God, she needed a drink and screw Margaret! Maybe it was that damn migraine pill. Maybe this was the reaction it had if it had no headache to work on.

She sat down at the edge of the bed and tried to catch her breath. Her heart was beating very fast. If it weren't for the fact that last night was the first time Peter had made love to her for longer than she cared to remember, she would think she was pregnant. Of course, even if he had made love to her this month, she couldn't possibly be pregnant because of that marvelous little coil inside her. Sometimes she forgot about it. Peter had suggested that she have herself fitted for one after Peter, Jr., was born two and a half years ago. Beverly thought this was a rather odd suggestion considering the fact that he practically never fucked her anywhere but in the ass anymore, but then she further thought that perhaps his habits would change once he was reassured that conception could not possibly take place. Perhaps she would feel reassured, too. And since neither of them wanted more children, Beverly finally decided the coil was a good idea. Diaphragms were a drag and the pill was too risky. Her friend, Dee Dee, had been taking the pill for over a year when she developed a sudden blood clot and had to be rushed to the Nassau Hospital in an ambulance. Dee Dee's doctor told her that blood clots were a not so uncommon effect of the pill and he advised her to go back to a diaphragm or get an intrauterine device. Dee Dee had chosen the latter but it would not stay in, her system rejected it. Beverly was lucky. She had never had any problem with the coil.

At the moment she felt it was the only thing she was lucky about. Maybe if she opened a window. She was afraid to get up for fear she would faint. What was *wrong* with her? It was this house. She felt like a prisoner here. Imprisoned in the castle. She had to get out. If only it were later in the day, she would drive to Hempstead and see a movie, any movie to get her mind off her life. Coffee might help, providing she could make it downstairs to the kitchen without falling on her ass.

"Get going, get going!"

"I'm going," Beverly said.

At that moment the ivory princess telephone on the night table rang softly. Beverly managed to slide across the unmade bed and reach the receiver. It was Dee Dee inviting her to lunch at the country club.

"I'm not eating lunch these days," Beverly said. "I'm on a diet."

"Okay, so watch me eat. I've got to talk to you. It's about George."

George was Dee Dee's latest lover. He taught Renaissance

music at Adelphi. Dee Dee was forever repeating his tony remarks about the madrigal, the chanson, and the motet, admitting she understood not a word of what he was saying. But what did it matter whether she understood or not? She was getting laid twice a week. Tuesdays and Thursdays at noon.

"You have to say one thing for George," Dee Dee was fond of telling Beverly. "He's punctual. Remember all the anxiety I went through with that compulsively late spic bastard, Luis?"

Dee Dee's husband was impotent, or at least he was impotent with Dee Dee, who was convinced that he was screwing his secretary. She had found makeup marks on his shirt. When Dee Dee had first started taking lovers, Beverly asked her how she managed to carry on the affairs in her own home.

"It's easy," Dee Dee said. "The children are at school and the housekeeper looks in the other direction, particularly since I've started slipping her an extra ten dollars a week. Two screws a week are worth ten bucks to me any day."

"What's happened with George?" Beverly asked her now. "Can't you tell me on the phone?"

"I'm so upset I can't even talk on the phone. Oh, come on. Meet me for lunch."

"Is it good news or bad?"

"Bad? It's terrible! Shit. Wait until you hear."

Beverly did not think she could have beared to listen to someone else's good news, not in her miserable state.

"Okay," she said. "I'll meet you at one."

"Christ, make it earlier. I can't wait until one. Make it at noon."

Then Beverly realized that today was Thursday, George's day. It must really be bad news if Dee Dee wasn't seeing him today.

"Noon it is," Beverly said, "and try to take it easy. You sound like you're going to have a heart attack."

"I think I am."

Beverly started to say goodbye but Dee Dee had hung up.

Less than two hours to kill. Maybe after she had coffee she should try reading a book. She was still in the middle of *Herzog* and probably always would be since she could make neither head nor tail out of all those Jewish words Saul Bellow was forever using. The publishers should have printed a Jewish-English dictionary to go along with the book as a special consideration for gentile readers. Peter had brought the book home with him one day, saying that somebody at the office had loaned it to him. Probably that bitch, Lou Marron.

"We're all out of Edam," Margaret announced when Beverly finally made it down to the kitchen.

"Mr. Northrop must have gotten hungry in the middle of the night." Edam was Peter's favorite cheese. "I'll stop by the cheese store on my way back from the country club. I'm having lunch with Mrs. Baker at noon."

"In that case I don't suppose you'd want a slice of toast."

"No more toast, Margaret. I just weighed myself. I've gained a pound. Did Sally eat her breakfast?"

"Oh, yes, M'am. She had a big plate of corn flakes with sliced bananas and milk."

When Beverly was a child her mother used to make her eat cereal out of a plate that had a dog painted on the bottom. The dog was so terrible looking that she never finished anything so as to avoid seeing the dog's face. But Sally's dish had a daisy on the bottom and apparently Sally like daisies. She was a good eater. It was Peter, Jr., they were having trouble with. He was going to be a problem eater, he didn't like anything. He was in his room now undoubtedly rocking on his hobbyhorse that played "Jingle Bells," or pushing his Doodle Bug steering cart around with ferocious energy. Beverly had told Margaret that she was too irritable in the morning for her young son's boisterousness and that she couldn't quite face him until after her second cup of coffee, so Margaret made a point of having Peter play in his room during the early morning hours. Then usually about eleven he was allowed to come down and see his mother. He was an adorable child, Beverly always thought, when she saw him for the first time each day. She was stricter with him than with Sally because she loved him more, and she felt guilty about it. As a result Sally got away with murder and would probably grow up to give some deserving man a very rough time indeed.

Beverly managed to get through the morning without reading *Herzog*. She drank three cups of coffee *sans* sugar or milk, smoked three mentholated cigarettes, checked out Margaret on dinner, kissed and hugged Peter, Jr. (why did children smell so sweet?), and answered all his "why" questions to the best of her demented ability. Then she slipped into her belted camel's hair coat and drove the short distance to the Cherry Valley Country Club where Dee Dee was waiting for her.

"The son of a bitch is transferring to Ohio State next month," Dee Dee said, twisting her mouth in a particularly unattractive way. She was a thin, nervous blond with practically no breasts but an interesting angular face. "Ohio! Can you beat it? Oh, shit. Now what do I do?"

She was drinking vodka martinis at an amazing rate of speed and to keep her company Beverly ordered a Scotch sour, still bearing in mind that new extra pound.

"You'll find someone else," Beverly said, trying to look sympathetic.

"Do you think it's so easy? *You* should try it sometime! It will take me weeks, maybe months."

Dee Dee began to cry into her martini. "He called me this morning to break our date. I said why couldn't we meet today since he's not leaving for a month? No, George said, we're tapering off. Only Tuesdays from now on. Tuesday! That's four days away. What am I supposed to do in the meantime? Play with myself? He's probably fucking one of his Renaissance music students this very minute. I'll bet they talk about polyphonic composition afterward."

We're all screwed up out here, Beverly thought, all we women. All we do is drink, shop, meet for lunch at the country club, and in some cases grab the nearest available man whenever he's available. Or would we be the same if we lived in the city? Is it us? The place? Both?

"It's bad enough now," Dee Dee said. "But what happens when I get older? Who'll want to bother with me then?"

"Maybe Chris will have revived by then," Beverly suggested.

"My husband? Revive with *me?* Are you kidding? He hates me, he really does. Just the other day he told me I was a big fucking bore."

Beverly wondered whether that was what Peter thought of her. She wished she could take a lover, but she didn't have Dee Dee's nerve, not here in Garden City, not in the house she had shared with Peter for eight years.

"And you know something?" Dee Dee said, signaling the waiter that they wanted to order lunch. "The bastard is right. I *am* a fucking bore."

On the way back home Beverly stopped at the cheese store on Seventh Street for Peter's Edam. After selecting his favorite brand she did a very odd thing before she even realized she had done it. There was a package of Camembert sitting on the counter, apparently discarded by some former customer and not yet returned to the display case. In a moment of frozen compulsion Beverly reached out, while the clerk's back was turned, grabbed the cheese off the counter and slipped it into her calf shoulderbag. Then she paid for the Edam and left.

She drove home in a catatonic state. *I must leave Peter.* That was the thought that ran through her mind except that it was more of a prayer than a thought, more of a supplication. *Can I leave Peter?* As she approached the castle on Stewart Avenue tears started to stream down Beverly's face, blurring her vision. She hastily wiped them away. Her fingers touching her cheeks felt dead, cold, inhuman.

The doorbell awakened Anita early Thursday morning and for a second she thought it was the electric alarm clock signaling her to get up, brush her teeth, jump into the shower, and slip into her new cocoa pantskirt and visored helmet stewardess uniform and take off for—Madrid? Paris? Rome? London? Cairo? Munich? Hamburg? Or was she in one of those strange-familiar places right now, shortly about to return to her current home base of New York?

Often before Anita removed her sleep mask she was confused as to her surroundings, momentarily disoriented. The sleep mask was a soft green and had the words, "Goodnight, Chet, goodnight, David" running boldly across it in a strong right-handed script. Sometimes Anita did not know what she would do without the mask, her hours being as erratic as they were. Then she heard a faint whining sound, remembered Chou-Chou in the tote bag next to the radiator, and knew even before she opened her sleepy eyes that she was indeed in New York, in bed with Jack Bailey, and the person at the door had to be Simone stopping by on her way to work to pick up the dog.

Jack had thrown all the pillows on the floor, an old habit of his, and was sleeping quietly as Anita padded barefoot through the littered living room to open the front door. In the early morning light Simone looked flushed and disheveled wearing last night's party clothes, but radiant as though the preceding hours spent with Robert Fingerhood had turned into a great success after all.

"I'm sorry if I woke you," Simone said, somewhat breathlessly (had she been running?), "but I didn't want to abandon poor Chou-Chou any longer than necessary. Also my keys and everything are in the bag."

Anita groggily handed her the tote. "He was a very good boy. I gave him some warm milk before going to bed and he didn't make a sound all night long. How did things go with you and Robert?"

"Marvelous. Just marvelous. He's really wonderful. What about you and Jack? Did he stay over?"

"Yes, he's asleep in the bedroom."

"Do you think you'll see him again?"

"I don't know," Anita admitted. "I can't tell with Jack. He's very noncommittal about things like that. That's what makes it all so painful, the uncertainty. Are you going to see Robert again? Did he say anything?"

Simone beamed. "I'm not going to see him again, I'm going to live with him! Can you imagine? He asked me to *live* with him!"

"Do you think that's a good idea?" Anita asked, suddenly very wide awake, and wondering whether the size of Simone's breasts had anything to do with her great success.

"A good idea?" Simone regarded her ex-roommate with stunned annoyance. "Are you kidding? Have you lost your marbles? Do I get offers like that every day in the week? I mean what are you talking about?"

"I was thinking of your apartment. You know, getting rid of it. I assume you do have a lease."

Simone's annoyance seemed to deepen visibly and Anita knew exactly what she was thinking: how can you be so impossibly dull at a time like this, so practical and uninspired, how can you stand there in your baby doll pajamas and talk to me about boring things like apartments and leases when I'm so deliriously happy? But that was precisely why Anita had mentioned those boring things, they were a decoy to divert Simone from suspecting what her true reaction was—painful, unbearable jealousy at this show of her friend's sudden happiness.

"I suppose what I really mean," Anita said, "is that maybe you should wait until he asks you to marry him. If you move in with him now, he might never ask you."

"He's mad about me," Simone said proudly. "I know all the symptoms. I really turn him on."

"But I'm talking about marriage."

"That's all you ever talk about. There are other things, you know."

"Like what. Getting screwed in the sink?"

"There's no need to remind me of my past. Everything has changed, everything is going to be different from now on. I've finally met a N*O*R*M*A*L man. Can you imagine? After all these years of scrambling around New York?"

"I'm glad to hear it. The next thing I know you'll tell me that you even had an orgasm."

At mention of this, Simone's mouth tightened and she looked very angry. "You really are a big pain in the ass. Did you know that?"

Then turning around she walked rapidly to the elevator, the tote bag swinging from her hand. Not once did she look back or bother to say good-bye, bother to thank Anita for last night's party or for keeping an eye on Chou-Chou. Anita did not understand rude people, they were an eternal mystery to her. Perhaps it was her airline training with its repeated emphasis upon graciousness and courtesy under all circumstances, even the most trying ones, that accounted for her inability to comprehend the nature of rudeness. Perhaps she should not have made that remark about Simone having an orgasm, but Simone had never been touchy on the subject in the past. In fact, it was Simone who at the beginning of their friendship told Anita all about her inadequacy and kept telling her of it as her adventures with men colorfully unfolded. Why she should take offense at this late date Anita could not imagine. She was baffled, rude people not only baffled her, they depressed her, and if depression was truly stifled anger (as the experts claimed) then Anita was very angry indeed at being treated in such a curt and peremptory fashion by someone she had considered to be a friend.

Heaven help us from our friends, she thought, for she did not basically believe in friendship among women but rather saw it as an intermediate step, a halfhearted gesture, a substitute for a husband and wife relationship. Women were always sneakily trying to do each other in anyway, even the most noble of them. None of them genuinely wished for each other's happiness, at least not at the expense of their own, women were finally not that generous. Anita certainly was not. Goodnight, Chet, goodnight, David. Spanky and Our Gang were singing *Sunday Will Never Be the Same* (he won't be back again), which could only mean that Jack had gotten up and turned on his favorite rock and roll radio station. Anita had seen Spanky and Our Gang once on "The Johnny Carson Show" and wished she hadn't. They made her nervous. Someone like Spanky eluded her. What did she think she was doing in those strange Bowery clothes with that squashed, dried mushroom hat on her head anyway? The lyrics made sense, though. Not only would Sunday never be the same but neither would any other day in the week, the days of the week were all mixed up for Anita as they were for

Jack. One of the reasons she remained so interested in him was because being in the same crazy business they tacitly understood each other's peculiar way of living, the odd hours, the dazed fatigue after a trip, the travel compulsion, and although none of them ever talked about it—the old-time romance of flying. Anita suspected that they were not unlike actors who could sympathize with and excuse certain modes of behavior that to the uninitiated would require a great deal of explanation, if not apology for the idiosyncrasy of it all.

And yet Jack did not seem to find a great deal of virtue in this mutual bond of theirs, for if he had, he would not have walked out on her so casually last October. Still (Anita reminded herself) many pilots did marry stewardesses, many flight engineers did marry reservation clerks, many airline people kept it in the family. She tried to bear this significant fact in mind whenever she lost faith, as she so frequently did, in the possibility of anything permanent coming to pass between her and Jack Bailey. *Do you think you'll see him again?* Simone had shrewdly asked. Anita's stomach went sour just contemplating that simple, yet all-import question. It was the height of misery not to be able to answer it, even to oneself, *especially* to oneself.

When Anita returned to the bedroom Jack had put on his pilot's cap and was lying in bed with only the top sheet over him, through which it was easy to see that he had a huge morning erection.

"Is this hotel on the American or European plan?" he asked.

"European, darling. And why does *that*—" she pointed to his protuberance, "—always happen to men in the morning?"

"I don't know but a Navy barracks at 7 A.M. is quite a sight to behold, I can assure you."

"I believe it."

Anita did not like to make love in the morning, she did not feel at all sensuous then, the morning was for other things like talking, drinking coffee, reflecting upon yesterday, planning for the day ahead, and somehow sex just did not seem to fit into what she felt should be a quiet, orderly, dispassionate, and yet productive time of day. Sex for Anita was a highly compartmentalized activity rather than an integral part of her life, and as such it was all mixed in with dates and low-cut cocktail dresses, formalized restaurant dinners, and if in New York, perhaps a hit Broadway play or a first-run foreign movie at Cinema II or one of the Trans-Lux houses. Sex had to do with having one's hair done earlier in the day and later putting on a honey-almond facial mask to tighten the pores of one's skin, and while they were obediently tightening Anita would give herself a manicure and a pedicure. Rituals like that were preparatory to sex, indispensable, the whole cleansing routine, daintiness and cleanliness, Jean Naté *friction pour le bain* and then aromatic dusting powder, a splash of Réplique, all of it ending with Germaine Monteil's super moist strawberry lip-dew. Moist and clean. Those were the prerequisites for lovemaking. Could it possibly be any other way? So that seeing Jack Bailey with an erection now in the cruddy morning aftermath not only failed to excite Anita, it rather repelled her.

A faint stubble of a beard had appeared on Jack's face overnight. He needed to shave, brush his teeth, take a brisk shower. As for her, she needed to bathe too, brush her teeth, put on a deodorant, clean up the living room mess, rejuvenate herself with energizing orange juice and a cup of creamy yogurt, then black coffee and a filtered cigarette. Anita liked to drink champagne in the morning, it was not like hard liquor, it was so bubbly and refreshing, so sparkling clean. There was an innocence about it that made it an appropriate breakfast drink. Of course, if she had a flight that day, she never touched anything intoxicating. It was strictly forbidden by the airline to do so and even though she knew stewardesses who blithely disobeyed the rules, she would never dream of taking such a risky chance. The rules were there for a reason, a perfectly good reason, she felt. They were there to protect both the passengers and the stewardesses. Passengers were entitled to an efficient and gracious stewardess, it was one of the things they had paid for when they bought their ticket, and how could anybody be efficient and gracious if she was loaded on the job?

However, when Anita pointed out this twofold logic to one of the girls who was a notorious sneaky drinker, the girl laughingly replied, "What I don't understand is how anybody could be efficient and gracious in this lousy business if she's *sober*." Her name was Lisa. She was a tall, healthy-looking Austrian girl with a throaty laugh. One imagined her outdoors on skis, her cheeks flushed with wholesome exercise. Lisa used to keep a bottle of chlorophyl mouth spray in the gally and squirt her breath with it every time she swung by to pick up a tray of food for one of her hated passengers. But one day fate caught up with her. Maybe she had run out of the mouth spray or maybe children had extra sensitive noses but when she leaned over one afternoon on the flight to Munich to give a six-year-old his hamburger and mashed potato luncheon tray he gleefully blurted out, "You smell just like my daddy when he's been drinking cocktails!"

Several passengers turned around, a few frowned, a few smiled, all went back to their food, but the boy's mother glancing suspiciously at the guilty Lisa (she was plastered on stingers, she had admitted to Anita when they checked in with Crew Sked that morning) saw that her son's accusation was not without warrant and later sent a blistering written complaint to the president of the airline, singling out the offender by name. Lisa was subsequently brought before a review board and fired for inebriation and insolence. She was drunk when they questioned her and after a few fretful moments told them without hesitation to take the crummy job and shove it up their puritanical assholes. Anita had since received several postcards from her from a town outside Los Angeles called West Covina where she had rented an apartment with a swimming pool and was getting ready for a screen test being arranged for her by a young film director she had met during a flight to London. "I'd rather be a whore than a stewardess," she had written in the last card, "except that a pro could starve to death out here, what with all the furious amateur competition. See you in the movies."

"There are a couple of them with every airline," Jack had remarked to Anita when the incident became known to all the personnel.

"A couple of what?" she asked. "Drinkers?"

"No. Hookers."

"What do you mean?"

"What do you think I mean? What do you think our Austrian friend was doing during her European layovers? Playing cribbage with the cabin crew?"

"But she seemed so nice," Anita said, utterly confused. "Even when she was drinking. She had . . . she had . . ." Why couldn't she finish the sentence? Perhaps because the thought she was about to express seemed too blatantly disparate with her new found knowledge about Lisa. "She had a great life force."

"Coupled with a great death wish."

Anita felt suddenly obliged to defend the condemned girl. "I liked her very much."

Jack smiled one of those faraway smiles that seemed so typically enigmatic of him. "That's funny. I loved her."

Anita had promptly pushed the entire conversation out of

her mind, it was amazing the way human beings could forget things that were too painful to remember, it was known as self-preservation. Jack being in love with anyone would have been too much for her to bear, but Jack being in love with a girl who was as different from Anita as two people could possibly be was more than too much to bear, it was like a direct negation of her, an utter dismissal, rattattat you're dead, you never even existed. That finally was how Anita perceived the whole business even when she was so busy perceiving nothing at all. She wondered why she should think of it now, why it was all being dredged up this hungover Thursday morning, her first chance at reconciliation in months with the man she was crazy about. But some blind force drove her on.

"Remember Lisa?" she asked him.

He did not answer, only looked at her with barely a nod of recognition, a disinterested nod.

"Did you really mean it when you told me that you were in love with her?"

"I meant it."

"Are you still?"

"In love with her?"

"Yes."

"No."

"What happened?"

"Time passed."

"Is that how you get over things?"

"Do you mean me or people in general?"

"Both."

"Well it's one method. It's not the easiest method, but it's always guaranteed to work."

"Wasn't she in love with you?"

"Obviously not or we'd be together this very minute.

He had wanted her that much. And Lisa's breasts weren't even anything to write home about. Just two small points through her stewardess blouse. Anita felt tears come to her eyes but they would stay there, she was much too sad to actually cry. Maybe in a week she would be able to cry. Then the tears might find release but now they just burned in her eyes and her throat felt thick, constricted, numbed. All this time she had been in love with Jack he had been in love with Lisa. Why she had never known him at all, never seen him except through her own distorted lenses. The shock of revelation hit her in the stomach, that was how she felt, as though someone had just clenched his fist and jammed her in the stomach with all his might. She wanted to double over. She wanted to sleep. Cry. Scream. Anything but this sick, mute sensation of misery. She opened her mouth and for a minute nothing came out.

"I . . ." Finally. "I'm sorry. I wish I had known."

The minute she said it she realized that she had known, he had told her he was in love with Lisa when they had their conversation early last fall, but she hadn't believed it, his words at the time meant nothing to her, they were words, not language, abstract, meaningless, they stood for nothing. Abracadabra. He might as well have said that. He could have recited Einstein's theory of relativity for all the difference it would have made. She would not have listened. Why then was she listening now? Because it suddenly seemed very important to listen, perhaps to learn. Irony. For he apparently had nothing more to say on the subject. In fact, he was changing the subject.

"Is there anything left to drink in this hotel?"

"There are a lot of leftover drinks, if you call that something to drink."

"With cigarette butts in the glasses?"

"Right."

"Good for flavor," he said, getting out of bed and disappearing into the living room.

When he returned several minutes later he was carrying Anita's cut glass pitcher filled to the top with an orange colored liquid that had at least one tray of ice cubes tinkling around in it. The liquid glistened gayly, cheerfully in the cold morning light.

"What on earth is it?" Anita asked.

"A very esoteric concoction known as LPD, not to be confused with you know what."

"But what does it stand for?"

"Leftover Party Drinks."

"Oh, no. You mean you emptied all those dregs of whiskey?" The something gay and cheerful had in one second turned into something downright disgusting, "—into that nice, clean pitcher?"

"And added orange juice and lemon juice for flavor. The lemon juice is very important, almost indispensable you might say to LPD. Do you have any baby bottles lying around?"

To someone not connected with an airline it might have sounded like a bizarre question but stewardesses were known to frequently swipe baby bottles which were standard equipment on all planes, and use them at home as water sprinkler bottles for pressing their uniforms when time was too short to send them to the cleaners.

"I have one in the kitchen," Anita said. "I'll get it."

"There's only one way to drink LPD," Jack informed her when she handed him the plastic bottle. "And that's from this. For germicidal reasons, obviously."

He then proceeded to pour some of the pitcher's contents into the bottle, replaced the rubber nipple, and lying back against the pillows that he had retrieved from the bedroom floor, stuck the nipple into his mouth and without the slightest trace of self-consciousness started to suck for all he was worth. The scrambled egg insignia on Jack's dark blue pilot's cap gave off just the right military glow to be in the same surreal snapshot as the baby bottle filled with last night's dirty booze. Five months ago (five minutes!) Anita might not have appreciated it, but she realized now that Lisa had something to do with her shift of view. She did not know what. Maybe it was that Lisa would have appreciated it. Yes, she could hear Lisa's throaty laugh permeate the room and she laughed, too.

Unloved women frequently get the notion that in order to win the love of the man they want all they have to do is emulate the style of their beloved predecessors. Unfortunately, that is not how it works. Even the most dismal kind of originality is preferable to a bad imitation. At first it might not be more palatable than a bad imitation, but it eventually creates its own aura, demands equal space, stands up better in the long run. Not knowing that, Anita buried the vestiges of herself beneath superimposed layers of another girl's personality. Later she would wonder why she was unsuccessful, but Jack could already feel the insincerity of her role at his nerve endings and he withdrew more than ever into solitary LPD drinking.

It was obvious to Anita that he had no intention of making love to her again and she felt both relieved and rejected. She did not want to make love just then but she wanted to be desired. Jack had lost his erection and seemed to have no intention of regaining it; he seemed quite oblivious to her presence now. She might have been a mute object in the room, a vase or a lamp, for all the attention he paid her as she picked up the bedside telephone and called the beauty parlor to make an appointment for that morning. Luckily they were able to take her at ten o'clock.

"I'm flying to Hamburg tonight," she told Jack after she had hung up.

"Oh?"

"I'll only be gone two days."

As though on cue he got out of bed and began to get dressed.

"I'll call you later in the week," he said.

"Simone is moving in with Robert."

He looked at her sharply but she could not tell what he was thinking. "That was fast."

"She stopped by earlier when you were asleep to pick up the dog. She was all worked up about Robert. Apparently they had quite a successful night together."

"Apparently."

Anita felt the onset of a familiar desperation take hold of her. Soon he would be dressed, out the door, gone, perhaps never to return. *I'll call you later in the week.* When? Which day? What time? But there was no point in pressing the issue, it didn't get you anywhere, it only made your anxiety that much more visible, more pitiable. If Anita had learned one thing, she had learned to keep her mouth shut in such instances and hope for the best. No. Pray.

"Think of me under the hair dryer," were Jack's last words to her as he kissed her on the cheek and made an unhesitating exit out of the apartment, a style of departure extremely typical of pilots whose lives were geared to the fast reflex action. Pilots did not linger, they had an acute sense of timing, they were trained to act first and think afterward. There was no point in spending hours trying to interpret or console oneself with a chance remark from them, a hurried message of goodbye. So that when Anita went to take a shower several minutes later and found a scribbled note from Jack lying on the bathroom sink, she accepted its contents as casually as she knew they were intended.

"You're running out of toothpaste," the note said.

Underneath the words he had drawn a heart with an arrow through it. On one side of the arrow it said, "Love," on the other side, "Hate."

Lou Marron's Thursday morning was different from Simone's, Beverly's, and Anita's, mainly because its immediate emphasis was not upon a man but upon work.

Marshall's dark body beside her when she opened her eyes in the mauve wallpapered bedroom did nothing at all to shift that emphasis. True he was a man, they had made love last night, and by sheer virtue of his physical presence he was still to be reckoned with, but at that point any resemblance between her and the other three girls came to an abrupt halt, for where Simone awakened with bleating love sounds for Robert Fingerhood, Beverly with the timeworn desperation of a nightmarish marriage, Anita with sinking sensations that Jack Bailey might fly off into the stratosphere and never be heard from again, Lou awakened with the words, *Cossack in the water,* spinning around in her head and the subsequent realization that she had yet to write the Steve Omaha interview, that she had yet to prove conclusively to Tony Elliot how much more qualified she was than Peter Northrop to be rewarded with the column, that she had yet to prove herself professionally even to the faintest degree of her own satisfaction.

Even as a child she had been a hopeless perfectionist, a straight "A" student, the only girl to graduate from William Cullen Bryant grade school in Philadelphia with an unsullied punctuality record. (I was never a day late to class, Mommy), and the pattern had continued through high school and college, NYU, her runaway to New York, the best journalism bet out of thirty-five competitors, but straight news reporting soon bored her, it was so metallic and uninspired.

No, it was in the realm of feature writing that Lou had hit her stride in college. She liked to interview people, she found it easy to talk to strangers and get responsive answers, people responded to her . . . an old Italian man who sold ices on MacDougal Street in the summertime, a tassel-breasted girl who danced at the Metropole on Seventh Avenue, a dentist who specialized in extractions and admitted to a predilection for tap dancing after two martinis. Also she had an easy style of writing, the finished product read easy because she worked hard to conceal the effort that had gone into it.

She worked hard to conceal all her efforts. Basically she did not want anyone to know what she was really like and she knew why: because if they found out, they might not like it. Sometimes she wondered whether she should have gone in for acting, she was such an excellent role player, but ironically she was too shy ever to get up on a stage. She could talk to absolute strangers with unfluttering confidence, but to emote publicly was quite beyond her scope. Her nature demanded a more quiet style of showing off. Writing was showing off but it was backhandedly quiet, more impersonal than face to audience (or even face to camera) acting, more controlled, the control was more in your hands. An editor had less control than a director. A director could really chop you up. She was undoubtedly afraid of being chopped up.

Why else did axes and knives figure so prominently, so ominously in her dreams?

She had only been chopped up in love once, with the boy who had gotten her pregnant at seventeen. He was killed in an automobile accident when she was still pregnant (drunk at the wheel he crashed headlong into a telephone post: was anything accidental?). When he died a certain well of tenderness within her had died, too, and even though she went through the motions of being in love with David, it was half an act. The fact was that she did not want her emotional virginity tampered with ever again. It hurt too much.

Marshall was talking in his sleep, his face buried in a pillow, the words strangled. "Your co-signer is not acceptable to us, Madam."

Mr. Crazy sat at the far end of the bed, curled up into a concentric black and white fur ball. Last night he had watched Marshall make love to her, his great yellow eyes widening in the dimly lit room. She wondered what sensations cats had when they saw two people going at it, what they actually felt. Mr. Crazy certainly displayed a very keen interest in the spectacle, he always had, and his fascinated presence had finally gotten on David's nerves so that when David made love to her now she saw to it that the cat was kept firmly out of the bedroom.

"He gives me the creeps," David said.

It had taken Lou a while to realize that it went farther than that. David was somehow afraid of the cat, although he was too ashamed to admit it. She wondered what precisely he was afraid of and she managed at last to get the truth out of him.

"If you really want to know," he said in a belligerent tone of voice that was not at all typical of him, "I'm afraid he's going to claw my goddamn balls."

Men were strange creatures, incomprehensible to her, and that was one of the reasons she preferred to concentrate upon work. There was finally much more satisfaction to be gained from work than from men. THE COLUMN! IT WAS LIKE SEX! IT WAS BETTER THAN SEX! The sex last night had not been bad once things belatedly got going, not bad at all, and even though she had no intention of seeing Marshall again (except in a similar erotic emergency), she felt thankful to him for having come so crucially to the rescue. Sex for Lou was indispensable to writing. Without it she felt dead, dried up, nothing flowed. Sex opened the door. It had occurred to her once, years ago, that she would sell her own mother down the river for a good feature piece. Writers were merciless on that score. They needed people to feed the creativity machine. They used up people just as she had already used up Marshall, who was dreaming about unsatisfactory co-signers. The narcissism of writers was not to be believed. Steve Omaha had called the painter David (Dahveeeeed) a monster. But did Steve Omaha think he, too, was a monster the morning he stole those nylon stockings out of a dead buddy's pocket in the waters of Normandy? Undoubtedly. It takes one to know one, Lou thought. Lou got her best writing thoughts almost but not quite upon awakening, when she was still in that twilight state between sleep and waking. There was even a word for it: hypnopompic. It was a magic state of superawareness, as though all of her half-formulated ideas and semifinished concepts had been put into a slow oven hours before to emerge gradually hours later in tender, baked perfection.

Cossack in the water. Sidney Greenstreet on horseback.

Just as she was about to get out of bed and head for the typewriter in the living room Marshall opened his eyes and looked at her with the kind of odd expression that she recognized as momentary lack of recognition.

"It's only me," she said. "The girl you picked up at the Jewish Museum. Remember?"

His smile revealed quite small teeth. For some reason she had not especially noticed them last night. His hair was brillo clipped and now that he knew where he was he looked quite happy to be there.

"Did I snore?"

"No. Why? Do you usually?"

"I've been known to cause pictures to tremble on the walls. But it only seems to happen when I'm very tired."

He had a nice body, long, lean. Somehow he struck her as more attractive this morning than he had last night, more self-confident now that he had proved himself as a satisfactory lover. If she didn't have to write that damned article, she would not mind making love to him again, particularly since the chances were that she would not be seeing him again, or if she did, at least not for a long time. Last night when he had been inside her she pretended he was a pimp from Harlem and she was one of the girls in his stable. He would have three Negro girls and two white girls, the other one, of course, being a honey blonde who specialized in blow jobs. At the same time she wondered what notions he was unconsciously entertaining about her.

"Where are you going?"

She had gotten out of bed and was stepping into her Ban-Lon leopard lounging pajamas. She made stealthy clawing motions at him from across the room.

"I'm going to my typewriter and write a funny story, darling baby honey sweetie cutie angel. But first I'm going to bring you a tall glass of orange juice so you won't be lonely."

"What kind of story?"

"For my paper. Remember that painter I told you about? The one I interviewed yesterday? Well, yesterday is when I should have written the piece but I became self-indulgent instead and seem to have picked up a man, so I'm paying for it this morning."

"I'm paying, too."

"Why? Would you like to make love to me again?"

She was smiling, flirting, but it was all a game. He didn't mean anything to her. In fact she wished he would put on his damn clothes and trot off to the personal loan department of The First National City Bank where he could spend the morning doling out pitiful sums of money to Puerto Ricans who were behind in their car payments, secretaries shrewdly investing in convertible sofas for their one-and-a-half-room flats, budding promotion managers who ran up bar tabs that the little woman knew nothing about. It was all her fault. What was? Getting involved with weak men. She drew them like a magnet, always had. Peter Northrop's blue eyes swam into view, dominating, commanding.

Lou frequently found herself wondering what his wife was like, what kind of woman a man like him would have chosen to marry, and although she had made several stabs at guess-work she never felt any sense of conclusion about any of her guesses. Knowing a man in an office situation more often than not left her utterly unprepared for his choice of a wife. Even the most attractive men had a way of surprising you with a perfect drudge who had driven into the city that day do a wee bit of shopping at Saks. There was a strange washed out quality about many businessmen's wives that Lou had met. For one thing their hems were too long and their shoes were from hunger. And then, their shoes and their bags always matched, but always, count on it.

That was just one of the many things Lou planned to go into in more detail if and when Tony Elliot let her do the column: all this matching compulsion that unimaginative women went in for. Black patent pumps and a black patent bag, their hems below their knees, and a sudsy smile on their faces. No wonder their husbands seldom left them. They weren't significant enough to bother leaving, they didn't get in the way, they just stood around their washing machines debating between Salvo and Bold while Mr. Two-Face was busy picking up cute tricks at The Cattleman and lying about his income bracket.

"I'd love to make love to you again," Marshall said.

She must have looked at him oddly because he then added, "A second ago you asked me whether I'd like to and I'm now giving you my honest, absolutely biased answer."

A Flip Wilson or a Godfrey Cambridge he would never be. What did she want of him anyway? Nothing. That was the whole point. He was the one who wanted something, not just sex either. He liked her, he expected to see her again, he didn't know that this was cutoff day, did not vaguely suspect. Last night he told her that he lived on West Fourth Street in the Village and she wondered whether he ever went out or went to bed with Negro girls, or whether like so many of his compatriots who had escaped the ghetto he concentrated most of his efforts upon blue-eyed blondes. Being a brown-eyed brunette, Lou found that Negro men were seldom drawn to her (her best bet was to go to Sweden and be elected king). Negro men had spent all their lives looking into other brown eyes, staring at other black hair, they were no doubt fed up with the tedious monochrome. Was that why they were so frequently seen walking proudly down the street arm in arm with garish blondes in bulging stretch pants (she wouldn't do badly in Denmark either)?

"I'd love to, too," she half-lied, "but work comes first in this case. You see, the paper goes to press tomorrow afternoon."

"We could do it fast," he said, hopefully.

"That's no fun, now is it?"

"I suppose not."

Get dressed, *schmuck*, was what she really felt like saying, but on the other hand it was early, only a few minutes past seven, and he probably planned to go straight to work in last night's clothes without bothering to go home first. In that case, why should he get dressed? He had plenty of time. Maybe he would go back to sleep. Actually she didn't give a damn what he did just as long as he didn't get in her way. She could bang out the straight news stuff in the office, surrounded by clamor and confusion, and it did not bother her in the least, because there was not much to think about, it wasn't really writing, it was more like the mechanical recording of an event, very factual and uninterpretive, but something like the Steve Omaha interview was another matter entirely. Tony Elliot had intimated that if it were well done, he would run it in Monday's paper in the coveted centerfold pages. With that kind of incentive staring her in the face, she needed peace and quiet when she wrote.

"Back in a minute," she said.

Mr. Crazy followed her into the kitchenette and promptly jumped up on the caned stool that sat next to the stove. Lou had trained him to sit there before she fed him. If he did not sit on the stool, he paced back and forth rubbing himself against her legs in ecstatic food anticipation, and for some reason that she had never bothered to explore that continual rubbing business irritated her terribly.

"Mr. Crazy is under arrest," Lou informed him, hoping that she had remembered to buy enough cat food the last time she went to Gristede's. Her life being what it was, her trips to Gristede's were few and far between, and one time when she was going through her canceled checks she realized that she spent an average of only eight dollars a week at the market, and much of that went for such inedibles as Kleenex and Clorox, not to mention food for the cat and kitty litter. Why, she spent more at the beauty parlor each week getting a set and a manicure than she did on food. As she so frequently told David, who was always trying to get her to eat more, food bored the hell out of her and she didn't understand why he made such a big deal out of it.

"It's because I'm Jewish," he said, laughing.

"Well I'm half Jewish and I don't have half your amount of interest, so it doesn't figure."

"Yes, but your other half is Irish and everybody knows they have no cuisine at all and consequently no food hang-ups. What does your father eat?"

"Cheese blintzes."

"An Irish lawyer?"

"He's not a very good lawyer. He mostly handles minor negligence cases. And besides my mother has a funny sense of humor. She gives him blintzes and bacon."

"Both on the same plate?"

She loved to tease David. "Of course. My family isn't kosher. But I'll bet you didn't know I could read a Jewish newspaper."

"Now I'm convinced you're putting me on."

She shook her head. "No, I'm not. I read the *Daily*

Forward every morning on my way to work. Honest. It breaks up the whole subway."

They had known each other only a short time when this exchange took place and Lou finally told David about her maternal grandfather, the Jewish Monte Wooley, who had lived in New York for forty years stubbornly refusing to learn English. One day her mother decided that since the old man was Lou's only surviving grandparent it would be fitting for her to learn how to communicate with him during the short time he undoubtedly had left on earth, since he was then going on ninety. Consequently, after regular school, which was bad enough, they shipped her off to another school to learn how to read, write, and speak Yiddish. She did not want to go but she was only eleven years old and her mother did not seem to feel that eleven-year-old children had veto privileges. So she went for two hours every day and after a while found it was fun. It was much less constricting than regular school, and with her usual academic diligence she was soon the best student in the class. Also, writing backward tickled her, it did not seem real, it seemed like a game.

The irony of the whole business was that, unknown to her mother, they taught her a dialect quite different from the one her grandfather spoke, and the next time she went to New York to visit him she could not understand a word he said, although he seemed to understand her perfectly and thought it was all very amusing. He died shortly after that, and now, sixteen years later, Lou felt grateful to him for having unwittingly made it possible for her to create subway havoc every morning with the *Daily Forward*.

"Mr. Crazy has been under arrest for weeks now and nobody is going to get him out on bail either."

Luckily the cupboard contained one can of Puss 'n Boots. It was the kidney and gravy flavor (*a gourmet food for cats*, it said on the label). Lou opened the can and scooped half the contents into Mr. Crazy's dish, added his vitamin powder, a handful of crunchies, and set the dish on the floor. She also refilled his water bowl.

"Mr. Crazy is wanted for armed robbery in five Southern states. Isn't that a fact?"

Then she proceeded to take her morning vitamins. David had a habit of gagging discreetly whenever he watched her go through what he referred to as "the morning vitamin *megillah*," which consisted of the following: four dolomite tablets, four bone meal tablets, one kelp, six acerola, one all-day iron, and two B–complex capsules. These were washed down with a tall glass of orange juice and a prayer to keep J. I. Rodale, her health mentor, safe and sound at the helm of *Prevention* magazine. Actually, she felt guilty about the orange juice because Rodale disapproved of it. He said it eroded the teeth and caused your asshole to itch (anus pruritus), but sometimes Lou thought he went too far in his food condemnations. If she cut out everything Rodale was against, there would not be much left to eat, not unless she stayed home all day and grew organic fruits and vegetables in her garden. Of course there was still lean meat, eggs, and seafood. According to Rodale those were okay, but he was vehemently against all milk products, all canned foods, all chemically treated foods. On defiant mornings, Lou washed down her vitamins with Carnation Instant Breakfast (mixed with prohibited whole milk!) and prayed that she would not be struck dead by mysterious nutritional forces before the day's end.

Marshall was sitting up in bed, smoking a cigarette, when she returned with his orange juice.

"What time do you plan to leave for work?" he asked her.

"Nine-thirty at the latest."

He frowned. "I've got to be in by nine. You know how banks are."

"We don't have to leave together."

"That's true."

"I just don't know how long it's going to take me to do this story, so you leave whenever you have to."

She did not want to leave with him because she had to drop off some clothes at the cleaner's first and she did not want the cleaner to suspect that she had spent the night with Marshall. The cleaner and other neighborhood shopkeepers were used to seeing her with David and were willing to accept the semblance of a monogamous relationship, despite their glaring age difference, but she would absolutely lose her good customer standing if she showed up at nine-thirty in the morning flanked by an unfamiliar black man. One's neighborhood in New York was as small-townish as any small town in the country, and Lou had discovered a long time ago that it was best from the standpoint of service not to offend the middle-class morality of shopkeepers you had to do business with day in and day out.

"What's your phone number?" Marshall asked. "I notice that it's not indicated on the phone."

The round white circle in the center of Lou's telephone

dial was significantly blank for a good reason. Her number was unlisted (any woman with a listed number in New York was stark, raving mad), and she only gave it to people she wanted to give it to. Unfortunately, Marshall was not about to become one of those people. True if he turned out to be the persistent type, which she doubted, he could always reach her at the office but it was easy to get rid of unwelcome callers on the office telephone. You just said you had to take another call, or that you were dashing off to a meeting and didn't have time to talk. After a while people gave up.

"The number is LE 2-6370," she said, watching him jot it down in his address book. The number really was LE 2-6039. Let him figure that one out.

"I'll call you soon," he promised.

"Okay."

"Maybe we can take in a movie."

She smiled at him. He was really rather sweet and she had played a dirty trick on him, but what point would there be in letting him call only to turn him down repeatedly?

"That would be nice," she said. "By the way, what is your last name?"

"Rivers."

If she should ever want to see him again, she would call him. His number was bound to be listed.

"Be sure to come kiss me goodbye before you leave," she said, as she went out of the bedroom and closed the door softly behind her.

It was a quarter to ten when Lou got off the Lexington Avenue subway, the Steve Omaha piece tucked securely into her chained Morlé swagger bag. The piece was roughly typed and if she had figured correctly, it ran approximately twelve hundred words. With Cav's photos that was a good length for a double-page spread. She hoped that Tony Elliot would approve of the way she had handled the interview. She had a hunch that he would since she seemed to be quite in his favor lately, and he had shown hearty enthusiasm for the last two feature pieces she had done in recent months, one on a fabrics designer and one on the owner of an East Side boutique for children.

She was going to suggest to Tony that in addition to the shots Cav had taken in Steve Omaha's studio, they use a couple of actual D-Day invasion photos of American soldiers wading up to the beaches of Normandy. *Cossack in the water.* The invasion photos would make an interesting counterpoint to the canvas showing Sidney Greenstreet, Mary

Astor, and Peter Lorre on horseback smoking Tiparillos, not to mention the one of Sonja Henie twirling on black ice. The whole thing was just nutty enough to appeal to Tony Elliot's fey imagination. She hoped.

"You had a call from Mr. Swern a few minutes ago," the girl who took messages for the reporters said to Lou, as she got off the elevator on the fifth floor of the Lexington Avenue building that housed *The Rag*.

"Thank you, Betty. Do you know if Mr. Elliot is in?"

"He's in his office with Mr. Northrop, I believe."

"I see. Thank you."

The office walls were decorated with enormously blown-up photographs of all the top European and American fashion designers. Unobtrusive thin black frames held the photographs. As soon as Lou got to her desk, over which hung Marc Bohan of Dior, she rang Tony's secretary and asked if she could see their leader as soon as he was free.

"I'll ring you, Miss Marron," the girl said mechanically.

"Thank you."

The reporter who covered the handbag market had the desk next to Lou and was about to call down for coffee. "Want anything?" she asked.

"I'll take a container."

"Black?"

"Yes. Thank you."

Thank you thank you thank you thank you one and all. We're all so damned polite to one another, she thought. There was only one thank you she would truly like to utter, and that was: Thank you, Tony, for letting me do the column. She wondered if she would live long enough ever to say those magic words to her fickle publisher, or would they be spoken instead by her competitor, Mr. Peter Northrop III? She would give anything to know what Peter and Tony were talking about this very minute. It was probably just routine business, going over a story Peter had written or preparing for a future assignment, but Lou felt shaky these days whenever these two got together in private. Any conference between them could be the big one in which Tony informed Peter that he had been awarded the plum, thereby shattering all of Lou's hopes and plans.

"Handbags are going very cold-blooded for spring, in case you're interested," the other reporter said, looking up from her typewriter. "Like sueded python swingers and hippie frog clutches. They've even got a mottled boa theater bag for those evenings when you're really feeling *sauvage*, darling."

"I'm feeling pretty *sauvage* this very minute," Lou said.

"Love?"

"In a way."

Desiring the column as badly as she did wasn't that much different from desiring a man, was it? Both situations carried with them a similar degree of frustration and painful intensity, almost the same exact kind of desperate yearning.

"Is his wife giving him a hard time because of you?" the other girl asked.

"She doesn't know about me. At least that's what David says."

"Christ, don't tell me that he's losing interest. What a putdown that would be!"

"No, I don't think he is but he's in a tough spot. You know, trying to keep both of us happy at the same time."

Lou considered it infinitely more strategic to pretend that she was upset about David rather than about her lagging career. It was not smart to let your aspirations show until you had actually achieved something important, and then your achievement could do the showing off for you. In the meantime, the wisest course of action was not to seem too eager or too greedy in front of fellow employees, never lose your cool.

"It's Miss O'Hara," she said into the telephone to David's receptionist. "Mr. Swern called me a little while ago. Can I please speak to him?"

She thought it sweet of David to try to protect her reputation by ascribing a false name to her for the benefit of his personnel, but she wondered, too, whether they did not by now see through his little sham. It was hard keeping secrets in offices, as Lou knew only too well.

"Hi, honey. How are you?" David asked a moment later.

"I'm the one who should be asking about you. And Lillian. Is she better?" She must be better or David would not have come into work today. "Tell me what's happening on the home front."

"The doctor gave her quite a bit of sedation last night and apparently the medicine he prescribed is pretty effective. I think she'll be completely well in a few days. I told the maid to look in on her at least once an hour. Excuse me a second." His voice grew fainter, gruffer, he was talking away from the receiver. "No, Simone, the herringbone doeskin cape. Yes, the one with the vinyl band. That's right, dear." Now he returned genially to Lou. "Can you meet me for lunch, baby? I have a little present for you."

"You shouldn't keep giving me things, David. Really, you're spoiling me."

The handbag reporter sardonically rolled her eyes at the ceiling in response to Lou's token gesture of protest. Lou grinned and winked at her, as the dour face of James Galanos sneered down at them both from his black frame above the other girl's desk.

"I'd love to meet you for lunch, David, but it will have to be on the latish side. You know it's hectic spring market time. Is one-thirty too terribly late for you, darling?"

The handbag reporter had started to play an imaginary violin and was mouthing "Love in Bloom."

"No that'll be okay," David said. "I have some inventory to take care of anyway."

"Marvelous." Lou was about to hang up. "I'll see you at one-thirty."

"By the way, what did you do last night?"

"I'll tell you all about it at lunch, David."

"Goodbye, dear."

"What's he got for you this time?" the handbag reporter asked. "An ermine jumpsuit?"

"Who knows? Who cares?"

"*I* do. I'm jealous."

"But you've got Jason, and Jason isn't married to another lady."

"Jason doesn't give me Kohinoor mink coats either."

"As the man said, there's more to life than—"

Lou stopped in mid-sentence because the door to Tony Elliot's office had just that second swung open, revealing Tony and Peter Northrop frozen on the threshold. They were standing so close that their heads were practically touching. Peter wore a tan corduroy jacket with suede patches on the elbows, and Tony was immaculate as usual in English tweed, an ascot at his throat. For a moment neither of them moved. Then Tony said something to Peter, who cocked his head slightly to one side, then Peter nodded a barely perceptible nod. Tony fished something out of his trouser pocket and handed it to Peter who nodded again, a bit more openly this time. Blue eyes looked into blue eyes but nobody smiled and nobody spoke. Lou had the feeling she was watching a scene from an Antonioni movie, one of the those silent, mysterious scenes where two people encounter each other in mute transaction, the clarity of their physical presence in no way detracting from the distinctly amorphous nature of what has just passed between them. In a second the door to Tony's office had closed shut and Peter Northrup walked swiftly across the carpeted floor to his desk that sat beneath an impishly smiling Coco Chanel, wearing one of her famous pearl necklaces.

After that, the morning went sharply downhill for Lou. Tony Elliot could not possibly see her today, his secretary said. No, it was out of the question. He had two people coming in at any minute, then he had a lunch date cross-town, and after that he had to take the afternoon shuttle to Boston.

"Actually, I don't have to *see* him," Lou said. "I simply wanted to get his okay on a feature piece I just finished. I suppose I can do that tomorrow."

"He'll be in Boston tomorrow. He won't be back in the office until Monday."

"Monday! Are you sure?"

"Positive, Miss Marron."

"But he told me he wanted to use this piece in Monday's issue. It was tentatively scheduled to run in the centerfold pages."

"That's odd." There was an embarrassed silence. "I'm almost certain that he's using a story of Mr. Northrop's in that spot."

"Oh, I see."

"I'm sorry, Miss Marron."

"So am I."

She felt like bursting into tears but there was no time for such emotional indulgences, no time at all. She was late as it was. She had to dash out, grab a taxi, and go downtown to attend a brassiere showing at a leading manufacturer's show-room. She had never felt less like attending anything in her life. When she arrived several mannequins were already on the floor. The bras were very cleverly designed without darts or seams and were modeled exclusively in dainty floral pastels. The mannequins wore coordinated bikini briefs and illustrated to the smattering of out-of-town buyers how easily the bra straps could be moved and switched around to different positions, in order to adjust to any cut of dress or gown worn over them.

The next showing, several blocks away, was a sleepwear manufacturer's spring line, and again only a paucity of buyers were present. *Buyers cool on spring,* Lou scribbled in her notebook, *attendance down.* Some of the styles modeled were quite lovely, and as the narrator pointed out, "They can double as discotheque dresses if worn with suitable underclothes." He was one of the partners in the firm and looked distinctly unhappy about the poor attendance he had drawn.

"They think fall is all that counts," he grumbled to Lou, as she shook his hand before leaving to meet David at the 37th Street Hideaway.

It was the restaurant she always met him at whenever they had lunch together, which was not too often, which was just as well with Lou, the restaurant being as windowless and airless as it was. Located on Thirty-Seventh Street between Fifth and Sixth Avenues, it was a popular midday dining place for executives and resident buyers from the surrounding garment and nearby fur districts. The particular stretch of Thirty-Seventh Street on which the restaurant was located was narrow and grimy, cluttered with hand trucks, trimming stores, and glaucous luncheonettes that sent their frying odors out onto the broken sidewalk.

The Hideaway was up one flight of stairs and seemed to try to compensate for its windowlessness by pretending that it was perennial nighttime and therefore dark outside, anyway. It always took a second for Lou's eyes to adjust to the hazy, indirect lighting, the deep red tablecloths, the illusory sense of being at some strange New Orleans supper club on a moonless midnight.

David was seated at his usual banquette table at the far left side of the back room. When he spotted her, he politely began to stand up but she motioned him not to.

Kissing him on the forehead, she said, "It's much too crowded here to be gallant, darling. I'll sit down instead."

David had saved her the more comfortable seat against the wall. He faced her across the table. "What would you like to drink?"

"Campari and soda, please."

"One campari and soda," he told the waiter, "and one Dewar's on the rocks."

"You look marvelous," David said, reaching for her hand. "Even though I can tell you've been working like a dog."

"How can you tell?"

"Your mouth. Something happens to your mouth when you've been working hard. I can't explain, it just looks different."

"I shudder to think what it will look like when the day is over. I have three more showings to go to this afternoon. It's a good thing I had plenty of sleep last night. You'll never guess where I went for dinner."

"Elaine's?"

They both laughed.

"How did you *ever* figure it out?" she said. "And I ran into—"

She told him about the married couple they both knew and then about the Jewish Museum opening. "But I left after a few minutes. It was a carnival, you can't imagine."

The waiter placed their drinks on the table and handed them menus.

"Before we order," David said, "I want to give you this."

Removing the slender Cartier box from his inside jacket pocket, he placed the bracelet on the table. The jewels glistened magically in the flickering Hideaway light.

"I'm stunned," Lou said. "What is it? I mean, what are they?"

"Emeralds, rubies, rose quartz, and pearls. Do you like it?"

She slipped it on her slender wrist, afraid even to contemplate what it might be worth. "It's beautiful, David. It's truly beautiful. Thank you."

As she reached to press his hand, tears came to her eyes.

"Hey there," he said, "we won't have any tears at this table. They're strictly forbidden."

"It's just that I'm so terribly terribly happy."

The emeralds blurred into rubies, rubies into rose quartz, only the pearls seemed steady and unwavering, the impishly smiling Coco Chanel's pearl necklace was all that Lou really saw as she wiped the tears from her eyes and tried to smile happily at David.

Part 2

CHAPTER FOUR 

It was late February, the longest, dreariest month of the year, and Simone had been living with Robert Fingerhood for three weeks and four days. Ordinarily, if someone asked her what day of the week it was, she would have to stop and think for a moment, seriously *think* about it, because not only did she have the disgusting habit of being unaware of the day of the week, she often had to remind herself of the month as well. Once on a balmy morning in June she had dated a check January something or other. A man in the dim past (the midget?) told her that the reason she could not place herself in time was because she did not know where her vagina was (yes, it was the midget). He also said that was the reason she had such a lousy sense of direction.

"You mean, it's all because of my vagina?" she asked him, unconvinced, but passionately interested in his line of reasoning.

"Precisely."

He seemed very sure of himself, as though he had spent a lifetime delving into knotty problems like this and coming up with unusual, but unhesitatingly self-confident answers.

"You don't *want* to know where it is."

There was something almost gleeful in the way he made this last pronouncement.

"Why don't I want to know?"

"Isn't it obvious?"

"Not to me."

"The penis-envy syndrome, silly girl. If you knew where

your vagina was, you might have to look at it and there's really not much to see, now is there?"

She wondered what made him so sure that she was not in the habit of looking at her vagina at least five times a day just to make certain it was still in its proper place.

"I would say there's quite a bit to see," she replied, "providing you have a healthy attitude."

"I'll bet you couldn't put your finger on your clitoris this very minute if you had to," he said, spitefully.

"You're being terribly nasty and I don't know why. What have I done? Why are you trying to hurt my feelings?"

"Because you're beautiful and five feet five and I'm ugly and only three feet seven."

"You're not ugly," she said, meaning it.

"But I am only three feet seven."

There seemed little point in denying that. "You might be only three feet seven, but when you're not being nasty you have a very beautiful soul."

"I also have the clap on my big toe. Would you like me to stick my clappy toe up your vagina? That could leave a lifetime of a marker. Just think. Then you'd never again be in doubt as to what day it was, or what month, it might even improve your sense of direction, which, as we all know, is pretty pathetic at present."

"Thanks all the same," Simone said, wondering how anyone could have the clap on his toe. There was so much she did not understand (would never understand?). "I prefer to remain in my disoriented state rather than . . ."

The midget, who was a systems analyst, observed her shrewdly.

"At least you don't pity me," he said.

"I'm too busy pitying myself."

"I prefer it that way."

Simone had met him at an electronics show at the Coliseum and gone to bed with him mainly to find out whether his penis would be as small as the rest of him, but like most men his stature seemed to have no bearing upon that most vital of all vital organs. They spent a couple of weeks together and often when she woke up in bed beside him she thought for the first couple of seconds that he was her baby. It was only when he rammed it into her, which he did with all the powerful three foot seven force he could muster, that she lay back against the pillows, happy to be in the arms of a man again. Height made no difference at all when you were getting laid.

However, after he mentioned his diseased toe, she went straight to her gynecologist for a gonorrhea test which subsequently came back negative, and yet in spite of medical reassurance she could not bring herself to go to bed with the midget again. He probably was only kidding about his toe, she would tell herself late at night, alone in the upper bunk bed. It was precisely the kind of warped story he would dredge up. Still she could not erase it from her mind, and whenever she thought of him after that she visualized him at a restaurant table sticking his malignant toe up some unsuspecting dinner partner's panties, a glistening white tablecloth shielding his slimy act from the eyes of waiters and diners both.

But as soon as Simone moved in with Robert Fingerhood she became suddenly, surprisingly conscious of time. Was it because she suspected she might be living on borrowed time with Robert, that at any moment he was liable to tire of her and politely ask her to clear out? Perhaps. Or perhaps her time with him was so delicious that she wanted to be achingly aware of every fragile second. Three weeks and four days. In only three more days they could celebrate their first anniversary. One whole month together! She felt the sense of accomplishment of a young bride who wakes up one morning and discovers, to her vast satisfaction, that at last she has mastered the art of the perfect three-minute egg.

Before moving in with Robert, Simone, who had rarely, if ever, shown signs of practicality, gave atavistic evidence of her practical Norman heritage. Instead of getting rid of the Fifty-Seventh Street apartment altogether, she had sublet it to Helen, one of the other models at Mini-Furs, Inc. Helen was only too happy to take the apartment on Simone's casual terms.

"Maybe I'll want it back eventually," Simone said, "and then again maybe I won't. It all depends on how things work out with Robert."

Helen said that was okay with her because she was dying to get out of her present place, and the sooner the better. She was utterly fed up with her roommate, whom she described as a big pain in the ass. It seemed that roomie did slobby things like leaving stacks of unwashed dishes in the kitchen sink, not to mention douche bags scattered around the bathroom, so that Helen could never bring a date home without first taking the time to check out the cleanliness scene. Simone's apartment, being as inexpensive as it was, meant that Helen would not have to find another girl to help split the rent, which was a big relief to her.

"Women shouldn't live together," she said to Simone. "It's obscene. It brings out the worst in everyone. 'That was *my* Chinese vase you broke yesterday.' 'That was *my* chocolate chip ice cream you finished off in the middle of the night.' Ugh."

Simone did not tell Robert that she had merely sublet her apartment and could get it back whenever she wished, since she felt that that might strike him as a lack of faith on her part in any ultimate, permanent relationship between them. On the other hand preferring to avoid an outright lie, if possible, she simply said that one of the girls she worked with was "taking" the apartment, which certainly was true enough. The fact that the lease remained in Simone's name and that she was still legally responsible for any damage that might occur were minor technicalities she saw no reason to burden the overworked Robert with. In between trying to finish his Ph.D. thesis, *The relationship between the rate of the subject's maternal heartbeat and the rate of sexual intromission that is optimal in achieving orgasm,* and treating tricky mental cases at The Child Guidance Center, he had enough on his mind. More than enough, was Simone's feeling.

The first week that Simone moved in, Robert went out and bought something called a Conar Audio Color Set, which he proceeded to install in the bedroom in no time flat. It was a harmless looking thing, on the order of a television screen, except that the proportions were different; it was longer and lower than most television screens. As Robert hooked up the set to the two stereo speakers that were also in the bedroom, he informed Simone that she was about to witness a brand new concept in musical enjoyment.

"This little marvel," he said, "electronically translates music to color. Here's what happens. I put a record on the stereo and Audio Color paints the music on the screen. Varying color patterns, synchronizing with the record, move across the screen, the colors grow fainter, brighter, wilder, all in time with the music. Can you imagine? From now on, you're not just going to hear a particular melody. You're going to *see* it."

Being nervous about anything electronic, Simone said that that was very interesting. She was ashamed to admit that she still did not understand the concept of radio. When she was a child her mother owned a monstrously large floor model radio set and Simone used to peer inside it, in back where the tubes were, convinced that all the entertainers who were playing instruments and singing songs and announcing the latest news over the airwaves, were locked up in the bowels of the set, having been miraculously reduced to miniature size for the duration of their performance after which they would return to normal size until it was time for their next performance.

Simone liked making love while Conar Audio painted musical pictures on the screen for her and Robert's aesthetic enjoyment. In order to give him a chance to appreciate the vivid color spectacle, Simone considerately got on top at least once during the night and went through a series of frantic pelvic motions that finally resulted in Robert telling her to "slow down."

"Don't you like it fast?" she asked, disappointed that her efforts were not greeted with greater enthusiasm.

"No. Do it the way I do when I'm on top. That's right."

He guided her slender hips with his hands. "Slow. Easy. Now doesn't that feel much better?"

"Mmmmmmmm, yes. I suppose so."

Actually, it felt the same as when she went fast, it didn't feel like much of anything. The only times she really got excited was when Robert put his finger on her clitoris while he was inside her. That drove her a little wild, but to her anguish failed to produce the stubbornly evasive orgasm she had been searching for in recent years. Maybe she would never have one, *jamais jamais jamais*. It was a grim thought at best, shattering at worst, and the terrible part was that she could not stop thinking about it. She thought about it during the day when she was at work, and she thought about it even more when she returned to Robert's apartment in the evening and the moment of lovemaking drew imminently near.

In the past her affairs had been so haphazard, so fragmented, and often so peculiarly deranged that she found it easy to excuse her lack of orgasm on the grounds that no girl in her right mind could be expected to come under such abnormal conditions, and with such freaky men. And then as if to prove the validity of her reasoning, she would mentally go through the list of men she had been to bed with, re-evaluating each of them, one by one, until she had succeeded in striking out every last one of them from the arena of sexual gratification. In fact, after a while she had the strikeout process down so pat that she was able to reel off the culprits and their defects as readily as the alphabet and with about as much emotion:

1) The behavioral psychologist who trained chimps for outer space (impotent).
2) The computer programmer (he was so small he thought A&P hotdogs were big).
3) Her literary friend, Edwin L. Kuberstein (reading *Fanny and Zooey* while being eaten for six days was not her idea of eroticism).
4) The electronics engineer (if she felt nothing with a penis, was it any wonder she felt doubly nothing with a candle?).
5) The steel guitar player (peeing on someone in the bathtub definitely did not turn her on).
6) The two freaky hairdressers (they had kissed each other in bed, over her head—was that supposed to engender excitement?).
7) The dental assistant with the unfortunate stammer (if only he had kept his goddamn mouth shut in bed).
8) Stamos, the Greek businessman (his admiration for American technology in general, and electric toothbrushes in particular, made her asshole bleed).
9) The market research analyst (he came in about five seconds, then cried for five hours).
10) The man who wore Hawaiian shirts and shot Redi-Whip up her vagina (the fake whipped cream turned out to be laughing gas which made the bastard high as a kite as he licked it out of her, but did nothing to raise *her* spirits).
11) The pothead who screwed her in the bathroom sink (porcelain was cold, damn it).
12) And of course the bitchy midget (fear of coming down with the clap was not exactly conducive to a girl's sexual satisfaction, now was it?).

Simone could not strike out Robert Fingerhood, though, not on any of the counts just specified, and not on any that she could think of. Although she kept waiting for him to pull some freaky stunt, he never did, and it soon occurred to her that he was the first man she had ever met who seemed to be sexually normal without being a big bore at the same time. In face of this, Simone felt more inadequate than ever.

"What's wrong with me?" she asked Robert one night, not

long after she had moved in. "You're a psychologist. You're supposed to know about these things."

His smile was tender, contemplative. "We're working on your case," he said.

"Maybe you should give me those tests with the funny names that you give your patients at The Child Guidance Center. Do you think they might reveal the root of my trouble?"

"Most of them are designed specifically for children," Robert pointed out.

"But that's what I think is wrong with me. I'm specifically a child."

Ignoring this last remark, Robert said, "Besides, even if they weren't for children, it would be unethical for me to test you. You're not my patient."

"I wish I were."

Robert gave her a funny look, a pained look. "If you want to go to someone, I could recommend a good . . ."

"No, I couldn't talk to a stranger. I don't see how people do that. I would only make up stories about myself, I'd tell him beautiful lies. I'd wear my Rima, The Bird Girl, outfit and insist that I was Rima. What do you imagine he'd say to that?"

"Polly want a cracker?"

"That's not so funny."

"Neither are your fantasies."

"Meaning . . .?"

They were in bed and Robert leaned over and kissed her left breast. "Meaning I think you're a delicious girl, even if you do have a couple of strange hangups."

One of the things that amazed Simone about Robert was that he preferred the traditional man-on-top, woman-on-bottom position to any other. He was the only man she had ever known who preferred it, most of them went in for highly intricate acrobatic arrangements, usually the more intricate the better. Sometimes she used to wonder whether they had all gone to the same esoteric school that trained people to turn into human pretzels at a moment's notice, so deftly convoluted did their bodies become at the whisper of sex.

Robert Fingerhood said very little when he made love to Simone, as he did every night, but there was no need for him to speak, Simone quickly realized, since his body and his actions spoke so much more eloquently than any words he might have chosen to utter. After he had kissed her breast, he began to suck on the nipple which quickly grew hard despite the fact that Simone felt hardly any sensation at all in her breasts. As though to compensate for this lack of feeling she started to moan and thrash around in bed, then she convulsively switched his head to her other breast, saying at last, "Take them both in your mouth at the same time." Cupping both breasts tightly together until the nipples were only inches apart, Robert covered them with his mouth and let his tongue flit rapidly from one hardened nipple to the other.

Simone enjoyed this activity very much because her breasts were her pride and joy, they were so perfectly, so exquisitely formed that she felt like some lofty love goddess offering them as a heathen sacrifice to her thirsty lover. Yes, she saw this particular act as a beautiful pagan sacrifice to the dark power of sex, and only the fear of her breasts becoming deformed after years of being pulled at made her tremble a little. Mistaking the trembling for passion, Robert let go of her breasts and parted the lips of her vagina to see whether she was wet enough to be entered. She was not.

"Sorry about that," she laughed.

He began to stimulate her clitoris with one hand while with the other he gently flicked her left nipple ("Because you're right handed," he had explained the night before), and in several minutes she felt the moisture start to trickle out of her. It pleased Simone to be able to lubricate so readily, and yet on another level it seemed like one more of Mother Nature's dirty tricks: why allow her to become physically prepared for the act of sex and then deny her its glorious ultimate reward? *Il n'y a pas de justice,* she thought, as lavender, blue, and gold images began to flash across the Conar Audio screen in tremulous response to Jeri Southern singing, *Don't you know, little fool, you never can win, use your mentality, wake up to reality, but each I time I do just the thought of you makes me stop before I begin . . .*

Then Robert entered her and she felt a sharp, unexpected stab of desire sweep over her and for the barest of seconds she actually dared hope that maybe this time, but as usual sensation abruptly dissipated itself and while she remained open and moist, indicating all the trappings of sensuality, she was almost totally insensate. Only her breasts seemed alive and still quivering from their recent altar offering, and lying quietly on her back all of a sudden Simone reached for her twin prizes and copying Robert's earlier gesture she cupped them in her own hands and presented them to an oblivious

Robert who was wildly lost in his own world of throbbing, bursting, plunging eroticism.

"Here!" Simone heard herself cry. "Take them! They're yours!"

In response to her harsh command, Robert reached mechanically for her breasts which he then held as though they were dumb weights, nothing more. As Simone's words reverberated in her ears she felt foolish mouthing such inappropriate sentiments, as foolish and demented as the midget, Robert must surely think she was foolish. In fact she was just about to ask him when she recognized that familiar quickening of breath and pelvic thrust.

"Ohhhhh," he said, moving still faster. "Ohhhhhhhh."

Then he very unfoolishly poured it all into her, and as he did so Simone felt a bitter surge of hatred for him, an almost venomous desire to interfere with his deep, agonized enjoyment, an enjoyment that she probably would never be fortunate enough to experience, and in that wavery second she moved through infinite layers of despair to take her place beside her maimed soulmate, the midget.

The next morning as they were getting dressed to go to work, Simone said to Robert, "Doesn't it bother you that I can't come?"

"Doesn't it bother *you?*"

"Yes, of course," she admitted, snapping her tasseled garter belt around her diminutive waist, "but I'm used to it by now. I hope it doesn't upset you too much, that you don't feel, well, inadequate. Because it's really not your fault. It's just something, I don't know what, something about me."

"I'll try not to let it get me down," Robert assured her, running his hand lightly across her exposed breasts. "You have the most beautiful breasts I've ever seen. How many times have you been told that?"

"Fourteen million. But it never meant anything until you said it."

Robert had his shirt and trousers on now and was debating between a navy and white striped tie and a solid navy. Walking up behind him, Simone encircled his waist with her hands and rested her head softly on his long back.

"I love you," she said. "I really think you're wonderful."

Turning around, he took her in his arms and held her to him.

"You're a lovely girl and I'm very happy with you. Now don't you think you had better get dressed? You're going to be late to work."

She gave him a mocking, military salute. "Yes, master."

Being in love was a brand new sensation for Simone and she was still grappling with all the complexities of it. The fact that she knew Robert did not love her had not yet taken on the ominous proportions it soon would. She was too busy sorting out her own range of feelings to think seriously about this. At the moment his not loving her was like some kind of dim inconvenience that interfered with the smoothness of her life, but precisely how and in what way, she could not have explained. It was simply there—his not loving her—a faint, undefined ache in the body that she trusted would disappear altogether some day, either that or become so painful that she would be forced to treat and cure it. Since things had not yet reached that latter stage, Simone was still in that marvelous land where love was king and the lover his obedient, radiant queen. The sensation of being in love so overwhelmed and delighted Simone that she felt sorry for Robert who could not share her joy, she felt sorry for him and superior to him, she felt sorry for everyone who was not in love, how dull their world must be, as dull and tasteless as hers had been before she met Robert. It was as though she had been living under a dark cloud before she met Robert and hadn't even known it. He had caused the sun to break through.

Why him, she asked herself. He was not at all the sort of man she would have imagined she would fall in love with. True, he was attractive but not even in the way she preferred. His dark hair and eyes at times seemed almost alien to her, having grown up among mostly fair-haired blue-eyed people. She could not actually remember what her father looked like since he had died when she was so young, but her mother had shown her photographs of him and they revealed a rather stocky, sandy-haired man, with a thick moustache that her mother said was on the reddish side. Somehow Simone instinctively knew that her father had very few, if any, chest hairs. She did not know how she had arrived at that conclusion but it was as firmly entrenched in her mind of facts as any fact that she could easily lay a finger on. Who could be more physically different from her beloved father than Robert, with his lanky body, his smooth shaven face, and his curly black chest hairs?

Aside from the contrast to her father, Robert was unlike any man she had previously been involved with. The discrepancies were blatant. Robert was quiet, unobtrusive, studious, and kind. The men she had chosen in the past were more flamboyant in personality, their style of dressing was more consciously individual, more unusual than Robert's muted, conservative style. They made a bigger initial splash. They were much more eccentric than Robert and undoubtedly much more immature. Finally, Simone realized, they were more like her. Perhaps in choosing Robert she had made an important breakthrough in that dense stone wall of growing up. Simone had always hated Proust, but they made her read Proust anyway. She would always remember that marvelous Proustian illumination that occurred after Swann had tired of Odette, who by then had been his wife for many years. Swann thinks back to an earlier day of meeting the infamous Odette, when his infatuation had reached the inflammatory stage; he remembers how jealous he was of her, how miserable, how pained; he recalls the shameful levels to which he stooped in order to spy on her comings and goings; and in reminiscence of these long ago absurdities on his part, he ironically says to himself many years later, "And she wasn't even my type!"

And because Robert Fingerhood had not been Simone's type to begin with, it never occurred to her that she would become so quickly dependent upon him. When Simone said, "I love you," she meant, "I need you," and she had sensed that need the very first night she went to bed with Robert. Yet the need was based largely upon practical, everyday considerations, like having someone to look after her and not having to pay the rent, and to the highly romantic and fanciful Simone, this kind of love-need was fine, but it did not begin to approach the tragic Tristan and Isolde love concept that had long been her ideal. Because it did not, Simone instinctively withheld part of herself from Robert, a very cherished part, and sensing her holding back he was drawn to her more than ever. She aroused his taste for total conquest; he wanted to possess all of her, not because he would want her in the long run but so that he could be free of her. And as long as she continued to give him only a fraction of what she was (albeit a generous fraction), he would continue to haunt her for the remaining, tantalizing portion.

There is such a profound mystery at the beginning of a love relationship that all kinds of mistakes in viewpoint are made by both sides, mistakes that are seen only in later months and years when more information has been gleaned about the other person, and then the nearsightedness that has afflicted the viewer is suddenly cleared up overnight, as the undistorted person swims before a now unsmudged lens. Simone's mistake in those early days with Robert was not realizing the extent to which he was infatuated with her. She realized certainly that he cared for her but she had no idea how much, or what it meant to him (he was good at hiding his true feelings). Not needing her for the practical, everyday reasons that she needed him, his infatuation was automatically granted a greater degree of purity and selflessness that Simone failed to perceive. She inflamed his senses. He loved the way she looked, at the same time knowing to his regret that he did not love her. There was not enough there to love, not enough substance, not enough being. Yet he had to have her, her aura of elusiveness tantalized him, his passion far outweighed hers. Whereas Simone would say, "I love you," Robert, if he had chosen to speak, would have said, "I desire you." Rima, The Bird Girl, had found a little nest at last, a nest where she was fed, sheltered, and taken care of, and Mr.-about-to-be-Dr.-Fingerhood had found a fluttery wild bird with beautiful plumage and all the unpredictability of an airborne creature.

So that while Simone wondered when Robert was going to tire of her and ask her to leave, Robert wondered when she was going to tire of him and fly off into the horizon. (He loves me only for my body, she thought. She loves me only for my mind, he thought. Neither was far from wrong.) For the first month that they were together, tension and anxiety on both their parts intensified and glorified their relationship. Every day brought with it all the acute excitement of the last day on earth before the world blew up. There was a deliciousness for both of them about this kind of heightened living with its focus not upon the future but upon each exquisite, golden second. The days were very long, crammed with memories that might have to feed a lifetime. During the workday they thought of each other, and at night they lay fastened together hoping that morning would never come. Turning points are usually imperceptible. Something changes, but why? Frequently, one never knows, so subtle are the ways that people affect each other's deepest being.

To keep a lover on his toes, he must be kept discreetly in fear, and because Simone was the less complex of the two it did not take Robert long to realize that he had nothing to fear from her; she was going nowhere, she had nowhere to go, her dependency was far greater than he had initially realized. Without being aware of it, Simone had relaxed her anxiety-provoking effect upon Robert, the immediate result of which was that he began to wonder whether he did not love her after all. No longer threatened he could permit himself the gesture of love, but no longer threatened he also found himself growing curiously bored and restless with his little dependent bird.

From the start, Simone had been fascinated by Robert's profession. Seeing him at home in an old sweater and a pair of faded jeans, tinkering with the Conar Audio Color Set, made her hard put to imagine him successfully as a crisp and efficient psychologist, into whose hands parents continued to place the welfare of their children.

"But what is it that you actually do at the clinic?" she asked him one Sunday morning at breakfast.

"Among other things, I diagnose cases and I treat them."

"Among what other things?"

"Well, most people assume that the unique or primary function of a clinic like The Child Guidance Center is to provide individual psychotherapy, while in truth that's only one part of its function. We're also very much involved in parent education, teacher education, teacher training, sex education in the schools, and preventive mental hygiene for teenagers independent of the school."

Which left Simone more confused than ever. "But you do *treat* children?" she persisted.

"Yes, Madam. I have been known to."

"What do you treat them for?"

"Whatever is wrong with them."

"How can you tell?"

"For one thing, we test them."

"Oh, you mean all of those—"

He smiled indulgently, "—all of those tests with the funny names, yes."

Robert frequently brought home psychological evaluation reports that were ominously stamped, "Confidential & Privileged" in large block letters. It was in these reports, through which Simone occasionally glanced, that she had come across mention of the various tests Robert now alluded to. The reports contained sentences like, "Harriet's Full Scale WISC score of 95 falls in the average range of intelligence and above the scores of about 40% of the normative population," or in a report on another child, "John's projectives reveal a number of soft organic indicators, such as rotation on the Bender-Gestalt, and the need to use the edge of the paper in Figure Drawings," and on a third, "An oligophrenic detail was noted on Card 3 of the Rorschach Test, and the necessity to cover part of the blot on several occasions also reflected Nancy's difficulty in handling stimuli," and a fourth,

"Martin's lowest score of 7 in Block Design reflects mild-to-moderate indications of perceptual difficulties."

It was all gobbledygook to Simone, Alice in Wonderland chatter, and she could not bring herself to believe that it was possible to unearth a child's malaise by means of tests known as the Spiral After-Effect or Thematic Apperception. Even the ubiquitous WISC (Wechsler's Intelligence Scale for Children, Robert had interpreted) left her cold. In fact, that was what disturbed Simone most of all about this testing—the cold-blooded, mechanical aspect of it, the soullessness of it.

"Just think what would have happened if you gave your Figure Drawing Test to the author of *The Little Prince,"* she said to Robert. "Speak about soft organic indicators! Remember what you told me about Saint-Exupéry? How when he was six years old he drew a picture of a boa constrictor digesting an elephant, but when he showed it to grown-ups they thought he had drawn a hat? And then when he made his second drawing, actually showing the elephant *inside* the boa constructor they really got disturbed and told him to devote himself to geography? What kind of awful score would Antoine de Saint-Exupéry have gotten on your tests if you'd tested him when he was a child? I can just imagine what your conclusions about him would be."

"You can?" Robert said, looking amused.

Near the end of the Confidential & Privileged reports there was a section devoted to the presiding psychologist's conclusions and recommendations. Having noted some of these, Simone now said:

"While Antoine's visual motor coordination and sensitivity to details are seen as unimpaired, there are several evidences that more complex perceptual problems generate confusion. Antoine must be encouraged and his successes reinforced, and self-deprecation must be worked with in a creative manner rather than . . . bla bla bla."

"You seem to know all about it," Robert said, laughing.

"I can read, if that's what you mean. But I still ask, what about a person's soul?"

"What about it?"

"How do you diagnose that?"

"We don't try to primarily, but isn't one's soul affected by the well-being or the illness of one's mind?"

"Camus puts it another way. He says that when the body is sick, the soul languishes."

"When the mind is sick, too."

"I prefer his explanation."

"You're both somatically oriented."

Ignoring this, Simone asked, "Besides, how can you be sure if your diagnosis of a certain case is correct? Don't you ever think you might have made a terrible mistake? Aren't you afraid that possibly you've misinterpreted the test results?"

"Diagnosis isn't as cut and dried as most people seem to imagine. Actually, it's a series of modifiable hypotheses. In other words, any psychologist who waits until all the testing is over before making a diagnosis is either an incompetent boob or a moron. You make your first diagnostic gesture, your first hypothesis (which is *always* modifiable) with the first bit of input information you receive."

"You make it sound like a computer."

"It works like a computer. Your diagnosis is made as soon as the patient enters the room. The way in which he enters, the way he's dressed, his manner, the way he sits down—these are the first bits of information that come into your input channels, or your computer. And you keep feeding information into the computer as it becomes available. The tests, for example, are part of his overall information but only one part of it, and they either support the psychologist's initial diagnosis or modify it, and continuously. The tests by themselves mean nothing, no test data is worth shit if it's not supported and backed up by appropriate behavior. Do you understand?"

"Yes," Simone said. "Saint-Exupéry would have flunked the Bender-Gestalt."

"Nobody *flunks* psychological tests," Robert said, "and what you're unaware of is that they're designed to reveal and explain strengths as well as weaknesses. For example, any psychologist glancing at a drawing by Saint-Exupéry, without knowing who had done it, would immediately be impressed by the creativity, by the whimsical quality, and the very rich fantasy life reflected in it. So get off my back."

When two people live together, everything sooner or later reverts to money. Living with Robert was a great financial boon for Simone and at the beginning she firmly planned to take advantage of her fortunate position. Her original plan, upon moving in, was to use the extra money she would now have to pay off her Bonwit Teller bill as soon as possible. Instead of the paltry fifty dollars a month she had been giving them, starting February she would give them one hundred a month, which meant that before long she would owe them absolutely nothing.

At the same time she hoped to clear up her other smaller department store debts and be totally, completely paid off. The conglomeration of these bills had begun to weigh her down. Seeing the familiar store envelopes in the mail each month automatically made her go sick in the stomach until she had opened the envelope and found out exactly how extravagant she had been the preceding month. When she did find out, it was invariably worse than she had expected and she felt sicker than ever.

The reason Simone never remembered what she had charged or where, until confronted with the bad news, was because she went into a hypnotic spell the moment she entered one of the Fifth Avenue stores and from then on she was unaccountable for her actions. In her trancelike state everything she saw dazzled her, the entire glistening array of perfumes, scarves, sunglasses, gloves, Garbo hats, beaded bags, ropes of beads, earrings, crunchy bracelets, square-cut glass decanters filled with rosy face powder, earth-colored face powder, clown white face powder, a thousand pale lipstick shades, a million possibilities to be purchased. That was Simone's dilemma. She wanted it all. She had to control herself from flinging open her arms in an instinctive gesture of sweeping it all toward her, all the colorful, desirable, delectable, irresistible display of indispensables.

Did I buy all that? was Simone's shocked reaction each month upon receiving the various bills and scanning the list of purchases she had presumably made during the preceding thirty days.

But it's not possible.

The store made a mistake.

I don't believe it!

I won't pay it!

And frequently, in exasperation, she did postpone payment for months on end, which was why her debts continued to pile up. Simone had long ago begun to receive printed notes from the stores, at first politely asking for her remittance and apologizing for the reminder in case she had already sent in her check.

Sometimes these notes started, "Did you forget . . .?" or, "Just in case you've overlooked . . ." or, "A gentle reminder . . ." The last choice of wording was definitely Simone's favorite and she knew that as long as she was only at the gentle reminder stage she had nothing to worry about. It was when she graduated to the "This is our last notice . . ." stage, that she reluctantly took out her checkbook and wrote a check for a fraction of what she owed, indicating on the bill stub that she was sorry to be so late in her payment but she had just gotten out of the hospital after a serious abdominal operation. Sometimes her excuse was that business had taken her to Czechoslovakia in recent months, or to her chagrin she just discovered that her butler had been hiding all her mail for reasons best known to himself, the poor demented man. She felt this last explanation would go over very big with the snobby clerks who worked for peanuts in the store's credit department. And as though further to punish the store for daring to ask her to pay her bill, she made a habit of never putting a stamp on the envelope. Experience proved that if she also omitted her name and return address, the envelope would be duly delivered and the store would pay the postage they should have had the graciousness to pay to begin with.

Once in desperation she sent a Lord & Taylor bill for eighty-five dollars to her literary friend, Edwin L. Kuberstein, begging him to take care of it for her inasmuch as she now had to support her aging mother, who had recently become crippled by arthritis and could no longer work for a living. Ironically, the very morning she posted the bill to Edwin L., she received a gusty letter from her mother telling about a large wedding party she had waited on at the Hôtel de la Marine restaurant, some days before.

"It's a fortunate thing for me," her mother wrote, in her large, blunt script, "that sturdy legs run in our family. I must have walked ten kilometers serving an eight-course meal to a party of ravenous wedding guests. Don't stop drinking milk, *ma fille*. It keeps the bones strong."

The following month's statement from Lord & Taylor happily revealed a zero balance, which meant that her hunch had been right and dear Edwin L. had paid the bill. After that whenever Simone got badly stuck for funds she would send a bill to a hopefully sympathetic male friend, pleading insolvency and other dire afflictions. A long time ago a man had told her that possession was nine-tenths of the law and it was a remark she never forgot. Once the bill was in another person's possession, the disposal of it somehow became *his* problem, and the electronics engineer who went in for candle fucking had admitted to Simone that even though he told himself he was not responsible for a friend's debts, he felt guilty when he tried throwing the bill in the wastebasket. The next morning he retrieved the bill, and thinking, "Oh, what the hell," sent his check for thirty-two dollars to B. Altman.

Unfortunately, it was not a system that could go on forever. After a while Simone began to run out of hopefully sympathetic male friends, not to mention convincing excuses for her prolonged indebtedness, but it was the midget finally who prompted her to abandon the ingenious method she had devised for solving her bill problems. Apparently, he was not as easily threatened by possession as the others, because instead of dutifully paying Saks Fifth as she had expected he returned the bill to Simone, unopened, and on the Sak's envelope he had drawn a nasty picture of a girl resembling Simone, going down on a man who was meanwhile sticking a red and white striped candy cane up her ass. Underneath the drawing were the words, "Attention Credit Manager: As you can see, Madam, I am far too busy to pay my bills," and then he had forged Simone's signature.

On a separate sheet of paper, addressed to Simone, he promised to send a replica of this charming drawing (plus explanation) to any store she chose, should she ever again have the nerve to try to weasel a dime out of him. By way of P.S., he informed her that his large toe had been amputated recently.

Having led such a precarious financial life in the past, Simone decided to ask Robert right at the start how he felt they should handle household and other expenses.

"I'll pay for everything," he said. "By that, I mean rent, utilities, food, and liquor. But your personal debts are your responsibility."

Simone bravely replied, "That's very generous of you but under the circumstances I feel that I should buy most of the food, since I will probably be doing most of the cooking."

"Can you cook?" It was the first time he had asked her.

"In a way."

"In what way?"

"I have my own personal style," she said, remembering the victimized family she had worked for in Forest Hills. "I do interesting things with casseroles."

"That's good. Because I'm strictly a charcoal broiled hibachi man myself."

"I shall cook tasty and beauteous casseroles for you, my darling Robert Fingerhood. Wait and see."

The first casserole Simone attempted turned into a veal and cream of mushroom soup catastrophe. Robert vomited for an hour afterward and then patted her on the head, and said, "I'm sure there's a perfectly reasonable explanation somewhere." Simone's second casserole was a shrimp and cream of mushroom soup catastrophe. This time Robert did not vomit. That was because he did not eat it. When she brought the steaming dish to the table, a familiar smell hit his nostrils.

"It smells like the other one," he said warily.

"Oh no, darling. This one has shrimp."

"But something else is the same."

"The cream of mushroom soup?"

Pressing his nose closer to the dish, he said, "That's what it is. But why twice in a row? I don't get it."

"I cook all casseroles with cream of mushroom soup," she explained.

Looking at her with infinite patience, he said, "In the future please don't."

"Very well."

"There's no need to pout. I'm sure you can whip up all sorts of perfectly delicious dishes that do not contain cream of mushroom soup."

"But that's the point," Simone said, trying to hold back her tears. "I can't. Cream of mushroom soup is . . . it is . . . that is." The tears streamed shamelessly down her cheeks.

"Don't cry, sweetheart. Please don't cry."

"I can't help it."

"Sure you can."

"No." She shook her head miserably. "It's worse than you think."

"In what way? Tell me."

"Cream of mushroom soup is the basis of my cuisine," she sobbed. "What have you got against it?"

"It makes me vomit."

Simone gave this last remark a great deal of consideration, the upshot of which was that she switched to cream of chicken soup, but Robert's reaction was the same. After two bites of a chicken and cream of chicken soup casserole, he was back in the bathroom, his head over the toilet.

"From now on, I'll do the hibachi bit," he said, when he had recovered. "Either that, or we'll eat out."

"I just remembered something."

"What?"

"I also know how to make salmon croquettes."

"I'd rather you didn't."

"You're not giving me a fair chance," she protested. "I happen to make delicious salmon croquettes. I put grated onion in them."

Robert held his stomach. "Please. Let's not talk about food

at the moment. And let's not plan any future menus. Believe me, I won't hold it against you that you're a lousy cook providing you don't try to poison me again. Is there any Pepto-Bismol left?"

"I'll bet you never in your life ate salmon croquettes made with grated onion," she said spitefully. "If you had, you wouldn't talk like that."

"I just want some Pepto-Bismol, that's all."

"I worked as a cook, you know. I was paid for it."

"Where is the family buried?"

"I suppose you think that's very funny—"

But then she stopped, because it occurred to her that if she did not do the cooking in the future, she would not have to buy the food, which meant she would have that much more money left over from her paycheck to send to the department stores each month.

"Well, maybe you're right," she told Robert at last. "But don't ever say that I didn't try my best to be a real little homemaker."

"It's a deal," he agreed.

After that, mealtimes improved vastly. Charcoal broiled filet mignons and Moët *brut* became standard dinner fare. Robert let Simone set the table, otherwise he took charge of all culinary preparations and even though she had to admit that the food and drink were delicious, she found his exacting attitude a bit much for her taste.

"Mother Fingerhood cooks again," she would tease Robert as he carefully trimmed the steaks, a dishtowel wrapped around his waist.

Double-thick lamb chops were another hibachi favorite of his, as were chicken breasts and lobster tails. He loved baked potatoes with sour cream and chives, salads with tart vinegar dressing, garlic bread, fresh asparagus, dripping with butter. Sometimes they started off with escargots or oysters on the half shell, finished with luscious chocolate cheesecake. Simone had never eaten so well or so much in her entire life, and within a month she had put on seven pounds and all her clothes which were on the snug side to begin with felt obscenely tight.

As she was leaving for work one morning, she ran into Jack Bailey coming into the building. He looked very trim and military in his navy blue pilot's uniform, suitcase in hand. It was the first time she had seen him since Anita's party, even though he lived downstairs from her and Robert, and she was reminded once more of the absolute anonymity of New York living.

"Hi, neighbor," he said, giving her his mechanical welcome-aboard smile. "How are you?"

"Pretty good, Jack." She was pleased to see that his eyes were bloodshot. Boozing again. "What exotic places are you returning from this time?"

"Oh, the same old route: London, Paris, Rome. Say you've put on a little weight, haven't you?"

"I've put it on and I'm going to take it off," she said, wondering how Anita could stand him, and at the same time determining never to fly with his airline.

He laughed, showing neatly capped teeth. "Just so long as you're not pregnant."

What a dunce he was! Thanks to the pill nobody got pregnant any more unless she wanted to. "Give my commiserations to Anita."

"What for?"

"For being involved with a creep like you."

"What makes you think—?" he started to say, but Simone brushed indignantly past him without waiting to hear the end of his sentence.

"I've gotten so fat," she told Robert that evening as he was tossing the salad, "that I saw Jack Bailey today and he thought I was pregnant."

"He was probably only teasing you."

"He has an obnoxious way of teasing."

"If it's any consolation, you don't look fat to me."

"Thanks, but my only consolation will be to go out and buy some new clothes. My present ones are bursting at the seams and it's all your fault."

"How much do you weigh?" Robert asked, eyeing her critically.

"One eleven."

He made a wry face. "You're fat, all right. Have you thought about trying out for fat lady at the circus?"

"Only if you agree to be the two-headed man."

The next morning Simone fed Chou-Chou stale champagne left over from the previous evening's bacchanal, and then made sure she had all her charge plates with her before leaving for work. Just the thought of going to one of those delicious Fifth Avenue stores made her quiver with ecstasy. Maybe she should try for an orgasm in accessories at Bonwit Teller. Now there was a thought. Yes, doctor, I came when I got to the chain belts. Or, I found my thrill in Lord &

Taylor's paper boutique. Well, why *not?* There certainly was a sensuous quality about those stores that far outsexed anything else she could think of, and she could think of plenty. Even pot was a washout in her case when it came to sex. That was the way Helen said she had come the first time: turning on before making love.

"Haven't you ever used the stuff?" Helen asked Simone. She seemed quite surprised.

"A few times at parties, but not seriously. I mean, not for serious sex."

"It slows everything down," Helen explained. "You feel as though you're floating. You're completely relaxed. Believe me, you'll be so relaxed you won't recognize yourself."

"It sounds great," Simone said, thinking that would be the day. "Where do I get hold of some?"

"I've got a jar at home. I'll roll a few cigarettes for you and bring them to the office tomorrow."

"Mr. Swern would have a heart attack if he knew."

"Don't be silly," Helen said. "He probably uses the stuff himself."

When Simone showed Robert the two cigarettes that Helen had sold her, he asked whether she knew how to inhale.

"Well, of course, I don't smoke," she said, "but all I have to do is swallow. Right?"

"Wrong."

She began to see what he meant when they got down to business and she realized that whenever she had tried pot in the past, she had pretty much faked the whole inhaling process, which was undoubtedly why the weed never had much effect upon her. Now, try as she would, the smoke kept escaping through her nostrils.

"Hold it in, hold it in," Robert said. "Look. Like this."

"Where did you learn all about it?"

"In Mexico."

"Is it legal there?"

"No, but the Mexican attitude toward it is cool."

Then he gave her a quick, sucking-in-smoke demonstration and handed her the remainder of the skinny cigarette. The sweetish smell made her feel dizzy and five puffs later Simone was sound asleep and dreaming about Percheron mares in Normandy. Robert said later that it was the first time he had ever heard her snore.

"I didn't come," she told a disappointed Helen the next day, "but on the other hand, I didn't get laid. I fell asleep instead."

"You have to practice," Helen said solemnly. "I have the craziest orgasms with that stuff. Multiple orgasms. My head just about blows off."

Helen's multiple orgasm remark made Simone wonder whether perhaps there were only so many potential orgasms in the universe and that by cornering the field as successfully as she had, Helen might be personally responsible for depriving Simone of her share of the take. Somehow it did not seem fair for one girl to come several times and for another girl not to come at all, and she said to Helen: "Would you mind cutting down on your ecstasy quotient and giving somebody else a break?" "Ecstasy quotient" she had picked up from Fingerhood, just as she picked up most of her other lines from her various lovers.

Her charge plates stashed securely in her Gucci purse, Simone had an orgy (if not an orgasm) after work that day at Franklin-Simon. She had decided to shop there rather than at any of the other stores because she did not owe them any money. Since she was in the clear to begin with, she would be able to stall them until she finished paying off her other, more pressing bills. It was no mean feat, she often thought, juggling all the stores' credit unions and coming out on top, and frequently it surprised her that she continued to be as successful as she was. But then, her charge accounts meant so much to her that she had to be successful. Without them, she would surely die. To pay cash for something was beyond Simone and she had learned to charge as much as she could in whatever areas she could, and when she couldn't charge an item she wrote a check for it. She had even paid for a couple of taxis by check, pleading insolvency to the drivers. What could the poor men do? Besides, it wasn't as though the checks would bounce, they were good, and to make them look even better she added a handsome tip.

"It beats me," one of the drivers had said. "I suppose I could call a cop and put you under arrest, but somehow it doesn't seem worth the trouble for a lousy dollar ten."

"You don't have the right spirit," Simone told him. "Just think what a much nicer world it would be if *everyone* paid by check. Money is so . . . grubby."

"Yeah," the driver said. "It's the grub I love to touch."

Which made Simone realize that she felt the exact opposite: she hated to touch money, it felt dirty to the touch, there was something unsanitary about it. All those greasy coins and crumpled bills. Who knew how many hands they had passed through before ending up in her pocketbook?

Who knew what slimy, germy course they had traveled after their sparkling clean emergence from the Treasury Department? No. Charge plates and checkbooks were definitely the answer and the only thing Simone regretted was that her salary was not high enough to admit her to any of the credit card organizations, or she would have had it made on all counts. To be able to charge restaurant food and drink, airplane tickets, and rental cars, was her idea of total bliss and she had little doubt that when she died the doors to heaven would be opened jointly by Diner's Club, Carte Blanche, and American Express, all of whom would assure her that for the rest of her heavenly life she was free to enjoy the unlimited credit she had been so rudely denied on earth.

"The spendthrift returns!" she announced gaily to Robert when she returned home that evening, a Franklin-Simon shopping bag in each hand. It had started to drizzle when she left the store and her fall was slightly damp. Ordinarily that would have upset her because you weren't supposed to get them wet, but having just bought a replacement (for two hundred dollars), she didn't give a damn.

Robert looked up from the hammock where he had been reading Albert Ellis's book, *The American Sexual Tragedy*, and regarded her with disapproval.

"Deeper and deeper into hock the compulsive buyer marches."

"Now don't give me any lectures. I feel too happy, and besides, every item in these shopping bags is absolutely indispensable."

"I'll bet."

Looking around she realized that Chou-Chou had not come to the door to greet her and he was nowhere in sight.

"Where's Chou-Chou?" she asked, taking off her damp coat and rubbing her hands in front of the fire.

"He's in the bedroom. He's sick."

"Sick? What happened?"

"He's been throwing up. Did you, by any chance, feed him something unusual?"

Remembering the champagne she had giddily given the dog that morning, Simone said, "Only a wee bit of flat champagne."

"Champagne!" Robert said angrily. "What a dumb thing to do. Why the hell did you do that?"

"Because he likes it."

Robert closed the book and looked at Simone expressionlessly.

"I don't understand you," he said, at last.

"That's the nicest thing you've said to me for days. Who wants to be understood anyway? I think it would be very boring if we all understood each other perfectly. Where would the suspense be?"

"I didn't mean that I couldn't figure you out." There was an undercurrent of contempt in his voice. "You're not that much of a mystery. What I can't figure out is how you got to be the way you are."

Curling up on the sand-colored sofa, Simone threw a serape over herself for protection. She could smell an argument in the air.

"What way am I?"

"Irresponsible."

She smiled uncertainly at Robert. "Is that all?"

"Isn't that enough?"

"Oh, Robert." She tried to sound light, whimsical. "Just because I gave my dog a little stale champagne is no reason to start—"

"No, not just *because* you gave him champagne. That's only one incident among many. It's your general attitude. You don't think about consequences. You don't care. You swing along making a big mess and then you expect other people to clean up after you."

"What have I made a mess of?" she asked innocently.

"What haven't you?"

"Aside from the champagne business, what have I done that's so terrible? Go ahead. Tell me."

But as soon as she said it, she knew it was a mistake. She should have changed the subject. She should have suggested that they make love. Simone hated arguments.

"You have no core," Robert said, swinging his legs onto the floor as though he meant business at last.

"No *what?*"

"Core. Nucleus. Center. Ego."

"I have a great deal of ego," she said, trying to keep her voice calm even though her heart was beginning to pound. "You know how vain I am."

Robert shook his head in contradiction. "Vanity is hardly synonymous with ego. In fact, it usually indicates a tremendous lack of ego."

"I don't know what the hell you're talking about."

But she knew only too well. Like most people who are acutely aware of their defects but who still make no attempt to overcome them, Simone had lived all her life waiting to be convicted of the same crime. Whenever she became involved with a man, she knew that it was only a matter of time before her initial charm wore off revealing her for the disorganized, irresponsible, incompetent person she truly was. Some men took longer than others to wade through her appealing façade. Her attitude of "I don't give a damn" went a long way with some men, they were intrigued by it, they would excuse a great deal of otherwise inexcusable behavior because of it, but eventually even they became fed up and bored with Rima, The Bird Girl.

"You're one of the most scatterbrained women I've ever met," Robert said.

Confronted by his condemnation, Simone realized that she instinctively had been waiting for it ever since she moved in with him. It had to come sooner or later. It always did. Just when she thought that perhaps this man would be different, that this one would approve of her, the axe fell, chopping her illusions to pieces. In a sense it was a relief to be found out, she did not want to fool anyone, she wanted to be perceived and loved as she really was, and for that reason she knew she would continue to search for a man, who, after perceiving her, would be only too happy to accept her with all her faults, no, *in spite of* all her faults. When she met Robert that first evening at Anita's party and he told her the fable of the little prince, she hoped he might be that man. She had not even realized how much she hoped so until this very minute.

"I'm sorry that I don't please you," she said, as the tears started to build up. "I've done my best."

"I'm sure that you have," he said gently. Now that he had gotten it off his chest, he could afford to be kind.

"You needn't pity me."

"I'm not pitying you."

She knew he was, though. It was a familiar enough reaction, one that she had learned to recognize easily. The less secure men became angry at her, the more generous ones felt sorry for her. Simone found this latter attitude harder to swallow inasmuch as it confirmed her own worst estimation of herself. Pushing back the tears, she said:

"Well, what do we do now?"

"Let's go out to dinner for a change."

In the days that followed, Simone wondered what kind of woman would appeal to Robert. He was thirty-three and had never been married. Why? Was he too harsh in his estimation of all women? Would none of them finally do? Or was she really so hopeless?

That was the question that bit her soul. On the one hand, she wanted to think highly of Robert's judgment (after all, she had chosen him), but on the other, she needed to salvage as much as she could of her own fleeting sense of worthiness. As a result, her appraisal of him could find no anchor. Some days she told herself that he would never wholeheartedly approve of any woman, his standards were too impossibly lofty, they were unreasonable, and whether he knew it or not he was looking for a goddess. When Simone convinced herself of that (and at times it was easy), she felt a great deal better, her personal stock market value soared for hours only to drop swiftly to rock bottom hours later, due to the depressing realization that she could mentally elevate herself only at the cost of demeaning him.

It was a seesaw. If Robert was right in crossing her off, then she had to live once more with the bitter confrontation of her own flimsiness. If he was wrong, that made her a better person than she had imagined but by the same token it made him a worse one, a less wise one. Simone wanted Robert to be smart so she could admire and love him. She wanted him to be stupid so she could love herself. The battle that waged within her was doomed to failure. No matter which side won, she lost.

About a week later, when Simone was at work, she received a telephone call from Anita. It was lunchtime and the showroom was deserted except for one of the other models seated at the far end of the long room, religiously dieting upon yogurt and black coffee.

"I've been meaning to call you sooner," Anita said. "How goes the big romance with Robert?"

"The big romance goes just fine."

A few weeks ago it would have been the truth and Simone would have been only too happy to tell Anita all the glowing details, but the way things stood with Robert now she was not eager to admit her failure, not to Anita, not to anyone, not yet. It still hurt too much.

"I guess you might say that I was very lucky to have met Robert when I did." She had never before realized how hard it was to sound happy when you felt miserable. "And apparently, he feels the same way about me."

"That's marvelous," Anita said, without conviction.

"If you can keep a secret, I have a hunch that he's going to ask me to marry him."

"No!"

"Yes!"

"How wonderful." Anita sounded as though she were presiding at a funeral rite.

"The only thing is, I'm not sure I'll accept his proposal. I'm not sure he's the right man for me."

"Any man who proposes is the right man. Dope."

"That's only one woman's viewpoint. I'm not that desperate to get married."

"I can't imagine why not. What's so great about the way you're living now? Robert could get tired of you and kick you out any time he felt like it. What kind of security do you have?"

"He could kick me out if we were married, too."

"And he'd pay through his teeth. Just remember. You're a resident of New York State. The alimony laws are on your side, not his. But, of course, you do have to be married to collect, dear."

"Don't you ever think about anything except marriage and money?"

"I try not to," Anita admitted with a nervous laugh. "Although I have to confess that my morbid preoccupation doesn't seem to be getting me anywhere. Would you believe that Jack hasn't called me *once* since he stayed over the night of the party?"

"What do you mean?"

"Exactly what I said. I haven't heard a peep out of the son of a bitch in over six weeks."

Simone was startled. "That's funny. I ran into Jack the other morning on my way to work and I just automatically assumed that the two of you had been seeing each other all this time."

"What did he say? Was he alone?"

"He wasn't with a girl, if that's what you mean. He was coming in from a flight."

"Did he say anything about me?"

"No, but it was a very brief conversation. He hardly had a chance to—"

"How did he look?" Anita sounded pathetically eager for any scrap of information about Jack Bailey.

"He looked the same as always," Simone replied, trying to be diplomatic. Jack Bailey's looks didn't do a thing to her.

"He *is* attractive, isn't he?"

"If you like the type. Were his teeth capped when you were seeing him last year?"

"Are they capped? I didn't realize."

"Are they capped?!" Simone laughed. "When he opens his mouth, you'd think the sun just came out."

"Many of our pilots get their teeth capped. The airline makes them do it, so they look better. After all, they are in the public eye. But how did we get off on this track?"

"We were discussing my having run into your beloved."

"Some beloved."

Although Simone would have been ashamed to admit it, she was relieved to hear that Anita was having love problems, too, relieved that Anita's problems appeared to be even worse than her own. She was surprised that Anita had not called her sooner to tell her the bad news.

"I nearly called you any number of times before this," Anita said, as though reading her mind, "but whenever I picked up the phone I'd think that maybe if I waited another day I'd hear from him. I guess I didn't want to admit failure so I kept hoping. Every time the phone rang I nearly lost my mind."

"It must have been a hellish six weeks."

"Six and a half," Anita said, absentmindedly. "Then just the other day I found out via the grapevine that he's been dating one of our stewardesses. I don't know how serious it is, though. It might be nothing or it might be true love. That is, if Jack Bailey is still capable of true love. But the part that kills me is that he never bothered to call me again after that night, not once. He could have called, couldn't he? Just to say hello?"

"I told you he was a bastard the first time I met him. He's always given you a hard time. Forget the guy."

"I've been trying to. I've been going out with other men. When I'm in New York, I see that Englishman, Ian Clarke. Did you meet him? He was at my party."

"I don't think so. What does he look like?"

"He's tall and blond and very English looking. He's all right, but he's basically interested in landing a rich American wife and I'm basically interested in landing Jack Bailey, but since neither of us is getting anywhere, we cry on each other's shoulders in all the nice spots in town."

"How is he in bed?" Simone asked.

"Not terribly exciting. His hip bone juts out. But compared to Jack, no man excites me. I don't only mean sexually. It's more than sex. It's everything about Jack. Oh, what can I say? I'm in love, Simone, and it's lousy. You can't imagine how lousy it is."

"Yes, I can."

"It's the vacuum," Anita went on, ignoring Simone's remark. "It's knowing that he's in the same city as I am, that he's close by, and yet that he's not with me. *Why?* That's what I keep asking myself. Why is he with another girl and not me? What does she have that I don't? What can she give him that I can't? I've questioned Jack in the past about what he's looking for in a woman. Do you know what his answer was?"

But before Simone could say anything, Anita replied:

"He said, 'Who's looking?' Now what kind of wiseguy remark is that? I ask you."

"Maybe he was serious," Simone suggested. "He's been divorced twice. Maybe he doesn't want to fall in love again. It might be too painful."

"Everybody wants to fall in love."

"Every woman does, but I'm not so sure about men." She was thinking of Robert. "I have a hunch that men resist love as strenuously as women seek it, otherwise we wouldn't be having so much trouble. How's that for my insight of the week, Miss Norforms?"

"I wish you'd get off that Miss Norforms kick. And as for your insight it doesn't sound too profound to me, because from what you said before Robert isn't putting up much resistance to love. Not if you think he's going to ask you to marry him."

Simone was beginning to wish that she had not lied about the way things were going with Robert. That was the trouble with telling lies. Unless you were ultracareful you were bound to contradict yourself sooner or later. Besides, now that she knew how unhappy Anita was, it might have been comforting to spill out her own tale of misery. She and Anita could have comforted each other. But having trapped herself in the lie, she had to go along with it.

"He can *beg* me to marry him," she said, "and I'll still say no. Marriage doesn't interest me at the moment. I plan to go to Lima as soon as I pay off my Bonwit Teller bill."

"When we were roommates you were planning to go to Khartoum," Anita said disdainfully.

"Well, I've switched to the little Paris of South America."

"If you had half a brain you'd marry Robert, let him pay your Bonwit Teller bill, and you'd go to Lima on your honeymoon."

"All you Cancers have such disgustingly practical minds."

"I don't see what's so disgusting about planning ahead. Think of your future. One day you'll wake up and you'll be thirty, and then what?"

"I'll join the hippie movement."

"You're so batty, I'm surprised you haven't done that already."

"I will start a hippie movement in Lima, Peru. I will turn on all the ex-Nazis who are hiding there, and we will have psychedelic love-ins. Ami Tahba Om, Ami Tahba Om, Ami Tahba Om."

"Crackpot," Anita said, hanging up.

Simone liked to bait Anita, whom she felt was so gullible that at that very moment Anita was probably sitting in her Murray Hill apartment imagining Simone walking around Tompkins Square, barefooted, and with a wreath of flowers on her head, chanting Hindu melodies. Their friendship (could it be called that?) was a strange one indeed, each of them heartily disapproving of the other's mode of living, and yet there was a certain interesting spark in the relationship, a certain nose-to-nose hostility that incited them to keep in touch with each other, check up on each other's progress or decline, definitely a certain competitiveness which flourished beneath the surface of their amicable façades.

Simone recalled the day they had met. It was here in the showroom of Mini-Furs, Inc., over two years ago. Anita sailed in one afternoon to buy a German fitch coat that she later traded to Simone in exchange for a double-breasted hamster suit that Simone had gotten tired of. There was such an air of womanly assurance about the twenty-three-year-old Anita that Simone immediately felt sexless, skinny, ugly, and five years old. She could still remember in perfect detail the way Anita had been dressed that day. It was spring and Anita wore a soft pinkish-white coat over its own solid pink sheath that revealed an ample hipline. Being on the hipless side herself, Simone was impressed by hips, they seemed to symbolize mature womanhood, a state of being she knew she would never achieve no matter how long she lived.

Further, Anita's coat and dress ensemble was the sort of coordinated outfit that Simone would not dream of choosing for herself. It conveyed a message of straight, unadulterated femininity. *This is for real women,* it seemed to be saying, *there are no gimmicks here.* In contrast, Simone's own clothes were a potpourri of kooky sweaters and micro-mini skirts, the colors were nutty, the fabrics were wild, skinny

skinny poor boy clothes that Simone could zoom around New York in with all the freakouts she used to zoom with before she met Robert. After she and Anita became bitchy roommates, Simone realized that every woman instinctively chooses a style of dressing in which she feels the most natural, the most like herself, if not necessarily the most attractive or seductive, and just as she would have felt like an absolute idiot in Anita's clothes, she knew that Anita would feel equally idiotic in hers. Which stopped neither of them from secretly admiring the other's clever handiwork.

When Anita left the showroom that day in a trail of Arpège, David Swern said admiringly, "Now *that's* what I call a woman."

"What would you call me?" Simone asked. "A zebra?"

"I've seen you in those nut outfits you change into after work when you've got a date. You look like something that just escaped from the funny farm."

That struck Simone as pretty amusing months later when David Swern became involved with Lou Marron, who wrote for the fashion paper that specialized in nut outfits, the nuttier the better. She would have liked to ask Mr. S. then whether he still thought she looked like she came from the funny farm, but she was not supposed to know about the affair, nobody in the office was supposed to know (they all did), so much to her chagrin she had to keep her mouth firmly closed on the subject.

"Did you have an exciting day?" Simone asked Robert when she came home that evening.

"Thrilling. I went to two staff meetings, spoke to the mother of a schizophrenic child, and tested a new patient. Diagnosis: organic damage to be thoroughly examined in neurological consultation. And you?"

"Same old routine."

Simone had been debating on the way home whether she should tell Robert about her telephone conversation with Anita, and decided it was not such a smart idea to let him know that Anita was manless and miserable. She still remembered the way his attention had focused upon the shimmering Anita the night of the party, and that it was not until he'd been informed of Anita's consuming interest in Jack Bailey that he switched attention to her.

"I'm going to bathe," she announced.

"How would you like to go to that new Greek place for dinner?"

"Fine."

Now that things were strained between them, they had been going out to dinner more and more often. The machinery of a restaurant made it easier for them to resort to superficial topics of conversation and avoid painful references to their unsatisfactory relationship.

"I'll be out of the bathroom in fifteen minutes, in case you want to shave," she said.

"No hurry. Don't rush."

They had become so polite, too. Simone had terrible images of Robert getting rid of her and then proceeding to feed Anita one of his gala filet mignon and champagne dinners, after which they would both dive into bed and Anita would teach him Jack Bailey's secret method for making those intriguing plier marks on her soft, buttery skin.

Simone's own skin was on the dry side and every night she used a liberal amount of Relaxor bath oil in her bath. It was wonderful for dry skin and the aroma was heavenly. While soaking in the tub, Simone washed the windowpane nylons she had worn to work that day. She always washed her stockings in the tub because it seemed much less time-consuming than rinsing them out in a separate operation in the sink. Twice a week she took her garter belt in with her and gave it a good scrúbbing. Simone had a strong bent for cleanliness, a characteristic undoubtedly handed down by her mother who, in memory, was forever either washing the floor or washing herself. Showers were unknown in Port-en-Bessin when Simone was a child and she had never become reconciled to them even after eight years in the United States. Anita used to take showers, a very unfeminine habit, because to Simone's way of thinking showers were a man's domain, women needed to soak.

And douche. After Simone got out of the tub, she filled her Marvel Whirling Spray with a brand new peppermint flavored douche that came in cute, premeasured plastic packets. "No measuring, no mistakes," it said proudly on the label. What would those precious pharmaceutical companies think of next? She wondered what kind of market research they had done in this case to determine that the majority of American men liked the taste of peppermint. It would certainly never go over big in France, there it would be licorice hands down. But what was she thinking of? She had been gone from her native country for so long that she'd forgotten there they had bidets and didn't need the Marvel Whirling Spray, patented in January 1899. Anita had screamed the first time Simone showed her the bulbous contraption.

"You mean, you put that thing inside you?" she asked, staring in terror at the shiny black tubular end.

"That's the general idea."

"Doesn't it hurt?"

"Only if the water is too hot."

"This demonstration proves only one thing," Anita said with great conviction. "I'm sticking to Norforms."

"You're afraid of penises. That's your trouble."

"A little fear wouldn't do *you* any harm."

"Hurray for penises! Especially big ones. Hurray!"

Simone liked her own sense of humor. She thought she was a riot.

"Hurray for big penises!" she said that evening at the Greek restaurant.

And Robert laughed, a little embarrassed but holding up rather well considering the fact that two women at a nearby table gave them drop dead looks and a man behind them choked quietly on his martini. She knew that if there was one thing Robert admired about her, it was her nerve. She would be wise to exercise it more often, she reminded herself. Two glasses of ouzo and she was feeling on top of the world, in addition to which she looked absolutely marvelous. Several men had given her admiring glances when she entered the restaurant in her shimmer shirtdress with the neckline that plunged crazily to the waist. Even Robert had looked at her in a new way, as though seeing her for the first time.

"We should go out to dinner every night," she said over the stuffed grape leaves. "You're nicer to me when we're out."

"How am I nicer?"

"You seem to like me more. At home I think you forget how attractive I am."

What she meant was that *she* forgot. Her looks were no longer of that much importance to Robert, but they were all important to her. Being a manufactured beauty, rather than a natural one, she needed a public setting to reconfirm her physical charm. At home in the evening, minus makeup and the sparkle of libido-enticing clothes, she dissolved into a rather plain-looking girl with hair that didn't have enough body and eyes that were too small. Tonight they were made up with silver eye-shadow, eyeliner, her best fake lashes, and for good luck she had painted false lashes under her own lower ones. It was such an exquisite eye job that she decided to go to bed with it when they got home.

"Your narcissism is beyond belief," Robert said as the false lashes scraped across her pillow. "I'm surprised you took off your fall."

"It's not my fault that I need cosmetic help to look my best. If you like natural beauties, why don't you call up Anita? She's probably sitting at home this very minute, masturbating with a pencil."

"What makes you say that?" Robert asked in the darkness, a distinct note of interest in his voice.

She knew all along that she would never be able to keep still about her conversation with Anita. She simply was not the type for secrets.

"Because I spoke to her today and she told me that Jack Bailey hasn't called her since the party, and that other men leave her cold."

"No kidding."

"Of course she's so afraid of penises that if she got a good glimpse of yours, she'd probably have a congestive heart attack."

"How do you know she's afraid?"

"I have my ways of researching these things. And come to think of it, she's not as natural as all that because her hair is bleached. Her pubic hair too."

"You're a regular fund of information tonight, aren't you?"

"I'm just trying to protect my own interests, that's all."

"If it's of any reassurance whatsoever, let me say right now that I have no designs on Anita. Does that make you feel better?"

"It would if I believed it."

"Believe it."

"Okay," Simone said. "I believe it."

But she didn't and they both knew it. And then, as though this exchange had been an essential prologue to subsequent events, Simone started to find odd bits of feminine paraphernalia around the apartment. A pair of velveteen mules shoved to the back of the clothes closet floor. An unfamiliar lipstick wedged between the Pepto-Bismol and the Band-Aids in the medicine chest. A box of fragrant dusting powder in a bureau drawer. How could she have not seen the overwhelming evidence before this? At first she was simply bewildered and said nothing about her strange discoveries, trying to pretend she was an incipient archaeologist unearthing rare and wonderful treasures that dated back to prehistoric times, but when she came across an atavistic diaphragm that had managed to find its way into the kitchen cupboard behind a can of Pepperridge Farm Lobster Bisque, Simone decided it was high time to bring her findings out in the open, no matter what the consequences. Robert listened blank-faced as she accosted him one evening with her various relic discoveries.

"How many women have lived here before me?" she said at last when no explanation seemed to be forthcoming.

"Oh, one or two."

"You might at least have gotten rid of their personal effects. Or do you intend to keep them around to torture the next victim?"

"I didn't realize these things were still here. I'm as surprised as you are."

"You didn't *realize?!*" She waved the diaphragm hysterically in his face. "You didn't *realize?!*"

"That's what I said."

"Realize this, then, you bastard!"

She hurled the diaphragm at him, he ducked, it hit the machete that hung on the wall and caught onto one of the knife's sharp ends where it dangled in idiotic splendor until Robert thoughtfully removed it a moment later and dropped it into the garbage can.

"I'm sorry you're so upset," he said, "but I repeat, I did not know these things were still around. I'm really sorry this had to happen."

"Bluebeard!" Simone screamed, collapsing into tears.

They did not make love that night nor the night after and for once Simone did not care. Her attitude was: we do, we don't, so what? either way I don't come. She was fed up with the whole miserable situation, she was tired of Robert's disapproval, she was bored with feeling inadequate, yes, that was it, she was *bored*. They practically never went anywhere except to a restaurant for dinner, and as far as she could determine Robert had no friends other than his creepy associates at The Child Guidance Center. She met one of them on a Saturday afternoon when he stopped by at the apartment to borrow a book by Ferenzi. He was a balding young man named Arthur who wore white socks and black loafers, and kept talking about the early ego development in enuretic children when he was not talking about mini-skirters he had met with hot pussies.

"Do you mean to tell me that *that* treats children?" Simone asked Robert after Arthur had left.

"He happens to be a brilliant therapist and we're fortunate to have him at the Center."

"Are you kidding? I wouldn't trust that *schmuck* with my dog."

Ordinarily, Robert would have been angry with her for denigrating an esteemed colleague, but it amused him to hear the word *schmuck* pronounced with a French accent, a charming French accent, and he couldn't help smiling as he said, "Arthur doesn't treat dogs. He's an authority on enuresis."

"What's that?"

"Wetting your pants."

"I once peed in bed. Did I ever tell you? It was when I had my apartment on Fifty-Seventh Street."

At the rate things were going with Robert, Simone wondered whether she wouldn't be back there before too long, shivering in two flannel nightgowns in the upper bunk bed. The prospect of returning to her own apartment depressed Simone beyond words. It would be the ultimate, humiliating defeat. And yet she knew if she and Robert did break up it would be much more sensible to take the Fifty-Seventh Street bargain back from Helen than to look for a new place. Chances were that if she looked high and low for the next year she'd never find anything as cheap in such a nice neighborhood. The apartment situation was disgusting in New York, a real nightmare unless you happened to be one of the fortunate rich, and Simone wondered how many people who otherwise would have split up long ago continued to stay together because it was so difficult to move.

"Let's go somewhere festive tonight," she suggested, trying to get onto a more pleasant subject. "It's Saturday night. Remember?"

"Where would you like to go?" Robert asked.

"El Morocco."

"You know that nightclubs bore me."

"A discotheque then."

"But I can't do those dances."

"You can't do anything," she said, "except sit around here with your hibachi and your damn psychological books."

"Need I remind you that I'm working for my Ph.D.?"

"I don't know what I ever saw in you to begin with," she said bitterly. "If you hadn't told me the story of the little prince, I wouldn't be here this very minute, bored to death."

"That's right. You'd be on a motorcycle with some brain-damaged bongo player, having the time of your life."

"At least I'd be moving."

"That's action, that's not movement."

"Well, I don't see that I've progressed so much as a result

of having gotten involved with you. You don't even talk to me. All we do it eat, watch television, make love, and go to sleep. I might as well be living with a garage mechanic in Dayton, Ohio."

"I'm talking to you this very minute."

"Is it such an effort?"

"Simone," he said wearily, "what is it that you want?"

I want you to love me. But how could she say that? Either they did or they didn't. It was nothing you could force on a person against his will. And perhaps more than love, she wanted Robert to organize her life, tell her what to do, give her direction. She could live with a bully more readily than with a Robert Fingerhood, who seemed perfectly content to go about his own business and let other people go about theirs.

"What is it that you want?" he repeated quietly.

"A business to go about," she said, wondering whether her old friend, the midget, was still fond of discotheques now that he had only nine toes.

The next afternoon, as they were wading through the Sunday *Times,* Robert received a nervous telephone call from A. H. S. Duckworth, executive director of The Child Guidance Center. It seemed that an irate father, whose son was being treated at the Center, had managed to gain entrance to Mr. Duckworth's sumptuous Park Avenue apartment and was making abusive remarks about the treatment being given his son by the consulting psychologist, Robert Fingerhood. The outraged man claimed that his ex-wife had sent their son to the Center without consulting him first, and that as far as he could see such an action was completely unjustified. Nothing that Mr. Duckworth said could calm him down or persuade him to leave, in fact he was becoming more hysterical by the moment and had threatened the executive director with his life. The only reason that the police had not been called in was because the man in question was Billy Day, a popular television comedian, and if the incident got into the papers both Day's career and the Center's reputation were bound to suffer from unfavorable publicity. A. H. S. Duckworth wanted Robert to come over to the apartment as quickly as possible and try to bring the situation under control.

"Oh Christ," Robert said, as he changed swiftly from jeans and a T-shirt to a dark business suit. "These cases are the worst. Ex-wives and ex-husbands fighting to keep the upper parental hand, and meanwhile it's the kid who ends up with all the battle scars."

But Simone was intrigued by the fact that this was no ordinary ex-husband, this was Billy Day, whom she had seen countless times on television.

"Are you sure I can't come along with you?" she asked Robert for the second time. "I watch his TV show every week."

"This isn't going to be any comedy routine, I can tell you that. Mr. Funnyman sounds pretty worked up. Poor old Duckworth is quaking in his Sackville Street trousers. Probably scared to death that Billy Day is going to pull out a thirty-eight any minute."

"Maybe you should take a weapon," Simone said, following him to the door.

"Like what? My machete? Look, I'll be back as soon as I can. In the meantime, why don't you read the financial section and see how my GM stock is doing."

But as soon as Robert left, her interest in the paper evaporated. She needed somebody to share things with and once more the prospect of being shipped back to her old lonely apartment loomed unpleasantly on the horizon. The isolation there would do her in. Becoming involved with a new series of freaky men would be more than she could bear, and even though living with Robert Fingerhood left a great deal to be desired, it still seemed like her best chance for a relatively sane existence.

She started to rattle around the apartment, looking for something to do. After a few minutes of luckless wandering, she remembered that she had been meaning to set her new Franklin-Simon fall as soon as she had some free time. It was with an immense feeling of relief and renewed purpose in life that Simone went to get the fall, rollers, and plastic head form needed for the setting operation. Clamping the head form to the edge of Robert's dining table she started to work on the glistening hair, using a book called *Creative Hairdos Made Easy* as a guide. In less than fifteen minutes she was finished. She had put a net over the head and it was ready to go under her portable hair dryer and bake for a couple of hours. Because the head had been so vapid and faceless to begin with, Simone had pasted a movie magazine photo of Belmondo on the front of it, and now here was dear Jean-Paul, the usual cigarette butt dangling out of the corner of his mouth, his hair all neatly set in jumbo pink plastic rollers in creative hairdo number 42 (J–P frowned upon sculpture curls), ready to sit and bake. The pink bouffant hair dryer hood fitted nicely over him. Simone turned the setting to "very hot," plugged in the cord, and admired her handiwork.

A few minutes later, Anita called and asked whether she had ever seen the movie *Breathless*.

"I missed it when it first came out," Anita said, "and it's playing at the Thalia. Would you care to go?"

"Jean-Paul doesn't like sculpture curls."

"What are you talking about?"

Simone smiled at the face on the head form under the dryer. "*Rien de tout*. I've never seen *Breathless* either. I'll meet you at the Thalia in about—"

Before leaving the apartment, she wrote a note to Robert, which she Scotch-taped to the pink bouffant hair dryer hood. The note said: "Please turn off dryer by six at the latest, because otherwise my beauteous new fall that cost two hundred dollars will be ruined." Then she reduced the temperature setting from "very hot" to "warm" just to be on the safe side.

A. H. S. Duckworth's butler ushered Robert Fingerhood into the drawing room that was decorated with antique tapestries and rosy Persian rugs. In one corner of the room A. H. S. Duckworth sat huddled in a Louis XVI bergère covered in blue pressed velvet. His hands were clasped together and he stared down at the rug's scrolling branches and leaves. On the other side of the room Billy Day, a thin dark-haired man in his early forties, stood looking expressionlessly at a small Renoir that hung above a second blue velvet bergère. Apparently, all attempt at reconciliation between the two of them had come to a halt, pending Robert's arrival.

The butler said, "Mr. Fingerhood, Sir."

At that, both men seemed to leap to life, A. H. S. Duckworth getting swiftly to his feet, and Billy Day's face taking on the sharp, suspicious look of the outraged parent. It was a look that Robert had encountered only too often in the past and he was struck once more by the fact that it mattered very little, if at all, to what income bracket or social stratum such parents belonged. When they had come to defend their child's normalcy, all parents, from the poorest to the richest, the most obscure to the most well known looked exactly the same: as though they would like to kill the psychologist on the spot.

Upon A. H. S. Duckworth's introduction, Billy Day and Robert Fingerhood shook hands and remained standing.

"Now you listen to me," Billy Day said threateningly to Robert, "I don't know what kind of bee got into my ex-wife's bonnet, sending my kid to a nut clinic, but I'm here to tell you that there's not a goddamn thing wrong with him. Do you understand that? This is a perfectly normal, healthy kid, a little rowdy, maybe, a little on the boisterous side, okay, I'll admit that, but *perfectly normal*. It's my ex-wife who should have signed up for treatment, she's the one whose head you should be examining."

A. H. S. Duckworth gently said, "Now, Mr. Day, I'm sure that if you give Mr. Fingerhood a chance to explain our position—"

"Explain shit! What's there to explain? That when I'm two thousand miles away playing a club date in Las Vegas that dummy I married sends my kid to some fancy nut clinic and that as a result he's going to have to go through life with a permanent record of mental illness? What? That some four-eyed doctor is going to take a healthy eight-year-old boy who likes to raise a little hell from time to time and turn him into a weak-mouthed vegetable? Is that what you're going to explain to me?"

Without a word, Robert Fingerhood turned and started to leave the room. Billy Day ran quickly after him and stopped him at the door, the anger still on his face.

"Now just a minute, goddamn it. I asked you to come over here. Where the hell are you going?"

Pausing with his hand on the doorknob, Robert said, "I have to admit that I've gotten a charge out of meeting you in person, Mr. Day. I've watched your show on television many times. In fact, it's one of my favorites, and maybe I'm just square enough to enjoy meeting a real live celebrity. But on the other hand, I didn't come up here on a pleasant Sunday afternoon to listen to this kind of crap, not from real live celebrities, not from anybody. So if that's all you have to say, I'm leaving."

"Oh no you're not!"

Robert smiled at him. "I'll tell you something else. I'm so square I'd even get a charge out of meeting Liberace."

The anger drained from Billy Day's face and a new wariness came over it. "Okay, okay," he said more quietly, "I'm sorry I blew my stack. Maybe I shouldn't have shot my mouth off like that, but when you're two thousand miles away and something like this happens behind your back you're apt to get a little sore."

Robert nodded sympathetically. "That's understandable but

screaming and shouting isn't going to solve anything. Now if you want to sit down with me, I'll try to answer some of your questions."

Billy Day glanced somewhat self-consciously at A. H. S. Duckworth who had been listening to the exchange with the demeanor of a man who hopes desperately for peace but knows he is in no position to bring it about. Robert could see him worrying about the board of directors.

"Please excuse my outburst," Billy Day said to both men.

Relief was visible on A. H. S. Duckworth's strained features. "It happens," he said, "it happens to all of us. Why don't you and Mr. Fingerhood use my study for your little talk? It's right over here."

The study connected to the drawing room. It was small and comfortable and boasted A. H. S. Duckworth's prized collection of Chinese porcelains, which were arranged on a tulipwood commode that stood against a paneled wall. A tulipwood desk dominated the room. Robert Fingerhood sat down on the chair behind the desk, and Billy Day took the chair on the other side.

"Let's make it clear from the start," Robert began, "that nobody thinks or has implied your child is insane, nobody thinks he is *seriously* mentally disturbed. What we do think is that he has a problem he can't work out by himself, and that his parents with all their good intentions cannot help him to work out. We can look at this problem from any one of several angles. We can talk about your son's happiness or unhappiness. We can talk about the hell he raises from time to time. Or we could talk about the real and measurable gap between his very adequate intelligence and his distressingly low academic achievement—"

"Good marks aren't everything," Billy Day cut in sharply. "I never got good marks in school and I'm not exactly washing dishes for a living."

"I agree with you. Good marks aren't everything by a long shot, and frankly I'm much more concerned with your son's unhappiness and his emotional outbursts and what they could eventually lead to. But in a situation like this where we don't know each other too well and have a limited amount of time, it's easier to talk about something simple and measurable, such as his academic underachievement."

"You say unhappiness, you say emotional outbursts, but when I was in school I wasn't the picture of contentment, I had my rough times. Doesn't every kid? I mean kids have their troubles and yet most of them eventually make out all right. Look at me. I don't like to rub it in, but wouldn't you say that I'm making out all right?"

"Professionally, more than all right," Robert said.

Billy Day eyed him suspiciously. Robert was surprised at how much better looking he was in person than he appeared to be on television.

"Meaning what?" Billy Day said.

"Meaning I have little knowledge about your private life, Mr. Day, but just on the basis of public information and on the nature of your profession I'm willing to bet that your adult life hasn't been a three-ring circus no matter how jolly it may look on the picture tube. I'm willing to bet that you've experienced a lot of heartache and depression over the years."

The comedian now appeared trapped, almost furtive.

"Okay," he said, "maybe I have. So what?"

"So I think it fair to assume that if you're interested in your son's well being—and I'm sure that you are—you'd like to help him avoid some of the heartache that you know only too well. My point is that you *can* help him . . ."

Billy Day's mouth curved into a faint smile of admiration. "You're a real cutie pie, Doctor, aren't you?"

Anita loved *Breathless*, Simone hated it.

"He looks better with jumbo pink rollers," she said by way of explanation and then proceeded to tell Anita about her strange vaginal condition as they took the crosstown bus to the East Side. Lately her vagina had begun to burn and a milky looking discharge stained her panties, and made her feel constantly unclean.

"I'm burning and leaking this very second," she whispered to Anita as the bus raced through Central Park.

Robert had not made love to her for a week and secretly she felt that her condition was a direct result of being unloved and unwanted, but she couldn't say that to Anita who thought she was deliriously happy.

"You'd better go see a doctor," Anita said. "You might have something serious."

"And be examined with my legs in that humiliating stirrup position? I can't bear the thought of it. Also I'm not exactly crazy about my gynecologist. How's yours? Do you like him?"

"He's okay," Anita said grudgingly, never having forgiven the man for upping her diaphragm size. "He's old and harmless."

"What's so great about that?"

"You don't want a young, handsome one poking around in *there* with those cold metal instruments, do you?"

"Sure. Why not?"

"Doesn't it embarrass you if they're young and good-looking?"

"No, I prefer it. I get wet all over."

"You're cracked."

"When you've been trying to have an orgasm for as long as I have," Simone said archly, "you don't turn up your nose at any opportunity, no matter how far out it may seem at the time."

"Completely cracked."

They got off at the Lexington Avenue stop to take the downtown bus, each one wondering why she continued to associate with the other. In a store window next to the bus stop was a large sign that said: GOD IS ALIVE AND WAITING FOR YOU IN MEXICO CITY.

The lights in the living room were on and Robert was waiting for Simone, a drink in his hand and a weary look on his face.

"Hi," she said. "How did it go?"

He nodded. "Everything is under control."

She glanced at the head form which was still clamped to the edge of the dining table. To her relief, the hair dryer dial pointed to "off."

"Thank you for saving my fall," she said.

"You're welcome."

She searched his face for telltale signs of sarcasm but in his dark business suit, with his tie loosened, he seemed far too tired to be sarcastic.

"What is Billy Day like?" she asked.

"Like every other angry father."

He was miles and miles away from her, immersed in his own world of disturbed children and difficult parents, a world from which she was totally shut out. He was not thinking of her. He did not care about her. He hadn't even bothered to ask where she'd been. She might have been making love to a handsome stranger all afternoon for all he knew.

"Tell me," he said, surprising her, "how do you manage to justify paying two hundred dollars for a new hairpiece when you're up to your neck in hock as it is?"

He wasn't even jealous. "Merely because it costs two hundred dollars doesn't mean I've paid for it. If you must know, I charged it at Franklin-Simon."

He stared at her as though she were an idiot child.

"You're going to have to pay for it eventually," he pointed out. "You're going to have to pay all your bills one of these days."

"Maybe," she said, thinking how much she was beginning to hate him.

"What do you mean *maybe?*"

"I mean that one day all the department stores will burn down and then I'll be completely in the clear."

"I wonder why I never thought of that," Robert Fingerhood said, finishing his drink in one gulp.

When Simone got to work ten minutes late the following morning, because she had just gotten her period, David Swern was in a familiarly black mood.

"I should do what some of the other furriers do," he said, glaring at her. "I should dock your pay when you're late."

"I'm terribly sorry, Mr. Swern, but I wasn't feeling well."

"I suppose you got your period for a change."

"As a matter of fact, I did."

He shrugged his shoulders as if to say that it was no use, life was hopeless. Then he dropped a saccharine tablet in his container of coffee.

"I once had a model working for me who had periods every other week. Would you believe that? I was going to write to Ripley about her. Every time she walked in late, she had just gotten her period that morning. What could I do—examine her to see if she was telling the truth? I'll let you in on a little secret. If a young woman wants to get away with first degree murder in this country, all she has to do in court is look a little pale and say she didn't know what she was doing at the time because she had her period, and the jury will let her off scot-free."

He swallowed the coffee and made a face. "Just between you and me, saccharine stinks."

"*Trois* guesses who doesn't have a by-line in today's *Rag?*" Simone said to Helen as they were changing in the models' dressing room.

"Oh no!" Helen moaned.

"It's going to be another black Monday."

David Swern had a subscription to *The Rag*, which he read each Monday morning with great interest. It was common knowledge around the showroom that whenever there was a piece in the paper by Lou Marron, Mr. Swern became extremely cheerful and good-natured for the rest of the day, joking with the models and bookkeeper, treating everyone to cokes in the afternoon, and once when there had been a two-page picture spread on the growing popularity of evening pajamas, with a big Lou Marron by-line, Mr. Swern sent the models home half an hour early and told them what a swell bunch of kids they all were.

"He must have it bad for that girl," Helen said, slipping out of her work clothes and into the plain black work sheath. "Her career certainly means a great deal to him. Remember the time she wrote that dopey story about a dinner party in Southampton and Mr. S. walked around for a week looking as proud as though she were the author of *Moby Dick?*"

"I feel sorry for Mrs. Swern," Simone said. "Not only does she have those attacks, but I'll bet she never gets her periods any more."

"I feel sorry for Lou Marron. Mr. S. will never leave his wife for her. That girl is whistling in the dark if she thinks he's going to marry her."

"She's getting what she wants out of the relationship," Simone said, thinking of the emerald and rose quartz bracelet. "I wouldn't even be surprised if Mr. S. pays her rent."

Helen had started to brush her thick reddish-blond hair vigorously, as Simone repaired her eyeliner in front of the wide dressing-table mirror.

"For all we know," Helen said, "she might be very hung up on him. We don't know her. She might be dying to marry him."

"Never mind the marriage part. How can she go to bed with him? That's what I don't understand. That *stomach*."

Simone made a shudder of disgust and Helen looked at her in surprise. "What stomach?"

"The stomach Mr. S. tries to hide behind all those vests he wears."

"I've never noticed any stomach."

"Are you serious?"

"Well, I mean, he must be fifty-five, he's bound to have a little something there. But it's not very much."

"It looks like very much to me. I can't stand men with stomachs. And he's probably flabby too. I'll bet all his flesh hangs."

"I thought you liked Mr. S.," Helen said. "You're the one who's always defending him whenever he's in one of his rotten moods and giving everybody hell."

"I do like him, but that doesn't mean I'd like to go to bed with him."

"I wonder what kind of lover he is," Helen mused. "I'll bet he uses the cardiac position."

"What's that?"

"That's when a man lies on his back and lets the woman do all the work."

"Oh is that all?" She had been hoping to hear something new which she could try herself and maybe have an orgasm.

"Men who have heart conditions use that position in order not to exert themselves too much and drop dead in the sack.

"What makes you think Mr. S. has a heart condition?"

"I didn't say he did, but it's awfully common among businessmen his age who smoke a lot. You know, the ones who are always croaking at those boring banquet dinners."

"Except for that stomach, he looks pretty healthy to me. But have you ever thought about people's taste in other people?"

"What do you mean?"

"Well, like I couldn't bear to go to bed with Mr. S., and I'll bet that Mr. S. can't bear to go to bed with Mrs. S."

"Can you blame him? With that colitis of hers?"

"No, I mean, aside from the colitis. I'll bet he's just repelled by Mrs. S. It's a theory I have: everybody is somebody's ugly."

A second after she said it, she wondered whether she had not recently become Robert's ugly. When he made love to her now it was with infinite tenderness, as though he were substituting that for the excitement he no longer felt. One night in bed she said to him, "Don't you love me any more?" forgetting for the moment that he had never once said he did love her.

By way of reply he held her very close to him and stroked her hair. "I could be very much in love with you," he said, "if you didn't do such foolish things at times."

So even though she would not admit it to herself, she knew it was all over except the actual ending, which she managed to bring about a couple of weeks later. Using a recipe she had borrowed from Helen, she planned to surprise Robert with a choice meat loaf when he came home from a Board of Education meeting. Later she would say, how was she to know that you weren't supposed to use plastic bowls for cooking? And she would believe it, too. And maybe she really didn't know. Or maybe it was the one last straw that she sensed Robert needed to justify getting rid of her. At any rate, she put the prepared meat loaf in a large yellow plastic bowl and put the bowl in a 350-degree oven, just as the recipe said. Then she went into the living room and started to stuff toilet paper in the lining of all her hats.

When Robert came home he kissed her absentmindedly on the cheek and said, "What's that I smell?"

"That's meat loaf."

"I thought the only things you knew how to cook were those lousy casseroles and salmon croquettes."

"Well now I know how to cook meat loaves too. Are you surprised?"

"Very pleasantly."

But when he opened the oven door minutes later to take a peek and saw the yellow plastic bowl quietly melting onto the oven floor, he said to Simone: "Why are you putting toilet paper in your hats?"

"So that my head doesn't look flat."

"Your head is worse than flat. It's empty."

"What does that mean?"

"It means that only an idiot would cook something in a plastic bowl."

"Don't call me an idiot!"

"Then don't act like one! Haven't you ever heard that heat makes plastic melt?"

"Maybe I have."

"Then why'd you do it?"

"I felt like it," she said defiantly.

"Felt like what?"

"Felt like cooking a meat loaf in a plastic bowl."

"But why? What's the point?"

"Aha," she said, with a triumphant smile. "That's exactly my point: there is no point. But I wouldn't expect you to understand surrealism. You have no sense of the absurd. If I tell you that I did it because it amused me, what would you say?"

"That you have a rather strange sense of humor."

"Well, you have no sense of humor at all." She started to dance around the room. "I have a funny meat loaf, I made a funny meat loaf, tra la la la, I made a funny . . ."

She couldn't stop laughing. But several days later as Robert drove her to Kennedy Airport, she was feeling considerably more subdued.

"You'll see," he said, patting her gloved hand. "You're just going to love Mexico."

"I don't want to go."

"Of course you do. You've told me many times how much you've always wanted to visit Mexico."

"I meant with *you*."

"But I can't get away just now. I'm snowed under with work. Besides, it's only for two weeks. The change will do you good."

"What you mean is that it will do *you* good. You'll probably screw Anita while I'm gone. I know what you're thinking."

"You're wrong. I have no intention of starting anything with your best friend behind your back."

"She's not my best friend. She's a dumb, middle-class, marriage-obsessed moron."

"I still have no intention of starting anything. You can take my word for it."

"I know when somebody's trying to get rid of me," Simone said, crying into the travel Kleenex package she had bought at the notions section in Bloomingdale's.

She was amazed by the wide assortment of items there were on the market specifically designed for travelers; the variety was amazing, why it opened up a whole new shopping world. Tiny folding toothbrushes, sanitized toilet seat covers, compact sewing kits, nylon clothes lines with suction cup attachments, ingeniously designed cosmetic cases to hold all a girl's beauty needs, even a plastic cup that opened up like an accordion and could be folded flat when not in use. Simone's only satisfaction, as stretches of graveyard zoomed by on the Long Island Expressway, was that her new tomato red suitcase (a going-away gift from Robert) was crawling with traveler's delights that she had giddily charged at Bloomingdale's the day before.

They got to the airport an hour before her plane was due to take off, and did all the boring checking-in things that were required of passengers on international flights. Her suitcase weighed more than the forty-four pound limit and Robert paid the difference.

"I had to pack for two climates," she said in defense. "You told me that Mexico City is cold and Puerto Vallarta is hot."

"Don't worry about it," he said good-naturedly. "It only cost a few dollars extra."

They had a drink at the bar. Simone bought a copy of *Cosmopolitan* and a copy of *Art News* at a magazine stand. Robert promised to meet her at the airport when she returned in two weeks. Then suddenly a voice came over the microphone.

"Eastern flight number 212 boarding at gate 7."

"That's *me!*" Simone said horrified.

"You have to go through there." Robert indicated a narrow passageway leading to the field. "You get on that line. Where'd you put your ticket?"

"In my purse. Where did you think? You really think I'm an idiot, don't you?"

Tears were streaming down her cheeks and Robert bent over to kiss her wet face. "Don't cry, Simone. Please don't cry, darling. You'll have a good time. You'll see. And you'll be back before you know it."

"I'll have a miserable time. I don't even know how to speak Spanish."

"They speak English at the Maria Cristina. Now go ahead." He turned her around by the shoulders. "You're going to miss your plane."

She turned back to him, misty-eyed. "Wouldn't you feel terrible if my plane crashes?"

He seemed genuinely horrified by the possibility.

"Yes, I would feel terrible. But it's not going to crash. Now, go on."

Then she was caught up in the stream of people moving toward the immense jet that sat waiting to take them to Mexico City. A sharp March wind blew across the airfield and it had started to rain lightly. In her belted, black vinyl raincoat with its own matching kerchief, Simone already felt very much the experienced world traveler. It was a good feeling. She walked briskly up the ramp of the jet holding her two-hundred-dollar fall in a fake leopard case. Perhaps she would enjoy herself after all. Perhaps God really was alive and waiting for her in Mexico City. Then she realized that she'd completely forgotten to check her horoscope to see if this was an auspicious month for Libras to make extended trips.

"Merde," she said aloud, but the stewardess who welcomed her aboard only smiled and pointed to the coach section.

The plane was number 16 for takeoff but unaware of this, Robert Fingerhood headed straight for the nearest telephone booth and dialed information.

"Could you please give me the number of Anita Schuler on East Thirty-Eighth Street?" he said. "Yes, Schuler. S-C-H-U-L-E-R."

❀ CHAPTER FIVE ❀

Eastern's flight number 212 left Kennedy Airport at seven in the evening. It was a nonstop flight, scheduled to take five hours, but because of the time change it would be only eleven o'clock when the plane landed in Mexico City.

Beverly Fields Northrop III was seated in the first-class section of the airplane, her long red hair coiled into a neat chignon at the nape of her neck. One of the hairpins had gotten loose, she could feel it jutting out, trying to escape. She reached behind her and wedged it forcefully into the thickest section of hair she could find. In a little while it would probably start to jut out again, but for now it was secure. It was funny, she thought, how some of them stayed put and others just didn't.

She glanced apprehensively at her diamond bracelet-watch. It was exactly nine-thirty. Halfway there. She decided that she would set her watch back when they landed, not now; somehow she still wanted to be on New York time, perhaps because it made her feel closer to Peter and the children. She could understand about the children, but why should she want to feel close to the man she had just left? Had she really left him, though, or was she only running away for a little while?

The cute stewardess with the big, brown eyes removed Beverly's uneaten ice-cream and said, "Would you like the cheese and fruit course? That's next."

The memory of stealing that wretched package of Camembert from the cheese shop in Garden City still rankled in her mind. She had not been able to look at a piece of cheese ever since, not any cheese. And besides, cheese was fattening and she was supposed to be on her prisoner-of-war diet.

"No, thank you," she said, smiling automatically at the stewardess, who had a smudge on her serving apron. "I'll wait for liqueurs."

They were fattening, too, but soothing at least. Beverly felt nervous, clammy, cold. Perhaps she shouldn't have drunk those two glasses of champagne.

The stewardess smiled back, just as automatically.

"Yes, of course," she said.

Beverly shivered and pulled down both sleeves of her gold cashmere sweater, debating whether to get her suede coat and throw it over her. It was on the rack above her seat. Or, she could ask the stewardess for a blanket. The girl was standing only a few feet away, sympathetically listening to a passenger's complaint.

Beverly felt sorry for her, what a dismal job she had. Yet maybe she liked it, maybe she thought it was glamorous and exciting to serve meals in the sky while flying to foreign countries, maybe she even had a boyfriend waiting for her in Mexico City. Across the aisle a second stewardess was starting to serve the eighth course, in a nine-course meal, to half of the twenty passengers in the section.

Beverly had a window seat and the one next to her was unoccupied. Just before fastening her seat belt she had counted the number of passengers, and at the moment of takeoff she had a grisly vision of the next day's newspaper headlines. *Twenty die in jet crash.* It would be one of those terrible air tragedies, and authorities would proceed to investigate the cause of the fatal power failure. Just thinking about it made her shiver even more. In the past she had never been afraid to fly, but then she had always flown with Peter and his presence somehow made her feel safe, impervious to injury.

Seconds later, when the plane was safely off the ground, Beverly unfastened her seat belt and laughed at herself. How absolutely typical it was of her to have forgotten about the passengers in back, in the coach section. It was as if they did not exist merely because they had paid less than she for their tickets, and were sitting there now all squashed together, three abreast, eating some miserable, one-course meal, and wishing they had more leg room. Beverly instinctively stretched out her long, slender legs and admired her Roger Vivier crocodile pumps.

Peter had done a good job on her. She'd become as big a

snob as he, even though she had never wanted to admit it before. She remembered going to Europe on her honeymoon; they sailed on the *Queen Mary,* first class of course, and one evening, in the magnificent dining room over caviar and impeccable linen, she waved a toast point at Peter, and said, "Darling, what do you suppose they're eating down there in tourist class?"

Peter airily replied, "Fried nails, darling. I believe that's what they serve them."

But Beverly had misunderstood and thought he said, "Fried snails."

"Who ever heard of frying a snail?" she asked him, and he roared with laughter.

Neither of them had been able to eat snails after that without remembering the incident and smiling.

Nine thirty-five. The children would be tucked in, asleep. Well, hopefully, they would be. Margaret had said not to worry about a thing, that she would take care of the household just as though Beverly were there, and Beverly felt uneasy when Margaret said it, because she wondered just how necessary her presence was in the castle on Stewart Avenue. It was almost as though having married Peter and produced two healthy, beautiful children she was no longer really very essential to the entire domestic operation. She could be spared. She had oiled the machinery and it would operate very nicely without her from then on.

Don't be maudlin, she warned herself, don't be self-pitying. They were both unattractive qualities and she despised them in other people, perhaps because they reminded her so much of her own inclinations.

"Stop wallowing in your misery," she had told her friend Dee Dee only two days before Dee Dee died from an overdose of sleeping pills. "Okay, so you don't have a lover at the moment. You'll live."

But Dee Dee hadn't lived, hadn't wanted to live, and when Beverly heard about the suicide she sobbed for hours, alone in her room, while downstairs the hysterical myna bird continued to shriek, "Get going! Get going!" How could Dee Dee have done it was Beverly's feeling at the time, was still her feeling. How could she leave a husband (albeit a loveless one) and three children who needed her? Or did they? Did they need her any more than her own children, who seemed very casual when told about their mother's trip? Well, of course, Peter, Jr., was so young, she had reasoned, you couldn't expect a two-and-a-half-year-old child to appreciate the significance of being separated from his mother by three thousand miles.

Sally, on the other hand, well, Sally should have been more disturbed than she was, no question about it, and Beverly felt sharply let down by her daughter's nonchalance. Sally was going through the riddle period and instead of saying, "I'll miss you, Mommy," she said, "Mommy, why do birds fly south in the winter?"

"I don't know," Beverly replied, wondering whether she would have missed her mother when she was five.

Clapping her hand over her mouth to control the laughter, Sally blurted out, "Because it's too far to walk!"

Beverly made a feeble attempt to show her daughter that she thought it was very funny, too, which encouraged Sally to say next: "What is gray, has four legs, and a trunk?"

"An elephant?"

"No. A mouse going on vacation!"

Sally was laughing so hard that she nearly had a choking fit and Beverly thought to herself, Oh, Christ, I've produced a comedian. When she repeated Sally's mouse riddle to Peter that evening, he smiled, patently pleased that his only daughter could be so witty at the age of five.

"Mexico?" he then said, giving her his lowered-lid look. "Why on earth *Mexico*, darling? Isn't that where everyone gets that dreadful dysentery business?"

Beverly felt like saying that she'd rather get dysentery and be really sick than to go on the way she had been for the past few months: dead, frozen, unloved. She had to get away from Peter, be alone, think. Mexico seemed the ideal place. "So foreign, yet so near," was the caption of an ad for Mexico in the Sunday *Times* travel section, and Beverly suspected that Mexico would be far more foreign than, say, Paris or London, and it was its very foreignness that appealed to her the most. She wanted to go somewhere alien. In Mexico, she would not be a wealthy Garden City matron with a proper husband and two properly spaced children. In Mexico, she would be anonymous. In Mexico, she could be anyone she wanted.

"I've been reading a great deal about that new anthropological museum in Mexico City," she said in reply to her husband's question. "I'd like to see it. You know how interested I've always been in anthropology, darling."

Peter looked at her quizzically. "Oh really, darling? No, I didn't know that."

"And then," she said hurriedly, "I thought it would be

relaxing to spend a few days in the sun in Acapulco or perhaps Puerto Vallarta. That's where they filmed *Night of the Iguana.*"

"Well, darling, it looks like the Mexican bug has really bitten you hard, in which case . . ."

Beverly could see the conflict on her husband's face.

Although he was relieved to be rid of her for a while, he resented her sudden independence. She could at least have gone through the motions of asking him whether he wouldn't like to go to Mexico, too. Then he could have said no, it was impossible, he couldn't get away just then, Tony Elliot relied more heavily upon him than ever. She could have given him a gracious out, he would have done as much for her. Of course, he reminded himself, her family really didn't have any class so what could one expect?

"Liqueurs," the brown-eyed stewardess said, approaching Beverly with a cart that contained bottles of Drambuie, Crème de Menthe, Triple Sec, and Courvoisier.

"Drambuie, please," Beverly said, noting that the smudge on the girl's apron was gone.

Then she gazed out the window, out into the dark and chilly sky, and wondered who she was going to be now that she was free to be anyone she wanted.

In seat 27-E in the coach section of the airplane, Simone picked at her one-course dinner. She had one of the middle seats and was closed in on both sides, which made her feel morbidly claustrophobic. She loved to fly and had hoped to get the seat next to the window, but that was occupied by a middle-aged businessman who had drunk two martinis before dinner, looked at the tray, and made a face.

On the other side of her, on the aisle, was a boy of about fourteen whose parents were sitting behind him with a younger child.

"I could eat a horse, saddle and all," the boy exuberantly confided to Simone when the stewardess passed them their trays. He had a shock of straight red hair and plunged into the food as though he'd been on a starvation diet for days.

Simone was amused by the tray. It had shallow indentations for the food and looked like all the TV dinners she used to eat when she was living on Fifty-Seventh Street. She had not realized before how spoiled she had become by Robert's excellent cooking, how it had changed her standards. This food didn't taste like food. It didn't even look like food, not really, it looked like a painting of food.

Simone smiled. She had just finished reading an article in *Art News* about the school of magic realism. Maybe this was make-believe food that had been painted on the tray, in three dimensions, by some clever magic realist who was employed by all the airlines. The painter certainly had done a first-rate job, Simone thought, because the passengers were eating like crazy, even the double martini man, and looking as though they enjoyed it.

There was a small Salisbury steak so overly tender that it fell apart at the touch of her fork, a snow white mound of whipped potatoes, a nest of bright green peas, a muffin, a square of butter and a square of amber jelly, each individually wrapped in plastic packets. The packets reminded Simone of the packets her peppermint douche came in, and she wondered if they had been made by the same company. Perhaps the company also made the yellow plastic bowl in which she tried to bake that unfortunate meat loaf.

The United States was addicted to plastic, Simone thought, and she heartily approved. There was something so clean and disposable about plastic, it struck her as an ingenious invention. Why buy things to last? Who wanted things to last forever? That was an old-fashioned concept, like the French middle-class women saving their francs for that good little black suit which they would wear until it finally fell off their backs, practically threadbare.

Disposability. That was the idea. And feeling very patriotic toward her adopted country, Simone broke open the plastic packet containing the butter and proceeded to butter her make-believe muffin.

Afterward, as she drank her coffee, she thought wistfully of Chou-Chou, last seen in Fingerhood's hammock. She missed him already, wished he were with her, in fact at the moment she missed him more than Robert. But she had only known Robert a short while, whereas she had had Chou-Chou for five years, and considering how hectic her life had been during that time, considering all the freakouts who had come and gone, it was hardly any wonder that she now felt the loss of her one permanent companion. She suspected that it would take a few days before the loss of Robert set in. She was too busy blocking it now.

The plane began to shake and shudder and the "Fasten your seat belt" sign flashed on. Then the captain's voice came over the loudspeaker.

"Please fasten your seat belts, ladies and gentlemen. We're going into rough air."

A second later one of the stewardesses repeated the message in Spanish.

Simone remembered her parting words to Robert:

"Wouldn't you feel terrible if my plane crashes?"

It had been said at the time to make him feel guilty for sending her away, but now she wondered whether some intuitive preknowledge on her part was not responsible for the remark. The astrologist she had consulted last October told her that she was extremely intuitive. Simone noticed that the red-haired boy next to her looked frightened as he secured the belt around his waist. Simone was not frightened. She was too fatalistic to be afraid of death. Besides, thanks to astrology, she was a firm believer in reincarnation, and even if this should turn out to be her last day in this world, she knew she would be reborn at some future date and live another life, probably as a cockroach since they seemed to go on forever. The astrologist said that in her last life she was an Egyptian slave girl and had died in 1612.

The stewardesses were walking up and down the aisles to see that everyone had fastened his belt.

"As though it matters," Simone said aloud.

"Did you say something?" the fourteen-year-old boy asked nervously.

Simone smiled at him. He was cute. He would probably be very attractive when he grew up.

"Don't pay any attention to me," she said. "I have a habit of talking to myself."

Maybe he and she had been lovers in a previous life. Maybe she had had an orgasm in a previous life. It was the first time that possibility occurred to her. Now wouldn't that be something?

And then, as she reluctantly buckled herself in, she decided that if they made it safely to Mexico City she was going to do everything she could to find out whether Latins really were lousy lovers. Because if they weren't, well, anything could happen. She might even have her first orgasm in this life—in Spanish!

By the time Beverly got through customs, changed some of her traveler's checks into Mexican currency at the Banco Nacional counter, and taken the long taxi ride to the Maria Cristina Hotel, it was close to midnight. Her flight had arrived on time but was unable to land because an Aeronaves and an Air France plane were ahead of them, and so the pilot had to circle the airport and wait his turn.

Beverly found it all very aggravating. She twisted her diamond bracelet-watch thinking how much she hated delays of any kind, and in this case the delay only heightened her fear that they would not land safely. The headline, *Twenty die in jet crash,* again loomed before her eyes, as they finally swooped down and made a smooth landing at International Airport in chilly Mexico City.

The standard taxi fare to all hotels from the airport was seventeen and a half pesos, approximately one dollar and forty cents in American money. At the first red light a young Mexican boy, about ten years old, Beverly judged, came up to the automobile and put out his hand, palm up. Beverly's window was open and the hand almost touched her face. For a second she was startled, then she saw that he was supporting himself on crutches because he had only one leg.

"Mendigo," the driver said, shrugging his shoulders apathetically, as though he were not to be held responsible for the conditions of his country.

Before Beverly could decide how much money to give the crippled child, the traffic light turned green and the taxi sped off down the darkened and oddly deserted street.

But before long there were lights, dazzling, brilliant, hypnotizing, what seemed like a panoramic city of lights. They were on the Paseo de la Reforma, which Beverly remembered the guidebook had likened to the Champs Elysées in Paris, and indeed there was a resemblance. It was a beautiful, wide, tree-lined avenue, boasting the most expensive and elegant hotels in the city. In making her reservations, however, Beverly had bypassed these hotels and chosen instead the Maria Cristina, which was one block north of the Reforma on Calle Lerma.

The reason she decided to stay at the Maria Cristina was because it was smaller, more off the beaten track, not as showy. The travel agent told her she would feel less like an American tourist there than at the other, more lavish places. The Maria Cristina had a colonial façade and its lobby was imaginatively done in colorful Spanish tiles. There was a quiet understatement of good taste that appealed to her. It would appeal to Peter, too, she thought; he had always maintained that only the nouveaux riches went in for flashy things.

"I'm Beverly Northrop," she told the gray-haired man at the desk, carefully omitting the "Mrs.," and at the same time wondering whether she would ever be able to do anything, go anywhere, without thinking of what Peter's reaction would be under the circumstances. "I wired for a reservation several days ago."

She wondered whether the cocktail lounge was still open, but, of course, it must be, she had read that evenings started late in Mexico. When packing for the trip she had filled a silver flask with one-hundred-proof vodka, just to be on the safe side. I'm becoming a drunk, she thought. But her next thought surprised her even more: I don't care.

The bellboy picked up her matching Vuitton bags. As she followed him to the elevator, she caught a side glimpse of a very pretty girl in a black vinyl raincoat entering the lobby. Something about the girl's expression touched Beverly and she turned to look at her full face. Then she realized what it was. The girl's eyes, beneath the professionally applied makeup, seemed furtive, almost hostile as she appraised her surroundings.

She looks the way I feel, Beverly thought, not without some satisfaction: unhappy.

Beverly and Simone met officially at lunch the next day in the garden restaurant. Each was seated alone at a table, only a few feet from one another. Beverly recognized Simone from the night before, even though now, under the hot afternoon sun, Simone had pulled her hair back with what appeared to be the belt of her bright red sweater dress, and was wearing gigantic tortoiseshell sunglasses.

Ordinarily, Beverly would not have dreamed of approaching a complete stranger, man or woman, but this was not an ordinary situation. She was in a foreign country and the old, conventional rules that she had lived by for so many years no longer seemed to apply. And as though to give herself still further courage, she noted that they were the only two women in the garden who were by themselves. Everyone else was with someone.

Lighting a Del Prado, she walked the short distance separating them. A waiter had just presented Simone with a dish of eggs swimming in a thin, green sauce, saying that it was "*muy picante.*"

"Excuse me for intruding like this," Beverly said, amazed at how self-confident she sounded, "but I couldn't help notice you when you checked into the hotel last night. You arrived right after me. You were wearing a black vinyl raincoat."

Simone looked at her quizzically, but interested.

"Yes, that was me. But I didn't see you."

Beverly had not expected the French accent and it threw her a little. If she had not assumed that Simone were American, she never would have had the nerve to speak to her.

"I was getting into the elevator," Beverly said, wondering whether she hadn't made a stupid mistake after all, but deciding to plunge ahead now that she had gone this far. "Look, I'm sitting over there by myself and I've just ordered lunch. If you're not waiting for someone, would you mind terribly if I joined you? I hate to eat alone."

Over her initial surprise, Simone seemed quite pleased.

"Oh, please do!" she said, smiling to show Beverly that she meant it. "I hate to eat alone too. It's such a fucking bore, isn't it?"

Simone's choice of language startled Beverly, but she tried her best not to show it. Beggars can't be choosers, she reminded herself.

"Yes it is a bore," she agreed.

Then she went to collect the blue cardigan she had left at her table. It was part of the three-piece Italian knit suit she wore, the one that Peter had given her last month for her twenty-ninth birthday.

Over lunch both girls realized that they had been on the same flight from New York to Mexico City, and that each in her own way had spent the preceding evening pretty much the same. Worn out by the trip, they unpacked their bags, bathed, and called room service for a nightcap. The only difference was that in Simone's case the nightcap was a cup of hot chocolate, in Beverly's it was ice and quinine water to mix with her vodka. Both slept through breakfast that morning and had yet to see the sights.

"We could hire a car and a driver," Beverly speculated.

"Wouldn't that be awfully expensive?"

It had not yet occurred to Simone that Beverly might have money, or be married, or have children. She simply assumed that Beverly was a poor, single, working girl like herself.

"It might be worth the expense, unless you think it would be more fun to explore the city by ourselves," Beverly said.

As with Margaret, her housekeeper, Beverly always tried to maintain a perfectly democratic relationship with those in a less fortunate position than she.

"I doubt if it would be more fun, but it certainly would be cheaper," Simone said, hoping that the money Robert had given her would last two weeks.

Beverly took a collection of pamphlets and brochures out

of her baby crocodile satchel. She had gotten them from the travel agent in Garden City.

"Well now," she said cheerfully, "let's see what there's to see in this town."

After a brief discussion, they walked to the Reforma and took a one-peso taxi to the National Museum of Archaeology in Chapultepec Park, where they paid a three-peso entrance fee. Beverly's brochures described the museum as a monument to the vitality of ancient Mexican art and architecture. The museum itself was modern, spacious, airy. It was stunning in its proportions. The stone objects they had come to see were housed in galleries that opened on an impressive central patio, in the middle of which was a huge waterfall.

Beverly and Simone spent over two hours looking at pre-Columbian treasures that had been gathered from centuries of the past. They felt insignificant as they walked from gallery to gallery, impressed by temple façades, fire serpents, astronomical observatories, oval cisterns, huge jaguars, and carved calendar stones that seemed to have been an Indian obsession.

When the two girls came out of the dark Teotihuacán gallery into the bright March sunlight, each felt mysteriously linked with her own ancient heritage.

"*Formidable,*" Simone said, giving it the French accent and meaning.

"Yes it is," Beverly agreed.

"Maybe in one of my previous lives, I was a beautiful and powerful Mayan queen," Simone mused, as they walked across the immense, open-air patio to the Museum's restaurant. "Did you see that skeleton in the fancy tomb? The one with all the jewels? That might have been me three thousand years ago."

"Oh, do you believe in reincarnation?" Beverly asked, wishing she had taken the museum tour with Peter.

The need to share her emotions was very strong. Her emotions were mixed, poignant, troubled somehow by what she had just seen. Then she realized that she had not shared anything with Peter for a long time. She was thinking of the past, of Peter as he once had been. Tears came to Beverly's eyes as she felt overpowered by a double sense of loss: the recent one of Peter, the ancient one of herself.

The Museum's restaurant turned out to be a Mexican automat. Beverly and Simone slipped pesos into a machine marked "*refrescos,*" and Coca-Cola came out in white paper cups.

They were tired when they returned to the hotel. They planned to take naps and then meet for a drink in the cocktail lounge at eight that evening. Beverly informed Simone that it was not chic to go out to dinner before nine in Mexico City. Then she went to her room and meticulously set her hair, while upstairs Simone rubbed a moisturizing cream into her face. Both girls read, neither could sleep. Each strongly suspected the other of not being her cup of tea. Simone thought Beverly should lose ten pounds and shorten her hemline. Beverly thought Simone should gain ten pounds and use less makeup.

But they did admire each other's handbags. Simone spotted Beverly's baby crocodile satchel as being the real thing, probably from the Hermes shop in Paris, and Beverly gave status obeisance to Simone's Gucci with the bamboo handles.

When they met in the hotel's dimly lit cocktail lounge, both girls were wearing dresses with plunging necklines. Simone had on her shimmer shirtdress, and Beverly the black sheath that Tony Elliot had found so engaging the evening of that terrible Choucroute Garni dinner. It all seemed very far away to Beverly . . . Tony Elliot, the castle in Garden City, even Peter, especially Peter. Only her children remained in sharp focus, a connection to the life she had left a mere twenty-four hours ago. It shocked her that she could feel so estranged from the past so quickly. Out of sight, out of mind. Was she really as callous as all that? Was this sense of emotional remoteness common to all travelers?

There was a bar at one end of the lounge, and in the center was a small bandstand. The stand was empty, musicians nowhere in sight, but a lively, cheerful atmosphere dominated the room. Except for the fact that some of the conversation was in Spanish, it could have been the clatter of any bar in any large American city at cocktail time.

Beverly and Simone took a table near the bandstand and upon the suggestion of their waiter, ordered two tequila sunsets. After a few sips of the tart drink, Simone began to tell Beverly about her life and hard times with Robert Fingerhood.

"For all I know, I might find myself moved out—clothes, dog, and all—when I get back to New York," Simone said in finishing her unhappy story.

Inspired by that unexpected confidence, Beverly in turn confessed that she was married and had two children. Without going into clinical detail, she told Simone that her relationship with Peter was far from idyllic.

"In a way, we're in the same boat," Simone said, "aren't we?"

Beverly hesitated. "In a way."

They tacitly acknowledged what Beverly had not said—that their worlds of operation were too far apart for them to be really in the same boat, or even to understand the true nature of each other's problems. And because their understanding was purely superficial, they found it easy to sympathize with one another, to offer words of false comfort, sincerely extended.

"He might miss you terribly while you're gone," Beverly said about Robert.

Simone resolutely shook her head. "No, I don't think so. He's bored with me. But in your case, it's different. You're married to him and there are children. The bond is greater."

"It's love I want," Beverly insisted, even while she thought that Simone was absolutely right. "Not legal bonds."

After that they felt better, cleansed, purged. They felt like more noble people, particularly since each one was secretly convinced that her problem was less terrible than the other's. Just as they were about to order a second round of tequila sunsets to celebrate their new friendship, the men appeared at their table.

Neither Beverly nor Simone had seen them come in and they looked up, equally startled. There were two of them, slender, elegant, both wore dark, well-tailored suits and shirts with French cuffs. One of the men was several inches taller than the other, and had black hair and somber grayish-green eyes. He spoke first in heavily accented English.

"Good evening. My name is Eduardo and this is my brother, Jorge. Please do not think us rude, but we couldn't help noticing two such lovely women sitting here all alone."

Beverly felt like saying, "We're not alone, we're with each other," but undoubtedly to a Latin, two women together must seem very much alone. She had read all about that *macho* business.

Then Jorge spoke. "What my brother is trying to say is that we would like to join you, if we may." He had black hair, too, but his eyes were dark, playful, teasing. He appeared to be several years younger than Eduardo, perhaps thirty or thirty-one. "May we sit down and buy you girls a drink?"

Beverly did not like him, he struck her as too arrogant, too sure of himself, and although his words were courteous, she found his manner offensive. She looked at Eduardo who was definitely the more reserved, the more gentlemanly of the two. Eduardo smiled at her. It was a polite smile, faintly apologetic, and Beverly found herself smiling back. Then she turned to Simone to determine what they should do about the situation, but to her surprise Simone was blatantly flirting with Jorge. Simone's provocative expression made it clear that she had no doubt what *she* was going to do, no doubt at all.

"Oh, yes," Simone said breathlessly, in a voice that Beverly did not recognize, "please do sit down. Oh, how nice this is! How nice of you to rescue us. Isn't it, Beverly?"

Beverly had a strong urge to slap her silly face. Jorge caught Beverly's angry glance and grinned triumphantly as he slipped into the chair opposite Simone and took a cigarette out of a gold cigarette case. He had won the first round, the grin seemed to say, and there was nothing Beverly could do about it short of leaving. In that instant Beverly contemplated excusing herself and walking out, but where would she go? Across the street to the Continental-Hilton to eat dinner alone?

She did not look forward to dining alone; she wanted companionship, and perhaps this unexpected pickup was less irregular than she imagined. What did she know after all about mores in Mexico? Besides, both men were well dressed, obviously well educated since they spoke English, and perhaps were even from a distinguished family. Surely they could be counted on to behave decently.

"My name is Beverly Northrop," she said stiffly to Eduardo, who had taken the seat opposite her. "May I please have another tequila sunset?"

Three sunsets later, Beverly was feeling no pain. Nobody at the table was. Simone, who had never gotten accustomed to hard liquor, was plainly high and holding hands across the table with Jorge. Both Jorge and Eduardo had been drinking Scotch, which was astronomically priced in Mexico. Eduardo seemed more relaxed, and Jorge more brash as he looked deeply into Simone's eyes and commented upon her beautiful lashes.

"They're my new Frivolashes," she said giddily. "I bought them at Bergdorf's."

Neither of the men understood what she was saying and assumed it was some sort of joke. They laughed, charmed by the exotic appeal of American girls.

"Ah, American women!" Jorge put his fingers to his lips in an expansive, generous kiss. "I drink to wonderful American women. *Bellisima!*"

The long awaited musicians took their places on the bandstand and launched into a soulful Spanish melody.

"Jamas jamas jamas," crooned the handsome male singer into the microphone. *"Si quiere separar, jamas jamas jamas."*

For dinner the men took them to a restaurant with paneled walls, ceramic tiles, and flowers on all the tables. Beverly sat next to Eduardo, Simone next to Jorge, but a strolling mariachi band practically drowned out conversation between them. In order to be heard it was necessary to whisper into each other's ear, an intimacy that Beverly would have liked to avoid, and she wondered if that was why the brothers had chosen this particular restaurant, although in all fairness she had to admit that the food was delicious. Eduardo and Jorge ordered for them.

As an appetizer they had tiny, chicken-filled tortillas called *chalupas,* then a soup garnished with avocado, a main course of roast kid, a dessert of melon flavored with rum, orange juice, and sugar. Beverly realized that she had fallen off her prisoner-of-war diet and promised herself to resume it the next day. Dee Dee had told her about the diet.

"You go on a starvation regime," Dee Dee explained, "and then you pretend you're a prisoner of war, and that's all the enemy will give you to eat. It's simple and it works."

"Providing you can convince yourself you're a prisoner of war," Beverly had added.

When coffee was served, Jorge kissed Simone on the lips and she eagerly put her arms around his neck and kissed him back. Beverly found herself blushing.

"I'm afraid she must be very drunk," Beverly said to Eduardo. "Usually, she's quite shy."

"And you?" Eduardo asked with an enticing smile. "Are you shy, too?"

"No, but I'm married," she said, intending it to ward him off.

For a second it seemed as though she had succeeded. His face fell. "Married. Oh, I see. And your husband. Where is he?"

Without thinking, Beverly replied, "New York."

The minute she said it the relieved expression on Eduardo's face confirmed her suspicion that she had made a blunder.

"That's a long way off, isn't it? New York?"

And he laughed as though he had just managed to escape

with his life from the wrath of a deceived husband. At the same time he seemed to shed the air of reserve he had maintained up until now, his manner of looking at her was different, more insinuating. He suddenly pressed his lips against her hair, and whispered, "*Querida,* you are so lovely, so lovely."

The change in his behavior was so abrupt that an odd idea popped into Beverly's head. Could he have thought before that she might be a virgin, and that by admitting she was married she had successfully ruled out the possibility?

It was so long since Beverly herself had been a virgin, so long since she'd met a virgin, that the concept was strangely archaic, and yet in a country as fiercely Catholic as Mexico, there must be many virgins among the upper-middle-class girls, untouchable girls. Also, as a Mexican male, Eduardo would surely consider it unusual for her to have taken a vacation without her husband. It was probably unheard of in his society. She could see the way his mind was working: a married woman, sexually experienced, alone, on the make, and a husband safely three thousand miles away.

After dinner they went dancing at the Jacaranda Club, which was so dark that they could barely see one another. Perhaps it was all the tequila she had consumed, perhaps it was the protective shield of darkness, Beverly was not sure which, but she began to loosen up. She felt less restricted, less concerned about what Eduardo thought of her. He thought she was out for a good time. Well, wasn't she? Wasn't that why she had come to Mexico? Yes, in a way, and no, in another way. She had come here to escape from Peter, to think, to meet people she never would have met in Garden City, but not to find a lover (no? whispered an inner voice, mockingly).

"Are you enjoying yourself?" Eduardo asked, as they left the dance floor.

The frug seemed to be as popular in Mexico as in the United States, and Beverly was grateful to her five-year-old daughter from whom she had picked up the steps.

"I'm having a marvelous time," she said.

Then she realized that she was leaning drunkenly on Eduardo's shoulder. Oh, so what, she asked herself. What was wrong with that? Would she never escape this wretched straitjacket of morality? It certainly did not seem to affect Simone, who had returned to the table, breathless, her arms wrapped around Jorge.

Beverly admired Simone, envied Simone, would have liked

to change places with Simone . . . for a little while at least. Simone was not torn between right and wrong, should and shouldn't. Simone responded to the beat of the moment. Beverly wanted to respond, too. More than anything else she wanted to be desired. She had wanted that for a long time, and now at last her wish was being fulfilled. Eduardo's rapt attentiveness left no doubt in her mind that all she had to do was say the word and a new, exciting chapter in her moldy life would shortly unfold.

Say what word? How to say it? Beverly had been married for eight years and during that time she'd never once looked at another man (why not, she bitterly asked herself now), and she was out of practice. It was like trying to ride a bicycle if you had not ridden one for a long while; the ability was still there, latent, lurking, but the self-assurance was not.

"I think you're very nice," she said weakly to Eduardo, who gazed at her out of knowing grayish-green eyes, as if to say that she had no idea *how* nice, but not to worry about it, because he would soon show her.

"I think you're more than nice. I think you're wonderful, beautiful," Eduardo said in return, and as he leaned over to kiss her soft, white throat in the darkness, his eyes peered intently down the deep décolletage of her dress.

The four of them ended up back in Beverly's suite at the Maria Cristina. Simone had insisted upon performing Rima's Dance for them before the evening was over, and the floor at the Jacaranda Club was much too crowded for the leaping acrobatics that the dance demanded. Beverly's suite had a good-sized sitting room, and in spite of her inebriation she was still sober enough to realize that that would be a far less compromising choice than Simone's stark bedroom.

Jorge called room service for Scotch, ice, and soda to be sent up, and Beverly managed to get a Los Angeles station on her transistor radio. Then Simone began to leap and fly around the room to the tune of the Jefferson Airplane singing one of their latest hits. Eduardo and Jorge clapped and whistled appreciatively, and at one point as she made a particularly spectacular leap they jumped to their feet in unison, and shouted, "*Olé!*"

When the performance was over, Simone breathlessly downed a tall glass of Scotch and soda that Jorge had fixed for her. Then Jorge flicked the radio dial to a local station and strains of tango music filled the room. He and Simone began to dance to the soft tango beat.

"Come," Eduardo said, beckoning to Beverly.

Feeling shaky she allowed herself to be drawn into his arms and pressed against his lithe body. He guided her firmly through the sinuous dance, his lips close to her ear, and she could not help remembering a movie she had seen on the "Late Late Show," in which Carole Lombard played a society girl and in one scene did a snaky tango with George Raft, who played a Cuban nightclub entertainer.

"What do you do for a living?" she asked Eduardo as they slithered around the room.

"I'm an architect," he whispered in her ear.

"And Jorge?"

"He works for Du Pont. But why do you ask such questions when I hold you in my arms?"

"Because I'm a product of a capitalistic society," she whispered back.

It was only when the dance had ended, that Beverly realized Simone and Jorge had danced themselves into the bedroom. To her dismay, she could hear their hushed voices from behind the bedroom door, and the rustle of familiar sounds. Clothes were being taken off.

"Now just a minute!" she started to say, with great policewoman indignation.

But that was as far as she got because Eduardo stopped her with a sudden, smoldering kiss. It was so long since she'd been kissed that way, that she was not sure afterward whether it was shock or passion (or a combination of both) that made her succumb to Eduardo's wild embrace. All she knew was that a man's arms were around her, holding her tight, and the warmth from his body seemed to melt into hers, giving her a strength she had forgotten she possessed.

The strength was not to resist him, it was to join him, to match him in mounting excitement. Eduardo's mouth went from her lips to her throat to her breasts to her stockinged thighs. Beverly was beside herself as he put one hand on the throbbing mound. She thought she would faint with desire. He kept his hand there and began to kiss her on the lips again, he bit her neck, buried his head in her flaming hair, and flicked his tongue in her ear.

Then he threw her back against the sofa and removed her shoes and unclasped her stockings and rolled them down. He began to kiss her long, white legs with a frenzy that would have frightened her if she were not so lost in her own burning response. He reached for the catch at the back of her dress, loosened it, and unzipped her. The black sheath came off like a snake shedding old skin, ready to shed it because underneath was a smooth new skin partially covered by a plunging brassiere and a black lace half slip.

Beverly's hair was tangled and she looked half wild. Eduardo's eyes gleamed at the magnificent, disheveled sight of her.

"I adore redheads," he said hoarsely, idiotically.

Then the telephone rang. Eduardo tried to keep her from answering it and for a moment Beverly wavered, wishing the ringing would stop, wishing she could drown in the sea of desire that tugged at her every nerve ending. But the caller could be only one person—Peter—and she had obeyed his insistent demands for too many years to be able to defy them now with a panting stranger.

"I have to," she said, pulling away from him and getting shakily to her feet.

"Darling, are you all right?" Peter asked, after she said hello. "You sound a little strange."

"I'm all right. I'm fine." She pushed the hair out of her eyes and tried to steady her quaking heart. "How are you, darling? How are the children?"

"We miss you, but we're carrying on," he replied with a hearty cheerfulness.

Was it possible that he really did miss her now that she was so far away from him, so physically inaccessible? Beverly hoped so but she doubted it. He sounded more as though he were trying desperately to give the *impression* of missing her: the dutiful husband role that he played so badly.

She glanced at her watch. It would be a little after ten o'clock in New York.

"Are you at home, darling?" she asked.

"Yes, of course. Where did you think I would be?"

"I was merely wondering. And the children. Are they asleep?"

"Have been for hours. They send you their love. By the way, how was the flight?"

"Uneventful."

Across the room, Eduardo stood nervously tapping his foot on the richly waxed floor, tapping and waiting for her to finish her conversation and return to him so they could pick up where they'd left off. Beverly's seminakedness embarrassed her. She felt as though Peter had X-ray eyes and could see through the telephone wires. The fact that he could not was merely a technical fluke; it did not change her condition of undress any more than she could effectively change her nature by allowing a handsome stranger to make love to her.

And she realized that now that she could be anyone she wanted, she was still the same old Beverly, bound to her husband, her children, her wretched respectability. She did not know whether to laugh or to cry.

"I'll phone you tomorrow," she said to Peter before hanging up. "Kiss the children for me. And please be sure to tell Margaret not to let Peter, Jr., have dessert unless he's finished everything else first. You know how he is."

"Yes, darling," Peter said. "Goodnight, love."

"Goodnight."

She turned to face an expectant Eduardo who stared in astonishment as she calmly retrieved her dress from where it had fallen on the floor, and stepped into it, zipped it up.

"What are you doing?" he demanded, darting forward.

"Getting dressed."

"Dressed? But I don't understand . . . I thought . . . before the telephone rang you were so . . ."

She felt sorry for him, sorry for herself, sorry sorry sorry. It was perhaps her most familiar emotion. Would she never get beyond feeling sorry for everyone? The image of Dee Dee flared up again in her mind. Before killing herself, Dee Dee had written a farewell note consisting of three words: *Please forgive me.*

"Please forgive me," she said to the bewildered Eduardo. "I know how you must feel. You probably hate me, but I can't help what I'm doing now. I should have realized that I wouldn't be able to go through with it. I should have known."

He grabbed her roughly by the shoulders. "You don't know what you're saying. You can't dismiss me like this. I'm a man, not a schoolboy. And you, you're a woman, aren't you? A woman with feelings, a passionate woman? What has happened? Tell me."

Beverly made a gesture of despair. "It was talking to my husband—"

"Your husband," he said, contemptuously. "But your husband is thousands of miles away, thousands, and I'm here. What has this to do with your husband? Or my wife? It has only to do with us."

The fact that he might be married had never even occurred to her. Yet he admitted it now, openly, as though it were the most natural thing in the world that he should have a wife, and, no doubt, children, too. Beverly admired his simplicity. She wished she could be simple, too; she wished she could abandon herself to him and let him do exactly as he liked; she longed to have him rip off her clothes and attack her savagely. She wanted to lie underneath him and be consumed by him. She wanted him to put out the fire that raged in her body. Yet she knew to her regret that she would end up taking a cold shower and having bad dreams instead. She had never hated herself as much as she did that very minute.

"I'm sorry," she said, suddenly feeling very tired, "but I'm afraid that you will have to leave."

Then she remembered Simone and Jorge.

"And I suggest you take your brother with you," she added, thinking that Jorge was probably married, too.

"How can I take him with me?" Eduardo asked. "He's in *there.*"

"Precisely. He's in my bedroom and I would like to go to sleep. Now all you have to do is knock on the door and explain that you're leaving. That's not asking too much, is it?"

Eduardo stared at her as though she were a madwoman.

"I don't understand you at all," he said, at last. "Do you really believe I would interrupt a man when he is in the act of making love? Do you think that I would be so cruel? So heartless?"

It was his compassion versus her hysteria. "If you don't, I will," she said.

He grabbed her arm. "No. You can't. You mustn't."

"Oh, I can't? Is that what you think? I can't? We'll see whether or not I can't."

And before he could stop her, she had flung the bedroom door open. The lights behind her flooded the room illuminating the two figures on the bed (*my* bed, Beverly thought viciously) who were so immersed in what they were doing that they did not realize they were being watched. Simone's legs were wrapped around Jorge's neck, her dusty pink toenail polish glimmering in the streak of light that fell across the bed. Jorge was going at her at breakneck speed, as though he were about to cross the finish line any moment. Beverly could see beads of perspiration on his back, could feel the heat emanating from his charged up body, could taste the flavor of his skin.

She stood there, spellbound, until she heard the strangled words come out of his mouth.

"Me voy," he cried. *"Me voy."*

And the bed seemed to gallop triumphantly through the pale and starless night, coming to a halt at last as Jorge fell in exhaustion from Simone's wet, contorted body. It was only then that the two of them looked up in surprise and saw Beverly and Eduardo framed in the doorway. Simone giggled and pulled the covers over her, but Jorge just lay there, naked, grinning, exultant. Ignoring his brother, he addressed Beverly.

"So you like to watch other people make love? So that's what you like, is it? Maybe next time we'll invite you to join us. Would you like that, too?"

Horrified by Jorge's words, by his naked body, by the scene she had just witnessed, by the act that she had almost committed with Eduardo a few minutes ago, Beverly stepped backward. She had to get away. Simone's purse lay on the coffee table and she picked it up, her hands shaking as she fumbled around inside until she found what she was looking for—the key to Simone's room. Then, without another word, she ran past a bewildered Eduardo, out of her suite and into the hallway where she nearly slipped and fell on the smoothly tiled floor. Her head was beginning to throb and there was a familiar, acrid taste in her mouth.

It occurred to her to go back to the suite and get her pills, but she couldn't set foot in there now, she would rather die of pain. She would rather run than wait for the elevator. And she did run, up the circular staircase to room 412 where she flung herself down on Simone's unmade bed and let the violent waves of a migraine attack wash over her at last.

For the first time in her life, Beverly did not try to fight the waves. It was easier to succumb. Sweeter.

She managed to get through the night, alternately sweating and shivering, and by giving in so thoroughly to the demands of the waves, by morning she was cured. Exhausted, but well. At ten o'clock she phoned Simone, who sounded bright and cheerful.

"Guess what?" Simone said. "I screwed Eduardo too. But I liked Jorge better."

Beverly felt too tired to be shocked. "Oh?"

"Yes. Two brothers in one night. How do you like that for fast work?"

"I'm not sure, but let's have breakfast at Sanborn's and you can tell me all about it."

Minutes later they were strolling down the Reforma in the brisk, chilly, morning air. Simone wore a nubby tweed suit and scarf around her neck, Beverly her suede coat over a woolen dress.

"Isn't this air marvelous?" Simone asked. "It's so clean. I'd almost forgotten what clean air smells like."

Or clean living, Beverly thought, wondering how Simone could look so bubbling and innocent in view of what she had done the night before. The French really were decadent, she decided; it was in the blood.

They passed the Continental-Hilton, a glittering fortress for American tourists. A young boy on the corner tried to sell them lottery tickets, and when they shook their heads no, he ran after them for two blocks jabbering in Spanish and pointing excitedly to the number on the tickets.

"You have good luck," he finally called out in desperation as they left him behind, a defeated figure in a torn leather jacket.

At Sanborn's, Simone ordered scrambled eggs and bacon and a chocolate milkshake. "I'm ravenous," she admitted.

Beverly gave her a dirty look and, remembering her P.O.W. diet, asked for half a grapefruit and black coffee.

"How did it happen?" she asked.

"What?"

"Eduardo."

"Oh *that.*" Simone shrugged. "I don't know. Jorge got dressed and left. I must have fallen asleep. The next thing I knew Eduardo was in bed with me."

"Didn't you resist?"

"No. Why should I have?" Simone asked, smiling impishly. "I was in the mood."

Beverly scooped out a section of grapefruit. "I hope you don't get in that mood very often. For your sake."

"Don't be silly. I had a marvelous time. Incidentally, Jorge is bigger than Eduardo but Eduardo went down on me. Do you like clinical details? *Je les adore.*"

Absolutely decadent, Beverly thought. No shame, no guilt, no conscience. "What about that guy in New York? The one you're supposed to be so crazy about? Robert. Doesn't last night bother you when you think about it in relation to him?"

Simone swallowed a forkful of scrambled egg. "No. Why should it?"

"I would think you'd feel guilty cheating on him."

Simone burst out laughing. *"Cheating?"*

"Yes. Why is that so funny?"

"Because I don't look at it that way."

"So it would appear."

"Well, if you must know," Simone started to explain,

suddenly very serious, "I say to myself, what's the difference whether I cheat on Robert or not since I don't come anyway? Now do you understand?"

"No," Beverly said, just as seriously. "No, I don't."

And afterward as they walked over to the Niza shopping section to buy silk shifts for themselves and gifts to take back to New York, Beverly convinced herself that Simone had been pulling her leg.

When Beverly and Simone flew back to New York two weeks later, they promised to get in touch with each other soon. Beverly said that perhaps Simone would like to come out to Garden City some weekend afternoon and go to the country club for lunch. Simone said that if Beverly found herself in the city during the week, perhaps she would give her a ring at Mini-Furs, Inc. and they could have lunch somewhere nearby.

Neither really believed they would meet again and neither was particularly sorry. The impression they had gotten about each other's lives, during their brief encounter in Mexico, was that they were worlds apart and although each girl was far from satisfied with what she had, she was more than slightly repelled with what the other one was stuck with.

"I hope things work out with you and Robert," Beverly said when they were parting at the airport.

"Ditto for you and your husband," Simone replied, unable for the life of her to remember his name.

Then they kissed each other lightly on tanned cheeks and waved good-bye. The minute Simone was out of sight, Beverly promptly forgot that she existed; Simone was like Mexico, an interlude, a bit of fantasy. Reality lay waiting for her in the castle in Garden City, and it was with a great deal of trepidation that she gave the taxi driver her Stewart Avenue address.

Two surprises awaited Beverly at home.

In her absence Peter, Jr., had begun to stutter, and Peter Sr., had bought another myna bird that he'd taught to say, "Happy days are here again." Beverly felt that between a stuttering child and two shrieking birds, an ominous assault was being made on her auditory senses.

"Why can't we be like normal people?" Beverly asked her husband, "and get a dog or a Siamese cat? Why must we continue to live with these damn birds?"

"Because we are not like normal people, darling," he

replied with great disdain. "We're superior to normal people. Thank God."

"I'm not," Beverly said, "and apparently neither is your son. Doctor Spock says that stuttering is very common among boys between the ages of two and three. Still, it worries me. What if he doesn't outgrow it?"

"You should have thought of that before you went traipsing off to Mexico. Didn't it ever occur to you that children need their mother around when they're young?"

"Are you trying to blame his stuttering on *me?*"

"No, but I'm suggesting it as a distinct possibility."

She could have killed Peter for that (didn't she have enough guilts as it was?), yet according to Doctor Spock stuttering was often brought on by what he referred to as "separation anxiety." The way to cure the condition, according to Doctor Spock, was not to go away again for a long period of time and to make sure that the child had enough other children he liked to play with. The thing not to do was to try to correct the child's speech, as that would only tend to make him more anxious.

Up until then Peter, Jr., had been playing several times a week with the little boy who lived next door. It was so convenient that way, but now Beverly wondered whether her son really liked the boy next door.

When she asked him, he said, "H-h-h-h-e st-st-st-inks."

Unfortunately, Peter, Jr., was still too young to be sent to nursery school, that would not happen for another six months, so Beverly called every mother she could think of in the neighborhood who had children of approximately the same age. It took a little doing, but before long she had managed to arrange a daily schedule of play for Peter, Jr., the sessions taking place at a different home each day.

Beverly's day to receive the herd was Saturday. The first Saturday that they showed up, she came down with a migraine headache. The second Saturday she decided to go into the city and see a matinee, leaving Peter to supervise the children's play operation. Peter thought she was being irresponsible, but she told him that it didn't matter which parent was present; it was the therapeutic value of the play period itself that counted.

"And besides, darling," Beverly pointed out, "if it gets too tedious, Margaret will relieve you. She and Sally are going to bake banana bread on Saturday."

Peter disliked banana bread intensely. "Oh, lovely," he said, making a face.

"Happy days are here again," shrieked the new myna bird.

The musical comedy that Beverly went to see proved to be a disaster, and she did not return for the second act. It was four o'clock when she walked out of the theater, wondering what to do with herself until it was time to take the six thirty-one back to Garden City. If she had not disliked the Manhattan department stores so much, she might have tried to do some shopping, but she could not face wading through their labyrinthine depths.

Then she remembered Simone. Fortunately, she had her address book with her and Simone had put her telephone number in it. Beverly hurried to the public telephone booth on the corner of Broadway, thinking it might be fun to see how the other half lived.

Minutes later she was ringing the doorbell to Robert Fingerhood's apartment on East Twenty-Sixth Street.

"Beverly!"

"Simone!"

They fell into each other's arms like sorority sisters stumbling across each other in the Mojave Desert, twenty years later.

"How wonderful to see you!" Simone cried. "Come in. Come in. The apartment is a bit of a mess, but I've stopped worrying about things like that ever since Robert told me that Freud himself was a big slob."

Simone was wearing skintight pants with bell bottoms, a navy blue shirt, and a man's white tie.

"You look marvelous," Beverly said. "You're as thin as ever. I don't know how you do it."

"I vomit a lot," Simone confided.

Beverly did not know whether to take her seriously. Simone baffled her. Had she been serious in Mexico City when she'd said that she couldn't come? Afterwards they had gone to Puerto Vallarta to relax in the sun, and Beverly considered asking her about it, but she never quite got up the nerve. It was not that she thought Simone would be offended by the inquiry. She had not asked because she was afraid to hear that it was true.

"You're looking very chic," Simone said generously, as she gave Beverly's checked wool suit the once-over and decided that Chanel really had had it.

Beverly followed her into the cavelike Mexican living room where Robert Fingerhood was sprawled out in the hammock reading a book entitled, *Creativity and Pathology.*

He glanced up as Beverly entered, and took off his reading glasses.

"It's nice to meet you," he said, after Simone had introduced them. "Simone has spoken about you a great deal since she got back from Mexico."

Beverly could not imagine what Simone would have to say about her, except possibly that she was a prude and easily shocked by situations that Simone took for granted. Such as the situation with Eduardo and Jorge. Ever since returning to New York, Beverly had mixed feelings about that bizarre evening. Sometimes when she remembered herself talking on the telephone to Peter, wearing only a bra and half-slip, she blushed with shame, and at other times she hated herself for not having let Eduardo make love to her.

"This is quite a place," Beverly said, looking curiously around. "I've never seen anything like it. I feel as though I'm in a jungle."

Robert had gotten out of the hammock. He was tall, taller than Peter, Beverly thought, with large, bony shoulders. He had on bleached jeans, a wide leather belt, a striped shirt, and his hair was mussed. Without daring to look, something told her that he had an erection, and a strong wave of desire swept over Beverly, startling her by its intensity.

"Really," she wanted to say to him, "I'm not such a prude as you might imagine, I've probably done everything you've done—and more. In fact, I'll bet I could teach you a few tricks."

"Can I get you a drink?" he asked.

"Yes, I'd love one." She could not look him in the eye. "A Scotch, please."

She had completely fallen off her prisoner-of-war diet since she'd gotten back to New York, particularly in the drinking department. She simply could not stop. The more she drank, the more she wanted, and unfortunately she was cursed with a fantastic capacity for alcohol. She could drink almost everyone she knew right under the table and not even feel high. What was the point, though, if she didn't feel anything? Maybe if she left Peter, she would stop drinking so much. She liked to blame him for all her problems, but if she left Peter and still continued to drink, who would she blame then?

"The reason you're such a big boozer," Simone had informed her on the beach in Puerto Vallarta, "is because you're a Pisces. Pisces is a water sign and people born under it have a tendency toward addiction of all kinds."

At the time Beverly thought that was a lot of bull, but

what if there were a grain of truth in it, she asked herself now? If it were true, then she could blame her drinking on the stars, which was even better than blaming it on Peter, more satisfying by far, more scientific.

Robert was in the kitchen, taking ice cubes out of the freezer. The two girls could hear his movements.

"He's very attractive," Beverly whispered, with a nod toward the kitchen. "How are things going?"

Simone shrugged. "Oh he's nice to me, *très gentil.* We don't argue as much as before, but in a way it's worse. We live in silence."

"That's an improvement over the way I live," Beverly said, thinking of Peter, Jr., and the two myna birds.

"Are you still considering a divorce?" Simone asked.

"I consider it all the time, but it's a tough decision to make. The children are so young, you know."

What she really wanted to say was, "I don't want a divorce. I love my husband."

If only Peter would love her, as he used to. If only she knew what to do to make him love her again. She had tried every trick she could think of, except another man. But what if she went to bed with another man and Peter weren't jealous? What then? At least she might have some pleasure, there was that to think about, and since returning from Mexico Beverly had been thinking about it a great deal. In the seventeen days since she'd been back, Peter made love to her only once, and it was not very inspired lovemaking at that. He had gone through the motions mechanically, dully, as though he couldn't wait to get it over with. As a result her orgasm had been so unsatisfactory that it was not really like an orgasm at all, and the next morning she felt violently nauseated.

She remembered having that feeling when she was growing up in Salt Lake City and used to neck with boys in cars, but not let them go any farther. The morning after she invariably felt sick to her stomach and had to take an ice-cold shower to try to wash away the sickening sensation. And then to make everything worse, she would go downstairs to breakfast and be confronted by her mother's radiant good looks that seemed to boast of another night of well-spent sensuousness. There was a way her mother's eyes looked certain mornings, slightly glazed, filmy. Beverly often wondered what provisions, if any, her mother had made since the death of Beverly's father over four years ago. Had she taken a lover? Or did she no longer care? Her mother was fifty-two now.

Was she beyond sex? Somehow Beverly felt not. She did not feel that she would be beyond it at fifty-two either; she could not conceive of being alive and not having sexual desires. It was inconceivable to her, it would be the same as being dead. No. Worse.

When Robert returned from the kitchen, Beverly noticed that the drink he handed her looked particularly strong. Had Simone also told him that she was an alcoholic?

"Thank you," she said, feeling a tremor as his hand brushed against hers.

Still, she could not help wondering whether it was specifically Robert Fingerhood she was attracted to, or whether any reasonable man would fit the bill at this frustrated point in her life. She knew that things had reached the breaking point last week when she came in her sleep. That hadn't happened to her since she was a virgin, eight million years ago in Salt Lake City.

Robert put some records on the hi-fi and the three of them started to talk about mundane things. The play Beverly had walked out on, her impression of Mexico versus Simone's, why Robert had a stuffed owl over his hammock, why Beverly had two crazy myna birds in the music room, and finally why Beverly had to take the six thirty-one back to Garden City.

"I'm expected," she said.

"Couldn't you call and say you're going to take a later train?" Robert asked. "Why don't you stay and have dinner with us? I just put a leg of lamb in the oven."

"Oh no," she said, tempted. "I couldn't. Really. I have to get home. But thank you. Maybe another time."

His remark about the leg of lamb surprised her since Peter was absolutely helpless in the kitchen, did not even know how to boil the proverbial egg. She wondered why Robert was doing the cooking tonight. Perhaps he enjoyed it on weekends. It never occurred to Beverly that Simone could not cook any more effectively than she could come.

"Yes, do come back and see us another time," Simone said earnestly. "We'd love to have you. Robert and I are terribly *ennuyés* with each other's company. Aren't we, Robert?"

He gave her a condemning look. "Terribly."

Beverly sensed there would be an argument after she left, eight years of marriage had taught her the warning signals, and for what seemed like the millionth time she found herself wondering whether somewhere, someplace, somebody was not happy.

"*Ennui* isn't the word for it," Simone whispered, as she saw Beverly to the door.

There are cycles of life so sparse with living that later we look back, in retrospect, and ask ourselves how we ever managed to survive such painful aridity. That was what Beverly asked herself five days later when Robert Fingerhood telephoned her at home and invited her to have dinner with him that evening.

"Simone moved out yesterday," he added, almost as an afterthought.

How had she managed to hang on up until then, was Beverly's immediate response? How had she been able to stand it? The recent grayness of her existence, the deadness? For suddenly she was alive, her heart was pounding, she could feel the blood race to her head as she mentally ran through her wardrobe for the most appropriate thing to wear.

"Where did she move to?" The pink wool dress? No. The green.

"Back to her old apartment on Fifty-Seventh Street."

"Oh, I see." The green might be too tight on her, though. She would have to try it on first.

"The break has been a long time coming," Robert said, "and now that it's happened, I'm sure it's for the best. What's the point in living with someone you can't communicate with?"

"No point at all," Beverly replied automatically. "But how did Simone take it? Wasn't she upset?"

"Only at first when I suggested that she might be happier if she had her own place again. Then she seemed to adjust to the idea quite quickly. There were no tears, no scenes."

No regrets on Simone's part? Somehow Beverly found that hard to believe and she wondered whether Robert was not fooling himself, trying to ease any guilts he might have, but a second later she decided that it was not her concern. Simone was only an acquaintance, hardly a friend, she owed her nothing. Then with a clear conscience and renewed anticipation, she told Robert she would meet him at his place at seven that evening.

"You must be sure to give me Simone's new telephone number when I see you," she said before hanging up. "I hope she's all right. The poor darling."

Luckily Peter was having dinner in the city with Tony Elliot and a Wall Street investment broker, and had said he would not be home until quite late. Beverly told Margaret that she was driving into New York to visit Simone and would probably be back before midnight in case Mr. Northrop got back before her.

"What's worse than raining cats and dogs?" Sally asked when her mother kissed her goodnight.

"I give up."

"Hailing taxicabs."

Beverly slipped into her iridescent raincoat over the green wool dress (it had not been too tight after all), and went to get the Mercedes out of the garage. At the sight of the empty space next to the Mercedes, she thought for a moment that their Buick had been stolen and her mouth opened in a soundless scream. Then she remembered that Peter had taken it into the city that morning because he knew he would be coming home late. How silly of her to have forgotten, but then he almost always took the train to work. She was used to his taking the train. It was more practical, he said, and he hated to drive.

Beverly liked to drive. She liked it almost as much as drinking, and often thought what a shame it was that she couldn't do both at the same time and be doubly relaxed. She said that once to Peter who remarked that if she ever tried it, she would probably wake up doubly dead.

"I only meant it as a joke," she replied, annoyed.

He knew she had meant it as a joke, she thought now as she pulled out of the driveway. He knew she was a careful responsible driver. Still, he could not resist being caustic and deflating every chance he got.

"Turn on your headlights, lady!" a passing driver shouted.

To her chagrin, Beverly realized that she had indeed failed to do so. It was all Peter's fault. He was slowly but surely dragging her down.

But by the time she reached the cloverleaf intersection, twenty-seven minutes later, she felt considerably more optimistic about everything. Not far away Robert Fingerhood was waiting for her. He would be nice to her, would raise her spirits.

"Did you have any trouble parking?" Robert asked, as he hung her coat in the hall closet.

"I put my car in the garage down the block."

"I should have told you that it's easy to find parking space around here. You needn't have spent the money on a garage."

"It doesn't matter."

Actually, she had seen a parking space but was afraid to take it for fear her car would be stripped. She had heard about all the terrible things that happened to cars parked on dark side streets in Manhattan, and Robert Fingerhood certainly lived on a dark side street. When she had come to visit Simone on Saturday, it was light outside and the neighborhood seemed bland, almost homey with its nondescript shops and small, Armenian restaurants, but now in the evening it was another story. Walking the one block from the garage to Robert's apartment house, she had seen danger everywhere, and in the self-service elevator she was convinced that at any floor a desperate lunatic would get on and rape her.

A telephone rang softly somewhere in the apartment but Robert made no move to answer it. After it had stopped ringing, he said:

"That was probably my mother. She calls at least once a week to see whether I've broken down yet and decided to get married. She can't wait to be a grandma."

"You should have answered it," Beverly said, following him into the Mexican jungle living room.

"Why? And confess that I'm still a disgrace to my family? It gets tedious after a while."

The living room seemed even more cavelike than Beverly had remembered. Shadows played on the ceiling, reflections from two dimly lit, gourdlike lamps, and tall lush plants behind the hammock glistened in the still tropical night. Jaguar skins nailed to one wall lent an appropriately primitive effect. Beverly shivered, apprehensive but excited.

"The last time she called," Robert went on, "she asked me whether I was a homosexual."

"What did you say?"

"I was tempted to say *yes,* just to get her off my back, but cowardice prevailed. I had to admit that that was not my problem, which made her more confused than ever. Christ knows what funny ideas she'll come up with next."

Beverly wished he would stop talking about his mother and get down to business. She didn't have all night, or had he failed to take that small fact into consideration?

"There's something about this room . . ." she began, hoping to distract him.

"Yes?"

She let her eyes wander slowly over the various objects, dropping them at last to the green grass rug on the floor. "Something very seductive . . ."

"Go on."

"Well, my husband claims that inside every civilized woman, there's a wild pagan struggling to get out. Do you believe that?"

He took her gently by the shoulders, all of his mother problems apparently forgotten. "You might say that I've built one area of my life on just that premise. Now, how about a little champagne?"

At last they were getting somewhere. "Wonderful."

She loved the idea of drinking French champagne in a Mexican cave. It seemed appropriately decadent. She felt her clitoris twitch, and she raised her glass to Robert's in a toast of unspoken desire. They were standing facing each other, and he said, "I'm glad that you're tall. I like tall girls."

"Simone wasn't tall."

He laughed. "I've been known to make exceptions, but I'm invariably disappointed."

"Chin chin."

They drank the delicious champagne and Robert refilled their glasses. Beverly sat down on a low chair that looked as though its stone base were built into the wall. Robert sat at her feet. He was wearing a long-sleeved blue velour pullover, blue and white striped cotton pants, and thonged leather sandals. This time his dark hair was neatly combed. Beverly preferred it the other way, felt like running her fingers through it and mussing it up, felt like being rough with him, roughing him up. Then she noticed the whip wedged into a corner of the room, and remembered when Peter had tried to strangle her with his belt at Cambridge.

"What's that for?" she asked, pointing to the whip.

"Masochists like you."

"Don't tell me you're going to beat me," she said with a shaky laugh.

"Only if you beg me."

"Shall I get down on my hands and knees?"

"If you prefer it that way."

"Which way do you prefer it?"

"What? Begging?"

"No," she said, remembering Cambridge. "Making love."

"It depends on who I'm with."

"How did you prefer it with Simone?"

"I didn't after the initial attraction faded. That's primarily why we broke up. Simone jumps around a lot in bed, but she doesn't know what she's doing. It's very boring. All narcissists are sexual bores."

"I'm too overweight to be narcissistic."

"That's the first coy thing you've said."

"But I mean it," she assured him.

"You're not overweight. Is that what you want to hear?"

"What am I, then?"

"Voluptuous."

"Fat."

"You asked me my opinion."

"My husband thinks I'm fat."

"And, of course, that's why you're home in bed with him this very minute. Because you're so crazy about his physical evaluation of you."

"Some men are attracted to thin women," she persisted, holding out her glass for more champagne.

"I don't deny that for a second. I simply tell you that I'm not one of them."

"Simone was thin."

"And short."

"Yet you liked her. You lived with her."

"She had nice breasts."

"I know. I saw her in a bikini in Puerto Vallarta. I was jealous."

Robert placed his champagne glass on the floor and reached up and placed both his hands on Beverly's breasts, feeling the hidden scope of them beneath her chemise.

"Why should you be jealous?" he asked, starting to play with her nipples until they hardened at his touch. "You have nothing to be jealous about."

"I have to wear a brassiere or they tend to sag."

He took his hands away. "I'm crazy about your mouth."

"It's too big."

"It's beautiful. Juicy. I want to kiss it."

"Why don't you?"

He pulled her head down toward him so far that her stomach doubled over, as she put her arms around his neck and let herself dissolve into the longest kiss of her life. When he let her go, she was breathing so hard she could barely swallow. The stuffed owl's glass eye peered intently at her from his perch above the hammock. There was nobody to see them, she told herself, nobody to know, nobody except Robert and her and a stuffed owl. She could do anything she wanted. Anything.

"Would you like to eat dinner now?" Robert asked. "I bought some great filets mignons today. I'm going to charcoal them."

"Could we wait a little while? I'm not all that hungry yet. But I would like some more champagne."

If there was anything that interested her less at the moment than food, she couldn't imagine what it was. She had not been interested in food for a long time (then how come she was so fat?). Drinking as much as she did ruined her appetite. That afternoon she had had three double Scotches while writing a letter to her mother and paying some of the household bills. Beverly found most things so dull and tedious that without alcohol she did not know how she would ever get through the day, she did not know how people who did not drink got through it. Perhaps to them the day was not that bad, day stretching into day with no discernible goal except paying the household bills, planning menus with Margaret, talking to her children, writing to her mother, wondering why her husband continued to reject her. She drank so much that when she woke up some mornings her kidneys ached, and at those moments she solemnly swore that she would never touch another drop, but then in a couple of hours she would feel engulfed once more in a life that seemed so meaningless, a life in which *she* seemed to have no meaning, that if it were not for the comfort of Scotch, she was sure she would have gone mad long before.

Sometimes glimmers of sanity shone through the fog. Sometimes she thought that certain women needed to have a continuing erotic relationship with a man, that without it nothing else made much sense and they became a little crazy. Look at what happened to Dee Dee. Beverly had always thought that in many ways Dee Dee was a foolish and hysterical woman, yet in the long run she identified with her brand of desperation far more than she ever could, say, with someone like Simone who was able to hop into bed with any man who came along, go through the motions, and hop out, apparently unsatisfied.

In Puerto Vallarta, Simone had said to her, "I might not get as much out of it as some women, but it's great for keeping your weight down. Particularly if you get on top and do all the work. That position is good for knocking off at least eight hundred calories."

"It wouldn't knock anything off me," Beverly replied. "Sex is the only activity that makes me hungry."

"*C'est vrai?* It completely destroys my appetite, but completely."

Which, when Beverly thought about it later, did not appear to make too much sense. Judging by everything she had read on the subject, it should be the frustrated person who wante to eat afterward, not the satisfied one. She not only wante to eat afterward, she wanted to fly, run, sing, dance, shou for joy. Sex stimulated her on every level. To Simone it wa apparently like doing pushups.

"We can wait for dinner as long as you want," Rober said. "In fact, if you don't want to eat at all, we won't."

"Oh, I'm sure I'll want to. Eventually."

"There's no rush. I'll wait until you're ready."

"Will you?"

"I promise."

"Some men don't like to wait."

"Some men like thin women. Remember?"

"It might take a while," she said. "I'm slow."

"I told you, I would wait."

"You must have a great deal of self-control."

"I like to please. I would like to please you."

"Why?"

"You excite me. I was excited the first time I saw you."

"Then start."

"Now?"

"Why not?"

"Stand up."

She was shaking so that she could hardly get to her feet. Robert stood up too and began to unbutton the front of her dress. The buttons extended only to just below her waist and the dress slipped over her hips and dropped to the floor. Reaching in back, Beverly unclasped her brassiere which fell to the floor on top of the dress.

"I knew you would look like that," Robert said softly. "It's exactly how I pictured you."

He cupped her breasts in his hands and kissed her again, but more fiercely this time, pushing her head back until her neck hurt.

"Come on," he said. "Let's go into the bedroom."

"No. Here."

"But why?"

"I want to. I don't want to leave the jungle."

Seconds later they were both naked on the green grass rug. Robert was on top of her. He was much bigger than Peter and he rammed it into her with such force that she screamed out in delicious agony. His face above her was formed into a strange half smile. Then Beverly closed her eyes and let it all happen, she moved with him, against him, stopped moving altogether and simply received, then he stopped and she gave, and all the while she was only vaguely conscious of her own voice off in the distance crying, "Kill me kill me kill me."

She came first and with such intensity that she thought she had died, a corpse who still shuddered and shook seconds afterward, who still continued to cling. Then Robert started to come, the waves building up to a final galloping crash of ecstasy, and only one word escaped his lips: "Murder."

They were so immersed in the tremulousness of the moment that they did not hear the front door open, did not see Simone in her black vinyl raincoat enter the apartment and then stop dead on the living room threshold, stop and stare at them in dazed bewilderment, a key ring dangling from one cold hand.

"Bon soir, mes amis," she said a moment later.

They nearly collapsed with shock, their mouths agape at the sight of her poised like a wax statue, staring down at the two of them naked on the floor.

Beverly looked desperately for something to cover herself with, and being unsuccessful she rolled over on her stomach and hid her face in her hands, trying to blot out this hideous turn of events.

"Simone!" Robert finally choked out. "What the hell—?"

"I telephoned before, but you didn't answer. I came over to get my hair dryer. YOU FUCKING BASTARD!"

Then as the statue unfroze and tears started to stream down Simone's face, she blindly hurled the metal key ring in the direction of Robert Fingerhood, but it missed him by inches and landed instead on Beverly's large, white, upturned ass.

"Ouch," she said into the green grass rug.

Sobbing hysterically now, Simone ran out of the apartment and slammed the door so hard behind her that the stuffed owl nearly fell off his perch.

Beverly sat up and looked at Robert. "I have never been so humiliated in my life."

Robert nodded, still slightly dazed. "From now on I'll answer the telephone no matter how many crazy questions my mother comes up with."

"Did you know she still had a key?"

"It never occurred to me. What a shock."

"If we're shocked, think how Simone must feel. Not just seeing you the next day with another girl, but with *me* of all people."

"It serves her right for barging in unannounced, phone call

or no phone call. What a moronic thing to do! If I hadn't been so stunned, I swear I would have wrung her neck."

"Don't be so hard on her. She's undoubtedly still in love with you."

"Love?!" Robert shouted. "Are you kidding? She's in love with her hair dryer and her false eyelashes. You don't know that crazy French broad like I do!"

"I suppose not."

"I'm changing the lock tomorrow. God knows how many other keys she's had made. I don't trust that hysteric for a second."

"Maybe you should cook those steaks after all," Beverly suggested. "I'm going to get dressed."

She picked up her clothes and purse, and went into the bathroom to try to reassemble herself. She was still trembling as she pulled up her stockings and stepped into her pumps, combed her hair. To her surprise, it was not yet nine o'clock. She couldn't believe it, so much seemed to have happened so fast, she was still trying to sort out her jumbled feelings. She supposed she should feel ashamed of what had happened, but somehow she didn't, she felt almost pleased with herself. Robert had wanted her and she had satisfied him. Was there anything morally reprehensible about that? It was nice to know that an attractive man could still want her. Let Simone be ashamed that she meant so little to the man she loved that he hadn't wasted a minute, after getting rid of her, to bestow his affections on someone else. Perhaps that was finally the deepest moral shame a woman ever felt, Beverly thought, no matter what she said to the contrary: the shame of being undesirable.

Robert had cooked the steak very rare and chosen a nice Beaujolais to go along with it.

Beverly did not realize how hungry she was until she took her first bite of the steak and remembered that she hadn't eaten anything solid since early that morning when Margaret served her half a grapefruit with an obnoxious maraschino cherry in the center. Beverly had told Margaret weeks before that in addition to black coffee for breakfast, only four ounces of tomato juice or half a grapefruit were allowed on the prisoner-of-war diet, but nothing else. Margaret had taken Beverly's instructions very much to heart; although weighing close to two hundred pounds herself she did not have much use for any kind of reducing diet, not even the spectacular P.O.W. variety.

Beverly wished that Margaret could see her now, wading

through a thick filet mignon, salad with roquefort dressing, and a large goblet of Beaujolais. Margaret would be so happy to know that the war was over and all prisoners had been sent home to gorge themselves into caloric oblivion.

Just as Beverly was about to compliment Robert on the steak, the telephone rang. They exchanged a nervous glance before Robert went to answer it.

"What?!" he said into the receiver, his face tightening into lines of incredulity. "You did *what?* Oh, Christ." He glanced sharply at Beverly. "Now just stay there. Don't move. We'll be right over."

Replacing the receiver, he said, "Simone tried to kill herself."

Beverly laid down her fork and thought of Dee Dee.

"How bad is she?"

"I don't know. She was babbling like an idiot. Come on. We're going over there."

As Beverly grabbed her purse and slipped into the iridescent raincoat she wondered whether there was a full moon out tonight; strange things certainly had been happening all evening long.

They could hear Chou-Chou barking the moment they entered the small building on Fifty-Seventh Street, and climbed the three flights of winding stairs to Simone's apartment. The door to the apartment was open. They walked through the chilly living room, Chou-Chou on their heels, and found her in the bathroom behind an astrological shower curtain, lying naked in about five inches of water at the bottom of a bathtub on legs. She was curled up in a foetal position and her face was puffy from crying, but except for a slight tremor that shook her thin body she now seemed ominously quiet. A pale streak of pink colored the water in the tub, and on top of the soap in the soap dish sat a dull looking razor blade.

"Simone," Robert said, bending over her. "Let me see your wrists."

Simone obediently held up both hands. The wrists were slightly, almost neatly nicked at the veins, and a small amount of pinkish blood oozed out. For a second her eyes focused on Beverly, but there was no expression in them.

"You're going to be all right," Beverly said, wondering whether this unfortunate incident would get into the papers and ruin her life.

Model tries suicide, jealous of friend. (*Twenty die in jet crash.*)

How would she ever be able to explain to the police what she was doing lying naked on Robert's living room floor, when Simone pointed an accusing finger at her? Peter would have a fit. Beverly started to giggle, thinking of her husband's discomfort.

"Have you gone off your rocker, too?" Robert asked, glaring at her.

"I'm sorry. I didn't mean to—" She glanced guiltily at Simone. "I wasn't laughing at you."

In reply, Simone stuck out her tongue.

Robert removed the stopper from the bathtub and told Beverly to go find something warm to cover Simone with. There was a heavy plaid blanket on the lower bunk bed and Beverly pulled it off, thinking that the bunk bed arrangement looked exactly like the one in her son's room. Robert scooped Simone out of the tub and wrapped the blanket around her. Simone's teeth were rattling.

"Go see if there's any whiskey in the kitchen," Robert instructed Beverly.

On a shelf next to the dinky hot plate she found a pint of apricot brandy, half empty. Next to it was a Mexican TV dinner that had not been opened. The dinner consisted of a taco, a tamale, an enchilada, and rice, all of which were pictured in glaucous colors on the outside of the wrapper. If I had to eat that crap, Beverly thought, I'd kill myself, too. Then she poured a generous amount of brandy into what looked like an old jelly glass and brought it into the bedroom where Robert was trying to get Simone dressed, as Chou-Chou raced frantically around the room, alternately barking and crying.

Simone still seemed dazed as Robert persuaded her to drink the brandy and to finish dressing herself. A few minutes later they drove to Roosevelt Hospital in Beverly's car. A cheerful intern in the out-patient section put a band-aid on each of Simone's wrists, which had stopped bleeding by then, and said, "Now young lady, let's hope you don't try *that* again."

On the way back to Simone's apartment, Robert said to Beverly, "I think I'd better stay with her the rest of the night. You go on home."

"I feel terrible about everything," Beverly said.

"It wasn't your fault."

"I still feel terrible."

Beverly pulled up in front of Simone's building, and Robert kissed her on the cheek. "Drive carefully. We don't want two casualties in one evening. I'll phone you tomorrow."

"Goodnight—" Beverly was about to add, "darling," but something made her look at Simone who had just gotten out of the car, and when Simone looked away, wordlessly, Beverly said, "Goodnight, Robert," instead.

In the next few days Beverly had some interesting thoughts.

One thought was that perhaps she was not nearly so weak nor unresourceful as she had imagined. A while ago she would have said that both Dee Dee and Simone had more guts than she, were more alive, better able to cope with what they each had to cope with, yet when the chips were down Dee Dee killed herself and Simone had taken a stab at it (ha ha).

The second thought Beverly had was that no matter how bad things should get, she would not dream of taking her own life (I'd rather die than do that, she said to herself, amused by her humorous approach). She might weigh too much, drink more than she should, and suffer from migraine headaches, but suicidal she wasn't. There was comfort in the realization. And a kind of renewed strength.

Thought number three was simply that she had a good, if macabre, sense of humor, something that had never before occurred to her.

Beverly realized that all three thoughts were variations on the same theme—reaffirmation of her badly battered ego—and she couldn't have felt more pleased about it, or suddenly more optimistic. Maybe she was not such a hopeless case after all, maybe there was still something to be done about her wavering life, something constructive. The trip to Mexico, she now felt, had been a first step in breaking the mold. What would be the next?

That question was soon answered when she began to see Robert Fingerhood one night a week, Wednesdays, at his place. After thinking it over she told Peter she had joined an amateur theater group to which her friend Simone belonged.

"Darling, I didn't know you were interested in acting," Peter said.

"You didn't know I was interested in anthropology either," she reminded him, feeling appropriately witty.

She did not expect Peter to raise much objection to her Wednesdays, and he didn't. Why should he? It gave him one more night to pursue his own inclinations, whatever they happened to be. Now that she was going to bed with Robert on a regular basis, Beverly had stopped trying so hard to figure Peter out. In fact, it sometimes amazed her how seldom she thought of him these days. He was only her husband of eight years, father of her children, supporter of the household, the man who slept beside her at night.

"I mean," she said to her reflection in the mirror, "it's not as though he were anyone *important*."

And although intended to be sarcastic, there was a grim ring of truth in the denouncement.

Seeing Robert every Wednesday had become the focal point of Beverly's life, her week revolved around it, and she had rearranged her schedule accordingly. For example, she now washed her hair on Tuesday, instead of Friday, so it would be clean and shining for Robert the next day. And she switched her half-day of volunteer work at The Cathedral's Rummage Shop from Thursday afternoon to Monday, because Thursday, now being the day after, was devoted to rest, reveries, and reflection.

The worst time proved to be the weekend. Whereas before Beverly had looked forward to those two days of enforced closeness with her husband, she now dreaded them and tried to keep occupied any way she could. She started doing needlepoint, she took up golf, she decided to improve her French, using records. Peter was terribly impressed with her new activities, not realizing that her main objective was to remove herself from his company as often as possible. It pained her now just to lay eyes on him, he reminded her of her carefully planned and smoothly executed duplicity. Yet when they were inevitably thrown together she found herself treating him with much more charm and good nature than she previously would have thought she was capable of. But it was easy to be good-natured now that she could look forward to lying in Robert's arms the following Wednesday. Beverly had never realized how sweet deceit could be.

"Mommy, are you going to be an actress?" Sally asked her one Wednesday evening, as she was about to take off for the city, ostensibly to her theater group. "Are you going to be on television?"

Beverly kissed her daughter. "No, darling. It's just for fun."

"Little Miss Fussy made wee wee again."

"Stop giving her so much water to drink."

Little Miss Fussy was Sally's favorite doll. Beverly did not understand what was so wonderful about a doll that urinated, but apparently it meant a great deal to Sally, who was forever lugging the doll around with her.

Margaret viewed Beverly's Wednesdays with philosophic resignation. "I guess it's something you just have to get out of your system, Mrs. Northrop."

"I think that's what it must be," Beverly said, wishing she could tell Margaret how inadvertently right she was.

Her evenings with Robert had quickly fallen into a set pattern. Variance from that pattern was slight, since time was too limited to permit them the luxury of wasting a second. First they made love, then Robert cooked dinner for them, then Beverly drove back to Garden City, ready to face another week of needlepoint and charity work.

Their bodies had become attuned to each other's needs, and their main goal when they were together was to fulfill those needs with all the skill and resourcefulness at their command. Not too many words passed between them. What was there to say? The dark terrain on which they met had an exclusivity all its own, a rarity of atmosphere, a lush, hothouse quality that seemed to transcend the need for mere words. They were happy just to be together, Robert to be free of the frustrations he had felt when living with Simone, and Beverly to be free of her own frustrations, if only for a little while. There were no side issues to mar their pleasure, nothing at all to stand in the way of their pursuing that pleasure with single-minded abandon, and they plunged into each other's bodies with the ferocity reserved for warriors who know only too well that each battle may be their last. But when they emerged from combat hours later, the battle scars were invisible and the victory a mutual achievement.

Afterwards, across the dinner table, they would observe one another with curious interest. Robert would think: Can this be the same woman who only a few minutes ago—? Beverly would think: Can this be the same man in whose arms I—? As social creatures they barely recognized each other, hardly knew what to talk about, were even faintly embarrassed. Under certain circumstances physical intimacy makes strangers of people. Sometimes grotesques.

There were moments when Beverly tried to convince herself that Robert was falling in love with her. She would have liked that. It would have heightened the tension between them, made their lovemaking even more ecstatic than it already was, permitted her the possibility of falling in love with him. She did not seriously want to be in love with Robert, as that would have presented too many complications, but she felt the need to simulate a wild, hopeless passion ("Are you going to be an actress, Mommy?"), and once in bed, without planning it, she said, "I love you," in response to which Robert became even more ardently tender than before.

She never asked him what he did with himself the other six nights of the week. Although she felt certain that he went to bed with other women, she did not want to hear about them. And he, in turn, did not question her about her relations with her husband. When they spoke at all it was about general subjects: a movie one had seen, a book the other had read, politics, modern art. It was the purest and most dishonest of relationships, exquisite in its verbal omissions. They were lovers who knew everything about each other's bodies, and nothing about each other's lives.

Only once did the subject of Simone come up.

"How is she?" Beverly asked.

"Back to normal. Meaning as batty as ever."

"I really should call her."

"Why?"

"To see how she's doing."

"Do you care?"

"Yes. In a way."

"Then call her."

"I intend to."

But she never did, and they never spoke of Simone again.

Then one evening the outside world cut in on them, to their surprise. They had finished making love and were going to eat dinner, but Beverly had not gotten dressed first as she usually did. Instead, she was wearing Robert's blue terry cloth robe, and sipping champagne in the Mexican jungle while waiting for Robert to take the chops off the hibachi.

It was one of the moments in the evening that Beverly savored most of all. Still warm and tingling from the delights of lovemaking, all sensations were marvelously heightened. Champagne tasted better, a Mabel Mercer record sounded better. *Life is worth the living since you made it plain to see that lovewise you're perfect for me.*

Then the doorbell rang.

"Who is it?" Beverly whispered.

"I can't imagine."

"Are you going to answer it?"

Before he could reply, the bell rang again and a man's voice called out, "Hey, Doc, come on, open up, it's me and Anita."

"It's Jack Bailey," Robert said to Beverly, smiling. "You'll get a charge out of him."

Ordinarily, Beverly would have left the room and gone to get dressed, but she felt too contented to budge, too blissful to be so rudely disturbed. *Facewise attractive, smilewise appealing, this contented feeling isn't hard to understand.*

"Who's Jack Bailey?" she asked.

But Robert had already opened the door. A rather attractive and rather drunken man was standing on the other side, next to a rather attractive and rather drunken girl who was wearing what looked like some sort of military cap on her pale blond hair. They both saluted in unison.

"We're cruising at an altitude of thirty thousand feet," Jack Bailey said.

"And we're not even in an airplane," Anita added.

Jack waved a half empty bottle of Remy Martin in Robert's face. "How about a little drink, neighbor? Aren't you going to invite us in?"

"Sure, come on in," Robert said. "I'm with someone, but come in anyway."

"I have a feeling we're not wanted," Anita said.

"We're wanted, we're wanted," Jack said, preceding her into the apartment. "Didn't they teach you anything about self-confidence at that crummy stewardess training school you went to?"

Then he spotted Beverly with a champagne glass in her hand, her long red hair falling over the collar of Robert's terry robe, and he turned expansively to Robert.

"The mad doctor strikes again, I see. You're okay, buddy. I don't know how you do it, but you're okay."

"He's loaded," Anita said, giggling.

"I'm entitled," Jack said, "I'm off the job."

"He's a menace to air safety," Anita said.

"Beverly," Robert said, "I want you to meet a couple of friends of mine."

As he introduced them, Beverly noticed that Anita's eyes went directly to the wedding ring on her left hand and lingered there. Then Anita took the cap off her head and held it in her lap. Robert brought them glasses for the Remy Martin.

"So you two kids are back together again," he said.

Jack merely shrugged and laughed, but Anita quickly said, "I'd say that was pretty obvious, wouldn't you?"

"I'm delighted. Really delighted."

"You don't sound delighted," Anita said.

Beverly wondered what Anita meant to Robert. She felt a mystery in the air, something left unspoken. Perhaps Anita was the reason Robert had shipped Simone off to Mexico. Perhaps, while Simone was in Mexico, Robert had had an affair with Anita. Perhaps (even worse!), Robert was in love with her. Beverly did not like Anita, whom she felt was too attractive, in too serious a way. Simone was attractive, also, but she could be dismissed on kooky grounds. This one, Beverly saw, with her intuitive feminine eye, was no kook in spite of her drunken state. There was a sensuousness about her that threatened Beverly on the deepest competitive level. She felt that Anita's glow outshone her own, and she did not like it, not one bit.

Anita turned to Robert. "Have you seen Simone lately?"

"No. Have you?"

"We had lunch the other day."

"How is she?"

"Fine," Anita replied. "Not that you give a damn, you rat."

"Of course I give a damn. I've always been concerned about Simone."

Anita opened her mouth to make a remark, then stopped. Now Beverly was convinced that she was right about something having gone on between Robert and Anita. She wondered how Anita happened to know Simone. When they were in Mexico, Simone had never mentioned Anita's name.

"I'm terribly fond of Simone," Beverly said, speaking for the first time. "I met her last month in Mexico."

"Yes, I know," Anita said. "She told me."

Had Simone also told her about finding Beverly naked on the living room floor? Probably, knowing Simone. Beverly turned up the collar of Robert's robe, as though to protect herself from Anita's probing eyes.

Dreamwise so haunting, heartwise so giving . . .

"Jack," Anita said, "I think we should be going. Something tells me these people want to eat dinner."

"Sure enough."

Jack got up. He and Robert shook hands.

"It's been a great pleasure," Robert said. "Stop by any time, old buddy."

Jack thumped him on the back. "You're giving this building a bad name with all your carryings on. You realize that, don't you?"

"Next time, call first."

"If we can't trust our professional men, where the hell are we?"

"Jack," Anita said, impatiently. "Let's *go.*"

Robert handed Jack the Remy Martin bottle.

"Take me along with you," Jack Bailey sang as they danced out the door. *"If you love-a me . . ."*

Driving home that evening, Beverly did a strange thing. While waiting for the light to change on Seventeenth Street she took off her panties and threw them out the car window, then drove serenely on. Suddenly the world was filled with desirable men.

Five days later she told Peter that she was leaving him. He did not believe her until she said that she was leaving the castle too.

"I've rented an apartment in the city," she told him.

It was the first time she had ever seen Peter cry.

"Happy days are here again," shrieked the myna bird.

❁ CHAPTER SIX ❁

Anita did not like Beverly. She told Jack so after they had left Robert Fingerhood's apartment, the Remy Martin bottle passing between them as they went down the one flight of stairs to Jack's place.

"If it weren't for that bitch up there," Anita said, "Simone never would have tried to kill herself."

Jack Bailey listened, but, characteristically, said nothing. As Anita had long ago realized, he seldom wasted a word if he could possibly help it.

"I wouldn't like her," Anita went on, "even if Simone didn't try to kill herself."

The truth of the matter was that Anita's reasons for taking such an instant and overwhelming dislike to Beverly had very little to do with Simone, who was merely the smoke screen she threw up to hide behind. Beverly had certain assets that Anita would have sold her soul for, namely large breasts and a husband. Had Anita known that Beverly also had a considerable amount of money, she would not only have disliked her, she would have militantly despised her. Every once in a while a woman finds her nemesis in another woman, and Anita had found hers in Beverly.

"I thought she was sexy," Jack said, in one of his rare verbal outbursts. "She's got legs that go right up to her ass."

"And where do mine go? To my nose?"

He laughed and opened the door to his apartment, which was a hodgepodge of many different lives led in many different countries during the past fifteen years that he had been an airline pilot. A silk kimono draped across a chair was a relic from old days in Hong Kong. An elaborately encrusted beer mug from Munich sat atop a bookcase. A bullfight poster on a wall was not a reproduction purchased in a Village bookshop, but the real thing from a long ago Sunday afternoon in Madrid.

And yet nothing really worked, nothing looked right or seemed at home, Anita thought, without knowing why. She was accustomed to the same kind of nomadic hotel living as he, and any objects that either of them brought back from a foreign country remained just that—objects to be superimposed upon the essential bareness of their lives. It was the bareness that neither of them saw.

"What flight did you bid next month?" she asked, as he got some glasses from the kitchen.

"Tripoli."

"I bid Paris," she said, when it was plain that he had no intention of asking.

He had known that she was going to bid Paris, she had told him so first thing after they'd gotten back together recently. She had said, "Why don't you bid Paris, too?" and he tersely replied, "I might just do that."

But he hadn't. It was not crucial that she fly with him, so long as she knew he would come back to her. He had come back this last time, and just when she thought she lost him for sure either to the English mod girl or that other stewardess, or perhaps, oh, but that was the frustration of it, with an airline pilot as with an old-time sailor, who was to say how many girls he had stashed away in how many places across the globe?

Anita had flown long enough to have seen (and at times been part of) the multi-wheeling-dealing maneuvers of pilots when it came to women. Still, she liked pilots more than men in other professions. Doctors, actors, stockbrokers, newspaper reporters (ugh!), lawyers, football players, advertising executives. She had seen them all from the other side of the stewardess tray, looking down, and they did not hold a candle to Jack Bailey, who had helped her out of a nasty situation one of the first times she'd flown with him.

She was working the tourist section that flight; it was a rough one, too, and when she served cocktails a government clerk from Stuttgart slipped her a note in which he offered her his sexual services for the evening. When she proceeded to ignore him, he made it painfully clear what his heart's desire was by staring intently at her pantskirted crotch every time she walked by, and slopping his tongue around his lips.

"I'll bet it *shmecks gut,* Miss Schuler," he whispered, as she removed the cocktail glasses in preparation for dinner.

That was the last straw, Anita decided. Enraged, she went into the cockpit and told Captain Bailey what had happened. She would always remember how Jack had taken care of the Kraut creep in one big hurry, dumped the man in Paris instead of letting him continue on to his destination in Munich, and later that evening Jack took Anita out to dinner and tried to comfort her.

"You run across these jerks from time to time," he said. "Try not to let it get you down."

"The strange part was that he comes from the same section of Germany as my family. I kept thinking how ironic it would be if he and I were somehow distantly related."

"What if you are?" Jack said. "So one of your distant relatives is a creep."

"Yes, but . . ."

She realized that she could not explain the innuendoes to Jack, who was of Irish-Scotch heritage and had not been born in 1942 when the old country and the new were at war. After the war was over, she remembered hearing her father remark that no matter what they said about Hitler at least he had tried to create jobs for the masses and improve Germany's economy, and Anita's mother had sadly shaken her head in agreement.

Her mother sadly agreed with everything Anita's father said. She was a true German housewife, all the three *K*'s dutifully in order. Was that why Anita had felt the need to run away, to escape the sweltering confines of that 3*K* household? Because when the airline recruiters had shown up at her high school gymnasium one lovely spring afternoon, sporting colorful posters that promised TRAVEL! GLAMOUR! EXCITEMENT! Anita Schuler, just turned eighteen, was first in line, first to be tentatively accepted, first to run home and tell her dazed and bewildered parents what she had done.

"But *why?*" her father kept repeating. "*Why?* What's so terrible about Cleveland?"

(In later years, Anita would fondly mimic him for the amusement of the various stewardesses she roomed with from time to time. "What's so terrible about Cleveland?" All the girls appreciated the question, each of them automatically substituting the name of her home town in place of Anita's and simultaneously concluding, "Everything!")

Anita could not tell her father that it wasn't just Cleveland, although that by itself would have been enough even if Cleveland could boast the world's eighth tallest building and an impressive symphony orchestra housed in Severance Hall. Neither could she say that she was afraid she would end up like her mother, a submissive, compliant, provincial woman whose highlight of the year was a two-hour Cuyahoga River sightseeing tour although after having lived in Cleveland most of her life Anita could not imagine what sights her mother still hoped to see. She could not say that if she stayed put, she would surely wither and die. And the worst part was that, being a minor, she had to get written permission from her parents before the airline would agree to send her to stewardess training school.

Much to Anita's amazement, it was her mother who spoke up on her behalf. "Let her go, Paul, for my sake." That was all she said, but apparently it was enough, the way she said it, her dark, quiet eyes so accustomed to looking away, so accustomed to avoidance, now directly encountering the man she obeyed for so many years, imploring him. Anita would never forget her mother for that, yet it hurt to think of her as she so often did, wearing dresses that were always one size too large, and still making her own noodles. If Anita had had to give a congent, one-sentence description of her mother, she would have said, "My mother does not approve of Betty Crocker."

There were other things that Anita's mother subsequently would not have approved of, had she known about them. The oddball hours that Anita worked all too often with all too little sleep, the relatively low scale of pay, the scrutiny that stewardesses were put under by other stewardesses who doubled as spies and reported their nasty findings to the airline supervisors:

"Yes, I heard her talk back to a VIP with an ATC," or, "She let a passenger in tourist have a third martini," or, "She snapped at a mother of four," or, "I caught her cadging a cigarette in the galley," and so on.

Anita was used to these things. The hours, the pay, the spies. They were occupational hazards she had learned to live with. What she could not live with so readily was the repeated theory that the passenger was always right. Passengers could be rude, crude, obnoxious, insulting, demanding, degrading, and not only were you supposed to take it, you were supposed to take it with a smile. Sometimes Anita thought that her face would crack from smiling so much. "Yes, Sir." Smile. "No, Ma'am." Smile. It was only in extreme situations that a stewardess knew she could turn to the captain for help, as Anita had turned to Jack Bailey in trying to deal with the man from Stuttgart. The rest of the time, she took it. And smiled. Much as her mother had done all her life.

"You know how he met her, don't you?" Anita asked Jack, who had just presented her with a water glass half filled with cognac.

He raised an eyebrow, as though to say, "Who?"

"Beverly. He met her through Simone."

Jack waited for her to go on.

"Poor Simone! She innocently goes ahead and introduces the man she's in love with to a girl she's just met. Of all the naïve things to do. She didn't know anything about Beverly, but I'll bet she does now. Can you imagine how she must have felt when she opened that door and saw the two of them on Robert's living room floor? If it were me, I think I would have fainted on the spot."

Jack chuckled. "The mad doctor sure must have something the girls go for."

According to Simone it was a big penis, but Anita felt certain there must be more to Robert Fingerhood than just that. She had never told Jack that Robert called her from the airport and asked her for a date practically the very minute that Simone's plane took off for Mexico. She would have accepted if Jack had not beaten him to the punch by a mere day, having checked back into her life only twenty-four hours before Robert made his pitch.

"Jack and I are back together again," she had told Robert that day, "or I would love to go out with you."

"I'll put you in my come-up file," he replied, "pending the next time you two kids have another falling out."

"*If* we have another falling out."

"You will," Robert said, self-confidently.

She carefully avoided mentioning Robert's telephone call to Jack because she did not want to make him jealous. At least that was what she told herself. But, as with the reason she gave for disliking Beverly, it was not the real one. Robert was her ace in the hole. Should Jack Bailey fly away one day and not be heard from again, Anita now knew that she had Robert to fall back upon. The fact that he had called her on the heels of Simone's departure made it extremely clear that his initial attraction to her had not faded, and she wanted Jack to know nothing about that attraction, not because she feared he would be jealous (as she pretended), but because it was wiser by far not to put all of one's cards on the table.

Subterfuge and evasion. Those qualities marked all of Anita's relationships with men, her motto being: never tell a man how you really feel, it can only work against you. So she dressed herself up for men, tried to say and do the right things, tried to be gay and glittery, tried to be fun (wasn't that what men wanted—a good time?), and almost never revealed her true feelings about anything. Her conversation with men was as polite and impersonal as with the passengers she served, and behind it all lurked the same compulsion to appear cheerful, happy. "Yes, Sir." Smile. "No, Ma'am." Smile.

It occurred to Anita for the first time in her life that she was an emotional robot and a vast feeling of sadness came over her, engulfing her in its enormity. She put her head back against the silk kimono on the chair, as tears started to run down her face. Something was wrong with her, terribly wrong, and always had been. The salt of the tears tasted funny mixed with the cognac sweetness.

"What is it?" Jack asked.

"Nothing." She brushed the tears away with her hand. "I must have had too much to drink."

I'm upset, she wanted to say, *I'm confused, I'm miserable.* But to admit one's true feelings was to be vulnerable and Anita did not want that. At the same time she realized that without it, she would never have anything.

"I get maudlin when I drink too much," she said.

"Oh."

If only he would probe further, draw her out, get her to say what was on her mind. But Jack Bailey was the last man in the world to do that. He was as locked up within himself as she was. They made a cute pair all right—Detachment, Incorporated.

"Maybe you'd feel better if you ate something," he said.

She could not help smiling. Pilots were notorious for attributing all ills to physical causes, rather than to psychological ones, and yet she liked them for it. Their outlook was refreshing these days, if not always accurate. On the other hand, maybe she would feel better if she ate something.

"I could go for a hamburger," she said. "How about Max's?"

"Fine."

"We can go someplace else if you don't want to go to Max's." She could never tell how he felt.

"No, Max's is fine."

"Are you sure?"

"Yes. Fine."

As Anita slipped into her coat she realized that she was starting to feel better already; in fact she was even starting to feel hungry. It was a good feeling, reassuring. Her mother's hefty German cooking all those years she had been growing up had indeed left its mark on her, she thought, not without some degree of satisfaction. For while she might not have big breasts and a husband, like Beverly, and while she wasn't fashionably thin or chic, like Simone, she did have one asset that both of them lacked: a good, healthy, Midwestern appetite.

"I'm going to have french fries, too," she said as she preceded Jack Bailey out the door.

Jack insisted on walking to Max's.

"It's only nine blocks," he said.

Anita hated the idea of walking anywhere, it seemed so low and degrading, as though they could not afford a taxi. Her dream of utopia was to have a chauffeured limousine waiting for her every beck and call. Besides, Jack's neighborhood depressed her, she liked his old one much better, the East Fifties. After he had dumped her last October he'd moved here, and she still could not figure out why since he could easily afford something more expensive and fashionable. When she had asked him about it, he said, "This is cheaper and I'm not home that much for it to matter."

It would matter if he were married, she thought, then he would want a good address, a doorman, central air-conditioning, all the things that New York was all about. Now, as a bachelor, he was probably putting the money he saved into sound investments. The image of Jack Bailey's money busily making money that very second made Anita feel immensely better. There would be that much more for her when they got married.

"I'm glad we decided to walk," she lied, squeezing his arm.

Things were as noisy and hysterical as usual at Max's Kansas City, but they finally managed to get a booth and give their order to the mini-skirted waitress.

"Let's get a pitcher of sangría," Anita suggested after the waitress had walked away.

When Jack did not reply, she knew that it could mean one of two things. Either he had not heard her clearly and was too proud to admit it (jet pilots tended toward deafness at an early age), or he had heard her, mentally okayed the suggestion, but being as stingy with words as he was, saw no reason to say anything.

"He's the taciturn type," Anita once explained to Simone who had asked why Jack never spoke to her.

"Taciturn?" Simone said. "Personally, I think the jerk has lockjaw."

"He is not a jerk. He talks when it's important. He's very good in emergencies."

"It sounds like a thrilling relationship. What do the two of you do—sit around, waiting for the building to catch on fire?"

"That's not so funny."

"Or if things really get dull, I suppose you could accidentally manage to slice off your little finger."

"Just because a man talks a lot doesn't mean that he's intelligent," Anita pointed out. "It's *what* he says that's significant."

"Okay, tell me one significant thing that Jack Bailey has said lately beside, 'This is your Captain speaking.' Or does he let his passengers figure that part out for themselves?"

This exchange had taken place when the two girls were roommates last year, and Anita replied, "You're just jealous because I'm in love."

"You're in love with a rock."

"Jealous."

Still, Simone had a point, much as Anita hated to admit it. Simone had an unnerving way of verbally pinpointing people's flaws and weaknesses without displaying the slightest ounce of embarrassment or discomfort during the process. Her directness staggered Anita at times. Simone would say anything, no matter how horrible, if she thought it were true. Nobody was sacred, not even herself.

"You'd cut your wrists, too," Simone had said recently, referring to her abortive suicide attempt, "if you saw the man you loved fucking your married girlfriend on the living room floor. But, frankly, I lost my nerve after the first nick. They don't call it The Spoiler for nothing."

Although appalled by the suicide part, Anita was delighted to hear that Simone's big romance with Robert Fingerhood had laid an egg. She could not have stood it if Simone had gotten married before her, particularly since Simone did not even want to get married. It just wouldn't have been fair.

"Well," Anita said to her, trying to be philosophic about it, "now you can go to Lima in peace."

"Not until I've cured my vaginitis, I can't. Do you think I want to go around itching all over Peru?"

"Is that what you've got? Vaginitis? It sounds terrible, but at least you finally went to a doctor."

"No, I didn't. I looked it up in a medical dictionary that that shithead has."

"Which shithead?"

"Robert of course," Simone said impatiently.

"Why, *of course?* You've been involved with more than one."

"Do you always have to rub it in? Anyhow, the dictionary said that vaginitis can be caused by two types of orgasms—"

"Organisms," Anita automatically corrected her.

"I'm a little preoccupied with you-know-what," Simone said, laughing. "Okay, organisms. One is called monilia and the other has a long name like trichinosis. It said not to use a vinegar douche, but I don't. I use that peppermint crap."

"Aren't you supposed to go to the doctor and get something to cure it? It sounds serious."

"I've broken three appointments already with my gynecologist. I lose my nerve at the last minute when I think of those stirrups and that crazy position they put you into."

"You're just ridiculously self-conscious, that's your trouble. Your gynecologist is used to things like this. That's what he went to medical school for. You can be sure that yours won't be the first itchy vagina he's poked his nose into."

"Are you purposely trying to make me vomit?" Simone asked. "You know how easily I vomit."

"Then vomit. But go to a doctor."

"Frankly, it smells, too."

"I don't want to hear any more," Anita said. "Go to a doctor!"

"I'll think about it."

Anita had not spoken to Simone since their conversation and she wondered now whether Simone had ever summoned the nerve to submit to a gynecological examination, and if so, what the prognosis was. Perhaps Simone's days of getting screwed in bathroom sinks were finally over.

"It might be a blessing in disguise," Anita said aloud.

Instead of saying, "What might be?" like any normal person, Jack Bailey merely cocked his head at a certain angle and looked mildly perplexed.

"Simone has vaginitis," she announced, wondering whether she should mention the sangría again.

"Vagin-what?"

He really was deaf. But interested. In the past, Anita had noticed that any mention of medical terms brought a peculiar gleam to Jack Bailey's eye. All airline pilots had a morbid tendency to be obsessed with matters of health, since their job depended so much on their own physical well-being, but Jack was even more obsessive than most, and sometimes Anita thought that if she really wanted to land him, she should try developing a few exotic symptoms for him to dwell upon. Symptoms that could not be seen, so that he would just have to take her word for it. Like a strange taste in the mouth that wouldn't go away, or a funny feeling in the stomach. Maybe if she said that she walked in her sleep, that would grab him. She could say that she only did it when she slept alone.

"Vaginitis," she repeated more loudly. "She itches and burns *there*. And she's so stubborn she won't go see a doctor."

The angle of Jack's head became even more pronounced, indicating acute interest. Anita wished she could think of something more to add, but what was there to say beyond what she had already said? That Simone smelled? It struck her as too distasteful to mention, particularly when they were just about to eat, in fact the entire subject was distasteful and she was beginning to wish she had never brought it up, even if she had managed to capture Jack Bailey's undivided attention.

"I told Simone that she'd be a fool not to see a doctor," Anita said lamely, noticing that their waitress had walked by several times and Jack had made no attempt to call her over. Perhaps he had heard Anita's suggestion about the sangría, and vetoed it. It would be typical of him not to say a word. He would just continue to sit there, wordlessly, while she racked her brain trying to interpret his monolithic silence. Simone's comment about being in love with a rock had a painful ring of truth.

"How did she get it?" he said, at last.

Anita felt immensely grateful to him for having opened his mouth. If he had opened it, and said, "Duck soup," she would have felt grateful.

"I don't know," she replied.

Jack Bailey's head straightened. Did that mean the conversation was over, Anita wondered? Had his mind turned to other, more pressing things? She searched his face to see whether she could detect any sign of his planning to stop their waitress the next time she walked by, but Jack's steely blue eyes were somewhere in the stratosphere grappling with the unpredictability of clear air turbulence.

Anita returned to her first conclusion: he had not caught her mention of the sangría and was too proud to admit it. Perhaps he was waiting for her to mention it again.

"Who gets the very rare?" their waitress asked, balancing a tray over their heads.

Jack tapped his finger on the table in front of him. He could at least have said, "Me," Anita thought.

"And I get the medium rare," she said, as though hoping to make up for Jack's silence.

The waitress looked at her with contempt and walked off, revealing a run in her black ribbed stockings.

Anita decided to take the plunge. "Jack," she said hesitantly, "wouldn't you like a pitcher of sangría?"

His steely blues became perplexed, confused.

"Didn't I tell her we wanted sangría?"

Relief flooded through Anita. He had heard her after all, he had okayed the idea, he had simply forgotten to give the order to the waitress. It was a normal enough oversight, particularly for an airline pilot who flew internationally as Jack did. Those five time-zone changes were enough to scramble anyone's brain.

"I thought I told her," he said.

"No, you didn't, darling." She squeezed his hand to show that she understood and was not censuring him. "But I'm sure you meant to."

Jack looked around the restaurant, but the waitress was nowhere in sight.

"It doesn't matter," Anita said. "We can get her later. Let's eat. Don't these hamburgers look delicious?"

"I could have sworn I told her."

Anita smiled at him lovingly. He meant well. He had meant to order the damned sangría. Perhaps it was her fault for not having repeated the suggestion sooner, instead of waiting all that time.

"Please don't worry about it," she said. "It was partially my fault anyway."

"Waitresses are never around when you want them," Jack said, looking a little white at the mouth. "Have you noticed that?"

"Yes. Yes I have!"

She hopefully waited for him to say something further on the subject, something brilliant and penetrating, but he had turned his attention to his very rare hamburger and baked potato.

"Did I ever tell you that I have a habit of walking in my

sleep?" Anita asked, as she turned her attention to her medium rare hamburger and french fries.

Jack Bailey looked up, a familiar gleam of interest in his eye.

"It started several years ago . . ." Anita happily began, her earlier sadness gone. Communication, she thought. It was wonderful!

But after that evening it began to wear on her, the terrible strain of getting through to Jack Bailey, and although she did not love him any the less for it she became increasingly troubled by the communication hurdle she was trying to overcome. Jack's responses to everything she said and did were on such an abstracted level that she often felt as though she were dealing with the man in the moon, and she wondered why she had not been bothered by this particular problem of his before. Perhaps before she had not seen the problem with such painful clarity, whereas now it seemed to loom up whenever they were together. Even what should have been the most simple exchange, had begun to assume momentous proportions.

"Let's go to the movies," she might say one evening after she had cooked *Cosmopolitan*'s Ten-Minute Gourmet Dinner for him.

Instead of answering one way or the other, he would give her an ambiguous half-smile over the kirsch-flavored dessert.

"Don't you want to?" she would ask, wondering why *Cosmopolitan*'s desserts were either flavored with kirsch or Kahlúa.

"Sure."

But the way he said it was so unconvincing that she suspected he did not mean it. Maybe he was only trying to be polite.

"We don't have to go to the movies," she would say, feeling her stomach start to churn. "It was just a suggestion."

"Which movie did you have in mind?" he would finally ask, in a granite tone that would have done justice to Gary Cooper.

At that point, even if she had been thinking of a certain movie, she would nervously say, "Oh, nothing in particular. Is there anything *you* want to see?"

Whereupon Jack would get to his feet and without another word, head for the door. Bewildered, she would say, "But where are you going?"

"Out."

And it was only several minutes later when he came back

with a newspaper tucked under his arm and proceeded to turn to the movie listings, that Anita understood the reason for his abrupt departure, and sighed with relief. He had not been angry at her after all, he had not been bored, he had not walked out in irritation as she had so ridiculously feared. Still, she could not help but blame him for his inability to mouth the few simple words of explanation that would have spared her the terrible anxiety she had experienced while he was gone.

Then, as though Jack, too, understood how hard it was for him to get his point verbally across, he started to leave her notes. She never knew where she would find them, they turned up everywhere. On her pillow ("You're delicious"), Scotch-taped to her full-length mirror in the bedroom ("Pick up your clothes"), in the medicine cabinet ("You're out of aspirin, sweetie"), on top of the refrig ("Your cooking is lousy"), in her Oomphies bedroom slippers ("I dig your ankles").

Anita was by turns confused, bemused, amused, but mainly troubled. In their own way, the notes were sweet, and she felt flattered even when they were not at their most flattering, but finally they depressed her. Would she one day find a note in her diaphragm case that said, "Change your brand of jelly, or no more notes"?

Meanwhile May dragged on, May in New York, May in Paris, and once as they landed at Orly airport Anita thought how nice it would be, how corny and nice, to be a June bride. Early dreams die hard and in Anita's she had always pictured herself as a radiant June bride wearing a lacy, long-sleeved gown with a demure neckline, and carrying a small bouquet of violets. But whenever she gingerly brought up the subject of marriage, Jack Bailey said, "Forget it" in a tone that left little doubt he was serious.

Sometimes Anita wondered what she meant to him. He must care for her or he would certainly not go on seeing her. Unlike other men she had known who continued with a relationship out of a sense of guilt, long after it had ceased to interest them, she did not feel that Jack was the type to be motivated either by guilt or obligation. He was far too selfish to do anything if it didn't please him in some way, and as disturbing as it was, she had to face the possibility that her primary attraction for Jack lay in the area of sex.

Pilots were famous for their virility, even the older ones who should have been slowing down, and Anita and Jack spent much of their time together in bed, drinking champagne she had swiped from the airline and making love. There was one aspect about Jack's lovemaking that bothered her immensely. As opposed to some men who came too fast, much of the time Jack seemed to have trouble coming at all ("You and Simone should get together," she told him once), and he could go on for hours, pounding away in clenched desperation.

Frequently when he thought that at last he was going to hit home base, he would grab her so tight by the arms that she would be black and blue for days afterward, but just as frequently his expectation proved to be a false alarm, and instead of coming he would extricate himself from her, drink another glass of champagne, and then start again, this time trying a new position in the hope that that would do the trick. They had done everything except screw from the ceiling, Anita thought one evening, and she was beginning to feel like a professional contortionist.

Jack's difficulty in reaching orgasm made her extremely anxious. She knew that many women would have welcomed his slowness as a blessing, but Anita did not enjoy sex that much to want it to go on, hour after hour, particularly since it sometimes ended with no satisfaction on Jack's part.

"It's not your fault," he said once, but she believed that it was, that another woman would know what to do to excite him to the point of fulfillment. And she further believed that in spite of his reassurances to the contrary, he secretly blamed her for not being exciting or resourceful enough.

"I wish I knew what to do," she had replied, with a great sense of futility. "I feel so stupid."

Actually, she felt frightened more than anything else when Jack did not come. She felt the weight of his unspoken recriminations against her—or was she merely projecting her own sense of inadequacy? When he did come, her fear and anxiety evaporated at once, and she realized one night that she was afraid of all men, terrified, and had been ever since Terry Radomski. To surmount her fear of the enemy (yes, that was the way she perceived them), she tried to get close to them, physically close. If you were close enough, they could not hurt you.

Unlike Simone, Anita was not promiscuous but she had gone to bed with quite a few men in her twenty-five years, quite a few more than Simone suspected, and whereas Simone made love with the express purpose of trying to come, Anita (who took her own orgasm for granted), made love with the express purpose of seeing the man come. A man's orgasm warmed her. When a man came, Anita felt safe with him if only for a little while; he was too unarmed then to hurt her. Of all the men she could have possibly gotten involved with, Jack Bailey was her perfect torturer.

The weather turned unseasonably warm around the middle of May, and Anita telephoned Simone one day and suggested they meet for lunch. Simone named a dairy restaurant in the fur district, saying that the food was "very cooling."

But when they were finally sitting across the table from each other, Simone's thoughts were not on food.

"I don't understand why it should be so easy for you to come and so hard for me," she said, bitterly.

"I have a large clitoris," Anita whispered, so that none of the other diners could hear. "And it's very strategically located. That's why. Also I'm bored with this subject."

"Mine is on the small side," Simone said, ignoring Anita's last remark. "I've been looking at it a lot lately. Could that be the problem?"

Anita sighed. "Partly."

"Why only partly?"

"Because your whole attitude toward sex is screwed up. If you tried to forget about your own satisfaction for a while and concentrated more on pleasing the man, you might be happily surprised at the results."

"Do you really think so?" Simone asked, looking very interested. "I'm going to try that the next time with Stacey."

"Who's Stacey?"

"Stacey MacFaren. I picked him up at the Russian Tea Room. Don't ask me what he was doing there. He's a steel man from Detroit. Vice-President in charge of sales for one of those monster corporations. He likes to be tied to the bed with heavy chains." Simone shrugged. *"Chacun à son mishegas."*

A balding furrier at a nearby table winked at her.

"But you never told me what happened with your vaginitis condition," Anita said, trying to overlook the steel man from Detroit as quickly as possible, for fear that if she didn't, she would choke into her blueberries and sour cream.

"Well, it was a scream when I finally got up enough nerve to keep an appointment with my gynecologist. You wouldn't believe what was causing all the difficulty. I mean, it's just too *amusant.*" Simone looked up from her cottage cheese and dietetic fruit salad, and giggled. "I had a Pursette stuck up there."

"What?"

"Like for months."

"Oh, you're kidding."

Simone was laughing harder now. "No, I'm not. It got imbedded, I tell you."

"I can't believe it."

"Neither could I at first, but Dr. Resnick just pulled it out and dangled it in front of me. It had turned a sort of yellowish-brown."

"That's the craziest story I've ever heard," Anita said, realizing that she would never be able to finish her lunch now.

"Dr. Resnick said that judging by its color it looked like it had been up there for quite a while, and I had to explain to him that I have a habit of wearing Pursettes not just when I get my period, but in order to keep warm. That shook him a little."

"I just hope that this will be a lesson to you," Anita said. "Maybe from now on, you'll wear panties like a normal person."

"*Pas de tout*. I wouldn't give up my Pursettes for anything, but the next time I start to itch and burn I'll know what's causing all the trouble, that's for sure."

On the way out of the restaurant she winked back at the balding furrier. Then she said to Anita, "After I chain Mr. Steel to the bed, he wants me to sit on his fucking face. And people wonder why capitalism is losing the war in Vietnam."

Like most airline people, Anita and Jack kept on the move, either together or separately, whenever they found themselves in New York between flights. Idleness was distasteful to both of them.

Jack liked to go to museums, shows at the Coliseum, Broadway and off-Broadway plays, and most of all he liked to run around Gramercy Park to keep in shape. Because the park was so small he had determined that to run around it ten times would be the equivalent of running around the reservoir in Central Park once, and he did so every morning wearing an old sweat shirt and a pair of thermal leggings. Young mothers with baby carriages and elderly people sunning themselves inside the park had become accustomed to the sight of him.

Anita's activities tended to be more languid. She loved to window-shop along Fifth Avenue, have her hair done at one of the good salons, meet a girlfriend for lunch, preferably at the Palm Court (that dairy restaurant meal with Simone still stuck in her throat).

They both loved to dress up, go out, and be seen, and although they had not discussed it, they knew they made a striking couple. People had a tendency to turn and look back after them, as though they recognized them from somewhere, and Anita suspected that as a unit they emanated a movie-star quality. It pleased her that people never guessed what their true professions were; in fact, that part pleased her most of all, the successful masquerade they managed to pull off. One of her secret prides was that she was never taken for a stewardess, unlike most of the girls she worked with, who were immediately tabbed as such, no matter how they dressed in their off-hours.

One evening, after the theater, she and Jack ended up having dinner in the back room at Orsini's. Jack was wearing a fashionable white turtleneck pullover beneath a suit he had had made in Madrid. Anita had on an elegant mauve velveteen pantsuit, with a heavily encrusted gold cross strategically slipping down the front of the jacket. She liked the idea of appearing to be Catholic. Since the advent of Jackie Kennedy it seemed a rather chic thing to be. It was certainly more chic than Cleveland Lutheran.

She had had her hair lightened that afternoon and the gold of the cross seemed to be reflected in her ash blond hair, which was softly drawn back from her face with a thin mauve ribbon. She knew she had never looked better in her life, and there wasn't a better place than the dimly lit Orsini's in which to shine and shimmer. Even Jack, who was not given to compliments, had commented upon her appearance earlier, saying that she radiated "a Carole Lombard quality."

"I've only seen her once or twice on the 'Late Late Show,'" Anita admitted. "She was killed shortly after I was born."

"I keep forgetting how young you are," Jack chuckled.

"Young? I'm twenty-five!"

And not married, she silently added. Sometimes she thought that if she were still unmarried at thirty, she would shoot herself. To reach thirty and not have a husband seemed to Anita like the greatest failure imaginable, even an ex-husband was preferable to no husband at all, and she thought of Beverly going to bed with Robert still wearing her wedding ring. Simone had told her that when they were in Mexico, Beverly talked a lot about leaving her husband but was very unhappy with the prospect of getting a divorce.

"I don't feel sorry for her," Anita had replied. "Not for a minute. At least she's got a husband to leave."

"Well, *I* certainly don't feel sorry for her," Simone said. "She's not only got a husband, now she's got Robert, too. Who do I have beside that maniac from Detroit?"

"I thought you didn't care about getting married," Anita said.

"Even if I don't, it would be nice to be asked."

To be asked. How much that finally meant to a woman, Anita thought, more than any man could ever understand.

"My bid for Tripoli next month has been canceled," Jack said a moment later, over the fettucini Alfredo. "In fact, I won't be seeing you for a while."

The wine that had tasted so delicious only a second ago seemed to turn sour in Anita's mouth.

"Why not? Where are you going?"

"Indiana."

For a minute she did not understand.

"Back home again in Indiana," he sang softly, *"through the fields there comes the groans of aging pilots . . ."*

"Oh, no!" she said.

"Oh, yes."

Indianapolis was where the airline training school was located, and once a year every pilot had to go back for a three-week refresher course. A long time ago one of the pilots had written a new set of lyrics to the song, "Home in Indiana," describing the tribulations of the refresher course.

"When do you leave?" she asked.

"The twenty-eighth."

"That soon?"

He nodded.

That meant he would not be back in New York until late in June. It seemed terribly unfair to lose him so soon after getting him back.

"That's awful," she said, feeling the depression start to set in. "I'll miss you."

He patted her hand, an enigmatic smile on his face.

"There, there."

"No, I really will, Jack." She missed him already.

"It's only three weeks."

The least he could say was that he would miss her too, even if he didn't mean it, but he seemed to have no intention of saying anything further on the subject. She had noticed that about him in the past, his inability (or was it refusal?) to offer a word of comfort when it was most needed. He was really callous, she thought, hard and uncaring. Somehow that only made her care all the more.

"Could I please have another glass of wine?" she said, as depression closed in on her.

Later they went back to Jack's place. Anita would have preferred to go to her own, but she had recently taken a roommate to help share the rent, another stewardess, and unfortunately the girl was there tonight entertaining her boyfriend who shared an apartment with two other men. Anita had promised that she would not return until the following morning.

As soon as they got into the apartment, Jack turned on the television set to catch the last of "The Johnny Carson Show." Even when she was in a good mood, Anita could live without Johnny Carson, but when she was in a bad mood, she wished he would fall off a cliff.

"If he swings that imaginary golf club one more time, I'll scream," she said.

But Jack had fixed himself a vodka and water, after asking her if she wanted anything, and was planted in front of the TV set, oblivious to her considerations.

"I'm going to change," she announced.

Jack laughed appreciatively at an exchange between Johnny Carson and Ed McMahon.

"Nobody cares about me," Anita said, going into the bedroom where she kept a caftan for nights when she stayed over.

She removed Germaine Monteil's strawberry lip dew with a Kleenex, but left the rest of her makeup on. Then she carefully hung up the pantsuit in Jack's closet, took off her fiber-filled bra and bikini panties, and slipped into the Indian print caftan that she had picked up at a Paris boutique last year.

To compensate for the loss of her brassiere, she threw out her chest the way that magazine article had said to. *Project your bosom,* was how they put it, explaining that bad posture often made a small-breasted girl look even smaller than she actually was. Lately, Anita had cut down on the hydrotherapy treatments, which didn't seem to be getting her anywhere, and had begun throwing out her chest more often as well as doing daily bosom exercises.

One of the exercises had a double function. You were supposed to hold a hairbrush in each hand, bend forward from the waist, and start brushing your hair, using the brushes alternately. Presumably, if you did that for five minutes every day you would end up with shining hair and larger breasts. Anita had been doing it for a couple of weeks now and unless she was imagining things, it seemed to her that her breasts actually had gotten a little larger.

"I'll develop a cleavage if it's the last thing I ever do," she said to her reflection in the mirror.

Jack was watching the end of "The Johnny Carson Show" when she went back to the living room. Then the news came on, and after that a Western with Randolph Scott, which Jack seemed to have no intention of missing. He had settled down on the sofa with a fresh glass of vodka and water. If there was anything Anita disliked more than "The Johnny Carson Show," it was Westerns; the women's roles were always so insignificant and depressing.

"I'm bored," she said.

"Go visit the mad doctor upstairs. I don't hear his bed creaking for a change. It probably means he's soloing tonight."

"It's pretty late to go visiting."

"He's up. I heard him walking around a few minutes ago."

"You're just trying to get rid of me."

Jack shrugged. "You're the one who's bored."

On the screen, Randolph Scott said, "I reckon we're going to have to shoot this horse, Ma'am."

That did it.

"I'm off," Anita said. "If I'm not back in an hour, score another point for Fingerhood."

Jack sipped his vodka and water without taking his eyes off the set for a second.

"Surprise," Anita said, when Robert Fingerhood opened the door. "Did I wake you?"

"No, I was reading." He seemed pleased to see her. "Come in."

"I hope you don't mind my barging in like this," she said following him into the living room, "but Jack is watching a Western downstairs and frankly I was bored."

"I don't mind at all. Can I get you a drink?"

A few minutes ago the last thing in the world she had wanted was a drink, now it seemed like a splendid idea.

"Vodka and tonic, if you have it."

"Sure thing."

He was wearing the same blue terry robe that Beverly had had on the one and only time Anita met her. Simone must have worn the robe, too, when she was living here, and God knew how many other women. According to Jack, who had moved into the building only six months ago, there had been quite a procession of gorgeous girls in and out of Fingerhood's apartment during that time.

Yet to look at Robert, he certainly didn't appear to be a lady killer. He was nice looking in a rather studious way, although of course he did have that smile. Again, Anita could not help but wonder what it was about him that women found so immensely attractive. Perhaps kindness. Simone had said that in spite of the fact Robert shipped her off to Mexico and then prompted her to move back to Fifty-Seventh Street, in spite of finding him on the floor with Beverly, she had to admit that while they were together he tried to be considerate.

"He has a sense of responsibility," Simone said. "Even when he behaves like a rat, it's still somehow a responsible rat."

Anita could not help contrasting this with Jack's behavior. As captain of his Boeing 707, Jack was the epitome of responsibility, but on the ground she felt that she could rely on him for very little. There was an immorality about his attitude that frightened her.

"Whatever you do, don't count on me," was his favorite remark.

It was almost as though his total capacity for involvement had been relegated to the passengers whose safety was in his hands. Still, at the same time that she thought it, she knew it to be a false concept. A person's capacities were never that limited, it was a matter of extending oneself, of wanting to extend oneself, and apparently Jack did not want to. He found it easier, safer, to be concerned about the lives of one hundred and fifty passengers he would never lay eyes on again, than one woman whom he would wake up beside the next morning.

Yet instead of wondering why she still loved him, as another woman might, Anita accepted her love with the tremulous hope that in time things might improve. Hope and perseverance. Those were the guidelines she had always lived by.

"And how are you two kids getting along?" Robert asked when he handed her her drink.

"Fine, except for the fact that he's going to desert me for three weeks." She explained about the mandatory refresher course in Indianapolis. "Isn't that terrible?"

"Terrible," he agreed, smiling at her in delight.

"I think I'll sit in the hammock," she said. "It looks so comfortable."

He watched as she maneuvered herself into it, trying to keep her long, narrow skirt from riding up too far. She was very conscious of having nothing on underneath and she wondered whether Robert had guessed it. She certainly had guessed that he had nothing on underneath his blue terry robe, and she felt a bit peculiar being in a strange man's apartment at one-thirty in the morning, the two of them practically naked.

And yet, in another sense, it seemed very natural to be here, talking to Robert, much more natural than talking to Jack. There was a receptive quality about Robert that Jack completely lacked. She felt she could tell Robert anything and he would be sympathetic, but of course that was what he had been professionally trained for, just as Jack had been trained to fly airplanes.

"Robert, I wonder if you would tell me what you seriously think of Jack."

"What do you mean?"

"Well, for one thing, Jack doesn't talk if he can possibly help it. Getting him to open his mouth is like pulling teeth. Why do you think that is?"

"I don't know."

"But you're a psychologist. You must have some idea."

"Maybe the cat's got his tongue."

Anita laughed, then turned solemn again. "He's so strange, so detached, so . . . almost inhuman at times. How do people get that way? I mean, do you think there's any possibility that he may change? Loosen up?"

"Probably not. To answer your last question. How old is he?"

"Forty-four."

Robert nodded. "By now he's developed what we call character armor. Or, as my mother would say, 'He's set in his ways.' As to how he got to be like that, that's anyone's speculation. Any number of different specifics could have happened to him to make him build a steel plate around himself."

The mention of steel made Anita think of Simone's new boyfriend and she wondered whether she should mention him to Robert. She was sorry she had asked Robert about Jack. His comments depressed her.

"Have you spoken to Simone recently?" she asked.

"She stopped by the other day to tell me about her friend

from Detroit. I'm sure she's already told you. She wanted me to explain why a grown man had to be chained to a bed in order to get an erection."

"What did you say?"

"Among other things, I said I was curious to know why she assumed he was a grown man." Robert started to laugh. "Simone being Simone, replied that whenever she saw a man who was six feet two and had gray hair she took it for granted he was a senior citizen."

"Did she use those words—senior citizen?"

Robert was laughing more openly now, as though in fond recollection of the incident.

"That's my point. It sounded so comical coming out of her, with that accent, and her false eyelashes batting away in indignation at me for daring to question this guy's maturity."

"Poor Robert," Anita said, laughing, too. "Do all the women you know ask you for psychological rundowns on their boyfriends?"

"Not all of them, I'm happy to say. And the ones who do aren't usually too crazy about my answers, as I imagine you realize by now."

"Has Beverly asked you to evaluate her husband yet?"

He seemed momentarily surprised at her mention of Beverly, and Anita wondered whether she had gone too far. But then, he quite casually said, "No, she hasn't and I hope she doesn't. From the little I've heard about him, he sounds like bad news." And almost just as casually, but not quite, he added, "She's left him, you know."

"No, I didn't." Anita wondered whether Simone knew and had forgotten to mention it. "Are you glad?"

"It has nothing to do with me. She didn't leave him on my account. From everything she says, I gather that this move has been a long time coming. She's taken an apartment in Manhattan and he's moved to his club, and everyone is miserable. But money always comes in handy at a time like this, and both of them are loaded."

It was too much to bear, Anita thought. Large breasts *and* money.

"Anyhow, the thing with Beverly and me is pretty much kaput," Robert said.

"Oh? She seemed to be very fond of you. At least that was the impression *I* got when I met her."

"And I'm fond of her, but that's as far as it goes. Ironically, it turned out that just when she decided to leave her husband, he landed some column assignment that he'd been after for months. He's a newspaper reporter, you know. Now Beverly wonders whether he might have behaved differently had he gotten this big break months back. In other words, whether it would have saved their marriage. Because, apparently, it's had a very good effect on him."

"Then why do you hold out so little hope for Jack? What if something good happened to him? Wouldn't he change, too?"

"Probably, to some extent. But how large an extent? I don't feel he's very flexible any more. Don't forget that Beverly's husband is a good ten years younger than Jack. And for that matter, just because she says that he's acting like Mr. Nice Guy lately, it doesn't necessarily mean that it's anything more than an act."

"You're very pessimistic about people, aren't you?"

"Let's just say that I'm not wildly optimistic about their ability to turn into butterflies overnight."

Anita had finished her vodka and tonic. "I really should be going. You have to get up in the morning—"

The doorbell cut her off.

"It's Randolph Scott," a man's voice said. "Come out of there with your hands over your head."

"The movie must have finally ended," Anita said.

When Robert opened the door, Jack glanced quickly at the two of them, as though looking for a fast clue to what they had been up to all that time.

"I tried my best to seduce her," Robert said, "but she wasn't having any."

"I was playing hard to get," Anita said.

Robert and Jack exchanged a couple of quick boxing jabs.

"It doesn't hurt to keep in practice, does it, *amigo?*" Jack asked.

Robert looked at Anita who chose that precise moment to throw out her chest.

"The only time it hurts, is when . . . it hurts," Robert said. "*Amigo.*"

Back in Jack's apartment, he wanted to make love for a change.

"All right, Bailey," Anita said.

He liked it when a woman called him by his last name, he had once told her, it established a kind of friendly camaraderie between them. Anita did not like the idea of calling him Bailey any more than she liked the idea of making love tonight. Still she would do both pending the day she married him and could do whatever the hell she pleased.

"Aren't you going to remove that damn thing?" Jack asked, referring to her caftan. He had already gotten undressed and was waiting for her in bed.

"It's awfully light in here," she protested, glancing at the lamp next to the bed, which he seemed to have no intention of turning off.

"I don't know why all you stewardesses are so ashamed of your bodies. It's really a hangup with you girls."

Anita resented being lumped with the masses and to assert her individuality, she unzipped the robe and slipped out of it, standing up, then walked slowly across the room under Jack Bailey's unswerving gaze and into his arms. The only thing she said before he kissed her was, "I feel so fat," then she let herself dissolve into the warmth of his embrace, at the same time keeping her thoughts separate and distinct from what was physically taking place.

The reason she felt so fat and hadn't wanted to make love (she thought, as his hands began to explore her body) was because she suspected she was about to get her period. She had stopped keeping track of when it was due a long time ago. Those five time-zone changes completely screwed up the old monthly menstrual cycle for her, just as it made other stewardesses constipated, pilots absent-minded, flight engineers insomniacs.

A bulletin that the airline had circulated among its international personnel, to alert them to the possibility of such health hazards, pointed out that migrating birds never flew through more than four time-zone changes at once.

After reading the bulletin, one of the stewardesses who was bothered by chronic indigestion, said, "Can't you see all these sparrows flying south in the winter, being very careful not to travel too far for fear their stomachs will get upset? I mean, can a sparrow stop at a drugstore for Gelusil?"

"You're dry as a bone," Jack announced, after a few minutes. "It will never go in."

"Yes, it will," she said, without conviction.

"I have no intention of getting scraped. I didn't come from no Escondido on a bale of hay. I'm going to put something on."

But all he could find in the bathroom in the way of a lubricant was a tube of hairdressing called *That Greasy Kid Stuff*, which he proceeded to dab on his penis.

"Oh, this is ridiculous," Anita said, wondering what strange ingredients were about to be injected inside her. Certainly, a man's hairdressing could not be expected to contain anything beneficial to a woman's vagina, no matter how you looked at it.

"I'm against the whole business," she said, as Jack Bailey finally made a smooth and lubricated entrance into her unwilling recesses.

Several minutes later, much to her delight, he came with great intensity.

"I won't be able to add for a month," he said afterward.

Anita was thinking of all that grease and sperm swimming aimlessly around inside her, and for a moment she contemplated taking a bath in the hope of getting rid of some of it, then she decided to wait until morning.

"I'm too tired now to budge," she said to Jack, but he had already rolled over on his side and was fast asleep.

The following afternoon Jack took off for London and Anita called Simone at work to tell her that Beverly had left her husband and moved to the city.

"But Robert claims that she didn't leave on *his* account," Anita added. "In fact, he said that things between them were pretty kaput. Doesn't that make you feel better?"

In the background, a man's voice shouted, "Where the hell is that let-out muskrat poncho?"

"This whole business with Beverly is beginning to take on ominous overtones," Simone said, thoughtfully.

"What do you mean?"

"Well, my boss is flipping because his girlfriend didn't get some column assignment that she had her heart set on. Apparently, she's been crying on poor Mr. Swern's shoulder about it, and he in turn is taking it out on all the people who work for him. But here's the really weird part: Lou Marron lost the column to Beverly's husband!"

"I didn't know he worked for *The Rag.*"

"Neither did I," Simone said. "In Mexico, Beverly told me he was a reporter, but she never said for which paper, and frankly at the time I wasn't interested enough to ask."

"It is quite a coincidence."

"If you understood anything about astrology, you would realize that nothing is a coincidence. Do you know what I think it means?"

"I'm afraid to hear."

"I think it means that all of us—Beverly, her husband, you, me, Robert, Mr. Swern, Lou Marron—all of us knew each other in a previous life. We were all probably together in Atlantis. It makes me shiver just to think of it."

"You left out Jack," Anita said.

"I don't think he was with us in Atlantis. You can feel these things."

"I can't."

"You won't let youself, that's why. Stacey wasn't with us either."

"Oh, Christ, is that nut still around?"

"He's not only still around," Simone said, wistfully, "now he tells me that the chains we've been using aren't heavy enough."

On the twenty-seventh of May, one day before Jack's departure for Indianapolis, he and Anita had a big blowout. It all started when she started to cry about the fact that he did not love her. She hadn't intended to cry; it was the last thing in the world she wanted to do, mainly because she was convinced that not only would it fail to impress Jack, it would probably tend to make him contemptuous of her.

Anita knew all about the stringent demands that Jack made upon himself (and, consequently, upon other people) in the area of self-control. And still the tears had come.

They were at her place, watching an Ann Sheridan movie on television, when Anita began to cry. At first she said, "All the old Warner Brothers movies make me cry, they're such damn tear jerkers." But after Jack had glanced at her with characteristic lack of sympathy, she blurted out, "That's not really the reason. It's because you're leaving and you don't love me."

"Oh, shit," was Jack's answer. "Are we going to have a big, melodramatic scene?"

"Is that all you can say?" she asked, making no attempt now to hold back the tears, which seemed to gush out of her, as though they were the collective result of months of repression. "Is that all the comfort you have to offer?"

His mouth tightened and his eyes gave the impression of clouding over. He despises me, Anita thought, he wishes I would evaporate. That realization made her cry all the more. She simply could not help herself, the frustration was too unbearable, too painful. She felt convinced by now that her period was due any second, since it was invariably preceded by this kind of jagged, emotional tenseness, which needed only a specific trouble spot to cause it to break loose.

"You're always bitching about something," Jack said, getting up. "I'm tired of your damn bitching."

Anita was too busy crying to realize for a while that at some point he had walked out of the apartment, slamming the door behind him, and then when she did realize it, she was too miserable to care. But after she had cried herself out, it all hit her at once: Jack was gone and she did not know if it was for good.

"I wish I were dead," she said to the empty apartment. "I really wish I were dead and buried."

Then, she waited, as though for lightning to strike her, but when nothing happened she decided to eat a sandwich. She was not the least bit hungry, still she managed to convince herself that she would feel better if she ate. One thing was certain, she couldn't possibly feel worse.

That was what she thought until she found the note in the lettuce bag ("What if I hadn't wanted lettuce on my sandwich?" she would say later). The note, scribbled on a napkin, said: "It's all over between us, so stop kidding yourself about the future. See you around the hangar." It was signed with his initials, J. B.

Anita threw up for the first time in her life. Then, she vigorously brushed her teeth, choked down a straight Scotch, and called Jack's apartment but there was no answer. She visualized him sitting there in his living room, reading *Sky Fighters of World War I,* obstinately refusing to answer the telephone. If she did not speak to him tonight, she would not have another chance until he returned from Indianapolis next month, and even then he might be just as obstinate and obdurate (her new word for the week) in his refusal to have anything to do with her.

"In five years I'll laugh at this," she said.

That reminded her of an anecdote she had once heard, about a man whose wife dies very suddenly. The man was very much in love with his wife, and at the funeral he is heartbroken.

"It's a terrible thing," a woman relative says to him, sympathetically, "but in time you'll get over it. You'll see. In time, you'll be happy again."

The man looks at her with infinite sadness, and replies, "Yes, but what am I going to do *tonight?"*

Anita felt the same kind of horrible desperation sweep over her, a futility, an agony that she would not have believed herself capable of. For some reason, it was worse, much worse, than the last time he had left her, it was like compounding the nightmare. If only she could talk to him for a few minutes, hear his voice, if only she could get him to promise to call her when he returned from Indianapolis . . . if only she could be reassured that she had not lost him forever.

Forever. It was more than the mind could grasp, more than she could bear to consider. Her heart was pounding so hard that she was afraid she would keel over on the spot and die of palpitations.

She looked at the Matisse reproduction that hung over her living room sofa: the two languid ladies framed against a Moorish screen, talking to each other. One of the reasons the picture had always intrigued her was because she liked to imagine what they were talking about, and she knew that the various conclusions she had reached from time to time were a direct counterpart to her own mood of the moment. Now she was convinced that one of the ladies was telling the other about a tragic love affair of the past, and how it had virtually ruined her life.

It was nearly eight-thirty. She drank another Scotch and dialed Jack's number again and let it ring ten times, but there was no answer. Then, something occurred to her. Perhaps he had stopped off at Robert Fingerhood's apartment. Why hadn't she thought of that before? With renewed hope, she dialed Robert's number.

"No, I haven't seen our captain tonight," Robert said. "What's the matter? Did you two kids have another fight?"

Anita told him what had happened, then said:

"I feel so miserable that I want to kill myself. I've never thought of killing myself before, but now I know how Simone must have felt when she made that crazy attempt. I just can't face the possibility of living without Jack. At least if he would answer the phone, if I could just *talk* to him—"

"You don't know for sure that he's at home. Maybe he stopped off at a bar after leaving your place. He's probably sitting at Max's Kansas City this very minute, getting plastered."

"I'd get plastered, too, if I left someone a farewell note in a lettuce bag," Anita said, wondering whether she should call Max's after she hung up. "I mean, why a lettuce bag? I might not have found that note for a week. Don't you agree that that's a nutty thing to do?"

"It's pretty nutty," Robert said, "but in character."

"What if I call Max's and he's not there? Then I'm really going to want to kill myself. There's a bottle of sleeping pills in the medicine chest here, compliments of my roommate. Ever since I found Jack's note, I've had the most overwhelming urge to swallow the whole bottle and die."

"You wouldn't necessarily die."

"Oh yes, I would. There must be about thirty pills in the bottle. It's enough to kill a horse."

"I'll take you on a tour of a mental institution sometime and show you people who swallowed thirty sleeping pills, then unconsciously vomited them up, and lived, but as dribbling, brain-damaged idiots. And I'm not kidding or exaggerating, believe me."

"I never heard of that," Anita said, horrified by the picture he had evoked.

"The nuthouses are full of them."

"That's ghastly. I don't even want to think about it. But I could never slash my wrists, like Simone tried to do. The sight of blood makes me ill."

"I guess you'll just have to live," Robert said cheerfully. "Unless you plan to throw youself under a subway train, or blow your brains out with a shotgun."

"I never realized how hard it was to commit suicide. Oh, Robert—" she started to cry, "I don't know what to do, I just can't stand it. The pain. I just can't bear it, it's so horrible."

"I'm sorry, baby, I'm really sorry. Why don't you fix yourself a stiff drink and try calling Max's? Maybe you'll get him there."

"That's exactly what I'm going to do," Anita said, not bothering to mention the fact that she had already had two stiff drinks and they hadn't helped one bit. "And in case he should stop in to see you later on, please tell him to call me. Tell him you're afraid that I'll kill myself, if he doesn't call me. Will you do that?"

"I promise," Robert Fingerhood said, "providing you promise not to kill yourself."

"I promise."

Jack was not at Max's Kansas City. Anita telephoned Simone and said she wanted to kill herself.

"Don't do it," Simone cautioned her. "Eat hot hors d'oeuvres instead. Ever since I tried to slash my wrists in the bathtub, I've developed a new outlook on this business of suicide."

"What's your new outlook?"

"Well, I say to myself, what if I were successful and were just about to go under and the telephone rang, and it was Eddie Fisher asking me to run away to Grossinger's with him for the weekend? Wouldn't I be sorry that I couldn't make it?"

"I prefer your old attitude," Anita said, hanging up.

It turned out to be one of the worst nights Anita had ever spent in her life. She rang Jack's apartment every half hour all night long, and by morning he still had not answered and she had lost two pounds. Ironically, when she looked in the mirror, she looked fresh and vibrant, as though she had just awakened from a deep, restful sleep.

There was no point in trying Jack after eight in the morning because that was his departure time for Indianapolis, and unfortunately she did not know which hotel he would be staying at when he got there, since he himself had been uncertain. The prospect of calling him at the training school was a bleak one. Jack would resent being bothered when he was in the midst of proving his ability as a pilot to the airline authorities; in fact, he would probably be infuriated.

Three weeks. It was like a prison sentence, she thought, wondering not only how she would manage to live through it, but worse, was there anything to look forward to at the end of that time?

Despair makes people very alert, Anita realized during the next few days.

When she went to her bank to cash a check, she noticed a sign in the teller's window. It said: *A camera will film any holdup in this bank.*

"Is that a new sign?" she asked the teller.

"No, Ma'am. It's been there since last year."

"Where's the camera?"

The teller, a dark-haired girl with glasses, gave her an unfriendly look and cracked her chewing gum.

"It's here."

Anita wondered whether there really was a camera that could film a holdup, just as she had always wondered whether the speed of highway drivers could be timed by radar, or whether both signs had been put in their respective places to frighten off potential robbers and speeders.

The next thing she noticed was that the man at the dry cleaner's had a wart next to his nose. She had been doing business with him for close to two years now, and she had never seen the wart before. Only the fear of appearing rude and idiotic kept her from asking whether it was a new wart.

When the man handed her her freshly cleaned and pressed summertime uniform, she said, "I'll bet we're going to have a long, hot summer."

"What are you worrying about, Miss Schuler? You'll be in a nice, cool airplane."

He pronounced it air-a-plane, as so many New Yorkers did. When Anita had been transferred east from Chicago, she was amazed at first by the number of people who mispronounced that particular word, then she had gotten used to it. Now, for some reason, she was amazed all over again.

The next thing she realized about despair was that it made her very eager to please, she suddenly wanted everyone to like her. It was no effort now to smile at all her passengers, no request of theirs was too bothersome, no drunk too loathsome. Even when a three-year-old boy threw up all over her new couturier uniform, on a flight from Athens to New York, she was not disconcerted.

"Don't worry about it," she said cheerfully to the boy's mother, after she had cleaned herself off as best she could. "It happens all the time."

"In that case, young lady, can you tell me why your airplane doesn't stock Dramamine?"

"Yes, Ma'am, because Dramamine makes pregnant women very ill. It would mean we would have to ask every female passenger whether she was pregnant before giving it to her. And that could be a bit embarrassing."

The woman looked at her with disdain. "That's the most stupid answer I have ever heard."

"Yes, Ma'am."

"And that's the next most stupid." The woman smoothed her son's hair. "Pregnant women!"

But it was not until Anita went to bed with Robert Fingerhood, the day after her return from Athens, that she understood the lengths to which despair could drive a person. Because her motives for going to bed with him were all wrong, they all had to do with Jack, not Robert, Jack who did not love her, Jack who had abandoned her, Jack who would never marry her. And the moment that Robert put his arms around her, she knew she was doing something wrong but she had done it anyway. She desperately needed to be made love to by a man who thought she was desirable.

It was she who had telephoned Robert and asked him if he felt like taking her out to dinner.

"I'll cook dinner for you," he replied. "I'm sure that Simone has told you all about my hibachi-champagne bit."

"You mean, in the Mexican seduction den?" she asked, laughing. "Yes, she told me. She also told me that you're a first-rate cook. What time should I be there?"

"How about seven?"

"Fine. Can I bring anything?"

He hesitated. "There is something, but I'd better not say it."

"No, tell me."

"I can't."

"Why not?"

"I can't explain. Please forget that I even mentioned it."

"Okay, but . . ."

She could not imagine what he was referring to, and it was only several hours later after they had made love that he said, "I can tell you now what it was. The thing I wanted you bring."

"Yes?"

He kissed her ear. "Your diaphragm."

"Did you really think you would make love to me tonight?" she asked, looking at him in the semidarkness.

"Frankly, no. I mean, I was hoping I would. I've wanted to ever since I met you, but I didn't think you were interested."

"Why did you think I called you, then?"

"Because you were lonely and upset about Jack. And because you like me. And if that's all it had turned out to be, just a nice, pleasant evening, I would have accepted it on exactly that level. But now I'm glad it turned out to be something else. Aren't you?"

"Yes," she said quickly. "Yes, of course."

But she was not at all sure. Even coming into the building earlier in the evening made her feel uneasy, it seemed so strange to be coming here to see someone other than Jack, almost treacherous in fact. And particularly someone whom Jack knew, a mutual friend. It would have been much easier, she realized now, to go to bed with a complete stranger. There were too many crosscurrents with Robert, not only Jack, but Simone who had undoubtedly told Robert that she used a diaphragm, for why else would he have assumed that she did when practically everyone was on the pill? Anita was afraid to consider what other inside information Simone might have traitorously passed on to Robert.

"Your breasts are larger than I had imagined they would be," Robert said, turning on the radio behind the bed.

"Oh, really? Do I seem very flat chested in clothes?"

"Well, no, not exactly . . ." He looked embarrassed. "But Simone did once mention that you wore padded brassieres."

"Is there anything about me that she left out?"

Anita was furious with Simone, and yet pleased at the same time that Robert had not been disappointed in her shape. It convinced her once and for all that those daily breast exercises really worked, and she made a mental note to do them five additional times each day from now on. She also made a note to be sure to call Simone tomorrow and tell her to drop dead.

A rock-and-roll group on the radio began to sing:

Where will the words come from when I tell you I don't want you, I don't love you any more?

But if you were Jack Bailey, you did not ask yourself questions like that, you did not feel the necessity for appropriate words. You simply left a callous note in a lettuce bag and went on your merry way. Betrayed, betrayed, Anita thought. Where had everyone's sense of responsibility gone?

Then she remembered Simone telling her that in the final analysis Robert proved to be responsible, and indeed Anita could feel a ring of truth in the remark, for she already sensed that merely by virtue of having gone to bed with her, he had assumed a certain moral commitment. He would not crassly abandon a woman the way Jack had done. He might get rid of her (as he had gotten rid of Simone), but he would go about it differently. After Simone had moved back to Fifty-Seventh Street, Robert had come up one afternoon and fixed her shower. Anita could just imagine asking Jack Bailey to fix her shower.

"What do I look like?" he would probably reply. "A handyman?"

And again, the sting of Jack's granite unconcern brought tears to her eyes. A few words of kindness from him would have made all the difference in the world. Yet he was either incapable of saying them, or he was so insensitive that he did not realize they needed to be said. How could she love a man like that, she asked herself now? Was she really such a masochist? But the answer lay buried somewhere in the tangle of her confused emotions.

She and Robert made love one more time before going to sleep, and the last waking thought she had was that he was longer than Jack, but Jack was thicker. Then she put her arms around him and kissed him on the shoulder and fell fast asleep, exhausted and troubled.

In the middle of the night she had a dream about Jack, his airplane was going down in flames over the Atlantic, life rafts and fire loomed in the vast expanse of water, passengers were hysterically jumping out of the emergency exits, but during the entire nightmare Captain Bailey maintained a steely-mouthed pose at the controls, firm and unswerving, as though this particular catastrophe could not be happening to him.

Then, toward morning, Robert awakened and started to make love to her again, and somehow it was all intermingled, Robert's hands upon her, Jack's hands upon the controls. They were fused together into one unshakable grip, and she knew all over again that she should not have gone to bed with Robert out of despair, because the mechanics of physical satisfaction were never enough if the emotional satisfaction was missing. She had learned that from experience. She should have remembered that when you loved a man you brought to bed a quality of exhilaration that was its own exciting reward. It wasn't just what the man did in bed, it was how you perceived him before he did it that made the essential difference. And although Robert was a passionate and tender lover, objectively a better lover than Jack, it was Jack whom she loved, Jack whom she wanted at the very moment that Robert's body was pressed tightly to hers.

Anita called Simone the next day, and said, "You've got a big mouth. I'll never tell you anything personal again."

"What are you talking about?"

"I went to bed with Robert last night, *your* Robert, and he told me that you had told him about my wearing padded brassieres. Also, he seemed to know for a fact that I use a diaphragm, and I can't figure out how he could be so sure, if you hadn't filled him in."

"You went to bed with Robert!" Simone hissed. "How could you do such a thing?"

"Why not? You aren't involved with him any more. You've got Mr. Steel and all those chains."

"Stacey has nothing to do with Robert," Simone said indignantly.

"I should hope not."

"Don't be a sarcastic bitch."

"Look," Anita said, starting to feel very sidetracked. "I called *you* up to give *you* a hard time. You can't turn the tables on me just like that."

"Oh, really? Well, I'm turning them, Miss Norforms, and in case you're interested I told Robert about those little suppositories too."

"DeGaulle is a monomaniac," Anita said.

"There's a neo-Nazi movement going on in Germany," Simone replied.

"Bitch."

"Cunt."

Each girl hung up, feeling that she had had the last, definitive word. Then they proceeded to go about their separate, daytime businesses, looking forward all the while to the men they were going to see that evening. Simone was meeting Stacey for dinner at the Russian Tea Room, then they were going to try out the new, heavier chains that he had ordered, and Anita was playing hostess for Robert who had invited the staff of The Child Guidance Center to his apartment for their annual whiz-bang.

Three days later, Anita woke up on a layover in Paris and discovered that she had crabs. At first, she couldn't believe it. Things like that did not happen to nice, clean, immaculate, respectable, hygienic people who took two showers a day, but it had happened, she hysterically realized, as she managed to snare one of the midget beasties and stick it under the lamp light, where the tiny thing, shaped exactly like a miniature crab, confronted her in all its hideous transparency.

The next horrible thought she had was how many more of its brothers and sisters were crawling around in her bleached pubic hairs at that very moment. She lit a cigarette, controlling a strong urge to scream at the top of her lungs. At first, before she realized what it was that she had, she began to think (because of all the itching) that she'd come down with Simone's unfortunate vaginitis syndrome, but some instinct told her that she and Simone, being as different from each other as they were, were not apt to be afflicted by the same malady, not unless there happened to be a worldwide contagion of the bubonic plague running loose.

Anita just knew that whatever it was she had, it was in some way a reflection of her particular personality, just as Simone's Pursette-vaginitis was a reflection of hers. Then when she caught and inspected the wretched crab, she remembered that she was born under the sign of Cancer, which was symbolized by the crab, and she couldn't help wondering whether she had been struck by a kind of terrible, astrological misfortune. There was a certain comfort in thinking that the stars were to blame for this miserable, but perhaps inevitable turn in her life.

"I am not going to panic," she told herself, after which she let out a loud, first-soprano shriek that brought the chambermaid running.

"Qu'est-ce que c'est, Mademoiselle? Qu'est-ce que c'est le problème?"

"Rien," Anita said, shakily puffing on her cigarette. *"Pardonnez-moi."*

"Ils sont fous, les américains," the chambermaid mumbled as she left the room, shaking her head.

Anita crushed out the cigarette, lit another, and telephoned Robert in New York, praying that he would be home. To her relief, he was.

"You gave me crabs," she said, scratching and smoking as she spoke into the receiver. "I just want you to know that I think it's a terrible thing to do to anybody. Even your worst enemy."

He let out a long, low groan. "Crabs. Oh, no. Beverly."

It took Anita a second to understand what he was saying. "Did you get them from her?"

"I didn't even know I had them until this very second, but now that you mention it, I have had a peculiar itch these last few days."

"I thought you weren't seeing Beverly any longer. You told me it was all over between the two of you, so how could you have gotten crabs from her?"

Robert sounded reasonably embarrassed. "I'm not going to see her anymore, but I did see her recently."

"How recently?"

"About a week ago."

She felt cruelly betrayed. "Do you mean to say that you've been going to bed with both of us during the same period of time, you miserable bastard?"

"Now don't get excited," he said nervously. "I only overlapped twice. And besides, I told Bev that it was definitely finished last night."

"Last night?!" Anita screamed, scratching more vigorously than ever. *"Last night?!* Do you mean to say that the minute I turn my back you jump into bed with that blowsy broad—?"

"There's no point in getting hysterical. I have no intention of seeing Beverly again."

"I don't believe you. You're lying. You're in love with her."

"I am not in love with her, but even if I were, who are *you* to talk? You're in love with that tongue-tied lunatic downstairs."

"He is not a lunatic," Anita said, thinking nevertheless that Robert had a point about her objections to Beverly. "And actually this is a silly conversation because all I'm really interested in at the moment is how to get rid of these damn crabs. Do you know what I can take for them?"

"Go buy a bottle of Campho-Phenique at the drugstore

and pour it over the entire pubic area. That will knock them out in no time."

"Campho-Phenique? That's what I use for cold sores."

"Well, now you'll use it for pediculosis pubis."

"Is that what they're called?" She was thinking of that medical dictionary he owned. "You sound like you're an authority on the subject. Has this happened to you before?"

"Only once when I was in Korea, and luckily I learned about the Campho-Phenique treatment from my sergeant. He's a dentist now."

Anita failed to understand what the dentist part had to do with anything.

"When we went to Japan on leave," Robert said, "I got laid and he got tattooed. He said that for two bucks he wanted something permanent. The tattoo said, 'Mother' and he's been trying to get rid of it ever since."

Anita could feel the panic sweep over her at the thought of her most intimate area being infested with disgusting, foreign organisms.

"He specializes in porcelain jackets now," Robert said. "Apparently, there's a fortune in porcelain jackets."

"I feel like a leper. In fact, I'm going to hang up and go to Le Drugstore, but immediately. I sure hope they have Campho-Phenique. Come to think of it, if you got them from Beverly, where do you suppose she got them?"

"That's what I've been wondering for the last few minutes. Probably from her husband. She says she hasn't been sleeping with him lately, but I don't believe her. And Christ knows where he picked them up."

"Maybe from that girl reporter he works with on *The Rag*."

"Why do you say that?"

"I don't know. But if she's having an affair with Simone's boss, she could also be having an affair with Beverly's husband. From what Simone says about her, she hardly sounds like Miss Goody-Two-Shoes to me."

"I guess it's possible."

"For all we know, Mr. Swern gave the crabs to Lou Marron, and she gave them to Beverly's husband, and he gave them to Beverly, and Beverly gave them to you, and you gave them to me."

"We are all linked together in strange and mysterious ways," Robert said solemnly, starting to scratch himself for all he was worth, just as Anita began to wonder whether they all hadn't been together in Atlantis at that.

When Anita's plane landed six hours late at JFK two days later, she no longer had crabs and New York was in the midst of its first summer heat spell. The taxi ride into the city was suffocating. Anita thought she would faint for sure, and then when she got to her apartment, she did. Luckily, Nan, her new roommate, was there to witness the collapse and Nan later told her:

"You sank to the floor like a person doing a strange, slow motion dance."

"It must be the heat. It's overwhelming. I've never felt anything like it."

Still, the next morning she went to her doctor, who asked her when she had had her last period.

"I can't remember," Anita said. "I don't keep track any more."

And she explained about the menstrual irregularity that afflicted many stewardesses on international jet flights.

After the doctor had examined her internally, he took a blood sample and said, "I suspect that you are pregnant, young lady."

"Pregnant!"

It was the same reaction that Anita had had to the crab situation. Ridiculous, impossible, this could not be happening to her.

"But I can't be pregnant. I'm very careful. I always use my diaphragm, and I put plenty of that expensive jelly on it, too."

"I said, I *suspect,*" Dr. Koch said patiently. "I didn't say I was certain, but unfortunately all the symptoms are there. Your uterus feels rather hard. That's one of the first signs. Tell me, have you been nauseated lately?"

"Certainly not."

Then she remembered throwing up after finding Jack's farewell note in the lettuce bag. But who wouldn't throw up under the circumstances?

"I did have a bad moment recently," she admitted, "but I'm sure that it was brought on by a situation that I would rather not go into."

"Your breasts are swollen," the doctor said.

Anita felt herself blush. "I've been doing certain . . . exercises to try to make them larger, if that's what you mean."

"I should get the results of the blood test from the lab tomorrow afternoon, and then we'll know for sure."

Anita hated him. First, he had upped her diaphragm size and now he was trying to terrify her by implying that she was pregnant. He was a monster, she decided, a gynecological monster who enjoyed frightening vulnerable young girls like herself.

"I'm sure that you'll find you are mistaken, Dr. Koch," she said.

"We'll see soon enough. Call me tomorrow, anyway."

"If you want to know what I think, I think you're barking up the wrong tree."

"We'll see. And in the meantime, just to be on the safe side, I'm going to give you an injection to try to bring on your period. It would be very helpful, you know, if you could remember even approximately the last time you menstruated. The more overdue you are, the less possibility there is of this series of injections working."

"Series?"

"There are three injections in all. Unless this first one brings on your period overnight, I want you to come back tomorrow for another, and the day after that, too."

"But what if the blood test turns out to be negative?"

"Unfortunately, the negative result is not always one hundred percent foolproof. It might come back negative and you could still be pregnant. Sometimes it does not show up right away."

"What if it comes back positive?"

"Positive is positive," Dr. Koch said firmly.

"I think the last time I had my period was on a layover in Rome, but I'm not certain." Anita felt as though she were going to vomit any second. "I guess I could check with Crew Sked and try to figure out when that was."

"That's a good idea," Dr. Koch said. "And now please roll up your sleeve."

"Frankly, that layover in Rome seems like a long time ago."

"I'm sorry to hear that, but try to get the date anyway."

Anita left his office in a state of dismay and confusion, marched into the Palm Court of the Plaza, drank three Brandy Alexanders and picked at a lobster salad, remembering a remark attributed to Byron about the eating and drinking habits of women. According to Byron, there was something indecent about watching a woman eat or drink anything, unless it happened to be lobster salad or champagne, and Anita felt that if the eighteenth-century poet were still alive he would make a gracious allowance to include Brandy Alexanders in his list of exclusives.

In secret we met, in silence I grieve that thy heart could forget, thy spirit deceive . . .

The rosy pink lobster salad stared back at her as though in mournful recognition that Dr. Koch was right in his prognosis. She thought of the note Jack had left in the lettuce bag. She thought of Jack. Had he ever cared for her at all?

Then she remembered something about the layover in Rome. She was having a cup of espresso with another stewardess at the El Greco café, and the girl said:

"Are you cold, or is it just me? I'm freezing."

"It's cold for April," Anita replied, "and I'm doubly cold because I got the curse this morning."

It was near the end of April and the other stewardess said, "Well, May will be here soon and we'll warm up."

Tears fell softly, quietly onto the curled endive leaves of Anita's salad, as she realized that her period was approximately three weeks late. She wanted to scream. Robert Fingerhood had given her crabs, which she'd gotten rid of in twenty-four hours, but Jack Bailey had given her a child that she could not have, and it was going to take more than twenty-four hours to try to get rid of, and a hell of a lot longer than that to try to forget.

The body knows who's responsible for what, Anita thought, suddenly feeling very wise and very pregnant as she tried to hold back the mounting waves of hysteria against the gentle, *art nouveau* background of the Palm Court.

When she arrived at Dr. Koch's office the following afternoon, for her second injection, he said, "I regret to tell you, Miss Schuler, that the test came back positive."

And positive is positive, Anita thought, wondering whether it would be indiscreet if she fainted. It was just another day in June, everyone else was going about his routine business in New York, the sun was shining, and she was having a nervous breakdown. The dreadful reality of Dr. Koch's words hit her all at once. Words. Terrible words. They were so cold and unassailable.

The test came back positive.

Sir, you have cancer.

Madam, your child is going to die.

Sorry about that, but positive is positive. How did people go on, she asked herself.

"Please roll up your sleeve, Miss Schuler. There is still a possibility that this will work."

Anita did not tell Robert about her condition until the

third injection failed to bring on her period. Then she said: "Guess what? I'm pregnant."

At first he looked at her in an odd way, as though he resented being pointed to as the guilty party.

"No, no," she said, when she realized what the look meant. "It's not you, it's Jack."

That disarmed him. "How can you be sure?"

"Dr. Koch claims that my symptoms are too fully developed for it to have been a very recent impregnation. And I've only been going to bed with you very recently. Dr. Koch says that it looks to him as though I'm in my sixth or seventh week."

"What are you going to do?"

"Go to Puerto Rico. There's a hospital there which I understand is pretty good."

To her surprise, he said, "I'll go with you."

"Will you? Really? Oh, Robert, I—"

She was so stunned by his gesture that it took her a moment to finish the sentence. "I appreciate that more than I can say. It's very kind of you."

"That's me," he answered with a bitter smile. "Doctor Kindness."

"Incidentally," she asked, "what ever happened to Beverly?"

She had been so busy with her crabs and her pregnancy that she'd almost forgotten the competition. But why should she think of Beverly at a time like this? Why should she care? Could she possibly be falling in love with Robert?

"I told you I'm not seeing her any more."

He's lying, Anita thought, feeling very panicky.

"Is she back with her husband?"

"The last thing she said to me was that she was going to get a divorce, and that's all I know."

"You know something? I just happened to think of a guy she might like, he's an old friend of mine. His name is Ian Clarke. He's an Englishman. In fact you might have met him at my party, he's quite tall and he was wearing a black turtleneck sweater."

"No, I don't remember him. But why are you so concerned suddenly about fixing Beverly up?"

"Perhaps I just feel that one good deed deserves another. You're being so nice to me about the Puerto Rico thing I can't help wanting to do something nice myself for someone else. And Ian is very, very nice. He's in television."

She strategically left out the fact that Ian was a dedicated fortune hunter, which of course was what made it so perfect. Ian wanted money and Beverly had it. If Beverly got interested in Ian, it would serve her right for having big breasts, and it would also effectively keep her away from Robert.

"I'll tell Ian to call her," Anita said, "providing you don't mind. I really think they'll like each other."

"Why should I mind?"

The next day Anita made two calls. One was to Ian to give him Beverly's telephone number, but, unfortunately, he could not be reached just then, the studio told her. Anita said that she would call back. The other call was to Jack Bailey in Indianapolis to ask him to send her money for the abortion. The call to Jack was very unpleasant. For one thing, there was a bad connection, and that, combined with Jack's hearing problem, created a grotesque series of misunderstandings. Although when Anita thought about it later, she wondered how much of the mixup was due to technical difficulties, and how much to Jack's final unwillingness to comprehend what she was telling him.

For example, when she asked him to send her five hundred dollars for the operation, he replied:

"Why do you want five dollars?"

As the telephone static droned on.

But at last terms were clearly defined and he agreed to wire the money immediately. Then, he said, "I hope everything works out okay. I have to go back to class now."

"Robert is coming to P.R. with me," she said, feeling an uncontrollable desire to get in the last word.

"That's nice," Jack replied, as though he were talking about the going price for mushrooms.

Through the airline that Anita worked for, she arranged to fly to San Juan via Trans-Caribbean Airlines (the route of the tradewinds), but in order for it to cost her practically nothing, she also had to go on standby. That meant not having a firm reservation and going out to the airport on the designated day with the hope of getting on Robert's flight.

"I know it sounds like a risky thing to do," she told Robert who, of course, had to pay full fare for his ticket and was, therefore, assured of a seat, "but the odds are excellent that I'll get on. There's usually a cancellation, or else the plane isn't filled to capacity to begin with."

"You're in the business," he said. "If you're not worried, I'm not worried."

"Don't you think that's a beautiful slogan: the route of the tradewinds? It reminds me of old Hedy Lamarr movies."

On June fourteenth, exactly one week before Anita's twenty-sixth birthday, she was busily packing for the trip to San Juan when the telephone rang.

"You don't know me," a female voice said at the other end, "but my name is Lou Marron and I'm a reporter for *The Rag.*"

"Yes?"

Anita was staggered to realize that this was the woman who was having an affair with Simone's boss (and maybe Beverly's husband, too), but even more importantly, the woman who might have been instrumental in passing along those disgusting crabs to her.

"Yes?" she repeated.

"My editor wants me to write an article on airline stewardesses," Lou Marron said. "How stewardesses feel about the uniforms they have to wear on the job, how they dress when they're off the job, what their social life is like, the travel aspect. It holds a lot of glamour for a lot of women who can't travel, to think of someone like you eating dinner on the Via Veneto one day and strolling down the Ramblas the next day."

You don't know the half of it, sister, Anita felt like saying, thinking about the El Greco café.

"In other words," Lou Marron said, "I'd like to interview you for my paper. Are you agreeable?"

"Yes, yes, I am, but I'm afraid that it's going to have to wait a couple of days. I'm on my way to San Juan practically this very minute to take in a little sun. I'll be back on the seventeenth. Do you want to call me then, or should I call you?"

"I'll try to call you, but in case I miss you, here's my number. I certainly hope we can get together and I promise not to take up too much of your time."

"I hope we can get together, too," Anita said, thinking that she would like to meet the woman who went around giving innocent people like herself body lice.

Several hours later at the airport, Anita was casually informed that she could not get on the plane for which Robert had a reservation.

"I'm sorry," the desk clerk said, "but the flight is all filled. No cancellations."

"I'm being bumped," Anita said. "I can't believe it. This practically never happens."

It was decided finally that Robert would get on the plane

and Anita would follow later on one of the two more flights scheduled for San Juan that day. The desk clerk told her that she stood an excellent chance of getting on one of those flights.

"This is crazy," Anita told Robert, as she kissed him goodbye. "I'm the one having the abortion and I'm the one being left behind."

"I'll be waiting for you at the Hilton. Don't worry, you'll get there."

"Remember that route of the tradewinds business?" she asked. "Well, it doesn't sound like an old Hedy Lamarr movie anymore. It sounds more like Boris Karloff now."

"Take it easy," Robert said. "Everything's going to be all right. You'll see. We'll drink lots of Banana Daiquiris when it's all over."

"I'm allergic to bananas."

❁ CHAPTER SEVEN ❁

By the time Lou tracked down Anita and made an appointment to meet her, she had already interviewed three stewardesses from other airlines, and decided that they were a curious combination of the nurse and the courtesan. When she spoke to Anita about their meeting, Anita said:

"Oh, let's have lunch at the Palm Court. I just love it there, don't you?"

Lou not only didn't love the Palm Court, she actively despised it, but since she needed Anita more than Anita needed her, she knew she had better be gracious about it. Being a reporter taught one the strategy of graciousness. It also created a deep, underlying frustration best summed up by a remark that Lou had once heard Peter Northrop make in an unguarded moment.

"Sometimes I wonder why *I'm* interviewing *them*. You know what I mean. Why aren't they interviewing *me?*"

Lou was convinced that every reporter felt the same way from time to time, if not always. There was a terrible ambivalence in the profession. You felt both vastly superior to your subject, and vastly inferior, and all at once. Lou had realized quite a while ago that even when she thought she wasn't evaluating the other person in terms of herself, she most definitely was. And, of course, that was why so many reporters turned in so many bitchy interview pieces, just as she had. The blow to the ego was often just too damn hard to swallow.

The morning of the Palm Court lunch meeting, Lou put on her sleeveless purple tent dress, her chunky purple slave bracelet, her avocado T-straps, and ran a fast comb through her Sassoon cut, which was still very much with her. After Peter had landed the column assignment, she decided that if Tony Elliot ever mentioned changing her hairstyle again, she would tell him to go fry ice. So, naturally, being the creepily intuitive person that he was, he never said another word about it.

Losing the column to Peter was the second worst thing that had ever happened to Lou in her life, the first being the loss of her daughter, Joan. She had recently received a telephone call from her mother in Philadelphia, saying that Joan was having a great deal of trouble in school, her grades were way below what they should be, and teachers were calling attention to her academic underachievement.

Sometimes Lou wished that her mother would not tell her these things, yet she also knew that because she had never really gotten over the loss of her daughter, she provoked her mother into sharing the responsibility for Joan with her. It was an unfortunate relationship for all concerned. Since Lou's mother knew that she was not the real mother of Joan, she guiltily felt compelled to ask advice from the real mother, her own daughter.

And Lou, knowing that she had her mother over a barrel, continued to take advantage of the situation not only by giving advice, but by tacitly threatening reprisals if the advice was not taken. Only two women could play this sort of game with each other, Lou had often thought, each of them respecting and paying homage to the undeniable fact of biological motherhood.

The money that David gave Lou to send to Philadelphia for the care of her daughter was only one more weapon that Lou used in the competitive battle of motherhood she had been waging for ten years with her own mother.

Once she had said to David, "If only I could let go, everyone would be happier."

And David replied, "Perhaps when you get married and have another child, you'll be able to do that."

But what if she never got married, she thought, at the time. Would she still go on beleaguering her mother and interfering in a life that she had long ago forfeited? Then, when she lost the column to Peter her maternal demands had become more stringent, more hysterical. She was more concerned than ever about every detail of Joan's existence: what her grades were, who her friends were, how much she had grown, what she ate for breakfast, whether she had any cavities. If Joan had a cold, Lou would lie awake for nights fearing that it was going to develop into pneumonia at any minute. And then, when it finally cleared up, she would imagine something else about her daughter to make herself miserable.

"You've got to stop it," David told her. "You're killing yourself with guilt."

"I don't know how to stop it."

"Maybe you should give her up for once and all."

"I have given her up."

"No, I'm not talking about the legal aspect. I mean, emotionally."

"I've tried that and it doesn't seem to work. I've really tried. Once, for two years, I pretended that she didn't exist, that she had died at birth, then I lost out on a job I was up for, and I became hysterical all over again. Not about the job, about Joan."

She looked at David with tremulous anger: "Don't you see? Don't you understand? I've got to have *something*."

But that was the wonderful thing about David, he did understand, and Lou often thought that that was why she was still with him, that if anything should ever happen to Joan, it would automatically sever her relationship with David.

After Lou had given Mr. Crazy his breakfast of chopped lamb kidneys sprinkled with his granular vitamins, she fed the goldfish, then made an organic milkshake for herself in the Osterizer that David had sent her for Christmas. The milkshake was substantial enough to see her through the morning hours until it was time to meet Anita at the Palm Court at one o'clock.

Anita turned up at the Palm Court twenty minutes late, which infuriated Lou, who was punctual as usual. She had long ago come to the conclusion that it was her destiny to sit and wait for people who considered it fashionable to be twenty minutes late. Why they thought that she could not possibly imagine, but it came as no surprise to her when Anita made only the fluffiest excuse for her tardiness.

"Oh, I'm so sorry but I had to do my nail polish over at the last moment."

Lou sipped her iced tea and marveled once more at the peculiar lack of concern on the part of people who made other people wait for them. There was definitely something hostile about their behavior, she decided, rude and hostile, even when they occasionally pretended to be apologetic about it.

"That's all right," she said, with a false heartiness. "It gave me a chance to relax for a while. I've been on the go all morning."

"I know what you mean," Anita said. "Sometimes when I come back from a flight I'm so bushed that I want to sleep forever. But it's hard to relax after a flight, as much as you'd like to. You're too keyed up."

"It sounds very tiring."

"There's a lot of strain involved," Anita admitted.

Lou, who could not imagine being an airline stewardess any more than she could imagine being Albert Schweitzer, smiled sympathetically, then reached for a cigarette and gave Anita the once-over.

Anita was wearing a cream-colored baby bolero dress, cream-colored accessories, and shimmering pink lipstick that matched her nail polish. Her ash blond hair was tied softly in back with a thin, cream-colored ribbon.

"Would you like a cigarette?" Lou asked her.

"No, thanks. I'm trying to cut down."

"I wish I could," Lou said as she lit her Gauloise.

The chunky purple slave bracelet slid down her tanned arm and she became immensely conscious of the visual disparity between herself and Anita, the difference in their styles being so acute:

Anita was the melting cherry-vanilla ice cream cone, and she was the epitome of tough chic spoofing the harem girl mentality.

For one quivering moment, Lou would have given anything to change places with Anita and not have to fight so hard for every rung on the ladder, just relax, calm down, give in, be a girl in a cream-colored dress, be twenty minutes late and girlishly blame it on her nail polish. But it was like wishing to be the moon, if you were the sun, and a second later she forgot all about it. Then it occurred to her that Anita had just returned from San Juan and did not have a tan.

"How was the weather down there?" she asked. "Very warm?"

Anita contemplated her Brandy Alexander.

"Yes, quite warm. In fact, too warm for comfort. I'd never been in Puerto Rico in the summer before and I ended up spending most of my time either in shady places or inside where it was air-conditioned."

Anita laughed, but it hit a sour note. "I love the Spanish phrase for it: *aire acondicionado.*"

She probably burns and peels, Lou thought, with the mild contemptuousness of all people who tan evenly, beautifully, painlessly, and rapidly.

"I have a very delicate skin," Anita amended. "It's an unfortunate handicap."

"Yes, I can imagine."

For the first time their eyes met, really met, and it struck Lou that Anita was lying through her teeth. The girl had obviously gone to San Juan for an abortion, and in some backhanded way she was trying to convey this message to Lou.

"I'm sorry that you didn't enjoy yourself," Lou said, thinking that if she had had an abortion when she was seventeen, there would be no daughter now to complicate her life, but perhaps there would be no David either.

Anita shrugged, and Lou wondered whether she was imagining it or whether those were tears filming over Anita's eyes.

"Well," Lou said with her best professional smile, "shall we order and then get down to business?"

"I'll have the lobster salad," Anita replied, not bothering to look at the menu. "It's rather good."

To Lou's dismay, there were nothing but salads on the menu. In the Oak Room, in the rear, men were no doubt cutting into thick, rare filets mignons, and she felt strongly resentful that because she was a woman she was condemned to sit in a segregated dining area, along with forty or so others of her sex, and delicately break lettuce leaves with her fork.

"I might as well have the lobster salad, too," she said, wishing she were at a steak house with David, instead of this tea parlor with a dumb stewardess whose life had probably just been ruined for the fifteenth time.

The interview did not go badly. Anita turned out to be brighter and funnier than Lou had imagained at first.

"Our new uniform is more functional than it looks," Anita said. "The pantskirt is just great for rolling out of the plane during emergencies."

"Rolling?"

"Maybe you could call it sliding. When there's an emergency evacuation, you have to go out a long inflated chute and sort of bounce to the ground. It's only happened to me twice, thank goodness. The first time was when we were still wearing our old uniforms with the regular skirt. I remember that the skirt ended up somewhere around my head when I ended up on the ground at JFK. The second time I felt much more ladylike."

"That sounds terrible. Was anyone hurt?"

"The first time, nobody. The second time an elderly man broke his leg on the slide down. Actually, the whole operation would be pretty amusing to watch if it weren't for the fact that the plane is liable to explode any minute, and the passengers are in a state of panic."

"I can imagine that they would be."

"But aside from that, most of the girls aren't too keen on the new couturier uniform. It is a bit Batwomanish, you know."

Lou jotted down these last few notes. Then to her surprise, she heard Anita say:

"You work with Peter Northrop, don't you?"

"Yes." Lou looked at her curiously. "What makes you ask?"

"His wife is a friend of a friend of mine, and she just happened to mention one day that her husband was a reporter for *The Rag*. What's he like? She's terrible."

"Really? What's so terrible about her?"

Anita was thinking of everything she had disliked about Beverly right from the start, and not least of all the fact that she suspected Robert was still involved with her, even though he denied it.

"Without going into morbid detail," Anita said, "she's a bit of a bitch. I understand that they've separated."

"Yes, so I've heard."

"What do you think of him?"

"Very little," she said, sharply. "In fact, he's a rotten bastard."

Anita smiled at her with girlish complicity.

"You sound the way I sound when I'm talking about the guy I'm in love with. He's a bastard, too."

No doubt the bastard responsible for your abortion, Lou thought. "How can you love him then?"

"When you get right down to it, all men are bastards in one way or another, aren't they?"

Lou found it very interesting that here sat a stewardess who was professionally trained to please men, to be gracious and smiling, and who in her private life seemed not at all embarrassed to admit that she was smiling at the natural enemy. A line of Simone de Beauvoir's occurred to her:

Confronting man, woman is always playacting. With that psychology, De Beauvoir would have made a great airline stewardess.

"I don't agree with your opinion of all men, any more than if you were talking about all women," Lou said. "I don't believe you can deal with people that way. You can't lump them all together. You have to get back to the individual, otherwise you might as well be whistling Dixie."

"Tell me something," Anita said, with an odd smile. "Why do you dislike Peter Northrop so much?"

"He's not a very nice human being. Does that answer your question?"

Later, Anita would wonder how she ever had the nerve to say it. "You mean not as nice as David Swern?"

A chill went through Lou upon hearing an absolute stranger mouth David's name, a terrible premonition of fear, and at the same time a surge of respect for Anita, who was now cleverly one up on her.

"You seem to know a great deal about me, considering the fact that you and I have never met before," Lou said. "Or am I wrong?"

"No, we never met."

As a child, Lou used to watch horror movies with her hands over her eyes, but with the fingers wide enough apart so that she could peek at the fearsome spectacle from time to time. That was how she felt now: she both wanted to get to the bottom of this unusual turn of events, and she was afraid to. Don't be a coward, she told herself, this girl can't possibly hurt you.

"But you do know a great deal about me," Lou said.

"That's right."

It suddenly seemed to have gotten very quiet at the Palm Court, even though nothing had changed. All the tables were still occupied, all the women were still talking.

"Would you care to explain where your information comes from?"

This time it was Anita who lit a cigarette.

"I have a friend, a French girl, who's very interested in astrology, particularly the aspect of reincarnation. She has a theory about previous lives that people have led, such as in Atlantis . . ."

When Lou emerged from the Plaza some forty minutes later, she was in a state of semishock.

Instead of hailing a taxi, as she ordinarily would have done, she decided to walk to the hairdresser's for her weekly wash and set, hoping that the walk would help clear her head. Atlantis, the lost continent, people who had had crabs and thought that she, Lou Marron, was instrumental in having passed them along, traumatic abortion experiences in sunny Puerto Rico.

No wonder her head was muddled. Anita's outpourings at the end of their luncheon were like a travesty of every misery-laden soap opera on television. At first, Lou had been appalled by what she was being told, then sympathetic, then outraged, then appalled all over again.

On Fifth Avenue and Fifty-First Street, she bumped into a man.

"Excuse me," she said automatically, before she looked at him.

"You're a very pretty girl." His bloodshot eyes were staring at her with religious ferocity. "Now you mustn't be ashamed of that. *Do you hear?!*"

Another nut, the city was crawling with them. No wonder people walked so fast in New York. It wasn't just because they were in a hurry to get somewhere, they knew it was hard to hit a moving target.

Louis XV, said the discreet brass plate on the side of the discreetly expensive building, just off Fifth. The uniformed doorman smiled at Lou with polite vagueness and she smiled back, as she did every week.

"Good afternoon," he said, holding the door open for her.

"Good afternoon," Lou said.

Habit was a comforting thing, she thought, and yet a dangerous one, too. By performing a familiar ritual you could deceive yourself into believing that all was the same as before, and that nothing had changed. But as a result of her luncheon with Anita, something had very definitely changed. She now understood the way other people, strangers, looked upon her relationship with David, and it was not very pretty.

After Lou had slipped into one of Louis XV's rose-colored smocks, she went into the salon where Philippe was waiting for her.

"And Miss Marron, how are you today?"

"A little rocky, Philippe."

"Anyhow, you are looking well."

"You always say that, Philippe."

"It is my *métier*. Did Rubirosa ever tell a lady that she did not look well?"

"No, but think of how he died."

Philippe seemed genuinely puzzled. "How?"

"I can't remember."

They both laughed and got on with her hair, which was a hairdresser's joy, since it was bone straight, thick, and had body. It had occurred to Lou sometime ago that childhood infirmities often turned out to be adult assets. When she was young, her mother used to roll her hair in rags to give it a wave, now all the girls with natural waves were trying to straighten their hair and look like her.

On the other hand, her legs, which had always been more shapely than most children's, the calf muscles more developed as a result of early ballet lessons, could now afford to be a trifle thinner. Lou felt particularly self-conscious of them in the summer when it was unfeasible to wear slenderizing, dark stockings, and she bitterly envied girls she saw on the street who had trim, even somewhat shapeless legs.

Instead of reading *Vogue* under the dryer, she thought of her conversation with Anita.

"According to my friend, Simone, everyone at the showroom knows about you and David," Anita said. "They all think it's pretty amusing that he refers to you as Miss O'Hara. They wonder who he thinks he's kidding."

"He's just trying to protect me."

"And himself, too."

"There's nothing wrong in that, is there?"

"Not if you don't think there's anything wrong in being kept by an older, married man."

"David doesn't keep me. Nobody keeps anybody anymore. That went out with Colette. And, as I'm sure you realize, I do have a job. But I don't know why I have to defend myself to you. I don't see that my private life is any of your business."

"Oh, that's where you're wrong," Anita said quickly. "Because if David Swern gave you crabs, and you gave them to Peter Northrop, and Peter gave them to Beverly, and Beverly gave them to Fingerhood, and Fingerhood gave them to me, then I really have you to blame for one of the worst experiences of my life."

For a moment Lou thought she had lost her mind.

"Crabs? What are you talking about? Are you crazy?"

"Well, that's how they're transmitted, you know. One person goes to bed with another person who goes to bed with another person . . ."

"Crabs?!"

"They had to come from somewhere and there seems to be

a very peculiar link among the people I've named. Very peculiar indeed."

"I'm not sure that I follow you correctly, but aside from this crab business that you seem to be obsessed with, are you implying that I went to bed with Peter Northrop?"

"Didn't you?"

"That abortion you just had must have scrambled your brain."

Anita looked as though someone had thrown a pitcher of ice water in her face. "Who told you that?"

"Nobody. I figured it all out by myself."

"I'll bet that Robert told Beverly, and Beverly told Peter, and Peter told you."

"I'm beginning to think you really are crazy. And who is Fingerhood? Aside from the man who gave you crabs. I assume it's a man. Maybe I should say, '*What* is a Fingerhood?' "

"It's a man, all right. It's my current lover. But I'm not in love with him. I'm in love with Jack Bailey. He's the one who got me pregnant."

"You sound like a perfectly charming group."

"Except that Simone says Jack wasn't with us in Atlantis. Stacey wasn't there either. Simone has a hunch they were both in Pompeii."

When Lou got back to the office to write the story on Anita, there was a message for her from David. The message said, "I will pick you up at eight. Let's eat afterward."

They were going to see *Cabaret* that evening and Lou had been looking forward to it ever since she read the reviews, although after her unsettling luncheon with Anita, she was not at all in the mood for a musical comedy. If she told that to David, he would say it was just the ticket to help cheer her up, but Lou had never operated on that particular theory. She liked to see musical comedies when she was in a good mood, just as she only enjoyed getting high if she was happy to begin with.

David had long ago called her a masochist for letting her moods get the better of her, and perhaps by his standards she was, but the happy-go-lucky approach left her cold, mainly because it seemed so unrewarding. Lou preferred her own peaks and valleys of elation and despair; she might sink lower at times than other people, but she also was capable of soaring higher.

At her desk, underneath the blownup photograph of Marc Bohan, she began to type:

She's blonde, lovely, and aims to please. Her name is Anita Schuler. She's an airline stewardess with some very definite opinions on clothes, men, and the dubious benefits of travel.

Not to mention crabs and abortions, Lou thought, immediately blocking out such extraneous ideas, just the way she blocked out the noise and chaos that reigned all around her. To be a successful reporter, you not only needed the proverbial nose for news, but a head with a steel door inside it, as well.

About the airline's new couturier uniform for their stewardesses, Anita had this to say: Actually, it's more functional than it looks. The pantskirt is terrific for rolling out of the plane during emergencies."

The girl who covered the handbag market breezed in as Lou was finishing her story, and began to type up a storm. She had once told Lou that she despised handbags, all handbags, and suspected that her antipathy toward them was the main reason Tony Elliot had assigned her to that particular market.

"Tony Elliot invented perversity," the handbag reporter had said. "Just let the son of a bitch know what interests you the least, and you can be sure it will turn into your next big assignment."

Now, months later, Lou suddenly remembered the girl's advice. Yet she knew it was no accident that she should remember it at this particular point, because experience had taught her that people were like squirrels storing acorns in that regard. When the propitious time presented itself, they dug into their memory banks and pulled out the exact prescription needed for survival. Assuming, of course, that they were the survival type.

"Watch out for fur handbags," the girl at the next desk said, without looking up. "That's what all the ladies are going to be toting come the winter. Aren't you glad you're not one of the ladies?"

Lou knew that the girl did not expect an answer, it was just her way of talking to herself. She leaned back in her chair and reread the piece she had written on Anita Schuler. It was not bad. If Tony liked it, he would send Cav or one of the other photographers around to take a few shots of Anita, and then run the story and pictures in next week's paper.

"Me?" the handbag reporter said. "I'm sticking with my black calf satchel like I have for the last ten years."

Lou placed the story in her out basket and began to think about why she had lost the column to Peter Northrop, *really* why. Up until now she was firmly convinced that she lost it because Peter and Tony had become lovers. Others in the office were convinced of that, too, but what if they were all wrong? They had been wrong about Tony Elliot before. What if Tony had perversely given the column to Peter because Peter acted as though he didn't give a damn about it one way or the other, whereas for months she had acted as though it were a matter of life or death?

Lou looked at her watch and was surprised to see that it was five after five. Where had the day gone? She felt tired but strangely restless, as though some kind of secret, nervous energy were busily fighting off her body's attempts at relaxation. All of her muscles ached. Reason said that she should go home and take a long, hot bath before David came by to pick her up at eight. Why, then, didn't she cover her typewriter, put herself in motion, and go?

"Am I interrupting?" a voice said.

It was Peter Northrop standing across from her, his palms flat on the edge of her desk.

"Oh, it's you," she said, feeling idiotic the moment she had said it.

"Yes, I'm afraid so. You look so far away that I feel like the stranger from Porlock."

Despising forced literary references, she said, "I thought you were from Garden City," and then felt doubly idiotic.

"I wanted to give you back the book I borrowed. I have it at my desk."

"Oh, *Herzog*. Did you like it?"

"Frankly, I never got around to reading it. My wife requisitioned it as soon as I brought it home."

"I'd nearly forgotten about that book. David loaned it to me ages ago. I think he's probably forgotten about it, too, but I should return it to him."

"Yes, you should."

To her surprise, he continued to stand there, his blue eyes gazing directly at her. "The other thing I was going to say is, why don't you have a drink with me?"

"Now?"

"Yes, if you're free. I was thinking of the Stork Club."

The Stork Club was the name everyone in the office had given to the dump downstairs.

"Well," she said, "I do have to go home and change eventually. David and I have tickets for *Cabaret* tonight."

"There's plenty of time for that, isn't there? It's only five o'clock."

"I suppose so."

Lou could not tell which startled her more: the fact that the aloof and arrogant Peter Northrop was asking her to have a drink with him, or the fact that she had accepted.

The handbag reporter said, "Muffs will be next. Just wait and see."

"I'll go get the book," Peter said. "Are you ready to leave?"

"As ready as I'll ever be."

It was an answer she would remember with great interest in the months ahead.

"This place certainly fills up fast," Peter said when they were seated at the bar.

He had suggested they take a booth, but Lou voted for the bar, saying she preferred it there. The bar seemed more impersonal than a booth. Surrounded by other drinkers, she could convince herself that she was not alone with Peter Northrop.

"People must come here for the air-conditioning," she said. "It can't be the décor."

"Or the free hors d'oeuvres."

"I don't see any free hors d'oeuvres."

"That's what I mean. What would you like to drink? I'm going to have a Dewar's on the rocks."

"I'll have the same."

"Two Dewar's on the rocks," he told the bartender, who looked like Gilbert Roland.

"Do you come here often?" Lou asked.

"I think this is my second time. It's a terrible place, isn't it? I wonder who did the murals."

"An out-of-work brick layer."

"I have a hunch you're right."

They both laughed self-consciously, as though they had come to some profound stage of mutual agreement. A man wearing a commuter's hat, with a plaid band, dropped a coin in the jukebox.

You're just too good to be true, can't take my eyes off of you, you'd be like heaven to touch, I want to hold you so much.

"That's the loudest jukebox I've ever heard," Lou said.

"This bar lacks only one thing."

"What's that?"

"A television set tuned to a baseball game."

A girl sitting on Lou's right began to sob into a Kleenex, as the man she was with tried in vain to comfort her with words. The more he tried, the harder she sobbed. Lou caught only one remark of his:

"It's not quite as hopeless as you imagine."

At long last love has arrived and I thank God I'm alive.

"Why is it?" Lou asked Peter, "that other people's catastrophes never seem quite real?"

She was thinking not only of the couple on her right, but of Anita's tale of woe about her abortion experience. In both cases, Lou felt a mild sense of discomfort, nothing more.

"They seem very real to people who like catastrophes," Peter replied. "Otherwise why would soap operas be so popular? Look at all the empathy they generate."

"Not in me. They make me want to laugh."

Peter was wearing an attractively rumpled cord suit and needed a shave. Also, his eyes were green, not blue, Lou realized. She wondered where he was living, now that he and his wife were no longer living together.

"If you laugh, you don't have to cry," he said.

"Is that what it is?"

"It's a possibility, wouldn't you say?"

"Yes, I guess so."

"Perhaps you're afraid to cry."

Her old feeling of hatred for him flared up at that precise moment, for he had touched off a sore spot of hers. Tears frightened her. They represented a total loss of control.

I love you, baby, and if it's quite all right I need you, baby, trust in me when I say, oh pretty baby.

"If the cosmetic companies hadn't come up with waterproof mascara, I could say that was the reason I didn't like to cry. All that black paint streaming piteously down my cheeks."

She glanced at the girl on her right and noted that she was wearing no mascara at all.

"Revlon has taken away your last defense," Peter said. "Now you have to state the real reason you don't like to cry."

"Perhaps I have nothing to cry about. Did that ever occur to you? Or would you like me to manufacture a quick tragedy?"

He ran his hand over the stubble on his face. "My wife is a cryer."

"Oh?"

"She seems to gain comfort from tears. Apparently, they soothe her."

Lou wondered which one of them was responsible for the recent separation. Probably Peter, judging from his distinct tone of condemnation. And again, Lou found herself thinking about his wife and what she was like, really like. The fact that Anita thought Peter's wife was a bitch meant very little to her, since she herself thought very little of Anita. She wished now that she had asked Anita for a physical description of the lady; her height or the color of her hair would be more meaningful at this point than any personality evaluation Anita had to offer.

"I was sorry to hear about the separation," Lou said. "I'm sure you know that everyone in the office has heard about it by now."

Peter laughed. "They probably knew about it before I did, offices being the gossip factories that they are. Sometimes I wonder who gets these things started, not that I really give a damn. In my case, it was hardly a top security secret."

Tony Elliot's secretary was the one who had been instrumental in spreading word of Peter's separation around the office, just as she had circulated other bits of inside information in the past, but Lou would cut off her tongue before she told that to Peter. If Peter told Tony, Tony might fire the girl and she would feel responsible. It was Tony's secretary who had let her know that Peter was definitely going to get the coveted column assignment, and the advance notice had saved Lou several weeks of painful anxiety before Tony himself made the news public. Other people on *The Rag* relied on Tony's secretary for similar tips, so much so in fact that the girl had secretly been dubbed The Informer.

"Where are you living these days?" Lou asked.

"At the Harvard Club while I look for an apartment. My wife has taken a place on Eighty-Fourth Street off Lex."

"What happened to Garden City?"

"We sold the house. When we separated, Beverly decided she wanted to move to the city."

His wife lived only ten blocks north of her, Lou thought, and again she wondered what she looked like. Then she remembered a remark an actress had made during an interview. "When you're interested in a man, and you're not sure he's interested, too, there's a natural curiosity to check out the most recent competition. It can give you a clue to what he likes in women, or, very often, what he used to like and now can't stand. But either way, it's indicative."

"Shall we have another drink?" Peter asked.

Lou glanced at her watch. It was almost six o'clock. There was still plenty of time for a long, hot, relaxing bath, even a nap before David was due.

"I'd love another drink," she said.

The couple on Lou's right had left the bar, and the man wearing the commuter's hat was stoned on martinis, when Peter said, "Have dinner with me."

"But I told you, I'm going to the theater with David."

"David who?"

"David Webb."

Another couple moved into the vacant spot on Lou's right. The man said, "I'm divorced, rich, and sterile."

The girl said, "No, you're not."

"Would you believe separated, poor, and impotent?"

"Yes."

Lou and Peter started to laugh, then stopped, then looked at each other.

"It's the beginning of summer madness," Peter said.

"And I can't even start to have an affair with a married man whose wife goes to Southampton, because I've been having one for two years and she never goes anywhere except Ocean Beach."

"Would you believe Ocean Beach?" Peter said to the couple on Lou's right.

But they were drinking Tom Collinses and did not deign to answer.

Life is a cabaret, old chum, come to the cabaret, sang Joel Grey hours later, while David held Lou's hand, and she thought of the man in the commuter's hat, the man who had said, "It's not quite as hopeless as you imagine," and the man who was separated, poor, and impotent, and Peter Northrop, who, hopefully, was none of those.

After the play, David took her to the Blue Ribbon where they ate steak tartare and drank a lot of Beaujolais.

"I don't feel well," Lou announced halfway through the meal.

"What's the matter?"

Earlier, Peter had said, "I'll call you at midnight," and she had said, "You mean, when I turn into a pumpkin?" and he had said, "Precisely."

"It's been a long, terrible, depressing day," she now explained to David, meanwhile feeling very excited and exhilarated.

"You work too hard."

"It's all I know how to do."

David gazed at her tenderly. "Why don't you ever give yourself a chance as a woman?"

"Because I don't know how to do that."

"If you ever said that you would marry me—"

"—you would divorce Lillian."

"Yes."

"No."

"Do you mean, no, I wouldn't, or no, you wouldn't marry me?"

"Both," Lou said, meaning it.

"You'd distort the truth for a glib remark. Any glib remark. Why is that?"

"It's an occupational hazard."

"Another glib remark."

"But true."

Lou speared a caper with her fork. "I just thought of something. I despise steak tartare. I've always despised steak tartare. It's only taken me twenty-seven years to realize it."

"Actually, you're right," David said, getting back at her, "I wouldn't divorce Lillian."

Peter had hit the nail on the head, Lou thought, it was indeed the beginning of summer madness. But later, after she kissed David goodnight, she undressed, got into bed, and did not answer the telephone when it rang at midnight.

It only rang four times and she respected Peter for that. Then she fell asleep and dreamed about crossing paths with his wife at Louis XV. In the dream, Philippe confided to her that Mrs. Northrop's hair had no body.

The following morning Peter stopped at Lou's desk and took a small dart out of his jacket pocket. Then he threw the dart at the photograph of Marc Bohan above her desk. It landed on Bohan's left nostril.

"You didn't answer the telephone," Peter said.

"I couldn't. I wasn't there. I didn't get home until almost two."

"Oh?"

"David and I ran into some people we knew at the Blue Ribbon and got involved in one of those long conversations that seem very meaningful at the time. Today I can't even remember what we spoke about."

Peter removed the dart from the photograph and put it back in his pocket. "Does David really mean so much to you?"

"Yes," she said quickly, "yes he does. I'm very fond of him."

"Fond." That seemed to amuse Peter. "I guess that's as good a word as any. Exquisite, in fact."

Lou felt herself starting to get angry. "Look, I don't have to explain or justify my relationship with David to you. And I resent your attitude. It's snide."

"I imagine that it is. I'm sorry. Still, I have to confess to a certain puzzlement over what you're doing with the man."

Thinking of Anita's cynical reaction, Lou said:

"I'm sure that by now you've boiled it down to a simple matter of money."

"No, that's where you're wrong. If I thought it were money, I wouldn't be puzzled, now would I? It's not money, but it's obviously not love either."

Lou had always felt guilty because she did not love David, and she disliked being reminded of it.

"Obviously?" she said. "How can you be so certain? What the hell do you know about it?"

Yesterday, at the bar, she had liked Peter for the first time since she'd known him, but now, overnight, he seemed to have reverted to the old, arrogant person she had always thought him to be.

"Maybe the keynote is comfort," Peter mused. "Like an old sweater. Maybe you find it safer to be with a middle-aged man who worships you, than a younger man who—"

"—who what?" she cut in, really angry now.

"You should have let me finish my sentence. Or were you afraid of what I was about to say?"

"I have a great deal of work to do." She took out a folder of p.r. releases and pretended to look them over. "You'll have to excuse me."

Peter put his hand on her bare arm and a tremor went through her. It was the first time they had ever touched.

"Behind that tough, career girl barricade of yours," he said, "I see a frightened, sexy woman struggling to get out."

"Oh, really? Well, Mr. Northrop, you're wrong on both counts. I'm not frightened, and I've never considered myself particularly sexy."

"I know," he said, "but I have."

A few minutes later, as Lou was about to go into the conference room for *The Rag*'s weekly editorial meeting, Tony Elliot's secretary buzzed her and asked if she were free for lunch.

Sensing that something was up, Lou said, "Yes. Fine. Shall we make it at noon?"

The Informer had worked for Tony Elliot for close to eight years and during that time was reputed to have never once gone to lunch at any hour except noon. It was the kind of consistent behavior that completely baffled Lou, and she knew that even if she lived to be a very wise, old lady, she would still not understand it. The other thing that she didn't understand about The Informer (whose name was Enid) was how she managed to eat at Schrafft's every day without losing her marbles.

Actually, Lou got a kick out of Schrafft's because she went there so seldom. It amused her. The antiseptic food, the Irish waitresses, the blue-veined ladies drinking weak Manhattans. She had a sneaking suspicion that all Schrafft's devotees were chronically constipated, yet she could not have explained why she thought so.

When they were seated, Enid ordered the Tomato Surprise and iced tea. Lou ordered the cheese omelette and iced coffee.

Then Enid said, "I spent the entire morning making arrangements for Mr. E.'s trip to Paris next month and I'm not through yet. Every time he goes over to cover those damn collections, I get stuck with a job that I wouldn't wish on my worst enemy."

The Informer had been known to turn into The Complainer upon occasion, and Lou realized that this was going to be one of those occasions.

"It sounds rough," she said.

"Rough? It's a nightmare. If people only knew what I go through twice a year!"

In July and January, the leaders of the French *haute couture* dramatically opened the doors of their salons to show new trends in women's fashions. The audience at these showings consisted of buyers, designers, manufacturers, private customers, and the ubiquitous press. Tony Elliot, who had personally covered the collections for as long as he had been publisher of *The Rag,* frequently said that for his money Paris put on the best theatrical show in the world.

"I should have thought you'd have all the mechanics down pat by now," Lou said. "I mean, if anyone is familiar with the ropes, Enid, it's you."

Enid looked at her blandly from behind blue-tinted granny glasses. "I wasn't referring to hotel and transportation arrangements. Those are nothing. It's the rest of it. The social engagements, for example. Do you think it's a snap to set up a dinner date with Pierre Cardin?"

"For you or me, no, but for Tony Elliot . . . ?"

Enid sliced a cross section of her Tomato Surprise.

"You have no idea what it's like talking to French secretaries. They can drive you up a tree."

"It sounds frustrating."

"It's worse than that, it's disgusting. You should see the list of names Mr. E. gave me to make appointments with. The only person he left out is Charles de Gaulle, and I'm not sure that that wasn't a mistake. I'll never finish any of my other work, if I don't get off that damn phone."

I hate whiners, Lou thought. "He can't expect you to do everything at once."

"Sometimes I think he does."

"You're too hard on yourself. After all, if these appointments mean so much to him, then he probably doesn't care if you neglect your other work. At least for the time being."

"Oh, they don't mean so much to him any more. He's just going through the motions."

It was the way she said it, the tone of voice, something. Lou felt a piece of cheese omelette stick in her throat.

"I don't understand," she said.

"Mr. E. is getting fed up covering the collections. He doesn't enjoy it the way he used to."

"Oh?"

"Well, you know how he feels about fresh approaches to everything."

"Who doesn't?" Lou said, still being very careful.

"Mr. E. really believes that people grow stale and jaded if they work at any one job for too long a period of time. And he doesn't consider himself an exception to that rule. In fact, that's just what he was saying to me yesterday. He said, 'Enid, I'm getting stale covering these damn collections twice a year. A fresh approach is needed, a new slant.' "

"But he's still going to Paris next month."

"Oh, yes. Next month."

Enid patted her mouth with the napkin and took a sip of iced tea. "Strictly off the record, I have a hunch that he's going for the last time. Something tells me that next January I will not be knocking my brains out trying to set up a zillion appointments with French secretaries, thank the good Lord."

"Who does he plan to send in his place?"

Enid finished her iced tea, and said, "How should *I* know?

I only work for the man, I can't anticipate every thought in his crazy mind."

Two interesting things happened over the July Fourth weekend. Tony Elliot fired his secretary, and Lou Marron went to bed with Peter Northrop. Lou later remarked that neither event would have occurred when it did, if it weren't for the fact that *The Rag*, being a newspaper, was not closed over the Fourth like practically every other office in New York.

David Swern was in Ocean Beach with his wife for the weekend, and Beverly Northrop and her two children were in Martha's Vineyard for the month of July. Even the Stork Club was closed. The skeletal crew that got stuck working on *The Rag* during each legal holiday felt a strong bond of kinship with one another, a mutual sensation of being both privileged and deprived, not unlike the sole survivors of a ship that has sunk off the coast of Greece, stranding a few staunch passengers on a primitive island to fend for themselves.

Actually, Tony Elliot fired his secretary on July Third, but nobody in the office heard about it until after the long weekend, because for once The Informer wasn't talking. And it was on the evening of the Third that Lou and Peter ended up at her apartment, a little sorry for themselves and more than a little drunk. They had not eaten dinner and lunch was only a dim dream.

"Let's sit in the garden," Lou said.

"I didn't know you had a garden."

"It's what I have instead of a doorman."

"My wife has a doorman."

It figures, Lou thought, wondering what Beverly was doing in Martha's Vineyard at that precise moment. A second later she wondered exactly when she had begun to think of her as Beverly. David's wife was Lillian. An hysterical giggle welled up inside Lou as she contemplated future catastrophes of nameless proportions if she should ever verbally confuse the two names. It was really very comical. She could see herself marching through life, desperately trying to come up with the right name for the right wife in front of the right husband, and praying that she did not make an embarrassing mistake. Oops. Sorry, dear, that was another lady. Index cards might help.

"It's very pleasant here," Peter said when they had gone into the garden.

"I love it, particularly on weekends in the summer. I sit out here and read. I pretend I'm in the south of France."

"The table is amusing."

"It thinks it's at a restaurant on a *plage* somewhere."

It was a white, circular table that she had bought in the garden furniture department at Bloomingdale's. In the center was a hole for a striped beach umbrella that shaded the entire table. Three ice cream chairs sat alongside the table, waiting for customers, and at the moment Mr. Crazy lay stretched out underneath the umbrella, his yellow eyes fastened upon Peter.

"Am I in or out?" Peter asked the cat.

"He hasn't decided yet."

"Have you?"

The suddenness and directness of the question startled Lou. She had not been at all prepared for it (why not? she asked herself). She was lying on a white chaise and she closed her eyes, Peter's question lingering in the air, unanswered, for what seemed to her like a very long time. Actually, it was only a matter of seconds.

"In."

Peter was lying on a chaise, a green one, and again for what seemed to Lou like a very long time nothing was said. Or done. Until Peter got up and kissed her. The kiss was so intense that Lou felt as though her head had been shot off. It was a reeling sensation. She had not been kissed with such intensity for years and she had almost forgotten what it felt like, in fact she *had* forgotten. David never kissed her that way, not even at the beginning, but of course David was older. Fatter. Weaker. Flabbier.

The minute they were in bed and she felt Peter's hard, lithe body against hers, the two years that she had spent with David dwindled into dust. She must have been crazy during those two years, out of her mind to have denied herself this exquisite magic. Because the second that Peter was inside her, she knew she was not going to deny herself anything for a long time to come.

"I love it," she moaned. "I love it."

"I love you."

Had she imagined it, or had he said it? Did it matter? She was so beside herself with mounting excitement that everything else became lost in the sound of their bodies smacking against each other. After minutes they were dripping with perspiration and now the sound was a wet one, everything was very wet, too wet to feel right.

"I'll get a towel," Peter said.

"Yes. Do."

He brought back a towel from the bathroom and she wiped them both.

"Do you think we'll get pneumonia if I turn on the air-conditioner?" she asked.

"If you don't, I'm afraid we're going to develop jungle rot."

She giggled idiotically, and with shaking legs went to turn on the Fedders. She was still shaking when Peter began to make love to her again. Her fingers felt as though there was electricity in them, a feeling she had never had before. He's plugged me in, she thought. For minutes she lingered on the brink of orgasm, bodiless, and yet bursting at every pore, deliciously crazed.

"Come on," he whispered very softly.

His words brought her over the brink, and with such a violent crash that off in the distance she heard a low, guttural sound and only afterward did she realize that it was her own voice.

Later when they were lying in bed, smoking, Peter said to her, "You have very nice breasts. Neither too big, nor too small. You're lucky."

Lou had never been particularly crazy about her breasts because they were not high enough. They didn't sag exactly, they just lacked character. Also, she didn't like her nipples, which were on the brownish side. Still, she knew that compared to a lot of women she was not doing too badly in that department. At least she had something there. Those button-breasted women she ran into so frequently in her work were for the birds.

"The mistake I made," Peter said, "was that I married a brassiere."

"What do you mean? Does your wife wear padded brassieres?"

"Hardly. In fact, it's quite the reverse. She has enough natural padding for two women."

"A lot of men find that very attractive."

"Well, you see, this business of marrying a brassiere finally involves a great deal of travel."

"Peter, what are you talking about?" Lou asked with a laugh.

"Travel. It took me eight years to get from Beverly's nipple to her brain, and when I did I decided the trip wasn't worth it. I demand a refund in full."

"You're really very nutty, you know," she said, pleased that he liked women with medium-sized chests and large-sized brains. "But sweet."

"Yes, I married a 36–B and I'm divorcing a 36–C. That's what it amounts to. In another few years she will probably graduate to 38– something or other. The last time I checked, she was bursting out of the 36–C."

"When was that?"

"About six months ago. Roughly. We hadn't been sleeping together, as they say, for quite a while before we broke up."

Lou remembered Anita's remark about Peter giving crabs to Beverly, who gave them to that Fingerhood character, whatever his first name was, who then gave them to Anita. If Anita were right in her theory as to how the little monsters had been passed along, then not only was Peter lying about not having slept with his wife recently, but there was also a possibility that he had no idea Beverly was involved with another man.

Peter stayed the night. They slept with their arms around each other, his soft breathing in her ear. Toward dawn, Lou woke up dying of thirst and went into the kitchen for a diet coke. As she switched on the light she wondered where she had ever gotten the notion that Peter and Tony Elliot were lovers.

"I must have been demented," she said to Mr. Crazy who had followed her in.

The cat thought it was time for breakfast and jumped up on the caned stool, waiting to be fed.

"Later," she told him.

Then she went back to the air-conditioned bedroom, hoping that when Peter woke up he would make love to her again. She needed to have it happen once more in the clear light of morning to believe that last night had not been a miraculous dream.

It did happen once more. She had imagined nothing.

"What a fit," Peter said.

Lou had an appointment at ten o'clock that morning with a designer of at-home clothes, and she did not get to the office until after eleven. When she sat down at her desk, she kept her sunglasses on, dreading the moment that she came face to face with Peter and was unable to look him straight in the eye. Earlier, before parting, they had agreed to make a concerted effort not to let people at the office know that anything between them had changed.

"We'll act just the way we did before," Peter said. "Friendly enemies."

"We weren't even friendly."

"Cordial, then."

"I hated you."

"Why?"

"You always seemed so snotty."

"And you so Mother Superior."

"Me?"

"Yes, darling, I know. Little old shy modest *me?* Maybe that's the way you felt, that's not the way you behaved."

"I have a terrible premonition that I'm going to blush like a lunatic the first time we run into each other."

"You're not the type to blush."

"That's what makes it even worse."

"They won't suspect a thing, not unless you come in with a sign spelling it out in big, block letters, and even then I'm not sure some of those idiots would get the message."

"I still hope I don't blush."

"Think of it as an exercise in self-control," Peter said. "That's the way to approach these situations."

It was not until after lunch that they actually encountered each other. Peter had been locked up all morning with Tony Elliot, and when he came out of the meeting Lou had already gone downstairs for a quick sandwich. When she returned to the office, Peter was not at his desk and his typewriter was covered.

Perhaps he was not coming back that afternoon, she thought, perhaps he planned to call her from the outside. Then it occurred to her that that might be a bit sticky since the switchboard operator would certainly recognize his voice. What of it? They were business associates, there was no reason in the world why he shouldn't call her for perfectly ordinary business reasons. But when the hell had he ever called her? How often? Three times in four years?

"It's none of their business anyway," she said to herself, envisioning the switchboard as one great spy network out to snare and trap her.

So that when Peter quite casually walked up to her desk after lunch and said, "Good afternoon," she was so surprised that she just as casually said, "Hello, how are you?" and then realized that she wasn't blushing at all.

"You see?" he said. "I knew you had a great deal of self-control."

"And I'm not even wearing my sunglasses any longer."

"Are you free tonight? I thought we might have dinner."

"That would be nice."

"I'll pick you up at seven. I have to go back to the club first and change my clothes."

"Okay."

They ate at a darkly lit Italian place on Third Avenue, where they had spinach soup, veal *piccata,* zabaglione, and expresso, all mixed together with half a bottle of Orvieto. It was the same wine that Lou had so foolishly ordered at Elaine's months back, when that obnoxious off-Broadway playwright, whose name she never could remember, had offered to buy her a drink at the bar. And later she had picked up Marshall at the Jewish Museum. If anyone had told her then that she would be having an affair with Peter Northrop in July, she would have concluded he was crazy.

"Don't you like the wine?" Peter asked her during dinner.

"Yes, very much. It's one of my favorites. Why?"

"You made a face when you tasted it."

"I was thinking of something else."

"Something or someone?"

"Both, actually."

Peter's eyes rested on her for a moment, with that intense, searching gaze of his, then he discreetly changed the subject and neither the wine nor her memories were mentioned again.

After dinner they walked languidly back to her apartment in the breezeless summer night. The minute they stepped inside the door, Peter took her in his arms and said, "I've been thinking about you all day."

They undressed very quickly and got into bed, but once there they took their time about everything. Now that they knew how nice it would be, there was no need to rush. Words were unnecessary, too. What was there to say? And yet, every once in a while certain isolated words would be spoken, by one, by the other, words that asked for no response, words that simply forced their way out of dry mouths and hovered silently over wet bodies.

"Oh yes," Lou might say at one point.

Many minutes later Peter might say, "Right there."

Or, "I can't."

"Do you like that?"

"Ow."

"Incredible."

"Listen."

"Electricity again."

But neither had any idea who said what, or in what sequence, or how much time passed between these words, and tomorrow no one would remember them. The words were part of the spell, and would be remembered again, in varying combinations, only when they were under the spell again. The language of eroticism is as peculiar to itself as is the language of any highly specialized field of endeavor, and as meaningless once the endeavor has been completed.

The next day, July Fifth, everyone at *The Rag* learned that Tony Elliot's secretary was no longer Tony Elliot's secretary, and Lou realized that David was back in town. She had forgotten all about him. And so quickly. Only a flippant person could forget someone so quickly, and Lou had never thought of herself as being flippant. Now that she did, it saddened her and yet gave her a feeling of great exhilaration, of freedom, power. Perhaps she did not need David as badly as she had led herself to believe, perhaps she never had.

Later in the morning, David phoned her.

"I missed you," he said. "How was your weekend?"

"Very dull."

"How was the weather in New York?"

"Very warm. I ran up a nice air-conditioning bill. Con Ed will be delighted."

"It's a shame you couldn't get away."

"Oh, I hate going anywhere on those holiday weekends. The traffic is terrible and everyone is frantic. Besides, now I have a couple of vacation days coming to me, which I can take during the week, so it's not too bad."

"At least if you'd gotten that column," David said.

"The column was yesterday," Lou replied more abruptly than she meant to.

"It's still a damn shame."

"Frankly, David, I wish you would forget about the column. Peter Northrop is doing it, and that's that."

"I'm sorry. I was only trying to . . ."

He was trying to show how much on her side he really was, the poor man. He had become the poor man the first moment that Peter Northrop began to make love to her, but he did not yet know it. What am I going to do about him, Lou wondered?

"Is tomorrow okay?" he asked. "I told Lillian I was going to the Turkish bath."

Spending the night at the Turkish bath was David's alibi to his wife for spending the night with Lou, and long ago, when the affair had just started, Lou used to kid him by saying, "I never thought I'd live to see the day when I'd be grateful to the Turks for anything." Now she felt the shoddiness of their arrangement, the lies, the indignity of it all. How dare he treat me this way, she thought, conveniently forgetting that for two years it had not bothered her in the least. Her next thought was: his flesh hangs.

"Tomorrow," she said, regretfully, "is fine."

"I'll call you tomorrow afternoon. Don't work too hard."

Had he always been so banal? "I'll try," she said. "So long."

As she replaced the receiver, she realized that her fingers were clenched tight. She looked at them. They were the same fingers through which electricity had run when she made love to Peter. Then she had loved her fingers, now she hated them.

"I'm seeing David tomorrow night," she told Peter that evening after they had made love.

"Oh?"

"He asked to see me and I didn't know how to get out of it."

"Why should you have gotten out of it?"

They were in the garden and except for the glow of their cigarettes it was very dark. Lou squinted in the darkness, trying to define the expression on his face, his mood of the moment. Was he being sincere? Sarcastic? Defensive?

"Because I don't want to go to bed with David any longer," she said, wondering whether she had ever wanted to, or whether it was just a nice arrangement. "I really don't want to, and yet I don't want to hurt him either."

"You're going to have to do one or the other, aren't you?"

They were wearing matching seersucker robes that Lou had bought some years back at the men's shop at Lord & Taylor. She originally bought two robes so that when David stayed over, he would be comfortable, and it occurred to her now that Peter was too smart not to realize that David had worn the robe before him. Did it bother Peter? He certainly did not appear to be bothered, but then he never did, not about anything.

"I'm going to make myself a drink," she said, suddenly feeling very nervous. "Can I make you one, too?"

"Yes, a drink would be nice."

As she went into the living room to pour the Scotch she realized that what she wanted from Peter was a show of jealousy and she wasn't getting it. She needed to feel that he cared whether she went to bed with David; she wanted it to upset him. Perhaps it wouldn't upset him at all, perhaps she meant nothing to Peter. And then Beverly came to mind.

"Did you ever hear of a man named Fingerhood?" she asked, as she returned to the garden with their drinks.

"Fingerhood?"

"Yes."

"No, I can't say as I have. And it's not a name I'd be likely to forget. Who is he?"

"The man who's been having an affair with your wife."

"My wife?!" Peter leaned forward in his chaise. "What are you talking about? What do you know about my wife?"

"Plenty." Lou was pleased to see that she had gotten a rise out of the son of a bitch at last.

"Are you trying to tell me that you've met Beverly?"

"No. Never."

"Then it must be this Fingerhood person whom you know. Right?"

"Wrong again."

Now she could see the expression on his face very clearly. It was one of trapped animal fear, and she wondered whether that was the way she had looked at the Palm Court when Anita mentioned David's name.

"I must admit that I'm intrigued," Peter said. "Would you like to explain what the hell you're talking about?"

Lou took a long drink of her Scotch and soda. "It's a rather involved story."

"I'm listening."

"Well, actually, the whole business started ages ago in Atlantis . . ."

The next evening Lou went down on David, since that seemed to be the only way he could get an erection lately.

As she was going down on him, she thought of Peter and his bewildered reaction to the story she had told him about Beverly meeting a girl named Simone in Mexico, Simone who worked for David and who was having an affair with Fingerhood, Simone who made the mistake of introducing Beverly to Fingerhood, and then the Anita part, because (as she carefully explained to the dazed Peter), Simone was a friend of Anita's, and Anita was having an affair with Fingerhood at the same time that Beverly was, and . . .

"Fingerfuck!" Peter shouted. "Who the hell is this Fingerhood character anyway?"

"He's a clinical psychologist."

"I'm glad to hear that because for a minute there he was beginning to sound like an oversexed postal clerk."

"According to Anita, he's very substantial. He works for The Child Guidance Center on Park Avenue."

"Oh, really? How can he spare the time?"

After David had gotten an erection and stuck it in her and come, Lou went to the bathroom and discreetly vomited.

Then she came back to David and said, "I can't see you any more."

David thought she was joking at first.

"No, I'm dead serious," she told him. "I feel too guilty about Lillian." (Thank God she hadn't said Beverly by mistake.)

"Lillian is my problem," David firmly replied. "Not yours."

"But I think about her."

"Don't."

"I can't help it. Like right now. What if she had another attack while you were here in bed with me? How do you imagine I would feel?"

"What if she had an attack and I really were in the Turkish bath? What's the difference?"

"The difference is that you're not in the Turkish bath. You're with me."

After a moment, David predictably said, "Is there someone else?"

"Of course not."

"If there's someone else, I wish you would tell me."

It was going to be a terrible night, she could see that. Perhaps she shouldn't have broken it off with David until the morning. That certainly would have been a more practical move, but it was too late now, goddamn it.

"I know that you don't want to hurt me," David said, "but I assure you that I would rather know the truth."

"There is absolutely and positively no one else. Now are you satisfied?"

She might be impractical, but she wasn't crazy. The truth! What a laugh. Only an idiot would tell the truth in a case like this, only another idiot would want to hear the truth. She had been an idiot to tell Peter that she was seeing David tonight. What had she gained by it? Well, tomorrow she would tell him that she had seen David all right, but had not slept with him. And Peter would believe her, just the way David was going to believe her about there being nobody else. Because they both wanted to. There was absolutely no doubt about it. The truth was for the birds. Deny everything.

"How could there be anyone else after all we've meant to

each other?" she said softly, feeling another vomit coming on.

In the morning she watched David get dressed and thought instantly of Peter. David put his shoes and socks on first, then his trousers. Peter put his trousers on first, then his shoes and socks. Peter's trousers were far too skinny for him to get dressed the way David did.

Watching David in the mauve wallpapered bedroom, Lou realized that she preferred Peter's style, and she wondered whether that was because she was starting to fall in love with him, or whether she was starting to fall in love with him because she liked his style. It was a subject that interested her. The way a person looked, the way he dressed, the way he walked across a room. Only a very superficial person would consider such things superficial. What was it that the man had said? Style is character. An external manifestation of innumerable internal decisions.

"I don't believe you," Peter said the next day, when she insisted that she had not slept with David. "I know damn well that you screwed the son of a bitch but I appreciate the gesture."

"It's not a gesture, it's the truth. After going to bed with you, I just *couldn't*."

"It's a good thing you never took up acting. You're rotten at it, darling."

He was laughing. To show how upset she was at not being believed, she began to cry. That only made him laugh all the more. The possibility that he might be too smart for her made her cry all the more. She could not bear being outwitted, it was just too much to take, she was going to have to change her approach with Peter since it was obvious that he would not swallow the crap that David swallowed. In between her sobs, Lou made a mental note to rethink the way to deal with Peter in the future.

"You're a bastard," she said.

As soon as she said it, she thought of Anita and her pilot. Hopeless, dependent love. Was she going to fall into the same dumb trap?

Almost as though he had read her mind, Peter said, "I want you to become dependent upon me."

"Why?"

"So I can get rid of you."

"That's not a very nice thing to say. But if you really mean it, why not get rid of me now?"

"Because now I'm the one who's dependent."

They were both naked but had not made love yet.

"I don't believe you've ever been dependent upon anyone in your life," Lou said.

"Not until I met you."

Suddenly she began to shiver. "I'm frightened."

"Of what?"

"I don't know. You. Us. You're going to kill me, I can feel it. I've never had this feeling before."

"You never had electricity in your fingers before."

"That's right. It's all connected. I want you too much."

"Good."

She did not know how it happened, how or why she ever said it, but a moment later she heard herself say:

"Slap me."

Without any hesitation, he slapped her across the face.

"Once more."

After the second blow, she said, "Okay, that's enough."

"I'm not very good at it, am I?"

"You're better than you think. You didn't waste a second. I mean, another man might have refused to do it altogether."

"Do you generally ask men to slap you?"

"I never have before."

"Another first," Peter said, putting his arms around her shivering, electrically charged body.

After that night, Lou became physically obsessed with Peter; he was practically all she could think about, and she began to live for the evenings they spent together in her mauve bedroom.

They saw each other about four times a week. The evenings that Lou spent alone were devoted mostly to catching up on her sleep, washing out her underwear, creaming her face, and reading. When she slept alone now, she tossed and turned a lot, and once reached out her hand to touch Peter's body before realizing that he was not there. His not being there at that particular moment disturbed her so much that she lay awake the rest of the night, staring up at the ceiling and wondering why she had become involved in this madness. She no longer felt like herself, she was out of control, and she didn't like it, not a bit, yet she couldn't seem to do anything about it either.

That had happened to her only once before, and as she stared at the ceiling she reluctantly remembered the other time. It was shortly after she'd come to New York from Philadelphia and was a student at NYU. The man was her journalism teacher, married, and not the least bit handsome.

Yet he had something. When he touched her, she went to pieces. For days after being with him, her body felt like it was on fire, her nipples were continually hard, and her brain was paralyzed. She would walk around in a daze, living only for the next time they were together.

He was not in love with her and did not pretend to be. He called her Louise. She hated her given name, but when he said it she did not mind. He could have called her Agnes or Priscilla for that matter, and she would not have minded. She used to try to figure out what it was about him that she found so irresistible and could only conclude that it must be his unavailability, although at times she wondered about that. What if it were just plain old, strong old biochemistry? She liked the way he smelled without being able to explain what he smelled like. It was a subtle, almost lemony scent and yet that didn't describe it either. Perhaps it was like trying to describe a color, impossible. How could you? *Can blaze be done in cochineal or noon in mazarin?*

Her grades deteriorated because her mind was elsewhere, and one night he said to her, "You've got the hottest cunt I've ever felt." She replied, "It isn't, usually." Which was true enough. He thought she was a nymphomaniac and was putting him on, and after a while she stopped trying to convince him otherwise because she had begun to think that maybe he was right, maybe her true nature was just starting to come through at the age of nineteen.

She would have done anything he wanted but fortunately for her, he wanted very little. At the end of the semester she lost him as a teacher, and he excused himself as a lover, saying that he had decided to remain faithful to his wife from then on, because of the kids, etc. It was only months later that she learned he was making it with a seventeen-year-old freshman with long, blond hair. Subsequently, he divorced his wife and married the girl, who, it seemed, was going to have a baby.

Now Lou's work at *The Rag* began to suffer and one day Tony Elliot said to her, "You haven't been your old sharp self lately. Is something wrong?"

"Maybe I'm getting an early menopause."

"If there's anything I can do . . ."

She was surprised. It was the first time she had ever seen Tony drop his patent leather façade and look truly sympathetic. Perhaps he's human after all, she thought, wondering why he had fired his secretary.

"I'll try to do better in the future," she said. "I've been having some personal problems."

"I'm sure you'll try. You're a damn good reporter."

Lou smiled. "You mean, *when* I'm a damn good reporter."

"That's what I mean."

Then he picked up the telephone, a cue that she was being dismissed.

That night she said to Peter, "Are you still in love with your wife?"

"I don't think so. But perhaps after eight years and two children something happens, perhaps it's not love, perhaps it's just habit or familiarity, and yet I don't want to live with her again."

Hating herself for persisting, Lou said, "But you think of her."

"Occasionally. No. More than occasionally. I think of those eight years and then I wonder whether we weren't happy after all. Not deliriously happy, but okay in our own way. Still I don't want to go back, it's too late for that. But I wonder. I even wonder about that brassiere business I mentioned a few weeks ago. Was I exaggerating about Beverly not being too bright?"

"You mean in trying to justify the separation?"

"Yes, something like that."

Men who were recently separated from their wives were impossible, Lou thought. They were neither here nor there. It was the most dismal time to get mixed up with them. A married man like David had the option of returning to his home and a soothing, domestic routine he was long accustomed to; a man who had been divorced for a while would have created a new kind of life for himself, made certain important adjustments, bridged the gap; but someone like Peter was wildly and inevitably transitional, caught between two divergent worlds, yet belonging to neither.

She should not have told him about Beverly and Fingerhood, probably the knowledge that Beverly might be interested in another man had rekindled Peter's interest in her. Why had she told him anyhow? No doubt out of some stupid, bitchy desire to prove that she knew a thing or two about his own wife that he did not know. Stupid was the word, all right. She should have kept her mouth shut. The thought that Peter might return to Beverly was driving her crazy and as a result she became even more sexually frantic and obsessive. It was as though she could hold him by the sheer intensity of her sexual needs, which, objectively, she knew was a lot of crap.

At the end of the month she received a check for one hundred dollars from David, along with a note that said, "Please accept it. For Joan's sake." It was just like David to be considerate and unselfish; it was just like her not to be. Still, she distrusted unselfish people, she could never believe they were on the level. She sent David a thank-you note in return, saying that he was a darling and that she hoped Lillian was feeling okay these days.

"Lillian is fine," David said when he phoned her shortly after receiving the note. "But how are you? I've missed you terribly."

What should she say? That she missed him, too? It would only falsely encourage him. "I'm okay."

"Would you like to get together for a drink some evening, or dinner?"

It seemed almost too rude to say no. "No, I don't think that's a good idea." Then, she added, "Under the circumstances."

"We can be friends, can't we?"

The bedroom loomed up between them. "Of course, David. Friends."

"I'll call you again."

"Take care of yourself, David."

"You, too, baby."

Meanwhile, other conversations were about to take place.

Conversation #1: Beverly and Anita

Beverly: This is Beverly Northrop. Do you remember me?

Anita: Oh yes, of course. How are you?

Beverly: Pretty good. My children and I have just gotten back from a month in Martha's Vineyard.

Anita: Lucky you.

Beverly: No sooner did we return than I received a phone call from a man who says he's a friend of yours. An Englishman—

Anita: Ian Clarke?

Beverly: That's the man.

Anita: I hope you don't mind my having given him your number, but I thought the two of you might like each other.

Beverly: That was very thoughtful of you. We haven't met yet, which is really why I'm calling. I wanted to ask you what he's like.

Anita (eagerly): He's very sweet, very reliable, and very attractive.

Beverly: What does he do?

Anita: He works for that television show, "Quiz."

Beverly: "Quiz"? Isn't that the one where all the contestants are high school dropouts?

Anita: Yes, yes, that's it. Ian is an assistant director. He recruits the dropouts.

Beverly: It sounds like a charming job.

Anita: Well, you see, being a foreigner it wasn't easy for him to break into television, so he took what he could get. But he'll go on to other, better things. He's very bright.

Beverly: What does he look like?

Anita: Tall, blond, you know, *English.*

Beverly (giving up on that): I saw that piece on you in *The Rag.* What did you think of the girl who interviewed you?

Anita: Lou Marron? I think she's a dyke. Well, not really a dyke, but definitely AC/DC.

Beverly: Oh? How could you tell?

Anita: She's screwing your AC/DC husband, isn't she?

Conversation #2: Anita and Simone

Anita: Hi, I just got a call from that cunt, Beverly Northrop.

Simone (eating a new meat-loaf TV dinner that featured a nut brownie for dessert): You're beginning to talk just like me. Has Robert told you that yet?

Anita: Don't get bitchy just because Stacey went back to Detroit. You'll find another freak, you always do.

Simone: Thanks for the compliment, but it has nothing to do with Stacey. In fact, I'm glad he's out of the picture. He was starting to get on my nerves. I kept hearing chains rattling in my sleep. But let's not talk about me all the time. How are you getting on *avec Monsieur* Fingerhood?

Anita: Frankly, not so good since my abortion. It really took a lot out of me.

Simone: I should hope so, because if it didn't you'd be in your third month by now.

Anita: I'm going to overlook these insults, Simone. We've been friends for a long time and I can tell when you're upset about something. I can always tell when you're upset.

Simone: How?

Anita: You invariably sink to a low Gallic level.

Simone: It's preferable to sinking to a low Germanic level, isn't it, Fräulein Norforms?

Anita: I'm just going to overlook you for the time being. What I called to say is it appears that I might have fixed Beverly up with Ian, the fortune hunter. Wouldn't that serve her right?

Simone: For what?

Anita: You're a fine one to ask that question! Don't you remember finding her screwing Robert on the floor two days after he kicked you out? Don't tell me you've since become friends with her again.

Simone: As a matter of fact, I have. Beverly is okay. I've forgiven her.

Anita: Well I haven't.

Simone: You don't have anything to forgive her *for*.

Anita: That's what you think. She has large breasts and a lot of money, doesn't she?

Simone: It's not her fault.

Anita: I know and that makes it doubly worse. She didn't even try to get them and she's got them. Look at me. I've been trying for twenty-five years and I'm still flat-chested and broke.

Simone: Twenty-six.

Anita: If it weren't for the fact that you've never had an orgasm, I wouldn't be so forgiving, but frankly I feel sorry for you, Simone. That's why I don't get angry.

Simone: I'd prefer it if you got angry. Who wants your lousy sympathy anyway? Besides, I'm working on something new in the orgasm department and one of these days I'm going to have a great *succès fou,* I can tell you that.

Anita: I'm not going to ask what it is because I'm afraid to hear. But I thought you'd like to know that your darling David Swern is being two-timed by his girlfriend.

Simone (impressed for the first time): Who is she two-timing him with?

Anita: Beverly's faggy husband.

Simone: How do you know he's faggy?

Anita: You told me so yourself when you got back from Mexico. Dope.

Simone: Why would you believe anything I say? You know what a notorious liar I am.

Anita: That's the last straw. I hope you never come.

Simone (wistfully): It's a combination of reverse psychology and yoga restraint. You keep saying to yourself, "I don't want to come, I don't want to come, I don't want to . . ."

Conversation #3: Simone and David

Simone: Mr. Swern, there's something I think you should know.

David (bored): Yes?

Simone: It's about Miss O'Hara.

David (not bored): Is something wrong? Is she in trouble? Has there been an accident?

Simone: She's in trouble, all right, but I wouldn't call it an accident. It sounds pretty deliberate to me.

David: What the hell are you talking about?

Simone: Miss O'Hara is fucking Mr. Northrop, Mr. Swern.

David (turning green): You're fired, Miss Lassitier.

When Peter asked Lou why she had a cat, Lou said:

"Because he's not really a cat. He's a prince. That is, he's going to turn into a prince one of these days."

"Or a frog."

"Sometimes I hate you."

Peter sang, *"And when I hate you it's 'cause I love you, so what can I do, I'm happy when I'm with you."*

"And I'm miserable."

They had run into each other on the way to the office and Peter suggested they stop for coffee at an Automat a few blocks from *The Rag*. It had been three days since they'd slept together.

"Are we on for tonight?" Peter asked when they had taken a table.

"We're on if you're on."

"I'm turned on."

"Who did it? Another girl? Beverly perhaps?"

"You're very prescient this morning."

"No, not prescient, darling." She was even beginning to talk like him. "Prescience has to do with the future. I'm talking about the immediate past. Like the last three nights."

He laughed, but made no attempt to deny the charge.

"You can't kid me," Lou said bitterly.

"Would I try to kid a kidder like you?"

"You'd *try*," she said. "Please pass the sugar."

But as they were leaving, he said, "There's one slight catch about tonight. I have to go to my daughter's birthday party first. She's six today. Would you like to come with me?"

The invitation startled Lou. "Won't Beverly be there?"

"Of course. She's Sally's mother."

"I'd love to go." Her stomach was starting to churn already. "Thank you."

The first thing that impressed Lou that evening was the apartment building that Beverly lived in. It was not one of those brand-new, chrome-plated, potted-palm, Miami Beach catastrophes, as she had expected. It was an older, more dignified building with an unprepossessing lobby, a disinterested doorman, and a self-service elevator.

Peter pushed the PH bell, and up they went. The symbolism was not lost upon Lou, who immediately thought of her own ground floor, garden apartment.

She had received a letter from her mother that morning, saying that Joan was becoming more rebellious by the minute. The latest thing was that she now refused to eat breakfast. Lou became infuriated when she read this. As a child, her mother used to practically force-feed her lumpy oatmeal, after which she would proceed to gag and throw up. In the summertime, it was Grapenuts. No wonder Joan had rebelled. She was undoubtedly getting the same forced breakfast treatment. The only thing that had ever made Lou gag faster than thinking of oatmeal and Grapenuts, was going down on David.

When she had gone to bed with Peter, four days ago, the first thing he said was, "I haven't had a good blow job in ages."

Her first reaction, which she did not express, was "Oh shit," but as it turned out, Peter was another matter in the going down department. She liked doing it to him, perhaps because she knew that his getting an erection was not dependent upon it, the way David's was. With David she had always experienced it as a kind of social welfare practice, which was enough to turn anyone right off.

Lou had written a letter to her mother that afternoon when she had some free time at the office, telling her to stop forcing Joan to eat breakfast if she didn't want it. "You used to do the same thing to me," she wrote. "Remember? And I haven't been able to eat breakfast since, thanks to you." But after one of the copy boys had picked up the letter, she became depressed. Did one hundred dollars a month entitle her to dictate terms?

"Here we are," Peter said, ringing the doorbell.

A heavy Negro maid, decked out in a white ruffled half apron and matching cap, opened the door. Lou was intrigued to notice that instead of wearing any semblance of a traditional maid's uniform beneath the apron, she had on what looked like a geometric Ungaro in flaming red. Lou had the distinct feeling that the woman was going to break into the African Jerk any minute, instead of which she very calmly said, "Good evening, Mr. Northrop."

"How are you, Margaret? This is Miss Marron. Lou, this is Margaret."

"Hello, Margaret," Lou said. "That's a pretty snappy dress you're wearing."

Margaret gave her a suspicious look. "Thank you, Ma'am."

"Stop putting on the hired help," Peter whispered into Lou's ear as they went into the living room, where, on one wall hung a huge, blown-up photograph of Adolf Hitler, minus the moustache.

"I had Cav do the blow-up," Peter said.

One blindfolded little girl, holding a paper moustache in her hand, was being spun around by a little boy, and when the spinning stopped she marched unsteadily in the direction of the photograph and tried to pin the moustache above Hitler's mouth. It landed, instead, on his ear and all the children at the party laughed.

"It's an educational game I devised for children," Peter said. "Instead of pinning the tail on the donkey, they pin the moustache on Hitler, the cigar on Winston Churchill, the eyeglasses on FDR, etc."

"Isn't it a bit anachronistic? I mean, the personages you've chosen for the game? Why not a Mao Tse-tung or a Lyndon Johnson?"

"That will be another series. This is the World War II series. I have various series planned, covering different periods in world history."

There were crepe paper streamers and balloons all over the room, and in the center of a long table, covered with a glistening white cloth, sat a frothy whipped cream cake with six pink birthday candles in it.

"Daddy! Daddy!"

It was the little girl who had just pinned the moustache on Hitler's ear. She threw her arms around Peter and hugged him tight. Her dress lifted up as she did so and Lou caught a peek of flowered underpants in the same pattern as her dainty summer dress.

"Daddy, I was afraid you weren't coming."

"Now, sweetheart, you know better than that. Would I miss my baby's birthday party?"

"Maybe you would," Sally said, glancing at Lou, "if we're going to be divorced."

"That kind of talk is silly. I'm surprised at you. Parents don't divorce children and sometimes they don't even divorce each other. Happy birthday, sweetheart."

After he had introduced Sally to Lou, Sally said:

"Oh, I know who you are. You're the lady who writes about brassieres and girdles for my daddy's paper."

"That's right," Lou said, struck by the resemblance between father and daughter.

"I don't think you should do that. I think you should write about baking contests instead."

Lou and Peter laughed, Sally returned to her guests, and then Beverly appeared. She was taller and much better looking than Lou had expected, and her hair was beautiful. It hung down well below her shoulders, which were freckled and lightly tanned. She wore a romantic lime chiffon dress, with a very low-cut, ruffled neckline that revealed a generous portion of the breasts Peter had said he was tired of. Lou wondered what kind of brassiere Beverly had on. She had a sudden, overwhelming urge to suck Beverly's breasts.

"Darling," Peter said to his wife, "I want you to meet . . ."

Beverly was drinking something out of an opaque glass, almost the same shade of green as her dress, and Lou noticed that beneath the tan her eyes were bloodshot and she looked tired. Margaret and another thin Negro maid had started to bring dishes of food out of the kitchen and place them on the long table. There were huge vases of red and yellow long-stemmed roses all around the room, and in one corner sat a baby grand. Lou thought of her daughter gagging on Grape-nuts on Spruce Street.

"I'm so glad you could come," Beverly said to Lou. "I've heard a great deal about you from Peter. He thinks you're a wonderful reporter."

"Thank you, but I'm afraid your daughter doesn't approve of my subject matter. She's of the opinion that I should write about baking contests."

A look passed between the two women. Empathy? Animosity? Despair? Lou was not sure. She had come here prepared to dislike Beverly, but now she was not certain how she felt about her. As a rule she could define her emotions rather quickly, yet there was a complexity here that she did not understand. If it weren't for Peter, we might be friends, she thought. Something about Beverly appealed to her. Beneath the healthy, well-groomed exterior was a lost woman.

"Where are the presents?" Peter asked his wife.

"I put them in Margaret's closet. That seemed like the safest hiding place."

"Shall we give them to her now?"

"I was just wondering the same thing."

But Lou had stopped listening. She felt like a gauche intruder in this little domestic scene; she did not belong here at all. Whatever had possessed her to accept Peter's invitation? Only the curiosity about Beverly. Now that she had met her, though, she could barely remember what she had expected her to look like or be like, and a moment later she realized why. It was because Beverly never existed for her, not really, she was a phantom figure, blurry, vague, a person whom Peter referred to as his wife, but, who, to Lou's mind, had always been a nonperson, a nonbeing.

And it was also how she thought of Lillian. She would probably like Lillian, too, if she ever met her, which seemed pretty unlikely at this point. David. She missed him already. She did not want him back, not on the old physical terms, but she missed him. He had been her friend, a relationship she knew she would never enjoy with Peter. Did Peter have friends? She wondered. Then she wondered whether she was able to be friends with David because passion had been at a minimum. Why should friendship preclude passion? Or passion, friendship?

"I guess I had better give Sally my presents now," Peter said, "because we have to be running along pretty soon."

"Where are you going?" Beverly asked. "That is, I'm sorry you can't stay longer. You haven't even said hello to your son."

"I was about to, darling. I just walked in."

"And you can't wait to walk out."

Lou started to say, "I feel somewhat responsible for—"

"It's not your fault," Peter cut in.

"It's nobody's fault," Beverly said, without rancor.

Just then Margaret approached Beverly and told her that a Mr. Clark was on the telephone.

"I'll take it in the kitchen," Beverly said, excusing herself.

When she returned, there was a distinct frown on her face. "My dinner date just conked out. He has to go to dinner with his producer. Business. Is that all men in New York think about? I don't know how any of them find the time to get laid, they're so obsessed with getting ahead. Wouldn't you say that's true, Miss Marron?"

"I wouldn't know. I'm too busy trying to get ahead myself."

"Yes, the competition must be pretty rough."

"You get used to it."

"I never could," Beverly said, sipping her drink. "Men in New York frighten me. I didn't realize how insulated I was when we lived in Garden City. Now I see that it was like living in a cotton candy world."

"Then you don't miss it."

"Too much cotton candy makes you sick." Beverly took another sip. "Too much Scotch, also."

"In that case, why don't you knock it off, darling?" Peter asked.

"I enjoy being a caricature. It amuses me. You know, the upper-middle-class, bored housewife whose husband doesn't love her any more, so she guzzles herself to death while watching soap operas on television."

"Your well of self-pity has never ceased to amaze me."

"Ditto for your appalling lack of compassion."

"There's no point in trading insults," Peter said. "Let's go get Sally's presents, shall we?"

Later, after Peter and Lou had escaped to the bar at the Carlyle, Lou said, "I liked your wife."

"You mean, you felt sorry for her."

"Not entirely. I never feel sorry for people who are attractive."

"Yes, she is attractive, isn't she?" He looked at himself in the mirror over the bar. "In spite of all her boozing."

"Does she really drink that much?"

"Only when she's awake. The woman is a fish. She has one of those unusual alcoholic capacities that you have to see to believe."

"Was she always that way? When you were first married, for instance?"

"She didn't drink so heavily the first few years but the proclivity was there right from the start. In looking back, I wonder why I didn't see the warning signs."

"You were in love with her then."

"I guess that's what it was."

Despite the fact that he was in part disgusted by his wife, Lou felt that an attraction for her still existed. Or was it just pity? Lou did not genuinely pity Beverly, she suspected there were hidden resources to the woman, ones that perhaps Peter knew nothing about, wanted to know nothing about. He's partially done in his wife, Lou thought, and now he's started on me.

Peter said, "Beverly is going to join us here as soon as Sally blows out the birthday candles."

"Here?"

"Yes, I hope you don't mind. She feeling pretty down in the dumps. That fellow breaking his date with her for tonight, and all."

Lou felt like saying, "But I do mind, I mind very much. How could you think that I wouldn't? Murderer."

Instead she made the mistake of trying to be civilized. "It should be an interesting evening."

It was.

Beverly was considerably higher than she had been when they'd left her at the party, and her mood seemed to have gotten worse, she seemed more sullen than before, alternately more abject and more abusive.

One minute Beverly would say, "My whole life is ruined, nobody cares whether I live or die, I might as well kill myself."

But the next minute she would look around the richly appointed room with glaring, angry eyes, and say, "This is a filthy place. Let's get out of here."

They went to a bar in Harlem called Lots of Momma and ordered the house special, a Black Mother, which turned out to be nothing more exotic than Kahlúa and milk with shaved ice. But that became boring too after a few minutes, particularly since nobody paid any attention to them and the air-conditioning was on the murky side.

"Where to now?"

It was Lou who asked, knowing even as she asked that if she had half a brain she would leave the two of them and go home to her garden and her cat. But not being used to drinking, she was high and could not face either the garden or the cat, she wanted to get higher, go farther, do something to break the spell she'd been living under since she had become involved with Peter. Sexual obsession was not a happy state of affairs; Lou wanted to be able to take sex, or leave it, not be dominated by it, as she now was. Extremes of feeling frightened her, she did not want to care that much about anybody. If she did not care too terribly much, then she could have the upper hand, as she had had with David. But she had left David for Peter (she bitterly reminded herself), Peter had made her become bored with the moderation she'd enjoyed with dear David.

And she had enjoyed it, because David proved to be good for her. With him, she worked well, felt a certain amount of pride in herself, slept soundly. With Peter, she was a wreck, and for what? Love? What a funny word that was, anyway, what funny misconceptions had been built up around it. Like love equals misery, anxiety, uncertainty, ecstasy. Proust had said that a person could only recognize the person he loved by the amount of pain that person caused him. That's why Proust lived in a cork-lined room and slept in a heavy overcoat and ran out in the middle of the night to talk to the headwaiter at the Ritz. Because he had such hot ideas.

As they were leaving the bar in Harlem, Peter said, "Let's drink some opium," and both girls drunkenly nodded. So he took them to a town house in the East Sixties to which it seemed he had a key.

"How do you drink opium?" Lou asked once they were inside the house.

There were three floors to the house but upon Peter's advice they remained on the ground floor where there were two rooms and a kitchen. The large room was filled with immense constructions of plaster people at a party. Some of the people were dancing with each other, some were standing at a real bar waiting for the plaster bartender to mix their plaster drinks, some of the people were embracing, one plaster man stood with his hand cupped around the breast of a plaster woman in a pantsuit, some of the people were eating plaster hotdogs painted to look like the real thing, and there was a plaster policeman with a plaster holster containing a plaster revolver. The policeman was talking to a plaster man in a motorcycle jacket and crash helmet.

"It's very simple," Peter said. "I'll show you."

He went into the kitchen and began to boil water in a tea kettle. Then he took three mugs off the cupboard shelf and filled them about one fourth of the way with sugar, added a tea bag to each mug, and poured in the boiling water.

"The sugar cuts the bitterness of the opium," he explained to Lou, who had followed him in.

From somewhere upstairs came the muted sound of a man singing a jazz record. *Hey Miss Bessie, you sure have some fine barbecue, I'll be around to get some tonight about a quarter to two.*

Beverly had remained in the large room and was dancing solo to the music when they returned with the three mugs of steaming tea. Peter took an aspirin box out of the plaster policeman's jacket pocket and removed three tiny, paper-thin pieces of what looked to Lou like truffles. Beverly paid no attention to anything except her dazed dancing, but when she nearly crashed into one of the plaster dancers, Peter told her to sit down.

Against the wall were a few cheap, metal folding chairs and she sat down heavily in one of them. "Is this where you take the children on alternate weekends?" she asked her husband.

The other, smaller room could be vaguely seen from the room they were in because the door to it was open. There was a bed in there, with a highly polished brass headboard and a cover that faded into the blackness of the room itself. Several gold-fringed pillows glistened in the blackness.

"What you do," Peter said, addressing both of them, "is put the opium under your tongue, but don't swallow it. Then you take a sip of tea and hold it in your mouth for a couple of seconds, swallow the tea, and take another sip. But don't swallow the opium. The point is to let the tea gradually dissolve the opium."

"What happens if you swallow it?" Lou asked.

"It takes much longer to work."

"What does it feel like when it works?"

"A very pleasant warm sensation starts to infuse your entire body. It starts in the stomach."

"I'm hungry," Beverly said.

"Shut up," Peter told her, "and drink your tea."

A moment later, she said, "I swallowed you-know-what. Now what?"

"Look at your watch and wait twenty minutes. If nothing happens by then, I'll give you more."

Peter became high first. They were all sitting on the metal folding chairs, lined up like wallflowers at a dance, waiting for the strains of "Goodnight, Ladies" to relieve them of their misery. The record man upstairs continued to sing:

I don't want it too hot, don't want it too cold, I want to eat the meat right down to the bone.

Afterwards, Lou would not remember who went into the bedroom first, who second, and who third, but it all happened in a hazy dream. She was floating far above the universe. She remembered the initial feel of the cover on the bed, it was some sort of soft black fur and it tickled her back, then her nipples, because she had turned over, or was that Beverly?

They were suddenly, but slowly all enmeshed, Peter was inside her, she had rolled back on her back and he had shoved one of the gold-tasseled pillows underneath her, and she lay there outstretched with her arms behind her head, and with Beverly, eyes closed, nibbling at her breasts, then Beverly kissed Peter on the mouth above her head, Lou tried to kiss them both at the same time but it became mixed up, and all the while she was lying there, she floated way above the bed, bodiless. Nothing but body. The dream was real. Tongues crossed. Faces were immersed. Lou's mouth was buried in Beverly's cunt, flicking buttons, as Peter, the sultan, observed until observation wore thin and he buried his mouth in Lou, the tips of his toes grazing Beverly's long red hair.

Not a word was exchanged, only muted animal sounds that lingered in the heavy air, refusing to vanish, waiting to be uttered again by one of the three madnesses. It was a slow-motion dance. Lou felt drugged. Peter was the choreographer. Now he would arrange them so, now in still another strange stance, but it would only seem strange to Lou the next day, because all the time it was happening it followed a natural unity of bodies. She felt. She was nothing but one extended mass of sensations. Her worst fears had been realized. Here was the final hedonism (she felt, not thought), and it would not kill her, she absolutely was not going to die as a result of being eaten alive by two other madnesses.

Don't want it too fat, don't want it too lean, Hey, Bess, you know what I mean.

The record must have been playing over and over again, and it was still playing when the three of them emerged from the black bedroom much later, and wordlessly began to dress themselves. Peter straightened his tie and tightened his belt. Beverly's breasts went back into semihiding behind her lime chiffon ruffles. Lou fastened the top of her beat orange summer stockings to her garter belt, which was embroidered with the words, "*Je me'en fiche.*" As she reached to the side for the back garter, she saw a man's leg, a real leg among the plaster people. It stared her in the face.

She opened her mouth, but no sound emerged. It was Tony Elliot in a double-breasted, pinstriped gangster suit, holding a plaster drink in his hand, and wearing a long blond wig on his head. Their eyes met like pieces of glass. Lou turned to Beverly in mute supplication, and Beverly turned to Peter. With the beginnings of a smile on his thin lips, Peter turned to Tony, who drew a piece of the blond wig above his mouth to simulate a moustache. Peter laughed.

It was the sound of his laughter that set Lou off. She walked to the plaster policeman, removed the plaster revolver from his holster, and pressed the gun to Peter's moist temple. Then she pulled the trigger. A trumpet blast from the record upstairs filled the silence for a moment, the next sound being Peter's fall to the floor, the next his continuing laughter, even as he clutched his stomach and writhed like George Raft.

Lou and Beverly continued to get dressed, but Tony Elliot had begun to tug at the policeman's arm to show him the plaster murder that had just taken place.

Part 3

CHAPTER EIGHT

It was a Wednesday morning in mid-September and Simone was getting dressed for David Swern's funeral.

At least she was trying to. The combination of shock, grief, and her usual clothes disorganization had considerably slowed down her efforts. She had started to get dressed at nine o'clock, over an hour before, and was now still debating between a black crochet mini and a black Arnel dress slip. The crochet seemed more dignified, and therefore more suitable for the occasion, but it had a peculiar spot in front that neither water nor rubbing would remove. She could not imagine where the spot had come from nor what had caused it: food, drink, sperm. The last man to come on a dress of hers was that nutty behavioral psychologist, but that was ages ago, and a different dress altogether. Oh well. She reconsidered the dress slip. It was really more for evening than for a funeral, it reminded her of those dresses that Italian actresses used to sit around in in the old Rossellini movies, when they were supposed to be portraying prostitutes.

Simone could have kicked herself for impetuously throwing out the three black work dresses she used to model in. Any one of them would have been perfect for a funeral, but when David Swern had fired her last month she'd been so upset that after she got home she stuck all three of them down the incinerator in a moment of spiteful fury. At first she had thought he was kidding about firing her, she just couldn't believe he was on the level.

"And just because I told him that Miss O'Hara was fucking

Mr. Northrop," she had cried on Helen's shoulder in the dressing room.

The other model found her naïveté incredible.

"How could you think you'd be able to talk to your boss like that and *not* get fired?" Helen asked.

"I was only trying to do him a good turn. Clue him in on what was happening behind his poor, innocent back."

"You clued him in, all right. How much severance pay is he giving you?"

"Two weeks."

"What are you going to do about another job?"

Simone dried her tears. "I guess I'll go to work for Dr. Hocker."

"Who's he?"

"He's a nice little chiropodist I met at the Russian Tea Room. His office is right around the corner from where I live, and he said he was looking for a girl to help him out."

"What will you do? Cut dirty toenails?"

"We didn't go into the morbid details, but what's the difference? He's a very sweet man and the location is terribly convenient. I could go home for lunch."

"Providing you still had an appetite left after sniffing all those old feet for hours."

"I have a lousy sense of smell. So does Dr. Hocker. He said that after three days I won't smell a thing. Look at the men who work on the city's sanitation trucks. I'll bet they think their garbage smells like Arpège."

"Why not get a job modeling for another furrier? You have good experience."

"No. I need a change of scene."

Helen shrugged. "Dr. Hocker sounds like a change of scene all right."

"Besides, he said I could wear one of those cute white nurse's uniforms. White will be refreshing after all this gloomy black, day in and day out. I have a hunch I'll feel happier in white."

"It's hard for me to visualize you in a nurse's uniform."

Simone laughed. "Yes, it is a fucking riot, isn't it?"

The funeral was to take place at 11 A.M. at the Riverside Chapel on Seventy-Sixth Street and Amsterdam Avenue. Helen had telephoned her last night to tell her the tragic news.

"He died right in the showroom before everybody's eyes. One minute he was sitting there with that creepy buyer from Louisville, talking about muskrat flanks, and the next minute he was slumped over on the table. By the time the ambulance arrived, he was cold as a fish. Heart attack, just like I predicted."

"I wonder how Miss O'Hara is taking it."

"I don't know about her, but his wife is pretty shook up. She started to scream on the phone when she was told what had happened."

"It's ironic," Simone said. "All those years she was the invalid, and then he goes ahead and kicks off. Well, the funeral should be interesting."

Helen was amazed. "You mean, you're *going?*"

"Of course. Aren't you?"

"Not on your sweet life. Have you ever gone to a Jewish funeral?"

"No."

"They're maudlin, Simone. They're unbelievably maudlin, no restraint at all, and particularly in a case like this where the death was so sudden. You'll see. They'll be gasping and fainting in the aisles."

"Well, you can't expect them to act like it's the Chinese New Year, can you?"

"I admire your courage. Let me know what Miss O'Hara looks like."

"I shall take copious notes," Simone promised.

Dr. Hocker had very kindly given her the morning off so she could go to the funeral. Working for a chiropodist was not bad, not bad at all, Simone decided as she made one last attempt to remove the stubborn spot from the crochet mini. Corns and ingrown toenails. She never would have believed that so many people, who otherwise looked perfectly okay, were suffering from either corns or ingrown toenails. Dr. Hocker was raking in a small fortune in feet. Her only direct contact with feet was to wash them afterward and gently sprinkle a little talcum powder between the toes. The rest of the time she answered the telephone, made appointments, and sent out bills. At noon she went home and heated a TV dinner on her hot plate, and took Chou-Chou for a walk along Fifty-Seventh Street. No, it was not bad.

But the spot would not come out and Simone finally decided to pin a cameo brooch over it. The brooch looked a little odd sitting there near the bottom of the dress, but maybe people would think it was a new fad. The other dress was really out of the question, it just would not do for a solemn (and maudlin) occasion like this. It would be an insult to the memory of Mr. Swern, for even though he had fired her she still retained fond recollections of the dear man.

Guilty ones, too. Perhaps by telling him about Miss O'Hara's extracurricular sexual activities, she had inadvertently driven him to a premature death.

Simone took the Seventh Avenue subway to the Riverside Chapel ("That's where all the rich Jews end up," Helen had said). She had not taken a subway since she stopped working for Mini-Furs, Inc., and she found it just as distasteful now as then. Despite all the years she had spent in New York, it never ceased to amaze her how many ugly people there were in the city, and how many of them talked to themselves. When she got out on Seventy-Second Street, a Puerto Rican in a short-sleeved, brightly striped shirt asked her whether it was warm enough for her for September. Simone felt sorry for the Puerto Ricans, but wished they would go home where they would not be looked down upon and treated so shabbily. It amazed her that they continued to hang on in New York.

The Riverside Chapel was a large, impressive building, and Simone felt her heart pounding as she approached it. When she had told Helen that she never attended a Jewish funeral, she failed to add that she never attended any funeral at all in her entire life. The idea of death was too horrifying for her to want to come face to face with it, as she was about to. And yet she had come here today, driven on by a combination of guilt, remorse, and curiosity.

There were a number of people standing in the street outside the chapel, talking to each other and looking at their watches. Simone did not own a watch but she knew it was before eleven, because she had seen a clock in the subway. When she entered the lobby of the building, a tall, solemn, gray-haired man in a black suit darted forward to greet her. He looked like one of the Addams family.

"Can I be of assistance?"

"Yes, I'd like to know where the service for Mr. Swern is being held."

"On the fourth floor. It hasn't started yet."

"Thank you."

The elevator operator was very solemn-looking, too, very soulful. Simone suspected that at the end of the work day they all went bowling together and drank beer.

As she stepped out of the elevator three young men, resembling ushers in a movie theater, beckoned to her. She had the feeling they were going to suggest a good front-row seat at the double feature she was about to witness, but where were their flashlights? They showed her into the high-ceilinged, stained-glass chapel where a fair amount of people were already gathered.

"The deceased is up front," one of the young men whispered. "The service will start in ten minutes."

She wondered who the people were standing outside in the street. Perhaps they were waiting for another service, or perhaps they did not want to see the deceased any more than she did. Still, it was too late now.

They had put too much rouge on Mr. Swern's cheeks, trying to make him look healthy and lifelike, which struck Simone as most peculiar since he was cold, stone dead. A quiet procession of people walked in single file past the open coffin of David Swern, some of them with tears in their eyes, some with terrible anguish on their faces, some with a seeming bland curiosity. After they had observed the dead man, they stopped and spoke to a woman seated in the front row, directly behind the coffin. Simone recognized her immediately as David's widow, because of the photograph that he used to keep of her in his office.

Mrs. Swern was small, with curly brown hair and brown eyes that showed no sign of tears. In fact, her entire demeanor was composed and dignified, not at all what Simone had expected after listening to Helen's account of her reaction to her husband's sudden death. Also, to Simone's amazement, Mrs. Swern looked unbelievably healthy. Was this the semi-invalid who suffered all those colitis attacks and had to be bedridden for days at a time?

Simone approached her and said, "We've never met, but I used to work for Mr. Swern. My name is Simone Lassitier."

Mrs. Swern smiled at her. "Yes, he mentioned you to me. You're the little French girl who modeled for him. He liked you very much. He was sorry when you quit."

Simone felt flattered that Mr. Swern had even referred to her departure, and yet annoyed that he had misrepresented the facts. On the other hand, he could hardly be expected to tell his wife that he'd fired an employee because she knew too much about his girlfriend.

"He was a wonderful man," Simone said. "I was terribly sorry to hear about his . . . passing."

She hated words like *passing*, they made her want to choke.

"Thank you, my dear. We shall all miss him a great deal."

Simone thought of her own father being killed by the Germans, when she was just a baby, and suddenly she had to go to the bathroom in the worst way. One of the movie ushers showed her where it was. There were several women in the outer room, combing their hair and dabbing pressed powder on their noses before the mirror. One of them said, "I hope the service isn't too long. I have to meet Florence at Longchamps at twelve-thirty."

In the other room, with the toilets and sinks, a girl could distinctly be heard throwing up behind one of the closed doors. Simone cursed the lack of privacy in public American bathrooms, because she knew that in a minute she too would be distinctly heard, and there was nothing she could do about it, there was no way to hold back the attack of diarrhea she felt coming on. Nerves. They would be her undoing yet, although working for Dr. Hocker had certain advantages like unlimited supplies of Miltown, as well as a weekly screw (for her nerves) in one of his nice, reclining chairs. Dr. Hocker proved to be very concerned about her orgasm problem, but since he looked like Charlie McCarthy she tended to laugh, rather than come, when he was doing it to her.

Simone came face to face with the vomiter, minutes later, when she emerged to wash her hands. The girl standing at the next sink had straight black hair, geometrically styled, and was wearing a black crepe shimmy dress reminiscent of the twenties, but it was the bracelet on her arm that made Simone stop and stare at her with great interest. The bracelet was composed of emeralds, rubies, and rose quartz, and Simone remembered only too well the day last winter when Mr. Swern had sent her to Cartier's to pick it up.

"Excuse me," she said, "but you're Lou Marron, aren't you?"

The girl stopped washing her hands and observed Simone with quiet amazement. "Who are you?"

"I used to work for Mr. Swern. My name is Simone Lassitier, and I remember that bracelet very well. I was the one who picked it up for him at Cartier's."

There was barely the trace of a smile on Lou Marron's angular face, but it did not strike Simone as a particularly pleasant smile. She dried her hands in a hurry.

"Simone. Yes, of course. You're the little girl with the big mouth, as I recall."

"I don't have the vaguest idea what you mean by that," Simone said, nervously recalling the exchange she had had with Mr. Swern that led to her being fired.

"Would you like me to refresh your memory?"

Simone wished she had brought a Miltown with her, something told her she was going to need it very shortly.

"It's not necessary," she said. "I'm really not interested."

"Listen, you miserable little troublemaker, do you know all the damage you've caused? Or perhaps you don't care. People like you usually don't. All you care about is destroying innocent people's lives with your vicious gossip."

"It's been very nice talking to you," Simone said, "but I have to go to a funeral."

She got as far as the door when Lou Marron grabbed her by the shoulders, with wet hands, and whirled her around. Simone was so startled by this physical assault that she made no attempt to defend herself, as the other girl smacked her across the face and screamed, "This is for telling David about Peter and me, you miserable slut!"

Simone burst into tears. "You broke his heart and you call *me* a slut."

"You killed David by telling him that."

"It wouldn't have killed him if it weren't true."

Lou looked trapped for the first time, and some of the anger drained out of her face. "You also told your friend, Anita, that I was indirectly responsible for giving her crabs."

"It was just a theory," Simone sobbed. "Why do you take everything so seriously? You must be a Capricorn."

Lou had calmed down to a state of quiet trembling.

"I'm a Leo," she said.

"I'll bet you have Capricorn rising. Mr. Swern was a Capricorn. That's why he wore vests all the time."

"I don't know what you're talking about."

"If you have Capricorn rising, it would explain why you were attracted to him. It would mean that your unconscious was equivalent to his conscious."

"Is that another one of your theories?" Lou asked, with unconcealed contempt.

"It's not a theory, it's an astrological fact. But you're too busy writing about underwear to be interested in the deeper aspects of life. Of course, being a Leo you were too strong for poor Mr. Swern. I'm only a Libra. A Libra could never do a Capricorn in. Leave it to a Leo to commit murder. Look at Castro, if you don't believe me."

"You're obviously insane," Lou Marron said. "Also, your fall is on cockeyed."

They walked back to the chapel together and sat side by side near the back of the crowded room. The service had already started, but Simone was so shook up by the strange bathroom incident that she barely listened to the rabbi's eulogy, although now and then she would emerge from her meditations to hear several of his comments about Mr. Swern.

"... he had a kind and generous heart."

"... he died with a startling suddenness."

"... his memory will be long revered by all who knew and loved him."

From among the congregation came sounds of people softly crying, and to Simone's surprise she realized that Lou was one of them. She instinctively reached out a hand and patted Lou on the arm, as though to reassure her of her sympathy. Lou looked at her with wet and surprised eyes.

"I think it's going to be over soon," Simone whispered. "Do you want a Kleenex?"

Lou nodded miserably.

As Simone pulled a Kleenex out of her purse, one of her ubiquitous Pursettes, which had been lodged inside the Kleenex, fell on the floor of the Riverside Chapel and started to roll down front toward the principal mourners.

"The family of the deceased will sit shivah at 960 West End Avenue," the rabbi announced.

Then the organ music swelled up and the velvet-covered coffin came down the aisle, carried by two men in stiff black suits, wearing black skullcaps on their heads, as did all the men in the room. They were followed by the rabbi, who intoned the Twenty-Third Psalm as he went.

"Yea, though I walk through the valley of the shadow of death, I will fear no evil, for Thou art with me, Thy rod and Thy staff, they comfort me, Thou preparest a table before me in the presence of mine enemies ..."

Behind the rabbi came Mrs. Swern, crying profusely now, supported on one side by a woman of her own age, and on the other by a young man who wore a string tie and had an enormous black moustache. Simone significantly poked Lou.

"That's *her*."

Lou nodded, but her eyes were riveted to the man with the moustache. "Steve Omaha! What the hell is he doing here?"

"He's sort of cute," Simone said, wondering whether anyone had picked up her luckless Pursette, and if so, what he made of it. "Even with that thing on his head. Do you know him?"

"I did a story on him some months back, but they never ran it. He must be a relative of David's. How absolutely weird."

Steve Omaha's moustache fascinated Simone. It was one of the bushiest moustaches she had ever seen and she had a creepy suspicion it might prove to be the answer to her stubborn orgasm problem. However, she didn't think this was the time to mention such things, particularly to Lou Marron, whom she barely knew, so she forced herself to keep her mouth shut as she and Lou silently followed the rest of the congregation downstairs.

In the main lobby, it was immediately apparent that something had gone wrong with the arrangements for driving out to the burial grounds in Queens. People were standing about in groups of two's and three's, whispering excitedly to each other, shaking their heads, shrugging their shoulders in disgust.

"Maybe Mr. Swern has come to life and stepped out of the casket," Simone suggested. "Wouldn't that be a fucking shock?"

"They're talking to one of the chapel officials," Lou said.

"Who is?"

"Mrs. Swern and that other woman."

"What if Mr. Swern just stepped out and said, 'Hi, folks. Fooled you, didn't I?' "

Lou was looking at Mrs. Swern. "I'm curious to know what's going on."

It took Simone a moment to realize that what Lou was curious about was meeting David's widow, this was her last chance.

"*J'ai une idée,*" Simone said. "Why don't you introduce me to the moustache? He's standing there all by himself. I have a hunch he might be able to help me with my problems."

Lou glanced at her suspiciously. "What problems?"

"I don't know you well enough . . ."

"You have something up your sleeve, don't you?"

The Leo personality tended toward paranoia, Simone reminded herself. "Yes, I have something in mind, if that's what you mean, but what I'm thinking about is quite a bit farther south than my sleeve. Come on. Be a sport. Introduce us. *J'adore le visage.*"

"If you insist."

At first Steve Omaha did not recognize Lou, but after a few reminders it all came back to him, that day at his studio, Cav photographing his painting of Sonja Henie twirling on black ice, the taped interview which *The Rag* never printed.

"How come?" he asked Lou.

"But I sent you a note explaining what happened. Didn't you receive it?"

"I never open my mail if I can help it. Takes too much

time. The telephone. That's the medium of communication for me."

"It's quite a coincidence running into you here," Lou said. "I had no idea you were related to David."

"He was my uncle, on my mother's side. But what about you?" Then he turned to Simone. "And you? Which side of the family are you girls on?"

"We're not on any side," Simone replied. "We're just friends. Tell me, why is everyone whispering? They look so upset. Is something wrong?"

He grinned. "Yeah. Would you believe it? A classy place like this, and the limo that was supposed to take us to the cem just blew a tire!"

"They must have other limousines," Lou said indignantly, her gaze still upon Mrs. Swern and the other woman, who had now stopped talking to the official and were heading their way.

"That's just it," Steve Omaha said, obviously enjoying the confusion. "Every single limo they own is presently in use. Somebody told me that they do a thriving death business in September, particularly among married men. You know, the end of the summer and their wives returning to nag them for another year. I don't mean Aunt Lil, of course. She's a doll. Anyway, they'll fix the flat in a few minutes, but it still kills me. You can't even get buried without something screwing up the works."

The other woman with Mrs. Swern turned out to be Steve Omaha's mother. After Steve had introduced them, his mother asked if she could speak to him alone for a minute.

As Simone watched Steve Omaha saunter off, she thought wistfully of all the years she had wasted trying to find a N*O*R*M*A*L man. What a fool she had been! First of all, he didn't exist, and second, even if he did, she had recently begun to see that she would not be interested. Anita was right about one thing, even if it hurt to admit it: she liked freaks. The realization had liberated her, and she no longer felt as though she were trying to swim upstream against some crazy, impossible tide. Maybe that was what maturity was all about. Giving in to the inevitable. Of course Robert Fingerhood would never go along with that theory, but what did he know about life, torturing all those poor children with his filthy Rorschachs and Bender-Gestalts and Thematic Apperception Tests? The Little Prince and Rima, The Bird Girl, swam into view. She had not thought about either of them for a long time and she had missed them. Remembering them now was like coming home.

"Perhaps David purposely misrepresented certain facts about my health, or perhaps he believed them himself," Mrs. Swern was saying to Lou.

Lou looked at the older woman tremulously, and Simone wondered whether another Kleenex (and another Pursette catastrophe) were going to be called for shortly. Lost in her own thoughts, she had nearly forgotten the strange connection between these two women who were now confronting each other for the first time in their lives.

"You see," Mrs. Swern went on, "I was quite sick at one time, many years ago. When I recovered, I didn't entirely recover. I found it more expedient that way, Miss Marron. I'm sure that you understand what I mean."

"You've known about me all along," Lou said.

"Do you think you could live with a man for thirty-two years and *not* know?"

"So you pretended to be an invalid in order to keep David from divorcing you?"

"A semi-invalid. An ailing wife. It wasn't such a lie. I did ail a little. You don't think you're the first one, do you?"

"You're trying to trick me," Lou said, her mouth tightening into an ugly line, "just the way you tricked David all those years with your phony attacks."

"I'm not sure he didn't want to be tricked. Frankly, I don't think he relished the prospect of being free to ask you to marry him. Maybe he couldn't bear the possibility that you might turn him down. Maybe he couldn't bear the possibility of your acceptance, which he would have construed as pity. Or maybe he really preferred to see you once a week, as opposed to being married to you and having to see you all the time. At any rate, I felt that it was better for all concerned if a divorce were out of the question."

"Better for you, too."

Mrs. Swern smiled. "Naturally, Miss Marron. I didn't want to lose my husband. Now it's too late. We've both lost him."

All the time that Simone had worked at Mini-Furs, Inc., it was Mrs. Swern whom she felt sorry for, but after hearing this exchange between the two women, her sympathies shifted to Lou. It struck her as oddly ironic that in the long run it was the girlfriend, not the wife, who should have been more cruelly betrayed. The sense of betrayal clouded Lou's eyes, she seemed visibly shaken by what she had just learned. Simone wished there were something she could say to her, some comfort she could offer, but she herself felt a little shaken. David Swern was the last person in the world Simone would have ever suspected of deviousness, which only went to prove how little anyone really knew about anyone else.

Steve Omaha and his mother rejoined them.

"The flat's been fixed, Aunt Lillian," he said. "We can leave now."

"Let's get the hell out of here," Lou said to Simone. "I feel sick."

"I don't feel so hot myself."

Steve Omaha excused himself from his aunt and his mother and took both girls by the arm, much as he had taken the two older women before.

"I have to go out to the cem," he said to Simone. "What a gory business. I hate it, but what can I do? My mother's pretty shook up."

"Why don't you call me later?" Simone said. "I'm in the book. I live on Fifty-Seventh Street."

"Lassitier?"

"Yes. By the way, what zodiac sign are you?"

"Sagittarius, the archer."

"Oh, that's marvelous! I'm a Libra. I get along beauteously with Sagittarians."

"I think I'm going to throw up again," Lou said. "It's very stuffy here."

"I'll talk to you later," Steve told Simone. "Take care of our friend."

Simone blew him a kiss by way of farewell.

"Let's get a drink," Lou said when they were out in the street.

"Sure. Do you really feel that bad?"

"I feel worse than bad."

It was hot and muggy, summer's last stand, and Amsterdam Avenue seemed particularly oppressive beneath the relentless sun. They went into a working-man's bar and took a booth. Lou ordered a double cognac, and Simone a cup of coffee.

"It's lunchtime, lady," the waiter said to Simone. "We have a thirty-five-cent minimum between twelve and two."

"In that case I'll have a sandwich with the coffee. Tuna on toast, please."

"We don't toast bread here, lady. This ain't Schrafft's. White, rye, or a hero?"

"White."

Lou swallowed the double cognac in one neat gulp.

"I feel as though a horse just kicked me in the stomach. Did you ever have that feeling?"

Simone thought of the time she had walked in and found Beverly and Robert on the living room floor.

"Yes, and I tried to kill myself as a result."

"Kill yourself?! My reaction is to kill *them*."

"Who?"

"Whoever has made me suffer. It's a little too late to think of killing David, but if he were alive and I knew what I know now—" She made a fist and jabbed at the air. "I'd knock the son of a bitch clear across the room."

"Why him? Why not Mrs. Swern? She's the one you're really angry at."

"I've been a fool. What a fool I've been. When I think of it, I—" She beckoned to their waiter. "Another double cognac, please."

Simone picked at her tuna sandwich, which was on the oniony side, and wondered what Steve Omaha would be like when she finally got him into bed. Painters were not exactly noted for their great finesse or sensitivity in lovemaking. She just hoped that he didn't come too fast. That really drove her up the wall, and New York seemed to have a preponderance of minute men. It was one of the qualities she had been grateful for with Robert, he took his time, he could control himself. Most men either couldn't or didn't give a damn. They were so involved with their careers and getting ahead in the world, that they didn't try to stretch it out as long as possible. Creative people were usually less in a hurry. They didn't have sales meetings and client conferences and all that crap on their minds. She once had a brief fling with a pop artist who was only nineteen, and as soon as he came he got hard again. He was gauche but there was something to be said for nineteen-year-olds. Definitely.

"He loved me," Lou said. "I know he did. And he would have married me if it hadn't been for her. I don't care what she says now. She can say anything she feels like. He's not around to contradict her. She can pretend that he loved her and didn't want a divorce, but I know better. He felt too guilty to ask for a divorce." Lou finished the second double cognac. "Mostly guilty about their son."

"What son?"

"Didn't you know? I thought that people who worked in offices knew all the gossip."

"So did I until now," Simone replied, thinking that she had better get down to Dr. Hocker's pretty soon or she'd be in trouble, and at the same time having no desire to spend the afternoon looking at corns and ingrown toenails. Maybe she should call Harry and tell him that she was too overcome with grief to be able to work effectively today, but that she would make it up to him by putting in an extra day next week (or agreeing to an extra reclining-chair screw).

"They had a son but he died at birth. It had something to do with his blood. After that, they never dared have another child. They were afraid the same thing would happen again. The doctor said it was one chance in a thousand, but they were too afraid."

"I never heard that."

"It happened a long time ago. David rarely spoke about it." Lou looked at Simone apologetically. "I'm sorry about that business earlier in the bathroom. I shouldn't have slapped you. *But why did you do it?* Why did you tell David about Peter and me?"

"I felt sorry for him."

"Sorry?!" Lou shouted, causing several men in coveralls to turn around and regard her with amusement. "When you feel sorry for a man, you don't kick him in the balls."

"I didn't realize it would have that effect. He seemed so unhappy that I thought if he knew you were involved with someone else, he might forget about you and feel better. He loved you so much."

Lou's tone changed to soft, girlish complicity. "He did love me, didn't he?"

"He worshiped you. Everyone at the showroom was aware of it. He was very proud of you, too. You should have seen the way he'd go through *The Rag* every Monday morning to see if there were any stories written by you. Whenever he read anything you wrote, he'd glow with pride for the rest of the day."

Lou lit a cigarette, smiled, and leaned back against the cheap, plastic booth. "She was lying today. There were no others before me. She made that up to hurt me because she was jealous. You worked for him. Did you ever hear of his being involved with anyone else before me?"

"I wouldn't know. I was only there a short time. Less than a year."

"But you would have heard rumors, gossip. I know what offices are like."

"I never heard anything," Simone said truthfully.

"Of course not. Because there was nothing to hear. There weren't any others. She's lying. Just the way she used to lie to

David about her health. You saw her today. Did that look like a sickly woman to you?"

Simone was on the verge of saying that David Swern hadn't looked sickly either, but then she thought better of it and shook her head negatively.

"She's got the constitution of a horse," Lou said. "She'll outlive us all, that terrible woman. In recent years David couldn't even bear to make love to her. They had separate bedrooms. She hung onto him right up to the end, but a lot of good it did her!"

"Maybe you should try not to think about it," Simone suggested. "You're only making yourself sick. Try to forget about it. Think of the future. Think of Peter."

"Peter?"

"Peter Northrop."

"*Peter?*" Lou repeated, incredulously. "What are you talking about? You don't think that after this I could—?"

Now it was Simone's turn to be incredulous. "You can't blame yourself for David's death. It wasn't your fault if he had a bad heart."

"David didn't have a bad heart, you fool. He died of a broken heart." Lou buried her face in her hands, the bracelet from Cartier's flashing in the murky overhead light. "I killed him! I killed him!"

The men in coveralls winked at each other and ordered another draft beer.

After Simone called Dr. Hocker and made her excuses, she called Robert Fingerhood who was on page 64 of his Ph.D. thesis, *The Relationship Between the Rate of the Subject's Maternal Heartbeat, and the Rate of Sexual Intromission That Is Optimal in Achieving Orgasm.*

It had suddenly occurred to Simone that Wednesday was Robert's day off from torturing small children at The Child Guidance Center, and since she was not going to go to work and didn't have anything better to do, she asked him if he would like to buy her a cup of coffee. If it hadn't been for the Steve Omaha encounter, she would not have had the security to call Fingerhood; knowing that S.O. was going to call her later in the day was like having an ace up her sleeve.

"Come on down," Robert said. "I just happen to have a bottle of Taittinger *brut* in the frig."

"Since when did you start talking like a faggot?"

"Since you left me, Rima."

"I didn't leave you. You threw me out. Remember?"

"Come on down, anyhow. We'll have a good time."

"I doubt it, but I'm on my way."

Lou was well into her fourth double cognac when Simone returned from the telephone booth.

"I'm going downtown to visit an old friend," Simone said. "What are you going to do?"

"Go back to the office."

It was interesting, Simone thought. In times of distress everyone reverted to the most familiar person or place they knew. With Lou, it was work, and with her it was, ironically, Fingerhood. Early dreams died hard indeed.

"Who's the old friend?" Lou asked.

"Fingerhood. He's got some champagne on ice for a change."

"One of these days I'm going to have to meet that son of a bitch."

"Why?"

"I don't know. His name has come up too often by now."

"He might be very involved with your karma," Simone said thoughtfully.

"I'm not even going to ask what that means," Lou replied, gulping down the last of the cognac.

"You both probably knew each other in Lemuria."

"Where's that?"

"At the moment it's under the Pacific Ocean, not far from Lima. It's a sunken continent like Atlantis which is right under Bimini. You know, at first I used to think that Robert was with the rest of us in Atlantis but recently I've had cause to change my mind. I now think he might be more Lemuria. Maybe that's why he can't finish his Ph.D. thesis."

"I don't get the connection."

"You don't know the thesis."

It was pleasant to be in the nice, secure confines of a taxicab once more, Simone decided moments later, as she was heading south to see the man who had once almost ruined her life and who now meant nothing to her. That she could have ever slashed her wrists because of Robert Fingerhood astonished her. He seemed so remote now, so trivial in retrospect, just another man in her crazy life, and yet she had nearly killed herself on his behalf. She doubted if she would ever care sufficiently for anyone again to endanger her own life. Or maybe you learned to care in a different way, a more self-protective way. She had *loved* Robert. That was the astonishing thing. She had had such great hopes about their future together. What a naïve fool she had been!

The taxi swung over to Lexington Avenue and Simone wistfully remembered going to collect Chou-Chou at Anita's, the morning after the party, and how exhilarated she had been, much to Anita's envy. But what did that kind of exhilaration mean? It was a girlish fantasy, a longing for a fairytale romance. Robert had told her the story of The Little Prince and she had fallen in love with him. He'd also informed her that Dostoevski said love was a pastime for the middle classes. Harry Hocker and his reclining chair, the midget with clap on his toe, Steve Omaha and his yet to be revealed (but count on it, they would be there) hangups. Those were real.

The taxi had one of those sliding glass windows to separate the passenger from the driver, and Scotch-taped to the window was a handwritten sign that read:

> Sneezing and coughing
> are infectious and offensive.
> Cover them up.
> It is also right and proper.

It was one of the dizziest signs Simone had ever seen and she was glad that she had a package of Kleenex in her purse, just in case she should start to sneeze violently. Her nose tickled already. The driver was obviously a germ nut.

Then he said, "Is it hot enough for you for September?"

Simone looked at the cameo still strategically pinned over the peculiar spot on her black crochet mini and said, "I'm really not interested in the heat today. I've just come from a funeral and I have other things on my mind."

"I hope it was nobody very personal."

It had just occurred to her that she did not have enough money for the fare; that tuna fish sandwich had wiped her out.

"Only my father," she replied.

As it turned out, the cab driver was very nice about accepting a stranger's check, even though he would not accept their germs.

"I'm just so confused," she started to say, with a neat catch in her voice.

"It's okay, kid. Don't give it another thought. It's not every day in the week that your old man kicks off."

"You're a very sweet person," Simone said, as she got out in front of Fingerhood's lousy apartment building, wondering whether the driver would lose faith in all humanity when the check bounced, as it surely was going to, since the last time she looked she only had one dollar in her account.

Jack Bailey was leaving the building as Simone entered. He had on his navy pilot's uniform and she could smell chlorophyl on his breath. Anita once told her that before a flight he always chewed chlorophyl tablets, anxiously trying to negate the telltale signs of any drinking or going down activities he might have been up to the night before. His eyes were familiarly bloodshot and Simone vowed once more never to fly with his airline if she could possibly help it. According to Anita, he had been desperate when his second wife walked out on him and sued him for alimony, and in a drunken moment had confided that at times he felt a strong urge to take all one hundred and fifty passengers down in the Atlantic Ocean with him.

"Of course he would never do it," Anita assured Simone, but Simone was not so certain.

There was an unhinged Irish quality about Jack Bailey that would have been appropriate if he were reading free verse in a cellar club in San Francisco, but was definitely inappropriate in his role as the airborne custodian of innocent people's lives.

He tipped his cap to Simone, smiled his blinding smile, and said, "Be good now."

"Thanks for the penetrating advice," she replied, swinging past him in disgust.

Robert Fingerhood was sipping champagne in his black bathing trunks and working on his Ph.D. thesis, by black candlelight, when Simone arrived.

"There's a short in the wiring," he explained, "and I'm waiting for the electrician."

His papers were spread out on the dining table in the small room off the Mexican seduction den. The lights in the rest of the apartment were working, but not in the room with the dining table which served as his desk.

"I just think you enjoy working by candlelight," Simone said. "All you need to complete the tableau is a raven."

"I'm not going to say 'nevermore.' "

"Mr. Swern is dead."

"What?"

"Yes, I've just come from the funeral. He died *hier* of a heart attack."

"I'm sorry to hear that. He sounded like such a nice guy. Are you going to keep on working for his company?"

Simone had not realized how long it had been since she'd

been in touch with Robert. She now told him about being fired and about her new job with Dr. Harry Hocker. Robert was amused by the Hocker stories, particularly her favorite one.

"Last week a patient came in," Simone said, "a woman who had never been to Dr. Hocker before. I didn't have a card on her. I showed her into one of the booths and said that the doctor would be with her shortly. He was in the next booth just then examining a transit worker's bunions. I went back to my desk and the next thing I heard was a hysterical scream from Dr. Hocker himself. Well, it seemed that when he went in to see the woman she was completely naked. Naturally, Dr. Hocker was pretty shook up and asked her exactly what she thought she was doing, taking off all her clothes like a lunatic."

"I'd like to know, too," Robert Fingerhood said, staring grimly into the black candlelight.

"*C'est complètement amusant,*" Simone giggled. "The woman thought that Dr. Hocker was a chiropractor. She'd gotten chiropractor and chiropodist mixed up in her poor, demented head, and she was just sitting there waiting for him to crack a few bones in her back. Dr. Hocker explained that he was most emphatically not in the bone-cracking business, but since she was undressed he took a fast look at her feet and saw that she was cutting her toenails wrong. You know, curved instead of straight across. So actually her visit wasn't a total loss, because Dr. Hocker very kindly explained the proper toenail-cutting procedure to her and didn't charge her a dime. But later he told me that he could live without free shows, and besides she had hair on her nipples."

"He sounds like a charming fellow."

"You don't understand how much strain he's constantly under. You should see some of the weirdos who march into that office. If it weren't for tranquilizers, I don't know how he'd be able to go on. He takes one before breakfast and one before lunch, and then nothing bothers him. Except naked women, of course. 'My patients can't get to me,' he once boasted. 'I'm floatin'.' "

After two glasses of champagne Simone felt utterly intoxicated and realized that even though she could never again be seriously interested in Robert Fingerhood, he still was most attractive. She would probably always find him attractive, despite the fact that he no longer had anything to do with her aspirations. It was sad, in a way. The physical response persisted (bodies had their reasons), but the emotional response was just about zero. She had not been prepared to find him attractive any longer, and her own reaction upset her. It made her feel like an animal rather than a relatively civilized human being. In the taxicab she had thought that they would sit around and have a glass of champagne and reminisce about old times, instead of which she now wanted to go to bed with him. And desperately.

"Don't think I'm interested in reviving anything between us," she said, after he had kissed her.

"I'm not thinking that for a second."

There was a certain look Robert used to get on his face before making love, and he looked that way now. Slightly glazed, as though his body had already taken over, leaving his mind far behind. All men looked different prior to the big act. She wondered how Steve Omaha would look. She wondered how she looked. Eager, no doubt. Hopeful. Maybe this time she would crack her stubborn inability to come.

"I feel like such a pagan," she said as she stepped out of her black crochet, letting Robert feast his eyes on the skimpy black lace chemise she was wearing underneath. The chemise was designed in such a way as to barely cover her breasts which were slightly swollen because her period was due in a couple of days.

"Isn't it pretty?" she asked, doing a little pirouette before pulling the chemise over her head, secure in the knowledge that although Robert did not love her any more than she loved him he was still moved by the sight of her exquisite body.

At that moment Simone felt sorry for ungainly women; they would never know the pleasure of sheer physical pride in oneself. Dr. Hocker often commented on her marvelous symmetry. Sometimes he just liked to look at her naked for a few minutes before he threw her back on the reclining chair. But actually what he liked most of all was going down on her, and whenever he did he would hold her feet in his hands. She had small, delicate, perfectly shaped, size 5½ feet, and they really turned him on. His own feet were very wide and pink, there was definitely something babyish about them. He had once told her that his wife had feet like an infantryman, and Simone realized how upsetting that must be to a man with such highly developed aesthetic tastes. One day she must be sure to ask him why he had married a woman with infantry feet, although she was not so sure she wanted to hear his strange, orthopedic explanations.

Robert had closed the blinds in the bedroom and was

starting to caress her all too willing body. She had nearly forgotten what a gentle touch he had, and how excited he became in anticipation of actually putting it in her. His mouth now closed on her right nipple, while his left hand provoked the left nipple until they were both very taut and erect, and she could feel a familiar burning sensation in her vagina. Her clitoris twitched beyond belief. She hoped he was going to do something about that, and soon. If only someone would save her from her terrible orgasm problem, she would be grateful to him for the rest of her life, which was not going to be a long one if she had to continue like this.

"Play with me a little," she said, feeling that if something did not make contact with her clitoris in another minute she would go right through the ceiling. She had not been this excited in years and she vaguely wondered whether it was in any way connected with poor Mr. Swern's funeral. Death was supposed to have an erotic effect upon some people. Robert had once told her that. She was breathing so hard now that her throat felt parched, and she asked him if she could have a little champagne.

"I feel as though I can't catch my breath."

"Back in a minute."

She gulped down the champagne and some of it tickled her nose. Robert had brought back a fresh bottle and two stemmed glasses, and he poured another glass for her as well as one for himself. Simone dipped a finger into her glass and moistened both nipples with the ice cold champagne.

"Look," she said, "they're cringing."

"They can't take it."

"I have cowardly nipples. Who would have thought it?"

Robert licked the champagne off her nipples.

"I'd like to rub it all over my body," she said. "Then when you stop drinking from your glass and begin to make love to me, you'll still have a taste thrill in store. Would you like that?"

"It sounds delightful," he said, with a laugh. "But don't get yourself too wet or it will be uncomfortable."

"It's refreshing in this warm weather."

She rubbed the champagne on her arms, her legs, her belly, and did her best to saturate her pubic hairs with Taittinger *brut*, without getting any on the sheets, at the same time making sure to stick some of it on her throbbing clitoris. It cooled it immediately. Maybe if she couldn't come, this would at least calm her down, but what an expensive solution to the problem. She could see herself going through life, ordering cases of champagne for erotic purposes. Who knew? It might just be worth it. She could cut down on other expenses.

When Robert put his tongue inside her and began to suck out the champagne, Simone very definitely started to feel convinced that it *was* worth it. Maybe she could find a cheaper brand of dog food for Chou-Chou than the one she was currently buying. Robert had never gone down on her much when they lived together and at the time she had not particularly minded, but since the advent of Dr. Hocker she realized that she liked it a whole lot. Still, as excited as she now was, the orgasm eluded her. At moments she felt it was close, but then it stole away like a *voleur* in the night, leaving her as frustrated as ever. If only she could stop thinking about it, maybe it would happen. She would be twenty-five in a month. SHE HAD TO COME!

Robert had stopped going down on her and was strategically and subtly wiping off his mouth on her stomach as he kissed it and traveled upward to meet her for the grand conclusion. Simone did not like to touch men's penises, they frightened her, and Robert's was so long that it doubly frightened her, so she let him put it in. It felt good when it went in, very warm and satisfying. She felt like a baby, whatever that meant.

"Put a pillow under me."

It was better that way, it raised the clitoris and felt more exciting. Robert had a nice, slow rhythm, very steady and regular, soothing, but it was not what Simone wanted. She wanted a man to really bang it into her, hard, she wanted to feel the hysterical force of two bodies pounding against each other, thrashing, she wanted someone to grab her by the ass and whisper obscenities into her ear, bite her, hurt her. Maybe that would make her come. This never would. Robert Fingerhood could make love to her for twenty-four hours and she wouldn't come, he was too tender, and while she liked him for it, it wasn't the ticket in her case. An approach that was more on the *sauvage* side was required, but definitely.

"Hold on," Robert said, his body starting to vibrate with preorgasm tremors, his pace quickening, and as he poured it into her Simone thought vivid thoughts about Steve Omaha's mean, black moustache.

They were still in bed, finishing the champagne, and Simone was about to ask Robert how he was getting along with

Anita when an ominous smell hit her nostrils and she sat up, frightened.

"Robert, I smell something funny."

The same look of fear planted itself on his face.

"Smoke!"

Simone's initial reaction was to lie down again, pull all the covers over her head, and pray for deliverance, but since she had been trying lately to get over her wretched cowardice she followed Robert out of bed, trembling, as the two of them raced in the direction of the smoke. It was in the small dining room where Robert had been working earlier on his thesis. One of the black candles had fallen on its side and half the table was severely charred, the flames still spreading toward the other half, consuming Robert's thesis as they went. Many of the pages were in cinders, although some still remained, only inches away from being swallowed up. Simone had never witnessed a fire at such close range and in such confined quarters, and the sight of the flames magnetized her into immobility. Robert had gone into the kitchen to get a pail of water. She dimly heard him shout at her to help him put out the blaze, but she could not move, and continued to stand there in naked fascination.

One page of Robert's manuscript began to curl under the flames which had just reached it. Simone saw the last line on the page disappear into ashes. It had said: "An inadequate erection and *ejaculatio praecox* had always made *immissio* impossible."

Then Robert returned carrying the huge pot that he used for boiling lobsters and said, "Remove those papers, idiot!"

As she did so, he threw the water in the pot on the flames, there was a loud sizzle and then silence. Simone looked at the pages which she held in her hand. Another line on the top page caught her eye: "With regard to the already mentioned foot-and-shoe fetishism, the therapist submitted to an exact analysis the patient's free associations to this theme, with the result that the following memory-images emerged which he had long forgotten and which were most painful to him."

The foot-and-shoe-fetishism phrase made her think of dear Dr. Hocker and how much better off she would have been if she'd gone to work after the funeral instead of coming here to visit Fingerhood. What had she accomplished by it, anyhow? Her body felt sticky from all that champagne and Robert was infuriated with her because of her immobility. Sex just wasn't worth the bother. Maybe she should give it all up and turn into a celibate. If she weren't so busy trying to come, she might have time for something constructive, like taking ballet lessons or learning how to paint with watercolors. Visions of a glistening career as a prima ballerina raced through her head, made particularly attractive by the knowledge that dancers had no time for sex, no interest in it, they were too consumed by the strict discipline their work required.

"You're a great help in an emergency," she heard Robert say.

"When I star with the Joffrey Ballet, you'll be sorry you talked to me like this." She handed him the remains of his manuscript and realized how wretched he must feel. "What are you going to do about your thesis?"

He stared at the cinders on the badly demolished table. "Try to reconstruct. Luckily, I still have my notes."

"You must feel terrible, I'm sorry I wasn't more of a help. I panicked. I've never seen a fire at such close range."

"I should have blown out the candles before we went into the bedroom."

She could tell what he was thinking: *and for what?* She felt the same way, disgusted, tired, it had been one of the worst days of her life. She never should have gotten out of bed that morning. Sometimes the stars were all against you, but she refrained from saying that to Robert since she knew how contemptuous he was of astrological explanations. She would have to consult her tables when she got home and see where the moon was: its position might be illuminating in view of the day's events.

"I guess I'll get dressed," Simone said.

When she was ready to leave, she asked him how his affair with Anita was progressing.

"Anita is still hung up on Captain Bailey," Robert said.

"Oh, I forgot to tell you. I ran into Smiling Jack as I was coming into the building before."

"Otherwise we get along fine."

"I'm glad to hear that." Simone was really glad to hear that Robert was no more happy than she. "*Dites-moi quelque chose*. What ever made you and Beverly break up?"

"One, she drinks too much, and, two, I couldn't stand her children."

"In other words, you were the one who broke it off."

"That's what I just said."

"Interesting," Simone mused.

"What's so interesting about it?"

"Well, according to Beverly, *she* dropped you. She said you always wanted to stay home, she couldn't get you to go anywhere, and it got to be a big bore after a while."

"Her drinking got to be a big bore. However, I don't doubt that Beverly believes her own fantasy. Drinkers usually do. That's why they're so impossible. They can't separate fact from illusion. It's one of the consequences of alcohol's damage to the brain."

Simone decided that she despised Robert Fingerhood and his cold, clinical approach to life. "How would you like to meet a new girl?"

Robert seemed to perk up for the first time since he had put out the fire. "Who do you have in mind?"

"Lou Marron. Mr. Swern's ex-sweetie pie. I had a sandwich with her after the funeral, and she says she's through with Peter."

"Peter?"

"Peter Northrop. Beverly's husband."

"I didn't know there was anything between them. Isn't she the girl who did that stewardess article on Anita?"

"That's right. She's really shook up about Mr. Swern's death. She feels she killed him because she betrayed him with Peter."

"Did she say that she wants to meet me?" Robert asked nervously.

"Not exactly. I mean, you can't expect her to be all steamed up about a new man in her present state of shock, but she did get interested when I said that the two of you were probably together in Lemuria."

"Where the hell is that?"

If anybody could put Fingerhood down, it would be Lou Marron, Simone thought, with a marvelous feeling of vindictiveness.

"Under the Pacific Ocean. *Schmuck*."

The first thing Simone did when she got back to Fifty-Seventh Street was to check the price on top of one of the cans of dog food in her cupboard. To her chagrin, it was only thirty-one cents. She found it hard to imagine how she could possibly cut down on that to the extent that she would be able to afford a bottle of champagne every time her clitoris sent her a telegraphic twitch. Also, as she was contemplating the can (which had a picture of a simpering cocker spaniel on the front), Chou-Chou regarded her with wet, licorice eyes, as though imploring her not to do anything rash about his favorite diet.

"I guess there must be another way," Simone said, giving the toy poodle a big hug and a kiss. "Another area I haven't yet contemplated."

A moment later it hit her. If she stopped going to bed with men who couldn't make her come anyway, she wouldn't have to go on buying those expensive birth control pills, and then she could afford *cases* of Taittinger *brut*. She could both drink it and pour it over herself, get high and cool off. It was a fantastic idea. Why hadn't she thought of it before? Then she remembered Steve Omaha and his mean, black moustache, which somehow seemed to promise mysterious satisfaction. He would be the last one, she firmly decided, the last in a long line of hopeful orgasm-makers, and if she didn't make it with him, out went the pills and in came the fucking champagne. Poor Dr. Hocker. He would have to find another reclining chair victim with small feet.

Simone removed her clothes for the second time that day and changed into a one-piece tricot romper that had an easy drawstring neckline. Then she turned on the air-conditioner that Dr. Hocker had given her as a present when she'd first gone to work for him and told him how miserably hot the summers were in her apartment. She still regarded the air-conditioner as a luxurious novelty, having lived without one for so long. She had to cool off before bathing and getting rid of Fingerhood's nasty sperm, which she envisioned as coursing madly through her system in their blockheaded attempt to connect with, and fertilize, one of her well-protected eggs. It would certainly be a relief when the entire quest for sexual satisfaction was over and done with, a truly blessed relief, for there was a reasonable doubt in Simone's mind that Steve Omaha (moustache or not) was going to prove to be any more of a savior than any of the freaks who had preceded him.

While she was in the shower, the telephone rang, and convinced that it was Steve she stumbled out with an astrological towel wrapped around her, dripping water over everything as she dashed to pick up the phone.

"Hello," Beverly said. "You sound out of breath. Did you just come in?"

"No, I just came out of the shower. I thought you might be someone else. I met a new man."

Something tinkled in Simone's ear and then Beverly's blurred voice said, "I really can't keep up with you any more. Every time we talk, you tell me you've met a new man. Who is it now?"

"His name is Steve Omaha. He's a painter and I met him this morning at a funeral, of all places. My ex-boss died. Mr. Swern. Steve is his nephew and we were introduced at the Riverside Chapel where the service was held. In fact, it was your old nemesis, Lou Marron, who introduced us. You know, I come from a small village in France but New York turns out to be absolutely microscopic. Sometimes I can't believe it."

"I can," Beverly said grimly.

"Meaning what?"

Simone could hear Beverly take a deep swallow of whatever it was she was drinking. Scotch, no doubt.

"Meaning nothing," Beverly said.

But thinking of Lou and Peter together, Simone smelled a rat. "Did you ever actually get around to meeting Lou?"

"Only once."

"And what happened?"

"We had a bit of an orgy."

"Now really, Beverly—"

"Really what?"

"You're drunk."

"Sure I'm drunk. I'm drunk and we had a bit of an orgy. Can't you entertain two possibilities at the same time?"

Simone remembered Robert's remark about alcoholics and their fantasies. "It's just that I find it rather hard to believe."

"It's true, nonetheless."

Something about the way she said it. Something. Simone believed her, perhaps because she did not want to believe anything that Fingerhood said.

"Well," Simone said, "you've certainly come a long way from Mexico City."

"From Garden City, too. I'm presently leading a double life which should interest you. I dash between my husband and a very nice Englishman who your friend, Anita, fixed me up with."

"Oh yes, Ian."

"Do you know him?" Beverly asked eagerly.

"No. I just met him once, briefly, at a party that Anita gave. Are you fond of him?"

"Yes, yes I am. He's been very sweet which is more than I can say for that bastard I'm married to. It was generous of Anita to introduce us. I can't imagine why she did it."

"I can."

There was a pause.

"Well, go *on*," Beverly said.

"He's looking for a lady with a lot of money and you have it."

"*Ian?*"

"No, Harry Belafonte."

"Stop playing games, Simone."

"Of course I mean Ian. Ian Clarke. He works for that dopey TV show, 'Quiz.' "

Beverly's glass smashed against the telephone.

"I don't believe it," she said. "About the money."

"That's okay. I don't believe you know what an orgy is."

"Ask Lou Marron. I'll bet she doesn't know either."

Now it was Simone's turn to be surprised. "What does she have to do with it?"

But Beverly had slammed down the receiver and the dial tone began its infuriating ring in Simone's wet left ear.

By 11 P.M. Steve Omaha still had not called and Simone felt like booting herself around the tiny apartment, because she suddenly remembered a line from her favorite astrology book: "Sagittarius may promise the world in a weak moment, but not have the slightest intention of keeping his promise." Or was that said about Leo? Unfortunately, Chou-Chou had chewed up the book several months ago so it was impossible to check it out. Disgusted, she decided to go to sleep and dream about all that champagne that was shortly going to enter her deprived life.

In the middle of a dream where she was bathing in champagne, the telephone rang and Simone staggered out of the bottom bunk bed (bottom in summer, top in winter—she had learned) to answer it.

"I'm sorry I didn't get you earlier," Steve Omaha said, "but first your line was busy, then I ran into some friends from Paris, then I gave up. What are you doing?"

"Sleeping. What time is it?"

"About two. I realize it's late but can I come over for a cup of coffee? I'll even bring the coffee and some cheese danish. Do you like cheese danish?"

"Sure. Where are you? I hear sounds in the background."

"I'm right across the street in the Russian Tea Room. I'll be over in a minute."

Chou-Chou had started to race around the apartment, barking in excitement. Then he lay down on the floor, turned over on his back, and put his feet up in the air, and started to whine for attention.

"That's right," Simone told him. "A man is coming over and there's nothing you can do about it, you jealous animal."

Feeling very wide awake and excited, Simone ran to her closet and took out the ostrich-plumed gown that she had charged at Lord & Taylor just before the summer when they were having a clearance sale. Slipping out of the skimpy romper she changed into the ostrich outfit, which was Chinese blue and languorously exotic, with wide ostrich collar and cuffs that made Chou-Chou sneeze.

"This place is freezing," Steve Omaha said when he came in. "How can you stand it?"

"I forgot to turn off the air-conditioner when I went to sleep. I'll turn it off now."

He was really smashingly attractive, she thought, sort of wild-eyed and crazy looking. In addition to the two containers of coffee and two cheese danishes, he had also brought a pint of cognac with him. Simone got out a couple of jelly glasses, one of which still had telltale traces of plum jelly on it, and she poured the cognac into them.

"Here," she said, "this will warm you up."

"Thanks. Say, this isn't a bad apartment. Do you have heat in the winter?"

"Yes, but it goes off at ten o'clock. Why?"

He glanced around. "Just wondering. My loft is like an ice cube in the wintertime."

"What are you trying to tell me?" Simone asked. "If anything?"

"You may think that I'm discussing comparative temperatures, but actually I'm talking about my aberrations of which I happen to have quite a few."

She had a strong urge to bury her face in his moustache. "You suddenly sound very different."

"Only because I've been faking up until now."

"Please go on," Simone said, taking a delicate sip of her cognac, at the same time that she began to feel a familiar twitch in a certain lower region.

"Well, to look at me you'd think I was perfectly normal, wouldn't you?"

"No."

"Then perhaps you've guessed."

"Guessed what?" Simone asked, more confused and more excited than ever.

"What is it I like to do with women."

"I know you'll think this is a strange remark, even possibly a putdown, but it isn't. Honestly. It's just that due to certain circumstances earlier today I decided to give up sex altogether unless you . . ."

She blushed, unable to finish the sentence, and tried again. "Unless you . . ."

"Unless I what?"

It was now or never, she thought. "Unless you make me come."

"You mean, you never have?"

She shook her head timidly. "*Non.*"

A very stern look crossed Steve Omaha's face.

"*Never?!*"

It was more an admonition than anything else.

"No, never."

"That's terrible. That's the worst thing I've heard in my life."

"Yes," she agreed, "it is pretty crummy."

"It's worse than crummy."

"Well, it's not my fault."

"Ah, but it is. That's exactly what it is. It's nobody's fault but yours. Don't you understand that? You've done something bad, very very bad."

"But how could I, when I haven't done anything at all?"

"Negative reactions can be as bad, and I would like to point out, as punishable, as positive reactions. You understand what I'm getting at, of course?"

"No, I don't. In fact, I'm beginning to think that you're a little crazy and perhaps you should take your cognac and your cheese danish and go home. *Vite.*"

"I will," Steve Omaha said, "but not until you've been properly punished."

"I told you, I've done nothing to be punished for. *Rien de tout.* Can't you get that through your head?"

"If you don't want to be punished, I suggest that you start to apologize. Now, all you have to say is that you've been a bad girl and you're sorry."

"I have not been bad," she insisted, "and I'm not sorry about anything!"

"Oh, no? We'll see."

With that, he put down the cognac, stood up, and lifted Simone's ostrich gown above her knees before she could stop him.

"Good," he said. "I see there's nothing to take off."

"What are you talking about?"

"Panties, of course. I'm going to give you one last chance to admit that you've been a bad girl and that you're sorry and ready to repent. Okay? Are you ready to repent and apologize?"

"I most certainly am not. And you can go right to hell!"

Steve Omaha nodded in quiet understanding. "Yes, I can see that my initial appraisal of you was right to begin with."

Then, grabbing her, he threw her across his knees, and with her long skirt still lifted high he began to slap her across the ass, the blows being very slow, hard, and deliberate.

In between each stinging slap, he said, "Are you ready now to admit that you've been a bad girl and that you're sorry? Are you, Simone?"

And each time Simone screamed, "No, you motherfucker, I am not!"

"Very well then. Here's another one to teach you your lesson."

"*What lesson?*" she shrieked.

"You'll find out."

Finally she could stand it no longer, not that the blows were that painful, they were in a way, but that wasn't the point. She was confused as to what they were leading up to and some peculiar instinct told her that they were definitely leading up to something most unusual.

"*C'est suffisant,*" she said. "I'm ready to admit."

Whereupon Steve Omaha took her off his knee and stood her before him on the floor.

"Let's hear it," he said.

"I've been a bad girl and I'm sorry."

"You're sorry *what?*"

She stared at him, uncomprehendingly, thinking that she had done what was demanded of her.

"I don't know what you mean," she said.

Then she remembered her mother and the Nazi sleeping downstairs on the living room sofa.

Steve Omaha's voice was very tender, very gentle, as he gave her the secret password.

"I'm sorry, *Sir.*"

"I'm sorry, Sir," Simone obediently repeated, and as the long-awaited apology came out of her seemingly unwilling mouth, the orgasm that she had been praying for for almost twenty-five years at last swept over her, an unbelievable storm of ecstasy that washed away all peripheral visions of cases of Taittinger *brut* cooling upon twitching clitorises.

A moment later she fell into his arms, her ostrich hem dragging on the floor. She was still Rima, The Bird Girl, but at last some of the feathers had been plucked.

❁ CHAPTER NINE ❁

A familiar throbbing pain above her left eyebrow heralded the October morning for Beverly. Outside it was sunny, but in the bedroom a pleasant darkness prevailed and still she did not dare to move for fear of confirming her worst suspicions: another migraine headache was on its way. To move would be to shake the precarious boat and feel the onslaught of that hideous pain which promised (*promised,* Beverly thought, the word implied a gift, something nice, hmmmm) hours of unmitigated release not only from the pain itself, but from the chills, nausea, dizziness, and loss of depth perception which accompanied the pain and virtually necessitated staying in bed, as motionless as a corpse on a slab, until the attack had run its course.

Why she asked herself. Why so many lately? For ever since moving to Manhattan five months ago, she had started to get the wretched attacks with increasing frequency, until it reached a point where she was afraid to wake up in the morning for fear that another one was about to strike.

Waking up in general had become a dirty business for Beverly, since even without the headache she invariably had a hangover, the kind that took hours to get rid of, and just when she succeeded she would be well into another drinking session that could only lead to the next day's hangover. All in all, life had become pretty intolerable, or as she said to Margaret, her housekeeper, recently, "It's really a pile of shit, and if it weren't for the children, well . . . bang bang." And played at pointing a revolver at her head.

Margaret no longer slept in, but now lived with her family,

or some portion of it, in Roslyn, and came in on the Long Island Rail Road each morning in time to dress the children, prepare their breakfast, and take them to the Dalton School where they had been enrolled for a month. The Dalton School was Peter's idea.

"It prepares one," he had told Beverly.

"For what? Exclusivity? Hypocrisy?"

"I suppose you would like to send them to some Puerto Rican school in East Harlem where they wouldn't learn how to read until they were nine years old, and would then spend the rest of their lives moving their lips over monosyllabic comic books?"

"There are other things to be learned at school beyond simple academics."

"Name one."

"Survival."

Just as Simone was trying to conquer her cowardice by following Robert Fingerhood into a burning room, Beverly was trying to conquer her snobbishness by voicing sentiments that she deemed liberal and progressive. Actually, she would have fainted if she ever had to send her children to a grimy public school.

"I think it's a mistake to protect children from the harsh realities that they are going to have to face sooner or later," she staunchly added.

Peter became infuriated and called her a nitwit, said she would be marching to Washington next with a bunch of frustrated housewives who had nothing better to do with themselves than sit on the lawn of the White House, screaming about civil rights.

"I can think of worse ways to spend my time," she told him, quite unable to imagine herself participating in any such noisy and ill-mannered effort.

"You are still my wife, separation or no, and my children are still my children, and as long as you all remain so, I have a word or two to say in this household, which I might add I am handsomely supporting."

"A word or two? You're so modest, darling. You always were. Right from the start."

"You liked it!"

The knowledge that he was right, that she knew it, that he knew she knew it, killed her. She had liked it at the beginning, had liked everything about Peter, his snobbishness, his snideness, his so-called shyness, which was only an aggressive front for the burgeoning power drive that would shortly reveal itself. When they were alone his very immodest superiority had made her feel superior, had saved her in a way from the isolation of being in the East, in a strange Wellesley world, the girl in the tower at Tower East. Christ, what a mistake her parents had made, they should have sent her to Sarah Lawrence with all the rest of the outcasts, but Wellesley was so healthy, so athletic, so damned normal, with its Tree Day celebration in May, its picturesque Lake Waban, so sweet, so bovine you could vomit. In despair, Beverly had taken up tennis.

"It's either that or ping-pong," she had written her parents, hoping they got the message, since they knew how absolutely unathletic she was. "Of course, darlings, there's always squash and marbles, but somehow . . ."

She let the sentence wander off in her new affected style, just as the "darlings" was an affectation she had picked up in the East, although not from the creeps at Wellesley but rather from the couple of snappy Radcliffe girls she met at mixers. The difference between the two schools was simply explained. At Wellesley you set your hair before a Harvard man took you to Bailey's Ice Cream Parlor for a banana split. At Radcliffe you ignored your hair and dashed off, man or no, to catch a W. C. Fields film festival at the Brattle. But did her parents understand such important distinctions? Certainly not. One Peter Bennett Northrop III did, however, and that, among other things, led to this miserable October morning, eight years and two children later.

Even their separation was no longer a statement of fact, for Peter had come crawling back last month after Lou Marron broke off their affair (count on Simone for the bitter details involving David Swern's death, and Lou's reaction to it). Of course, Peter denied that his return to the fold had anything to do with Lou Marron. Instead he pretended that he couldn't live one second longer without his loving wife and wonderful children.

"I'm a family man at heart," he had confessed.

"Family men aren't in the habit of drugging their wives and submitting them to orgies with their girlfriends in their employer's townhouses, now are they?"

Typically nonchalant, Peter said, "Oh, we all have our little quirks."

Which certainly was true, except that Beverly would hardly call them little. She often thought that the townhouse incident was to blame for many, if not all of her heartaches, for she could not get it out of her head and her head was letting her know about it by immobolizing her to such an exorbitant degree. Guilt and punishment. Orgies and migraines. Oh, yes.

From the adjoining bathroom came the sound of running water. Then a man said, "Damn."

"Peter, are you shaving?"

"No, I'm doing the Funky Broadway."

"What's that?"

"A new shave lotion."

"Then what do you mean you're *doing* it?"

"Because it's a new dance, dummy."

"Peter," she called out, even though every vibration hurt, "did you come back to torture me?"

"Isn't that what marriage is all about?"

"I hope you cut yourself to ribbons."

"So do a few other people I know. Sometimes I think I'm not well liked, syndication possibilities or no."

She did not want to hear him go into that again. Tony Elliot had recently received offers for nationwide syndication of Peters fashion column, entitled *From Peter's Perspective*, but Beverly did not give a damn. Peter's career no longer interested her, Peter no longer interested her. And yet she had let him move back. Why?

A Larry Rivers bicycle painting on the opposite wall caught her eye for the first time in weeks. It was a strange thing about paintings—after you hung them, you stopped noticing them. Since moving to the city Beverly had taken up collecting. Well, it was something to do, the gallery circuit was better than drinking yourself to death, although there was time enough in her life for both activities. She liked to go to the galleries. They made her feel sophisticated, even though she didn't understand much of what was being shown these days and at times felt convinced that the whole thing was some sort of elaborate joke.

Peter, freshly nicked and shaven, stuck his head under the chintz canopy. "Are you all right, darling?"

"No, I'm getting another headache."

"Do you want one of your pills?"

"No, I don't take them any more. They make my heart beat too fast."

"I didn't know that."

"Yes, Dr. Rodgers says they have that effect upon certain people."

"Perhaps if you didn't drink so much, you wouldn't be

bothered by these damn things. Drinking dilates the blood vessels, you know."

"It's also the only thing that keeps me relatively sane, and please don't give me a lecture about the importance of will power."

"It's too early in the morning for lectures."

"Thank goodness."

"By the way, shouldn't Margaret be here by now? I don't hear any of the usual activity out there."

A pang of fear went through Beverly and she shuddered to herself. "Darling, I completely forgot about it, I'm afraid, but Margaret is going to be late today. She's having a tooth extracted. Would you mind taking the children to school?"

"Of course not." There was an unpleasant edge to Peter's voice; he could not tolerate mistakes. "I simply wish you had told me sooner. I have an early appointment at Bergdorf's."

"I'm sorry, really I am."

"If Margaret isn't here, that means the children haven't gotten dressed or had their breakfast yet."

He walked out of the room to return several minutes later with a deep scowl on his face. "They were in Sally's bed, having a pillow fight. You've been efficient in one area, I'll grant you that. They don't dare disturb their fragile mother in the morning, no matter what. You must have really drummed that lesson into them. Sally said, 'Mommy doesn't like us to bother her until she's had her coffee.' I laid out their clothes. Sally will help Peter get dressed, and they will just have to do without breakfast today, thanks to your lack of memory."

Reproaches, reproaches. And yet, this time Peter was absolutely right, she had neglected her own children. Tears of distress and confusion came to Beverly's eyes, but she tried to choke them back.

After a moment she said, "Peter, why did you insist upon a reconciliation? You know you don't love me."

"That's ridiculous. Of course, I love you. You're my wife."

"Yes, that kind of love. That's not what I mean."

"Really, Beverly, we've been married for eight years. You can't expect me to behave like a passionate high school boy."

"I wonder how you behaved with Lou Marron."

"Oh, God, are we going to go into that again? That was different. I've told you a thousand times. It was an *affair*. An affair is not a marriage. That's why married men have affairs. Because the two situations are so different."

Beverly thought of her own affair with Ian. After Peter

moved back she had stopped seeing Ian, but only for about a week. Peter's presence soon became unbearable to her and she telephoned Ian and asked him to take her to lunch. Suspecting what was on her mind, he invited her to his apartment for lunch. He lived only a few blocks from the TV studio where he worked, and they now met at his apartment twice a week, Tuesdays and Thursdays at noon. Thinking back to that day at the Garden City country club, Beverly remembered that Tuesdays and Thursdays had been Dee Dee's arrangement with the man who taught Renaissance music at Adelphi. At the time Beverly had been shocked by Dee Dee's intrepid infidelity, now she was doing the same exact thing. Dee Dee must be laughing in her grave.

"You're thirty years old, Beverly, and the mother of two children. Don't you think it's about time you started acting your age, remembering your responsibilities, and stopped lying around longing for Heathcliffe?"

"Yes, yes, you're right," Beverly said wearily.

She knew what Peter meant about affairs and marriage being so different, and it was a very depressing thought. Before Peter moved back, Ian asked her to get a divorce and marry him. If she had done that, then they would no longer be having an affair and a great deal of the clandestine spice would be gone. Then Ian would be her husband and she would probably end up having an affair with someone else after a while. She wondered whether any long-married couples managed to surmount the daily attrition of wedded life, or whether they were all pretty much in the same boat as she and Peter.

"I hate this damn bed," Peter said, still in his robe and slippers. "Why on earth did you ever buy a four-poster canopy? I feel like an idiot sleeping in it."

Beverly loved the canopy, which was predominantly a soft orange, as were the curtains.

"When I bought the bed and took this apartment neither of us thought you'd be living here. Remember? Besides, I think the canopy is romantic."

There was a closed-in feeling of safety and security about the bed and Beverly often lingered there, reading the *Times* or a new novel until lunchtime. Unfortunately, today was only Monday, which meant that she would not be seeing Ian until tomorrow. Peter had made love to her last night, but she hadn't had an orgasm. He really did not excite her any longer, in fact he rather revolted her, and yet he didn't do anything different than before. Apparently, it was no longer what he did, but what he was, how she now perceived him. Her change in attitude stemmed directly from that day at Tony Elliot's townhouse. Those terrible plaster people at a plaster party, and the taste of Lou Marron still in her mouth.

Peter removed his robe. "I'll get dressed and bring the children in to kiss you good-bye."

"Yes, please do."

The children were darling looking, Beverly thought, in their neat Cerutti outfits, Peter, Jr., in his Eton jacket, and Sally in her buttercup yellow coat with the Peter Pan collar. Beverly opened her arms to them and kissed each child in turn.

Sally said, "Every man has his woman, but the iceman has his pick."

Peter, Jr., giggled in delight.

His sister pinched him, and said, "You don't even understand the joke."

Beverly wished she had had Peter, Jr., first so that he could take care of his sister, the way her brother Howard had taken care of her when she was young. Dear, dull Howard. She forgot about him now for years at a time, and yet once they had been very close. Howard was the one to tell her about sex and describe his friends' favorite pastime, "Circle Jerks." The adolescent boys in Salt Lake City sat around in a circle and jerked off in front of each other, the winner being the one who came first, great sport, and it had made Beverly jealous that she couldn't do it, too. Howard had been very sympathetic and explained that it was different with girls because they didn't have a "thing" to jerk off with. Beverly was sad that she didn't have a "thing" and asked Howard whether he thought she might eventually grow one. Howard said not unless she was a freak or a lesbian (Beverly had never heard the word lesbian and Howard had to explain what that was), but that when she became older she would find out what it was that girls did, and it was really very nice. So considering the solace she had received from Howard, it was no wonder that she felt regretful her firstborn had not been a boy, and lately she'd begun to worry whether Peter, Jr., might not turn out to be a homosexual.

"Like his father," came to her mind, but she pushed it away. Peter obviously was not one hundred percent homosexual, or why would he stay married to her? Still she was now quite certain that he and Tony Elliot had been doing more over the years than turning out a fashion newspaper, much more, but she never drummed up the nerve to put it to

Peter directly. She was afraid of what his answer might be. With Peter, you could never be sure. He was liable to tell her the most shameful details, if he were in a mood to shock. Although she hated to admit it, even to herself, her husband frightened her, he was unpredictable, and despite their eight years together at times she felt that she did not know him at all.

"Margaret will pick you up at school," Beverly told the children.

"Why isn't she here now?" Sally wanted to know.

"She's having a tooth extracted, darling."

"What does extracted mean?" Peter, Jr., asked.

"Your father will explain it to you on the way to school."

Peter brushed his lips against Beverly's hair and she caught his eyes peering down the loose neckline of her white batiste gown. Her long hair was tied back with a thin, white ribbon. In the ghostly darkness of the room she felt very young and girlish, not like a wife or mother at all.

"You look like a little girl in her mother's bed," Peter said, as though reading her thoughts.

The children had gone out into the foyer. Beverly had the strangest feeling that Peter wanted to make love to her, right then and there, perhaps to compensate for last night's fiasco. He was looking at her in a most peculiar way.

"You might have waited until I came," she said.

"I tried. It was one of those things."

"You fell asleep immediately afterward."

"It was a long day. I was tired."

"Were you tired with Lou Marron, too?"

Peter straightened his tie even though nothing was wrong with it. "I won't be home for dinner tonight."

Beverly waited for the explanation, knowing all the while that Peter was too smart to go into fraudulent details if he didn't have to. She had learned the secret of the wise businessman: keep the lie short, don't explain anything unless absolutely necessary, and then lie through your teeth with a straight face.

"And just when I was going to cook another one of *Life*'s Great Dinners," she said.

"Take care of yourself, darling. Try to go back to sleep."

"Yes, darling, I'll do that."

The minute they were gone, Beverly got out of bed, put on a pale blue and white breakfast coat over her short gown and went into the living room with its John Hultberg landscape above the W & J Sloane sofa. The painting appealed to

Beverly because the bleak landscape was seen through a window, it was seen indirectly, not firsthand, and the day Beverly had bought it from the Martha Jackson Gallery she was blindly drunk and felt that she had gone through life seeing everything through a window, from a distance, detached.

She felt that way now as she went to the liquor cabinet and poured herself a very stiff Dewar's, straight, which she gulped down in two swallows. Liquor was terrible if you had a migraine; it only intensified the pain, and Beverly often wondered why she persisted in torturing herself like this. The Scotch made her shudder. She shook her head in the involuntary gesture of all alcoholics who seem to be saying, "No, no," even while their actions tell them, "Yes, yes."

Beverly no longer cared that she was a drunk, or at least she cared much less than she had when she was living in Garden City. There was no attempt now to hide her drinking from Margaret, for example. As for Peter, she knew that he would not seriously attempt to criticize or stop her. He was good for an occasional, "Perhaps if you didn't drink so much, darling . . ." the mildest of reprimands, and that was about all, and Beverly knew why. He would let her go her way without too much interference, if she let him go his. The pact had been tacitly sealed. No recriminations, no condemnations, just the quiet understanding between two friendly enemies that each would hold to his dirty bargain.

"Get going, get going!"

"Happy days are here again."

Yes, she still had the miserable myna birds and they were another manifestation of her bending to Peter's will, because she hated the birds, had from the start, and yet had not gotten rid of them when she moved to Manhattan.

Peter had said to her, "The children are very fond of them, you know."

"No, I don't."

"The children are going to be transplanted to a new environment. It won't be easy for them. They'll be confronted with enough unfamiliarity without your taking away the few familiar things they have left."

Beverly knew that neither Peter, Jr., nor Sally gave a damn about the birds, but she didn't have the nerve to defy Peter. She felt guilty as it was, uprooting her children and leaving them without a father, to make an issue over two orange-beaked birds who couldn't shut up.

"If only they had a repertoire," she said now to her reflection in the living room mirror.

In her short gown and breakfast coat, the little girl impression was rudely shattered by the closeup of a haggard and drawn face. Beverly saw her puffy eyes, the sallowness of her skin, the general note of despair, and thought to herself that the blood was definitely running in the wrong direction. Elizabeth Arden had failed again. Their revolutionary night cream, Beauty Sleep, had not held the moisture content in her skin, as promised, had not held back the little lines and wrinkles that took over (the ad warned) where moisture left off. Looking at herself in the rococo oval mirror, Beverly decided that Beauty Sleep had failed to wake up one woman's tired complexion, but absolutely. She stuck out her tongue. It was coated white.

"I'm a wreck."

And she had only turned twenty-nine in March, seven months ago. Twenty-nine going on the dreaded thirty mark. The prospect of never being in her twenties again horrified Beverly more than she would ever have admitted. There was something unreal about being thirty, unreal and yet inevitable: youth and all its inflated promises gone forever. She started to sob, remembering Peter's remark that her self-pity would be her undoing yet.

"But why shouldn't I feel sorry for myself?" she asked him. "What do I have? What have I been trained for? Nothing except to be a wife and mother and play tennis when I'm not too smashed."

"You're young. There are still things you could learn if you were interested."

"No. The dream is gone."

"Only if you want to be a loser."

Well, that was Peter's answer to her hysteria, but what did he know? Peter was stronger than she. He did not have her exorbitant emotional needs. She had read his column in last week's *Rag,* its fashion message boring her to tears. Peter had raised the issue of skirt lengths, saying that it looked as though the mini was on its way out, and the midi and maxi were on their way in. He blamed it all on American designers like Norman Norell and Bill Blass, who sat around in their zebra-lined apartments watching Lupé Velez on "The Late Show" and trying to figure out ways to disfigure as many women as possible.

"They'll be bringing back Joan Crawford's plastic wedgies next," was Peter's last line in the column.

The reason that it bored Beverly so was because she found it hard to get excited about a few inches of material here or there, when men were being blown to shreds in Vietnam and the world trembled on the periphery of nuclear disaster.

"Who gives a damn about hemlines?" she had said to Peter after she read the column. "Or plastic wedgies? Or any of it? Do you think that in Salt Lake City they're still not wearing spike heels, seven years behind the fashion times?"

Peter became acutely contemptuous. "Nobody cares what they're wearing in Salt Lake City, darling. That's what *you* don't understand."

"Nobody in New York or Paris cares. But nobody in Salt Lake City cares what the people in New York or Paris think. That's what *you* don't understand."

"You're a fool," Peter said.

Then he went to his club.

Still looking at herself in the rococo mirror, Beverly suddenly ripped off her breakfast coat and gown, and stared at her reflected nudity. Her body was in good shape, better than ever in fact. Drinking always hit the face first. Her old prisoner-of-war reducing diet was a thing of the dim past. She had lost ten pounds since moving to Manhattan without having to pretend to herself that she'd been captured behind enemy lines and was only being fed a bare subsistence diet. Yesterday, all she'd had was one hard-boiled egg and two frozen egg rolls (and fifteen Scotches), yet her stomach was firm and her breasts were still flying at relatively high mast, considering their size.

"Some days you can't even give it away," she said, wishing it were Tuesday instead of Monday.

Beverly went back to the bar, picked up the bottle of Dewar's, tipped her head back, and took a long, dizzying swallow. God, it was filthy stuff, alcohol, really despicable. Her headache was getting worse by the minute, the nausea swelling up inside her at a frightening rate of speed. Soon she would be in the bathroom, throwing up, and wondering what all the sane, healthy people in the world were doing at that moment. Beverly tipped her head back again.

"Mrs. Northrop!"

She had not heard Margaret's key in the door. It was the first time that Beverly had ever seen Margaret look shocked.

"Mrs. Northrop, what are you doing? It's only nine-thirty in the morning. You're drinking and you're not dressed."

"What the hell is the difference? Who's there to be soberly dressed for?"

Margaret held an airmail letter in her hand. "It's from your mother."

"Great. Just what I need this morning, a missile from the old witch. I can't see a thing, Margaret. I have a blinding headache. Would you open it and read the good parts, providing there are any?"

Margaret tore open the envelope. "You mother has taken up golf," she said after a moment.

"Do you call that a good part?"

"She plays at the Mountain Dell Golf Course where the scenery is so dazzling that she had to wear blinders to putt."

"I'm enchanted."

"She's just broken eighty," Margaret droned on, "and her swing is getting better every day. She takes lessons."

"*Margaret!*"

"Yes, Mrs. Northrop?"

"I am not even remotely interested in my mother's golf progress. If that's all she has to write about, please don't bother to read the rest. Just throw the damn letter away."

Margaret turned the page over. "She asks how you like living in Manhattan and whether the children are in good health. She thinks you should bring them to Salt Lake City for Christmas or they'll forget they have a grandmother."

"Does she mention Mr. Northrop?"

Margaret read further. "Yes. She says, 'Really, dear, I must admonish you for considering a divorce. As you know, I was never very fond of Peter, but a marriage is a vow to God and not something to be taken lightly.' "

"I've heard enough. Dump it in the garbage can."

"Don't you want to hear about your brother, Howard?"

Howard had always been her mother's favorite.

"Let me guess," Beverly said, closing her eyes. "He's running for city council president."

"No, he's running for state legislature."

"There's no telling how far a man can go after Circle Jerks."

Margaret confronted Beverly's tall, white nakedness, trying her best not to stare at the reddish pubic hairs. It occurred to Beverly for the first time that Margaret had probably never seen any other than the black variety.

"Mrs. Northrop, don't you think you should put your robe back on and get into bed? You don't look well, not well at all, no Ma'am."

Beverly picked up the white batiste gown and slipped it over her head. She was starting to shiver; after the shivering stopped, she would become feverishly hot. The hot-cold syndromes would alternate for hours, putting her body through an enervating temperature bout that would leave her weak even after the migraine itself was gone.

"Don't you think you should leave that bottle of Scotch here, Mrs. Northrop?"

"No, I don't. By the way, Margaret, how is your tooth? I mean, the hole in your mouth?"

"Things feel a little vacant in there."

Beverly smiled. "That's the story of my life."

"Happy days are here again," screamed the myna bird.

Beverly got into bed with the bottle of Scotch and turned the electric blanket dial to nine. She was shivering so badly that she nearly dropped the opened bottle on the bed. It was almost two-thirds full and she wondered what Peter would say to sleeping on a Scotch-perfumed mattress. The pale green princess telephone next to the bed buzzed softly.

Beverly removed the receiver and said, "Yes?"

"Hello," said Ian. "How are you this morning?"

"I'm home and I'm drunk."

Ian had a cheery laugh. The Englishman's typical resistance to any form of unpleasantness.

"Would you like to meet me for lunch?" he asked.

Beverly was surprised. "But it's only Monday. It's not one of our days, darling."

He laughed again. "No, I really mean *lunch*. Come on. You sound as though it would do you good."

"Something else would do me better."

"I'll tell you what I'm going to do. I shall make a reservation for two at The Ground Floor at twelve-thirty. Will you join me?"

"I'd rather make love."

"There isn't enough time today, darling. I have a hellish afternoon."

"Then why is there time to go to lunch?"

"Because there's something I want to discuss with you," he said patiently.

"We could discuss it in bed."

"Darling, you know I'm not very good at bedtime discussions. Besides, it sounds to me as though you could use a spot of food."

A spot of food was the last thing in the world Beverly felt she could use, but she was curious as to what Ian had on his mind.

"Twelve-thirty it is," she said.

After she hung up, she realized that she should not have agreed to meet Ian, not in her condition. She would never be able to dress, put on makeup, or walk out the door, without experiencing the most excruciating agony. If only she could sleep for a little while it would help so much, but like practically every other normal activity sleep was also denied to the migraine sufferer. Beverly started to cry in sheer frustration.

"It's not fair, it's not fair, it's not fair."

The flowered Porthault sheets were damp with her tears. She took another drink of Scotch, shivered, and wondered what was on Ian's mind. When she had seen him on Thursday, he was visibly disturbed that not only had Peter moved back with her, but that she seemed to have no intention of asking him to leave.

"You can't go on living with a man you dislike," Ian had said.

"On the contrary, I can go on forever."

"I don't understand your attitude, Beverly."

"When you're married you will."

There was a soft knock on the door.

"Come in," Beverly said.

Margaret stuck her head into the darkened room.

"Mrs. Northrop, can I get you something? A cup of tea perhaps? Or some real breakfast?"

Margaret had recently been expressing concern over Beverly's fierce disinterest in food.

"You know I can't eat when I have these headaches, but perhaps a cup of tea. With honey and a lot of lemon, please."

Lemon was a good idea, it might help alleviate the dreadful nausea. Most of the migraine pain was centered above Beverly's left eye. She could open the right eye without too much difficulty, but the left one had to be kept shut or it felt as though someone had stuck a knife through it. She put the bottle of Scotch on the floor and turned off the electric blanket dial. The chills had started to subside, and a slow, deep warmth was beginning to pervade her entire body. When Margaret returned with a tray, a few minutes later, Beverly was feverishly sweating.

"Thank you, Margaret. You're optimistic."

Next to the cup of tea, Margaret had placed a dish containing one slice of light toast (the way Beverly liked it) and a generous portion of apricot preserves.

"Toast is good for nausea," Margaret pointed out before closing the door behind her.

At moments like this, Beverly wondered what she would ever do without Margaret. From time to time she had considered becoming actively involved in civil rights as a gesture toward Margaret, but somehow she could not visualize herself toiling away in some sweaty office, say, two afternoons a week, for a cause so complex and convoluted that it was quite beyond her ability to understand. Beverly felt sorry for the plight of the Negroes, but she did not know what the answer was. For her part, she paid Margaret well, treated her kindly, and gave her all of hers and Peter's castoff clothes. Beyond that, she could not cope. After all, people had to help themselves. The Mormons had been driven from the midwest, their prophet murdered, and their homes attacked, but they had crossed the Rockies in dusty wagons and created a thriving metropolis out of a desert. Beverly's upbringing dictated that people should not ask for or expect handouts. Charity diminished the dignity of man. It was one of the few points on which she and Peter agreed.

She took a sip of the lemony tea, a small bite of dry toast, and placed the tray on the floor next to the bottle of Scotch. Then she ran into her expensive bathroom and vomited.

At noon she had decided upon a plan of action. She would meet Ian at The Ground Floor, as agreed, but really to get dressed and really to put on makeup were feats she was incapable of. A garter belt, stockings, panties, shoes, and the purple sweater coat (from Paraphernalia) to slip over her white batiste gown were all she could manage. As drunk and deranged as she felt, she realized that the gown was terribly transparent and that she would have to keep her coat on during lunch, but that seemed a much more desirable alternative than going through the arduous process of getting completely dressed. To shield her eyes from the painful sunlight, Beverly wore wide-rimmed lavender sunglasses (from Bloomingdale's) that had a green snake slithering from one end of the rim to the other.

She had told Carey Limousine to be in front of the building at twelve-twenty. Under ordinary circumstances, she would have asked Henry, the doorman, to get her a taxi, but the way she felt now even a three-minute delay would be unbearable.

"I expect to be home shortly after lunch," she informed Margaret. "And you needn't bother about dinner tonight. Mr. Northrop is eating out and I shall not be eating at all.

Please call the florist and order three dozen daffodils and arrange them in the living room. This apartment looks like a tomb."

Margaret nodded, sighed, and went back to her weekly Monday chore of giving the General Electric oven a thorough cleaning job. She wore rubber gloves and used a new oven cleaner that Beverly had recommended after seeing it advertised on "The Mike Douglas Show." Margaret preferred the old cleaner she had used for years, but she knew Beverly well enough not to say so.

"Mrs. Northrop is like a child, a real little child," Margaret was fond of telling her sister-in-law in Roslyn, "and you know how some chldren just got to have their way. Particularly when they're spoiled and have been used to getting it all their lives."

It was cooler outside than Beverly had expected, or was that another attack of chills coming on? Henry held her arm during the few steps from the building to the curb where the limousine was waiting. The chauffeur stood holding the door open to the long, black Cadillac, a polite smile on his face.

"Good afternoon, Ma'am," he said.

"Good afternoon," Beverly replied, gratefully slipping into the darkened interior of the car.

"I hope you feel better, Mrs. Northrop," Henry said.

"Thank you, Henry."

Then she grasped the hand pull next to the left window and leaned her head back against the smooth leather cushioning, her right hand resting on her status baby crocodile purse. She might be only half dressed, she thought, in a sudden, giddy moment, but her accessories were impeccable.

The thirty-block ride to The Ground Floor was more pleasant than Beverly thought it would be. Fifth Avenue was crowded with lunchtime people, and Beverly was surprised to see how chic and well dressed the young working girls were. Ordinarily, if she had to go to the stores for something, she never ventured out until after two when the *paparazzi* had returned to their offices, clearing the way for the leisured ladies. As the driver stopped for a light, two girls caught her eye. They were just coming out of Bonwit Teller's, each holding a shopping bag with Bonwit's distinctive flower design. They were laughing and talking about something. Beverly wondered what it was: their new purchases, where to eat lunch, last evening's date. They appeared to be in their early twenties, fresh, vibrant. They probably were secretaries earning one hundred dollars a week, and Beverly envied them.

They were free. They had not yet made the important mistakes.

Beverly had never been to The Ground Floor before and she was starkly unprepared for it. She would have been unprepared for it under the best of circumstances, but in her migraine condition the restaurant was nightmarish. The lights! One step in the door and she stared unbelievingly at the ceiling, which looked as though some maniac from Con Edison had taken one thousand brandy snifters, turned them upside down, screwed in one thousand light bulbs and flicked on the master switch. The glare was blinding, even shielded as she was by her lavender sunglasses.

"Mr. Clarke's table is in the rear," the maitre d' informed her. "Please follow me."

It disturbed Beverly to see John Fairchild and two of his key henchmen sitting at the very first table in the front room, their three heads poised together in muted conspiracy. There was something about those three heads, they seemed perfectly sculptured, almost beautiful in their perfection, and strangely still.

Beverly nodded and smiled at John Fairchild before moving on, on eggshells. She had met the publisher of *Women's Wear Daily* upon various occasions over the years, his paper being the only competitive thorn in the side of *The Rag*. The reason that it disturbed her to see the *Women's Wear* people at such close range on this particular day was because they reminded her that somewhere, not far away, Peter and perhaps Lou Marron and Tony Elliot were similarly lunching in muted conspiracy. Lunching and plotting the latest fashion madness. As much as Beverly felt contemptuous of their world, she also envied it if only because it *was* a world, a cohesive force, a unity from which she was excluded. At least Lou Marron had that: her work.

It struck Beverly as terribly ironic that she should envy someone like Lou Marron when most women, given only the surface facts, would have envied her, her attractive, successful husband, her children at a good private school, the house in Martha's Vineyard, the lovely apartment in New York, money, social status, the best kind of respectability. But what did it all finally mean when she slept side by side at night with a man who did not love her, when she was surely drinking herself to death, when here she was on a cool and sparkling

October afternoon wearing a flimsy nightgown beneath her coat, on her way to meet the second of what might prove a long line of lovers?

She thought fondly of Fingerhood, her first infidelity, and the voluptuous meals he used to prepare, which reminded her of the meals served at Durgin-Park in Boston. Peter used to take her there for dinner on Saturday nights, then drive her back to Wellesley in time for the rotten curfew.

The women lunching at The Ground Floor were mostly wearing trim little fall suits, and they either had just had their hair done or were wearing trim little hats, too. A well-known movie actor seated at a banquette caught her eye. He was with two other men, both of whom were baldish and overweight. The actor was much better looking than he appeared on screen, but what surprised Beverly were his glinty eyes, Peter's eyes. They looked as though they could cut through steel. Peter's eyes gave away nothing.

"For the last time," he had said days ago, "I tell you that the thing with Lou Marron is over and done with."

But Beverly was not so certain, despite the fact that Simone insisted Lou would have nothing to do with Peter after David Swern's death. Simone had become friendly with Lou since the funeral last month and now called Beverly on the average of once a week to give her what Simone termed, "the friendly detective report." According to Simone, Lou was leading a very chaste life these days, although Simone intended to rectify that by introducing her to Fingerhood. The only hitch was that Lou claimed it was too soon after dear David's death for introductions, and out of respect for his memory she would have to wait a decent amount of time.

"Your friendly detective report, number four," Simone said on the telephone yesterday, in between discreet bites of her Mexican TV dinner, which contained refried beans among other indigestibles. "Lou Marron says she is so turned off sex that she's even stopped taking the pill."

Beverly was surprised to hear that someone as ostensibly intelligent as Lou had been taking the pill to begin with. There was no discussing the pill with Simone who called it the greatest invention since penises, but then Simone was not exactly a deep thinker and refused to listen to factual accounts of women who had died of blood clots because of the oral contraceptive.

"You know what my opinion of the pill is," Beverly said to Simone, "so let's not get started on that."

"Your opinion doesn't mean a damn when you think about

Anita. If she'd been able to take the pill, she wouldn't have had to go to San Juan for an abortion. They didn't even give her an anesthetic."

"An abortion?"

There was a momentary pause and then Simone started to gasp. "I think I'm choking on a taco. It went down the wrong way."

"I didn't know Anita had an abortion."

"It was a tamale," Simone said, after she had drunk a glass of Perrier.

"You never told me that Anita had an abortion," Beverly said, stunned by the news. "When did that happen?"

Simone became conspiratorial. "It's supposed to be a secret. Me and my big mouth. Please, I beg you, don't mention it to a soul. Anita would burn my fall if she knew I told anyone, let alone you."

"I only met the girl once. What does she have against me?"

"Your money and your breasts," Simone promptly replied.

Beverly could no more believe that Anita disliked her than she could believe that Ian was interested in her because of her money. She felt that she was too unhappy to be disliked and not wealthy enough in her own right to be financially coveted.

"You know, Simone, sometimes I think you're a bit batty."

"I've never denied that. But you won't tell anyone about Anita, will you? She's really touchy on the subject."

"My lips are sealed," Beverly said, wondering what Ian's reaction would be when he heard the thrilling news. Ian had always claimed that he and Anita were never more than friends, but Beverly doubted that as much as she doubted Lou Marron's current chastity.

"When did she have the abortion?"

"This past summer. Dr. Kindness went to San Juan with her."

"Who's Dr. Kindness?"

"Fingerhood, of course," Simone said, impatiently. "But he wasn't the responsible party. It was Smiling Jack who knocked her up. And she even had her diaphragm in at the time."

"That was very sensible."

"Sensible?! And you call me batty? She got preg, didn't she? What was so sensible about it?"

"Don't get excited," Beverly said. "You'll choke on another taco."

"Tamale."

"Remember when we went to dinner with those two brothers in Mexico City? Remember what a prude I was that night?"

"That's okay. You're making up for it now."

"I know. But when I think of all those wasted years . . ."

"What about me? All those years of fucking and not coming? Sometimes I could die. Which brings me to an interesting point. Do you realize that I had my first orgasm the day of Mr. Swern's funeral?"

"I'm afraid I don't get the connection."

"*Tu es complètement folle* if you don't get the connection," Simone said. "Death. Life. Don't you see? Mr. Swern went and I came!"

Beverly nearly walked into the dessert cart, which would have looked quite luscious if it weren't for the fact that the smell of food was rapidly bringing back her nausea full force. God, how could people eat so much? Simone said the reason that New Yorkers were consumed with food was because New York came under the sign of Cancer, which happened to be the food sign of the zodiac. Simone's astrological interpretations were lost upon Beverly who had long ago concluded that certain people were basically pigs at heart, and that was all there was to it.

"Excuse me," she said to the startled waiter manning the cart. "The strawberries look wonderful."

"They were flown in from France this morning," he said with a touch of pride.

Beverly made a mental note to be sure to tell that to the chauvinistic Simone when she received the next friendly detective report. She hurried to catch up to the maitre d' who was paces ahead of her. The heat in the restaurant seemed insufferable. Beverly could feel her underarms wet with perspiration and she wondered how she would ever live through this luncheon. It was a relief, finally, to catch sight of Ian waiting for her.

"Darling." Ian stood up, blond, beaming. "You're right on time."

"I took a Carey limousine."

The maitre d' pulled out the table and Beverly sat down next to Ian on the soft banquette. She despised the banquette arrangement because it made conversation so awkward; she would probably have a stiff neck for days.

"Why not a taxi?" Ian wanted to know.

"I have a dreadful headache. I really shouldn't have come at all."

"You do look a bit *gênée*," he admitted.

Beverly wondered why the English liked to sprinkle their conversation with French words and phrases when for the most part they disliked the French so much.

"*Gênée* is nothing compared to what I *feel* like."

"Would you like to order cocktails, sir?" the waiter asked.

Ian turned to Beverly.

"A Scotch sour on the rocks. No sugar and a lot of lemon, please."

Ian repeated Beverly's request to the waiter and added a Scotch and soda for himself. Then he said:

"I'm sorry you're feeling badly, but tell me—how are things on the home front?"

Ever since Peter had returned to the roost, that was Ian's favorite question.

"Status quo."

He looked at her in disapproval. "You certainly don't seem troubled about it."

The perspiration was starting to drip down her arms. "Troubled? I feel too rotten at the moment to be troubled about anything."

"We can't go on much longer like this, you realize."

"Oh? Why not?"

"I don't consider Tuesdays and Thursdays at noon the basis for a satisfactory relationship."

"We could try Mondays and Wednesdays in that case."

"Your sense of humor fails to amuse me."

"Does it?" she said, thinking that if the waiter did not bring their drinks in another minute, she would vomit all over the impeccable tablecloth. "I thought I was being quite witty."

Ian cleared his throat and took a different tack. "You know how I feel about you."

"Please, darling, not now."

He sighed in exasperation and it occurred to Beverly that there was a peculiar reversal of the male-female roles in their exchange. Traditionally, it would be she, the woman, who would have complained about the limitations of their affair, and it would be he, the man, who held firm to not being able to do anything about it. Beverly felt a not so small satisfaction in having the upper hand with Ian; it partially made up for Peter having the upper hand with her. Across the room a popular gossip columnist was jotting something down in his notebook, as he listened to an elegant blond woman whom Beverly did not recognize. The restaurant was packed. On the banquette, to Beverly's left, a man and a woman were being served a fillet of white fish garnished with pale green grapes.

The woman said, "Christopher sent me a postcard from Delos."

The man replied, "The sole is overcooked. What did the dear boy say?"

Beverly did not bother to wait for the woman's answer. It seemed to her that the majority of relationships were extraordinarily tedious. Still people went on with them, they went on eating and drinking together, and endlessly talking about insignificant details. What was the alternative? Her own case was a good example. She could have stayed home in bed today, silently sick beneath the orange canopy, and yet in spite of a pounding head she had chosen to come out into the world of eating and drinking and talking. Killing time. She often thought that that was about all most people's lives amounted to, not least of all her own, for in the back of her mind she must have known that Ian really had nothing to discuss with her that had not already been discussed. He had nothing new to say; it was just a rehash of what had gone before. Still, like the man on her left mentioning the overcooked sole, she, too, found a soporific comfort in inessential conversation. The human species had to talk. Jabber jabber jabber. Even nonsense talk was better than silence. Lewis Carroll had the right idea.

"At last," Ian said, as the waiter finally placed their drinks before them. "Cheers, darling."

Beverly's hand was shaking as she reached for the icy drink. Why did the damn fools fill the glass to the very top?

"Cheers," she said, taking a deep swallow. "They put sugar in."

"Shall I send it back?"

The sole is overcooked. They put sugar in. Jabber jabber jabber. Ah, but the immense solace of one's own voice.

"No, I'll drink it as it is this time. I'm parched."

"As you like."

Ian was wearing a dark blue Mao suit with a lighter blue turtleneck.

"You look very dashing today," she said.

"I'm a dashing fellow, but it doesn't seem to get me anywhere with you."

"I'd say it's gotten you pretty far."

"But not far enough. I want to marry you, Beverly. You know that. Or perhaps you don't believe me."

"I believe you."

"Well, then?"

"I'm already married."

"You don't love him."

"What makes you think I love you?"

"You've said so," Ian replied, hurt.

Had she indeed? She could not remember when. It must have been when they were making love, but who took such remarks seriously? People constantly said things they did not really mean when they were in a state of sexual abandon. She considered it very childish and unreasonable of Ian to hold her responsible for words spoken in the dark. It revealed him to be much less sophisticated than his façade would indicate, but then Americans were forever being fooled by the English accent, which had a way of making even the most innocuous statement sound impressively intelligent.

"Of course, I love you," she amended, thinking that only a few hours earlier Peter had said the same exact words to her. But Peter did not love her any more than she loved Ian. Peter did not want to lose her, though, and she did not want to lose Ian. She was Peter's cushion of safety, and Ian was hers. Peter needed her to come home to, and she needed Ian in order to be able to go on living with Peter. She could well understand Ian's sense of frustration, for he was the outsider in the situation, he was the one being used by the wife, who, despite her protestations did not truly want to give up her husband. Beverly was unhappy with Peter but it was a familiar kind of unhappiness. She was used to it, and during the few months that they had lived apart, she'd missed it. To divorce Peter and marry Ian (or anyone else for that matter) would be to chance an unfamiliar kind of unhappiness, and what was the point in that? At least with Peter she knew what she had, and even though it was far from perfect, it was also far from being fraught with the kind of intense anxiety that accompanied the unknown.

"I love you," she repeated, "but I can't marry you. That's the way things are."

"It's a hell of a way."

"We can't always have what we want," she said, feeling very pretentious.

"You seem to have what you want. Your nice, comfy marriage and me on Tuesdays and Thursdays."

"Ian, you're being petulant."

"Only because you put me in an unfortunate position."

He was really very weak, Beverly thought, to whine like this, without pride. Peter would never stoop to such depths. Or would he? Perhaps he, too, had whined and nagged when Lou Marron said she wouldn't see him any more. It was difficult to imagine Peter in that role, but then it would probably be difficult for Peter to imagine her in the forcible role she assumed with Ian. With Peter she was the weak one, and with Ian she was the strong one. Which one was she?

"Ian, please, let's not argue. Not today. My head is killing me."

He finished off his Scotch and soda and noted that her glass was empty. "Would you like another drink?"

"Please. And no sugar this time."

"I shall exert my powerful influence upon the waiter."

He said it sarcastically, he said it self-deprecatingly, and it occurred to Beverly how little power or influence he had in competitive New York where those were the measures of a man's worth. Poor Ian. He was, after all, only an assistant director of a daytime quiz show. She wondered how much money he made, but dared not imagine the exact amount for fear that it would turn out to be even more paltry than her dimmest estimate. This luncheon was undoubtedly an extravagance for him unless the network gave him a small expense account that he could write it off on. She wondered where Peter was having lunch, what he was eating, who his companions were. An unexpected feeling of affection for her husband swept over Beverly, sharp and poignant in its suddenness. At that moment she knew she could never leave him again, no matter what he did. The knowledge had a strange effect upon her: it made her want to go to bed with Ian worse than ever, and immediately.

"Aren't you warm, darling?" Ian asked, composed once more. "Wouldn't you like to take off your coat?"

"Yes. Thank you."

Ian helped her off with the coat and stared in amazement at what she was wearing underneath.

"Is that a nightie you have on? Or am I going mad?"

Beverly looked down at herself, as though noticing her apparel for the first time. Her breasts were clearly visible through the transparent batiste, the nipples lending a rosy glow to the stark whiteness of the gown.

"I was too sick to get properly dressed," she said. "But actually, what's the difference? No one will notice. You'll see."

"I think you should put your coat back on," Ian said nervously.

"Don't be ridiculous. No one cares. Do you see anyone in this room batting an eyelash?"

"That's not the point."

"Then what is?"

"You're . . . you're . . ." He could not seem to go on. "You're not *dressed,*" he said at last looking furtively around the restaurant to see whether anybody else had made the same observation.

"Nightgowns go everywhere these days," she pointed out. "And I should know. My husband is in the business."

"But not nightgowns like that."

"Well, perhaps I'll start a new fad. Peter would be so pleased."

"Beverly, I implore you. Put your coat on."

"No, I won't. It's too warm."

Ian lit a mentholated cigarette and began puffing away with ill-concealed anger.

"I'll give you an example," Beverly said, tickled by the novelty of the situation. "I'll ask this couple on my left whether they notice anything unusual."

"You'll do nothing of the sort."

Beverly turned to the couple on her left. "Excuse me, but would you say that I look unusual in any way?"

They glanced at her with blank disinterest and after a moment the man said, "Thanks the same, dear, but I'm not a breast man. Ankles. That's what gets me."

The woman merely shrugged and went back to her dessert. Pear Helène.

"You see?" Beverly said triumphantly to Ian. "I told you. No one gives a damn."

"Well, I do."

"Only because you're being foolishly conservative."

"Everyone can see your breasts, you fool."

"So what? They couldn't care less."

"This is absolutely ridiculous."

"You're the one who's ridiculous. You're the one who's making a fuss over nothing."

He ground out his cigarette, lit another one, and hissed, "I don't consider it *nothing.*"

Beverly was starting to feel better for the first time since she had gotten up that morning. Count on a good laugh to win the day. That was the trouble with her, she decided. She was too gloomy as a rule, too maudlin; she should learn to see the humor in life. Maybe this incident with Ian would change her entire outlook.

"Ankles," the man on the left said. "But definitely."

"Beverly. Please," Ian said.

The waiter placed a Scotch sour in front of her. "No sugar."

Beverly turned to face Ian, giving him a ringside view of herself. "What are you doing this afternoon that's so important we can't make love?"

"I have to line up more dummies."

"Quiz." It was really a terrible show. Beverly had watched five minutes of it once, wincing at the contestants who were all high school dropouts. According to Ian, the reason the show had such a high rating was because it gave mothers all over the country a chance to watch kids even dumber than their own.

"Yes," Ian said now, "we're running terribly low on dummies."

"I don't consider that more important than making love."

"A lot of dummies don't want to go on 'Quiz' and be publicly humiliated, you know."

"We're talking at cross purposes."

"It's not worth a high school diploma to them to make television fools of themselves."

"Make love, not fools."

Ian seemed to hear her for the first time. "I'm sorry, darling, but it's out of the question today."

Beverly took a sip of her sugarless sour. "Anita Schuler had an abortion a couple of months ago."

"What?"

"Yes. Simone told me. It was a D and C."

The man on Beverly's left said, "There's a new process that's much better. They use it in China where it only costs ten cents."

Not only would her neck be stiff for days, but she was having lunch with two total strangers to boot.

"Was it that pilot chap she was running around with last winter?" Ian asked.

"That's the bum. But Fingerhood went to San Juan with her. And they didn't even give her an anesthetic. Simone said they just stuck some Novocain up you-know-where. So she screamed for twenty minutes."

"It's a suction machine," the man on the left said. "It works on the same principle as a hand vacuum cleaner. Just sucks the foetus right out."

"That's very interesting," Beverly said, "but we would prefer to have our own conversation. If you don't mind."

"Ten cents in China. I'll bet they charged your friend five hundred dollars."

"Four fifty. Fingerhood bargained him down."

"That's the way it is with those Puerto Rican horse traders. You've got to bargain, or you're nowhere."

Peter wouldn't allow two total strangers to butt in on his conversation, Beverly thought, wishing that Ian weren't so weak and yet realizing that she wouldn't have him any other way.

"Please don't ever tell Anita that I told you about the abortion," Beverly said. "She pledged Simone to secrecy."

"Some pledge."

The couple on the left were finally leaving. As the man stood up, he said to Beverly, "Breasts are definitely out, dear. Believe me, I know."

"It's been fun lunching with you. Let's not do it again sometime."

The woman merely gave her a stony smile, and they were off.

"Charming couple," Ian said with a scowl. "Shall we look at the menu?"

After lunch Ian put Beverly in a taxi and said that he would call her later.

"Why?" Beverly asked.

"Just to say hello. See how you're feeling."

"I know how I'll be feeling. Even more rotten than I feel now."

"Don't despair, darling. Tomorrow is Tuesday."

"*Our* day." She blew him a kiss as the cab drove off. "I want to go to the Leo Castelli Gallery on East Seventy-Seventh Street," she told the driver. "And don't hurry. I'm in no rush at all."

"I've got to hurry. That's my business. Seventy-Seventh between what and what?"

"Fifth and Madison. And do you want to know something?"

"Not particularly."

"It's not so easy to get laid in New York."

When Beverly got to the gallery the only person there beside Castelli and Ivan Karp was a man in a loden corduroy suit. He had a big, black moustache and was seriously contemplating a diptych of John Payne and Carmen Miranda on horseback. The painting puzzled Beverly slightly because the bananas and oranges were on John Payne's head instead of Carmen's, but being a hardened gallery goer by now she knew that the thing to do was never to look puzzled about anything. And actually, why shouldn't they be on John Payne's head? What difference did it make? She turned to the man with the moustache.

"As Baudelaire said, 'This life is a hospital where every patient longs desperately to change his bed.' "

The man gazed at her impassively. "Where do you think you are? At the Modern?"

Beverly chose to ignore what she did not understand. "Whose show is this?"

"Mine."

"Oh. Who are you?"

"Steve Omaha."

"It's nice to meet you. I'm Beverly Northrop. I understand you have a neat way of giving women orgasms."

For a second it appeared as though his moustache was going to fall off. "Wait a minute. What did you say your name was?"

"Beverly Northrop. I'm a friend of Simone's. In fact I'm shattered that she's never mentioned me to you."

"Northrop. Northrop. Oh yeah, you're the crazy lady with all the dough."

"She calls *me* crazy?"

"I guess I made a *faux pas.*"

"I'm surprised you can even pronounce it."

Steve Omaha put his hands in his pockets. "What do you think of my show?"

"It's very unusual."

Betty Hutton and Eddie Bracken were on horseback in one painting, as were Vera Hruba Ralston and John Carroll in another. Also on horseback were George Brent and Merle Oberon.

"I know this is probably a dumb question," Beverly said. "But why is everyone on a horse?"

"You're right. It is a dumb question."

Merle Oberon had Steve Omaha's moustache, but after Rosenquist, Rauschenberg, and Oldenburg, Beverly figured, so what? Yvonne DeCarlo and Turhan Bey rounded out the show. There was a red star next to the John Payne and Carmen Miranda painting, and also next to George Brent.

"Did you really sell them?" Beverly asked. "Or is it a put-up job?"

"Why don't you offer to buy one and find out?"

It was a brilliant idea. If Peter persisted in having the screwy myna birds, she could have George Brent (or John Payne) on the wall. Either one would lend an appropriate contrast to the Hultberg landscape. Beverly felt full of quotations. She hadn't taken the weekly Tuesday art tour from Garden City all those years for nothing. The art guide had said that a surrealistic painting was as beautiful as the chance of coalition of an umbrella and a sewing machine upon a dissecting table.

"As a matter of fact, I would be very interested in purchasing one of your paintings. I'll speak to Leo tomorrow."

"Why not today?"

"I have a splitting headache. I don't like to talk about money when my head hurts. But I'm really quite interested in your work."

"Good. For a moment there I thought it was my body."

"I haven't ruled out the possibility."

"I think you should," Steve Omaha said, "because look who's coming to dinner."

It was Simone wearing the same black vinyl raincoat she was wearing when Beverly spotted her in the lobby of the Maria Cristina Hotel in Mexico City.

Simone said, "What are you doing here?"

"Trying to pick up your boyfriend, but I can't seem to get to first base."

Simone and Steve Omaha smiled blissfully at each other.

"Stevie is no Robert Fingerhood in that department," Simone said. "This one you can't have."

"I can't have anybody these days. You don't know what I go through. I just had lunch with Ian at The Ground Floor. I wanted to make love and he had to recruit dummies, so that was that."

"Beverly is interested in buying one of my paintings," Steve said, putting his arm around Simone's waist.

"She's got the do-re-mi."

"I don't think that's what Ian is interested in," Beverly said. "I really don't." (Secretly, she did. He wasn't interested in the money per se, but more to the point, the built-in life, the ready-made children, the easy set-up. Oh, yes, indeedy, he would love to move right in and take over another man's domicile. In fact Beverly was convinced that if it weren't for Peter, Ian would never have paid any attention to her.)

"I have very fond memories of that coat," Beverly said to Simone. "What are you wearing underneath?"

"Nothing."

Beverly was annoyed that Simone could beat her at her own game. After all, how could a nightgown ever begin to compete with nothing? Still—

"I'm only wearing a nightgown." And she opened the purple knit coat to prove her point.

"You can get into trouble that way," Steve said, staring at her prominent nipples.

"Want to bet?"

"Are you still leading your double life?" Simone asked Beverly.

"If you consider two half-men a double life, the answer is yes."

"Let's go have a drink," Steve said. "How about the Chez Madison?"

Both girls nodded in agreement.

"Sometimes Pursettes don't protect you from the cold," Simone said as they started out the door, "even when it's not all that cold."

After three more Scotch sours, Beverly went home. Henry, the doorman, asked her if she was feeling better.

"Yes, Henry, much better. Thank you."

She really felt much worse, her head still hurt like hell and Peter would not be home for hours. When she got upstairs, the chlldren were in the kitchen talking to Margaret about sex education.

"If eggs hatch, what will come out?" Sally asked.

"Baby chickens," Peter, Jr., said.

"Other animals have babies, too," Margaret reminded them. "But you never see their eggs. Where do you think they are?"

"In the barn," Peter, Jr., said, erupting into hysterical laughter, as his sister pinched him to keep quiet.

"Mother is going to have a little martini for a change," Beverly announced, "and then we are going to wait for a phone call from our Uncle Ian."

"Who's he?" Sally asked.

"The new one, darling."

❁ CHAPTER TEN ❁

Anita poured a premixed martini into a glass for one of her first-class passengers on flight #431 returning from Cairo. She remembered her last Cairo flight and the passenger who had subsequently taken her to dinner in New York. He was an attractive man in his forties, unmarried (he said), and extremely polite. Over shad roe at Maud Chez Elle he suggested that she could increase her income "substantially" if, the next time she had a Cairo run, she would agree to bring a small package back to New York with her.

"Containing what?"

"Oh," he said blandly, "just a little heroin."

"You can go to prison for things like that."

"There's really not much danger, not for a stewardess. And even if you did get caught, which is unlikely, you could always say that some unscrupulous passenger planted the stuff on you."

Anita found it difficult getting the shad roe down.

"Thanks all the same, but no thanks. It's not worth the risk."

Mr. Politeness did not push the matter. "Whatever you say. It's your bank account."

Anita was about to point out that she had no bank account, but then reconsidered the remark; it might encourage him to repeat his proposition, which frankly shocked her. After six years with the airline she thought she had encountered everything, but although she'd heard vague stories of smuggling by crew members, she had never run into the situation first hand. Even Lisa, the stewardess who had done a little hustling on the side, according to Jack Bailey, could not begin to compete with trafficking in narcotics for sheer shock value. She wondered whether she should report her dinner companion to the FBI, but dire visions of being murdered by an international crime syndicate immediately banished such thoughts from her mind.

"Besides," she told Simone the next time she spoke to her, "how did I know he wasn't pulling my leg? Trying to make himself sound ominously important?"

Simone had recently switched from Mini-Furs, Inc., to Dr. Harry Hocker's foot emporium where she was earning one hundred and two dollars a week, seven dollars more than before.

"Think of all the money you could have made," Simone said. "Think of the intrigue. Remember Zorina in *I Was a Jewel Thief?*"

"Dope is more dangerous than stealing jewels."

"Richard Greene made her go straight at the end."

"It's a Federal offense. I could wind up in Sing-Sing for twenty years."

"You would only be forty-six when you got out. With all that money in a bank in Switzerland, you could have an expensive face lift and spend the rest of your days sipping pink champagne in a villa in Cannes or Biarritz."

"Must you always remind me of my age?"

"Don't be so touchy. If it makes you feel any better, my birthday was yesterday. I am now twenty-five."

"Must you always remind me that you're a year younger than I am?"

"You might at least say, 'Happy birthday,' " Simone suggested.

"Happy birthday. How does it feel to be heading rapidly toward thirty?"

"I never thought it would happen to me."

"Thirty and not married?"

"I might become Mrs. Steven Omaha, for all you know."

"I might become Mrs. Robert Fingerhood," Anita said.

"Well, at least you've given up on becoming Mrs. Jack Bailey. That's progress."

"I keep seeing engraved invitations that read: *Dr. and Mrs. Robert Fingerhood cordially invite you to attend . . .*"

"Are you still planning to have a walnut poudreuse in your bedroom?"

"Yes, and I will buy all my maternity clothes at Bendel's. They have a wonderful boutique."

"Children!" Simone said in disgust. "Why do you want to have children and ruin your figure?"

"Every woman wants to have children. It's natural."

"I don't care if I never have a child. Chou-Chou is enough for me."

"The only problem is," Anita said, lost in her own thoughts, "what religion to bring them up in. Robert is Jewish, you know. And I'm Lutheran."

"Why not raise them as Hindu mystics? That would be a happy compromise."

"My family is morbidly anti-Semitic. Can't you see me bringing Robert home to Cleveland to meet them? I'd have to be sure to warn them in advance not to make any terrible remarks about lampshades, and things like that."

"*Peut-être* you should wait until Robert asks you to marry him before you get all worked up about your family and what religion to raise your kids in."

"Are you implying that he's not going to ask me?"

"You must admit that he does seem to have a peculiarly evasive quality in the marriage-proposal department."

"Just because he didn't ask *you*—" Anita heatedly began.

"I'm not going to trade bitchy remarks, but my advice is not to get too worked up about any walnut poudreuses you happen to run across in your travels. Fingerhood is a fuckup and we all know it."

"And I suppose that that screwball painter of yours isn't?"

Simone sighed ecstatically. "We have a new system now. It turns out that if I salute him when I say, 'Yes, sir,' I come twice as hard."

"You're abnormal."

"Sticks and stones will break my bones, but a good orgasm never hurt anybody."

That exchange with Simone had taken place a little over a month ago, and to date neither Robert Fingerhood nor Steve Omaha had come up with any proposals of marriage. Anita was not discouraged, though. At least Robert insisted that he did want to get married eventually whereas Jack had always insisted that he did not. In spite of the sarcasm, Simone was right in saying that it was progress to have given up hopes of becoming Mrs. Jack Bailey. To go on harboring that fantasy would have been foolishly self-defeating, and Anita often wondered why it had taken her so long to believe that Jack meant what he said. He had not tried to deceive her; she had deceived herself by her stubborn refusal to accept no for an answer. There would always be a soft spot in her heart for

Jack Bailey, rat that he was, but in the five months since her abortion Anita had grown to love and depend upon Robert Fingerhood to an extent that she would not have believed possible before going to Puerto Rico with him. Simone did not refer to him as Doctor Kindness for nothing, even though she said it in her usual deprecating manner.

Robert had indeed been kind both before and after the terrible operation through which she screamed for twenty minutes. Without him to take care of her and comfort her, she did not know how she would have ever survived. The sense of loss and defeat in the aftermath was worse than the pain had been. Pain, Anita discovered, could be easily forgotten, but the depression was something else again, gray and unyielding in its insistence. To her dismay, it lasted months longer than she thought it would, and at one point she began to wonder whether it would ever leave her. Often she would start to cry for no reason at all, her body shaking with uncontrollable, shuddering sobs, and then as quickly as the tears had started, they would subside and she would go about her business for the day, but with a tired, worn-out feeling of hopelessness. It was only in the last few weeks that the crying had ceased and the grayness had begun to dissolve, and a flicker of optimism could be felt once more. She had even stopped blaming Jack Bailey for making her pregnant and then abandoning her.

"To forgive is divine," she kept telling herself whenever she remembered his leaving her that farewell note in the plastic lettuce bag, before taking off for the airline training school in Indiana.

"This here isn't the driest martini in the world," Anita's first class passenger complained. "Can't you be a nice girl and slip in a little more vodka?"

Anita smiled her professional stewardess smile.

"I'm sorry, Sir, but they're premixed."

"You'd think that in first class you could get a dry martini, now wouldn't you?"

Anita smiled again, wishing he would drop dead.

"I'm sorry, Sir. We try to do our best."

"Yeah. Sure. Well, it's not your fault. Do you know whether we're going to get to New York on time?"

"I believe that we're right on schedule, Sir."

The man narrowed his eyes as he looked at her.

"They sure got you girls trained, all right. I'll say that for the sons of bitches."

Complaints, sneers, dissatisfaction. She was used to all of

it. Yet, hours later when the passengers were deplaning at JFK, the same man patted Anita on the shoulder and told her to be sure to eat her share of Thanksgiving turkey the next day.

"Thank you," she replied. "I certainly shall."

Robert Fingerhood was giving a Thanksgiving dinner party, which Anita had been dreading for weeks because of the people who'd been invited, but she was too tired and sleepy just then to worry about it. The layover in Cairo had been a brief one and she tossed and turned for six hours, unable to give in to fatigue. Now all she wanted to do was get back to her apartment as quickly as possible and flop into bed, shutting out everyone and everything in the whole damn world.

In the middle of the night she had an upsetting dream. She had taken Fingerhood home to Cleveland to meet her family for the first time. It was Thanksgiving and they were all seated around the table, watching her father carve the turkey. As he placed two slices of dark meat on Fingerhood's plate, Anita noticed that engraved on each slice was a small, but clearly visible swastika. Robert, however, seemed not to notice anything unusual and complimented her father upon his fine carving skill. Anita looked in horror at her father who winked gleefully at her.

She woke up in a sweat and went into the kitchen for a glass of warm milk, her body trembling. After she drank the milk, she tried to go back to sleep but couldn't. She spent the rest of the night smoking, reading *Cosmopolitan*'s new mystery novel, but most of all wondering how she was ever going to reconcile her parents to the idea of having a Jewish psychologist for a son-in-law.

Robert had asked Anita to come over early the next day in order to help him with the preparations. When she got there he was trying to fit a turkey and a suckling pig into his rather narrow oven, but there wasn't enough room for them both side by side.

"Why don't you put one on top of the other?" Anita suggested.

"Good idea."

He mounted the turkey on the pig, the turkey's legs wrapped around the poor pig who stared up at his strange oven companion, an apple stuck in his gaping mouth.

"By the time they're done roasting, they'll be madly in love," Robert said, closing the oven door.

"They're a queer-looking match."

"Who isn't?"

Anita wondered what he meant by that, but cautiously decided not to inquire further. "I brought you a present. Four bottles of Moët that I managed to swipe off the plane."

"Good girl. I was running low."

"When is the catastrophe scheduled to start? I mean, what time is everyone invited for?"

"Five. We have an hour. Do you want to make the salad?"

Anita was afraid he was going to ask her if she wanted to make love. She did not want to because her makeup would get all smeared, and, also, she was still quite bloated from yesterday's flight. Beneath her two-piece leopard print, she was wearing the sexiest panty girdle she owned, a black net affair, to hold in her protruding stomach. Simone maintained that there was no such thing as a sexy panty girdle, that it was an obnoxious contraption designed to turn off any man, but Anita felt that it was easy for Simone to talk since she did not have a bloating problem. Nevertheless, she sure wished that the Air Force would get on with its study as to why so many stewardesses tended to bloat after jet flights.

What with her bloating problem, her small breast problem, and her having-to-use-a-diaphragm problem, Anita sometimes thought that she was one of the most unfortunate girls alive. Every once in a while, though, she would inadvertently catch a glimpse of herself in a passing mirror and be amazed to discover how radiantly attractive she was, how greatly admired she must be by less attractive girls who had no idea that she suffered from problems, too, that she was nowhere near as self-confident as she appeared. Coping with the needs of passengers had a way of giving stewardesses an outward air of assurance which very often had little, or nothing, to do with their basic inner strengths.

"I'd love to make the salad," she said.

Actually, she would have been more than delighted if Robert had taken care of all the food preparations himself. She was so busy preparing and serving meals in the air, that it was a luxury to be out of the galley when she was on the ground. In fact, one of the qualities that appealed to her about Robert was that he loved to cook, thereby relieving her of the unpleasant responsibility. What appealed to her even more, had been Jack Bailey's habit of eating out. Jack's refrigerator rarely used to contain anything except a fifth of vodka and a dried-up lemon, whereas Robert's was invariably stocked full of food. But, as Anita kept reminding herself, the refrigerator contrast between the two men was also a pretty good indicator of their respective inclinations toward domesticity, and men who were domestic had a charming tendency to get married sooner or later. It bothered her that Robert had not yet popped the all-important question, yet whenever she thought of the inevitable confrontation between him and her family, she felt ironically grateful for his hesitancy.

"I hope you don't mind my inviting Jack," Robert said, "but I felt sorry for the poor bastard having nowhere to go on Thanksgiving. And he does live right in the building."

As though she could forget a salient fact like that.

"Why should I mind? It's been over with us for a long time now."

Six months, to be exact, and although Anita had flown a couple of trips with Jack Bailey since then, they'd exchanged little more than the usual captain-stewardess pleasantries. Only once did they have a real conversation, and that was when they ran into each other in Operations before a Madrid-Tunisia flight.

"How did the abortion go?" Jack asked, taking her aside.

"Fine."

"Do you feel okay?"

"Yes, I'm fine."

"I hope Fingerhood didn't get all shook up in P.R."

"If he was, he didn't show it. He was very sweet to me, very comforting to have around at the time."

"I'm glad. I would have gone with you if it were possible."

It was easy for him to say that in retrospect when the whole dirty business was over and done with.

"I doubt it," she said, "but if it makes you feel like less of a rat to think so, be my guest."

Then spotting one of the stewardesses who was going to be on the same flight, she picked up her suitcase and walked off without another word.

"Is there anything else I can do?" Anita asked Robert after she had mixed the salad.

"Not a thing. Why don't we open a bottle of Moët and go into the living room?"

"Okay. If you're sure."

"I'm sure. Simone is going to bring a sweet potato casserole, and Beverly said she would bring the pie."

"Beverly! How did that bitch get into the act?"

"Simone begged me to invite her," Robert Fingerhood said feebly.

Anita felt like strangling her ex-roommate. Simone knew that if there was one person in the world she could live without, it was Beverly Northrop. She dreaded seeing Beverly even more than Jack because she had never completely conquered her suspicion that Robert might still be interested in his old flame.

"This is going to be one hell of a party," Anita said, downing a glass of champagne in two gulps. "And since when does Simone know how to cook a sweet potato casserole?"

"She doesn't, but it seems that Dr. Harry Hocker, chiropodist extraordinaire, does."

"Don't tell me that nut is coming, too."

Robert shook his head in the negative. "He's the only one who's *not* coming."

"He's smart. He doesn't want to eat sweet potatoes sprinkled with old toenails."

Simone arrived at a quarter to five in a state of tears, hysteria, and confusion, minus the sweet potato casserole. Robert took her by the shoulders.

"What's wrong?" he asked. "What's happened?"

"I hate painters! I hate painters! I hate painters!"

Anita poured a glass of champagne for her and said, "As I recall, you also hate computer programmers, behavioral psychologists, midgets, electronic engineers, dental assistants, steel men from Detroit—"

"Oh, shut up," Simone said, accepting the champagne. "Must you always dredge up the past?"

"In your case, I find it irresistible."

Simone drank the champagne and took off her guanaco coat. To the surprise of Robert and Anita, all she had on underneath was a black body stocking and four flesh-colored band-aids holding up her window pane nylons.

"You'll have to excuse my lack of attire, but I left my dress outside Stevie's door."

"Doesn't everyone?" Anita asked, thinking that there was no hope for her ex-roommate, no hope at all.

Robert suggested that Simone sit down, try to relax, and tell them exactly what happened. Simone chose the hammock and waved to the stuffed owl overhead.

"I see you still have the *hibou,*" she said to Robert, her eyes filling with tears. "Everything reminds me of something. It's awful to be cursed with a sentimental memory. Could I please have some more champagne?"

"You know you have no capacity for alcohol," Anita said. "You'll be smashed in five minutes."

"I have never really liked you, Anita, and I like you even less at the moment. You're such a fucking pain in the ass."

"Why? Because I'm reasonable? Because I don't get involved with madmen and perverts? Because I don't indulge in bizarre sexual experiments?"

"Because you have no imagination."

"Girls, girls," Fingerhood said nervously. "Don't get into an argument. Not today. Please. Just cool it."

There was a momentary silence in the room, then Simone said, "The reason I'm in this disturbed state is because Stevie and I had an argument a couple of days ago. It started when I criticized a painting he was working on. Dennis Morgan and Joan Leslie on horseback. All I said was, 'Why the hell is everyone always on a fucking horse in your paintings?' You wouldn't think a simple question like that could drive a man into a state of violence, now would you?"

The only thing that constantly used to amaze Anita about Simone was that considering all the wild chances she took, and all the nuts she got involved with, nobody had ever beaten her up, but Simone maintained that the worst thing that ever happened to her was being held captive for six days by Edwin L. Kuberstein, the novelist, and having to read the collected works of J. D. Salinger while Ed chewed up her clitoris.

"Did Steve hit you?" Anita asked, hoping for the worst.

"Only twice. I mean, he's Jewish. Jewish men don't go in for fisticuffs. They consider that sort of thing beneath them. Can you imagine a Jewish prizefighter, for instance? In between rounds he'd read *The New Republic*. No, Stevie just slapped me twice across the face. It didn't really hurt. Then he burst into tears and said he was hung up on horses and couldn't help it."

"Steve Omaha doesn't sound so Jewish to me," Fingerhood said.

Simone finished her second glass of champagne and placed the glass on a jaguar skin on the floor.

"Omaha's not his real name, stupid. His real name is Silverstein. I thought I told you."

"You told me he was David Swern's nephew, but you never mentioned the Silverstein part."

"You never mentioned it to me, either," Anita said, thinking that Simone was lucky her mother lived so far away. If Simone and Steve should get married, at least she wouldn't have to take him home to meet her family.

"After Stevie stopped crying, he became very cold and detached, and asked me to leave," Simone went on. "I said I was sorry that I had hurt his feelings, but there was no reason for him to be upset about his horse hangup because it suddenly occurred to me that he probably had been a Cossack in a previous life. I also pointed out that he has Jupiter in the house of creativity, and his Sun in the house of money and possessions, so he's bound to be a raging success and has nothing to worry about."

"I'll bet that reassured him," Anita said.

"It would have if he knew anything about reincarnation and astrology."

The doorbell rang and Robert went to answer it.

"I understand you invited Beverly," Anita said to Simone. "That was cute of you."

"There's nothing wrong with Beverly. The reason you don't like her is because she's a Pisces and you're a Cancer, and the two signs are too much alike."

"I don't like her because of her money and her breasts. How many times do I have to tell you that?"

"That's your story."

"I hope Ian takes her for all she's worth."

"Good will toward others was never one of your shining attributes, Anita. Could I have some more champagne?"

The new arrival was Lou Marron in a gold mole knicker-dress. Simone had previously told Anita that she was going to invite Lou to the party in the hopes of getting her interested in Jack Bailey, and Anita said it would serve Lou right if she did.

"I thought you liked her," Simone had said, surprised by Anita's reaction. "She wrote a very nice piece on you, I thought."

"She also gave me crabs."

"You don't know that for a fact."

It was Anita's turn to be surprised. "But you're the one whose theory it was. Remember?"

"A theory isn't a fact. Maybe it was her fault and maybe it wasn't."

"Let's put it this way. I'm not crazy about her, but she's certainly better than that bitch, Beverly."

"Be nice to her," Simone whispered, as Lou came into the room. "She's gone through bad times recently."

Observing Lou, it did indeed strike Anita that she had changed considerably since their first and only meeting that past summer. Her face seemed softer and less constricted than the day she had interviewed Anita at The Palm Court. Perhaps Simone was right about David Swern's death having had a devastating effect upon her.

"Simone was in the middle of telling us about her catastrophic love life," Anita explained to Lou who had sat down, legs astride, on one of Fingerhood's whalebone vertebrae. "You should be interested since I understand it was through you that she met Steve Silverstein. I mean, Omaha."

Lou smiled, rather wanly, it seemed to Anita, and replied. "Yes, I did introduce them. I hope nothing too terrible has happened."

"That remains to be seen," Simone said, picking up the thread of her story. "After the fight with Stevie, he refused to answer the telephone, so just before coming over here today I went to his studio to try and persuade him to come with me. He was working on the Dennis Morgan—Joan Leslie painting when I got there, and although he let me in he wouldn't talk to me. I pleaded with him not to be so stubborn. I told him what a nice time he'd have, and how everyone was bringing something for the dinner. I even showed him my contribution, Dr. Hocker's sweet potato casserole. Something about that casserole must have rubbed him the wrong way, because suddenly he grabbed the whole thing and smashed it on the floor which was all splattered with paint. Poor Dr. Hocker! He worked very hard on that casserole. It had melted marshmallows in it."

"Not to mention old toenails," Anita said, but nobody paid any attention to her remark.

"When I saw what he did to the casserole, I really got mad. I marched out, slammed the door behind me, and started down the stairs. But then I had a brilliant afterthought. I went right back upstairs again and took off my dress outside Stevie's door, and set it on fire."

"You did *what?!*" the other three cried in shocked unison.

"It was a dress I didn't care for anyway, and I thought that a small blaze would be a fitting lesson to Stevie for having destroyed Dr. Hocker's work of love." Simone turned to Lou. "That's why I'm sitting here in my body stocking."

Fingerhood shook his head sadly. "How come I know all the crazy ladies in the world?" he said to no one in particular.

Then everybody started arriving all at once.

First, came Jack Bailey in a Cardin-styled suit that he'd had made in Madrid. He was looking better than ever, Anita thought, exuberant, self-confident, on top of the world. His attractiveness dazzled her almost as much as it had the first time she met him, and she realized that it always would. There was a magnetism about him, a glamour. He seemed to promise something when he smiled at you from behind those deep-set eyes, something that he would never fulfill. His concern for himself ruled out any real concern for another person, and Anita knew she should be grateful that it was all over between them. She even felt grateful to Jack for having ended it as he did, because inadvertently he had paved the way for his successor, Robert Fingerhood, who would make a far better husband than Jack ever could.

Anita turned lovingly toward Robert only to realize that he appeared to be absorbed with Lou Marron's legs, which could only be seen from the calf down, the upper part being covered by her gold mole knickers. Lou's legs were hardly her best feature, and Anita could not imagine why Robert was so interested in them. A feeling of dread shot through her as she thought of Simone and Beverly, her predecessors. Was she about to join their unlovely ranks? To her relief, Lou seemed blatantly unaware of Robert's attention, and was talking to Jack. Six months ago Anita would have been horrified if it were the other way around. Were there no constants at all?

"I'm glad you enjoyed the series," Lou was saying to Jack. "I enjoyed writing it. Airline people are a strange breed."

Jack gave her his best Gary Cooper chuckle. "We're even stranger when you get to know us."

"Isn't everyone?"

"Of course. The longer you know a person, the less familiar he or she becomes."

"Why is that?" Lou asked.

"New facets reveal themselves. Ones you hadn't been aware of before. The person becomes more shaded, not so black and white as you'd imagined at first."

"Do you think that's true of everyone?"

Jack chuckled again. "Everyone worth knowing."

Anita perceived this last remark as a veiled insult. Was that why Jack had dropped her? Because she was not sufficiently shaded? It never before occurred to her that he could even entertain such thoughts, and then she realized that she was only proving his theory of familiarity. How little she knew him after all. Making love, finally, was not a very good way of getting to know someone. In two minutes Lou had learned more about Jack Bailey than she had in nearly two years.

"Where the hell is that crazy cunt?"

Everyone looked up, startled, as a man came barging into

the room, wearing a pair of singed jeans and a paint-stained sweat shirt with the number forty-one on the back.

"Stevie!" Simone rushed up to him. "Are you hurt?"

Before anyone could stop him, he punched Simone halfway across the room where she landed on one of the jaguar skins, her head in Fingerhood's lap.

"Two years of 1940's movie stars have gone up in flames, thanks to you!" Steve Omaha shouted. "Two years of work burned to a crisp. You'd better stay there, on the floor, because if you get up I'm going to break your fucking jaw."

Fingerhood removed Simone's head from his lap and introduced himself to Steve.

"I'm sorry about your paintings," he said, "but I'm not going to stand for women being physically attacked in my apartment. So you can either pull yourself together, or get the hell out."

"Don't you dare speak to Stevie like that," Simone said rubbing her cheek where she had been struck. "You don't know what I've done. I've ruined his life!"

"So you're Robert Fingerhood," Steve said. "I've been wanting to meet you for a long time now. Simone has told me quite a bit about you. Like you're the creep who nearly drove her to suicide last winter."

"It wasn't entirely my fault," Robert began, but he got no further because Steve Omaha knocked him to the floor with two fast blows.

"Anybody else looking for trouble?" Steve asked.

Jack Bailey stood up. "If I get my hand broken, I don't fly. If I don't fly, I don't get paid. If I don't get paid, I get anxious. Oh, screw it. We've all lost our reflexes."

He hauled off and punched Steve in the nose causing it to bleed. Anita quickly came between them.

"Please," she begged. "Please stop this stupid violence immediately. It's barbaric. I think we should all have a glass of champagne and try to calm down."

"Good idea," Fingerhood said from the floor. "Would you open another bottle?"

"I'm all for champagne," Jack said to Steve. "What do you say?"

"Sure." He removed a handkerchief from his pants pocket and pressed it to his bloody nose. "I don't like violence any more than the next guy."

"I'll bet you don't," Anita said. "*The New Republic* indeed."

When she returned from the kitchen with the champagne,

Steve Omaha was sobbing loudly, his hands over his face, and everyone was trying to comfort him, everyone except Simone, who was in tears herself.

"I didn't mean to burn down your studio," she kept repeating. "Please forgive me. I'm sorry."

"You're sorry *what?*" he asked in between sobs.

"I'm sorry, Sir."

"If she goes on like this," Anita whispered to Fingerhood, "she's liable to come on the spot."

"When I see it, I'll believe it."

After a few minutes, Anita managed to coax Simone and Steve to stop crying long enough to gulp down a glass of champagne.

"Hey, that's pretty zippy stuff," Steve said, brightening. "I feel almost sane again. How about a refill?"

"*Moi aussi,*" Simone chimed in.

Anita was starting to feel the effects of the champagne, and looking around the room she had a strong hunch that the others were, too. All excitement had subsided and in its place a kind of lethargy prevailed. Everyone seemed to be talking and moving in blurry slow motion, as though they were being restrained by some invisible weighty force. The doorbell rang twice before anyone heard it.

"*Entrez,*" Simone called out.

And in walked Ian Clarke, looking somewhat confused.

"Ian!" Anita said, happy to see an old friend. "I'm surprised, but delighted. No one told me that you'd been invited."

"I wasn't, at least not officially. I hope I'm not intruding, but Beverly asked me to meet her here."

Lou Marron turned pale. "Beverly Northrop?"

"Yes." Ian glanced at Robert, then Jack, then Steve, apparently undetermined who his host was. "I presume that one of you gentlemen is Robert Fingerhood."

Fingerhood identified himself and introduced Ian to the others. "Beverly should be along any moment. Can I offer you a glass of champagne?"

"Delighted."

"I'd like another glass, too," Lou said, nervously.

Anita was startled to see the change that had come over Lou in the few seconds since Ian arrived. Her previous calm was gone, shattered, replaced by a highly charged intensity which reminded Anita of the Lou she had met at The Palm Court. As though on cue, Lou took out a cigarette, flicked her lighter before anyone could offer her a match, and started to puff away like Bette Davis whose fiancé had just been stolen by Miriam Hopkins. Anita had been dreading Beverly's arrival all along, but it was clearly apparent that Lou dreaded it even more, and why shouldn't she? What woman in her right mind would want to come face to face with her ex-lover's wife? Anita felt a sudden compassion for Lou, a sudden superiority, too, a sudden lightness of heart. She began to smile to herself. The evening might turn out to be more interesting than she had expected.

When Beverly arrived minutes later, she had nothing on beneath her belted Russian Crown Sable coat.

"I brought the pie," she said, handing it to Fingerhood. "Coconut custard."

Then, kissing Ian langorously on the cheek, she handed him her coat and asked him to hang it up for her. Stunned by her nakedness, for a moment nobody in the room spoke.

Finally Lou said, "It's a body without the stocking."

Beverly twirled around on unsteady feet and said to everyone, "Well, what's the consensus?"

"You look pretty good to me," Jack replied. "I'm ready any time you are."

"Oh, I remember you," Beverly said, pointing a finger at him. "You're that cute airline pilot who knocked up Anita. Simone told me all about it, you bad boy."

"I did not!" Simone protested, turning red. "That's a terrible thing to say. That's—slander!"

Beverly grinned. "Don't bother denying it, darling. Everyone knows what a compulsive gossip you are, but we love you all the same."

"I don't love her," Anita said, all lightness gone. "In fact, I'd like to strangle her this very moment."

"Beverly, I think you should put your coat back on," Ian said, still holding the sable.

"Oh, Christ, we had this conversation at The Ground Floor and I tell you now what I told you then, Ian, my sweet. I have no intention of putting anything on. Why should I? I'm proud of my body."

"You're drunk."

"I'm drunk *and* I'm proud of my body."

Anita observed Beverly with envy. Her breasts were just as big as Anita had feared and she could well understand why Beverly was proud. She would be proud, too, if she had a body like that. It gave her some satisfaction, though, to note that Beverly's face was beginning to show the wear and tear of excessive drinking. The skin had started to lose its elasticity. Why on the face and not the breasts, Anita wondered? It wasn't fair.

Jack Bailey seemed as intrigued as Anita by Beverly's shape. "Just give me the high sign," he said to her, "and you're on."

"I wouldn't continue in that vein, if I were you," Ian reproached Jack. "Or, as I believe they say in this country, can it. Contrary to how it may appear, Mrs. Northrop is not trying to be suggestive by her nudity."

"Do you have another word for it?" Steve Omaha asked.

"I am so trying to be suggestive," Beverly said, sitting down as close to Jack Bailey as she could possibly get.

"You're succeeding, honey," he said.

"You wouldn't believe that I'm a respectable married woman with two children, now would you?"

"If you say so."

"It's true. Ask anyone in this room." Her eyes stopped on Lou. "Well, practically anyone."

"Beverly!" Ian said, visibly shaken.

"Oh do be quiet, Ian. You'll louse up your inheritance." She pressed herself against Jack, her heavy breasts disappearing into his Cardin jacket. "I understand you fly boys have a fantastic reputation for virility."

"We try to please, Ma'am."

"But you don't always succeed," Anita said, "and if anyone should know, it's this little girl right here."

Beverly gave Anita a perfectly sweet, perfectly contemptuous smile. "Make way for a big woman, little girl."

"Dinner is served," Fingerhood announced, but nobody moved. They were too busy watching Jack take Beverly's right breast in his mouth.

"It's not much of a dinner." Fingerhood's eyes were glued to Beverly and Jack. "But it's served anyway."

"Yes, I think we all should eat something," Anita said without enthusiasm, wondering whether Jack was going to be Beverly's next big romance. She was jealous already.

"Your jealousy is showing." Simone had sized up Anita's reaction to the situation. "You don't want Jack anymore. At least that's what you keep telling me."

"That doesn't mean I want Beverly to have him."

"Selfish pig."

"Please. Don't use that word. You know how sensitive I am about my father being a pork butcher. Besides, you're a fine one to talk about jealousy. How did you feel when you found Beverly and Robert fucking on the floor? You only went home and tried to kill yourself."

"True, but I didn't have another man at the time. You have Robert."

Anita recalled her dream of last night. "I could just murder Hitler. If it weren't for him, I'll bet my parents wouldn't be so damned anti-Semitic."

"Everyone's anti-Semitic," Simone said cheerfully. "Especially the Jews. They're worst of all."

"I'm not concerned about everyone. I'm concerned about my parents. You don't know my father. He still sings *Deutschland Über Alles* in the shower."

"Maybe he'll have a heart attack and drop dead soon, like poor Mr. Swern, and then you won't have anything to worry about."

"Your solutions to knotty problems have always fascinated me. Sheer genius. That's what they're the product of."

"I think so, too," Simone agreed, rolling her eyes as she did for Chou-Chou in the morning, and making her imbecile face. "That's how it is with us idiot-savants."

Jack and Beverly finally drew apart and joined the others in the next room. Above the table was a large oil of people in evening clothes sitting down to dinner, a butler poised on the threshold.

Simone poked Steve who was seated next to her.

"See? They're not on horseback."

"Are you asking for another shot in the nose?"

She laughingly saluted him. "No, Sir."

Fingerhood lit the tall, black candles in the center of the table and brought out three bottles of champagne, and individual crab cocktails on beds of lettuce. The crabmeat was cut in large, shimmering chunks, and each portion was more than generous.

"Mother Fingerhood cooks again," Simone said. "This looks absolutely yummy."

Jack and Beverly were in a feverish embrace which everyone pretended to ignore while stealing surreptitious glances at the uninhibited lovers.

"Let's go in the bedroom," Beverly stage-whispered in Jack's ear.

"Roger."

"You'll do no such thing!" Ian said firmly.

Neither Beverly nor Jack paid any attention to him.

"We'll see you later, folks," Jack said as they left the

room, their arms wrapped around each other. "*Bon appétit.*"

Anita was enraged by their exit. "Robert, you're the host. Are you just going to sit there and allow this . . . this . . . this terrible immorality to take place in your own apartment? In your own *bed?*"

Fingerhood had started in on the crab. "What would you like me to do? Suggest that they screw in the bathtub?"

"I suggest that you ask them to leave."

"Why? They're not bothering anybody."

"Oh, yes they are. They're bothering me." She looked desperately around the table for a sympathetic face, but except for Ian the others seemed blandly disinterested in her diatribe. "It's a disgrace! They have no right to carry on like this in front of everyone. It's degenerate!"

"They're not carrying on in front of everyone," Lou pointed out. "They've gone in the bedroom so they can carry on in private."

"You're as degenerate as they are!"

"Shut up," Steve told her, "and eat your crabmeat."

"I despise crabmeat." She glared at Robert. "You served this on purpose, didn't you? To remind me of that nasty disease you gave me last summer."

"It wasn't my fault. Beverly gave it to me."

Simone and Anita exchanged triumphant glances.

"So now you admit it. And I wonder where Miss Big Tits got it."

Lou looked up. "She got it from Peter, who got it from Tony Elliot, who got it from the United States Marines. Now are you satisfied?"

"Tony wasn't with us in Atlantis," Simone said thoughtfully. "But the Marines were. *From the halls of Montezuma to the shores of Tripoli* is a symbolic way of saying that in a previous life these men lived in colonies of Atlantis, like Africa and Mexico. The largest colony of Atlantis was ancient Egypt. Not that I expect anyone here to believe me."

No one spoke for a couple of minutes, then Ian said, "They certainly are taking a long time in there."

"It's hard for Jack to come," Anita admitted, before she realized that she was giving away intimate secrets that were no one else's business. "I mean, he likes to hold back for as long as he can."

"*Ejaculata retardata,*" Fingerhood said.

"I'll bet she's going down on him," Simone giggled. "I'll

bet we're not the only ones who have a mouthful this very minute."

Ian turned white. "Beverly doesn't do that sort of thing."

"Want to bet?" Fingerhood asked.

"Are you implying—?"

"Implying, shit. I'm the one who saved her from the Garden City humdrums. I was *numero uno,* buddy, I should know."

"I agree with you," Ian said to Anita. "They're all degenerate. I can't understand what I'm doing here."

"You're waiting for Miss Money Bags to stop going down on Smiling Jack," Simone said.

"That's enough," Steve told her. "Let the guy alone."

"Yes, Sir."

"Maybe Jack is going down on Beverly," Lou suggested.

"I hope she used a Norforms recently," Anita said. "Jack is very meticulous when it comes to feminine hygiene."

Lou laughed derisively. "Feminine hygiene? You sound like a copywriter for a pharmaceutical company."

"At least I don't screw faggots who screw other faggots who screw the United States Marines."

"When Atlantis rises above Bimini, you'll all realize that Simone isn't as crazy as you think," Simone said.

"Peter Northrop wouldn't screw you with a ten foot pole," Lou said to Anita. "You're so antiseptic you probably douche with Mr. Clean."

"Degenerate," Ian repeated.

"I'm the only one here who's having a good time," Fingerhood said, pouring more champagne. "Everybody else just wants to bitch. Atlantis. Degeneracy. Who's blowing who. Who gives a damn? Don't you know how to enjoy yourselves?"

"I'm enjoying myself," Steve said.

"Then why do you look like you're going to burst into tears any minute?"

"If you lost two years of work in a fire, you'd look that way, too."

Fingerhood glanced at Simone. "I did. That's why I didn't break your nose when you belted me. I felt sorry for you."

"That particular fire wasn't my fault," Simone protested.

"What fire?" Steve asked, very alert now.

"Oh, Robert and I were in bed one day and his Ph.D. thesis burned up. It was all about orgasms."

"One day when?"

Without thinking, she said, "The day of poor Mr. Swern's funeral."

"That was the day I went to bed with you for the first time," Steve said, putting down his fork.

"Yes, that's right."

"You mean, you screwed both of us the same day?"

"Yes, I guess you could say I did."

"You *guess?!* What do you mean *guess?!*"

"I mean I screwed both of you the same day."

"Utterly degenerate," Ian said.

"Boy, am I having a good time," Fingerhood said.

Steve pushed his chair back from the table. "I don't think this is very funny at all, Simone."

"I didn't say it was funny."

"Then how could you do such a thing?"

"What do you mean?"

"Screw him and me the same day, you dumb broad."

"What's the difference if it was the same day or different days?"

"She's got a point there," Fingerhood said.

"You keep out of this," Steve told him.

"I've decided I don't feel sorry for you any longer. You're an obnoxious prick. Stand up."

The minute Steve got to his feet, Fingerhood knocked him to the floor.

"I guess I deserved that," Steve admitted, checking to see whether his nose had started to bleed again.

"You deserve more than that, but fortunately for you I'm not overly vindictive. If I were, I'd beat the shit out of you, wise guy. Now that that's settled can we go on with our Thanksgiving dinner?"

"Violent as well as degenerate," Ian observed.

Anita and Robert started to remove the crab cocktail dishes from the table, as Beverly and Jack emerged from the bedroom with beatific smiles on their faces. Now Jack was naked, too, which immediately aroused speculation from the others.

"He's thicker than Fingerhood," Simone said.

"But not longer," Anita pointed out.

"Thickness is more important."

"Who says?"

"Moi."

Beverly and Jack paid no attention to this exchange, so lost were they in ecstatic reverie.

"One of his balls is smaller than the other," Steve said.

"Degenerate, degenerate, degenerate."

Fingerhood brought in more bottles of champagne and Anita brought in the salad, which glistened lushly in a gigantic Mexican bowl. The salad consisted of Boston lettuce, endive, and halved black olives, tossed with the tart oil and vinegar dressing. Then Fingerhood brought in the stuffed turkey, while Anita brought in the suckling pig, whose apple had roasted to a crisp. Anita scooped out the stuffing from the turkey and piled it on a separate plate.

"I could cry when I think of poor Dr. Hocker's sweet potato casserole," Simone said. "It would have been a perfect accompaniment to this meal. Aren't you sorry it's lying on your studio floor, Stevie?"

"It is not lying on my studio floor."

"*Pourquoi?*"

"Because there is no more studio."

"That's right. I forgot." Tears streamed down Simone's face as she was reminded of the disaster she had caused, and suddenly she shouted, "I want to be beaten!"

"Sado-masochistic degeneracy."

But Simone was not to be stopped, and a second later her body stocking was no longer on her body. The only people who seemed oblivious to her sudden nakedness were Beverly and Jack, who were eating turkey and pig for all they were worth, but eating with one hand on each other, fondling each other, lost in their own particular world of food-sex sensuality, and not wishing to be diverted from two good things.

"Ian is right," Anita said. "You are all degenerate. And disgusting, too, I might add."

"Degeneracy *is* disgusting," Ian said.

"Not necessarily," Lou corrected him. "It depends upon one's personal sense of morality."

Lou removed her gold mole knickerdress. Not only did she have nothing on underneath, but her breasts were painted a pale green.

"Breast makeup is very in," she said. "The cosmetic industry is going to give the lingerie industry something to think about in the very near future."

"Won't that put you in an awkward position?" Anita asked. "Since you're lingerie editor of *The Rag?*"

"Not if I become cosmetic editor."

"I INSIST UPON BEING BEATEN!" Simone shouted, feeling very ignored, abused, and taken advantage of.

Anita had become violently nauseated. She saw her world lying on the floor in pieces and shreds, broken, crumbled.

The disillusionment was more than she could bear. Why didn't Robert put an end to this horrible striptease? Why didn't he protect her from it? Wasn't that the man's role? Or were there no familiar roles between the sexes any longer? A sense of dread set in.

"I INSIST UPON BEING BEATEN, BUT WHO'S GOING TO DO IT?"

Fingerhood confirmed Anita's worst fears. "I have the whip."

"You're not supposed to act this way," Anita said. "You're Jewish."

"What's that got to do with it? I'm as depraved as the next guy."

"But you're not *supposed* to be."

"Who says?"

"*Moi.*"

Steve Omaha stood up, a good-natured smile on his face. "I'll beat the shit out of you, Simone, you know that. I just don't understand why you have to pick unlikely times for these things to happen. You might have waited until we went home."

"Your stupidity is beyond belief," she told him. "I don't want *you* to beat me."

"Why not?"

"Painters are really stupid. *Stupide!* If you did it, it wouldn't count. Don't you understand anything except horses? It's got to be someone who doesn't want to, someone who's revolted by it. My goodness, do I have to explain every fucking motivation?"

"I'm amazed that you even know the word," Fingerhood said.

Anita wanted to cry but the tears wouldn't come. She felt them swelling up behind her eyes, waiting to be released, blessed release, if only it would happen. She looked around the room, trying to place herself in perspective, but nothing made any sense, it was all a mad disaster. Lou's green breasts were only one projection of the disaster. They were no more shocking (or less shocking) than Simone's wanting to be beaten, than Beverly's left hand upon Jack's right ball, than Robert's offer of his whip to whomever cared to use it, than Steve's admission of sadism, than Ian's iceman act. She was in a nut bin: the world.

"I nominate Anita," Jack said dispassionately.

"For what?" she asked.

"Beating Simone."

"Don't be ridiculous."

"I'm not being ridiculous."

"Yes you are." But he had hit a responsive chord, although she could not yet admit it.

"You've always hated that French cunt," Jack said, swooping down upon Beverly's reddish pubic hairs for a fast kiss. "Why keep your hatred in a closet? Bring it out in the open. Be a *mensch*. Beat her!"

"I will not."

"Oh, go ahead," Fingerhood said, looking bored with the entire business.

Anita swallowed a forkful of turkey stuffing and wondered why it tasted so strange. Marjoram? Tarragon? Sage? Thyme? A Pepperidge Farm recipe? No. It was something quite different, an evasive taste thrill she could not define. Then she noticed that Robert had become very interested in Lou's green breasts and for a moment she did not know what to do about it. She was confused because Lou's breasts were not exactly something to write home about. They were medium-sized, a little low, okay in a strictly unfabulous way, but she had to admit that the green makeup made sense. It upgraded very ordinary looking tits, and not the least of it was the fact that the nipples were green, too. Here she had been doing all those lousy breast exercises, not to mention the hydrotherapy, and where had it gotten her? Nowhere. Although she hated to admit it, Lou had hit upon a far smarter solution: if you can't change them, fantasize them. Then she realized that she was the only clothed woman in the room and she became doubly frightened because there seemed to be but one solution left, and she didn't like it, not a bit.

"I'M NOT GOING TO HANG AROUND ALL DAY. COME ON!"

Anita's two-piece leopard print suddenly seemed old-fashioned. Still the prospect of taking off all her clothes made her nervous. It was that rotten lower-middle-class background of hers that perpetrated this old-fashioned inhibition. She should have been really low class, and then she wouldn't be so cautious. Or really high.

"Robert," she said. "Do you love me?"

He swallowed a leaf of Boston lettuce. "Yes, I love you. Now why don't you go beat Simone?"

"Be a *mensch*," Jack said.

Lou's green nipples dipped into the turkey stuffing as she

leaned over her plate. Only because they're on the low side, Anita thought gleefully.

"THIS IS BECOMING RIDICULOUS."

"It must have been like this when the Third Reich was in business," Ian said.

Then he went down on Lou as she continued to dip and eat.

"You never went down on me," Beverly said. "Not once. I take it as a personal insult."

"It's only because I mean nothing to him," Lou tried to tell her. "He probably cares about you."

"I resent the *probably* part. Of course he cares about me. Don't you, Ian?"

But Ian couldn't answer with any coherence, his face being buried in Lou's steaming recesses.

"I'M WAITING."

Nobody paid any attention to Simone. Her exquisite body was vying for attention with Beverly's and Lou's, which were far less exquisite, and, consequently, far more exciting. It was only when Anita came to that realization that she had the courage to take off the top of her two-piece leopard print.

Lou became immediately contemptuous. "Look. She still wears a brassiere. How quaint."

"I wear a brassiere, too," Beverly said.

"In your case, I'm afraid it's a dire necessity."

"I resent that."

"*J'ATTENDS QUELQU'UN.*"

"If you didn't wear one," Lou said to Beverly, "you'd look a little silly flopping around in the wind. Ian, you're doing it too hard. Silly boy. It hurts."

"This sure is a great dinner," Fingerhood said, helping himself to another slice of suckling pig, as Anita carefully laid her Hollywood Vassarette bra on the floor, inches from Ian's feet.

"She not only wears a brassiere, she wears a padded brassiere."

Lou felt immensely superior, what with the green makeup and Ian's unexpected attention. She didn't even know the man.

"Aren't you going to take off the bottom half?" Steve asked Anita who had come to a standstill in undressing.

"Eventually."

The bottom half seemed more significant to Anita and she had not yet summoned the courage to reveal that. She was terrified that if she did, Simone would make a crack about her bleaching her pubic hairs, and then where would she be? So humiliating if that should happen. She got up from the table and grabbed the whip that stood in a corner of the room and gave Simone a resounding whack across the stomach.

"YOU FUCKING FOOL. YOU WEREN'T SUPPOSED TO ACTUALLY DO IT. YOU WERE ONLY SUPPOSED TO THREATEN ME. DON'T YOU UNDERSTAND ANYTHING AT ALL ABOUT PERVERSITY?"

Feeling put down because of her lack of perception, Anita whipped Simone again, on her thighs. "That was for old times' sake."

Simone cringed appropriately. "IT HURTS."

Steve was the only one who continued to watch the two girls; in a few seconds the others had become bored with the whipping repetition and were concentrating upon their food. Even Ian had stopped eating Lou and was eating turkey again, his clothes removed, his very white English skin an interesting contrast to Lou's darker tone. For some reason, she began to think about Marshall, the Negro who worked in the personal loan department of the First National City Bank. He suddenly seemed very sweet, very long ago, part of the David Swern era. She still could not believe that David was gone. Somehow she had always felt that he would be around forever and his death continued to strike her as a cruel and unexpected abandonment. She wondered how his wife had adjusted to the loss. Did one ever adjust to death? She suspected not; it was simply too much for the human brain to absorb. Nothingness defied the imagination. No wonder Simone chose to believe in reincarnation.

"I want to get fucked again," Beverly announced.

"I'm forty-four years old," Jack said. "I can't get it up every minute. Try someone else. I'm shot for the night. Try the mad doctor."

"Wait until I stop eating," Fingerhood said, helping himself to more roast pig.

Steve looked at Beverly. "I've stopped eating. Let's go."

"Oh, no!" Simone screamed. "You're not going to fuck Beverly."

"What do you care? You're busy being beaten."

Anita had worked herself up to a frenzied state and was gratified to see welts beginning to show on Simone's curvacious body. She would never have believed herself capable of this degree of sadism and it made her feel slightly proud to know that she could be as cruel as the next person. Secretly she blamed her new-found capability upon the airline: all those years of forced stewardess smiles and having to warm putrid baby formulas had taken their inevitable toll. The whip made a gratifying sound.

"*ÇA SUFFIT.*"

"Simone is right," Fingerhood said to Anita. "You're getting a bit carried away."

"I'm enjoying myself."

"Well, we certainly don't want that."

Beverly and Steve left the room.

"I don't see why they have to do it in private," Lou said. "You'd think they weren't among friends."

Chastised by Fingerhood, Anita regretfully relinquished the whip and she and Simone rejoined the others at the table.

"You certainly are a mean bitch," Simone said to Anita. "I don't know how I ever was a roommate of yours. I don't know how I stood it for even one second."

"Beverly steals all your men, doesn't she? First Robert and now Steve."

"She won't steal Stevie for long. He's only doing this to get even with me for having burned down his studio. I hope he doesn't come."

"*Ejaculata retardata,*" Fingerhood said.

Tears had started to stream down Ian's face. "I love that girl. I don't understand how she can do this to me."

"You don't love Beverly," Anita said. "You love the aura of her money. Who are we kidding?"

"No, I really love her."

"I wish I were forty-one thousand feet over Barcelona and happy," Jack said, a faraway smile on his face. "I'm flying a Boeing 707, #6748 these days. A friend of mine crashed with it a couple of years ago. You remember Happy Gonzales, don't you, Anita?"

"I flew with him the trip before he crashed. He was a sweet guy."

"Lousy pilot, though. Those Latins don't understand precision. Never fly with a Latin, folks, and never let one operate on you. That's my motto. The English have the best airports."

"Thanks," Ian wiped his eyes.

Anita took off her leopard print skirt.

"My God," Lou said. "She wears a panty girdle. I really don't believe it."

"It's easy for you to sit there with your green breasts and talk. You don't fly in jets three or four days a week. You don't know what it's like to be bloated all the goddamn time. Incidentally, didn't the green come off on your gold mole?"

"No. It's smear-proof."

"Where do you buy it? I mean, what is it called?"

"Toujours Avocado. I get it at my beauty parlor. I understand that it's selling like mad. You can use it as eye shadow, too."

"How interesting." Anita observed the curve of her belly. "The bloating is starting to go away. Jack, won't the Air Force ever hurry up with their study?"

"They're working on it. A breakthrough is expected any minute. Happy knew one of the VIPs on the project."

"Poor Happy. I kind of miss him. He always used to goose me when I brought him his coffee."

"Sure. That's probably why he crashed. If he was looking out the window, like you're supposed to, instead of sticking his finger up stewardesses' assholes, he might be around today."

"You're really disgusting, Jack."

"I always said he was," Simone told her. "But you used to defend him. Now you see his true nature. Beast. I'm going to make doubly sure never to fly with your crazy airline."

"No fighting, no fighting," Fingerhood said.

Anita noted Simone's welts with immense satisfaction.

"We wouldn't want you with us, anyway. You're probably one of those passengers who vomit all the time."

"I do not."

"And not even in the barf bag."

"I don't see how you can criticize Jack," Simone replied, "when you're so disgusting yourself."

"No fighting, I said."

"Oh shut up, Robert," Anita snapped. "You know that Simone and I are only happy when we fight."

"We don't want anyone to be happy around here."

"Happy was never really happy," Jack said. "I know. He had a terrible hemorrhoid problem. Man, that stuff must be murder. Happy used to buy Preparation H like other people buy aspirin."

"You're obsessed with assholes, buddy," Fingerhood said.

"The mad doctor has a clinical outlook. I'll give him that."

"He's saner than you are," Anita said to Jack. "And if you want to know the truth, he's a better lover, too."

"I never said I wanted to know the truth. I'm with O'Neill. 'As the history of the world proves, the truth has no bearing on anything. It's irrelevant and immaterial.' "

"That's all this country needs," Ian said. "A pilot who's a poet, too."

"It's better than being an Englishman who lines up dummies for a living," Anita said, coming to Jack's defense now that someone else was attacking him. Actually she hated them all, all four men. One was worse than the other, and the worst of all was Robert Fingerhood for proving himself to be as immoral and corrupt as the others. He had been her last bastion of hope for an old-fashioned life of marriage and motherhood, but she could see now that, as with Jack, she'd made another crummy mistake on that score.

"I just realized that I'm the only girl present who hasn't been to bed with Fingerhood," Lou said, looking at him. "Would you care to rectify that?"

"As soon as I get through eating."

"If it's not one orifice, it's another," Jack observed.

"I also just realized that Fingerhood is the only man present who still has his clothes on. Would you care to rectify that?"

"As soon as I get through eating."

Simone held out her glass for more champagne. "I sure wish that Beverly and Stevie would finish up in there. I'm starting to get jealous."

"Starting?" Anita asked. "Your face turned the color of Lou's tits about fifteen minutes ago."

"They haven't been in there that long, have they? Steve can't last for more than five minutes tops."

"*Ejaculato praecox.*"

At that profound point, the doorbell rang.

"Come in," Fingerhood called out. "It's open."

"Who could it possibly be?" Anita asked.

"It could be Peter Northrop," Peter Northrop said, entering the room. "And it is."

He stopped in his tracks, slightly stunned by the scene before his eyes. He and Lou exchanged glances, and then he said, "Has anyone seen my wife?"

"She's in the bedroom at the moment," Simone replied. "Getting fucked by my boyfriend."

"Oh, that's okay. Just so long as she's not drinking herself to death for a change."

"It might be okay with you, but I don't like it one bit. Stevie never screwed me for more than five minutes tops, and they've been in there for at least fifteen."

"What do you do? Keep a stop watch under your pillow?"

"I heard all about you in Mexico City. And you turn out

to be as big a *schmuck* as I'd imagined. Not to mention the limp wrist business."

"You must be that French gossip-monger, Simone."

"And I'm Robert Fingerhood," Robert Fingerhood said, shaking Peter's hand. "I don't remember inviting you, but have a chair. This is Anita Schuler, Jack Bailey, and Ian Clarke. I believe you know Lou Marron."

"Yes, we've met. Well, what an interesting little group. What was the turkey stuffed with? Pot?"

"We don't need artificial stimulants to be uninhibited," Anita replied, wishing she were dead. "We just take our clothes off when we feel like it. And I don't mind telling everyone that my pubic hairs have been bleached. I use Born Blond."

Simone pouted. "I was going to tell them that."

"I know. That's why I decided to beat you to the punch."

"If you want to know the truth," Peter said, "I'm not even vaguely interested in your pubic hairs."

"Irrelevant and immaterial."

Ignoring Jack, Peter turned to Fingerhood.

"Is there any reason that you're the only clothed person in this wretched group?"

"Yes. I haven't finished eating yet."

Ian, who had finished the second Peter identified himself, said to Fingerhood, "And it doesn't look as though you're ever going to, old-boy."

"Knock off the 'old boy' crap. I have an aversion to chauvinistic expressions."

"I sure wish my wife would hurry up in there."

Then Peter took off his clothes in two seconds flat.

"Look," Simone said. "He doesn't wear shorts. That's a serious sign. And by the way, where are your children on this festive occasion?"

"Beverly shipped them home to her mother for the holiday. Our housekeeper went with them. Not that it's any of your damn business."

"Your balls are on the soft side. I find that very unattractive. Stevie's are tight and hard."

"Is Stevie that crackpot who paints old movie stars on a horse?"

"He is not a crackpot."

"My wife actually bought one of those monstrosities. Fifteen hundred dollars for Don Ameche and Alice Faye on a brown nag. Alice has the moustache."

"That was one of Stevie's best paintings."

"Really? You could have fooled me."

Simone was about to say something when footsteps were heard coming from the bedroom. Everyone looked up as Beverly and Steve entered the room, seeming not too happy.

"Hello, darling," Peter said.

"Oh, it's you, darling. What are you doing here? I thought you were having dinner with Tony."

"I did have dinner with Tony. We ate fast."

"In more ways than one," Simone said.

"It's not my fault if I'm pan-sexual."

"Fucking faggot."

Beverly patted Simone on the shoulder. "There, there. Everything is going to be all right. I've brought your boyfriend back to you, and, frankly, darling, he can't screw his way out of a paper bag."

"He sure can give commands, though."

"Would the Nazis have come to power if they'd spoken French?" Anita asked. "*Nein! Nein! Nein!*"

"Well, I'm through eating." Fingerhood got up from the table. "And ready for a little diversion. Can I offer my superior services to any of the crazy ladies present?"

Lou felt a bit miffed. "I thought you were going to offer them to me, inasmuch as I'm the only one here who's unfamiliar with them, except through hearsay. Simone tells me you're a real superman in the sack."

"And very Clark Kent when it comes to his professional life," Simone said.

Peter turned to Fingerhood. "Before you honor Miss Marron, let me give you a fast blow job because to tell the truth you're highly desirable."

"Irrelevant and immaterial."

"Degenerate beyond belief."

"Have you lost all contact with reality?" Fingerhood said to Peter. "I'm not queer."

"Of course you're not. That's why you appeal to me so much. The gay boys are par for the course, but to get a real heterosexual's cock in my mouth—"

He stopped, carried away by his own projected ecstasy.

"This is the most absurd thing I've ever heard," Fingerhood said. "You *have* lost all contact with reality."

An undercurrent of tension had gripped the room and Anita was afraid of what would happen next. Yesterday she would not have believed any of this possible, today she heard herself say, "Oh, Robert. Go ahead. It's only a joke."

"It's a joke all right because I could never get a hard-on if a man went down on me."

"Want to bet?" Peter asked, unzipping Fingerhood's pants before he could be stopped.

After much discussion, the dining room table was cleared and all the girls said they would stay close to the now naked Fingerhood while he underwent his tremulous ordeal.

"I tell you, I'll never get it up," Fingerhood said as he laid down on the table, and suddenly felt a finger zoom up his asshole. "Cut that out. That's not playing fair."

"Hooray for Robert Fingerhood," they all chanted in unison. "Hooray for Fingerhood."

"He's good to his word," Simone said. "It's still soft."

The girls hovered over Fingerhood, giving him sustenance, as he gritted his teeth in disgust. Their breasts dangled over his unhappy face.

"It's still soft," Simone said.

Then Lou leaned down and kissed Fingerhood on the lips, at which point he developed an enormous erection which he promptly withdrew from Peter's mouth.

"You rotten bitch," Peter said. "Just when things were going so nicely."

It was only when Fingerhood pushed Peter away and began to fuck Lou on top of the table that Anita grabbed Ian in a feverish embrace in the hammock in the next room. Ian was lying underneath her, looking up at the stuffed owl, and as he got it into her, he said, "It's degenerate, but it's better than jerking off in a bag of Planter's Peanuts."

In complete desperation, Peter began to make love to his own wife on the sofa, as Simone, Steve, and Jack formed a three-way chain across a couple of jaguar skins on the floor.

Minutes later, after Anita had come, she looked around the room and started to laugh hysterically. Robert paused in his table activities long enough to ask her what was so funny.

"I find it highly amusing," she said, "that only a few hours ago I was worried my parents might not like you because you're Jewish."

❁ CHAPTER ELEVEN ❁

There was another table now, but instead of being on it, Lou and Robert Fingerhood were solemnly seated at either side of it, across from each other, in Fingerhood's private office at The Child Guidance Center. Lou had come to discuss her daughter's problems with Fingerhood, who had seen and tested the eleven-year-old Joan several days before.

It was the first time that Lou had seen Robert since his memorable Thanksgiving party the previous month, and in her Kohinoor mink and dark dress she hardly felt like the same girl who had gotten laid on top of a dining table in front of seven other people. She wondered whether Robert, in his conservative gray suit and striped tie, felt a bit strange, too, a bit whacky, in fact, to be talking to her in serious, professional tones about her daughter's academic underachievement.

The tableau that they presented amused Lou. She, the concerned mother. Robert, the dedicated psychologist. And yet, they were that, too, just as a month before they had been two sweating, thrashing, exhibitionistic maniacs.

"I think I can speak to you more clinically than I do to most parents." Fingerhood had a typewritten report on the desk before him, which he kept referring to as he spoke. "I do that when it's appropriate. I don't translate from the technical to the idiomatic unless it's necessary. If I can speak clinically to parents who understand, I find that it's more efficient and illuminating, and precludes the unfortunate possibility of their feeling talked down to."

The room they were in was relatively sparse, with no

pictures on the walls, no carpeting on the floor, no attempt at decorative embellishment. Near the window that overlooked Park Avenue was another table, a repository for what looked like a variety of children's toys. Lou knew that those were the tools used for testing purposes by the clinical psychologist, and yet she could not help feeling that she was in a child's room somewhere; no, not exclusively a child's room, but one used by both the child for play, and the father for work, perhaps because space in their house was unduly limited. The room had a contradiction about it which appealed to her. It was as though Fingerhood's orderly desk had been set adrift on a sea of multicolored blocks and haphazardly piled construction games, the whimsical vying with the scientific for attention, fantasy juxtaposed with clinical detail.

Lou felt herself caught between the two moods that the room conveyed, caught between the two different guises that she and Robert now wore.

"Joan entered the testing situation casually," Robert said, reading from the report before him. "She related easily and appropriately. There were several occasions during which she experienced confusion and became very passive and uncommunicative. These occasions were limited to the Rorschach, but otherwise she was quite cooperative and verbal."

Lou wondered what it all meant. She was confused, unable to reconcile the cold, blunt terminology that Robert employed, with the tender, maternal feelings she had about the child she had given up at birth. Given up legally, and yet, emotionally, had continued to cling to. Like all parents, she resented hearing her child reduced to a patter of psychological jargon, and at the same time that she resented it, she knew she was behaving true to parental form and she felt embarrassed. In all things, Lou wanted to be superior to the norm, but the longer she lived, the more she wondered whether she wasn't, in fact, quite ordinary after all. Sometimes being ordinary held a distinct appeal for her: to give in, succumb, not to have to try so hard, abandon the struggle. But where would she be without the struggle? Push, fight, win. Even when she was not sure what she was pushing or fighting for so hard, she still knew that she had to win, excel, stand out from the crowd. It was her identity, and consequently, her destiny.

"Joan's Full Scale WISC of 96 falls in the average range of intelligence," Fingerhood resolutely went on, "and above the scores of about 37 percent of the normative population. Her score is made up of a verbal component of 97 and a performance component of 94, with interest scatter ranging between 6 and 12. Her lowest scores suggest some perceptual difficulties, and the disorganizing effects of anxiety. Her highest scores make it clear that her intellectual potential is, conservatively, higher in the average range."

Normative population. Average range. Lou felt bitterly disappointed. Had she given birth to a dull child? Thinking of Joan's father, who had been killed in an automobile accident before Joan was born, Lou reluctantly conceded the possibility of inferior genes from the other side. Although Hank had been personable with the typical easygoing charm of the Irish, he was hardly a brain. She remembered his keen interest in baseball and his often-repeated ambition to pitch for the major leagues some day. But at seventeen he crashed drunkenly into a telephone pole on the way home from a high school dance that Lou could not attend because she was five months pregnant. The girl in the car with him, a classmate of Lou's, had lived but was permanently paralyzed from the waist down.

Lou decided to verbalize her apprehensions.

"Your report. What does it mean?"

"For one thing, in terms of academic achievement, Joan appears to be functioning somewhat below grade level." Fingerhood looked pensive. "She expresses a dislike of school and a generally negative attitude toward it."

"Why is that?"

Lou wondered about the sparseness of the room. Was it some sort of administrative policy that the walls at The Child Guidance Center be kept bare, and decor held to a minimum? Or was it the personal choice of the psychologist who occupied the office? She recalled, with interest, the very decorative walls in Fingerhood's own apartment.

"Joan is fearful," he said. "In fact, she admits to a variety of fears. She seems to feel that both parental figures, most particularly the mother, from whom she seeks security, are inadequate sources of it."

"You mean, *my* mother," Lou said, more sharply than she had intended to.

"That's the person Joan believes to be her mother, doesn't she?"

"Yes."

"You told me that she has no idea you're her real mother, that she's always thought of you as her older sister. That's correct, isn't it?"

"Yes. Do you think that was a mistake?"

She had not meant to ask him that. The question seemed a shameful admission of failure.

"In terms of Joan's welfare, it would only have been a mistake if you couldn't reconcile yourself to assuming the role of the older sister. In other words, if you continued to interfere with the way your parents chose to bring up Joan over the years."

"And you think that I have interfered?"

"Let's say that you appear to have taken undue responsibility for Joan, over and above that which an older sister generally would be expected to take."

"Like what?"

"Well, I notice that it's you who have come to consult me, not Joan's parents."

Lou nodded. "You're right. I have interfered. I've tried not to, I've tried to stay out of the way, but I'm afraid that I haven't been very successful. I've never been able to keep my nose out of anything that concerned Joan. I didn't want the responsibility for her, and yet I couldn't give her up either. Not entirely. I felt too guilty."

"Your parents—her parents—have apparently felt guilty, too, about enforcing any kind of disciplinary control, as a result of which the most salient feature about Joan is her persistent evidence of insecurity. She seems to seek out the security of control by attempting to exert it herself. For example, by constantly playing with younger children. The point is that Joan needs the security of reasonable control, she needs it very badly. Her parents have been far too indecisive and permissive with her, possibly because they felt that as a result of your influence they didn't have a free hand with her. In a sense, you've tied their hands."

Everything that Fingerhood said was known to Lou, albeit in a different language, had been known for years, yet it was with relief (as well as regret) that she heard the charge against her expressed in such unemotional, clinical terms.

"What should I do?"

"You can speak to your parents about our conversation today. Or, if you like, you can bring them in and I'll speak to them. Or, perhaps even better yet, I could recommend a psychologist in Philadelphia for them to see. That might be more practical under the circumstances."

"Yes, I think it would."

"Fine." Fingerhood wrote down two names on a slip of paper. "I highly recommend both of these men, and I'll send my report to whichever one you decide upon."

"Does that mean you think Joan needs treatment?"

"Yes, I would definitely say so at this point. She needs treatment, her parents need counseling, and unless you decide to become a fulltime mother, I strongly suggest that you begin to reconcile yourself to the far less influential role of older sister."

Lou shivered inside her Kohinoor mink, and stood up. "Thank you. I'm glad we had this talk. It's been very helpful."

"I know how you must feel." Fingerhood stood up, too. "It's difficult to relinquish someone you love, but you have to remember that, in this case, it's for her own good."

"That makes it even more painful."

"Why?"

"I feel like a bit of a monster. The dragon lady who can only help matters by not helping, whose influence is destructive, whose interference over the years has only served to harm the person she loves most in the world."

Even as she said it, Lou wondered how much she really did love Joan, or how much she pretended to love her in order to ward off the terrible feelings of guilt that were engendered by the abandonment of her daughter eleven years ago. She suddenly seemed to have lost everyone in the world she cared about: David, Peter, Joan. An agonizing vacuity stretched before her, pitiless in its sense of condemnation. All she had was her work, and perhaps for the first time in her life it struck her as a paltry substitute for the warmth and comfort of a close human relationship. Tears came to her eyes as she shook hands with Robert Fingerhood and thanked him again.

Lou left the Center with mixed feelings of relief and foreboding, grateful not to have to listen to further analyses of her daughter's problems, but dreading the steps she knew she had to take in order to cope effectively with those problems. It was cold and clear on Park Avenue, with only the most discreet of Christmas holly wreaths adorning the apartment buildings that lined the avenue like giant, gray fortresses. On Sixty-Fifth Street a woman emerged from one of the fortresses. She had grayish-blue hair, similar to the color of the building, and wore a flowing cape above gray suede boots. She looked through Lou as if she were made of glass.

At Fifty-Seventh Street, Lou turned west and wondered whether it was going to snow. There was a muted taste of snow in the air, tempting, teasing the city with its evasiveness. Originally, Lou had planned to spend these four leftover vacation days skiing at Stowe, but at the last minute she canceled her reservations and persuaded her parents to let Joan come visit her instead, with the thought of taking her to Fingerhood's clinic for testing. According to Lou's mother, Joan had become "wild" and "impossible" lately, and they did not know how to cope with her. They said that at school the teachers called her "belligerent" and "hostile." When Lou met her at Penn Station she was prepared for an eleven-year-old hellion, instead of which a very reserved and reticent Joan emerged from the train, carrying a weekend case in one hand and a gift-wrapped package from Menagerie (Philadelphia's answer to Paraphernalia) in the other.

"Merry Christmas." Joan shyly handed the package to Lou. "I hope you like it. I didn't know what to get you. You're hard to shop for. I mean, you have such kinky taste."

They kissed self-consciously. It had been several months since they'd laid eyes on each other, and it always took them a while to reestablish their tentative sister relationship. Since Joan's birth, Lou had seen her only four or five times a year and always in Philadelphia, never New York. This was Joan's first visit here and she seemed dazed by the hurrying Christmas crowds outside on Seventh Avenue.

"It isn't usually this frantic," Lou explained. "The holidays are murder in New York. I hope we can get a taxi."

Joan was suitably impressed with Lou's apartment, particularly the see-through plastic sofa and armchair. Mr. Crazy sniffed at Joan's shoes, rubbed against her legs, then retreated to his wicker basket in a corner of the room.

"Oh, you have a garden, too." Joan peered out at the naked patch of land, then plopped down on the see-through sofa. "This is fun. I've never seen a sofa like this before. What would happen if I stuck a pin in it?"

"I'd kill you."

"No, I mean, it looks as though the whole thing would go whoosh."

"Let's not test it. Okay?"

"Okay," Joan said, good-naturedly. "Aren't you going to open my present?"

"Of course."

Joan watched with trepidation as Lou waded through wrapping paper and tissue paper and finally held up an oval linen purse in bright summer colors of orange, pink, and purple.

"It's called a kookaburra bag," Joan said. "Do you like it? I think it's fun to give out of season presents, don't you?"

"Now that I've gotten one, I do. Thank you, love. It's beautiful. Those are my colors, all right."

She wondered whether Joan had picked out the purse by herself, or whether her mother had helped with the selection. In choosing a Christmas gift for Joan, Lou consulted the children's wear editor at *The Rag,* who suggested something on the grown-up side, like culotte pajamas or a jewel box filled with cologne, bath oil, and hand lotion.

"At eleven they're practically going on fifteen these days," the children's wear editor said, knowingly.

Lou took her up on both suggestions and was gratified to see the pleasure on Joan's face as she opened her presents.

"They're very sophisticated, aren't they?" she asked Lou, holding the pink culottes up to herself.

"Very."

"Oh, bath oil! Yummy. I *adore* bath oil."

Lou smiled. "I thought you might."

"What did you buy for the folk?"

"That's a secret."

"I know what the folk bought for you."

"Don't tell. I want to be surprised."

"The folk" was their own private name for Lou's parents, their own private joke, and it tickled them both to refer to "the folk" as often as possible; it made them feel closer to each other than they actually were.

"Well, you'll be seeing the folk in a couple of days," Joan had said, "so I guess the suspense won't kill you."

"I'll try to hold out."

The shops on Fifty-Seventh Street were very festive for the holidays. Lou caught a fleeting glimpse of herself in the window of the Hotel Buckingham and was hardly surprised by the constriction on her face. Tonight was Christmas Eve and she had planned to go back to Philadelphia with Joan later that afternoon, but the conversation with Fingerhood had changed her mind. She would send Joan back by herself and she would visit her parents the following week, or possibly the week after that. She was too upset now to talk to them about the things she had learned this morning. She needed a breather to let it all sink in. Most importantly, she needed to be separated from Joan as soon as possible. Letting Joan return home alone was not that significant a step by itself, but to Lou it marked the beginning of a new relationship she planned to have with her daughter. She corrected herself. Her sister.

She stopped in front of a small, undistinguished building in the middle of the block and checked the names on the bells for *Lassitier*. Lou had never before visited Simone, but earlier that morning she'd sent Joan over there in a taxi and said she would pick her up after her appointment. Since Dr. Harry Hocker had fired Simone for incompetence the previous week (she inadvertently stepped on an old lady's bunions), Simone said she would love to go see the Radio City Music Hall's Christmas show with Joan and Lou that afternoon.

The man who sold thrift furs stood in the doorway of his shop. "Looks like it's going to snow, doesn't it?"

"Yes, it certainly does."

"You a friend of Frenchie's?"

Lou waited for Simone to ring back. "That's right."

"She's a cute kid, but—" he made a circling gesture around his head, "a little *meshugah* upstairs."

It never failed to amuse Lou that people in New York automatically assumed everyone understood Jewish words and expressions. She should have been carrying her copy of *The Daily Forward* to give the thrift shop man a real thrill.

"*Mon ange!*"

Simone stood in the doorway of her apartment, as Lou came up the rickety staircase. There was a small poodle wagging its tail at Simone's heels, and squealing.

"I've just made a delicious TV dinner for Joan. Fried chicken with apple and peach slices for dessert."

The two girls pecked at each other's cheeks.

"You didn't have to bother," Lou said, touched nonetheless. "We could have gone somewhere for lunch."

Joan was seated at the drop-leaf table, finishing the remains of apple and peach slices as Lou came in.

"I never had a TV dinner before," Joan said enthusiastically. "It's good. I mean, it's fun. It's not like eating real food."

"That's why I like it, too." Simone sat down on one of the rockers with faded car seat covers, and motioned Lou to take the other. "Who can bear the thought of eating real food? It's so disgusting."

Simone was wearing a sheer blouse, a man's striped tie, and orange velveteen bell-bottom trousers. It seemed to Lou that she looked radiant, absolutely glowing, then Simone blurted out:

"Stevie has asked me to marry him! Isn't that *extraordinaire?*"

"Did you accept?"

"Of course. Everyone should get married once, if only for the experience. I told Anita and she's ready to throw herself out of the airplane. She and Robert have broken up, you know."

"Really?"

(At that very moment Anita was wistfully contemplating a full-page brassiere ad in *Life*, the caption of which read, "If nature didn't, Warner's will.")

Simone went on. "Robert told me he couldn't stand her any more, with her Norforms, and her fucking breast exercises, and all that Born Blond crap cluttering up the bathroom. But, of course, with him, if it's not one excuse, it's another. After a while, he can't stand any girl. Sometimes I wonder exactly what he's looking for."

"A paragon, like everybody else."

"He told me that I was irresponsible and scatterbrained. He told Beverly that she drank too much and that her children were impossible. Now it's Anita and her hygenic practices. I'd love to know what he'd say to Jackie Kennedy."

"Probably that her feet were too big and she was a chain smoker."

"I've never seen a picture of her smoking."

"And you probably never will. The American press has been told to protect her public image."

Simone rocked back and forth in the creaking chair.

"Actually, I feel sorry for Anita. She wanted to get married so badly and I didn't, and now I'm going to and she's not. I hate to get philosophical, but do you think there's any justice in the world?"

"I hope not." Lou thought of David Swern, "If there were, I might be in a lot of trouble."

"Anita is really discouraged," Simone said. "So much so that the last time I spoke to her, she said she was asking the airline for a transfer back to Chicago."

"I didn't know she used to live in Chicago."

"That's where she flew from before she asked for a transfer to New York."

"I wonder why she did that."

"She thought she would find love and happiness in New York. Can you imagine anyone being so fucking naïve?"

"You found love and happiness here."

Simone laughed. "I found Steve Omaha. That's a different thing."

Lou could not help laughing, too. Simone was so casually honest, in such a casually self-deprecating way that it was hard not to admire her.

"Anita is only a year older than me," Simone said, "but she's still living in a fantasy world. She still believes that the junior executive of her dreams is going to come along and whisk her away to a life of blissful domesticity."

"But it does happen."

"Not to girls like Anita, not in New York. What does a pretty face mean in this city? *Rien de tout*. A girl here has to have something more. Talent, money, position, exoticism, but *something*. With me, it's being French, the accent and all. That's what Stevie is intrigued by. Besides, Anita has an uncanny ability to pick men who are sure to reject her. Look at Jack Bailey and Fingerhood. She didn't stand a chance with either of them. Jack and Robert aren't interested in blissful domesticity. Jack is too jaded to get married again, and if by some fluke he did, I'll bet it would be to a wealthy widow. As for Robert, he might play the field forever. He knows what the situation is in New York. All those desperate, unmarried girls ready to flop into the sack at a moment's notice in the hope that it will lead to the altar. The men in this city have it made."

"I guess you're right. I never thought about it that way."

"That's because you've always been concerned with your career. If marriage had been on your mind, you wouldn't have gotten involved with David and Peter."

"Who's David and Peter?" Joan asked.

"Friends of mine," Lou replied, signaling Simone with her eyes to drop the subject.

"Boyfriends?" Joan persisted.

"Yes."

"Were they good looking?"

"In a fashion."

"What does that mean?"

"It means that I thought so, but that not everyone necessarily would."

"Why is that?"

"Because people have different standards. And since when did you start asking so many questions?"

Joan looked startled by Lou's sharpness. "I just never knew you had any boyfriends. That's all."

"Okay, now you know."

But why was she getting so angry? Joan's questions were harmless enough. Any eleven-year-old girl would naturally be curious about her older sister's love life. Lou glanced around the room, at the two bunk beds covered with inexpensive throws, the two peeling lemon yellow bureaus, the poodle now asleep on the bottom bed, at Joan still seated at the drop-leaf table, looking hurt and bewildered. The apartment was in a state of unmistakable decay, and Lou wondered how badly someone as attractive and fashion-conscious as Simone minded living there. Like so many other single girls in New York, existing on a limited budget, Simone had apparently chosen to sink whatever money she had into her own personal façade. It was one of the curious things about girls in this city. When you met them outside of their apartment, it was hard to tell on what kind of scale they lived. With their charge accounts and their hair rollers, a ninety-five dollar a week receptionist could appear at a cocktail party looking like an heiress.

"When is the wedding going to take place?" Lou asked. "Am I invited?"

"Of course you're invited. It will be next month. Everyone's invited. It's not really a wedding, you know. It's more of a wed-in."

"A what?"

"Well, a wedding ceremony is performed by a chaplain and you go through all the formal motions, but you don't use a marriage license. It's the latest thing. Civil disobedience comes to matrimony. I plan to wear a white paper maxi and carry a bunch of white paper roses."

"And live in a white paper house."

"No, we're going to live right here for the time being," Simone said, very seriously. "Stevie is living here now, but he paints at a studio that he's sharing with another guy. He can't afford a studio of his own yet, and I can't afford to move to a larger place until I find a new job. I'm having a tough time, because there aren't too many things I can do."

"How about modeling?"

"Are you kidding? I never want to see another fur coat again as long as I live, not unless I own it."

"I was thinking of lingerie. I might be able to get you a job. I know quite a few of the manufacturers."

"You mean I'd be running around a drafty showroom all day in a skimpy bra and bikini panties?"

"Something like that?"

"It sounds *merveilleux*. Will fat, ugly buyers pinch my bottom?"

"Probably."

Simone grinned and rolled her eyes. "When do I start?"

The movie at Radio City Music Hall was a soapy Doris Day comedy which even Joan was contemptuous of, although the theater itself impressed her by its luxuriousness. She snuggled happily in the plush chair, and more than twice flicked on the small light next to the seat in order to read her program.

"I could sit here forever," she whispered to Lou.

Lou kissed her on the cheek and in the protective darkness of the theater felt an overpowering surge of love for the daughter she now realized she had truly to give up, after having only tokenly given her up at birth. Her parents would be surprised when she telephoned them in a little while, saying that she was going to send Joan back to Philadelphia by herself that afternoon. She would tell them that her editor had called with a special assignment which she could not turn down and they would understand. They always understood when she spoke about her job because it made them feel proud of her. Years ago, when she became pregnant, they'd been so ashamed, so worried about what would happen to her in the future. Now they knew. By turning into the hard-working, successful career girl, she had exonerated herself in their opinion. She had desperately wanted to exonerate herself; they'd made her feel so guilty about the illegitimate pregnancy. Was that why she never spoke to them now about her personal life, about men? *I just never knew you had any boyfriends*, Joan had said minutes ago, and she'd become inexplicably angry, resenting Joan's remark because it made her feel as though she were some kind of work machine, with no softness, no desire or need for love, possessed by only the hard drive of ambition. Surely there was more to her than that, and yet that was what she had let herself appear to be in her parents' eyes in order to justify her existence and atone for mistakes of the past. Perhaps without realizing it, she had convinced herself over the years that she did not deserve love, otherwise (and Simone had pointed it out) why did she continue to become involved with married men who had no intention of leaving their wives?

Joan was dazzled by the Rockettes, so much so that she wanted to stay and see the movie another time just so she could see the Rockettes again.

"Not on your life," Lou told her.

"I wonder how they can dance that way when they have their period," Simone mused. "It must hurt."

Snow had begun to fall lightly on the holiday crowds along Sixth Avenue, as they started to walk to the Russian Tea Room, which Simone insisted they stop at, because it was her favorite restaurant in New York. They took a circular booth in the front room and ordered tea and assorted pastries.

"It's too bad Chou-Chou isn't here," Simone said. "This is his favorite restaurant too. Capricorns are such status seekers."

"What's a Capricorn?" Joan asked.

As Simone was about to tell her, Lou stood up.

"Excuse me a moment. I have to call my office."

When she returned to the booth, Simone was just finishing her explanation of the heavens to a captivated Joan. Lou then told Joan that she would have to go back to Philadelphia alone that afternoon.

"But tonight is Christmas Eve." Disappointment flooded Joan's face. "How can they make you work?"

"It's a newspaper, darling, and one of the other reporters has just come down with the flu. I have to cover a charity ball in her place."

"They're a bunch of slave drivers," Simone said, waving to a middle-aged man with a small, pointed beard.

"Who's that?" Lou asked, absentmindedly.

"One of the regulars here. I met him at the bar last winter."

"I still think it's not fair," Joan pouted. "It being Christmas Eve and all."

"I thought he had a pulmonary disorder at the time, but it turns out that he plays the cello and is in love with one of the dancers in the Joffrey Ballet. I spent a rather interesting evening with the two of them once." Simone looked significantly at Lou. "If you know what I mean."

Lou finished her tea and suddenly felt very tired. It was only a little after three, but all she wanted to do was put Joan on the train, go back to her apartment, and go to sleep. A certain panic was starting to set in. She prayed that it would not be too difficult to find a taxi.

"Ballet dancers are able to assume rather tricky positions that would be quite beyond the power of the average man," Simone said, as Lou beckoned to the waiter for their check and Joan stared glumly into her half-eaten apricot pastry.

When Lou left Penn Station after seeing Joan off, her

heart was pounding so fast that she could barely catch her breath. Instead of getting better, the panic had gotten worse. All she could think of was: David, Peter, and now Joan. Dead, lost, gone. Within a year she had forfeited them all, and never in her life had she felt so very much alone. The raucous holiday gaiety only served to emphasize her sense of aloneness, and she wished that she did have a charity ball to cover for the paper tonight, something, anything to take her mind off her galloping panic. She would never be able to go home and go to sleep, not in her condition, but what was the alternative? Where to go? The children's wear editor had invited her to a party tonight, but at the time Lou thought she would be in Philadelphia and she'd turned down the invitation. She could still call the girl and say that her plans had changed. Yet the last thing in the world she was in the mood for at this point was a party, the prospect of having to face a roomful of cheery people made her shudder. No. It was out of the question. What she needed were a couple of tranquilizers, a glass of warm milk, and a good night's sleep. Then she thought of Robert Fingerhood.

"Yes, I can let you have a few Miltown," he said when she got him at home on the telephone. "Come on down. You know where I live."

"I'll be there shortly. And thanks."

It was with a tremendous sense of anticipated relief that Lou hailed a taxi and gave the driver Fingerhood's address. Then she leaned back against the cold leather seat and watched the snowflakes fall dizzily to the ground. Next weekend she would definitely go up to Stowe.

When Robert opened the door to his apartment, Lou thought to herself: so we meet for the third time in still a different guise. The wild orgiasts of Thanksgiving, and the doctor-patient relationship of that morning, now gave way to the softer, more subtle tone of two old friends, who, having seen each other at their worst and at their best, were about to strike a new middle ground.

"I hope I didn't get you at an inconvenient time," she said.

"No. I'd just gotten home when you called. Would you like a drink?"

"I'd love one."

He opened the liquor cabinet in the dining room.

"What will it be?"

"Do you have any cognac?"

"Remy Martin okay?"

"Yes. Fine."

"Why don't you sit down?"

She went into the living room and perched precariously on the hammock. Robert came in carrying the bottle of Remy Martin and two glasses, which he set on the whalebone vertebrae that served as an end table. Lou remembered sitting on the vertebrae in her gold mole knickerdress at the Thanksgiving party. Although that had only been last month, it seemed like last year, another lifetime altogether.

Robert picked up the bottle and started to pour.

"Tell me when to stop."

After a second, she said, "Stop."

"I find something interesting about the way you're sitting on that hammock," he said, as he handed her the drink.

"What's that?"

"It's curious, but I've noticed that slender girls, like you, tend to sit on it very gently, as though they're afraid the hammock will cave in if they put their full weight on it. Whereas big, heavy girls just jump right in without giving it a second thought."

Lou finished off the cognac in one gulp, but the pounding in her heart still continued. "What does it mean?"

He laughed. "I'm not sure."

"Did Beverly jump right in?"

He reddened somewhat. "As a matter of fact, she did."

Lou envisioned Beverly's large, voluptuous body sprawled self-confidently in the hammock and it made her feel less confident than ever, which immediately produced a combative reaction.

"Perhaps big women act that way in order to delude themselves that they're really delicate, fragile creatures after all," she said.

"It's possible."

"You know, the way girls with heavy, unattractive legs and thighs tend to wear the most eye-catching stockings, as if to prove that they don't have heavy legs and thighs."

"That still doesn't explain why the small, slender ones are afraid the hammock won't hold their weight."

Lou hated to lose any argument; her father wasn't a lawyer for nothing. "Well, because they, on the other hand, are trying to delude themselves into believing that they're tall, statuesque, and terribly powerful."

"Who's the psychologist around here?" Fingerhood asked.

"I guess I'm trying to be."

"Do you like to think that you're terribly powerful?"

"All the time, but frequently I have to admit I'm wrong.

Like now. I'm afraid I don't feel too powerful. In fact, I feel pretty lousy."

"I have the Miltown right here." He crossed the room to the fireplace mantel on top of which was a small plastic bottle. "I only had eight."

"That's more than enough."

"Do you want to take one now? I'll get you a glass of water."

"Please."

The cognac had hit her like a ton of bricks and then she realized that she hadn't had a thing to eat since toast and coffee early that morning. A wave of nausea rose up within her, vying for attention with the waves of panic. Her head started to throb. She hoped she wasn't coming down with a virus. January was always a big month on the paper, what with news of the Paris collections being wired in daily to New York, and if there was one place she did not want to be in January, it was home in bed drinking liquids and taking her temperature while fashion history was being made.

When Robert returned with the water, she gratefully swallowed one of the Miltowns, hoping that it might take her headache away along with the pounding of her heart.

"You shouldn't drink when you take that stuff," he said, as she poured herself another cognac.

"One more won't kill me. Besides, I can't imagine feeling worse than I do right now."

But she was wrong there. Several minutes later she felt infinitely worse, an emergency vomit was coming over her, forcing her to her feet.

"Quick. Where's the bathroom?"

"First door on your left," he said, as she dashed out of the room.

The hallway was darkened and she pushed open the first door. That room was darkened, too, and she could make nothing out clearly. It didn't matter. It was too late for clarity, too late for discretion. With relief she vomited into something. Seconds later when she managed to find the light, she discovered that the something was an opened bureau drawer. She was in a dressing room and she had thrown up all over Robert's socks. What a blunder. What a mess. Where was the bathroom, anyway? She stepped out into the hall and realized that the bathroom was on the opposite side. Scooping up the soiled socks, she took them into the bathroom and filled the sink with hot water. After she had thoroughly washed the socks, she hung them on the towel rack above the tub and started to giggle, imagining Robert's startled reaction the next time he came in there and saw his socks neatly lined up, drying on the rack. She was smiling when she returned to the living room.

"Well, you look better," he said. "How do you feel?"

"Much, much better."

It was true. Gone was her headache, her nausea, her panic. She felt like a reasonable human being for the first time since she'd awakened that morning.

"I can't believe that I was in your office only this morning," she said. "It seems like at least yesterday, if not longer ago than that."

"I hope that what I had to say didn't upset you too much."

"I can live with it. In fact, I've already begun to."

Then she told him about her decision concerning Joan, adding, "David Swern left a trust fund for Joan, as well as a bank account in my name to be used for her until she reached eighteen. Up until now I've been sending my parents money each month for Joan, but since speaking to you I've decided to turn the account directly over to them. If they're not financially dependent upon me for her care, it might help alleviate their emotional dependence. That way they should feel more confident about coping with her problems themselves. I think it should make them more authoritative, more able to exert—what was it you called it?"

"Disciplinary control?"

"Something like that."

She paused, waiting for his appraisal.

"You've made a constructive start. And very quickly, too."

"I just hope I can stick to my guns. I know it won't be easy, but I'm sure as hell going to try."

"It's never easy to admit you've made a mistake, but it's never too late either."

Lou was struck once more by the proliferation of paintings and artifacts in Robert's apartment, and the absence of any note of personal taste in his office.

"Do you like your job?" she asked, wondering about it for the first time.

"Let's say that I can't easily imagine any other job as being more satisfying. But let's also say that, as in most businesses, I'm up against a collection of policy-makers who seem to specialize in resignation and apathy. I'm referring to our Board of Directors, in case you're interested."

"That's odd. I never think of clinics as having the same type of problems as other businesses."

"Most people don't, but we have them, all right. We have an Executive Director who could compete with any VIP *schmuck* in any top corporation for sheer gutlessness and mediocrity. A. H. S. Duckworth is the son of a bitch's name. Ah Hate Sincerity Duckworth. Have you ever met a man who is able to maintain his position by accomplishing virtually nothing of value, by antagonizing everyone who works for him, and yet at the same time is able to hypnotize the Board into keeping him on?"

Lou thought of Tony Elliot. "He sounds like my boss, only worse."

"Christ, it's frustrating to have your hands tied by hypocrites like that. He's the sort of guy who makes pious speeches to the staff one day, and then beats the shit out of his wife the next. He hospitalized her once with a fractured arm. And this is the great decision-maker for a clinic devoted to the advancement of better mental health, if you'll pardon the expression."

Fingerhood glanced at his watch.

"Am I keeping you from something?" she asked.

"I have a date at six-thirty with Anita."

"I thought the two of you broke up."

"We did, but she asked me to take her out tonight, it being Christmas Eve, and foolishly I agreed."

"Why foolishly?"

"Because it's over between us and I really have no desire to see her tonight. Or any other night, for that matter, but since she's transferring to Chicago after the first of the year I said she could count on me during the holidays."

"Robert Fingerhood: Mr. Good Guy."

"It happens to be a role I detest."

"You seem to do very well at it, though."

"Who says?"

"Don't look so horrified. I won't tell anyone. I know that you want to be considered a rat."

"But I am a rat in certain ways. Ask Simone, if you don't believe me."

"Simone doesn't think you're a rat. She thinks you're confused. She can't understand what you're looking for in a woman."

Fingerhood turned on a slow, gorgeous smile.

"Maybe I'm looking for you."

Was this his typical approach? The dazzling smile. The message of secret adoration. She had not run across this particular come-on in a long time: you're-the-answer-to-my-every-prayer-cha-cha-cha. It was sweet, in a way, it was so blatantly obvious that Lou could see where a girl might wonder whether there wasn't something to it at that.

"No," she said. "You're not looking for me."

A film seemed to have descended over his eyes, giving them a dreamy, romantic character. All semblance of the Angry Psychologist of a few minutes before had completely vanished. Now he was Fingerhood, the Aspiring Lover (oddly, she believed him in both roles).

"How do you know what I'm looking for?"

"I don't," she admitted, "but I doubt very much that whatever it is, I'd fit the bill."

"Why?"

"I have no desire to get involved with you, or any man at this point in my life. I'm just not interested in that now."

"Who's talking about involvement?"

"That appears to be your pattern. Simone, Beverly, Anita. You were with each of them for a period of time, you went through the motions of exclusive involvement." She thought of the stories she'd heard about all those champagne and hibachi dinners. "I don't want to do that. I don't have the time."

"You don't have to."

She laughed. "You mean, we can just jump into the sack and no strings attached?"

"If that's what you like."

She stood up. "It would be preferable to the other. I'll tell you what. Why don't you call me after the holidays, when Anita is out of your hair, and we'll see how uninvolved we can become? I'm in the book."

"I will. In fact, I'd love to."

He helped her on with her coat and walked her to the door.

"Have a nice time tonight," she teased him.

"It might amuse you to know that we're going out with Beverly and Ian."

"I thought Anita hated Beverly."

"She used to, but now that Simone is getting married Anita has decided she hates Simone even more, so she and Beverly are well on the road to becoming fast friends."

"What do you think about Simone and Steve? Isn't that wonderful?"

"I couldn't be happier for her. I just wish she hadn't suggested that I wear a plastic tuxedo to the wedding. And beads."

"You mean, the wed-in. I'm going to tell my boss that I think the paper should cover it. Do you know where it's going to take place? I forgot to ask."

"At Steve's studio."

"Oh, that's perfect." Lou clapped her hands. "I can just see them being joined in unholy matrimony against a back drop of old movie stars on horseback. Tony will love the idea. I'm going to twist his arm to let Cav and me do the story."

Robert kissed her lightly on the mouth and ruffled her hair. "I'll be speaking to you soon. Take care of yourself."

When Lou got outside the snow was several inches deep and it looked as though it was going to continue all night. Luckily, she had put on boots before taking Joan to the train, or the shoes she'd had on earlier would have been ruined. The first thing she did when she got home was to feed Mr. Crazy, who had become violently jealous of Joan during her three-day stay, and who now purred in delight, realizing that his despised rival was gone. The second thing Lou did was to change into her favorite lavender slacks and art nouveau pullover and try to ignore the Christmas tree that she'd bought expressly for Joan's benefit. Now that Joan was gone, the tree seemed out of its element sitting alongside the plastic, see-through sofa, on the zebra floor. Just as she had settled down with a copy of that week's *Rag*, the telephone rang.

"Hello," said Peter Northrop. "Happy Christmas Eve or whatever it is you're supposed to say tonight."

"Where are you?"

"Just finishing up at the office. Can I buy you a drink?"

She thought of Beverly off with Ian. "Why not?"

"Good. Where would you like to meet?"

As though he couldn't guess. "Why don't you come over here? It's not very nice outside, in case you hadn't noticed lately."

"I've noticed. I'm on my way."

She hung up without saying good-bye, her hand trembling. It was the first time that Peter had called her since she told him not to call her, after David's death. Several times in the office he offered to buy her lunch, and each time she firmly said that she was sorry, but she was busy.

"Can't we even talk about it?" he asked her once.

"There's nothing to say. You know how I feel."

"I know how you feel, but it doesn't make any sense."

"It does to me."

"A man you were having an affair with kicked the bucket.

Okay. And everyone is very sorry about it. But you didn't kill him by cutting out with me. So why can't we go on seeing each other?"

"Because David is dead, and I don't want to."

"Great. That's what I love. Exacting female logic."

That conversation had taken place months ago, and shortly afterward Peter went back to Beverly and stopped asking Lou to have lunch with him. She had thought about their affair many times since then, and although she remembered that he excited her in bed, she could not remember what he specifically did that excited her. She only remembered liking it, and she wondered whether Peter's memory was more extensive than hers, or whether, he, too, harbored shadowy impressions. It seemed to Lou that the aura of lovemaking with any given person could only be reinvoked by making love with that same person again.

She opened *The Rag* and leafed idly through it, looking for anything she might have missed when it came out earlier in the week. There was her page on the new Mexican and Spanish influence upon loungewear, with the brilliant caption of *OLÉ*. And there was Peter's column devoted to the anticipation of which couturier was going to steal the show when the Paris collections got under way in January. Next week's issue of *The Rag* would carry pages of discreet block ads placed by the various *haute couture* houses. Lou remembered them only too well from the previous year.

Gres, 1 Rue de la Paix
Chanel, 31 Rue Cambon
Castillo, 95 Faubourg Saint-Honoré
Philippe Venet, 62 Rue François
Jean Patou, 7 Rue St. Florentin
Christian Dior, Paris

Marc Bohan apparently did not deign to give the Avenue Montaigne address. *Paris* was sufficient for him.

Lou got up, put on her ski boots, and went out into the garden, which was blanketed with snow. Scooping up a handful of it, she made a tight snowball, and when Peter Northrop arrived several minutes later she threw it in his face. It hit him in the forehead and he reeled back, stunned.

"What the hell—?"

"It serves you right, you rotten bastard."

"For what?"

"For stealing the column out from under my nose and leaving me with that lousy underwear section."

He brushed the snow off his face and coat.

"Isn't it a bit late to be talking about that now? Tony made the column decision months ago."

"I would have hit you with a snowball then, but I couldn't. It was summer."

"An empty coke bottle would have done the trick."

She stared at him from across the room, all of her pent-up resentment at last out in the open, not just the column resentment (although that was hardly the least of it), but the resentment about David, and the resentment that he had gone back to Beverly.

"Why shouldn't I have gone back?" he said now, when she accused him. "You didn't want me. You wouldn't even have lunch with me. What was I supposed to do—live out the rest of my days at the Harvard Club?"

As though that were the only place to live in New York. As though she and Beverly were the only available women in New York.

"Why are you so stupid?" she asked.

He was about to say something nasty in response, then he caught himself. "Look, Lou, I didn't come here tonight to be hit by snowballs and yesterday's accusations. I think I had better leave."

As he turned to go, she suddenly said, "No. Don't. Please don't. I'm sorry."

She walked over to him and wiped the snow wetness from his forehead, then put her arms around him and kissed him on the lips.

"I'm sorry," she repeated. "It's been a dreadful day. Come on, take off your coat. I'll give you a drink."

"Just so long as you don't throw it at me."

They both laughed and kissed again. Later, in bed, it all came rushing back to Lou in an avalanche of tremulous detail. What it was like with Peter, his lemony scent, the perfect fit, the way his eyes changed from blue to green, the charge of electricity through her fingers. How could she have forgotten?"

"It's as wonderful as ever," he said.

"I know. I'm surprised."

"I'm not."

"How come?"

"Because I remembered how good it was before. Things like that usually don't change."

"I suppose they don't."

In a way, she'd almost been hoping that they would have changed, that it would not be good any longer with them. It did not seem right for it to be that good now that they no longer meant anything to each other. We're animals after all, she thought, rolling over on her stomach.

"Don't you have to be getting home soon?" she asked after a while.

"Yes. Pretty soon. Beverly put the presents under the tree before she went out. I just hope the kids haven't opened them when Margaret wasn't looking."

Lou wondered whether he knew where Beverly was, and with whom.

"She's getting worse by the minute," Peter said, as though reading her thoughts. "The drinking is getting worse and the running around with that asinine Englishman is getting worse. I don't know what to do about her any more. She refuses to see a doctor."

"Get a divorce."

Peter had a far-off look in his eyes; they did not see Lou. "No."

"Won't she give you a divorce?"

"I don't know whether she would or not. I haven't asked. I don't intend to ask. Actually, I don't think she wants a divorce any more than I do. Beverly is twenty-nine and it frightens her. The thought of turning thirty and being without a husband frightens her even more."

Lou thought of all the women she knew who dreaded turning thirty, not least of all herself. Two more years to go.

"Beverly and I have to stay together. We don't always have to be together, but it's important that we don't get divorced."

"Why is it so important?"

"Men don't like to lose their children."

"Neither do women," Lou said, thinking of Joan.

But Peter did not know about Joan; she had never told him, and he assumed that she was referring to Beverly.

"Beverly knows I would never take the children away from her, not unless she became . . ."

"Became what?"

His lips tightened. "Nothing. Never mind. I shouldn't have started on the subject. It's not fair to you. It really has nothing to do with you."

She remembered David saying that she should not concern herself with Lillian, that Lillian was his problem. But if you cared for a man, how could you not be concerned about what troubled him? How could you remain indifferent?

"I'd better get dressed," Peter said, swinging his legs over the side of the bed.

Lou did not move. She was thinking about the strength of marital and parental bonds. She had never before realized how powerful they were, how binding, how difficult and painful to break. Even Peter, who could hardly be considered anyone's concept of the ideal father and loving husband, was saying in effect that he *was* a father and husband, and even if he performed both functions in a haphazard fashion, by most standards, he preferred that to not performing them at all.

"I have something to tell you," he said, knotting his tie in front of the dressing table mirror. "I've saved it for last."

"Yes?" But now that he was leaving, she felt numb inside, dead, cold, alone.

"Well, since The Informer is no longer among us I thought that someone should be appointed to relay the good news. So in a moment of immodesty I appointed myself."

She was barely listening. "What good news?"

"It's about the Paris collections. Guess who's going to cover them for us next month?"

"Tony Elliot, for the thirtieth time."

"No, darling. You."

This time Lou did not move because she couldn't. Her mouth opened, then closed. She just sat there, the sheets at her feet, and stared at him. Peter began to laugh.

"You should see yourself. I swear, even your nipples look surprised."

"You're kidding," she said when she could finally speak.

"Certainly not. Tony plans to break it to you on Monday, so be sure to look properly surprised, but I thought you might have a more pleasant weekend if you knew the good news tonight. You know what a bastard Tony is when it comes to making these announcements. He'd wait until it was time for your plane to take off for Paris, if he possibly could, before letting you in on the big secret. Strange man. Strange mind."

"Peter. I just don't know what to say. I still can't believe it. I feel dazed."

"Don't say anything. Have another drink. Go to sleep. Everything is going to be all right. You have a great career ahead of you."

After Peter had kissed her and left, she thought that she damn well better have a great career ahead of her because at the moment she didn't have anything else. It was a rotten realization. Now that she was about to land the most coveted assignment that any fashion reporter could dream of, she suddenly felt frightened, apprehensive, more alone than ever before. Simone had once said to her, "Be careful of what you want. You're liable to get it."

She thought of the photograph of Marc Bohan above her desk. She thought of the House of Dior on Avenue Montaigne.

Paris.

Lou threw back her head and laughed. She was getting it, all right.